The Never-Time Girl

Copyright © 2014 by Ron Horsley

Cover by: Ron Horsley
(stock images supplied by BigStockPhoto.com)

ISBN-13: 978-0990391005
ISBN-10: 0990391000

"If I Had No Loot" by Tony! Toni! Toné! ©1993 Polygram Records
"A Whiter Shade of Pale" by Annie Lennox, ©1995 SBME Special Markets
"Black" by Pearl Jam ©1990 Polygram Records
"Over the Rainbow" ©1993 EMI Feist Catalog Inc.
"Fish Head" by Barnes & Barnes
"No One is to Blame" by Howard Jones ©Songs of Kobalt Music
"Don't Dream It's Over" by Crowded House © Lasora Ltd.

www.Everything-Under.net
Printed in U.S.A

The Never-Time Girl

An Everything Under Novel

For my grandmother, Barbara Ann Horsley. Who taught me the right way to scramble eggs and make flour dumplings.

For my grandfather and father, Ron Horsleys I and II. When you see me deep into telling a story, and I stop to adjust my glasses and look you in the eyes...it's my Grandpa looking out of them. And when I open my mouth and tell you something hard to believe, that's my dad talking.

And for Jerry Williamson, my literary grandfather.
            ...Jerry, I think you would've really dug this one.

"*...fear in its way is a comfort for it means that somewhere hope is alive.*"

-Theodore Sturgeon
More Than Human

"*Friends like you and you I gotta leave behind.*"

— Tony! Toni! Toné!
"*If I Had No Loot*"

Ever heard a clock crying?

Neither had I.

A friend of Lyneisha Battelle had called her with a somewhat unique problem. Lyneisha wanted some special assistance from us on this problem. Which is how I got called to sit in a townhouse dinette area on a Friday afternoon in Reynoldsburg, a suburb of my glorious hometown of Columbus, Ohio.

The somewhat unique problem: a grandfather clock Lyneisha's friend recently inherited from a deceased great-uncle back in the Ukraine. The clock wouldn't stop issuing a loud, pervasive weeping when it struck each new hour. Seeing as it was a family heirloom going back at least a good century or so, and a fantastic piece of French Comtoise clockwork made somewhere in the vicinity of 1860, this friend couldn't see simply taking it to the dump or selling it to some sucker on eBay. It certainly wouldn't sit quietly on some dais in an auction house.

But take a weeping clock to the local repair shop? Not an option.

Picture this clock for a moment. Comtoise are also known as 'potbellied' clocks. Not the same as your longcase, Gothic-styled, hard-angled and sharply peaked-top grandfather clocks. You probably are more familiar with the Shaker and English styles, all split finials at the top, fat toe moulding at the base to support massive swinging pendulums and counter-bobs cast in dull brass.

This is more something you would think at home in a King Louis, Versailles-weekend-chateau setting. The top casement for the clock face was roughly rectangular, bowing out at the sides but with a narrow cello neck that came down gracefully for the first foot or so, finally ballooning out with a graceful eggplant curvature to the 'potbelly' part. This middle column of the whole affair held what looked like a giant brass-cast skate key or teardrop-shaped plumb bob. Roses and carved ivy leaves leading down from the cornice-dressed neck to swoop out and around, cradling and framing the brass pendulum works. Then a thumb-wide shelf separated the bottom section from the harmony of the rest of it, bearing the potbelly weight. The base itself was an afterthought, a miniature pastoral scene within a gilded frame its centerpiece. The whole thing made out of a rich, cherry-rubbed-to-gleaming mahogany.

The silhouette makes you think more of some sort of Art Nouveau streetlamp from the *Metropolitain*. The mood and character of its decoration makes you think in a sexist vein of a prim woman from the turn of the 20th century with a bit of a flat chest but plenty of make-up-for-it in the lower pelvic region. All dressed in prudish schoolmarm chocolate tones yet allowing a little vanity in the embroidery of those roses and ivy. The clock face looked a hairs-breadth too small for the huge, square head but showed beautiful, blue-enamel faces with gold inlaid Roman numerals. Frail, spider-thin chased-gold hands giving you the hours, minutes and seconds in graceful, looping turns of their arrowheads. The whole thing a good seven feet high, weighing in the neighborhood of several hundred pounds when taking into account all the gearworks and weights inside its cabinetry.

All of this gilt-and-wood-and-metal sitting in the shadowed corner between the living room area and breakfast buffet board of a two-bedroom townhome. Back behind the table-set-for-four done in tubular chrome, a tacky eighties-modern style that some people never learn was never cool. The new arrival had already settled in thoroughly, crushing flat the bland taupe carpeting that ran wall-to-wall through the whole apartment.

If the clock was a tall, graceful and somewhat flirtatious turn-of-the-century lady, then she was sitting in the corner of a rather boring furniture store display of out-of-stock sales items, waiting for a ride home.

We waited forty-two minutes after arriving, sitting at that tacky dinette set.

The clock announced it was five o' the clock by first tonging a gentle, bell-like chime five times.

Around the middle *clang-ting* of the third chime, from its midsection a sawing, viola-sounding reverberation began. The sound choked off each sobbing finish, moving to take a whispery gasp like an inhaled breath. A faint crackle, a pneumoniac static on the inhale, then it emitted the sawing-whine-sob again. After the five chimes of the hour had finished, the saw-whine-sob-choke-gasp went on a good ten more minutes before fading out. As if whatever was emitting the sound had decided to walk out of the apartment and left the door open behind it, the Doppler fade rapid and dying away within seconds.

"Wow," Lyneisha breathed.

"Yeah." I stared at the clock. "Wow indeed."

"It *really cries*. I almost thought Staci was pulling a gag on me."

"I was pretty sure *you* were pulling a gag on me."

She took her gaze off the clock to look at me. She let her hair remain natural and let it grow out, never one for heavy styling. It extended in rope-braided, ebony starfish arms around her long face. Large almond eyes were the main emphasis of a handsome face. Good smile full of bright teeth set into topaz-toned skin. A dark blue denim jacket over a torn V-necked "London Calling" t-shirt and gray corduroy overalls.

"So?" she asked.

"So what?"

She tilted a corner of that smile into a close-lipped smirk. "So you *know* what. Do you see anything?"

I see something but I have no idea what it is.

Ah yes. The voice in your head. The whisper that tells you the bad jokes you know not to utter out loud, or remind you that what you're about to do is supremely stupid and you know it, or basically doesn't shut up on those worrisome nights you can never go to sleep.

For you, that's normal. For me, it's an actual voice, belonging to an actual person. The personality which we refer to as Soul, the intangible and invisible half of this existence called a *doppelgeist*. A 'double-ghost'; a person who has died yet their body and spirit remain walking the world. One half the aforementioned Soul, and the other half being me. The physical remains of a local bookstore owner named John Flicker.

Body & Soul, John Flicker redux in stereo. Same man's memories and thoughts and feelings, now photocopied by the universe into two separate viewpoints.

So what are you seeing, then?

A faint shiver of air across my nerve endings, primarily in my shoulders and arms, flowing down my forearms, fingertips, away and hovering somewhere in the vicinity of the space between Lyneisha and me, over the table.

It's like there's a sort of spiral shape made of...fuzzy orange light that keeps dimming and almost dying out. When the clock was going at it hardest, I saw the spiral shape unwinding, expanding...then disappearing a few feet out from the clock's body. Like the opening credits of "The Twilight Zone."

"Anything?"

"There's a sort of orange spiral shape, fuzzy-edged, coming off the clock. But it spins out and fades."

She pursed her lips. "That could be funky."

"Funky how?"

"Does it only do it during the crying jag?"

Soul confirmed it did. I relayed this to her.

"What about right now? While it's ticking away?"

There's normal air disturbances. Some dust mites clouding around the base—whoever this friend of hers is needs to vacuum more often—and the air shivers a little each time there's a pendulum or a gear tripping over a notch. But no, no orange-fuzzy spiral. Although…

What?

…there's a blurry element…I can't focus on the clock face like I should be able to. That same dull-orange seems to haze around it.

I repeated all of this to Lyneisha. She frowned deeper. "I was afraid of that. It's Time."

"Time for what?"

"No, that distortion, that hazy spiral. It's Time. The clock's bleeding it."

Lyneisha is a telemetrist, sometimes joking referred to as a 'groper-feeler' in Under circles. She has a low-level ability to interact with objects and, in some manner nobody fully understands, pick up on what she calls 'resonance' with other objects, events or individual people.

It's not as useful an ability as you would think (hence the day job at an office where her co-worker Staci met her). It's not like in old novels where the psychic grabs the knife, melodramatically puts a hand to their forehead and declares to the whole sitting room *"Ah-ha! The killer was YOU!"* Then points histrionically at the butler or the heiress or whomever and everything else is simply anticlimax.

All it truly consists of is hearing the 'speech-hum' of objects. Which is a way of saying that if you could talk to animals, Doctor Doolittle style, you would have anything interesting come out of a sparrow's beak or a fat, old beagle's muzzle. Objects are even stupider, so to speak. Akin to the phenomenon of scientists using a fine-calibrated laser beam in the manner of record player's needle, picking up faint acoustic traces embedded in the clay of pottery that was thrown and fired seven thousand years ago. Very faint echoes and embedded whispers in the world of the inanimate.

Interpreting what you pick up is a much more difficult art, which is why many people with Lyneisha's tickle of ability don't always realize or bother developing it. It doesn't provide nearly as reliable or legally-binding a body of evidence as more established forensic methods. It doesn't give you lottery numbers. Like most realities in Everything Under, there are no silver bullets to dispatch problems, no magic wands or potions to cheat your way to resolution.

But Lyneisha is excellent at consulting with local art appraisers and auction houses as to the authenticity of something, when the provenance of a given antique is in doubt and the money in question is quite high. Which is why Lyneisha only has to work at that same office job part-time.

"Correct me if I'm wrong, but Time's not a real thing that clocks store or leak or whatever," I said. "It's a human construct to describe the passing of change. This fine piece of wood-mongery here is basically a useful toy." I held up a hand to the clock. "No offense." The clock gave no indication if it was hurt by the comment.

"So say the quantum physicists, sure," Lyneisha replied. "But Time is change, as you said. And change is very real and very powerful. Time is real, though I don't have nearly the PhDs to get to the real nub of the matter." She scratched at her temple, eyes slanting right-wise in that way that many con men say is a liar's tell but is simply creative thinking. "It's real. Maybe Time is an expression of space getting bored with monotony." A chuckle. "My guess is, this clock is resonating with something bad in the time stream and the weeping is how it expresses its distress about it. Some objects, if they're old enough or in the vicinity of a given owner long enough, get very settled into place, and settled into time. Clocks are very susceptible to it because they're partly inanimate embodiments. They're seen as physical manifestation of Time to many people, even if they really are simply 'toys' as you put it, man-made and man-defined."

"You lost me around the point that a clock has feelings."

"Not feelings. This clock doesn't have any thoughts, no stake in whatever it's picked up or soaked in from its past owners. What it's like is more…a brainless parrot, mimicking that something bad is going to happen in the quantum-flood of Time that very lightly brushes against it as it tocks away the hours."

"It ticks, it doesn't tock. Wrong clock model. So what's the orange spiral supposed to be, then? Time spinning out and dying away from the clock?"

"In a way. That haze you described over the clock face can also be a manifestation of how Time obscures things. One second to the next is pretty much the same, but the overall flow and feel of Time is a turbulent thing. It's not a river or a stream or a string like many people picture. It's more like a bomb that is constantly exploding, blowing outwards in every direction, then some piece of stray shrapnel goes off in one particular way and sets off the next bomb, which blows in every direction, collapses against one trail of shrapnel, and repeats."

"Picturesque way of saying 'time flies.'" I stood up and ran a hand along the smooth side of the clock. Up to down, then down to up. *Nice varnish finish.*

Stop that.

I jerked my hand back.

Lyneisha caught the movement. "Are you okay?"

The curve-shapes…the whole thing turned blank for a second. Like a television switched off. And a bird noise.

What?

It tasted like Italian wedding soup mixed with furniture polish, then it stopped when you pulled your hand off. And it made a sound, like a robin being interrupted in mid-chirp. Now it's back to the orange creamsicle spinning again. But for a moment, it was like it was because of you. Pulling away from you. Like…the wood cringed?

Lyneisha repeated her question. I shook my head. "I'm fine." Sat back down at the table.

"You looked like something was wrong when you touched it."

"Just a feeling."

"Something wrong with it?"

More like something wrong with us. The underside of my hand where I'd touched it didn't offer any special sensations. No unique coldness or flush of heat. The usual room-temperature meat and bones.

"Are you having problems with Time and change yourself, lately?"

Hrm.

Yes and no. My problem wasn't with Time. Time was no enemy of mine. After all, it seemed these days I had no true friend *but* Time. Time and Time and Time and Time.

But change? Yeah. Change was kicking my ass for the nonce. Particularly change in the form of having Trina, our friendly neighborhood neophyte vampire, living under the same roof with us.

"Want to talk about it?"

I shrugged.

"It could help. Especially when you're talking to somebody with no stake in the matter. Except to help."

I considered it.

****

The first night Trina stayed with us.

Lying across the cot, shoes and socks off. Reading some randomly-chosen book on the details of over five hundred artificial varieties of roses. I had gotten to the pictorial on the Chrysler Imperial Rose and the description of its deep-crimson, teahouse-shaded petals when Trina cleared her throat, the esophageal equivalent of the tap of the fork to the edge of the champagne flute at wedding receptions.

Looking up, I saw a mirror of my posture, resting on the cot kitty-corner to mine. I'd shoved aside some of the bookshelves that had lined the interior brick wall of the shop to give Trina her own partition of space in the makeshift apartment that was once the rearmost landscape-and-gardening section of The Nookery, my former-bookstore-now-oddball-residence. She sat widthwise on the cot, shoes off, legs straight out but feet demurely together in a sweet-but-funereal position.

Vampires don't age in an appreciable fashion. Her hair was still the jet-black bob it had been when we'd first met, though she'd made some attempts at variety by bleaching and coloring a pale blue streak in the forelocks that dangled like fragile raven tail feathers over her forehead. A face made from that kind of pale off-white plastic used in inexpensive kids' beginner chess sets, even the semi-elliptical of its contours combined with her petite size making me think of a pawn sitting alone on a line of otherwise-captured fellows.

It was the eyes. Their occasional flashes of weak violet light like the afterimage of summer lightning on your inner eye. Those gave away to the most casual observer that she was something other than human.

How had I ended up here?

I closed the book on my right thumb, saving the page on the full-page pen-and-watercolor of the Chrysler Imperial. "Yes?"

"It's four in the morning."

I glanced at the alarm clock she'd brought with her, sitting on my desk across the room and giving out a hot glare of LED digits, every minute that passed looking accusatory. "So it is."

She smiled.

I stared back.

A tilt of the head. That summer lightning afterimage, for only a heartbeat. "So can I go to bed, or do you want to keep reading?"

"Oh." I let my thumb slip from the book. "Sorry. Totally lost track of time."

"S'okay." She drew her legs up, curling around on her backside, pivoting to match the lengthwise position of the cot. It was one of those classic institutional models, cast-aluminum with a chipped gray enamel finish, those curved-arch head and foot bars terminating in rubber-toed ends just like my own.

I regarded her movements in silence, and then the action and implications struck me. "Wait, you need to sleep?"

She was halfway through pulling the topsheet and blanket out from under her and swinging it over her lower body. She stopped when I spoke. "Not exactly, but rest. Yeah. They taught that the best way was I should lie down and close my eyes when I start to feel out-of-it. You know, like when you're up all night buzzing on caffeine, an energy drink kind of thing?"

"I can recall the feeling. But you're not physically tired?"

She seesawed her hand. "They said it's all in the head, not the body. But yeah, I feel a bit zonked so thought I'd lie down. Let the brain cells clear out, you know?"

"Sure. Sorry I kept you up. I didn't know."

She smiled. The off-white plastic softened and was the malleable flesh of a girl at last, matte-flat but a longer-lasting impression than any piece on a board. "It's all right. I didn't say anything for a while because I didn't want to interrupt you reading."

I clicked off the small clip-on lamp attached to the head-bar of my cot. Blackness draped the room.

I settled into the thin mattress. Let my thoughts relax. Stared up into the dark where I knew the chipped plaster of the ceiling was. My eyes adjusted, and I could make out the faintest impressions of the room thanks to the weak streetlight that trickled through the soap-paint whorls of the old store windows.

We should consider getting the ceiling in here re-done.

Is it that bad?

My opinion might not be the most useful. A shush across the beams. *I mean, without thinking about it, I can look at this surface so minutely each crack is like a mosaic laid out in the Sistine Chapel for all the sense of scale I could keep in mind.*

Maybe next month or so.

It's not like we need to worry about the expense for once.

I shifted on the cot, frowning into the dark. *I don't want to spend any more of the money than is necessary. So far we've been good about getting the necessities addressed. Let's keep it at that.*

I'm all for necessities, but have you noticed how much plaster dust is getting on the tops of the book piles in here?

Not lately, no.

Next time it's light, look.

"John?"

"Yes?"

"Are you tired?"

"Not really."

The silence of a record player needle when it hit the blank radius of the album, spinning on its turntable. The Nookery provided the soundtrack with its clicks and cracks. Faint hums of water sloshing through some pipe buried deep in the walls. The only sounds missing from the room were the breathing of the occupants.

"Are you going to sleep too?"

"I don't sleep."

I heard a shift in bedclothes.

"Really?"

"Really."

A creak of floorboards under her cot's legs. "You said you could control all that stuff. But you really don't need to sleep, like the no-eating and no-breathing stuff?"

"Really."

"But I thought…I mean, I remember in health class in school sometime, they said that people *have* to sleep or they go crazy. That's what I have to rest for, like sleep but not all-the-way dreaming stuff."

"That's true."

Another pause. "So are you crazy?"

She sounds only half-kidding.

"No more so than anybody else I know."

"How do you do that?"

That pressed my own pause button.

Then: "I don't know. Never gave much thought to it these last few years."

"How is that?"

"Not sure. I guess my attention wavered. I didn't need to sleep, so at some point I stopped noticing that I wasn't."

"But you don't feel off at all?"

Another thought on it. "Not that I can tell, no."

Quiet again. But now awkward.

It was all neuroses of course. As the physical half of a doppelgeist I don't need any of the usual requirements a living body needs to survive. I knew it was all psychosomatic, couldn't be anything else.

But lying there as I'd done countless times since our death a few years prior, it suddenly felt wrong with Trina's commenting on it. The way you can have tics, a twitch of your mouth when you laugh or drumming of your fingers on a desk that only feel embarrassing when someone else remarks on it.

Why was I lying there, staring up at the ceiling in the pitch black? Shouldn't I be up and about, always active at some task if I didn't need to be lying down or pretending to rest? The old, internal hectoring, as habitual and established as anything. Mental hangnails like college football cheers and motivational speaker seminars: *Be active, Be doing, Be somebody!*

It occurred to me as a vague but sizable figure, how often in a given week I could find myself lying down or sitting in the blue nubbly-textured armchair nearby, reading book after book or leafing through illustrated portfolios like that collection of roses. If I went online and discovered some latest hit television series or podcast, I could sit and absorb it utterly...only to get a phone call or finish watching its entirety and realize it had been days and nights without stopping, uninterrupted in the monomania of distraction.

I never paid any attention to that either.

I wouldn't have expected you to think of it. Neither of us needs sleep these days.

Yeah, but I'm still conscious, such as that is. A mild shiver of air like the last gasp of when you've opened a refrigerator door, as your skin goosepimples at the touch. *And I never noticed that I just...don't stop. Or you, either.* A bodiless shifting, somewhere near my stomach and below the cot. *Do you think you could? If you* wanted *to?*

I closed my eyes. Tried to remember the feeling. That hypnagogic, almost drunken feeling of succumbing to sleep. Letting your eyelids take on twenty pounds as they dragged and glued firmly shut over your eyes. Your mind uncoupling, a rocket ship floating free from its dock in the spaceport, drifting out into the darkness of dream. How it would pass like nothing, and you would open your eyes to find the clocks had all betrayed you, tricking the world into jumping hours past what you remembered.

Nothing. Not even a twinge of tiredness. Still as aware and capable of movement, of decision and action, as I recall being any other moment.

I guess you can't will yourself to feel something you don't. I adjusted my position on the bed, letting my legs completely stretch out. *On the plus side, I don't seem to suffer sleep deprivation.*

Yeah, suppose that's a good thing. Another shift of air in my ear canals, the prelude to your ears popping from a sea pressure change, but the pop never comes. The voice-sensation in my head elevated…the ceiling, somewhere to the left. *Good thing you don't have sleep issues. I mean, like the old Bard said, 'what dreams may come?'*

I rolled over, facing the brick wall. Let my fingertips play at the rough mortar, as if I was trying to decipher some masonic braille.

But after a few minutes of restless scrabbling I sat up, moving as quietly as I could to pivot around and get my feet back on the floor.

"John?"

A wink of pale amethyst, as a cigarette lighter's spin-wheel sparking briefly.

"Yeah?"

"Why did you ask Justin to let me live with you?"

I've been wondering that myself.

Shut up.

Sorry, Touchy. Feel free to field this one.

"I wanted to help. You're going through a tricky time right now with the transition. Even with the training they've given you…I figured you might want to be around someone who appreciates what it's like. Dealing with big changes."

"Oh." The dark shape on the other cot swallowed the

response and digested it for a while. Then in a smaller voice, barely audible: "Thanks."

I waited another couple of minutes to see if the dark had any more questions. But there was only one isolated sigh.

I didn't feel comfortable anymore. I put my shoes on and went deeper into the store's depths, hunting around for science fiction novels or a travelogue that would interest me. After fruitless hunting and sifting as long as I could stand, I gave up and used the abandoned front entrance to go outside.

I went walking in the early morning hours. What Robert Frost would've called the lonely watches of the night. Everything smelling of leaves and the first pastry bread baking from one of the patisseries along Third Avenue.

Soul followed along, making meandering paths through fence rails or along the pavement. Occasionally mumbling about details in the cracks or the leaves blowing in the skinny oak trees. For the most part, we were silent. Rocket ships sharing trajectories in space, cut off from radio communication.

When I reached the corner at Schiller Park, a Columbus *Dispatch* newspaper delivery van passed me. Like an idiot, I found myself waving at its passing as if I knew the driver or thought he saw me as he went by.

After that, I simply stood at the corner. When a smeary gray-blue dawn began leaking into the world, I returned to find Trina sitting in a corner by the windows, reading an old collection of Calvin & Hobbes comic strips.

That was the first night.

****

Lyneisha sneezed and excused herself.

I shook my head. "No. It's all right. No need to have a bitching fest about minor housekeeping issues."

She nodded, said nothing.

"So how do we stop the clock from going all orange and sobby every hour and driving your friend nuts?"

She stared up at the clock, tapping a bubblegum-pink

nail on the table. "These objects are delicate. The connection probably wasn't prominent or aligned this way until it was shipped overseas and put here. It might've stayed dormant for decades at her great-uncle's home."

"Can it be repaired?"

"That's probably the best way to deal with it." She stood up and touched a fingertip to the clock face, as if to caress the hands under the glass frontispiece. "It's gorgeous, isn't it?"

"They don't make them like this anymore, that's for sure."

"That's it, then."

We left the apartment, Lyneisha locking the door behind her as I stood a few feet away on the tiny porch-step, waiting to walk her to my car.

She gave a sigh as she pocketed the keys. "I'll tell Staci to call a specialist who does heirloom clock repair. I know a guy through one of my auctioneer friends. She doesn't have to say what, just ask him to come out and do a cleaning and check of the gearworks inside. He'll do some spritzing with lubricants, wipe down the pendulums with mineral spirits. Re-hang the counterweights, most likely. It should disturb the internal atmosphere of the whole thing enough to stop it doing that."

We walked to where my car was parked at a little concrete island, the designated visitor's parking in the center of the lot.

"You sounded almost disappointed."

She gave a shrug that jounced the ropes of dark hair on her shoulders. "In a way." A wry smile twisted at the last second into an out-of-level frown. "Kind of, yeah. I mean, annoying or not, that thing in there is *unique.* Or at least, it will be until Staci gets some repairman to go fumbling around in it with some bronze polish and pipe cleaners and take that away."

"A repairman won't change that it's a beautiful piece of work, right?"

"Maybe." We arrived at my time-beaten '77 Vega and I opened the passenger door for her. She hesitated before lowering herself into the passenger seat. "Are you sure you don't want the usual fifty-fifty cut? I mean…you really helped me out. Before I thought of calling you I was feeling a total idiot because all my readings on it came up clean."

"I'm fine for money right now."

"I couldn't get any reading off it, and what you showed me makes sense now. It wasn't anything in the clock's history or interactions before affecting it, so telemetry was useless in this case."

"No. Thanks though. I mainly appreciated the chance to get out of the house."

"But you live in a bookstore."

"Ha-ha. Get in the car."

As I climbed into the driver's seat I discovered her looking at me the way people do when they're not sure if they want to come out and ask if you stole something of theirs or not.

"Seriously, is everything all right? When you touched it, it looked like it burned you, or you got a splinter or something."

"Nothing. When I touched it…it felt like I was doing something wrong, that's all. I trust my instincts."

"I doubt the clock is dangerous."

It wasn't the clock that I was thinking of in that way. But how to explain that even inanimate objects had the right idea nowadays? That we were a quantity to best be avoided rather than encountered?

As I started up the engine and pulled away from the townhome, I couldn't help ruminating out loud.

"Interesting thing to consider though."

"What?"

"Well, I mean…it's all good to get it to stop crying." I signaled to make the turn to leave the complex, looking both ways before pulling out. "But it raises the question: what was it crying *about*?"

2.

"I'd like to have a washer and dryer. You have a cellar where we could put those, so it wouldn't be in your way."

Crap.

I never had aspirations of owning a home.

Back in the breathing-and-eating days I was fairly happy renting the small townhouse a few blocks north of my bookshop. I was relatively content with a desire to not bother with any major home maintenance that couldn't be solved by calling the management and letting them worry about the details.

Ownership of a home was, for me, tied to a lot of other things that seemed to go with it in a total package of prerequisites: marriage, kids, small dog and/or cat, two-point-one fuel-efficient mini-vans with turn-back easy-carriage seats and lots of trunk area. And cupholders. Lawnmower comparison-shopping at the Sears Outlet store.

A house suggested the kind of stability that would—I presumed—never permeate my life.

If I'm to be completely honest about myself, it was also held to largely high-school-stunted ideas of being the slick urban bachelor, living in my suave Victorian-fixed-up-run-down townhome in cramped German Village. Maintaining my own business, living fairly fancy-free, as the saying goes. Not rich, but not bogged down either.

I still have no desire to own a house. Though now that could be due to being a disembodied Soul with no need for physical lodgings or the usual trappings of clothing, food, sleep and so on. I doubt any realty office is swarming to beat down the door to check a dead man's credit rating for a large mortgage and swollen annual percentage rate, either.

Trina sat on the overstuffed nubbly-blue-upholstered chair we reserve for our rare guests. She'd dragged it across the room closer to her cot where her feet were propped, ankles crossed.

"I can't keep sponge-bathing out of the sink in your little bathroom day after day."

Body put his hands behind his head, resting back against the wall as he sprawled across his cot. He closed his eyes as I pulled my attention away from the dust mote cloud that hovered in the light coming through the store windows.

She's got a point. It's not like I get off on watching her do it every night, either.

When you want absolute privacy in your own mind, there's nothing like having your disembodied Soul around. Flittering around your physical form, sharing much the same thought processes, memory and viewpoint as you, only intangible and invisible, utterly inaudible to the rest of the world.

No, seriously. There's nothing like it. Because it's neither absolute nor private.

She saw his attention was not entirely lost and pressed the point. "And not always having to dig for clean clothes at the bottom of my overnight bag would be nice, too."

I know she's right, Body replied. *I'm not looking forward to having a bunch of people in and out of the place.*

All we had done to accommodate Body's minimal living needs was clear the rearmost storeroom of the free-standing bookshelves in the middle of the floor area. Then a cot from Army-Navy surplus, a dollar-store clip-lamp affixed to the cot's steel crossbar, a couple of salvaged chairs, desk, a dorm microwave and fridge in a corner, and an area rug on the hardwood flooring left open in the middle.

That was it. Less overall furnishing than you'd find in some of your cheapest hole-in-the-wall motor lodge rooms.

The Nookery being the collection of decades that it is, a lot of sensory input and memories have had time to clutter, degrade, mix and blow around like any dust and dead termites would in such a ratchety refurbished shop.

Some parts of The Nookery taste like leather and lemonade. Leavings of when it was a tannery. Sometimes I can smell bootstrap oil and cherrywood tobacco. Head shop days from the sixties when they sold 'water pipes' and other thinly-veiled marijuana paraphernalia.

Other afternoons there can be a single beam of sunlight from one of the few skylights down into a room of books and I see jigsaw puzzles in the dust motes.

The building amuses itself. We have been firmly convinced of that since our first months making it our permanent home. When I ran the shop, making what razor-thin profit margin I could, the place was a great novelty. Several buildings crammed together and bridged and connected with various knocked-down walls and interconnected wooden hallways almost like fistulas forming in a human body, incorrectly connecting one organ with another completely unrelated one, all becoming a hodge-podge gestalt of spaces and cramped crevices.

Not sure whether it was always hiding itself from our full awareness…or whether becoming what we are somehow catalyzed its newest behavior. Either way, there's no question The Nookery has some sort of nascent awareness, an energy that has nothing to do with the kilowatt hours from AEP flowing through the outlets.

I've learned since becoming disembodied that the older some buildings get, the more the structure doesn't feel a need to be inhabited by anything but time and air. People are incidental at best to its construction…after that, a lot of buildings can take or leave the bipedal intrusions. Do oak trees spend a lot of time wanting to talk to the acorns on the ground around its roots? And how much sentimentality do you get about the gloves used by the doctor that delivered you? People are ultimately seen by a building as necessary functionaries, otherwise to be ignored or let on their way.

Trina ignored the hints of exasperation coming off Body like radio signals.

"Why don't you have a regular apartment? With a bathroom and bedroom and kitchen and all that?"

A sigh drew out from Body's mouth. He rubbed his eyes so he wouldn't have to look at her while he talked. I knew the trick. It'd been mine too, once upon a time.

"Because point number one." He held up an index finger, "it is more expensive than moving into the bookstore. Or at least, it was when I first came to this setup a few years ago. Point two." The middle finger went up to join the index, "it is a difficult thing to maintain any property in your name after you're dead. The Nookery, unlike my old duplex rental down the road, is so tangled in a bizarre real estate and probate limbo that nobody seems to've gotten around to noticing I'm no longer a living tax-paying citizen. Point three, and this is most key for this discussion." The ring finger joined the middle and index, like an umpire declaring the batter out, "I no longer eat, sleep, breathe, drink, shed dead hair or skin cells, get drunk, get hung over, throw up, or in any way effectively still do the things that living people do, therefore do not need all the different facilities under one roof to do them in or on." He let the hand completely drop to his chest with a thump.

She tilted her head to the side, a pout protruding from her lips. "I don't need to eat or sleep or most of that either, you know."

"Not the same."

"How is it not the same?"

"You're still…we're not the same way. You still technically function in some ways like a living person, just not the same as your former metabolism did. You can still do things like cut your hair, meaning it can be shed or changed. If I try to shave what stubble I have off, it's back on my face within the hour. You still feed, in a manner of speaking. You can still feel pain or injury."

As he made the remark, it struck me how true it was: Christ, even direct-breed vampires were closer to living than we were now. It was a sobering thing to have splashed into your thinking, like dishwater tossed out a windowsill as you're walking beneath it.

"Do you realize," Trina grinned, "that you just gave the best argument for why I need these things put in here instead of simply leaving the store the way it is?"

He lifted the hand that had been over his eyes and raised his head to look at her. No smiles or frowns or smirks or glares.

"*Hnn.* Fine. You're absolutely right. We need to make some changes here if you're going to live here."

"Or we could simply go look for an apartment…"

The coquette voice, the little extra twist of the tilted neck so the chin demurely near-touched the collarbone, eyes askance.

"No, we are not getting an apartment."

"Why not? It'd be easier than having to renovate parts of the store, wouldn't it?"

"In the short term, yes. Have you ever had an apartment of your own?"

"Not entirely. I had roommates. But if you mean have I moved out of my parents' house and lived on my own, yeah. I've paid my own bills and such."

"Never mind that we don't have endless supplies of money—"

"Justin would—"

"Justin would expect you and I to eventually fend for ourselves if we're to fend at all."

Not to mention there's no way we want to be any more beholden to the vampire community than we already are.

Agreed. "Look, we'll have the work done and I promise you will be made more at-home soon."

"So about the washer-dryer thing? I'm sure we could get those put in right away even while waiting on everything else. Are there at least water hookups, like maybe in the cellar?"

The moment she said 'cellar' I felt cold. More like I suddenly and involuntarily had a memory of what cold felt like, similar to having the spine tickled with the tip of an icicle.

Body sat up from the cot.

"Don't go into the cellar, okay? I mean it, not even to look for water hookups."

"What," she laughed, "are there bodies buried down there you don't want me to find?"

Body simply stared back. "I wish I could tell you 'no' with absolute certainty."

She stopped laughing, inspecting his expression for a moment.

"You're screwing with me."

"I wish. This building is over a century old and in its time all these different buildings that were hollowed out and joined up with weird little corridors and staircases has been all kinds of different things. Flophouse, tannery, apartment buildings, a head shop back in the sixties, who knows what else. I don't know much of anything beyond a sketch about The Nookery's history. And I haven't been to the cellar since I first started coming in to create the bookstore. It's a lot like the upper part: made up of all the different spaces that have had walls knocked down or corridors carved through them to make it all one thing, but nowhere near all neat and planned out."

"What, you're scared?"

"Not so much 'scared' as 'owing a respectful distance.' The Nookery sometimes has a mind of its own. Think of the cellar as its subconscious."

She didn't shiver, but there was a visible discomfort in her posture. "You're trying to mess with me."

"No. But in the unlikely event that you'd get me to go down there with you, odds are good this building is too old to have proper modern-day-compatible fixtures down there anyway."

I moved over to Body and momentarily sluiced through his vocal chords, a whistle through fan-blades in that freaky metallic-warble note that always marks when I attempt to communicate with him as my medium.

"*If it helps discourage you any further in exploring down there,*" I said in my shaky burble, "*even I don't go floating around down there.*"

She looked up at the ceiling. Looked down at the floor.

"Crud. Was hoping to get a washer and dryer in at least."

"We'll get things fixed up, I promise you, all right?"

He gave her a smile and she finally returned it.

"Hey, come to think of it," another tilt of the head, "where is the door to the cellar anyhow? I at least want to know which door is off-limits in this place."

"Good question. And if you ever find it, be sure to let me know where it is too."

She let this settle in the air for a few silent minutes.

"Are you serious about getting some things done so we can live here?"

"I promised. I wasn't bullshitting you."

She got up and went to her little black leather purse sitting on our desk. Dug into it and pulled out a business card, which she walked over to Body and held out to him.

I huddled closer to his shoulder so I could look at it as he took it from her. Before he turned it so he could see it, he paused in mid-reach.

"Wait a minute. Bathroom is one thing. Washer-dryer is another thing. But why am I having a kitchen put in this bookstore for you?"

Her eyes narrowed.

"Because I'm a vampire I don't deserve even a basic place where I can have a few things?"

"But you don't really eat anymore. Not like regular cooked meals and foods needing heating up or anything." He narrowed his eyes. "Do you?"

She frowned. "That's considered a personal question."

He sat up as she went back to curling up on the nubbly blue chair. "Sorry. You're going to have to teach me some of the rules so I don't screw things up too badly with you." A sigh. "But you're living here with me now, so I think we have to share a few personal things between each other, if we're going to get along."

She looked at her nails as if checking for a burr or a hangnail somewhere, though filing these was like an obsessive-compulsive tic with her. Proof in point, she reached behind her to the desk for a stray nail file and began to whisk it across the tip of an index finger as she spoke. Another one of Justin's habits she'd apparently started aping. "There are...ways to prepare things. Would you want to eat the same thing over and over, even if you could or needed to?"

He shrugged. "Fair enough." Turned over the card to look at the print. A rich cream-bond...heavy stock, it looked like.

"Justin said to give this to you. It's a contractor company to do the work. Apparently they're really good, and they know about this stuff."

"Never knew a contractor to have embossed print on a linen business card."

"Justin says they're the best people to hire for this, and I guess he was going to tell them to expect you to call them anyways."

Great. Glad to know Justin's keeping tabs on us even now. I sidled away towards an upper corner of the room, near the top of the bookshelves. Body tucked the card into a jean pocket.

After another minute or so of Trina's whisk-scratching at her nails with the file, I floated over the desk to peruse the various bills and junk mail lying around.

"Did Justin say anything else? Give you anybody else's cards to call in case of something?"

Trina didn't look up from her nails. That faint violet, not quite a reflective glitter like a cat when you look at it from the right angle of a light shining in its eyes, flashed in her own orbs for a split-second as I moved past her towards the front windows. She had a similar flit in the air around her, something like winter rain and bitter coffee grounds that I've come to associate with some people as uncertainty crossed with a species of frustration.

"Nope."

Our relationship with the local vampire community is an odd one. We are, in the larger picture, on good account with them. Especially after our most recent little escapade dealing with a maddened demon-god-wannabe that had killed one of their esteemed local pillars of the bloodfeeder community. As nominal chairman of their board, the nightclub owner we know as Justin considered us on friendly terms enough to ask for our help once in a while.

New vampires like Trina represent a danger to the established order, feeding rampantly or without regard for merit of target. Risking exposure of the community to the day-to-day world. My overall impression is that in most cases it would be less a danger nowadays, in the age of "vampire hunter" novels and books about hunky, pouty-lipped vamps glittering like Bedazzled Levi jeans. There would be some media rumbling, but mostly public dismissal as hoax or some other banality. More an embarrassment, an inconvenience of public relations for the community. But still a problem.

Vampire societies are wary of 'outsiders,' defined as anyone other than themselves. They have their contracted employees and networks. Nobody works entirely in vacuum. But even 'friendlies' amongst the Under are not considered part of the real fold. Werewolves and related 'thropes get along with them all right. Some other vampire varieties like nosferati and lamias also can coexist with them okay.

A *doppelgeist* is considered something of an oddity. Think of a Chinese finger trap that may or may not have a miniature mousetrap spring loaded in its center. You can stick your fingers in, play around with it, have a laugh…but you're never sure if there isn't going to be something that suddenly chomps down and costs you a fingertip or two.

Whether it's fear or the predator sense picking up that we're not acceptably vulnerable-enough prey to bother with, I don't know. Maybe both.

****

Another handful of days passed in which we did our best to avoid Trina. Our ready-made excuse was the frequent intrusion of workmen going in and out of the bookstore.

It only took a phone call to the number on the card she'd given us. An exchange of numbers, The Nookery's address. A time for the main foreman to come out and take a look at the property.

"This place is a mess."

His professional estimate was concise. He spent half an hour walking the perimeter of the property, another half looking through some of the larger rooms.

"It was originally a bunch of different buildings on this one block." Body sounded like he was apologizing for it.

"I can see that." He was a sand-haired, rawboned amalgamation of a person but had surprisingly pale skin and a gawky-teen way of walking that shifted his shoulders more than related to his arms swinging at his sides. He asked to see the Liliputian bathroom that had once been allowed only for employees and paying customers, barely large enough to house a single toilet crammed next to a wall-mounted sink. It was reminiscent of one of your more 'luxurious' coach-class airplane johns.

He glared at the light fixtures. Peered up a couple of staircases. Back into the bathroom. Ran the tap. Flushed the toilet. Listened at the walls while making perfunctory knocks of his knuckles against them.

"Going to be a bitch bringing in stuff with some of these smaller rooms between the back and the bathroom. You sure you don't have water lines a little closer? I could empty out one of those other rooms back towards the street access. Make you a nice full bath there without having to traipse through your space so much."

"I don't mind that so much. I'd like to keep as much of the building intact as we can manage."

"I'm still gonna have to knock out this one wall here." He knocked knuckles against the wall where the sink was mounted. "Re-route the plumbing and give it more floor space, so you can have a full shower and bath, a new set of water-efficient fixtures. You'll need to empty out the room right next to this."

"That was one of the closets when I first moved in. I used it for storing posters and some remaindered half-off book sale stuff. That's fine. But the bigger rooms down the way, near the alley side...those are a little tougher."

"Why? You've got door access to two of them that I could

see, right off the little side garden you have down there."

"Those doors were nailed and painted shut. From the 'I Like Ike' pin I found lodged in one, I think since the Korean War. They might as well be decorative walls."

He looked at Body as if in disbelief, shook his head, and resumed to knocking on walls. He took out a stud finder to check the struts on the load-bearing walls to the bathroom. A couple of terse, competent-looking measurements noted in a small notebook that emerged from another pouch of his tool belt.

"Huh." He re-checked the stud-finder. He crossed something out in his notebook, wrote a revision in with a stub of pencil. "Weird. Different strut counts on the second pass-through."

Body didn't say a word.

I spent most of my time listening but otherwise staying in other rooms within hearing. The stud finder made an irritating electronic bird-chirp/hum to me. Living ears didn't pick it up but it was like a broken dog whistle for me when I got too close. Some battery-operated devices are like that; though for some reason newer devices that use rechargeables don't make noises. Maybe it's something to do with older disposable batteries.

Finally he was done examining walls and counting fixtures. He shook hands with Body and left, shaking his head all the way back to his large Navigator (another thing we had never noted a contractor to drive, shiny and looking totally impractical for hauling so much as a single two-by-four on its kid-leather backseats).

The next morning there arrived a half-dozen Ford and Chevy pickups, a small caravan that parked along the street at the back of the shop. The travails of renovation had begun.

****

They used the back entrance for bringing in the lumber and other materials, which meant they were regularly tramping through our makeshift apartment as the foreman had warned. They made sure to stay on the plastic hall-runner that one of them had thoughtfully taped down before work began.

We trusted that Trina would oversee things to her satisfaction. For our own part we didn't care much how it went either way. In this way, we managed to get through five days without incident. Or by avoiding incident, which anyone can tell you isn't the same.We stayed in the living-space of the backroom while the workmen did their thing, operating a rough and hectic schedule of dawn to dusk. None of them stayed any later than the first touch of the sun to the horizon, though we never thought to ask if this was a labor union thing or perhaps some of the workers needed to go before it got dark.

Two days into the job, one stocky-built and beard-stubbled fellow, bearing a massive armload of lumber, almost fell down a staircase during one of his runs for materials.

"Damned thing wasn't there all the other trips in before," he insisted after Body gave him a bottled water while he wiped his face with a red plaid bandanna. He looked utterly bewildered. The staircase he pointed to was only a few steps downwards between rooms that had started in adjoining buildings. The boards he'd dropped lay like a scatter of giant, unsharpened pencils along the steps. But I couldn't say definitively that the room hadn't been on the same level with the short hallway before.

I noticed he dabbed the bandanna at his lip where a small dot of green pooled, like a tiny emerald.

Check the lip, I remarked.

"Do you need more water?" Body offered a second unopened bottle.

The workman looked into Body's eyes, wiped at his mouth, made the dot disappear. Took the bottle with a nod of thanks.

Maybe a *tarbh usige.* Sometimes called tarbells or—with the classic tasteless humor of the Under—'tar babies.' An old Scottish thing, though by now most in the Under have become part of the great melting pot that America once promised to be and only the Under truly has made manifest. Also known as a 'water bull.' Powerfully built, muscled types. Husky and able to carry great loads, but tend to get dry-mouthed pretty quick. Not absolutely certain, but it's rude to ask things like that in the

Under. Like when you ask an overweight woman when her baby is due, only to have her frown and respond with "*What* baby?"

"If you need any more, there's a fridge there in the back room. Help yourself."

He tucked the unopened bottle into one of the sizable open holster pockets of his work belt.

"I'm John. Flicker. I own this place."

"I know." He took a glance around at the bookshelves, the posters and few hanging paper mobiles advertising outdated paperback sales from years ago. "This place is huge."

"Our motto used to be 'Get Lost!'"

"I believe it." He seemed to consider something, then the mental coin flip was finished and put out his hand. "Scotty. Craig. I work for the crew here."

I smiled and accepted his hand. "I kinda figured. Either that or you're a guy with a fetish for carrying tons of lumber through strangers' stores."

He smiled nervously and was quick to relinquish the handshake.

From there on, Scotty Craig made sure to carry a few less boards so he could see the space ahead of him as he trudged through the building.

****

Five or so days in. The news relayed through Trina was that another day or two to put in tile and finish grouting the edges of everything, and the bathroom would be finished. The kitchenette had also had its bare bones laid down in lumber and wiring, and would be done within another week.

"It's really cool," she effused. Trina sat on the nubbly armchair in the apartment. Body was tossing some old bills into a trash bag, trying to straighten up some piles of books near his cot. "They brought in all these chunks of plastic and shells and put the tub together. Like it was a jigsaw puzzle."

"That's cool."

She continued with details of the renovations, mentioning

something about blue tiles for the bathroom. Somehow *blue* struck a chord, setting off a chain of little mnemonic bells in my thoughts that woke me up.

Blue. Blue like baby clothes for a boy. Newborn. Bris. A bris ceremony. Shit. We're late to meet with Loewenstein.

That was today? I thought it was tomorrow.

It was *tomorrow. Now tomorrow is* today. *You better get your coat and let's get moving.*

Body shuffled around Trina to get across the room for his coat draped on one end of the desk.

She got up from the chair to face him.

"I really need to talk about all this stuff with you!"

He shrugged, giving that familiar 'sorry-shucks' face as he pulled on the lightweight London Fog trenchcoat. "I'm sorry, Trina, but I forgot that we have an appointment to meet with a friend about some research we asked them to do for me. I'm already late."

"You promised you'd take this seriously."

"And I do. Believe me. Listen, you just brought all this stuff up now. It's only bad timing, I promise, it's not me avoiding you on this subject."

She was a good head and a half shorter than Body's six feet in height. But putting her hands on her hips and tilting that onyx-hair-framed pale face to one side, she reminded me of being a kid, getting tongue-lashed by my mother. "This is not *new* stuff. I've tried to bring it up like three times this week. There's always some reason why you can't talk to me about it."

That's true. She's picked up on that much already.

Crap.

"Look, I promise we will sit down and talk about it when I get back, okay? Absolutely and totally promise."

"I'd threaten to kill you if you don't, but that wouldn't make a difference, would it?"

He smiled, going from sorry-shucks to guilty admission but still moving to the door. It clunked against his hand as he tried the knob.

"I locked the door."

Another sigh. Body started to fumble into the coat pockets—

"I took your keys and hid them, too."

He started to hunt through the desk drawers for a long-ago set-aside set of duplicates.

"You gave me the other house keys, remember?"

He slammed the desk drawer. "Damn it, what is the *problem*?"

"I'm asking you the same thing!" She shifted, from the cot to right in front of me, pressed in close and blocked our path to the door. "You've been avoiding me this entire week, acting like I'm barely here, going out all the time! You *asked* Justin for this...this *thing* with you and me, but you've acted like I'm some crappy houseguest, like some mother-in-law you're always avoiding! What is going on?"

"I'm working on something, that's all."

"That's crap."

"It's not. I'm doing research on a problem, that's all. And I've also been doing some shoots for my friend Hal, you remember him? For some extra money."

"You told Justin you would look after me, you *promised*."

Christ on a cracker what have we gotten into *with this girl, what the hell are we even* doing *here in this?*

"I haven't forgotten you or avoided—"

She slammed her fist down on the desk. The blow dented the edge of the pressed steel top, sending half the junk mail and old bills into the air to *flap-plap* to the floor around the desk.

In the silence after, all that could be heard was the faint twanging of the desk's structure reverberating from the blow. The Nookery's walls and ceilings seemed like the scared only child, waiting with held breath to see what its parents would yell next.

She raised her fist, popped out the index finger to point into Body's face. The air around her looked like a heat-shimmer haze filled with dark blue-black champagne bubbles that felt like minor bruise-throbs and tasted of sour wine.

"I showed up with everything I have. You tossed my bag onto a cot, put my boxes in another room of junk. Ever since then, nothing. When I try to find you, you're not here or even when you are you're like a million years away."

"I'm sorry if it seems like—"

"*Bullshit.*" Violet sparks in the backs of her eyes. Those champagne bubbles popped into gluey, amorphous shapes that settled to the floor and faded like rose petals made of dry ice. "I *know* you're not working for that guy Hal doing video shoots because you haven't needed the money."

"That's—"

"He called here the other day when you left your phone at your desk, wanting to know where you'd been."

"I'm sorry—"

"I don't care about that." A bitter smirk. "Apparently neither does he. After I told him you were busy he remembered who I was and asked if I was interested in doing a girl-girl shoot he has planned next weekend. I told him I wasn't in the business anymore, and he said to tell you to call him when you get a chance and hung up."

That sounds like Hal all right.

"What's going on?"

Tell her.

I don't know what I would tell her right now.

The truth. She's seen enough at this point that maybe it won't shock.

It's still a shock to us.

True. But no point in adding sitcom misery to this by trying to hide it from her any longer.

I don't like the idea of getting her into this.

We already did that. If we're not going to treat her like an adult or another person what the hell is all this for anyway?

"I *hate* when you talk to yourself!" she snarled.

"Actually I was arguing in your favor."

She blinked, the weak sparks fading to dull lavender embers at the backs of her eyes. "S-sorry."

Body swallowed.

What the hell are we doing here? Why did we ask for this? We knew better. We should've known better.

The common wail of the human condition, whether you're

technically human or not: the desires and intentions that override good sense. The practicalities get washed away in a hail of gunfire optimism, only to slowly bleed and hemorrhage their painful way back into the picture under the glaring x-ray of mounting evidence. Reality does not allow much leeway for pretense, once it's begun with the best hope for the most illogically wonderful outcome.

What *had* we wanted to do here, asking Justin to make us Trina's blood partner? We had…what? Hoped to distract ourselves? Feel less alone in the big empty bookstore? Have someone to play mentor to? Some half-assed romantic aspirations straight out of a bad young adult fantasy novel? What did that say about my part in this partnership? I didn't have any stake in any romance here.

The quickest way to respond on that particular quiz was to simply check off "all of the above." There were percentages representing all of those possibilities.

Discovering there was something dangerous, something potentially nasty lurking between us in this dual existence…it hadn't factored in. Not enough. Not nearly enough.

Recent events had been a confusing whirlwind. Like winning the lottery as you get a terminal cancer diagnosis all in the middle of a Rio de Janeiro *carnevale* parade. Color and confusion, pain and calamity all mixed in with a tango-citrus flavor of thrilling discovery.

Had it *ever* occurred to Body or me, for more than a token minute? That this whole potential-for-destruction thing we found in our make-up wasn't something to blithely ignore? Or compound the error in judgment further by inviting someone else along to share the ride?

So stupid. Were we *that* lonely? Meghan had shunted us out of her life, clean and sharp as a cartoon villain hitting the trapdoor button and sending us shooting into the dark. Was that justification for dragging Trina in to…what? Surrogate our need for company? Quasi-romance in the making, a fledgling effort like the fumbling of a teenager trying to reach a girl's bra strap under the shirt in the backseat of a parked car?

So sure. Welcome the nubile, neophyte vampire into your sort-of bookstore-turned-maybe-haunted home. With your personal ghost/immortal dead-undead body status that's treated as pariah by the rest of the Under. Welcome her then completely piss all over her presence as you go back to brooding over your own navels.

What's the R.E.M. line? *Another prop, to occupy my time?*

Or worse than some sort of pubescent-hormonal desire for romance…had we invited her to life and home simply to give ourselves someone to *ignore?* Someone who needed us so we could in some parasitic, inverted way blow her off and thus feel wanted, feel more important and angst-tinged in this pathetic autobiographical melodrama wherein we pictured ourselves the hero?

Again: check off 'all of the above.'

And go to hell.

Introspection only gets you useful insights so far into the game. After that, it's repeating old sins of arrogant self-overvaluing.

Just because you discover a dragon, and it lets you take a ride on its scaly back, doesn't mean you should wave your friend to get on behind and join you, gripping your hips and hoping you know what you're doing. Discovery is not always a tandem bicycle ride. Having someone else there is not a safety valve, a backup gesture.

Trina was worth more than that circular, self-aggrandizing bullshit. But more embarrassing than us knowing that: she did, too.

"I'm sorry. It's not something wrong with you or you being here. It's about us. We recently—not to get crazy about it—need to do some research. Try to find out more about ourselves."

"I thought you'd settled all that."

He shook his head, staring at the floor. "Not by a long shot. What happened was, we started hitting walls and dead ends. Other things came up that distracted us, so we dropped it. But lately…we needed to pick it up again, this time try to get real answers."

She sat on her cot, leaning towards him conspiratorially. "Is it bad? Are you dying or something?"

"I wouldn't know if I was, at this point. I don't think so, though, don't worry. But we've had...after our dealing with that mess last month for Justin...some stuff happened that we need to understand. Get a handle on it. More about what a doppelgeist is, why we're so rare. What-all we're about."

"Have you found anything out?"

"We have some friends who are pretty much born to research. They're looking through old records and legends. Even so, they're not yet coming up with more than some theories and rehashed speculations."

"I kind of thought you guys would be found in some sort of monster's Wikipedia and boom, you're all explained."

"I wish. With what passes for a Who's Who and What's What of Everything Under, doppelgeists are barely a footnote entry. I'm beginning to suspect that might be as much because people don't *want* to know anything as they don't know anything to begin with."

"I don't get it." She frowned. "I mean...I don't mean to sound like a jerk or anything, and you do that spooky voice thing perfect, but...you don't seem all that scary."

You ought to see what we can do with any stray paper or old soda cans when we're pissed, dear.

"I didn't think we were all that much to speak of either. Before recent events."

"I mean...you can't be hurt, you don't sleep or eat or...any of that other stuff. You have a ghost copy of you—"

"Indelicately put, but okay."

She froze. The vampire equivalent of shivering, when involuntary muscles no longer react. "But what else can you guys do? Turn into a werewolf or something?"

Our thoughts, so often our own trains and on their own tracks, momentarily shared and crashed on the same flashed image: a spiral of dirt and road dust, a spiral of lines of force flowing directly towards Body's feet as we were standing on the sidewalk. In a dazed fugue at realizing something very,

very unsettling about ourselves after the Jennyripper incident.

It felt good. For a moment, a moment without apology and shame and regret coming in to make us feel more civilized and embarrassed... for a moment it had felt good to be cold yet burning, tearing and shredding away the world with simple rage...

Body shrugged it away. "Nothing as glamorous. Truth is, I don't entirely know what it is that makes us so weird amongst the weirdoes. That's what we're trying to find out. And we're doing it this way while we have a chance to...I don't know, keep it under control? Keep it mostly secret? I don't want to find out that we're radioactive or something walking the streets and only finding out when people around me start getting sick, you know?" She nodded. He gave a pat on one shoulder, quick and businesslike. "I don't think it's anything we can't come to grips with if we take the trouble to learn about it. But better to find out than learn the hard way."

"I'm sorry I jumped down your throat."

"It was justified. I didn't realize how much I've been avoiding it without admitting to myself that's what we were doing. We'll talk when I get back."

She gave a sharp nod.

"Now," he clapped his hands, "any chance you could tell me where you hid the keys?"

****

I followed as Body walked towards the end of the block, around the corner and in the midst of a row of old shotgun houses. Our former neighbor still lived there and let us board our '77 Vega in her garage shed.

The day had turned out warmer than expected. Shortly after stepping outside, Body took off the coat and carried it draped over an arm, hands in pockets.

Body was looking mostly at his feet.

I think we lied to her just now.

I moved along with the swing of his arms. *Quite likely.*

I don't feel an abundance of control these days.

Same. I hope Loewenstein has something.

He won't.

You're more pessimistic than usual, even for me, if I say so yourself.

Maybe we should find some warehouse. Or old missile bunker a mile below the soil. Bury ourselves. Box ourselves up and make sure nobody knows where to find us so we can't let this thing out.

I don't generally focus on where Body walks, like some dog on a leash. He almost walked directly into the man who had stepped into his path.

Body caught himself up short. "Oh…sorry, sir."

"Not at all." The stranger beamed. He was Body's height which put him at an even six feet. Stocky-built, a shaved-bald head with a pair of slightly clipped earlobes, giving him a sort of pointed-ear-devilish look. With his dark goatee and wide grin, he looked like Anton LaVey, the former leader of the Satanic Church who had always been a talk show fixture in the eighties when I was a kid, doing the Geraldo and Donohue circuits whenever scared parents wanted to talk about Black Sabbath and Judas Priest driving their kids to suicide. That, or Max Von Sydow in *Flash Gordon* playing Ming the Merciless.

He wore a buttoned-down white long-sleeve shirt, throat unbuttoned, tucked into the waistband of a pair of faded blue jeans. Ratty and worn-down Nike sneakers. Almost a casual Mormon or Mennonite look, neat and clean but not strict. That smooth skull was shiny with a fine sheen of sweat in the warming weather.

At his side he carried what looked like a toolbox only it was a little deeper and longer, resembling a sort of toolbox/briefcase hybrid, done in dented stainless steel flecked with black paint and corners chipping with rust spots.

He hadn't been bothered by Body almost walking into him. He didn't move aside either.

To my 'eyes,' he had a strange 'beaming' around him. As if he had his own personal sunshine. It was dim, weaker than reflected sunbeams coming off the parked cars. It made me think of lemons coated in artificial sweetener, the smell of Clove cigarettes…but it wasn't entirely alien, either. Little kids often have a similar sort of internal fusion generator of happy that comes off them when they're really running and rarin' in a happy daze with some toy or balloon. It's like watching joy as a casual, smooth engine all its own. Whatever this guy was about, he was genuinely happy and okay with it.

"I'm sorry," Body repeated, making a short wave to indicate he was going around.

The stranger remained unmoved. His happy-beam-lemon-sweet fluttered, like birds nervous from a chill wind. I moved closer and got a whiff-taste of something that made me think of the smell of baking plastic off an old rotary telephone…like worry or something communicating purpose and fear from a long, long ways off.

"You're Mr. Flicker?"

Body grinned politely. "Uh, yeah. Do I know you? Do you live around here?"

A happy shake of the shiny head. "No, we haven't met before. My name is Bill Arrundale. I was hoping to meet with you." The plastic and lemon smell-tastes shifted…his light pulsed brighter, the lemon-light coming out from behind its momentary cloud. He was still upbeat but it was wrong…what was *wrong* with it?

Was he something in the Under, not an everyday person but something new? I let myself slough down to the ground, taking in those shoes and blue jeans…what *was* this…?

Body looked at the toolbox. "Oh, yeah, the renovations." Another workman from the crew. Maybe like that water-bull; that could explain the unfamiliarity. "Of course. Sure. I'm sorry, what can I do for you?"

Bill Arrundale frowned for a moment, eyebrows pulling in with puzzlement. Then he broke a fresh smile back out of its sterile package and plastered it up on his lips. Another pulse of hot plastic happy-lemon-light and the fake sugar taste became caramel…the touch of sawgrass digging its teeth into the palm a little…something not bad but not good either…

"Oh, no, sir, I'm not a contractor. I don't mean to take up your time, but I needed to meet you and address something."

"What can I do for you?"

Hey, watch—

The hand that had been in the pocket came out with snake swiftness. The hand held a boxy, nasty-matte-black-finished Beretta 9mm. Was the barrel really that long? No; there was a fatter tube around an inch and a half beyond the little nub-sight on the end of the barrel. Perforations drilled along the tube length: a suppressor. A silencer, fitted to the end making it look more absurd.

The gun barrel came up to meet squarely against the middle of Body's chest, a few inches above the diaphragm.

He pulled the trigger.

Firing point-blank into Body's chest.

No time to drop. No time to fight.

In the real world there is no dramatic and convenient movie-gimmick slowing down of the film, a lot of hero swats and sweeps and karate *hai-yah*'s to save you. In the real world you don't get any moment to think things through and form a plan.

There was a sharp *puh-chwoong*, almost a silly mimic of a hard car door slam. A muzzle-flicker of light.

Cordite wisp in the air. It mixed with the lemon-sugar-sawgrass and was cloying, bitter. I could see the shockwave of the bullet's velocity in that brief distance, distorting the air like water with a heavy stone dropped into it. Air molecules shoved aside, violently rippling away from the end of the barrel.

"I'm terribly sorry about all this, Mr. Flicker. As I said, my name is Bill Arrundale. I am doing this as a member of the Believers in the Second Freedom. I hope you appreciate this despite the inconvenience of dying."

3.

I heard a harsh, flat bang. Felt a punch from a length of steel dowel going through my left breast, above the nipple. I was forced a step back to keep my balance. A hard *fwuh-crack!*, the shot reaching subsonic speed then hitting me, in the space of nothing.

All that movie nonsense is nonsense indeed: most bullets don't grab you and throw you with some big dramatic transfer of kinetic energy.

Startled, I could only look at this guy, this Bill Arrundale from Out of Nowhere, USA with a wide-eyed, glassy lack of feeling.

It was my first time being shot.

I do not recommend it like bungee jumping or skydiving as something you just *have* to try for the adrenaline.

Cold. A wet, cold feeling. The nerve endings went into conflict. They wanted to transmit, they wanted to scream and run, to play Paul Revere riding horseback as fast as possible to all points and yell out the town crier news that something was damaged, something was wrong.

But the horse was lame, the crier had lost his voice, and the nerves knew that this was more news than the system could readily handle. The violated neurological connections tried to shut down, to get everything put in black-out mode. The arm wanted to swing. The shoulder wanted to buckle.

There was a faint whistle-blubbering noise, like bubbles percolating from a hole in an inner tube held down in a bathtub. An inner tube filled with gelatin and broken pocket watch parts.

I opened my mouth to try and speak. But as I willed the act of air, bellows-lungs pump, vocal chords vibrate…I couldn't. There was a sickening lack of pressure. No power to the mouth, lips flopping. The tongue lifted and slapped like a dog with broken legs trying to still pathetically get up to the sound of its master's whistling. *Damn it.* A punctured lung? Possible injury to the diaphragm, maybe hydrostatic shock doing further damage as it dissipated out from the shot just from being at point-blank range…I tried pushing a hand against the place where a gunpowder-ringed hole had been socked through my shirt and into my flesh.

I sensed a chill wetness down my back, counterpoint to the front feeling dry and hot and slack, a hot water bottle feeling.

"Again, sir," Arrundale was saying with sincere resignation, "we apologize for the necessity of this. But in a few moments all should be clear and everything brought back to equilibrium." The flat, odd toolbox of stainless steel was revealed to be a gun case as he popped it open and carefully returned his weapon to the little molded foam indent that it slotted into, latched the case shut again and resumed staring at me as I dropped to the ground.

I tried to push a breath and nearly passed out from a wave of sick-feeling. Gray crowded in on the edges of my vision with furry, cotton-wad ease. I blinked. Fought somewhere in the middle of my brain to remember that I didn't need this, it didn't have to feel like anything…the pain fought back. It had supremacy, it had first call on my meat puppet body… but I was still fighting it. A crunch, bubbly feeling there in the wound…*oh god*…a thin trickle of dark, dark fluid staining my shirt front now…no heart pumping to make it really spurt, but…where he had hit…a major vein there? I couldn't talk if

I couldn't properly take air into my dead throat to make the lungs inflate, will them to work, speak as a normal person... my face still gawped...oh that pain was a raptor made of icicles, spreading out across my chest, my back, the tail feathers billowing against my lower spine...

Crazy...what I was thinking in my head for a beat was the first few guitar-strums that open that song by Apache Relay, "Home is Not Places."

Some part of me wanted to raise a fist, raise an alarm, punch this guy and be the movie hero, take the slug shot like it was a flesh wound, like it was nothing at all. Shrug it off and kick some ass, real hero-style stuff.

Instead, my body wanted far less heroic, more primitive, early-animal stuff. It wanted to stumble, fall back against the tree. That would feel a little better, wouldn't it? I could rest, let my knees go soft...my other hand reached behind me, groped air as the fingers tried to find the bark-rough surface...

It's gonna be okay, I heard Soul speaking. *Christ, man, I know that's gotta suck but it's gonna be okay, you're going to recover from it, remember that.*

It was an impossible thing to remember. The world was sliding away. I cracked my knees as I fell to the ground and succumbed.

I can heal from anything, as far as we have learned in the last few years. But it doesn't mean my body is bulletproof and can withstand anything any more than you or the next guy can. A bullet had torn through me and that meant damage, injury, shock. That meant my body was going to have to have a moment to collect its thoughts, so to speak, before it could muster any sort of useful reaction.

Arrundale's imp-Ming features were calm. He was neither gloating nor remorseful. Simply patient, curious. A man who might as well have been waiting for a bus to arrive at his stop.

The whole world tilted...no, it was me falling over...cold and sluggish... nerve endings were getting weary.

The brain wasn't processing signals correctly. I thought I smelled something oily and yet fruity. Like oranges dipped in motor oil.

I closed my eyes. Tried to gasp a breath. Call for help. A slow-blooming nightmare. Nobody else but the man and me on the street in this moment. It was insane. Darkness crept up around the edges of my sight, black ivy steadily growing up and clouding the wall of my vision…

I wanted to cry.

Oh god this is it. I'm actually going to die this time. I'm going to die.

No you'll be okay—

No I can't breathe I can't—

My brain rolled the reel back to a time when I was a kid. Maybe ten or eleven, horsing around with my dad and one of my uncles. Wrestling around and feeling my uncle trap me underneath him, pinning me in the dark and the breathless space. Crying out that I couldn't breathe, that I couldn't *breeeeathe*, and hearing a high-pitched mimicking of my voice from my dad and my uncle. Finding it funny, knowing from the safe perch of adults that there was no real danger but I couldn't know that. I only knew real terror: they would pin me and hold me and I would suffocate and panic…I couldn't breathe and now I was really going to die, it was finally going to happen.

The world was still moving and people were still going along their own paths and I was laying on the ground on a calm day with the man putting away his gun, calmly walking off. I couldn't breathe, I couldn't *breeeeathe* and this was all that was going to be of me, I was going to be gone forever—

I swallowed something hot and solid. A tear squeezed out from the corner of an eye.

Not now, god not now.

As I surrendered to the black becoming total and felt my back slam into the sidewalk, I heard a faint sigh from Arrundale, then a few dull clumps as he walked away. Not hurried, not worried at all. The bus hadn't arrived, *oh well it's a lovely day I'll walk.*

Then I couldn't see or hear or anything again for a while.

****

—gotta get up.

The tail end of a frustrated, hoarse draft in my skull.

I can't breeeeeathe. Let me up let me up I can't—

Fingertips. The very distant satellites of sensation, reporting back with laggy radio wave frequencies to the brain's central space station. Light leaving the sun, at its fastest still groggy and time-delayed.

Sidewalk. Air. A breeze made the leaves overhead hush and hiss lazily.

Still here. Not gone forever. Somehow there was a dull iron shame in my stomach at that. Like I had wet the bed or crapped my pants in some busy supermarket.

I tested out the door in my head, the one that I picture as the portal by which pain comes and goes. The door opened a crack, and through the crack snuck a little sleek whippet who nipped at me in the small of my back, and barked up my spine with eager but dwindling energy.

What the hell?

I didn't go after him, I thought I should stay and keep an eye on you. All he did was walk off and disappear around the corner on Beck Street. Are you okay?

Opening my eyes. Blinked to adjust to the light. More blinking. This seemed comfortable. If I just stayed here, that sleek dog would stop yapping in my nerve endings and I could enjoy a cool, relaxed, blue-sky day. Stay down, everything's better when you're lying down looking up. No place to look but up.

Oh man. I sent a new radio transmission down to the fingers. Join with palms, combine at wrists. Like a Japanese cartoon, one of those featuring various robots that change and combine to form bigger robots. Join and form arms. Pressure. The sidewalk pushed back. I sent other signals, commands to the muscles in the lower back.

The door cracked open wider and now the whippet was joined by a bigger pit bull who started gnawing and thrashing at the bunched muscles there. I slammed the door shut and pictured a board nailed across it. Sensation dulled away and became nothing, a radio signal with no receivers dialed in to receive it, white static in the nothingness.

Pull. Tug. Leverage. Push with the hands. Crook at the elbows…bend…rise…

I sat up slowly. More blinking. As I sat up, my arms did a fumbly fan-sweep to come around and support my weight…

I heard a *tunk* as that something flop-rolled on the concrete. Looked down.

On the sidewalk next to me was a lump of metal a little bigger than an oversized pencil eraser. It looked like a dull-shiny turd, some woodland animal's spoor.

Hand reached out, the signals commanded the robot claw to open, reach, close, bring up for closer inspection. It was a game. The two-quarters-a-try Chuck E. Cheese crane-and-arm game, with my fingers at the dangling end of the nerveless prosthetic…

A bullet. Deformed by impact, the head flattened in a lopsided way, as if it had dinged off something and come to a stop here. A half-chewed pencil eraser cast in a pewter-dull metal. Coppery-speckled lead.

Copper-jacketed? Not an expert enough to know.

My other hand groped at my shirt, down at my abdomen…

A hole. Ringed with faint gunpowder burn. And beyond… skin. A dimple deep enough that I could put my thumb down against it, press the pad into the depression, flush with the rest of the skin. Nasty red-pink flesh there, filling in the holes and burns. Tissue healing and regenerating. Doing it fairly quick, but then the skin is always the fastest, the shallowest and easiest to accommodate. The deeper damage…the stuff you would need X-rays to see, that was probably still torn up and would mend at a much slower rate.

But a glance over a shoulder didn't show any other damage…the bullet…hadn't it gone through-and-through, a quick and close shot? Why was…this wasn't…

Connections made. No other damage. No other strike-point. The bullet felt greasy.

It was greasy because it hadn't traveled through-and-through.

The bullet hadn't bounced off like some Superman comic book. It hadn't gone through and moved on to some other object to stop it.

It had gone in and struck and stayed in there somewhere. Somewhere deep and bloody and hemorrhaging.

Now here it was, in my hand.

My body had spit out the bullet.

Well, that's something new.

Soul quickened as if woken up. *Are you okay?*

I put the bullet in my shirt's breast pocket. Blinked.

Yeah. I don't want to experience that again anytime soon. Like ever. But I'm…yeah, it all seems…

I reached a hand, snaked it around to my back. No tearing of shirt fabric back there, but a fat pimple-bump on my back…a near-exit wound. *Yeah, all seems accounted for.*

That was utterly insane.

A lot of things seem to fall under that description lately.

Can you get up?

I'm sure four out of five doctors wouldn't have recommended it, but I did it. A slow crawl forward to get my balance, my gravity set right. Then a sort of swimming grope of air up to my wobbly feet.

There was a pressure down near the wound. Probably clotted blood that was going to take a while to re-liquefy. I swayed a few times before steadying.

We have to deal with this.

Soul, from above my head and playing lookout: *What do you want to do, call the cops? Report an attempted murder that never was going to be more than 'attempted'?*

You should at least call Pinney and say something, maybe he could find something out about that guy.

My coat. Dropped to the ground. I bent over—feeling that pressure shift with a low gurgle, the way you might associate the gurgle of feeling hungry—and recovered it. Patted off some dirt, swung it around and over me.

If I kept my shirt tucked in and the coat mostly closed, nobody would pick up on the hole with burnt edges.

We need to see Loewenstein. This doesn't change anything right now. We'll deal with it after we meet with the man.

No argument. But a sullen-feeling swirl of air around my neck.

****

I walked the couple of blocks over to the old Victorian house converted into a duplex, where I lived before relocating to The Nookery. My former neighbor still lives in her half; a retired schoolteacher who doesn't drive so allows me to use her garage shed in the back of the property to store my wheels. A '77 Chevy Vega that boasts what we generously refers to as Vintage Birdshit & Lime Green Duotone.

Are we going to find yet another reason to not be home this evening?

I shrugged the voice off as I got into the Vega's driver seat and started up the coughing, putt-sputtering engine. The Vega gave that kind of friendly welcome-growl that you get from dogs that only like their masters and bite everyone else, as we pulled out of the garage.

I felt Soul flutter to the backseat and wander amongst the old candy wrappers and receipts that were nearly as much floor covering as actual carpet for the ancient vehicle's floor. *Why do we persist in keeping this thing? Especially now that Justin's cash means we have the capital to get new wheels? You probably spent three times what it's actually worth to get it all fixed up, and the engine still sounds like an old man trying to decide whether to fart or cough.*

"I dunno. I asked you about getting a new car when the first estimate came in."

I know. The sigh of air in the back meandered around the back window as I pulled onto one of the main roads to head towards I-71 North, out of downtown and heading into suburbia.

"But when you talked about replacing it, you said it simply

felt…wrong."

This car is as old as we are and it's never crapped out on us, despite its issues.

"Exactly. We don't leave things behind that haven't done the same to us."

Don't bother calling ahead, the voice reminded as I started one-hand fumbling in my inner pockets for my cell phone. *He doesn't keep a phone at his office, remember?*

"Crap. Yeah. That's why he specifically said *not* to be late."

He's a rabbi. Even a retired one has commitments on his time.

4.

Heading north, getting off on the 670 and heading westward, then onto the 315 and once again moving towards compass north. We were silent for the rest of the drive to the tiny former synagogue, tucked away at the end of a sycamore-shaded drive in the Olentangy River area.

Getting out of the car I could see the slow, lazy waves of dank, earthy smell of the Olentangy running on the other side of the main road we'd arrive along, down an embankment and running white-green-dark in splashes and tiny waterfalls. It was early spring for Ohio, which meant nothing if a freak snowstorm decided to hit anyway; they've been known to come as late as April in some years. But for now at least spring had decided to get an early shift and make up for lost productivity from the prior winter's interference. There were hesitant green buds on many of the trees, and shoots of weeds threading their way out between the pine needles. Dead leaves carpeted everything around the property that wasn't paved.

The former Congregation Beth Emet N Chesed built a much larger, more modern synagogue and facilities out in Dublin. When they stopped actively using the original building there were debates about selling it, leasing it, keeping it as some form of local Judaism studies and community rec center. Or even allowing a nearby Korean Lutheran group have the building when their church burnt down.

The Korean Lutherans ended up deciding to rebuild instead of relocate. Rabbi Loewenstein prevailed on the trustees for the synagogue to allow the building to remain in the congregation's management as a Talmudic studies site.

Although a lot more goes on than just reading and interpreting Talmudic law, under Rabbi Loewenstein's volunteered supervision. It's true a few younger rabbis and rabbinical students come to him at the location for assistance and guidance...more people come to Loewenstein because he has a reputation amongst the Under for being an amazing archivist and researcher. As discreet as, well, any priest, he never reveals the details of any client's requests. With three master's degrees in archaeology, library sciences and ancient language and semiotics thrown in for good measure, and most likely enough knowledge in mythology, religious comparative studies and anthropology to earn a few more master's if he wanted them, he is about as formidable a mind as you can find in the Midwest when it comes to reconciling history and the Under to myth and outright bullshit.

All that in consideration, when we'd first been recommended to seek his help with our little query, our skepticism had been at an all-time high. Nobody before him had gotten anywhere in finding more than a bunch of suspiciously-apocryphal nonsense about doppelgeists.

But in our first meeting with him, he was engaging, warm, funny yet stern in an oddly patriarchal manner. First impressions being what they are in any scenario, it went a long way with us in entrusting him the secret of trying to find out whatever he could about us.

As we neared the door, I whispered near Body's ear: *Maybe we should've kept in better touch the last few months.*

We were somewhat busy with dragons and demons, if you'll recall.

Yeah, but even aside from all that...we weren't exactly

burning up with excitement anymore about this line of research.

Are you suggesting there isn't something of an urgency to this now?

Not that...just it seems kind of rude, manipulative. To only call this guy up last week after months of no communication. All because we've got a new burning itch to find out what the hell is up with us.

Doesn't change that we need to find out if he has anything new.

You know, I'm thinking this might not be a hot idea. Might be a good time for a rain check.

Why?

Why? *Because you got* shot *not an hour ago! Shot, man. As in bullet-and-gun-and-shot. By some nut with a silencer, no less. Somebody or something wanted you dead, and maybe if they discover they weren't successful they're going to be trying again. This might not be safe for anyone around us.*

Body stopped. *You have a point.*

Damned straight.

But what else can we do? Lock our doors and I hide in the cellar forever?

No response. I didn't have any answers for myself, either, so couldn't blame him.

He pressed the buzzer and waited.

The intercom speaker set into the wall to the side of the black steel security door clacked on.

"Yes?"

"Rabbi?"

"Yes? John?"

"It's me."

"Come in."

I really hope like hell he's got something for us.

I remembered the look on the face of a weasely little man that we'd burned. Body and I together had integrated in a brief but violent moment...and nearly killed someone with barely a thought.

Hence, the renewed desire for new information.

"Here's to hoping," Body whispered back. There was an alarm clock buzz and the door lock clicked free.

You take a series of circles and make them into Mickey Mouse's silhouette. You take a few more circles, soften some edges, melt them in an oven, you get the Pilsbury Doughboy. Now you take those circles, put some flesh tone over them, a faint blonde-brown indication of beard around the edge that suggests a separation of chin and neck. Widen the smile a little, put some age crinkles at the corners of the blue eyes. You get Rabbi Jonathan Loewenstein. He only comes up to Body's chest but bounces with the springs of a man who needs to always be in motion. The academic decades haven't dampened that internal mattress-spring enthusiasm that echoes in every motion and twirl of his limbs when he turns, speaks, jumps to attention, anything.

He jounced and smiled ahead of us as he lead the way back to his small office at the back of the building.

"I was beginning to think you wouldn't come."

"Sorry. Was distracted with things."

"You've always been good about coming on time, I wasn't offended."

Great. Way to get the immediate guilt-trip for almost canceling this appointment entirely. Or the months of 'no-call, no-show' between us. Neither of us said anything as we moved behind Loewenstein towards the back of the building where his bare-cinderblock office was located, like an afterthought janitor's closet converted grudgingly into an office.

A single narrow notch of window, only a few inches wider than a medieval archer's slit but running from drop-tile ceiling nearly to the floor, let in mid-afternoon western sunlight. Flits of dust-mote and the pulp cells of old books floated in his motion-wake as he cleared thick volumes of leather-bound history from a fold-out chair, then invited Body to sit as he took his own creaky office chair on the other side of the gunmetal Army-issue desk.

"How've you been keeping?" he asked.

"Fine. I wondered if you had anything new for us."

A pursing of those smile-hinting lips. "Not entirely new, perhaps. I don't want to give you any fool's gold hopes."

I'll take Naugahyde hopes at this point.

"I'm sure whatever you have will be informative."

"Your status, this dual-and-singular in the same instance…I warned you when you first commissioned me to find anything I could about doppelgeists that it's already a little-known phenomenon."

"I wasn't hoping you could find a who's-who directory or anything."

"But you'd be surprised, when someone like me goes digging and tries not to let any tidbits distract him into wandering off, how difficult it can be to find such specifics in the history books. At least in a case like yours."

Body sighed and sat back against the folding chair's support. "You couldn't find anything?"

"The most direct correlation I could find was in Egyptian mythology." He tilted his head. "This is going to be one of those 'longwinded tangent' moments. Are you up for me going into this? It could be little more than curiosity-piquing trivia."

"Even if it's irrelevant, I like tangents. They make for good storytelling when you want to not think about yourself for five minutes at least."

His eyes twinkled as his cheekbones rounded with his smile. "Suit yourself. *Caveat listener* and all. The *ba* was seen as the spiritual double of a person, featuring all their original memories and feelings." Loewenstein tilted his head the other way. "Of course, as in all these avenues of research, there are elements that don't line up. Most prominently in the case of the Egyptian ba, there's nothing in the texts about the physical body surviving past death, much less having its own consciousness." He frowned over the thought. "Although again, there's some leeway for interpretation. Do you know the Egyptians also thought the body was itself an entity by itself, apart from the ba?"

"No. But it sounds like it might be our ballpark."

He gave the seesawing *maybe-maybe-not* gesture of his

hand again. "It was the *ha*, as they called it. Or if you get more poetic, there's the flesh-spirit. They referred to it as the *ib*, or the human heart. It all comes down to metaphysics and metaphoric interpretations of course, but the lifeblood of a human being was believed to be separate from their soul, and the *ka*, the lifespark, was itself also separate.

"Basically the Egyptians broke the human being down into the relative components, almost like a chemical or alchemical equation. A body, or heart, plus soul, bringing in the lifespark to ignite their joining and functioning, and you ended up with the human being. Define them with their *ren*, or name, which would define the person throughout life. And the *sheut*, their shadow. Which, as they saw every day looking at the ground, never left someone. So they assumed it meant a person could not live without their shade, and the shade itself must be imparted with some element of themselves."

"You're not describing us. You're describing Peter Pan."

"Consider James Barrie's many-varied interests, perhaps he came across some monograph about Egyptian mythology and got the idea from the same source."

"Sounds like the Egyptians were really busy cataloguing parts."

"In a manner of speaking."

"So the idea here was that the body could be intelligent separate from all the rest of a person's spirit?"

"Yes. It's not all that unique, if you consider that there are many religious or spiritual ideologies that clearly define the spirit as separate from the corporeal flesh. Even more interesting is the Chinese dualism tradition of *hun* and *po*." He gave a shrug. "Here we go. I warned you. Here's a switching of the tracks to another tangent."

"That's another new one on me."

"They mean the 'cloud-soul' and 'white soul.' Not good and evil, rather a philosophy that argues there is an intangible soul, the *yang* part of the universal dualism that leaves the body upon death to join the rest of the universe. Then there is the *yin* soul which is a consciousness grounded and remaining with the corpse of the deceased. Does that sound like anyone you know?"

I felt a little cooler despite the sunlight still bathing the room. That felt too close to the mark in so many respects. *Hun* and *po.* I was going to remember that one amidst my mental filing cabinet of trivia.

I pooled around Body's shoulders: *I don't exactly feel One With the Universe lately, though.*

Body rubbed his chin, frowning. "The only things I ever found about bodies with their own consciousness after death were zombies."

"Have you considered the possibility of the *nzumbe*? The earlier form that the word derives from?"

"I'm not familiar with it."

"I don't know how relevant it might be…" the Rabbi gave a lopsided smirk at his notes. "A *nzumbe* is the traditional idea of someone being raised from the dead, or from a hypnotic state where they've been induced to believe they are dead."

Like that weird Wes Craven movie years ago. The Serpent and the Rainbow.

"But that involves the intervention and command of a *bokor*, or sorcerer." A tilt of the head as he regarded Body with narrowed eyes. "But you haven't been commanded or been under the constant supervision of anyone since you arose, have you?" Body shook his head. "No…no…so no bokor to raise you…"

"There's no such thing as magic anyway. And if I was raised by some hypnotic drug that only made me *think* I was dead, that wouldn't explain Soul, or explain how it is I can heal from any damage."

And it sure wouldn't make us a walking incinerator.

"Mmm-hmm," Loewenstein nodded over his notes. "Plus of course, any drug that had such potent effects would have to be re-administered from time to time…but you don't sleep or eat, do you?"

"I eat occasionally. Matter of habit, I guess. Sleep? No."

While he spoke, it had me thinking back…I found it fuzzy and difficult to clearly recall the last time I'd lain down and felt my eyes close with that pleasant, heavy weight of sleepiness. Or had eyes to close.

"Mmm-hmm." He pored over another pile of notes. "There's still primarily the legend of the *doppelgänger* to go on. Did you know John Donne, the Romantic poet, was fabled to have seen his wife's doppelgänger on the same night their daughter was stillborn?"

"Gah."

"Sorry, I know that's distasteful, but it does owe something to the idea of a double-spirit being the source of many people's idea of menace or bad omens."

"Hey, can I ask you something that's more a tangent than a direct inquiry?"

His eyebrows hiked up. "Go right ahead."

"Do you know of any sort of religious group called the Believers of the Second Freedom?"

"Nothing comes readily to mind. Why?"

Body tugged his coat a little tighter, not wanting to let him see the burn hole in his shirt. "I have a concern that they might be after me for some reason. I'd never heard of them but I got approached by one of them earlier today."

"Are you all right?"

"Yeah, I'm fine. But do you think you might ask around, see if you can come up with anything?"

"Certainly. Are you in danger?"

"I couldn't rightly say."

"Is this about someone you...associate with?"

"Couldn't rightly say."

"Are you prevaricating with me?"

"I couldn't rightly say."

A sigh. Joviality faded a degree as his eyes bore into Body. "You've mentioned that people like yourself...aren't entirely welcome in all homes. Is this something to do with a conflict? Some problem with an associate in the Under? Why do you think you have such issues with others in the...communities?"

"I've had a slight theory of my own on that."

"Which is?"

"I'd rather not going into it."

"We haven't spoken in some months, John. If you don't mind

my noseying for a moment...why all of a sudden did you want to renew my research into your situation so much? So recently?"

We should say something. Try to lay it out for him.

No way, Body snapped. *We don't need yet another person to think...*

...what? That we're not popular? That we weren't really the Prom King in high school? What are we going to tell him that he can't handle?

This isn't exactly the same thing.

Yeah, but he needs to understand. *Maybe...I don't know, maybe a little more means he can find out more for us.*

There was more than that to it, and we both felt it.

Things seemed to be continuing their usual track to Crapsville that we'd come to expect in the last few weeks was going to be pretty much the perpetual after-life-life we were living together. We'd narrowly managed to help get rid of a major monster that had threatened the city, not even the first time we'd necessarily done such a thing.

But there's no newspaper headlines for a hero in the Under. Usually there's only a grave marker with an empty coffin to bury under it.

More than that, elements of our strange lifestyle had pushed someone away that we'd thought was growing closer and accepting of my strange existence. She'd left a note at our door, and we'd respected her enough to not call or try to see her to bypass her blunt request that we leave her the hell alone.

We felt like a freak. More than ever.

Even this diversion, having the rabbi try to find anything useful out. Mostly meaningless in the bigger picture of things. As if we hadn't begged, cajoled, bribed and favored our way to any bit of information the first three years we were loose, and come up with nothing.

The latest in a long line of disappointments.

I'm tired of being formless, helpless, of not knowing what to do and feeling like a leaf in every breeze, and still wanting things. Things and people and touch and people accepting, smiling to see us.

A strange and familiar rusty-throat feeling lodged past Body's tonsils. The feeling of childhood humiliation in front of an adult. I could share the sensation as we were overlapped.

Loewenstein's watching Body reminded me of something.

Meghan, staring out of the door of her store at us. Faint twilight blue light on the glass. Knocking on her door, shaking the doorknob a little. Telling her it was okay, it was safe to come out.

Shaking her head. Drawing away from the door.

Freak. Stay away freak.

She knew about us and still shook her head.

The memory sparked a small chain of other bit-pieces.

Being laughed at in a classroom.

Being turned down for a date. Numerous times.

Saying the wrong thing at an old job and getting fired by a petty boss.

Dad, red-eyed and turning away from me.

You don't give a damn about me anyway, Dad, you don't understand half of my life to be telling me how to live any of it.

Dad, not wanting me to see him crying, closing his door to me.

He was wrong.

He was right.

We never really felt like we fit in…even at home. The last place you're supposed to always fit.

Home is the place that when you go there, they have to try and crucify you.

Freak. All my life, it didn't matter what I could do or who we were.

A cold electricity was running across our hands. Our fingers were the same, our eyes looked at the paper and saw a faint echo-sheen of something like oil and the sunlight drawing around it, like another hand of light—

As frighteningly easy as that, with a hiss-whisper, like the low-pressure eardrum pop of takeoff in an airplane…the wastebasket next to the desk made a dull gonging noise. It was a battered, rivet-seamed steel wastebasket, a real old school office piece of work.

Its sides caved in.

It went from looking like a solid, metal-made thing to a sort of giant dull-grey Dixie cup sculpture crunched by an unseen fist.

A *crunch-crang* noise echoed a little inside it before dying away.

Loewenstein jerked back as if he'd been dented in as well, a squawk from his mouth like a bird falling out of the sky when its wings stop working. His eyes were wide, staring; I sensed that same feeling even as his better nature as a counselor and spiritual man was quickly rushing in to fill that vacuum of fear. *Freak. Get out. Get out and don't say anything, don't do anything more.* Get out before you really hurt somebody.

I'm sorry Dad. I wish I'd been more what you wanted.

Meghan why did you close the door? Why leave that note? Why leave at all?

Body shook his hands weakly, unfolding the fists and letting the fingers droop.

A tendril of foul smoke, thinner than a hair, rising from the trash inside the can. It dissipated.

I don't think Body noticed the last thing, but I couldn't avoid seeing it.

In the failing sunbeam, the dust motes were faintly lining up in pale lines of energy, only hints of an order…then broke up, resuming their random flits in the light.

The hiss of the last of the smoke made me think of my mother's last breath as she'd passed away in her bed, lips hanging open.

Loewenstein groaned back in his overtaxed office chair. The sound of its grinding, like unoiled metal teeth in a giant's dentures, brought me back to the here and now. His eyes were still wide, his breathing audible.

"I hope…that's all there is."

We didn't reply.

"Are you…are you all right, John?"

At that I wished I could cry. We just completely wrecked this guy's moment, made him feel terrified in the depth of his own space, his corner of the world where he felt sacred and protected and warm...and he was concerned about our reaction to having done it to him.

"I'm sorry," Body whispered. Loewenstein waved a hand. *Okay, okay.* But his eyes kept darting to the crushed wastebasket.

"You know..." Loewenstein wiped a hand across wet lips, "you've told me often that there's no such thing as magic, but..."

"It's *not* magic." Body put his hands back in his pockets and leaned back into his chair. "I'm not sure *what* it is. But a laser pointer looks impressive to a caveman, and that's not magic."

"That was a bit more than a laser pointer and a playful cat on the carpet."

"I know. But a nuclear warhead isn't magic either, rabbi."

He stared at Body for a minute before speaking. The air seemed to hold itself still between us.

"Are you saying you believe you're *that* dangerous?"

Body lifted his shoulders in a very slow shrug. "I'm not sure."

"John..." he leaned forward, another squeal of the chair. "I have to ask, whether I want to know the answer or not...have you hurt anyone with this ability of yours?"

"Yes."

Couldn't even hesitate. Couldn't even hem and haw for a half-assed lie. It came out and that was it. "I didn't consciously want it to happen."

Bullshit.

Body ignored me. "Not entirely. We...we both were somewhat out of control...by the time we realized what was happening, it was already happening."

We didn't try very hard to stop it though, did we?

"Did you—?" The question was obvious.

"No. They're still alive. Injured, but alive."

Loewenstein read Body's face a few more heartbeats. I couldn't tell if he genuinely accepted Body's answers or not, but he didn't probe further.

"Are you able to control this thing?"

Body looked away.

"Can you control this?"

"The first couple of times…we didn't even know what it was to stop it. Now at least I know it's there, under the surface."

"That's not an answer to the question." Another glance at the wastebasket. His foot nearest to it twitched. He wanted to shove it against the wall, away from himself.

"How do you call it up? How did you do it just now?"

"I can't entirely explain. It involves…invoking feelings. A sense of…wanting to do it. Wanting something to happen that's…I don't know. Feelings. But it can't be that alone, or it would…it would've come out a lot more often. Sooner, maybe."

He stared for almost a minute before his next question.

"Violent feelings?"

"They can be. They were. Now it's more…than simply anger. Or frustration. It feels like…almost like picking up an instrument you played. One you're out of practice with, but there's still some memory of how to do it."

"Frustration is a pretty violent feeling on its own, John."

"I can't lie to you and say we have control of it. I didn't…I'm really sorry, I didn't mean for that—"

Loewenstein held up his hands, palms out. "Calm down." A tic in his eyes. He was keeping contact on Body, trying not to succumb to looking at the wastebasket anymore. "It was only a wastebasket. Maybe you meant to force it…to channel it that way. So it wouldn't…hurt anyone. That's a step in the right direction at any rate."

"I don't want to 'control' it. We want it gone."

The stare didn't break or change. "If I'd known this is what it was, I might've spared you giving me this…demonstration." He folded his arms and leaned back. "If this is something you can be provoked into calling forth, 'control' is a very flimsy term."

"I didn't meant to let it loose in here."

"But were you sure as you did it that it would stay on the wastebasket?"

Tell him.

Body shook my head. "Not entirely, no."

"Is there anyone that can help you with this?"

Not that she's ever going to answer our calls, no. I held that one back. Body heard it anyway. I could hear a faint back-of-the-head sigh.

The rabbi immediately picked up on the hesitation. Hunching closer in with Body, his hands clasped together between his legs. He looked like a coach who was asking the player on the field if he thought he could get up and walk back to the sidelines under his own power after being at the bottom of a horrendous scrimmage pile-up.

"This problem may not even entirely be related to your... particular state of being." He tilted his head as his eyes bored harder. "Not to insult you or offend, but have you considered that this could be an issue that, unusual dangers aside, is a very human problem? A psychological one?"

"You're suggesting I've got some subconscious issues, some Freudian screw loose?"

A shrug. "I wouldn't refer to it so cynically, but yes. What about the possibility of not seeking some otherworldly answer but rather a more baseline, internalized one? Do you know anyone who is a therapist? Someone who can...I don't know... better identify with you in the Under? Someone you can trust to help get inside your head?"

Body and I had the same *twang-thunk* as the strings were plucked by the mutual idea.

Someone to get into our head.

There was someone we knew who could help in that area. Though they didn't have any sort of medical diplomas on the walls of their office. Or even an office, for that matter.

But they were enough off the beaten path to risk it without humiliation if it failed.

"There's someone," Body muttered. "I can't say as to if he's the guy for it, but he's the only one that springs to mind. Even if he's right for it, he may not be the most willing."

"You have no one else besides this prospect? I could

recommend a therapist who might—"

Body shook his head. "No."

"That's a big 'no' for something like this to be hinged on."

"I know. Look, this is new to me, it's not like we've been running around town flashing this at everyone that bugs me. But it's here and I have to admit to it."

"Other than when you...injured someone." A tinge of something to the air around the rabbi. Impatience? Disappointment? Or plain fear. "That adds a certain flavor of...priority? To the issue. If I were you, I'd want to know what was going on with me as well, if I were at risk for doing... something like that. Out of control. I'd say take the risk and go see this someone you think is the only one in a position to try helping you."

Body smiled. It wasn't happy.

"Is something funny?"

Body shook his head. "It's strange to hear you describe it that way. As something being urgent for a dead man. When I was a bookstore owner, I never felt any sense of emergency about anything. Nowadays though," he looked down at his hands. I knew he was wondering if the light on the palms were entirely sunbeams. If the shadows were quite as dark as they should have been. "It seems like everything has to be in a hurry. Crazy, isn't it? You're supposed to have all the time in the world *after* you die."

I'm going to die this time for real for all for ever god no—

"Frankly," Loewenstein remarked with a startlingly quiet voice, amidst the soft sighs of his office chair and the dust in the sunlight, "I'm pretty certain that most peoples' way of thinking is that it's when you die that you've run *out* of time."

****

I was already at the Vega in the parking lot when Body emerged from the synagogue to take his seat behind the steering wheel. I took up a place near the windshield on the passenger side, musing over the bits of dust making home on the sun-faded tan upholstery.

You think there's anything to the Egyptian stuff? Or that Chinese bit, that was fairly on-target.

He shrugged as he pulled out of the driveway and found his way back to mainstream traffic. *No telling. There's you and me, I haven't exactly noticed our shadow acting funny lately, have you?*

Heaven forbid.

And as little as we've learned in the last few years, we already knew there have been other doppelgeists in the world before, so for all we know any of these legends are just ways of explaining those others in history, not the other way around. No real use to us.

I noted the shift of the sun as it was finally gaining momentum down the kid's playground slide of blue sky, straining to hit the dirt of the horizon and make for sunset, running home at last for dinner.

Now would be a good time to take a moment and call Pinney. Tell him about that Arrundale guy shooting you.

Body shook his head as he pulled his smartphone (another new acquisition, though a finger-fumblingly awkward one for him; me, I liked the large screen that made it easier for me to do my parrot-on-the-shoulder thing and read or listen to a call once in a while). *It's important but not priority. The guy clearly didn't know what he was doing or he wouldn't have done such a ridiculous thing, trying to shoot me and walk off like that was all it took.*

Looked to me like he knew exactly what he was doing with that gun. This is crazy. Why risk him coming back and trying again, maybe with a hedge clipper to your neck next time?

I have to assume that risk.

I watched him open the phone's text message window, thumbing at the virtual keys, frequently having to stop, groan and go back to correct a typo or a misplaced period. Autocorrect was a cavorting word-demon, changing some innocuous thing like "depend" to "dwarf" when you weren't paying attention.

So we really are going to try and see Rod?

Body nodded. *He may not be in the best shape to help us even if he agrees to, you* know *that.*

Another acquiescent nod. He finished typing and hit the 'send' button.

Here's nothing ventured, nothing gained.

I watched the signal from the phone's transmitter make blue-pearl-glitter-and-burnt-rubber-taste shivers in the air; the shape of the cellular words in open air. Like a scatterbrained dove made of runny ink and trails of child's craft glitter, it went off on a wide arc into the sky. *Hopefully our friendly neighborhood mind-reader will answer us back today.*

Body put the phone away, started the car.

Some miles into the drive back, I couldn't keep my nonexistent mouth shut any longer.

We have to deal with Trina.

I know.

Any ideas?

None whatsoever. Justin didn't give any tips on how to handle this part.

Probably because he didn't have any inkling that 'this part' including our new concern that maybe being anywhere near anyone could cause us to go up like Roman candle.

His frown deepened. We got onto the entrance ramp for 315 South, heading back towards the Village and home.

Guess it's like improv theater. We'll make it up as we go along.

As it revealed soon enough, we had something of a script rewrite waiting for us when we got back.

****

Body parked the Vega back in the garage shed and got it locked up. Sunset conceded the field to budding twilight for a full game advantage. What stars were feeling ambitious were already peeking out as we traveled the few blocks to the backdoor of The Nookery. Twilight was lingering at this time of year, at least another good hour or two before full dark. He unlocked the doors while I observed a pair of robins arguing over a nest in the nearby oak tree.

Immediately, everything was wrong.

As noticeable as the door clunking into something three-quarters into the arc of its opening inward to admit us.

Same makeshift apartment space we had left. But it had been rearranged.

Violently.

Trina's cot was overturned. Its thin mattress on the ground, sheets spread out under it like a body with its arms and legs splayed out.

Books that had sat on the floor in knee-high towers were all dashed to ground level, some of them opened and resting with their spines up like the fins of small predator fish.

Body's cot was still resting up against the interior wall to the back. But the clip lamp that was mounted to the headboard was on the floor, its shade crushed flat and tiny chips of opaque white bulb-glass dusted around it where it lay.

The area rug that took up the most of the floor between the cots and desk was bunched, a rent through its shaggy middle like something had taken a carpet knife to it with savage abandon.

The office desk was upright but shoved away at an angle near the door. It was the something the door had thunked into as we came in.

Most damningly—at least for me—the air...the air had a disrupted appearance.

I could see the gnats-in-fury motion of molecules, the sense of energies that normally flowed in and out of the room as regular as the breathing of air through the heating ducts... jagged and disoriented.

I could sense in Body a brief panic. *That guy, Arrundale? Could he be waiting—?*

No. He didn't seem to be the wild-throw-books-and-toss-the-place type. And this doesn't feel-look like new energy...this is the regular feel of the place, but disturbed.

The door had been locked and we had nothing worth taking. It didn't truly occur to either of us at all that this had been some invasion or robbery.

Trina was nowhere to be seen. No conventional robber could've stood a chance against even a neophyte vampire if they'd tried anyway.

What the hell? Was she this *angry at us?*

Body shoved against the desk to put it back to its original place, then closed the door behind him. *I can't believe she'd just throw a tantrum after we'd already spoken earlier.*

I swirled around the disarrayed books. *Well it had to have been her.* I looked at the shattered and crushed clip lamp. *Oh man, if she is angry with you, this is* not *good. Whether she stomped on it with her foot or did this with her hands—*

This isn't anger. She would be in here if she'd been this angry for some reason. Body picked up a single book from the floor near his feet. The title was *Unto the Spheres*, a collection of William Ashbless poetry.

I think she would've waited to let us in on a piece of her mind if that's what it was about. Something's wrong. Period.

I won't argue the impression. He put the book down on the desktop as I circled near his head. *But I don't have a clue what to do regardless.*

Me nei—

A metallic, jangling crash distant in the depths of the store.

I could instantly recognize the sound though I'd never heard it before. *The postcard racks near the old front counter. Something's knocked one over.*

5.

"Trina?" I called out.

I stepped forward, squinting into the dim of the entryway that led to the rest of the old bookstore. It was too dark to see more than rudimentary shapes, bookshelves that lined that corridor on both sides, leading into obscurity.

There was another loud crash, punctuated crazily by a loud ding of a bell. The cash register.

A cry. Like an eagle being boiled. Sorry, that's the best I could possibly describe it for you. Crack-screeching in my eardrums, in that way you feel when a concert's speaker system is blasting so hard in the upper registers that your inner ears start to do that weird paper-wrapper-tender sensation, and you know you're a hair or two away from being struck deaf.

It died away. Leaving the air hanging in the sudden after-silence as the quiet that must accompany the squeal of train cars braking after the engineer realizes he's hit someone.

Moving towards the central room that used to serve as the cash counter for the bookstore, we passed shelves that had been emptied of books. The volumes were strewn about the floor. On a few twists I had to shove them aside with my toe to keep moving or risk stamping on them to get by. The contractors were definitely not finished— there was tile to be laid and spackled into place in Trina's new bathroom—and the smell-touch of freshly-cut lumber, newly-applied paint only just-dried floated in the gulfs between disturbed air currents.

I didn't call out again. We were both listening for any signs ahead.

We'd gotten to the room where we had once sold travelogues and poster prints of Old World maps and famous world landmarks. The posters mounted on one wall were mostly shredded; confetti lengths of them lay on the floor amongst destroyed Fodor's guides and photo collection books like pennants for the losing ball team.

Can you go ahead of me? Scout things out?

No good. Soul hovered around me. *Everything is in a total helter-skelter. If she's ahead, I wouldn't see her any better than I can make out a lot of this other muck.*

Great. I tilted my head slightly, a pointer dog trying to re-orient on the fallen bird in the brush.

Do you know at all the last time she fed?

That had both of us stopped.

Wrapped up in ourselves as we'd been of late, I hadn't paid attention to her amenities anymore than Soul had. And Trina had kept a lot of her personal habits to herself.

I honestly have no idea. I scowled in the dark. *I never saw her feed at any point, and we didn't ask after it.*

Let's be brutal here, man. We've been assholes and it didn't occur to us to ask because before now we didn't care.

Trina hadn't owned a lot of personal possessions to bring with her into The Nookery when we'd welcomed her in. Her clothes and similar needs were minimal.

Or we just assumed they were minimal.

But she had to have blood. That much we knew even with our rudimentary knowledge of vampires like her breed. Blood that in some way provided a metabolic booster to her quasi-dead body in a way that nobody—well, nobody except vampires—truly understand.

Yet you don't need all the details to comprehend the

larger truth: vampires feed.

How often? How much? Did it have to always be from a living subject or could she ingest 'cold' blood as could be stored for a time? Could she die, or go into some sort of blood sugar fit like a severe diabetic?

She hadn't kept blood in the mini-fridge in the apartment area, that much we knew. But what else? Justin hadn't given us those facts and we hadn't bothered to find out.

Justin's words fluttered up into my thoughts, like birds startled off a telephone line, sudden and filling me with a dawning dread.

This isn't like sponsoring someone in Alcoholics Anonymous, John. They don't call you at three in the morning and ask you to encourage them not to tip a bottle of cheap whiskey down their gullet. When a new conversion slips—and she will slip, it happens to everyone at least once—she will feel something unlike any other craving known. And she will be scared. And in pain. And she may not know her own strength. Or yours.

"Trina?"

The Nookery was clicking-and-creaking, an obscurely breathing body of rooms and caches. I tried to listen for anything different: a floorboard groaning, a faint patter of steps.

Then I realized that those were the things I'd be listening for if I expected an intruder to be human. *Maybe we should go back to the front room and wait to see if she—*

There's a movement in the air ahead—

I was flung back against the wall by a hundred-and-five-pound dark bullet that emitted the keening of a lawnmower crossed with a housecat purr.

****

I was scared of the dark as a kid, but not scared of the ocean. Not then.

I bring this up for a very particular reason.

I was allowed to watch all sorts of trashy horror movies such as would play late night on cable channels, or were broadcast by our local CBS affiliate's Friday night Chiller Theater. This gave me a healthy fear of going up to my room past the dark of the staircases, or the dim of a partially-opened door into what I knew was just the bathroom or another bedroom. But in the dark, these things have a way of becoming distrustful. You know even as a child, without having seen all those zombie and vampire and space monster movies, that the dark is the cloak worn by many things that want to get close, to get within reach. It's the cloth thrown over your face to blind and knock you out, for the hairy-knuckled Lon Chaney nightmare to then leisurely tug you back into the deeper shadows...

The dark. The space inside it. To get to you and beyond. To get past the point of escape where, once you finally see them in all their raw, quivering, drooling glory...it's too late to do anything but be taken.

But my summer vacations, when my parents would take me down to Myrtle Beach in South Carolina, I didn't mind splashing and rushing at first sight into the sunny green-grey glass and foam surfaces of the Atlantic Ocean. There was nothing wrong in the water under the sunny skies and salt breeze. I would wonder why so many of the adults would stay back on the sand, on beach chairs and under wide, striped umbrellas.

Then I got older, got into junior high school. At some point in my schooling I had biology classes that told me about Portuguese man o' war jellyfish. Millions-year-evolved sharks. Megamouths that looked in National Geographic photos like primordial dinosaurs still haunting the living waters. Megaladons that fed on other predators. Piranha that could devour a mammal in minutes if one should unfortunately go wading into their waters.

The man o' wars, though. Jellyfish. Those somehow were the worst to me. A shark you could conceivably see from a ways off, fin stuck up like an idiot's flag. Whales and other monsters of the deep were just that: deep.

But jellyfish...Christ, those could hurt you even when they were *dead* and dried bits of condom-looking plastic flesh washed up on a high-tide stretch of seaweedy beach. Jellyfish were casual, floating and placid, almost fetal in the horror they presented. Poison. Stinging, like a billion bees clutched in your fists.

Somewhere in all this maturity and growing up and learning about the world, my fears shifted. I still watched horror movies and had the occasional nightmares...but I was now afraid not of the dark but of the ocean. Of unknown waters. Even at Hoover Reservoir, an artificial lake of manmade dams and docks, I somehow thought the muddy waters might conceal some government-stocked Loch Ness plesiosaur that would lie in wait in the shallows. Long kraken arms that somehow looked less and less in my nightmares like sucker-laden octopoid things...and more like the fleshless, tendril-soft lengths of squishing, poisonous jellyfish strands.

I shifted fears from the dark which I learned in those innocent days was only the dark, merely an absence of light in otherwise known and familiar places, to the very real and uncharted darkness of the beach on a sunny day. It didn't need nightfall to get stung by jellyfish or stalked by a hungry shark. There was no silver bullet against the tendrils of a kraken reaching up and pulling you down, down towards that cracking, chitinous beak at the crux of all those wriggling arms...

Intellectual awareness that these things are so unlikely and things like piranha didn't exist anywhere near my northern climate didn't matter, anymore than knowing the geography of my house as a younger boy had dispelled the fear of the dark under the staircase.

More appropriately, I became convinced this was why so many of the adults stayed safely back on the beach. Because while they insisted there were no monsters under the stairs or in my closet...the ocean was definitely a place of monsters and harms waiting to leap on you and drag you down, and being the more educated adults they were more than happy to let the children frolic in the tides of danger and keep themselves nicely safe back up on the dry sands, well above the high tide watermarks.

It never occurred to me to wonder what sort of parents and adults would let their kids play where they didn't dare to endanger themselves.

This is what formed one of the strangely fundamental points of my development. I got rid of 'childish' fears like the dark, but instead of losing fear merely transferred it to the ocean, to watery depths of green and blue dying.

More than transferring fears, it became a rationale by which I thought I understood adult behavior as I left childhood in the queer corridor of transition into becoming one of them. That they didn't so much try to fight these fears as give in to them, and not mind so much relegating their children and friends to these risks while they remain safe and out of harm's way.

Did I come to resent adults under this assumption? I can't remember. My teenage years were fairly typical with the usual rebellions and miniature coup attempts to break from my parents' upbringing and restrictions. If any of that stemmed from this one particular shift in my thinking, I couldn't tell you. I only remember it happened.

And it still continues to happen now... though in the last few years, I've learned that it was the dark I should've been worried about all along. Dark under the waves, dark under the stairs, dark up in the sky.

Because in truth, the dark is the ultimate ocean. The one that truly does in fact cover all the one as one massive sea of night.

In the Under, that's not always the echoes of your own footsteps you're hearing behind you.

****

Violet-amber sparks from Trina's eyes blurred into trails as my shirt ripped. A blunt tug-tear at the belt holding my pants on that didn't break the belt but yanked at my middle so hard that my back felt like I'd fallen off a ladder and landed on it.

There was nothing sexual in any of this. Trina's hands were

barely-discernible, flaying claws. Ripping at fabric then trying for the skin underneath. The engine growls, the panting were ragged. Cold exhalations against my face and exposed abdomen.

I was too dazed to keep my bearings in those first few moments, cloth tearing and movements shaking me with doll-like ease…until I felt teeth sink into my right shoulder, clenching so hard that the collarbone knob there felt about to crack.

The sharp hole-punch of her fangs into me shoved a scream out from my lungs and pushed it ahead of the line of anything I could've said or uttered and burst from my lips, echoing into the distance of the rooms.

I shook myself hard, bringing my hands between us and trying to push. My hands were battered away.

At some point I think I yelled her name, for all the good it did.

SHE'S GOING TO TEAR YOU APART MOVE

I couldn't formulate a reply to Soul screaming in my skull. It all was a blend, like a fire hose of alcohol solution spraying all over me as I suffered open wounds, a thousand tiny nicks and cuts and big slashes across my flesh. Claws dug at my belly striving for more purchase as I was digging my hands back into the narrow space between us, trying to find leverage, any advantage.

She had shoved me back into a bookshelf. It shook and rattled, suddenly a torrent of hardcover books was falling, arcing down through the air and pummeling on top of us. Because my back was against the shelf most of them fell on Trina, momentarily freeing her bite as she squalled in animal fury and pained surprise, backing away from me.

As soon as I could take her in, I could see her face had a bestial twist to the lips. Her eyes seemed twice as large as normal, completely black with lightless, avid hunger.

A smell had risen from her, musky yet arctic…like the smell of meat lying out on a snow bank. Freshly killed and steaming but frigid with the breeze.

The pause was too brief. She was already coiling up her legs and crouched, claw hands gripping at the thin carpet and tearing it with loud, abrupt shredding sounds.

She jumped. Going for the throat this time. My whole body was a gigantic, singular pump of hydraulic fear and to her it must have been a beacon as clear as a road flare to night vision goggles.

That childhood panic rose in me. That strange but unique flavor that had made as a boy rushed me along the staircases when I went from the TV room to bed after a good scary movie. The fears that what lay in wait in the dark only needed me to be a little slower, a little overconfident, and then it would take me away and tear me apart at its leonine leisure…

…I was screaming as she jumped towards me I grabbed one of the thick hardcovers without a thought. I swung it, desperate and aimless.

The book made cracking contact with Trina's skull. If I'd been trying to time it I'm sure I would've missed or would've gone weak in the arm like those nightmares where you can't run away from the monster and all your limbs seem kitten-weak so you can't throw any punches to save yourself.

If I had tried some clever defense I would've failed. The only thing that made it possible for that swing to make contact and send her flying off to a side with a yipping snarl was that childhood fear of the dark, coming back. No intellectual jellyfish or krakens waiting to drag me down into the waters… simply dark, primal terror. The monster was real after all, and I would do anything with absolutely no premeditation to fend it off, get it off me, get it away, Christ *mom dad somebody get this thing away and make me safe again, PLEASE—*

GET OUT OF THERE!

She struck another set of shelves to my right and this time took a few seconds to shake her head like a defeated dog and recover. The violet light was brightening; it was like looking into twin lanterns distantly down a train track. A lonely track through dark woods. If my heart still worked it would've been beating in my chest hard enough to be audible to anyone in the room.

I was choking and hollering like a man at a campsite trying

to seem more menacing to the wildcat that has come slinking to his fire at the smell of food. I waved the book, tried throwing it. My luck ended. She easily moved aside as the book struck the shelves behind her.

She came at me again. A breeze drafted through my skull. The hairs on my neck and arms rose as stiff as bristles.

A wail, loud as the world but also between my ears alone. Like my voice, but run through a tunnel and charged with lightning.

Soul passed through me and that overlap of *presence* came back.

A new panic seized me even as I felt the rest of me go with the joining sensation.

"No no no NOT HERE WE CAN'T—"

A book leapt up of its own out from under my legs and flew at her. She tried to weave from it and the book *curved in the air* to match her, striking with a thunderous sound that made me wince.

More flew open, pages ripping free of their binding. A crick-crack shivered through the shelves at my back. I felt as though the carpet underneath us was shuddering…

"NO NO GET IT UNDER CONTROL NOW—"

The ripped pages shredded and flew like confetti, a draft strengthening and knocking books off other shelves. Some shreds blew against her and a pair of books crashed against her shins, forcing her onto her stomach with a *whoof.*

Two more hardcovers flew through the air before I could even try and mount any sort of way to stop it, dropping like stones and pounding the back of her skull into the floor, making a double *thwok* and *thunk* as her forehead met the boards under the thin carpeting, stopping her.

I felt fresh panic and it doubled as Soul gasped in my head and pulled back. All that kinetic energy stopped and there was the clattering-thunking crash as books and bits of pages all stopped being moved and fell to the floor.

The sigh of air, re-settling into its place.

Trina didn't move.

A book of Paris night scene photos was lying open on her back almost like a hand rubbing the base of her spine. It dawned on me that she was completely naked. Her hair was spread out around her head like a dark swirl of an octopus (kraken), crouched on her neck as she lay motionless. I began to collect my feet under me to look down on her.

I took a breath, a deep breath to try and steady myself.

And thought of Loewenstein. And our talk about being able to control this thing, whatever it was.

The ghost of a *krang*ing wastebasket, invisibly crushed by some hand, from a limb I wasn't aware I had, couldn't feel to control.

The worst part, that part of the childhood dark-fear that had struck me…the worst part was remembering how a moment ago the floor itself had seemed about to rip away to join the melee with the paper and more fragile things flying about.

How far could it go if we didn't control it, if we let go again like that in a moment of panic?

How far did we *want* it to potentially go?

I couldn't think of what to do. As my thoughts coalesced into real cognition once again, I looked around at the disaster of the room.

Most of the shelves had emptied themselves at the shaking climax. I didn't have anything like rope or chain to bind her if she was still a danger…I couldn't even conceive of what I could bind her with, if she recovered in the same furious state.

Her arms and legs were stretched out at her sides, with a few more hardcovers rested on top of one hand and against her knees. It gave me a moment's inspiration.

I carefully moved towards her, hunched and listening and watching for any sign of recovery. I took the risk of getting down on my knees beside her. I shoved the book off her back and replaced it with my hands, open and spread out across the small of her back. I carefully put my weight down, testing the resiliency of the surface. It felt tight, more durable than a small woman's body had any right to feel. I allowed more weight, felt less and less give and got no response from her, so finally trusted my full weight down onto my hands and directly on the small of her spine.

"Trina?" I tried speaking softly, said it again louder. "Trina, are you there?"

A whistle-moan came from the mass of dark hair.

I saw the sphere of her head under it rise, shift, turn to one side… felt unnatural muscles contracting under my hands. Trying to rise up, to bring her arms and legs to bear in going under her, tissue crinkling under the thin pale skin and it was wrong. So wrong that for a brilliant, horrified moment I thought of fibrous jellyfish tendons under the skin, poisoned and swaying…but I was defeating her with leverage. She could still buck and shift…but at least I'd have a moment before she could completely throw me, with her leverage reduced to practically nothing, lying prone on the floor with her limbs away from her command.

"J-john?" Small, meek. "Oh god, *John*?"

They all slip, Justin said. He'd said I wasn't really prepared or understanding of what I was in for.

He'd been right.

"Trina? Are you okay now?"

"Oh god, J-john I'm suh…suh-so…oh *GOD*…"

"It's okay, Trina," I soothed. She squirmed again. "Relax. I'm holding you down because I wasn't sure how you'd be when you recovered. Can I let you up?"

"G-guh..god…" She sobbed into the carpet, a muffled hitch-and-gasping. "I'm s-suh-so sorry…"

"It's okay. I'm going to back off you, okay?" A tiny nod of head. I leaned back onto my knees and released her.

She rose slowly, pulling in her knees and arms like ropes being pulled in on a sail, gradually finding her gravity again and rising up on hands and knees.

She didn't look at me right away, but crawled on all fours away from me, to the nearest corner. She fumbled herself around and on her ass, sitting in an upright fetal position with her knees tucked against her chest, her arms around them. Her head peeked over her knees like a princess in a castle under siege, her knees her only embankment against the hordes around her.

"J-john?"

I sat back Indian fashion. "Yes. Are you okay?"

A shake of her head. "N-nuh-no. No."

"What happened while I was gone?"

"They s-said it c-could happen, but I th…thuh-thought I'd *know* before. I thought I'd nuh-*know*…" Another wrenching series of sobs.

"Know what?"

"I should…" swallowed with a click in her throat. "I sh-should've told you, but they s-said to keep things to myself, to not suh-say too much about…about us…how…we live an' all…"

I kept my voice even and calm, but there was an edge of darkness fear creeping up my spine that I had to fight as I spoke. "What happened?"

"There are…if we don't…if w-we don't—"

"Feed?"

She nodded. "If w-we don't f-fuh-feed…for too long…they said it could cause me to guh…go c-crazy all of a sudden. That I'd try to feed on anything that came near me. I'd go nuts for a wh-while."

"Trina, when did you last feed?"

"Just buh…b-before I moved in."

"Oh Christ, *that was nearly three weeks ago,* woman! Why didn't you say anything?"

"You didn't…I muh…mean…"

We didn't ask, so she figured she shouldn't tell. God damn it. We are the biggest assholes in the world.

A pocket of cool air on the nape of my neck as Soul recovered.

We didn't know, I answered. *We didn't—*

Bullshit. We should've asked. We should've asked Justin more questions before proposing that she be our responsibility. We're more at fault for this than she is, poor girl didn't have a chance if this kind of thing was weighing on her and she could see we were already preoccupied with our own business, damn it.

I couldn't argue the point.

"Trina, how often are you supposed to feed?"

She rubbed her fists into her eyes like a child wiping away tears, but her eye sockets were dry when she pulled them away. Now the violet-amber light was low, barely two cigarette embers in the dim peering back at me. Without wanting to I thought of Tolkien's famous cave beast, Gollum, his lantern eyes looking out over his sunless underground lake.

"They s-said that as I got older, I wouldn't need to v-very often, but now I sh-shouldn't...I should feed at least once a week. No muh-more..." She took a breath to steady herself further. "No m-more than twice a week. For now."

"You haven't fed for over three weeks? How did you stand it?"

"I was stupid, okay?" she yelled back. "I'm s-*sorry*, alright? I wasn't really feeling anything, not hungry or anything. I thought for sure, if I didn't feed too long I'd start to feel it, there'd be some warning. It seemed fine, even with the training I thought it was somehow overhyped, that nothing was wrong. I w-was gonna say something if I felt it, but I didn't and th-then tonight while you were gone, I was trying to read something and thinking about when you'd come back what I'd s-say and..." She looked around as if trying to find someone else to speak for her, but found herself trapped in giving her own confession. "...oh god, I can't *remember*. Next thing I knew I was hearing you come in and...I wasn't th-thinking...I was in the dark here and moving around, hearing you step on the floor and every movement...I could hear everything but I wanted to hear your heart, I remember that little bit...I was somehow thinking I should follow the sound of your heart, the smell of you, but you don't h-have those...and I was hungry...it wasn't...no, it wasn't like hungry...it was more like...like that thing you mentioned one time, about the birds?"

She had been enjoying an Audobon photo collection the previous weekend. We'd talked about the habits of birds, particularly birds using their sense of magnetic north to navigate during migrations.

"You felt compelled? Like it was something you had to do and it didn't matter about anything else?"

She nodded. "I couldn't think of anything else, it was like it'd already happened. Like nothing else could happen at all. I came down from that other room where I'd been, I couldn't remember going all that way back into the store, but I heard you calling and came forward and then you were there across f-from me and…I can't remember anything until now. I c-can't…I thought I would *know* when it was going to happen."

"Trina…" I got up and crawled on my hands and knees towards her. She shivered and jerked when I placed a hand on one of her knees, but didn't run away. "You need to feed. Do you need me…"

I swallowed. I didn't realize until then how nervous I'd been contemplating this, though I knew this was what I'd mainly signed up for when I'd demanded Justin repay me by making me Trina's first blood-partner. "If you need to feed, you feed, okay? You tell me and let's…let's do it. You need to before any longer, so this doesn't keep happening, okay?"

Fear sparkled in her eyes. "I *c-can't!* What if—"

"You won't lose it again. It's not feeding that made you lose it, right?" She nodded more slowly. "Then you need to feed. Think of it like diabetes, like simply needing a regular shot of insulin to keep yourself from going crazy and sick, right?"

"W-what if I hurt you any…any-w-way?"

"Then the fault is mine for having neglected you all these days." I gave a faint smile. "And besides, remember? I'm not that easy to hurt."

She gave a weak smile and the light dimmed further, but she put her hands over mine and squeezed gently.

"Can w-we…can I get dressed first, please? I need…" another steadying breath. "I n-need to feel cleaned up first, before we…before we do it."

I nodded without a word and got up. When I reached the corridor back to the apartment space, I looked back. "I'll wait in the main room until you're ready, okay? You're not going to freak out again. We'll take care of it, this is my fault and we're going to fix it, all right?" She nodded and I left her to herself.

*****

Back in the rear storage room, I righted her cot and flattened out the area rug, noting that I was going to have to buy a new one with this one so torn up. I spread her bed sheets out on her cot. I found the hand brush and dustpan I kept in the large bottom drawer of the desk and swept up the mess of my clip lamp. Check another item I was going to need to replace tomorrow. I dumped the mess in the wastebasket, then sat on my own cot and wait.

This is wrong, Soul whispered to me. *If she can go apeshit when she hasn't fed and there's no warning signs or early symptoms to tell, we are so not qualified to do this.*

Maybe.

I looked down at my hands. At the tatters of my shirt hanging off my shoulders, spattered with my blood where she'd torn at me. I took off the shirt and balled it up, making a halfway decent rebound shot into the wastebasket. One of my black t-shirts was draped on the back of my office chair, so I pulled that on. I noticed as I pulled the fabric down over my stomach that the scratches and nicks were already pale pink lines, closing up. The bite in my shoulder was too close to my neck for me to see without a mirror. When I tested out touching the area there was nothing that felt too torn up, nothing that felt open and gaping.

Think I'm in danger of infection? Becoming a vampire?

At this point, you're more at risk of dying of a vicious paper cut.

Ha.

We need to call Justin. Call this off.

Maybe. We made a bad mistake. Luckily this time nobody was permanently hurt.

Don't play Saint Paul the Positive, Mister Sudden Case of Responsibility. This might not be the kind of mistake to learn from. A shudder of air overhead. *Except to learn to call it off and not risk any more such fuck-ups.*

Look, we basically treated her like she was furniture the last few weeks while we were all caught up in ourselves. We have yet to actually try this situation, so why drop it before we've truly tried it and make her feel worse for it?

A moment's silence. While he considered that, I re-piled the books scattered around my cot.

Finally: *You're right. It's not her fault so it shouldn't be her getting passed off.*

I sat on the cot again. Wandering the room felt stupid. *If something like this happens again—*

It will *happen again, the rate this is going.*

If something happens again, we'll get some outside help. But I'm not giving up on her because we were lazy.

This isn't about giving up or quitting smoking. She's a living...I mean, she's an intelligent person who deserves more than being our walking guilt-trip.

I know that.

Music crackled from the speakers throughout the store.

We'd shown her where the main stereo player was in the old cashier's area when she'd arrived. She'd discovered it wasn't compatible with her iPod and disdained using it. Throughout The Nookery crackle-blurted tinkling electronica music.

Annie Lennox. Singing her cover of Procol Harum's "A Whiter Shade of Pale."

"Trina?"

We skipped the light fandango...

"Trina?"

...turned cartwheels 'cross the floor...

All the messiahs I don't believe in, save and preserve me from a millennial-generation vampire girl's idea of an oldies 'romantic' song as soundtrack to a first feeding. I got up from the cot as she emerged from the corridor.

She stepped in from the next room, shadows parting in the manner of a curtain soft velvet as she allowed herself to be seen in the light.

She wore a black nightie that came down to her mid-thigh. The bra and panties were solid, the belly and fringe around the thighs was diaphanous. Against the pale skin, she seemed dressed in nightfall. There were glitters of gold and silver in the weave of the fabric.

She smiled to see me so astounded. A hand raised and flapped the lacing around one thigh in coquettish toying.

"Pleased?"

I nodded, though no smile or change in expression found its way on my face.

She's got a hell of a way of settling issues.

"Trina, I don't know—"

She held up a hand. "You wanted to make it up to me, and I realized…we hadn't yet done this. We need to."

I give up on the saints. Lazy bastards never show up when you really need them.

And never mind saving me from romantic overtures, what the hell *was* all this? What were we doing? This felt farcical, like any moment an English vicar was going to come barging in looking for his pants in a BBC teleplay.

She moved with sylph suddenness. Pressed against me. A lot of the farce and sense of comedy dissolved. Somehow her speed and litheness were more intimidating than having her tear me apart. She tilted her head up. Brought her nose an inch from mine. "I haven't…the last few days…I'm sorry—"

"What?"

She closed her eyes and bowed her head.

"I'm sorry. I know I should've said something—"

"You didn't know, it's okay."

I'm going to go now.

I felt the thinning of the air near my back.

Where the happy hell are you *going?*

I don't need to be a part of this.

What are you talking about? It's ok—

Just take care of her. I'll be back in a while. When you're done.

Not another word. He was gone.

Soul often hung around during my scenes with women when making adult films with Hal. Physical acts like sex don't represent much stimulation to either of us.

But intimacy. Different from physical act. He didn't care about witnessing me do whatever with a woman in some artificial setting. But something truly private...he left me to it.

We've gotten past the mutual pity partying for the most part...allowing for the lapses where it still gets to us, how we were. But I severely wished there was a way I could switch places so it didn't seem like he got the short end of the stick in things like this.

"It won't hurt." It drew my attention back to her. "There's something we do when...when we...bite...it's this stuff they said will..."

"A painkiller? You have a neurotoxin in your bite so when you bite someone it numbs the spot?"

"Yeah."

"Don't worry about hurting me. You need to feed. I won't feel it if I don't want to."

"Yeah."

I ran a hand up and down her back. She closed her eyes, relaxed against the motion. Each of my fingers felt that special pressure of her flesh against the pads of the tips. She was cool to the touch, but there was something...some energy that didn't pulse like a heartbeat but was so certainly present, so *vibrant.* Like trying to hold onto a hummingbird in a loosely-cupped fist.

She pulled me tighter. I heard a hollow hush of air as her mouth opened. That purr-growl sound far at the back of the throat.

Then the piercing...the hummingbird's beak lowered to feed.

6,

Stars look different than they used to. It's amazing what you see when you no longer have eyes.

I can look up through the light pollution of the city in full twilight throes, arc sodium and incandescents erasing much of the night sky our pre-electric ancestors took for granted.

To *your* eyes, the night sky over Columbus is a mauve-and-orange haze that breaks only at the utmost top of its dome to allow a half-dozen familiar constellations entry. Like superstars permitted into the VIP backroom of a club too crowded to hear each other talk clearly while the rest of the un-beautiful people have to loiter at the bar.

But when I relaxed and let myself view the skyscape over the capital city, I could see the stars...their X-ray halos, like irregular and shifting briar-crowns of radiation. Flickering and flashing out with octopus energy in a grayish-newsprint haze. Cosmic-ray arcs that lensed and warped with each others' gravity, white monochromatic rainbows that knifed through ray-storms of parti-colored waves from pulsars. Hydrogen, exotic gas clouds, continents-long and flowing in pastel smears...microbursts of meteors...

If I focused myself into a kind of incorporeal scrunching of my 'eyes,' relaxed further, there were radio lights. Ping-waves; a billion intangible rain drops hitting the milk-and-water surface of everything. Buildings disappeared. The geography of the world became a topology of rising and quavering cellphone songs and symphonies of lowjacks and GPS readers. Microwave satellite signals ricocheting with the echo-shards of car antennae.

Shift to infrared. Now everything was a heat-death-crazed dance. Everything pulsing to keep warm in the darkening infinite. Look: the ghosts of the living universe. Millions-of-years gone but still showing their fires and stellar petticoats of gamma rays. Like a museum display of the best gowns of European royalty and Indian Raj majesty. Silken colors melting into aurorae of amazing sparks, spitting comet bursts.

Try to go softer. Letting my sense of being dissolve further, almost-but-not-quite the brink of non-self…the last few cube-crystals of sugar at the bottom of a glass of saturated sweet tea…and all these spectra would crash and overlap…the world became a massive painting, splashed in the colors of the Big Bang and photographed, then lithographed and silkscreened into a final matted framework of life. Beating a tiny, tinny pulse against a universe of massive thermonuclear hearts and dark, dark matter.

Dark matter that was strangely…magnetic…to even look at…as if perception itself were the event horizon of a black hole that was encompassing everything…gravity merely a word to describe the swirl of space, falling with nowhere to hit bottom…

I had to stop somewhere.

In early days, I hadn't known this as a conscious act.

It took almost falling into that dark place, nearly getting dissolved all the way in that syrupy universal sweet tea, for some sense of 'me' to panic, jerking back into a stunted—but integrated—awareness once more.

Never mind that. Another story for maybe another time. Never again. Not if I could help it.

All that said: I may be dead and disembodied, but there are these compensations. A telescope nowadays would be anticlimactic.

I was half watching the stars, half watching ahead of my movements to see cars going by, the faintest bee-swarm of radio signals homing in on their antennae as moths to a bug-light, drawn in and reinterpreted into sound by the radio mechanisms within.

Pleasant, eldred trees along the street and in the backyards of the older brick houses...they swayed and spoke in the whispery language of the arbor. Telling each other the things that only trees notice and only other trees care to hear through their chlorophyll telegraphs. The glitter-glue flits as the day's last photons were being drained of their energy, fused into vascular threads of photochemical life-fire. Birds were flittering about. Squirrels were finishing up their diurnal tasks.

I swept around the block, taking in the water-wavery, fresh-paint-sunlight taste-touch senses of the Americana Bakery as I passed its yellow-lit front windows. Cream puffs and heavy, spicy tastes of sausage...sharp, pungent sauerkraut from Schmidt's Sausage Haus. Over everything a faintly smoky smell, carbon dioxide reek of burning leaves and woodsmoke from a fireplace somewhere in the Village. Cauliflower clouds of smell-chemistry, swallowing each other...I was reminded of Kurt Vonnegut describing those beautiful Harmonium creatures on the planet Mercury...life broadcasting to life a constant message...*so happy to be here...so happy to be here.* And other Harmoniums warbling back the calm reassurance: *we're happy to have you...happy you're here...*

Everything heady and distracting. I kept to a circle of a few blocks around the bookstore, not wanting to stray too far. I could feel the faint tether-sensation that always stays between us—I've traveled as far as the depths of the Columbus underground and still not lost my sense of direction towards Body—but the feeling could act thin like an infinitely-extensible thread that never entirely broke...but felt thinned the farther I got.

I saw a jogger with her huffing little Boxer dog, a partly-remembered neighbor. A man picking up an office's worth of coffees from Common Grounds, the local Starbuck's competition. He was trying to balance them in their cardboard carrier while using his free hand to get out his electronic key fob for his Acura. On my second pass around the Acura was gone and the jogger was well down the road to Schiller Park, dog still gamely alongside her.

And on this second pass I saw a pair of dim figures in the shadow of a large, ivy-coated red-brick privacy wall for the law offices across the street from The Nookery.

They seemed to be standing in quiet conference. I didn't initially pay them any significant attention because an asteroid streaked through the upper atmosphere, a Morse code dash-dot of its contrail as it skipped off the stratosphere, a big stone kipping across a huge pond.

But I was on their side of the street, peering at old brick pavement showing underneath the holes in the modern asphalt once the asteroid was gone. I was floating past them and noting dead leaves blowing across my path when the shorter figure's voice cut into my reverie.

"He returned to the bookstore a little while ago. No, he hasn't come out. Do you wish for us to proceed?"

I stopped, reversed, twisting and coming back as quick as I could. But the figures were separating, each going down a different length of sidewalk.

Smiling men with guns, blasting away in the late afternoon and walking off as if they'd dropped off your mail. I instantly disliked all of this.

I was about to follow the shorter figure when it disappeared from view. There was a shushing sound and the shadow-shape…melted.

A wind blew across the hedge that lined the sidewalk where the brick privacy wall had ended at some property line or other. They might have gone through the thick brush, but in that split second all it appeared to me was as if the figure… 'folded' in on itself and was gone.

Which left the taller one walking away with loping steps. One hand was raised to the side of its head. Rain-drop ripple-pings near the head. I regrouped and realized this was the traditional 'phone held up to the ear' pose. I sped up to flow after them, concentrating on hearing.

Shadows...stuck to this person. Mummy wrappings of darkness stubbornly defying my attempts to see this person better...what was this?

Heavy breathing as they spoke: "Yes, yes...no, there should be no problems." Another wheeze of breath. "Yes. No, no. Thank you. Should we—" A grunt. A clack of the phone being closed. Another easily-interpreted gesture: the reaction of someone having just been hung up on in mid-sentence.

I moved ahead and tried to take in the figure from a new angle. It was so damned *difficult*, in looking directly at them. Their shadows flowed like molasses syrup around them, puddling at the feet and trailing with tiny wisps as when you draw hot tar off a freshly-paved street with a stick.

The voice had seemed mechanically sexless, as balanced in the low tones and high glottals as a male or equally female gender. But something in the swing of the arms and overall carriage of the body suggested male. He wore a long coat buttoned primly along a row on the left breast like some sort of antiquated admiral's jacket that V-ed open at the waist. The pants were an unremarkable pair of khakis, the shoes a non-designer pair of working dress shoes, the kind made of cheap, black leather and lace up to look similar to wingtips. But with thicker and more durable soles. Traction treading imprinted on them; the kind favored by waiters and servers in better restaurants. Functional but still looking somewhat formal.

As he emerged from the tree cover the shadows partially slinked off, spooked cats with tucked tails. The light behaved more as expected, though there were lingering elements of obscurity that continued to confound.

Above the button collar of the coat...I couldn't make out a face.

If I'd had eyes I would've been squinting, trying to make features out of the murk. The man's face and head...were like trying to stare across smoke from a bonfire, identifying someone as through a smeared pane of old window glass. I could see the general suggestions of two eyes and a mouth, a faint smudge that could've been the shadow of a nose...but the geography of the features would melt, slightly shifting out-of-true with the movement of the whole body. His face was like it was on shock-absorbers, the movements always a beat behind the up-and-down lift of his walking. Springing back but the head already in motion to the next space. I caught indications that the skin was cheesy-white, and there was no change in the smears of color to suggest any hair on top of the head...but looking at his hands didn't help: these were similarly blurred and indistinct.

The impression was of someone who was every blurry photo or shaky video you ever shot at a family gathering, except walking and breathing right in front of me instead of captured on some other medium.

I relaxed. Tried to view him through another lens of sight... the way that X-ray and microwaves glowed for me. It felt like an old childhood optic trick...squinching my eyes shut on a bright sunny day, open them fast and for a *moment* everything is bathed in a blue Munchkin pigment...a similar shifting subtly settled across my sight as I willed it. His features came together into something more coherent as the murk clarified.

I wished they hadn't.

I could see that in no spectrum of a sane universe could this ever be remotely beautiful. A spider sucking dry a helpless beetle can be mesmerizing when viewed by an entomologist, or in a rainbow flash of ultraviolet.

But not him. Not him and not what he carried with him.

His features were still soft at the edges, now more of a Monet expressionist painting. His face shifted, overlapping views of him had suddenly focused, aligning to present a clearer whole as I zeroed in.

His eyes were wide and lidless, specks of light skimming across their surfaces like oil oozing across water. I couldn't see pupil or iris differences. They resembled the dead-predator stare of a beached shark, looking out with the emotional blank of a doll. His skin was a sour milk, highlighted with veins and bulges of cheekbones and chin. A blade nose that uptilted at the end to present a pair of pinprick nostrils. The unflattering bust of some long-dead, Roman patrician-general carved in travertine paving-stone. The mouth was a narrow slit like the gun-sight slot of a WWII Nazi pillbox. Nothing in the cheese-dull face had any lines suggesting misery, happiness or any truly lasting reaction. The skull was bald and had a thin layer of sweat or oil beading and dropping off it. Where the drops fell to the ground a faint discoloration was left momentarily on the sidewalk pavement, evaporating quickly. Spilled gasoline on asphalt.

It was no comfort that his was the lesser horror.

The air around him was lurid with squirming, verminous shapes. Something of centipedes crossed with brine shrimp, with tiny monkey heads, jaws distended out in a massive, deep-sea fish's underbite, jagged and glassy-toothed. Green-black bodies that, as they squirmed and rubbed against each other, put out spurts of that same viscous oil as on the man's skull. Bulge eyes glared out of those vaguely primate skulls as the things—barely the length of the last knuckle and tip of a grown man's pinky finger, some as small as a newborn baby's toenails—looped and dove in a lumpish sphere around the man's head.

Every few moments what I'd initially thought was his wheezing, out-of-breath sound was actually his lipless mouth opening in a brief purse like a dead whistle. With the inhalation one of the looping, diving centi-shrimp-monkey-fish would be sucked in, fine pearl teeth past the man's lips crunching and sucking its squealing, snarling form. It disappeared in a protest-filled rush, the vacuum of its absence immediately filled in with the seemingly endless supply that packed the air. All the crunching, smacking and devouring didn't bring any light or change to his lidless, expressionless eyes.

A few rogue centi-shrimp-monkey-fish things floated around his nailless hands. I could detect signs of faint movement under his coat and pants legs. More of them, nesting in the dark recesses of his clothes and the crevices of his body. Birthing from lightless eggs and finding the nearest opening or orifice to emerge into the spawning pool. Every one to eventually feed that chewing, smacking mouth.

The whole thing, watching him walk speedily along to the corner where our street intersected with Schiller Park, made me think of dark caverns and eyeless white grub creatures littering a cave floor. A cave floor clean of any bat guano or other signs of life since no decent mammals would live that deep, that cold and forever blighted. H.P. Lovecraft daydreams weren't as grotesque and unlovely as this man. A shark and a doll and altogether something not human. Not even close. He was unfamiliar to me. I didn't recall our encountering anything like this before. As soon as I realized what I was looking at I immediately relaxed my sight, reverting to a more human-normal spectrum. A relief to let it all go back to a flesh-pale blur of hard-to-see components.

He stopped at the corner and stood as if waiting for a chance to cross, only there was no traffic passing along the road.

I floated overhead, but at that perspective watching him left me disoriented. I moved down to his eye level. I was looking at him as if I were another pedestrian waiting with him to cross.

The jogger with her dog had done a circuit around the park and apparently cut back along one of the duck pond paths back to the northern gate that faced my street. She was an attractive young black woman with skin the color of freshly unwrapped butterscotch hard candy, hair curled and long but tied back in a purple sweatband-held bun. A pea-green sweatsuit with a bright pink racing stripe down the pants legs.

As she paused to re-tie a shoelace, I noticed Mister Sharkdoll's head tilt to a side with a birdlike twitch. The fat paint-blobs of eye sockets focused on the jogger. Another palpable wheeze-suck crunched the air in front of his jostling mouth-line. He chewed slower...almost thoughtfully.

His neck straightened, then slowly rotated his head.

Towards me.

Was he *seeing* me in some way?

So far in our various misadventures, we had yet to encounter any beings, high or low, that could actually see me. Believe me, I've tried. I've stared into a mirror, been right up against its cold silver skin...trying to see something. Radio waves, heat waves, ultraviolet shivers, anything at all...nothing.

And mythological vampires are supposed to be the ones who cast no reflection. It's not really fair, is it? A dead man should be able to at least look himself in the mirror.

Various beings with a bit better attunement to the world around them could very-nearly perceive me, usually as a faint static in the air or a very low whisper, but that was a cheap trick. Spotting Pluto by looking at how Neptune and Uranus were warped in orbits because of the unseen mass. Absence is not a form, and the invisible is not a shape. Even black is at least all the colors absorbed, swallowed whole and combined in the digestion of light...but me? Nothing.

Other than that, those few physical signs of my interference with the walking world, and without Body's mouth to act as my personal windpipe I couldn't be noticed by anyone.

I dared a half-notch of vision again as Mister Sharkdoll pursed his lips. This time he spat out rather than sucking in.

What came from his mouth was a noxious spray of broken bits of leg, carapace, all these pieces like hideous little pottery statues had been ground up in a garbage disposal. Bits of luminous-gray fodder from crunching up those things. The squirming mass parted to let the spray fly free for the two seconds he blew it out from the slit of mouth. His eyes remained wide open, betraying no mood whatsoever.

The first bits of the spray reached where I perceived myself to be...they passed through with a buzzing, electricity-burning sense that instantly made me remember the taste of hot, dry mouth on a muggy July day and the smell of rotten meat in an old garbage bag during a summer strike of garbage collectors when I was a kid. Piles of maggots pooled in the watery puddles that collected in the divots of the piles of black plastic when it rained.

I was mentally gagging as the swarm proceeded through, passed along...continuing towards the jogger and her dog. The target he'd been looking at.

I spun about to follow, feeling helpless as the jagged swarm undulated forward. A motion that combined elements of a flag unfurling in a wind and the sweep and tug of a breast-stroking swimmer.

They reached the jogger as she was standing up and doing a brief neck stretch. In the last moment the stream split into two lines, flowing in greasy-swift eagerness to her and her dog.

The higher stream struck her in her chest. As it made contact, the bits and pieces didn't splash or blow back from the impact. They stuck, spreading from the contact point resembling not a flag or a swimmer but a gooey fluid, more of that slimy oil substance such as Mister Sharkdoll was sweating out. The material seemed to gel further and lose that limbs-and-chunks appearance as the substance flared and disappeared, a gray-white flash like the last pop of a light bulb when you flip the switch and it goes bad in the last surge. I didn't have to blink away the flash, but in that moment the substance disappeared.

On impact, the jogger coughed, an expression of complete shock on her face as her fist came up to muffle the cough, doubling over for a few hacks. A few more gasps and her throat seemed to recover.

The second stream struck the dog against its chest and a similar phenomenon occurred in a brief burst. The dog made a plaintive yowl, clearly experiencing more intensity than his mistress, and used one of his paws to bat at his nose. Then he did that frantic motion of a dog with fleas on its jowls, rubbing its face against the pavement for several moments while the jogger tugged at his leash and husked out coaxing words between her coughs. In less than a minute the pooch recovered with his owner.

She moved as an old arthritic woman, crossing the street and heading straight to Mister Sharkdoll. Wincing every few steps as if stepping on tacks while the dog followed with a dispirited whimper burbling out of his throat.

This was more than I could control. I blurted out a cry for

her to stop, instantly feeling the complete jackass. *Of course she can't hear you, dipshit.*

The jogger stumbled her way to the curb, and at the last second before they would have collided Mister Sharkdoll smoothly sidestepped to his right and completely clear of the jogger's path, letting her and the dog go by without any movement or seeming threat in her direction.

Those creatures thickened for one clutching moment, the shadows masking him with those eager, sticky-tar finger wisps around his limbs.

She obviously didn't see or sense him at all. No movement to increase the distance away from him as she went past, no comment or anything passed between them. Even the dog didn't react, moving as placidly in that defeated droop alongside the woman.

Watching this, I considered how my normal vision saw him as a fuzzy blur, an abstract paint-smear walking around… but could it be even harder for living people to perceive him? Maybe that was the reason for his constant intake and crunching away at those disgusting things…perhaps they permitted him that hazy state sufficient to fool human senses in a way, letting him move about unmolested. Like hunters smearing musk on themselves to be undetectable to deer or bear.

Unseen or not…as he finished his step aside and she came even with him…I could see the skin on the nape of her neck, under the bun of her hair…a faint bulge appeared, shifted with an under-the-bed sheet grotesque ease, disappearing as quick as it manifested. She reached up without thinking, scratching at the spot, not stopping her walk to do so. She turned at the next corner and was gone.

The mechanism seemed fairly basic and horrible for that simplicity. As I'd begun to ask certain questions of this creature, like where the centi-shrimp-monkey-fish things originated from for Mister Sharkdoll to feed on, here seemed to be the answer. He implanted them on periodic passer-by, maybe to hatch at some point later…gutting free of a helpless host the way desert wasps impregnate living spiders with their eggs...to later join up with his ever-present feed-sphere.

God only knew what ways those things would demonstrate their presence in that woman or her dog. What could nurture and fatten them to maturity? You didn't have to be a genius to see Mister Sharkdoll and his tiny ecosphere of beasts weren't of any sort of wholesome stripe.

When I was a teenager I once read a novella by Dan Simmons called "Metastasis." A tale about a man who, after a traffic accident, had the ability to see alien 'cancer vampires' who spit-planted these nasty gray slugs into people without anyone seeing or sensing them. All cases of people getting various kinds of tumors and malignant cancers were actually these things hatching and giving birth to more slugs, at which time the cancer vampires then returned to the victim's body and sucked up the matured slugs in their long, mosquito-like funnel-mouths.

I had a couple of nightmares after reading that story; after all, half my family were a veritable cancer cluster of breast, ovarian, colon and pancreatic flavors.

Not everything in the Under is necessarily good or evil. Many things are as amoral as any other things of the natural world. The wolf feeds on a deer. The lion brings down a gazelle. The praying mantis snatches at a passing beetle. Despite Disney attempts to sanitize the natural world and make it cute, Rudyard Kipling had it more right. That business about *Nature, red in tooth and claw.* Even those Disney people filmed poor, helpless lemmings being purposefully flung to drown into a flowing river, all to create the myth of their driving themselves to death in droves.

Don't believe that last one? Look it up.

But Mister Sharkdoll definitely was not anything operating in an amoral world. Those things looked hideous and so did he. When more of those things eventually found their way out of that woman and her animal or grew to some suitably gluttonous size, I had the feeling it was going to be nasty and painful. And in the case of the smaller animal quite likely fatal.

As I was mulling this over, Mister Sharkdoll decided he'd

had enough fun for the evening. He crossed the street and came to one of the many cars parked along the western curb of the park, a silver Honda Accord. I made note of the license plate as he peeled off, quickly accelerating down Third Avenue and off to merge with the rest of downtown traffic. Nothing bizarre here: he used a key fob and put his hands at ten-and-two on the steering wheel like any other driver.

I considered following him all the way...but telling Body as soon as possible seemed more sensible...no, I tell a lie. The truth is, I didn't want to ride shotgun in close quarters with that...walking menagerie of horrors.

So Mister Sharkdoll, and whoever had been the other figure he was loitering with, were clearly quite interested in our comings and goings. Who was on the phone?   Was it something fairly passive, merely curiosity?

No. Nothing passive nor innocent. That much I felt I could safely presume. Nobody has something as coldly loathsome as Mister Sharkdoll prowling at your doorstop for sheer curiosity.

Time to go home.

Go home and share a little of the bad news all around. Unable to entirely push away the memory of that electrical sensation of meaty, squirming motion that the swarm had evoked in me during its brief contact, I didn't do any lingering the last few blocks back to home.

7.

When I was sixteen, about two months after I'd gotten my driver's license, I got the idea to spend the weekend visiting my grandparents living down in Chillicothe, an hour's drive south of Columbus.

I don't remember that specific visit. I remember the drive back home, coming up along one of the back roads out of Chillicothe to eventually join with Route 23 back to 71 North and home.

I was approaching a T-intersection near a large dairy farm, with two Tolkienesque humped hills flanking the road I wanted to turn onto. A dead-man's blind turn. It was overcast, cool and damp. As I approached the T-intersection, signaling like any good new driver of sixteen to make a right, my '86 Safari minivan (my '77 Vega came much later) decided it liked the road it was already on a *skosh* too much.

Instead of slowing down as I started depressing the brake, it started a hard judder-skid that was mostly straight, then jerked to the right...headed for the steep ditch that came before the far embankment of the road I'd meant to turn onto.

For what felt like forever—more likely three seconds—of my heart flattening out and spreading wide, shadowboxing against the back of my lungs, I froze up as the minivan finally chug-squealed to a shuddery stop. Two feet from the ditch.

The stereo was playing my cassette of Pearl Jam's *Ten*. Eddie Vedder quavered about how his *whole world was painted black*…while the van shook and shivered and my heart danced a drunken step or two along a crooked stone wall, the dam between the living and the abyss…finally stepping back. Weeping and giggling, but stepping back…my heart settling again…

Pearl Jam: *I can feel their* laughter..*so why..do I* sear?

I took a breath. Took another. Was amazed that I could pull off two in a row, so I let the trend continue. Un-hunched from the frozen lunge I'd been in, uncramped my white-knuckled fingers from the steering wheel.

Looked around at the zinc-white sky. The dull greenish-brown grass that coated the hobbit embankment I'd almost crashed into.

One cow in the dairy farm's pasture to my left. Chewing cud and eyeballing me with all the bored bemusement that defines the word 'bovine.' *Another idiot almost crashed into one of those big property-line-hill-y things? Damn, if only you'd gone all the way, I'd've had something to really enjoy watching. Ah well, back to milk-making.*

No other cars or witnesses. I got hold of myself again and resumed the drive home without further event.

Recounting it later that evening to my dad, him pushing out pizza dough for one of his homemade pizza experiments. I sat at the dining.

Dad paused pressing out dough to give me an amused, geez-look-at-you grin. "You were driving too fast."

"No I wasn't. The speed limit was fifty. That's what I was doing."

Now the grin swept side to side in that tight little shake of head, less amused than disappointed. "Not the speed limit. You were driving too fast for the road conditions. It's wet out there. The reason you skidded and almost crashed was because you were going the legal speed limit, not the speed that actually suited the type of road you were driving on. You can't always assume that what's posted and official and legal is the way things really are. You need to make sure you pay attention to the *real* world as much as the *rules*."

I felt chided. But I've never forgotten it. That was, as best I can tell, the first time I consciously felt like an emerging adult learning one of the biggest lessons of the adult world: the big difference between the real world and the rules we try to impose on the world, and how dangerous it is to trust too much in the latter to accurately reflect the conditions of the former.

****

But like a lot of things that people know better, the lesson slips my mind at times as other priorities impose themselves.

I'd let my mind wander a bit, into Trina's embrace, the feelings, probably even allowed myself a little semi-narcotic painkiller toxin pulsing out of her salivary glands and into my skin. I allowed my heart to beat a bit, I let my thoughts lag and trying not to think of anything too distracting or complex. Nothing but her standing with me in the middle of the space, taking each other in…

There were soft, barely-a-sigh sounds from her. Puffs of cold breath against my ear, the nape of my neck.

I inhaled an evasive ghost of scent…powdered fruit-drink or not-quite-bittersweet flower petals…I thought of popcorn balls, puffed and collapsing, popcorn balls collapsing in a breeze to become tiny white flower petals…dogwood. Flowering dogwood in a spring breeze, same as what grew near my house as a teenager.

Flowering dogwood…her skin like the white-white of those petals, but her hair…my hands were in her hair, and it was so *there*, intoxicating…

…suddenly my thought, rummaged from an old memory and adapted for the moment: *If I had grown up across the street from Mother Nature, and gone to grade school with her and one summer afternoon left to our own devices in that playroom above the garage, we played spin-the-bottle and it pointed to the two of us...Mother Nature leaning forward on her hands and knees, meeting you face-to-face and kissing you with that forever awkward, forever lovely sensation of your lips, your nervous tics of motion, the desire and the burgeoning understanding of what it was to be something adult, something to be* loved...

...I was thinking that that's what flowering dogwood in Ohio springtime was, what it was *exactly*. The smell of Mother Nature's teenaged, nervous first kiss on your lips. The sensation you would always thereafter compare any other sense of romance or unrequited desire against.

There was the gentlest push and tug of her eagerness, tempered by an only-slightly-more-in-control intelligence trying to keep the hunger-rush under leash.

Somehow the puffs against my neck, the shift of allowing myself to be helpless against this smaller body holding me in a grip as firm as a steel-banded safety harness...the feeling like being air-lifted out of an ocean of warm but cloying water into the cold, vibrating air of release in her feeding...it was making my mind think of the flight of starlings and robins in the sky. The shape of black wings and silhouetted, bullet-smooth flying forms against the white paper sheet of a winter sky. I was thinking of her smell, still taking in that ghostly dogwood odor, that red-beet-pollen-and-erotic lilt-of-peach like Tom Robbins might have meant in *Jitterbug Perfume*. Leather and flowers, the smells of a familiar room, a walk down the street. Cobblestones and blood, throbbing and shifting, falling apart and away into everything...

A thought bubbled up from the mindlessness: *Gravity is the whole universe falling, with nowhere to land. So it all keeps falling, in one direction or another...*

Very, very distantly, I could think of my body responding the way it once had. I was taking her in, my senses flooding with her, relishing the deluge...

...but nothing...it was pulling away. That description doctors give of how LSD was used to treat pain in patients with terminal illness, clinical phrases about how it did nothing for the pain except detach the brain from wallowing in it. Their detachment became analytical, the distance that of a scientist looking down at the body and its agony as a laboratory beaker shaped like their body beneath them…

…nothing.

No real joy.

All the sensations and glory and ache from her to me, but in that crashing instant it was distanced. There was that precious but adamantine millimeter between myself and my own feelings.

God damn it.

Trina squirmed against my neck. Her hands balled into fists against my chest. Pushing. My vision jerked to the left. Jerked again.

Another tug widened that gap. The floral dogwood scent evaporated. My flights of fancy wiped away as clashingly as smashing pots and pans off a countertop.

Another jerk. I could hear her crying out, muffled as if her head were wrapped in a woolen scarf—

Muffled by my flesh in her mouth.

I allowed feeling to intrude back. As it did, the mental door screeched open and cracked a hinge or two.

Sharp, burning. Someone had taken a knife to my carotid, sawing away merrily like a demonic lumberjack on the tree-trunk of my neck.

Trina was alternately growling, whimpering, then tore her face away from my neck.

Literally tore. A chunk of my neck, spraying droplets and sizzling out a few candle flames, went with her. I dropped to the floor as so much flour in a sack.

Trina, snarling, crouched back to the shadows in the corridor, the startled predator taking over in self-preservation.

I lay on the floor, bleeding out onto the rug. My lips moved. I tried to force the door shut again, but it was only moving grudgingly, the pain arguing against being evicted into nothing.

It was numbing, gradually but definitely. But I realized, as my vision was darkening though my eyes stayed open…I was bleeding to death, not gaining control over my pain.

What the hell?

It came before I totally blacked out.

I had forgotten dad's lesson. A slick road, but I'd only been paying attention to the posted signs, not the real world.

Damn it. I should—

8.

I had no idea how long it could conceivably take for a baby vampire to feed for its first occasion. I probably should've been gone longer, rather than risk floating back to the store and discovering anything going on that might've warranted more privacy.

But I figured to hell with it. I hadn't planned on encountering Mister Sharkdoll and his floating Fishbowl of Freakies, either.

As I wisped back into the apartment at the rear of the store, I discovered Body on the floor, a huge Rorschach flower of darkened blood spread out a good couple of feet around him. His hands were folded over his stomach. Eyes closed. There was no point in checking to see if he was breathing.

I hovered closer. And noticed in a rush of air there was someone sitting on the cot, hunched like a Notre Dame gargoyle.

Trina's eyes were wide open, showing no white around the pupils. Volcanic glass with violet flashes. Her head was tilted to a side, like a listening dog. But no movement. She could've been plastic poured and cooled in that position on the cot, curled up, legs and knees tucked against her midsection and arms wrapped around her to be as far away from Body as she could manage.

What the hell?

I tried touching along that thin thread between myself and Body. It's nothing I can outright visualize, but it's there. Faint and ochre-tinged in my mind's eye. I gave it an experimental twang of spider-web alarm. *Testing. Hey, man, you in there? Speak if you aren't dead. I mean permanently.*

Nothing.

I glanced back at Trina.

What happened? Christ, I leave you kids for five minutes…

No response from Body's prone form.

Another look at Trina. No movement.

God damn it, I can't speak with no voice, no lips, no head or throat or…Jesus…what the hell happened? *Wake up, you asshole, I can't…*

The crazy of it must've inspired me. I looked at Body's mouth, the lips parted to show a glimmer of overbite.

The stereo was still playing randomly-loaded tunes. Insanely, it was Judy Garland from the soundtrack to *The Wizard of Oz*. I was floating closer to Body's face as that sad-sweet child-woman's voice began to extol the virtues of Somewhere Over the Rainbow.

I remembered explaining to Trina that the way I communicate through Body doesn't work like humans talking. I don't press air through his lungs and make his vocal cords vibrate, using his lips to shape sounds into comprehensible words. The closest I've been able to describe speaking with Body as my medium has been using his throat and head like a sort of giant Edison conductor, a metaphysical and semi-solid human windchime that I buzz through when I need to.

…and the dreams that you dare to dream really do come true…

It occurred to me as I stared, frustrated, at that glint of overbite.

I didn't really need Body conscious to still do it, did I?

I flowed down, imagining funnels pouring beer into a fraternity kid's mouth. Drains of water flowing away into the dark of a pipe. Down into Body's throat, the impression of closeness from dry tongue, cold teeth set in the gums as ranks of growing enamel sculpture.

Vibrate…willing the thought of moving back and forth as sound, what I was wanting to try and make that dark and wet space do, the bellow in my mind's eye pumping…a skull made of stretching and contracting canvas, a giant tympanum...

"*Wwwwwwuhhhhhhhaaaaaaaaaa…*"

Christ, this was *harder* than usual. It was so easy when Body was awake and aware and willing. I didn't have to provide all the willpower, all the imperative for the cells to cooperate, the organs to line up, the bones to shiver in the skin and do their thing for me to be heard.

…*someday-I'll-wish-up-on-a-star-and-wake-up-where-the-clouds-are-far…be-hind me…*

And I was aware. I couldn't see out of his closed eyes or move so much as his littlest fingers…but I wasn't bound to his form, was I? I was the ghost in the smoke, less than a bubble in a glass of beer. I could still perceive Trina on the cot, the room around us, the cool of the motionless form as I willed some sort of thrum and shudder to form, to shape, using the inactive throat as my sounding pipes, my personal flesh-organ in a cathedral of skull and tendons and veins…

"…*wwwhaaaa..*"

I had to try picturing teeth clacking, a tongue tapping the upper palate…the old sensations of slowly, carefully enunciating a strange word so you get it right…the vowels turning into the stop-sign of a strong 't' sound.

"*wwwhuhaaT. WhhhaaT? What?*"

…*where troubles melt like lemon drops a-way above the chimney-tops…*

Good God, that was eerie! With Body awake, my voice sounded like I remembered it sounding, except with a more hollow, slightly electrical reverb underlying it on the bass notes.

But speaking all by myself, my own effort making it, it didn't sound like anything organic at all. It sounded like one of those electronic voice simulators, vaguely borrowing melodics of my old voice, the bass and the faint lisp at the end of some sibilants (damn overbite)...but otherwise more resembling one of those Stephen Hawking computer voices reading out a sentence over an automated bank phone line.

Trina's head straightened. She unclasped her legs, unfolded her body like an insect moving away upon the approach of a shadow, a bird's wing on the sky as it dove in, seeking the prey.

She flowed off the cot, going to all fours, silent as she approached Body.

"John?"

"*Nnnnnnuhaht. Not? Not kuh...kuhwhyyy...kuhwhite. Quite. Nuht kuwhite. Not. Quite.*"

Easier with more practice, but only barely. The sensation was not unlike the phantom of a muscle beginning to heat up and cramp with fatigue poisons from over-exertion. Was I doing some sort of damage, forcing my will into words through his unconscious form?

Do unreceived radio waves scream in silent agony, begging to be received and heard somehow?

"You?" Trina pulled away, curling backwards until she stopped at the edge of the cot, seated on the floor much as she had been retreated on the cot a moment earlier.

"*Yuhesss. Yeah. Me. What. Hhhhhap...*" Another exercise: picture pressing the lips together, holding a cloud of air behind the lips...use the tongue to push, like a hammer striking a very pillowy bullet...release the air behind the lips as they purse out...the plosive sounds. "*Hhhap. Puh. Pen. Hhappen?*"

"What happened?"

"*Yeee-uh.*"

"I don't... we started to, and it was okay, like I was told it goes when you...when I would feed. But..." She looked away, curling her arms tighter around her tucked-in legs. She bowed her head and bumped her forehead against her knees. Once, twice. Looked back up and I saw two maroon trails down her chin. Parenthetical tracks from the ends of her mouth. "He... it was okay, but after like a minute...it was wrong. I was *stuck*."

Oh shit. What stupid dumbasses we'd been. Well, really Body, since it's his carcass to deal with.

"You got...tuh..trapped...in his...fuh..ff..fflesh as it..sss... started to heal...*ffff*from *your bite, d...d-d..didn't you?"*

She nodded. "Not just that. It wasn't that I was...stuck... there was something else. I felt something...it was like I was falling into his neck, through my...through my teeth. Does that make any sense?"

"Nn. Nuh. Oh. *No.*"

"I had..." she waved a hand, not moving the forearm but just rotating at the wrist, the rest of the arm still clutched around her legs. "...he...you told me that he heals, that he can't be hurt, but you didn't...you never said it was like that."

"D-didn't...nuh...know."

"Yeah. Shit's unfair all around the world, isn't it?"

"Yuh...youuu...oh..oh-kuh..kay?"

Another curt nod of the head. Her eyes roved everywhere but at Body. Up to the ceiling, towards the bookshelves and the walls, to the dim street outside the soaped-over windows. Minute purple-white flickers of light punctuated the rolls of the eyes. She was panicked, trying to cover it. If she'd still been a living human she may have been shivering and her teeth ratcheting against each other. But vampirism doesn't allow any wasted involuntary movements. So: violet-pale sparks from the eyes, nothing else. Even her voice was fairly steady and calm despite the hesitations.

Maybe it was simply another aspect we'd learned in the last few years of our 'weirdmanship': in Everything Under, you get used fairly quickly to the odd and deadly. Or you end up oddly dead.

"I had...to get loose, I was stuck, and..."

"I...geh...get the puh..picture."

So she'd torn out his throat getting free. That fit with the insanity she'd laid out. Of course. His body didn't know the difference between a mugger's knife and a lover's bite. It had healed automatically, not caring that the weapon, so to speak, was still lodged in the wound.

I'd never seen Body injured in any way like this before. A few months prior, dealing with the would-be demon thing that had almost taken out the city in a metal-fiery blast, he had been severely injured but not in any prolonged manner. All those injuries that resulted, even while he'd been temporarily possessed by the 'ripper's blazing burnt-blood-and-copper-steam essence, had stopped when he'd been freed of its presence and his body allowed to do its normal repair.

But neither of us understood how it operated. That talk of hers, about 'falling into' him through her bite, about somehow being pulled at, drawn inside him…was it more than healing?

Did Body's physical form, the one I'd known as my own until our separation into these separate-but-single entities, actually…*ingest* foreign bodies? Make them part of himself? Maybe…*digest* them? The way a living body digested food to rebuild tissue and generate energy?

Disturbing thought. To say the least.

Here was a new twist. Over the years we'd made a few experiments, accidents. Piecemeal trial-and-error education of what we're capable of. Now this: the ability to apparently talk through Body when he wasn't consciously allowing me access.

But on the tails of that particular wonder, another discovery. One that yielded no real understanding but suggested unpleasant future possibilities if not careful. And it was…what? An instinctive defense mechanism against personal attack? That didn't fit. Why draw *in* something attacking you? More likely a defense would repel. No. This seemed more like the initial ingestion theory…and that was god-awful ugly to think about.

I didn't think it was going to be fun if we had to see Rabbi Loewenstein's face if we divulged these latest tidbits to him.

While I was rolling these thoughts back and forth, I was acutely snapped out of them by the feeling of that thread inside my mind, twanging.

…*god…my throat frigging* HURTS.

It should. About half of it is on the floor.

I felt a pushing, an eviction upwards back into the air and dust of the room. I let it take me up as I twisted my attention downwards, back at the tableau below.

Body's eyes roved under the lids. Back and forth, as if hunting for something forgotten, an artifact tossed aside in some room at the back of his brain.

You'd better snap it up, Trina is freaked out. And there's some other news you need to hear about.

The eyes slowed. Stopped.

Christ. Please tell me you're joking I can lay here forever being dead.

No such luck. Get up.

The head turned, only a millimeter or two to the right, but movement. Then back the other way. I could see that the flesh there was very raw, discolored and chalky compared to the surrounding tissue. As I watched, it was gradually but steadily filled in, ragged edges meeting then fusing, matching the surrounding skin. In minutes it would be completely restored, no sign of any injury having taken place.

The mouth closed. Tightened. The lips were pinked with restored vigor. The whole face flushed.

Trina pushed up on her feet, sliding away from him and back onto the cot.

How long?

I came back after about an hour and found you like this. I moved higher, towards the ceiling beams. *I think she folded your hands on your stomach for you. Otherwise she's been sitting on the cot, staring at you and I think deciding whether or not to go running off screaming into the night.*

Glad...she hung around...

Are you okay?

His eyes opened. With a hinged, pained motion, he folded himself upwards to a sitting position.

Rubbed his neck. The back of his head. Turned the head one way then back the other, testing the tendons and restored meat of the neck. Felt the injury site, gingerly. Looked down at his legs, glanced around at the floor.

"Well..." he croaked, "this...rug is definitely a write-off."

"Are you okay?" Trina and eyed him like a bomb that was ticking inconsistently. Maybe about to go off, maybe about to merely *pfft* some smoke and go kaput.

He peered in her direction, making out her shape in the darkness. "Can you…could you please turn on the lamp? The floor lamp, over there in the corner."

She obeyed, and with a click an elliptic pool of pale light flew from the floor lamp in the corner, falling on him harsh as a miniature prison spotlight. He winced again at the brightness, eyes adjusting, and pulled his legs in to an Indian sitting position.

Coughed. Swallowed. Popped his eyes wide open and shook his head to clear out any dust or detritus there. Rubbed them. Coughed again.

"Please…hand me a water from the fridge."

A *thump-whump* of the insulated door being opened and slammed shut. A bottle flew a short arc, landed with a solid *plump* on the rug next to him, rolled and stopped at his hip.

He looked up from the bottle to the shadows. "Something wrong?"

"*You didn't say that would happen!*" Her burst of sound was feral, bright as the lamplight. It made waves in the air underneath me, jagged and sharp-angled as the exclamation graphics around cartoon sound effects of a fight, something from the old '60's *Batman* show. "You didn't tell me."

He picked up the bottle of water. Unscrewed the cap. Slowly took a tentative sip of water. Found he could manage that, swallowed a deeper gulp of the liquid. Restored the cap to the bottle.

Swallowed. Coughed.

"I didn't know that would happen."

"*Bullshit!* You…you were trying to *swallow* me or something!"

"Trina, I swear: I had *no idea* that would happen. It didn't occur to me that my body…"

"You *said* you healed! You *knew* about that!"

"It never entered my mind beforehand…I thought…when I talked to Justin—"

"*Justin isn't here!* He's not the one who promised to take

care of me!" She surged out of the dark, inches away from his face. The optic flashes were lilac-blue as a fresh bruise. Her next words had the quality of a car slowly crawl-grinding over gravel in a dark parking lot. "Justin isn't here, and you should've *known*."

He didn't shy from her.

"You're right. I'm sorry."

"You didn't warn me or anything."

"I didn't know, Trina. That's not a lie."

She didn't reply for several seconds. Around them the air itself was filled with conflicts: her own anger and tension were green-yellow shifts of that same spiky, exclamatory pain. His air was subtler, softer. He barely registered any auras or effects on his environment at all. A few curlicues like lazy smoke that died off.

That reminded me of the recent spirals off a certain crying clock.

Time collects in us, I reflected meaninglessly.

"Trina. Nobody can promise to take care of you forever. Even if they sincerely want to. That's not how the world works."

And with that, the world apparently heard, decided it didn't like being spoken on behalf of itself, and announced it would work just any way it so pleased. It announced via three hard *thwaps* against the back door. From the other side, a female voice stridently called out, sharp enough to be heard through the thick door.

"I got a call for a vampire losing her shit?"

9.

At my back step was a slight-built, attractive young Chinese woman. She looked like a magazine advertisement for something alcoholic. Something with words like 'spiced' and 'dark' in its label description.

The shoulder-length raven hair that haloed her oval picture-frame face had a single forelock braid of interwoven blonde, ginger and silver hair, falling down and then tucked behind one ear. The fire-engine-red leather knee-length trench coat was cinched at the waist with a wide, fat-buckled belt of the same material. She stared back at me with spark-bright eyes flickering behind a pair of cat's-eye glasses, a single rhinestone set in the upper frame corners. Unlike Trina's these eyes were the amethyst tint of old, pressed flower petals in a scrapbook. A nightshade color. A pair of matching-red, ankle-high leather boots with two-inch heels completed the set, one of them tapping a foot with barely-concealed impatience.

Her skin was pale to the point of resembling late spring lily petals floating on a dark duck pond. Something balanced in her way of standing, like a cormorant on a fishing boat's prow.

I had all of a second to take this in and she was already into her question.

"Hey. Where's the lady of the house who called?"

The stereo was still on random play. Robert Johnson's guitar twang-strumming was the soundtrack of the moment, accompanied by his whine-cry about a hellhound on his trail. *Blues fallin' 'round like hail, blues fallin' 'round like hail...*

I took a step back, waved a hand to indicate inside. "She's in here."

"You'd be John Flicker?"

I held out a hand. She gave it a two-second glance, clearly intended to show me she was fully prepared to decide not to take it, then reversed and accepted it with a quick one-two shake-and-release.

Her nails are painted with tiny hypno-swirls of cerise, do you see that?

"Jennifer Yu. I'm a transitions counselor."

I looked back at Trina.

She gave a helpless shrug. "I was *supposed* to call them if anything went wrong. But only if things were really bad. Last resort. I couldn't think to do it while I was...out of it. I did it when you fell...on the floor and all. Sorry."

"Don't apologize," Jennifer said soothingly, sliding through the space to take a seat next to her on the cot, no invitation needed. Her boots clunked authoritatively on the floorboards, and it all gave me an immediate sense of embarrassment for the state of the place, my dress, the whole generally 'domestically disturbed' air that her attitude projected onto me.

"But I seriously screwed things uh-hup."

"It's okay, you did the right thing." She leaned in closer. "I'm Jennifer. I specialize in helping people in the post-animate community deal with the more troubling aspects of their transitions into functionality."

Post-animate? A vampire therapist? A faint chuckle-whistle in my ears. *This is good. A vamp-whisperer.*

Jennifer looked up at me. "She's in a fragile place right now, which is at odds with the fact that at this same time, her body is primed as a predator. She's walking around with basically Kevlar skin, adamantium fangs, and cast-iron talons.

Her body is pumping excitement over every little pheromone her enhanced senses inhale, second to second. She's pulsing and pounding, and with the younger transitions like this, that energy, all that pumping inside…it gets sublimated."

"I get it."

Jennifer turned back to Trina. "When did you last feed?"

Trina mumbled. "Three *weeks?*" Trina paused, then nodded in obvious embarrassment.

Jennifer glowered at me. The lilac glint brightened. "Why didn't you notice that she hadn't fed in so long?"

"I…I didn't know. I thought she'd say something. She said herself that she didn't even feel anything for most of the time."

"You're an idiot." She said as straightforward as remarking on my height or the color of my hair. A direct and immutable fact of who I was. "You're a neophyte's first blood partner. It's your responsibility to look after her so she doesn't slip so badly." A surveying glance around the room. "Is this place normally this much of a wreck, or was this some of what happened?"

"D-don't be…" Trina collected herself, "h-hard on him. It's nuh-not his *fault*, I didn't—"

"Sweetheart, take a pill for a second and shut the hell up, okay?" Jennifer offered sweetly, patting the hands resting on Trina's knees. "You need help and I'm here to give it, but your partner has clearly let you down."

I had to speak up. "I know that I screwed up—"

"You don't know your dick from a tin whistle," Jennifer snapped, silencing me. "Did Justin not go over any of these details with you? About savaging?"

"Savaging?"

That sounds like ten kinds of red-flag bad, there.

A sigh that conveyed elementary school-level simplicity was forthcoming, in deference to my stupidity.

"When a vampire metabolizes energy, it's treated similarly to how carbohydrates in a normal person's diet are converted to fats for long-term storage. If the personal doesn't eat and begins to starve themselves, first the muscle is cannibalized and then eventually the fats stored in the pockets around the body. Vampires don't work the same. In their bodies, when starvation occurs, their metabolism slows dramatically. Now if they're not all that active to begin with, they won't consciously notice the changes. Same goes if they're a relatively new conversion. When a vampire is first-changed…there's a mechanism…I can't go into it too much. Basically, not all the old blood and bodily fluids are entirely purged. A small cache of the body's original tissue is preserved in discrete packets around the body. Older vampires know to take care of the feeding, keep to a regular schedule to avoid the consequences. But if a young or newer vampire goes long enough without feeding—the remission periods get longer with age—the body only has so many resources of stored energy to draw upon. We don't store fat and we can't eat normal foods anymore. Our bodies are designed to feed, not store or cannibalize. The body reverts to that bit of stored old material. Like a form of avoiding transplant rejection, having that last bit of 'emergency personal stock,' I'm not the expert to explain it. That's what gets cannibalized if a newer conversion starts to starve. Instead of being aware of a growing hunger, there's a twinge for a short time. The hunger pangs fade out so it seems like it went away and you're okay again. But that old supply is tiny, it runs out quick. At some point the vampire…snaps. Goes from perfectly fine to animal in a blink."

The glint flickered as she tightened her mouth, a clear *moue* of disdain towards me. "That's savaging. A vampire's body overriding its brain in one giant bang. You're lucky that she still had some conscious control somewhere and didn't go out looking for someone. There'd probably be bodies in the street right now. For the stronger ones, when savaging hits they sometimes have a blip of comprehension. Like human toilet training, you're asleep but still don't wet the bed." She looked at Trina, allowing a smile to creep out. "You did good, girlie. You kept it indoors and nobody was permanently hurt. You learned a hell of a hard lesson in what not to do, but there have been much worse scenarios for how something like this has turned out."

"Okay…" I tugged open the door, standing at its side with a wave to indicate going out. "I think I need a moment with you alone, Miss Yu. We need to settle some things."

Jennifer's smile crept back behind a steel door, slamming it shut as her whole face went metallic-sharp.

"This can wait—"

"No. It can't."

"Are you going to be okay for a few minutes?" she asked Trina. "I can stay if you really need me to."

Trina shook her head. "'M'okay."

Can you stay here and keep an eye on her while I confab with this 'transitions counselor'?

My pleasure. If she tries to kick you in the balls, my advice is not to invite her back for dinner.

Funny. Float your ass in this general vicinity for the near-future, okay?

Will-do.

The air fairly crackled with the sound of the soft leather trench coat whispering past me and out the door.

"It'll only be a few minutes," I offered Trina. She didn't give any indication of hearing me, merely stared at her hands at rest on her knees.

****

Closing the door after me, I turned to find the counselor standing barely an inch away from me. The personal space between us was so overlapped I could feel the cold that was settled around her, very distinct from the late-spring chill that was in the outside air.

"What the hell is your problem?" Her voice was reined-in but had a grating at the end of each sentence belying how much anger was underneath. "I've only barely gotten here and you're having *me* step outside?"

"I'm sorry if I'm messing up you 'establishing rapport' with Trina or anything, but we need to get some things settled before we go any further. You clearly think I'm some thoughtless dick—"

"A theory supported so far by much evidence," she interjected.

"Which I've been behaving like, yes. But I *do* care about her. I want this to work out for her. But before we get all into this problem, I think you should know a few things about me so maybe you can make a more honest assessment of what she needs."

She moved back enough to allow her to fold her arms at her chest. Looking up at me, I felt like I was being glowered at by some strange wind-up doll. The kind that in some freaky movie the villain has loaded full of dynamite and sent into the hero's bedroom while he sleeps.

"I asked for this assignment specially. I wanted to help Trina because I was the one who first discovered her and sent her to be brought up by your community."

"That doesn't mean you get special leeway for screwing it up."

I held up my hands. "I get that. I'm not asking—"

"She should be going with me straight back to a facility for an emergency transfusion and help—"

"God damn it, are you going to let me have two seconds' to actually finish a sentence?"

That froze both of us.

It wasn't my voice.

It sounded like when Soul spoke through me. The same metallic wind-tunnel distortion that I thought only resulted from having our intangible half speak through me.

More shades of Loewenstein, warning us about keeping things under control. I bowed my head, forming a breath as a moment's recompose. None of the pebbles or bits of trash on the ground moved...a breeze shifted a candy wrapper slightly and almost induced a mental heart attack.

The breeze passed. I looked up at Jennifer. Her features were neutral...but that lilac light was shivering in her pupils.

"I'm sorry about that. I didn't know that would happen when I got too upset. I'm...look, I don't know how much you were briefed about this before coming over—"

"You're a doppelgeist." Spots of streetlamp light kicked off the rhinestones in the corner of the cat's eye glasses. "How long?"

"Few years, give or take."

"Mmm-hhmm. You're invulnerable, right? Her teeth shouldn't even be able to penetrate your skin. Why did you volunteer to be a partner?"

"No, no," I waved my hands, "you've got it wrong. I'm not invincible. This isn't Superman's-36D-chest making buckshot bounce off his nipples. I can be hurt, I can be cut and shot and just about anything else. But I heal. I heal fast. When she bit me—"

She worked the rest out. "She bites, breaks the skin, starts to do her thing, and your body doesn't know any better, treats it like any wound." Her eyes widened, more spots of light lens-flaring off the rhinestones. "You started to heal *around* the bite, with her *still biting?*"

"Exactly. It never occurred to me that it would act so fast in such a way."

A tapping of booted foot on the pavement. A few moments' musing. "Okay, here's the situation: if she can't feed, you're no good to her as a blood partner. We'll have to get her back to the dormitory and then find—"

"Whoa, whoa. Wait a moment. There's got to be a way to deal with this."

"I don't see how. You can't be bled, and she can't feed without getting the blood out of you, and a blood partner kind of has 'blood' right there in the front of the term, so—"

"Look, not all mothers directly breastfeed, right? There are milking devices they can use to lactate into and store up a supply of milk, right? Isn't there something out there that could be used like that, to...I guess...bleed me? So I can draw out blood without endangering Trina in the process?"

She stared at me. That statue stillness...it gets to me every time. It's the only truly disorienting attribute of vampirism for me: the total lack of involuntary body movement you normally look for in another person without totally realizing it until it's absent.

Finally: "You're crazy."

"So's three-quarters of the breathing world. And frankly..." I passed a hand across my eyes, rubbing at a perfectly dry forehead as if I could sweat out of panic. "…frankly it's horrible, the thought that what I put her through these last few weeks… that she literally was cannibalizing herself…the last parts of her old self, no less…I can't fathom that right now. When it hits me later, *really* hits me, I'm probably going to go out and drink half a bar so I'll have something to justify throwing up." I lowered my hand, leaned back against the doorframe. I cleared my throat and the rusty-hurt feeling didn't go away, but at least I could talk once more without my voice wavering. "You haven't answered the question."

"They have…there's medical equipment available to the community." She was considering it carefully. "I think someone might…*might*…be able to adapt one of their apheresis machines for the purpose."

"That's the thing they use at plasma donation clinics? The machine that separates plasma and platelets from blood and then puts the blood back into the donor?"

She nodded. "It could work. *Maybe.* Have you had blood drawn before? I mean, as you are now?"

"I have it withdrawn whenever I've needed a blood test for…work purposes. If the needle is in and out quick enough, I've never noticed any problems with it. Maybe the needle is smoother than teeth so if I was healing around it I just never noticed…but yeah, it works."

"The porn?" The look on my face was sufficient answer. "Don't look put-out. I have a dossier on you and her. She's one of my case assignments. I always get a call at least once in a transition period, so I figured inevitably I'd hear from one of you."

"I have to ask you something. I don't care who you work for. If you give even half a damn as you seem to for Trina, I need a straight answer."

Stillness. "O-kay."

"You're pissed at me for my negligence. I take that on the chin full-bore. It's my fault I didn't live up to my obligations and pay more attention to what she's been going through. I don't have any excuses."

"I'm with you so far."

"All right. So why did I not hear about you until you were knocking on my door?"

"And with that you lost me."

"I mean Trina has been too scared or worried or embarrassed to tell me things, and admittedly I haven't been asking to find out. But you guys could've warned me about some of these things. Could've given me your number? Obviously it was given to Trina to have in case of an emergency. All *I* got was a reference to some contractors to tear up my store and a few brief notes on where to buy modified S&M gear to restrain her if she got out of hand. Of course that particular ship has sailed and I have a half-dismantled ex-bookstore to prove it. Why the hell wasn't I given this kind of information up-front? Even the most tyrannical and stupid corporate office has a day's training and orientation when you get hired to answer phones. What's going on here?"

"Wait a minute." The boot stopped tapping. "Let me get this straight. You don't know *any* of this?"

"I don't even know what 'this' is to tell you yes or no, so let's go with 'no.'" Mental fatigue was congealing in my skull. "No warning about 'savagings' or anything else. Is this how you guys normally set up blood partners and new vampires? Is it really *this* slipshod?"

She tilted her head. Half-turned from me, gave us a few more inches of space. Looked at the street as a car went by. She looked back at me.

"No, now that you bring it up. They normally have a pretty decent system in place for new partners when they place a new conversion with someone. It's considered standard practice, virtually no exceptions ever."

"Yeah, well, you showed up for one of those 'virtual' exceptions, trust me."

"I don't...wait a second." She pulled out a smartphone from one of her jacket pockets and began taping and dragging her fingertips on its screen. "I have a case summary here..." she stopped. "This is ridiculous. I didn't notice it before. There's no listing for who discharged her to you. Who did you deal with?"

"Justin."

That brought about another lengthy stare, then a long look at the phone display. The phone screen reflected in her glasses, making the whole surface go flat and opaque; in the dim she looked like a comic book drawing, a Ty Wilson eighties-trendy wall poster of short-haired women with neon for eyes, or a stark black-and-white of a Frank Miller comic book *femme fatale.*

"Justin personally discharged her to you? And he didn't say anything about any of this? Or even tell you about contacting me if there was trouble?"

"Not a word."

"This is…crazy. I wouldn't imagine…"

"This is the part where you need to give me the truth if you can: in *your* opinion, is this how any new vampire is assigned to someone like me?"

"No." She lowered her phone. Her expression was as plain as outright nudity. "I mean, there could be other circumstances… the community doesn't usually require giving orientation information to someone if it's an experienced member being assigned…they're considered responsible for themselves if they've been converted long enough, but—"

"But this isn't that set of circumstances. Look, I get this weird feeling…either Justin had way too much confidence in my ability to deal with this, or…" I held my hands palm out, fingers down, with a weak shrug.

"Or he wanted you to fail? Is that what you're suggesting?"

"You suggested it. I shrugged."

"There's no good reason for Justin to have misrepresented this to you, or leave you to sink or swim."

"No good reason that you or I can think of," I countered. "But not necessarily one *he* couldn't think of."

"That's insane."

"Maybe," I shuffled a foot, scuffed the toe of a sneaker against the ground. "But fact remains: I was left effectively out in the boondocks on this, and both Trina and I nearly paid dear for that slip-up. Unless you want to consider the premise that Justin simply went total balls-up and forgot to mention anything to all this, something which I personally don't believe…then as the old master detective said: remove all the impossible and what's left—however improbable—is the truth."

My phone rang, the unmistakable ring tone chorus *Fish heads, fish heads, roly-poly FISH heads—*

I held up a finger for a minute's patience while the other hand dug out the cell phone from my jeans pocket.

"Hello?"

"Got a car comin' for you in about a minute, hoss."

Toneless. Straight remark, as inevitable as pronouncing the weather. Not messing around or telemarketing. Besides, telemarketers can't call my phone anyway, thanks to a favor or two owed me by a *voltwraeth.*

Don't ask. Another time, maybe.

Voice familiar but not one I associated with being on the phone. Scraping gravel vowels, cough-from-the-throat consonants. Yet somehow soft at the end, like a resignation to some bad news devoutly wishing never to be delivered.

"Need to see you, old son."

That made it all terribly clear.

"Bit rude of you, to be so out of touch of late. Hate these damned portables, but Cackler was able to get me one so I could try reachin' you." The mildest touch of reproach, like your grandfather shaking his head over your childishly kicked-and-spilled can of paint on the carpet.

Oh shit. Shit on a shingle and stuck on the shithouse roof. As my grandfather once said.

"So he'll be by with a car in about a shake and a half of the lamb's rear end, 'kay?" The call blipped off, no civilities or arguments permitted.

I put my phone away with the motion of backing away from a questionably-defused explosive.

Jennifer couldn't miss the cues. "You look like you just got called by your broker and told that you'd been invested in heavy Las Vegas real estate before 2002."

I shook my head, feeling punch-drunk and I hadn't even

felt the hit. Yet.

"Not a what. 'Who'."

"Who, then?"

"Please take care of Trina. Do whatever you ultimately think is in her best interests, okay?"

"Do you need help?"

I smiled. The smile a ride operator gives you when he's trying to assure you it's all okay, though he can't remember if he really tightened those last bolts the last time the fair came into town and put the ride up.

"I have been issued a royal summons. So it looks like I'm meeting with the Sexton King within the hour."

10.

I watched Trina sit on the cot from a ceiling corner. I wasn't avoiding her or being cute; I wanted to stay up and away for a time. She got up, fixed a few piles of books, then sat back on the cot.

It's easy to fall back into the pattern of thinking like I did when I was a child. When I could scrunch down under tables where adults were seated, talking. From burrowing past clothes on a sales rack, hiding in the hollow centers of those department store circular displays. Knee-and-hands shuffling through crawlspaces and balling up to sleep inside old trunks in my grandparents' house. My time now is a lot like being a kid again, being able to see the world from the viewpoint of the tucked-away and too-small-to-notice. You almost want to hold your breath, if you still had any, so as to be the fly in the rafters, the worm in the garden.

I listened to the click and tick of the building around us. The sigh of air disturbing dust. The faintest burr, buzz and clap of the voices outside the door. It was enough that in a minute I was feeling something like old drowsiness, relaxing into a bath of insensate 'non-think.'

The smell of high grass and timothy stalks...my

grandmother's backyard in Chillicothe, the small garden patch of herbs and tomatoes. The feel of cool, twilight-dim moss amongst the poison oaks.

Rough bark. Taste of lemonade lingering bittersweet on the back of my throat. Sweat on my neck. Chilly breeze.

Chill. Summer. Hilltop. Darkness in the woods...what did I see, that one summer I was alone? When I'd gotten away from everyone and gone into that copse of trees behind Hess House?

Slam-shudder as the back door opened to admit the counselor and Body coming in after her.

I need to tell you about—

We have to go—

I stopped. *Okay, I guess you first.*

Jennifer approached Trina. "Honey? Do you have a coat? A bag you can pack for an overnight stay?"

Trina looked at Body with a panicked face, unwrapping from her curled-up pose with a taut edge to the arms, hands gripping at the edge of the cot. "Do I have to move out? What's wrong?"

"It's fine." For what it was worth, I had to give credit: Jennifer had a hell of a voice for calming someone down. Very fluid and quiet without whispering or sounding condescending. "It's only for a night."

"I don't need to leave."

Jennifer looked to Body. "It really is fine, Trina," he offered, trying to match the counselor's tone. "I need to take care of some things. I got called for some help. It's a good idea if you go with Jennifer and she can help you take care of your needs while I get this other stuff settled."

Trina did another pass at glancing from Jennifer to Body. Without further protest she disappeared back into the depths of the bookstore.

I watched her go, seeing on Body's face the same expression of what I was feeling. Good intention seems to often end at a dead end of regret, and there's no one to blame except your sanctimonious self.

Jennifer pulled out a blank business card and wrote her

name and a pair of local phone numbers in a bluish-purple ballpoint ink: the same cerise shade as her fingernail polish. "Here. The first is my direct number. If you can't reach me, don't leave any messages. Hang up and call the second number. That's to the facilities desk. If I don't answer the first it's because I'm at the second, so one way or another you'll reach me."

Body nodded, pulling out his wallet and scrunching aside various receipts and other business cards to make room for the latest tenant of the battered black leather vortex. "I'll call you later tonight if that's okay, let you know if things are settled down any. If...anything significant happens...call me immediately, okay?"

Jennifer nodded. A hand rummaged into one of the deep front pockets of the trench coat. The hand emerged with a small plastic seal-lip bag, the tiny kind automatically associated with drugs. She used an exquisitely-tipped nail to split the seal, another fingertip reaching in to extract an assembly of loose change. Spiral-swirl-painted fingernails deftly selected a nickel and two pennies.

"Here." Body put his hand out and dutifully accepted the coins. "If you somehow can't reach me by phone, if something happens where you lose yours or there's no signal...whatever. If anything goes bad and there's no one else handy, use these."

"I haven't used a pay phone in a long time, but I'm fairly certain it costs more than seven cents to make a local call on one."

"They're not for a pay phone. And that's not a nickel."

We peered into his palm. Sure enough, the coin I'd mistaken for a nickel was nearly the same diameter as the traditional brown-copper coins next to it. Except this had a tarnished finished, with a slightly heavier edge-stamp. It glinted brighter than its fellows.

Holy shit, I snapped on the recognition. *That's a 1943 steelhead penny. That thing is worth about two bucks by itself, even dirty and used like that. If it was brilliant-uncirculated condition, I think...*

It'd be more like a hundred or so.

"You a numismatist?" Jennifer asked.

Body smiled. "Bookstore owners pick up a lot of useless information. It's what we get in lieu of wild fortunes and fame."

"Don't lose those and don't go accidentally making any wishes into a wishing well or anything." Her face gave zero suggestion of humor. "And if you drop one, pick it up right away or leave it where it falls."

"You need to illuminate me further, please." He plucked the steel penny from his palm and held it up, turned it to see both sides. The back, instead of the more modern engraving of the Lincoln Memorial, was text stating ONE PENNY and under that the heading UNITED STATES OF AMERICA with a pair of wheat sheaves curled around the edge like long, spindly hands cupping the words in the center.

"If you absolutely can't reach me by conventional means, try these. Preferably on open sidewalk or parking lot, a place like that. Open and public. Drop these on the ground and leave them. We're talking very much strictly absolutely three-alarm emergency, you got it?"

"How do these work?"

"Never mind. I don't entirely get it either, I've never had to use them before. Put them away from the rest of your pocket lint and loose change and remember them if you have to empty your pockets like for an airport metal detector or whatever."

"Should I have safety gloves when I handle them?"

"Very funny. Though I'd keep them away from your wallet if I were you. They have a way of destroying credit cards."

"I'm good, thanks."

"Do you understand?"

"Yes. And the code phrase is 'Klaatu barada nikto.'"

Faintest muscular quirk at the right corner of her mouth. "Smartass." A tilt of her head. "But better than the dumbass I came here thinking you were, at least."

"We aim to please."

I let my vision relax on the pennies as Body returned the steelhead to its kin and put them into his breast pocket. I was somewhat happy to see them put away.

Coins are like most inanimate objects: relatively dead

air. Objects like food, wood or feathers can sometimes have very frail, puffy after-image trails because they came from something alive that once fed them energy and sustenance. The ghosts of the chlorophyll network I saw in its live state earlier on the street, when looking at a block of wood. Metal objects, though, especially machined-produced and not unique or hand-tooled, give off virtually nothing except the slow, long waves of whatever body heat they might've gotten from handling, or radiation and other incidentals. I wouldn't go so far as to say metals are 'dead' but it's more that inherent properties are so atomically grounded as to make their qualities 'sleep' in their depths. Metal is a tough gig.

The three pennies in Body's hand, before he put them in his breast pocket, had a pale glow that made me think of the semi-transparent reflection of streetlights in a car windshield. It flickered, would seem to be gone completely, then slowly return like a light warming on a dimmer switch.

Those things are not just collectibles. They look...they feel-taste like soft velvet and radio static covered in bittersweet baker's chocolate.

They had the faintest—only faintest—feel like...a dark magnetism from above. Pass a strong magnet over iron filings, watch the queerly organic-looking fronds of the iron rise and wave upwards. Looking at the pennies had made me want to very gently...fall *into* them, somehow. Fall in and flow up...a reverse waterfall dragging me into a current flow, frond waving upwards to the Giant Magnet overhead.

Do you think she's giving me a Mickey? Some sort of booby trap?

The coins took their attraction with them when they were out of sight, out of (my) mind. *No. She reads honest about her surprise at this situation. I don't think she's giving you anything harmful. Still, I'd consider keeping them for very long very carefully.* I let the mental image of the pull-glow transmit to him. *I couldn't begin to guess what they glow on those things means, or even if they're necessarily real pennies or made to look like them.*

Jennifer pointed at Body's chest. "Trina didn't cause that."

Ooops. When you put the coins away your coat opened. It revealed the hole with burnt edges that marked your shirt. Body hastily pulled his coat shut.

"No, Trina didn't do that."

"Powder burns?" He nodded. "So someone shot you."

He relayed a brief description of what happened, leaving out Arrundale's name.

"Is that a regular thing with you?"

"If it was do you think I'd have asked for a housemate to move in with me?"

"They're not in the business of protecting people for the sake of their blood partner. Are you certain you can handle this?"

"Not certain at all." Body looked into her eyes. "But for her, I'll try anything." He swallowed. "Can I ask you a personal question?"

She cocked an eyebrow, and for a moment I was sure she was going to refuse. Then: "Your dime. Or pennies, as it were. Go ahead."

"You never talk about them as one of them."

"What?"

"I noticed a difference between you and Justin. When Justin talks about the community, he uses 'we' and 'our.' *Our* community, *we* can help. But every time you spoke about the community...you referred to *them* and *they* and *their.*"

"So?"

"So aren't you one of them? Am I misreading the signs or are you not a fellow member of the community?"

She glanced at the ground. Put a hand on one hip. Tapped the foot a few beats to a song I couldn't recognize with just the rhythm section.

Then a smile half-cocked her mouth, showing a little white of teeth. A very pretty woman when she wasn't snarling at you.

"You're an observant person. For once. Let's put it this way: there's *working for* something, then there's being a *part* of something. Being a part of something is when you feel it." The smile wilted. "Working for something is usually when you don't have much choice, if you expect to survive in your new situation."

I think I know why she's a transitions counselor for people like Trina. I felt Body's mental nod in return.

"I hope someday soon I'll be less of a dickhead to you, Jennifer Yu."

The smile came out once more, less guarded and more genuine this time. "We'll see."

Trina returned with a suitcase held in front of her in both hands, the image of a child waiting at the train station in some Norman Rockwell pastiche. Jennifer took the suitcase from her with a gentle but firm tug.

A faint shush of air, and Trina's arms wrapped around Body, head pressed against his chest like she was listening for a heartbeat.

"I'm sorry," she muttered.

Body's tear ducts are as the rest of his body: a semblance of living but for all practical purposes non-functional unless he's consciously choosing to make them so.

But there are moments where he responds the same way he remembers doing before.

And I could taste-feel a sensation of choking, of wanting to blink against a bright light and not having anything I could blink to shut it out. Things skewed slightly before I willed myself to regain focus.

His eyes were very bright before he squeezed them shut. A hand stroked Trina's head, the other giving a faint squeeze to one of her upper arms.

"You didn't do anything wrong. This is all my fault."

I moved forward and weakly whistle-buzzed: *"My fault, too."*

She gave a shuddery sniff mixed with a childish, teary laugh. "You guys together almost make a whole working brain, you know that?"

Through overlap...I could smell the lightest ghost of her. Leather and rose oil.

"Someday we hope to be a real boy, too."

Body grinned, wiping hard at his eyes as he opened them.

She stepped back, releasing him and looking up at us. "Is it going to be okay?"

We should have told her it doesn't work like that. No one can predict the future. Never could. I've met some fantastic guessers, even a time traveler, but no perfect fortune tellers.

But I'm not fabled for being a steely pragmatist.

"Of course it will," I replied. *"Right now is one of those stupid moments that get in the way of the good stuff. But the good stuff* always *comes back. You know it."*

She smiled. The violet flinting in her eyes went so low that for a brief second she was the girl we first met just after her conversion, when her body and mind had still been lingering in that semi-living limbo between who she was born as and what she was now, now and forever after. For a moment, I saw a smile that was something alive. And happy.

Only that smile was how we could have let her go on her way.

Body shut the door after her, standing for a minute with his hand still on the door.

The stereo had been left on. The random selection continued. Stevie Wonder. "My Cherie Amour."

We stayed by the door for a minute. Body's hand stayed on the door. Somewhere outside a car started up and pulled away.

I wished I could swallow. Ever have that rusty-metal-lump feeling in your throat? Like when you're being disciplined as a child and you want desperately to swallow because until you swallow, make it all fall away, go down into your stomach, that feeling seems to have the power to keep swelling and swelling and choke you off? You think that the pain will never go away, but part of you keeps at the throb of it because you also know that the second you manage to swallow, all the feeling and fear will come exploding out and you'll finally lose control, bursting into tears and your face boiling hot? Imagine all that, only picture that you're no longer the owner of a throat, a tongue, a face...so you can't simply swallow it all away.

"Okay," Body breathed. He went to the desk. "So let's see..." He opened the big main drawer and started to rummage.

What did you want to tell me?

"We're waiting for a car to pick us up." He shoved aside old papers, a couple of keyrings of keys long forgotten for their application. "Where is the pocket flashlight?"

O-kay. And our mystery driver is—?

"Cackler. Where's the damned flashlight?"

That sent cellphone-signal-quivering down and up my oil-on-water length. *Why?*

"We have been summoned by the King."

For what reason?

"He wouldn't say. He asked us to come out as soon as possible and he'd explain when we got there."

He called you? I mean, like on a phone?

"Yeah. He sounded less than thrilled about having to resort to such a 'modern' method." He started grabbing handfuls of the old papers and keychains and other bric-a-brac and dumped them onto the desktop.

Huh. Wonder what sort of minutes plan he gets.

Body didn't see the flashlight and in a bolt of exasperation swung an arm with a snarl, sweeping half the contents of the desktop onto the floor, pens and pencils clattering as the keychains made plink-clatter noise. "I don't feel like shits and giggles right now."

Neither do I. And that was before you dropped that particular stink bomb on my already-shit mood.

"What?"

Without further verbals, I let memories of the recent encounter with Mister Sharkdoll and his unidentified partner flow along the mental thread. He sat down in the nubbly blue armchair as he digested the impressions.

Finally he jerked up a hand. *Enough, enough.* "Good Christ, I wish you hadn't shared those little squirming things."

Tough luck. I wish I hadn't seen those little squirming things to begin with.

You didn't see any real detail of the other person. The one that got away first?

Mister Sharkdoll was the one in communication with whomever else is in this. I figure it worked out picking him to follow after all.

But those shadows...the way they moved...that's a new

one. Body rubbed his chin. This sucks all around like a Dyson upright. At least Trina will be out of harm's way for now.

Maybe Bill Arrundale has friends keeping watch?

The vampires have clearly been observing us off and on, as much as they seem to always know about our goings-on. I caught a whiff from Body in the thought-stream: Jennifer, remarking on a 'dossier' about us.

The list of who might have reason to tail us is fast getting intolerable.

Body rested his hand flat on his thigh and stared at the fingertips. *Do you sincerely think Justin would hire someone like* that *to shadow us?*

Times past, I would've said no.

Same. But times past, I would've said he wouldn't try and trip us up with Trina. "Damn it," he breathed, closing his eyes. The other hand came up to rub at his recently-restored neck.

I hovered up in the ceiling corner by the back door. *Maybe Pinney could run the license plate number. You need to call him about Arrundale anyway. This could be related, or it could simply be open season on our collective ass. By the way, the flashlight is in the right inside pocket of the coat you still have on.*

He reached absently into the selected pocket and confirmed the black palm-sized flashlight was there. Snapped the little rubber button to make sure it worked, turned it off and returned it to the pocket. Ran his hands through his hair.

Either way it's a problem. I hovered over the desktop, contemplating the remaining bits of notepad paper and old scribbled reminders.

"It's a thought. But we need to put it on the back-burner for now."

Agreed. I moved to the ceiling corner. *Change your shirt. The King is waiting.*

11.

I went and shut off the stereo and found a clean shirt to put on, returning to the apartment space in time to hear a whonking noise. Our ride had arrived.

Cackler pulled up to the curb outside The Nookery in something he'd stolen straight from a Big Daddy Roth cartoon.

It was a blindingly glittery-flecked custom paint job in a screamy "Florida orange rind." Running flames painted in acetylene-torch blues faded to white tapered tips at the rend ends of the suicide doors. The rear tires were at least four inches greater diameter than the front, and there were gaping cavities exposing spring shocks and chassis assembly over the front. The whole vehicle had a streamlined, balloon-soft quality to its low-slung, growling-leaned-back look. Like seeing a puma in the zoo during an afternoon doze, but with a bunch of birthday party glitter spilled into his fur.

I am not an autophile by any stretch. I've only owned three cars in my life. I was about as familiar with Blue Book Listings as you might be familiar with the Crimean phonebook. But I couldn't miss the cyclopean middle headlight that shone like some hell's lantern, dominating the lesser left and right lights the way and alpha wolf will lead lesser beta males on the hunt.

I opened the door and lingered, staring at the car by the illumination of the streetlights. Taking in the microsuede upholstery still crisp with faint vacuum-cleaned whorls in its weave. The interior was spilled-wine-on-damask burgundy, a stabbingly clashing tone with the blue-white-flame-and-orange-explosion exterior.

Wow. A shush of motion on my left, doing a circuit of the vehicle before me. *Just...wow.*

Wow, indeed.

"Is this a Tucker Torpedo?"

Cackler looked at me from behind the wheel. His greasy grub-dirt pallor seemed to provide its own light in the obscure cabin space. A lanky, soiled-clothed man in plain work dungarees, Frankenstein-soled work boots caked with ancient mud, and a hat as formless and clumpy as the rest of him.

A Deadjack: one of the least-liked humanoids in the Under. A sworn servant of the Gravedigger's Emperor, sent to collect us by royal summons.

He grinned with teeth that in the dim of the interior seemed to be both glowing and dingy, like grim spots on a chemical glow-stick.

"Ain't she a beaut?"

"That wasn't quite my first word for her, no. Why the hell butcher an already-perfectly-good classic car?"

A faint raspberry from rubber lips. "I just drive 'er tonight. I didn't tart her up like this. But she's got a nitrous hookup in the trunk, if you wanna siphon off a little giggle-time." The grin framing the remark was one you wanted to hit but you'd be afraid that somehow your knuckles would ooze on contact and be deflected with a waxy, rancid sliding off the skin. "I didn't have a chance to ask the owner his opinion on car paint. Get in. Time's a-wastin'."

I climbed in, feeling Soul shiver past me to the back window and stay back there, wanting to keep his own distance from Cackler as much as could be managed in the enclosed space.

"You been shackin' up with any—"

"Shut. Up." I slammed the door shut and didn't look at him.

He gave an exaggerated shrug of resignation and started the car with barely a whish-grunt of changing gears.

I was tired. Of all of it. I can't go to sleep, but I can still get exhausted of sheer circumstance. Trina, Jennifer, people trying to shoot me on the street in broad daylight, dealing with these twisted changes...it was all coming to a crashing, cacophonous head. Now topped off with this grinning jack o' lantern scuzzball driving me to a meeting I had no clue as to the reasons for.

Cackler didn't offer any further commentary, and I didn't try engaging him for the rest of the drive.

****

Greenfriars, if I haven't belabored the point enough to you, is huge on a scale that is hard to convey when you're walking around a boneyard the size of a small town where no structure is more than two storeys tall.

When the city fathers of Columbus in the mid-1800's wanted to create a true cemetery-cum-bird-and-picnic community park, in the grand Age of Urban Enlightenment that swept up the country and lasted well past the beginning of the 1900's, they didn't screw around. They also didn't skimp on giving their own family tombs and plots a lot of afterlife leg-room.

There are over 40 miles of roads, paths and walkways. Patina-green, wrought-iron bridges spanning empty, artificial creek-beds that make you think of Japanese abstract rock gardens as interpreted by Victorian landscape designers. There are official Audubon Society birdwatching spots around Quarry Pond, at the center of the whole place. A lot of the original stone that paved the graveyard was mined from that site, until a poor pick-wielder struck an aquifer that flooded the site in moments. You can easily get lost—even in a car— amongst the rows of crypts and semi-earth-bermed tombs. There are mausoleums the size of small housing developments dedicated to single families, these dynasties of old Columbus.

These even have their own trimmed lawns, hedgerows and marble sitting-couched ensconced with grinning gargoyles, like poor country cousins for the grand European cathedrals.

As Cackler took me past the more modern 1960's burials section where the current entrance gate is situated (and which I couldn't avoid noting was wide open, not closed and padlocked as it normally should be), I couldn't avoid the feeling that I was breaching a faint, webby membrane crossing into the property. It's psychological, not technically there. But when you know about the Under, you can't help but wonder if there isn't something to all the talk of 'cold spots' and ghostly emanations caught on blank cassette tapes, the things you usually (and rightly) dismiss as made-up or delusional.

Out of the corner of my eye I saw the faintest profiles of people in ectoplasmic finery, walking about or standing near stones and obelisks, quietly conversing or simply standing together, watching us pass. To you, in the same circumstances, you would turn, look to clarify what you saw, and catch a late-night squirrel. A scatter of dead leaves blowing in the wind.

Ghosts are generally not perceivable for what they are; nature's way of compensating, maybe, for certain things to stay invisible in their own way. The way certain elements never go critical in the universe because they start immediately bonding with the most attractive fellow atoms and stabilize. Table salt and water. The human race can't usually handle the truth about death and what it may entail, so ghosts are merely the imagination of your grandmother telling you horror stories over a campfire. The real ghosts? Just don't mind that hiss of leaves across your driveway. And don't look too hard at that shape in the tree bark you could swear makes you think there's someone peeking out from behind the trunk.

Some of the dead talk. I don't know the dialects, though. They seem to congregate pretty heavily in Greenfriars, and you speculate as you move amongst such a dense assembly, flickering in and out between perceptibility, that you are seeing them there out of some sense of tradition. As if they are saying *We're dead. You expect us in a cemetery with our remains. So here we are.*

Now *what?*

Do you ever get the feeling, came the whisper in my inner right ear, *that every time we come here, we might not be allowed to leave?*

Not the most cheery of feelings in common.

Cackler did what he had in previous such rounds, driving towards the rough geographic center of the cemetery and pulling into the semi-circular drive in front of the main Chapel Mausoleum.

We have visited Greenfriars before. Even as one of the largest of its kind in the Midwestern United States (maybe the largest anywhere, if you take into account the parts that don't obey any map or survey guides), it carries a certain 'hometown' charm for us. In daylight. It's outside the bustle and hustle of downtown, just south enough along 71 that most people can live for years in the city without even knowing it's down there.

But visits after dark had been confined to only a couple, and none of them desired or by our choice. A cemetery at night is one thing (again: all in your head). I am not afraid of ghosts for the most part. As transient as we all are in the bigger picture of things, how can you ultimately be that scared, one breeze or bit of dust to another?

But the Cemetery Lord, the Mausoleum Magnate, was somewhere amongst these cold stones and frozen angels. Waiting to meet us in his personal 'court o' bones.' That was something else altogether.

Then some of those breezes have winter teeth. Some of those bits of dust can chew as they nuzzle against your spine.

A flagpole stood out in front of the mausoleum, making lonesome, tinny ringing sounds against the pole every time the American flag dangling at its top shivered in the breeze and rang the lanyard lines against the metal. A foxfire echo with echo was staring up at the flag, making wagging, worrisome shakes of its head...a veteran upset about leaving the flag out on the pole at night?

Cackler put the car in park but stayed in the driver's seat, hands neatly at two-and-ten positions on the steering wheel.

All sadistic joviality was boiled out of him once we'd crossed the gate threshold. He wouldn't look at me.

"Go on. He's out there."

I got out. The sound of closing the Tucker's door was the slamming of a door in an empty theater, clack-booming into the air. More leaves stirred in the corner of my eyes. Another muttering glimpse by the flagpole that disappeared when I looked straight-on towards it.

The thing about the Sexton King is that, as best we've learned, he appears to have domain over the gravesites of the world. From a postage stamp churchyard in Tokyo to a Buddhist tomb in China, a royal mausoleum in England or the solitude of a sad, singular pet's final resting place in some backyard. The catacombs of Paris or the tombs of Capuchin monastery must be like summer and winter homes for him. He can be there, or in any of those other places, as easily as taking a few steps. I have no idea what exactly is his role beyond being apparently some sort of patron rule over those whose task it is to tend the places of final rest, but I've never felt inclined to argue any points of his job with him.

The King has only been an acquaintance for a few years. His was one of the first faces we saw when my eyes opened and I first moved as something other than the living bookstore owner I started out from. Why he seems to have taken any special interest in us I don't know. But I can't deny that he's been instrumentally helpful in certain bad gigs. And that type of obligation carried with it a sense of debt that was heavier than simply being in the presence of someone who may or may not have been one of the most powerful beings I know walking on the planet's surface.

I walked along the graveled road, away from the car. Not giving any thought to where I put my feet down with each step, allowing whim and wind to suggest my directions. It wouldn't matter to seek him out. He'd be wherever he wanted to be, and that would inevitably be where I was headed. After all: in the court of the king, you don't have to walk too far to bump into the throne.

This place doesn't feel the same as before. I keep expecting something to...grab us. Everything around us.

I don't think the Stone God is going to rise up again simply to slap us and run off giggling.

I still wouldn't put ten dollars' bet on it not happening. Uncomfortable air around my shoulders. *This place is...big.*

I passed familiar markers...the headless angel whose body appeared to be in some raised-arms supplication to heaven, minus the beseeching face it never had (a popular myth is that it was vandalized; you have to know a few folks working at the main trustee office up near the eastern gate to discover that the headless angel never had a head to begin with). I was about to pass a bulk of shrubs that were the dark crown around a Romanesque couch carved out of granite when I heard one of the shrub-shadows clear its throat.

"Jesus!" Soul blurted from my mouth.

"Evenin' Johnny-cake."

I didn't see him there!

I stopped. The shadows and leaf-blowing motions clattered and crackled, like watching reversed film of some sort of inverted flames burning paper, the consumption turning into mass and restoring into the clarity of the King sitting casually at one end of the stone couch.

A long, gaunt sketch of a man clarified as I stared harder. A figure of charcoals and faint smudged impressions of features on the lined plank of face with its wisp of goatee at the chin. A porkpie hat squashed in the fashion of a hobo Buster Keaton. His jacket and pants were black and fitted him with a secondhand clothing's ill grace, a little too short at ankles and wrists yet somehow looking for all the world like they could belong to nobody else. His beetled eyes took me in through a gauzy litter of smoke that was hatched from the ratty crooked cigarette at his lips. Resting beside him on the couch, like a fellow resting traveler, was his scepter of office. A good five-foot-long shovel, its blade against the soil and nearly as black and perfect as a well-seasoned iron skillet.

He plucked the cigarette from his lips after taking a rasping drag. The ember flared in the dim, momentarily giving a glimpse of eyes that looked heart-stoppingly like they were all pupil, no iris or whites but black straight through. The dark, shineless regard of deep-sea fish in caverns too deep for submarines.

Mister Sharkdoll.

Quiet.

"Good evening to you, too, Your Majesty."

A nod. "How you keeping these days?"

I shrugged. "About the same as usual, with the exception of maybe getting shot."

It is either a statement in his favor—or in some very ominous aspect of his character—that the King didn't react to this in any way I could detect. As if hearing his acquaintances suffering assassination attempts was an every-day-of-the-week sort of affair.

Another couple of long, thoughtful pulls on the cigarette. His fingers rolled the cylinder until he was holding it in that quaintly European manner, where the cigarette is held vertically, burnt end up, by the first two fingers pinching it against the thumb, treating the palm as the default ashtray.

"Suppose you aren't exactly accustomed to people making a play for your skin?"

"I'm caught up in a chaotic mess and I am having trouble beginning to comprehend how to sort any of it out."

"Then, as Lewis Carroll wrote in *Alice in Wonderland*: start at the beginning." He slowly lifted up one boot, folding over to stub out the cigarette against the thick sole, then depositing it into one of the breast pockets of the tattered jacket. "And when you reach the end, stop."

I relayed what I could in as succinct a way as I was capable, trying to use chronology to make order where I couldn't find it in the events themselves. The construction and renovations at The Nookery...seeing Loewenstein and the gist of what he'd had to contribute. Trina's lapse...the shooting by the Believer. The surveillance on us.

The only thing I left out of order I saved deliberately for last because it was the thing that seemed totally contrary to anything I could grasp.

"And we're experiencing...changes. Since the thing with the Jennyripper."

"Growin' new hairs n' thinkin' about girls?"

"That would be funnier if it wasn't capable of burning down our house from a temper tantrum."

Or burning down the city, maybe.

Shut it.

The King's face remained placid, unconvinced as of yet to show any obvious interest. He sat back, arms going up akimbo as he rested his elbows on the back of the couch. "All right."

"Things that could be dangerous. As bad as the 'ripper. Maybe worse."

Still no outward response. After a few moments, he looked down at the ground and gave a few slow nods of his head.

"Huh. Yeah. That's...I'll grant you that's something."

"As best as I can tell, yes. "

I woke up to realize several more minutes had sped by as my mouth, totally on autopilot, divulged the counseling with Rabbi Loewenstein in full detail. All the mythological and psychological mess came out of me like upchucking dirty wash-water on a Thanksgiving dinner setting before him. All sounding so stupid in the now and here.

After another minute or two of silence, the King straightened his back, lowering his arms to rest those spindly-fingered spider-hands on his thighs.

"You gone to a shrink then?"

"Not exactly. I called an acquaintance who might be able to offer...a more effective viewpoint. Hopefully he'll agree to help."

Not even a raised eyebrow, much less asking any further about who we'd called.

I don't like this. He's a cool customer, but this is Frigidaire interrogation here.

"Here's a wild long shot of a question for you, though, if you don't mind."

He chewed the request a moment. Then: "Shoot."

"Do you know anything about these Believers? This

guy who shot me?"

A long, considered thought on my query. Almost the feeling of watching an old tape-reel Univac computer, slowly grinding through its magnetic difference engine churnings before giving its response.

"Nope. Not a thing here." He looked out across the various lumps of stone. Eroded granite bleachers of silent crowds that I couldn't avoid feeling all around us. More leaves clustered and whisper-scratched close to us, eavesdroppers in the gloom. "Think these Believers are the same as the weirdoes who're watching your place?"

"Anything's possible, though I really hate to give in to the temptation to assume there's any connection between events simply because they happen close together. The ones that Soul saw watching The Nookery…different kettle of fish entirely."

The King scratched at the whiskers on his long bone shelf of a chin. "Hrm. Yeah. I can't say I recognize that fellow you described, what did you call him?"

"Mister Sharkdoll."

"Yeah. I won't argue with you: you have a hell of a handful of things to figure out, you're right on that."

"Gee, thanks."

The hands splayed out, a shrug of exaggerated apology. The growl came out regretful. "Sorry I'm not more service to you, Johnny-Go-Lightly. But I don't know what I don't know. It's a big world out there past the gates of twilight and all that poesy."

We need to get things rolling. We could be here all night with him playing Twenty Thousand Questions of Weird Stuff.

Agreed.

"Not to sound rude or ungracious or anything, sir…but why am I out here right now talking to you?"

His face betrayed no change. Somehow in his next few breaths…very measured, very careful and deliberate…I could read that he was either very pissed or very sad. Neither one was a situation I wanted to be close to.

"You play chess?"

That's…definitely not a question I was expecting.

"Learned to play as a kid with my grandfather. Tried playing in high school chess club but I sucked at it so I quit pretty early on."

"Why?"

"I don't have a head for memorizing a bunch of strategies. I would try to retain some gambit or defense or rally, and it wouldn't ever stick."

"Play kind of fast and loose, do you?"

"Yeah. I didn't play strategy, I played the pieces. Move a pawn here. Try to capture that bishop there. I could never plan more than a move or two ahead."

"Think that says something about you?"

I shifted weight from foot to foot. I didn't like talking seemingly without purpose when I also had a sense that there had to be some reasoning behind it. The man, as far as I knew, couldn't operate without one, not for the littlest action. "I have no idea. Where is this going?"

"Ever heard of the Benoni Defense?"

"I don't follow big-league chess. I know who Bobby Fischer and Kasparov were, that's about it. I know the horsey-piece is called a knight."

A shrug. His head straightened. Exaggerated mope of the lips pursing. "It goes where it goes. Benoni is Hebrew. It means 'son of sorrow.'"

"Doesn't sound like a smart move."

"Depends. Benoni is an opening strategy. Very risky to many players, even the best."

He plucked a silver dollar from a pocket and began to roll it, like quicksilver, across the scarred knuckles of his left hand. As idle as a man flicking mindlessly through keys as he talks weather and latest business figures.

Why are we standing in a cemetery in the dark talking about chess moves? What exactly in blue shitfire is all this about?

No clue. You want to holler at him a little to get a straight answer? Be my guest.

I felt the tickle-shiver at my neck calm significantly.

No.

"It's where basically you box up pawns right out of the gate." The hypnotic silverfish flash. "You force your opponent to take a pawn or two. You can end up shaking them pretty good. Fischer did it, funny that you mention him. He threw Spassky for a loop coming out like that."

"I would think another grandmaster would shrug it off."

"Yes and no. Spassky hadn't studied such risky playing. Two great masters of any art that meet up, they often assume that the other is going to play the best moves, use their toughest strategies. You don't start a judo match assuming the other guy's gonna lie down on the ground and invite you to kick him first, you dig?" I nodded. "Benoni's kind of like that. And Spassky got rattled. He didn't study to play against someone like Fischer who was throwing so much of his hand into the game right off. It threw Spassky off enough that Fischer was able to take him and win that game. That was how Fischer played a lot of the time. It's what makes people think he was a genius at it."

"That he was a gambler?"

"That he played his best by seeming to not really care about the game at first. That his playing style suggested he was always feeling out his opponent, like he was learning the game brand new every time. His genius was that he could disturb his opponent. Make them think he was throwing it away. And while they were surprised with his risk, he would rally a wagon or two around them and flanked their cleverness. People tend to assume the worst about an enemy. Meaning they assume the enemy's always going to try his best, every step, every gambit."

"Interesting. Are you…trying to say something about my problem? Am I overlooking an attack on us or something?"

Eyes downcast. Then…one, two brief shakes of his head. What was this? He was as unreadable as ever.

"Let me show you a game, Johnny."

He swept his hand to the empty space at the other end of the couch. A nod of his head as he held the hand out. I took the indicated seat across from him.

As I sat down, there was a bump against the knee closest

to him, to my left.

I looked down. In the faint moonlight I saw a scattering of black and white squares. At first glance I thought it was the parquet floor of an expensive dollhouse.

That wasn't there a moment ago, I know it wasn't. The sloughing air moved down and across my fingertips; I could sense Soul teasing about the shapes on the couch space between the King and myself, trying to comprehend it.

It's...I know *these shapes...wait...*the whisper blew out, flattening against the weird tiles...*this is...*

"It's chess." The peaks and ball heads were suddenly unmistakable in the partial light. "A chessboard ready to play. You want to play a game of chess with me?" I looked up at the King with a grin automatically pulling the strings on my lips.

The King didn't smile.

"This isn't King's Chess, Matchflick. This is *Emperor's* Chess. And you could say, when it matters, there's nothing else."

****

What I was looking at appeared to be a chessboard like I'd seen a million times before, set up and ready for play.

But there was an optical illusion incorporated into it, like the fork image with two-tines-becoming-three-tips.

Oh man. Count 'em up.

On longer stare, I realized the sense of optical illusion was because it wasn't sixty-four squares, eight to a side. It was an even hundred, ten to a length. And there were four more pieces than usual on the board.

Between the miter-topped bishops and the equine-headed knights was a piece I'd never seen before. The King picked up the queen-side new piece on his side of the board and held it up between thumb and forefinger. Rolling it a little to give me a good look.

"This is the Vassal. Sometimes called the Duke, or the Viscount." The piece looked like a tall Puritan, until I made out the shape of a tilted Guy Fawkes hat, the kind of pitched stovepipe with the wide, floppy brim you see in those oil paintings from the Elizabethan era on dukes and courtiers. The whole piece was equally as tall as the bishops, and the column sloped down from the base of its hat to the pediment of the piece the same as all the other major pieces, a simplistic Doric column affair.

"How does he move?"

The King restored the Vassal to its place on the board with the lightest clunk of stone to stone. "The Vassal represents the court of the Emperor, since the Bishop traditionally represents the Church and not the royal house. And the Knights, Rooks and Pawns are only varying degrees of soldiery. Only the Vassal represents the Emperor's court and interests where the rest are merely soldiers or dilettante religious creeps." I thought he was making a joke, but he wasn't chuckling. "The Vassal, therefore, is the bridge in moves between a Bishop and a Knight. He moves diagonally, like a Bishop, but only two over, one across in sequence. Like the Knights. There's a game out there similar, called Omega Chess. But it's not special, and in fact it's a poor man's interpretation of this very game right here. In that one, though, I think the Vassal is called the Wizard or some nonsense."

"That's bizarre."

The King considered the remark, gave a shrug. "No more so than any of the other arbitrary rules assigned. It's a game, remember. Now," he rested a thin, pale-nailed fingertip atop the pawn directly in front of the Vassal. "This is the Pawn."

"I'm familiar."

"No, you're not. This is the *Vassal's* Pawn."

"Right, like the one in front of the Queen—"

"Empress."

"—in front of the Empress is the Empress' Pawn, and so on."

A nod. "Yeah. But you don't know jack shit about the Vassal's Pawn. So *listen*." A shocking brunt of impatience to him, something I'd never heard before.

"Sorry."

"Emperor's Chess isn't about proving how smart at strategy you are. Thing about most chess is, you can get so good but play against someone just as good. Then it's wasted hours of stupid tic-tac-toe for grownups. What proves who the better player in regular chess is, is the guy who can make the other one a little stupider, just for a move. Just long enough that it makes a difference, breaks the even odds. You play long-term in chess, you have to set up goals and try to meet them, not only get through the next couple of moves."

"Okay."

"But Emperor's Chess is one step further. It takes into account, like a real Emperor's court, that long-term goals may be destroyed in a heartbeat, no matter how well-laid. You know about a Ninth-Row Gambit?"

"Is that the thing from *Alice in Wonderland*?"

Wrong.

Another frown and sigh from the King. "*Alice Through the Looking-Glass*. I thought I just mentioned Alice, or was that some other King here with you? You owned a bookstore, didn't you?"

I glared. "Yes. But that's where a Pawn can reach the ninth row and convert to a Queen, right?"

A nod. "Yeah. It's also called queening, or Queen's Promotion." An eyebrow raised to glare at me before going back down to the board. "Anyways, you get the gist of traditional chess on that score. Now the Vassal's Pawn, what it can do, if a player manages the trick of it, is pull off what no other Pawn or piece on this board can: he can get to the tenth row here and commit Court's Betrayal."

"Interesting."

"You wouldn't think so if you're the opponent."

"So what is it, you get the Vassal's Pawn there and can take one of the other guys pieces from him? Or force a trade back for one of your own?"

"You can choose any of the opponent's live pieces and make them one of your own."

Wow.

I gave a low whistle. "That's...potent stuff."

"No shit, Shirley Temple." He reached down, touched the Vassal's Pawn he'd tapped earlier, only now nudged the head enough to make it click over onto its side, effectively dead in the chessboard world. "Now you don't get two for the price of one on this move. The Vassal's Pawn is sacrificed once this is declared, and taken off the board. The popular way of telling it is, whoever betrays the Emperor kills the Pawn who paid him off, to cover their tracks. Court's Betrayal is ugly. It is how whole games of Emperor's Chess are lost even when the other guy is a better player. He might have a nice, cute defensive line set up around his own Emperor while he systematically takes you to the cleaners with his Pawns, Knights and other assorted jackanapes. All of a sudden, if he hasn't been paying attention or thought he was too cool for school, you get that Vassal's Pawn to the tenth line, right past all his stunts. You declare Court's Betrayal, and now the Empress Herself could be the traitor, sitting right there next to her Emperor. Who is locked in and can't go anywhere, can't call for help from any of his oh-so-neatly-placed other pieces. The game is immediately checkmated in one sweep."

"This version of the game sounds Machiavellian."

"Funny you say that. Who do you think invented it?" Again: no chuckle. No indication of irony.

"So you want to play a round of Emperor's Chess, is that it?"

"Nah." He tilted back his hat, looked down at the chess set as if surprised to see it. "Not the right evening for chess. Too much like rain and old postcards right now." He glanced up at the clouds, indigo framed against cobalt-black. "Yeah, not right at all for chess. But maybe you can brush up on your Emperor's, next time you come 'round." The face that turned to me was expressionless, the voice to match. "I hope to see you that next time, John."

The dismissal was clear. I couldn't escape feeling that I had failed in some important regard.

I tapped the top of the queen—no, Empress—Vassal that was in front of me. "You will."

A flap of a hand. The ghost grin returned to the living world on his narrow face.

"Promises, promises."

12.

What the hell was all that about?

Cackler was driving us away. I hovered somewhere near the glove compartment, a ghost approximation of a passenger. The Tucker with the souped-up paintjob had an interior that felt and tasted like roasting shards of walnut shells, burning locks of hair. Acrid. Uncomfortable. Probably Cackler's presence souring things. Yet I wondered if what I was reading might not mean that someone had died because of this thing.

No idea. Body frowned at the windshield. *But the King has yet to do or say anything where we're concerned that wasn't significant in some way.*

I don't entirely see how antique chess relates.

Neither do I. But presumably that's the point. Or part of it.

Cackler avoided the most frequented streets and stayed on the residential side-roads, signaling left as he slowly turned back onto High Street. The Tucker growled choppily in that healthy rev of a classic engine. Body shifted in his seat. *He never gives it away straight. I don't know if that's his style or that's some rule of the game or what.*

We don't know anything about him, aside from what we've learned the last few years. And what is that, really, except that he's the Monarch of Morbid?

He's a good guy.

Good is relative. We thought we were pretty good guys until recently.

Body bit at his lower lip for a long breath.

He saved us. That's important.

He was there at the beginning, sure. But what do we know?

Body shook his head.

The Jennyripper was a century-old monstrosity that tore through flesh and metal, made of the worst essences of both. A hybrid-thing that was also unfortunately the product of some sort of doppelgeist gone wrong. Like us, but different. That was what we wanted to think of it as.

The Sexton King had gotten involved. He hadn't himself stopped the thing, but he'd known how to call on elder powers, the power of a Stone God, that had stomped the Jennyripper into the earth like a lion stomping on a beetle.

But half-living, ghoul-slapping gigglers like Cackler as his servants didn't make an argument in favor of the Sexton King being all that great and cozy a guy.

It was easy to forget that for all his homilies and homespun asides, the Sexton King was not human. Not entirely. No human being can smile, tilt their hat back, and walk between cemeteries across the world in a breath. No human being can talk to the dead and have them *listen*. No human gravedigger wields a shovel as a scepter, or can command spirits to speak to you.

We could ask around, Body remarked. *But that feels... underhanded.*

If we trust him, we wouldn't ask.

Right.

Was he telling us not to trust anyone? Is that like the Benoni Defense he went on about? Is he trying to show us something lower, something vulnerable, at a time when we're expecting everything and everyone to be on guard?

No idea. Probably. Could be.

Coulda, Woulda, Shoulda. The Three Moron Brothers.

Body looked over at Cackler. "Can I ask you something?"

An eyebrow went up on the greasy-lit face. "Go right 'head, friend. Your dime and my time, that's all that's a-wastin'."

"How did you become a Deadjack?"

His face tightened, paper-fold-sharp along those mushroom-soft, gooey features. He suddenly seemed nothing weasel or rat, more a species of statue, a cemetery carving himself. Quixotically, his fast reticence and obvious discomfort gave him a dignity his otherwise odious attitudes usually lacked.

I still hadn't gotten used to how the space around Cackler looked. We didn't know any other 'jacks to compare, but Cackler didn't have the kind of living, breathing aura and disturbances of emotion and reaction like other people emit to me. His was a sobering, sort of decomposing space. It was as if everything that came into contact with him transmitted an atomic poison, killing off molecules in black spits of anti-light. These black-on-black spots ate into themselves, miniature imploding black holes that popcorned in the air around him.

The irritations of the air slackened, lessened... like watching a massive heartbeat slow to a drugged crawl.

"Don't talk about that," he whispered. "Don't ask, don't tell, and no angels fall to Hell. You *get* me sport?"

"I'm sorry."

He didn't say anything more, neither accepting the apology or anything else. Body kept quiet and I made sure to stay on my side of the car with him, well away from the eventually-accelerating pop-crackle-death of air around the Deadjack. The walnut-burnt-hair sensation intensified and for excruciating minutes I felt pinned inside the car. Cackler's simmering anger was an energy unto itself.

A servant of the King. So I trusted his loyalty as far as *that* went. But servants sometimes stage a coup. There is always intrigue at court.

And betrayal was, of course, our most recent lesson learned from the King himself.

✶✶✶✶

Doesn't feel right, does it?

Body stood at the doorway of the makeshift apartment in The Nookery, surveying the dark room.

"She even remembered to turn off the upright lamp before she left."

We are utter shits on the shoe-sole of life at this moment.

He swallowed deep and then entered, letting the door carelessly slam shut behind him. I barely avoided being half-caught by the door's matter—going through solid objects is doable, but I hate it because I often have this molasses-sticky sense that I'll be trapped permanently in a given substance—while he stood by the desk, contemplating the space.

Christ, this is a mood, isn't it?

"I don't care what it is."

There was a pile of books that had knocked over. He went and started to aimlessly pile them back up like a stunted Tower of Babel. As he was placing the last one on top, the phone in his coat pocket went off.

Oh I wish it was a telemarketer making a wrong phone call. I'd love to tear someone a new asshole via phone line.

No such luck.

"Hey, Jo-Jo, you got five to gimme?"

That voice. Light and bubbling. The effect of talking to a highly articulate drunk through a champagne bender.

Why do we get these things at the worst possible times?

Body closed his eyes. The fingers tightened on the phone.

"Hello, Ceyggan."

"Was wondering if you might be able to do me a solid, miracle-man."

"I don't know if I can quite—"

"Johnny." That stopped it cold. Ceyggan could barely remember close friends' names, much less dropped them into the running river that was his usual talking jag method of conversing. "Need you to give me five minutes of your time and some help here. You're the only one we could ask."

Slight emphasis on the 'we.' As in 'the royal We.'

Body hissed. "Sssssure, man. I can come by sometime."

"Is now a good time?"

He opened his eyes and took in the darkened room around us.

Might as well. I hovered near his shoulder, against the cool of the phone plastic. *Seeing as how it's not like there're any housemates keeping us at the moment.*

"Yeah, it's cool."

"Great!" No business, all happiness and buddy-buddy good feelings. "See you in ten? You know where I'm at, right?"

"I assume you're still at the gallery?"

"Got in one, man, you are the walking phonebook!"

"That's my day job."

Ceyggan bubble-laughed and hung up, cutting himself off in mid-chuckle.

Better clear your pockets. Check for any of the ole' metal.

Body went to the desk and started emptying his pockets, examining bits of paper, stray dollar bills. One old house key emerged. The YALE stamp was nearly rubbed away and it had the dirt-bronze color of a well-used key.

He dropped it to the desktop. *Okay, that's the only cold iron I think we might have on us. Let's go.*

I couldn't help being a bit sour as we went back out the door we'd so recently entered through.

Sure. Ceyggan wants five minutes of our time and some help. All we needed right now.

A sick newbie vampire.

A confused and pissed vampire counselor.

A cult of crazies surveilling or trying to kill us.

Now a call from one of the most prominent fairy families in Columbus.

13.

The Faede.

What you would traditionally mislabel 'fairy' folk.

One of the things that pass as a quasi-monarchist dynasty of powers in the Under. Faer beings from way, way back in the inhuman archives.

A few rules about the Faede.

You don't call them 'fairy,' for one. You don't give them attitude unless you carry a much bigger stick than they do. And if you're someone, like us, who can see past their pheromone-light trick (what more fanciful people have called their 'glamour'), don't remark or brag on that fact.

They aren't vain *per se*, but even the average person doesn't necessarily like having you point out that they don't look as hot as they think they do. The difference is that if you make one of the Faede feel a lack of self-esteem or offense, they have ways of making you into what Orwell would've called an 'un-person.' It's not Orwellian in terms of terminating you so much as actually erasing you from existence in such a way that even your own mother wouldn't remember having given birth to you.

I drove the Vega with Soul hovering in the passenger seat, sometimes wandering to the space between the dashboard and windshield. The topics for conversation were limited.

You're thinking we should call it all off, this thing with Trina. Let her go back to Justin and his people to find a better blood partner.

I'm thinking it because clearly you're thinking it, too.

Okay, then, Kreskin, read my mind further and tell me what else I'm thinking, then.

You're thinking 'screw Justin, if he and his people somehow set us up for this to fail.'

Damned straight. I squeezed the steering wheel in my hands, eliciting a small groan-squeal from the wheel cover. *I don't like people screwing with us. I like it even less when they do it through other people.*

I drove through the ghost-town ambience of downtown, heading towards that section of High Street known as the Short North, our capital city's district for various art galleries, expensive furniture shops, salons and cafes.

****

I finally got past the snarl of one-way roads and turns, through downtown to the gallery district, reaching the place Ceyggan owned: the Segal-Byers Avante Garden. A narrow two-story with Victorian brick facade, big glass windows in its front. Old pine flooring and tastefully weathered battered-tin-plate ceiling. Small spot lighting mounted in seemingly random places to cast spills of light on various works mounted to the walls or resting on freestanding pedestals.

For one of the rarest instances in my life, there was an open and legal parking space in front of the place I wanted to get to, right on High Street.

The gallery was closed until later tonight when, according to all the flyers taped to the glass of its front door, there was to be a showing of "Endless Artists," whatever that meant. I gave a few knocks and waited.

Does Ceyggan care about the difference between a Van Gogh or a spilled soda? I didn't think the Faede were into any sort of lasting culture.

I stared at the flyers. *You're forgetting how nuts they are for always being into whatever's new. I'll bet none of the work in this exhibit will be up in a few days.*

The door was answered by a silent, moon-faced black woman with a helmet of slicked-back hair and an inscrutably calm expression the entire time she led us to the backroom and the stairs to the second floor. She wore a modernized form of Chinese Mandarin blouse, the kind with the hidden front buttons and the priest-like rounded collar, woven from a brilliant aquamarine fabric, all above an almost tawdry-dull tan ankle-length skirt and plain pumps. The blouse fairly glowed up the dim staircase where she stopped and indicated we could proceed into the upper room without further assistance. A mutual nod—hers of completion and mine of thanks—and I went in. The door clacked shut behind me and echoed off the chamber walls.

I was in a long room that, unlike the downstairs gallery, was lit by a pair of stark bug-zapper-like lamps at the other end, fluorescent tubes sitting vertically on-end. That end of the building farthest from us featured windows thoroughly painted over to block all outside light. In front of these painted over windows was a pile of various throw-cushions, a mattress, pillows and bed sheets. All massed like a great, multicolored, Egyptian-cotton-and-satin model volcano. To one side of this mass was a small rolltop desk resting at a skewed angle near the wall. Opposite the rolltop desk was a free-standing entertainment center with a large flatscreen television and stereo system neatly mounted in the glass shelf supports, cables trailing out and away in various directions like baobab roots scrambling across the floor. Magazines and various package wrappers for electronics were scattered on the floor, with a few large and ornate area rugs like the rectangles of farmland you see from an airplane window after takeoff. Nearly every inch of the walls were papered in posters for rock shows, local bands, Comfests come and gone, even circuses and church bake-offs. Not so much an expression of love for any particular event or style, merely a packrat taste for anything printed on large-scale paper for gluing up indiscriminately on an otherwise-bare surface.

No bed. Where does he sleep? Does he sleep?

To the left and right of the 'pillow throne' were those two lamps. They gave off a pale blue light, constant and oddly warm.

Cripes what a mess. Soul stayed close, as if he were afraid he'd somehow come into contact with any surfaces.

It was all exaggeratedly slovenly. It was about enough to fool anybody.

But I noted that there was no smell. No incense, no lingering smell of pot or food, cologne or perfume. Even with the aged posters, no smell of dust, aging papers, wear and tear on the space. Most places that looked this haphazard usually had a pervasive scent that denoted why things were so scattered and discarded. But Ceyggan's nest was neutral, sharp with a lack of atmosphere. So much that I felt I'd walked onto a popular television show's stage, experiencing that momentary unreality where you see things that look so familiar because you've watched the show so much, but it's an entirely different thing to be walking through the reality... you can see where a wall is missing, where the stage lights extend above a ceiling that isn't there, and the doors that go to the bedrooms or the dining rooms actually open onto craft service tables and soundstage flats.

A flapping sound of paper. I saw that the mass of pillows and cushions had a tenant, stretched out with indolent ease to the point that his immobility had been camouflage against the riot of fabrics.

Ceyggan was flipping pages through a copy of Italian *Vogue* magazine. He only looked up as the door finally closed behind me, raising a hand to wave us towards him.

"Hey, Jo-Jo. Thanks for coming over, man."

I blinked a couple of times, feeling the faintest touch of dizziness, not unlike the vertigo joy of spinning around with your arms stretched out like when you're a kid, spinning until you drop to the grass and giggle, waiting for the world to stop rolling as well. A brief moment where I felt as though I was standing at some great height, looking down at an ant-sized Ceyggan grinning up at me. Another blink, and everything restored to its proper arrangement.

A curious bit of trivia, about that glamour in that blink: some brain chemistries react differently to it. The pheromone chemical they release affects certain perception and memory zones of the brain, not unlike a sort of willed LSD effect combined with hypnotic suggestion. As with most experiences of hallucinations, it's in the eye of the beholder. Literally. Those few percentage of human brains the glamour affects differently most frequently experience a loss of focal depth-of-field management. Their brains have difficulty properly perceiving the Faede in their proper scale.

It can make the Faede appear immense or ludicrously tiny and out-of-true with the surroundings. It's the reason why one of their mythic titles is "wee folk." From humans whose brains were enough out-of-whack to see tiny people simultaneously taking up the space of a normal-size-seeming person.

Apparently doppelgeists have the same chemistry issue as well. Though it only took that last blink or two to dispel it. Soul never sees it.

After blinking the glamour away and walking closer, I saw a man who was perpetually an early-twenty-something Japanese or Pacific Islander, though with fuller lips, a Brad Pitt variety of leering heaviness. Sallow skin that the blue lamps made look nearly like a soft, flawless marble. His hair was colored a henna-treated shade of ruby and indifferently cut with that choppy, irregular fashion known most popularly as 'bed-head chic.' He wore a long silk shirt printed in a pattern of ironically-meant, wildly retro Hawaiian print style of surfboards and wood-paneled Studebakers parked on a beach dune, top two buttons undone to give that needed hint of hairless, supple chest and indifference. Leather pants. No socks or shoes. His feet stuck out and the toes roamed various lengths of sheet or pillow while he talked.

"Have you heard this latest single from this group, Zero Point Vacuum?" Ceyggan didn't wait for an answer, but dug out a palm-sized remote, pointing it towards the entertainment center. A heavy beat started boom-thumping through the chamber. The music was somewhere between a song by One Direction and cats trying to group-orgy in a wood-chipper. I've never been a good judge of pop music. My last favorite single on the radio was by The Dave Matthews Band sometime in the late nineties.

I nodded, gave my best attempt at a convincing smile. "It's got a beat, that's for sure."

"Not into it?"

"I can enjoy new stuff. But it's getting fewer and farther between those happy discoveries."

"They're awesome." He relaxed back into his seat. In another week—probably less—he'd be crazy about some other group. Or several. Or none. He would just as likely be into extreme sporting, something with waxed boards or paraglider equipment involved, leaping off cliffs in the Rockies. The Faede have a mood swing frequency that puts any emo-wannabe kid to shame. "Really better than that crap out from Nerves of Real. You dig them?"

"Not into it. I'm an easy-listening type myself."

He gave a good-natured frown to disparage everything about my taste in music and the world related to it. Tossed the remote control onto the cushions. He waved a hand to indicate I could have a seat on my choice of cushion piles or laundry.

His dangling leg kicked out lazily. "So what can I do you for?"

My neck stretched a little. "What?"

"I asked what can I do for you?"

I pinched the bridge of my nose and gave a loud sigh. Another aspect of dealing with the Faede, one that can be way more annoying than breathing in their glamour-scent.

I swear if these guys weren't so good-natured most of the time I'd nominate them for a solid kick in the face with a steel-toed boot once in a while. Soul floated down to the magazines on the ground. *It couldn't make them any stupider.*

"Ceyggan…" I spoke slowly and was careful to moderate my tone to keep it patient. "*You* called *me*, remember?"

A puzzled knit of his brow. "Did I?"

"Yes. You did. On the cell phone. About half an hour ago. It's why I came here in the first place."

The eyebrows unknotted. A sunny smirk came up on his face. He snapped his fingers. "Just playing you."

Yeah, right.

"I called you because I need your help with something. You want a soda?"

Don't.

I remember, chill out.

"No, thanks. I had a soda before I came over."

A shrug. He didn't get anything for himself. "Hey, man, have you had any issues lately? I mean, like weirder than usual problems?"

Danger, Will Robinson, danger.

"Why do you ask?"

"Because there is a serious boom in crazy going on around town."

I looked down at the magazines at my feet. Used a foot to shove the top one aside so I could see the Olivia Wilde swimsuit shot on the on the cover beneath it.

The key thing about talking to the Faede was to never get too passionate. Never suggest too much value to what you're asking about. They're opportunistic for anything valuable. Because value is often the source of drama. And drama is entertainment. They're only absent-minded for things that are trivial: little courtesies, names of people that aren't important enough to them to remember more than a millisecond, that sort of thing. So you let them talk—which is not a problem, since they are more than happy to do so, and at length—until they slip what they want, rather than you fishing for it the other way 'round.

"Lead-heads around town are going postal."

I looked up.

"Lead-heads? Emotion junkies?"

"Yeah. Water bottles."

I frowned. "I don't get it."

"They suck up to the bottlers. But they're barely bags of water, you know?"

"Ah." A nod. "'Water bottles.' Not bad."

He grinned wider. "Cool. Hey, have a seat man, you make me nervous standing over me like that." He indicated a lower place in the soft quagmire of pillows and I managed to get partially balanced atop a large throw-pillow with little gold tassels swinging off its corners. I cleared a pile of *Maxim* magazines to do so. "Yeah, they're snapping right and left. We had one that went at one of us right outside a couple of nights ago."

That's *different.*

"They're like that movie, the one a few years ago, with that guy? The zombie one that wasn't really a zombie movie. With the virus? Where they run around screaming and tearing ass until they just drop?"

"I remember it."

"That's the ticket. These stupid water bottles are going out in some sort of sick blaze of glory, like meth addicts buzzing on a high feed when the cops show up."

"This isn't the only attack, I take it?"

He shook his head. "I have a buddy who works down at that bookstore, the 'alternative medicine and magic crystals' crap, what's it called?"

"Aquarian Books & Supplies."

"Yeah. Anyways, he told me that last night, as he was closing shop, a water bottle smashed its own head through the plate glass front window of the bar next door to him. Just smashed his head in and still tried to crawl through while he bled to death."

This doesn't bode well.

"Sounds pretty rough."

Ceyggan paused a beat too long for innocent response. "Yeah. Yeah. Bad enough. I own part stock in that store, too."

"Sorry about that."

"Just seems pretty crazy, out-of-the-blue stuff."

Watch it...

"I thought lead-heads are always around. They occasionally go a little crazy, one or two here or there. Why now all of a sudden?"

A shrug. "Who knows? It's the Under. Weird stuff suddenly blows up in peoples' faces all the time."

Why didn't we hear about this?

No idea. Probably any police investigation would have thought they were simple drug addicts. Nothing special.

Plus, lower down than this dialogue, I didn't want to admit that it was painfully obvious neither of us had been paying due attention to the rest of world the last few weeks.

I leaned back as far as I could without overbalancing off the cushion pile. "True enough."

"Still, though, kinda weird."

Play this straight. Blow it off.

"Eh. Lead-heads are a dime a dozen. Stupid people who get hooked on stupid crap."

"The buzz-peddlers are stupid, sure."

I gave a smirk, risking a test of his humor. "Really? I mean, not that it's not a waste, but I thought the Faede weren't above trying a little pharmaceutical recreation from time to time themselves."

A disdainful grimace. "That's *drugs*. A little coke, a bit of ecstasy? No big deal. Hell you could probably pump one of us full of *drain cleaner* and we'd get a buzz. But that's drugs." He tilted his head. "Lead-heads…that's not drugs. That's almost as bad as zombies." A forced shudder for emphasis. Then he peered at me. "Do you think you could do a little looking for us, Jo-Jo?"

This time it was my turn to shrug. Amazing how quickly the language of talking to the Faede was all shrugs and nods and barely-diffident gestures. If you haven't already picked up on it, the Faede are the only ones that I ever let call me 'Jo-Jo.' In part because they're the only people who do it. "Is that what this is about? Looking into the lead-heads going psycho?"

The tilted head straightened. He pulled his leg off the

rolled-up cushion that he'd been using like an armrest and sat up straight. Now you could see something of the historic element in that pose...you could appreciate why myth and legend made the Faede something intimidating.

"We don't feel cool with getting attacked. You feel me?"

"Sure."

Wait for it.

Ceyggan frowned, as if for a moment he suspected I was waiting him out.

"The one that I said, the other night? Did a little more than hassle us."

"Was somebody hurt?"

A measuring regard before answering. "One of my sisters. Diatha."

"How badly?"

"Not important." Too fast an answer, but I didn't push it. "But we want you to look into it for us if you could. We're not all that hot on detective stuff, you know?"

"I'm not a detective."

"Close enough for government work."

"I guess." No commitment, avoid showing too much interest.

If they want us, assume it was bad. Otherwise they'd've forgotten about it already.

"Is Diatha around? Could I ask her about it?"

A quick recovery. Not quick enough. "Nah. She doesn't want to get into it. But we would appreciate if you could do something, find out if there's something going on?"

"Probably just lead-heads losing their shit, like you said. No big deal."

"It's a big deal to us."

"Who's us? Your house or what?"

Maybe too much.

I shut up and directed my gaze to the magazines again. Let him think he had to convince me.

A long hold. I didn't dare break eye contact with the magazines.

Hope you remember where the exits are.

Have to wait him out.

"Look, the family wants to know if there's something bigger, okay?"

Hrm. With Faede, 'family' is a pretty hard wall to invoke butting up against. Their words for it go way past bloodlines. I'd never met any 'heads' of the families at all. As far as I could tell, Ceyggan and his like were all referred to as 'princes' or 'princesses,' maybe a half-breed with a human parent would be a minor 'lord' but that was as far as they went for anything approaching a hierarchy or titles. The terms meant nothing, really. An affectation like most things. A holdover from older times when that was how they liked being referred to and they still got a kick out of the tradition.

"There's another reason why I called you on this, why the powers that be want you in on this deal."

A cold that had nothing to do with the temperature of the room flicked its wet fingertips across my cheeks and neck, leaving prickly spots all over me. The blue of the lamp lights seemed to shift to a whiter, chillier luminescence. "Yeah?"

"I heard you got rid of Spam Tam."

There it was.

The most prominent local fear bottler. The primary local distiller and distributor of stolen human miseries who had supplied emotion-buzzes for his various clients. Spam Tam had made the mistake a while back of catching Soul and I in a particularly bad state. The result of said encounter was that he stopped his business and skipped town. Forever.

Here was the flip side of such a hasty—though satisfying and arguably moral—act. It made the Faede's logic a pretty straight syllogism: *You got rid of him, these things may have been his customers, so now you get to deal with the mess from his absence.*

Ceyggan's eyes pinned me on the spot.

"Is it true?"

No sense lying.

"Yeah. He didn't show me the proper courtesy the last time we met. I guess I overdid it on my response."

Ceyggan flapped a hand. "Don't get me wrong. Nobody's coming down on you for getting him out of town. But if him running out is why now there're these water bottles going apeshit around town…"

"I follow you. Then it falls on me to try and clean up."

"Yeah."

"Any other attacks?"

"I'd heard of a couple other 'unprovoked attack' deals. Over in Goodale Park a couple of women say they got attacked by some naked girl who scratched and wailed at them, broad daylight and all. But I only have a feeling that's another one, don't know for sure. The grapevine says it was a drug thing, somebody strung out on salts or whatever."

"Which wouldn't be an entirely inaccurate way for the day-to-day world to try and classify what happened."

Ceyggan leaned towards me, secretive and smiling. "I have to admit I've always been curious…"

"About what exactly?"

"Well…you're a doppelgeist, right?"

"Yeah."

"I've always wondered, some friends of mine and all…"

Here comes some strange question we'll either have to lie or act dumb over, Soul whispered.

"…what's it like doing porno?"

My mouth was half-opened, already forming some non-answer. I closed it.

"It's…interesting. Definitely has its perks."

The smile grew back. "Sounds cool. I don't know any Faede that do it. I know some lamia that're doing it out in California. But I've wondered if *I* could do it, y'know?"

"Well…yeah, you could probably do well."

"You think? What are the women like?"

I had to go along with it for whatever mileage it was worth to get him back to the subject. Faede are considered 'the beautiful people' but never let anyone photograph them. There are no Faede supermodels or movie stars. Their effect won't translate through an impersonal camera lens or on a big theater screen. They tend to be one step removed from such things. Press agents and talent representatives, sales people in high-yield entertainment fields and booking offices. Ways to stay tapped to the pulse of the world's leading pop culture plug-ins without being directly on its face.

"The women in porn? Kinda hard to say. I mean, they're hot in a lot of ways. There are a few of the older ones that are pretty smart and funny to meet."

The hiss in my right ear. *What the hell are you doing? Trying honey instead of vinegar. Shut up.*

"Yeah, I've seen enough of the final product to guess." Ceyggan allowed the smile to slide into a weak leer. "Do you get paid a lot?"

"It pays okay. Although I gotta say, a few of the girls aren't much far-removed from a lead-head, the way they act."

"Really?"

"Yeah. I mean, emotionally dead? You'd think they had a fear bottler on speed-dial, some of them. Not all of them, only the worst cases. To be honest, it's a business like any other. You'd probably get bored of the reality real quick. A lot of waiting around for cues and camera setup, people drinking coffee buck-naked and sitting on a couch reading magazines or going to the bathroom. It's about as sexy as your average office full of cubicles. Complete with a few stuck-up types, both men and women."

"Pfft." He waved a hand, shook his head. "I know stuck-up girls. My sisters are the queens of being queens."

"I don't know the girls in California. Haven't been there." It was time to bring it back to the rails and try to get back on the tracks. "So you really feel like the various attacks are all related?"

"Don't know. Like I said, with us it could be drugs but that's nothing. Water bottles, though…man, that's heavy stuff."

Spam had made a mistake in trying to tactically frighten us by sending a couple of lead-heads after me and a friend. Soul and I had sent them on their way with pretty hideous results… but I couldn't help recalling how sudden, how unfathomable the whole attack had seemed when it started, completely out of nowhere. A lead head attacking you might not have the superhuman adrenaline-crazed strength of your average PCP user freaking out, but a couple of them coming at you out of the blue, motivated by a hunger for more product…a formidable thing to simply have-at-you on the street.

"Did the one that attacked your sister do anything else after the attack, or just drop?"

"That thing? She was at the end. I don't know what she'd been into, but she looked like someone had dragged her behind their car about a hundred miles and then cut him loose. We were going out to a party, we were running the usual kind of late. I was taking this girlfriend of mine, Brit-Lee, and Diatha to that new place, the one under Skylab?" No clue, but I nodded. "So yeah, we're coming out, I'm holding the door for Brit, Diatha is already standing outside waiting for us by my car, and up comes this water bottle. Hair all patchy and pulled out at the roots in places. Eyes about five times too big, baggy and bruised. I've seen bum fights where the losers looked better even being worked over with a broken end of a beer bottle."

"Did it look like she'd come from anywhere in particular?"

"Who could tell? The street, that's all I would guess. It was around the corner, there in the alley where we have the parking spaces behind this building. It wasn't even like she'd been really coming at us. It was more like she'd been wandering around there and we walked into her and woke her up at that moment."

"You ever fight a water-bottle before?"

"I've had to deal with them." One of Spam's half-assed lead head agents had been so disoriented, he'd ground his own face off using the sidewalk pavement like sandpaper. It wasn't one of my more pleasant memories.

"They're not what I'd call a major threat, assuming you meet up with one when they're less-than-fresh. This one was past ripe and dead on her feet."

There didn't seem to be anything more to dig from him, and if I stayed longer there was a good chance that Ceyggan would go totally off-script and start asking about porn again.

Or if I listened to a new group he'd found that afternoon. Or any other of a number of irrelevant topics.

"Thanks for letting me know. I'll get on this and see what I can find out." I got up and he rose with me, holding out his hand. I gave a firm shake and a smile, then left.

The silent woman who had escorted me on arrival was nowhere to be seen. But I was able to figure out the lock on the front door well enough to leave and secure it behind me.

Why do I feel like we've been signed on to be a stunt-double for Evel Knievel?

I slid behind the Vega's steering wheel and started it up. There was a pop and grind under the hood for a second that quickly smoothed out. The Vega's engine growled with a little rev before going into idle.

"It's okay, gal," I patted the steering wheel. The Vega is temperamental about the most random things. She won't let me park her or drive too close to a White Castle restaurant. She doesn't appreciate being parked by more expensive high-end model vehicles. Apparently this was a newest addition to her vehicular shit-list: she didn't like being left parked in front of Faede residences.

The bit with not accepting any food or drink from the Faede when invited to do so. There's a twofold reason, neither of them being that like some Greek myth or old Irish folktale you become trapped in a fairy underworld or become their slave or anything.

The first reason is that it's always a risk that a Faede might think it's the height of hilarity to slip something into your food or drink. Anything from mild hallucinogens to outright poison, depending on the humor of the particular person you're dealing with. When I say poison as a joke, remember that we're talking about what the Faede would find funny, not necessarily you. It sounds hideous as an analogy—and I'm not going to argue it isn't—but you have to treat meeting them as if you were a single, seemingly vulnerable woman going for drinks out on the town. You don't leave your drink unattended and you don't let anyone you don't trust or know fix your food for you. There are dark things in the world without even getting into fairies and vampires, and while it's never the victim's fault that monsters prey on them, that's a cold comfort afterwards. The second reason is, to me, the more important one I always keep in mind. For all Ceyggan's casualness and absent-minded nonchalance, underneath it is a very solid steel layer of calculation and observation. It's not all conscious—like a praying mantis or a spider, instinct drives them more than intellectualism—but it's powerful. They test loyalty, politeness, deferral to their power. Things that the Faede take seriously as ways to give them a constant advantage, even in seemingly benign interactions.

Notice the occasional scandal that ruins a celebrity or figure of power? Think back to a celebrity who died of 'heart failure' that was revealed to be AIDS when that was the latest epidemic of terror for middle America. Sex tapes, child porn schemes...there's a solid chance that a Faede is somewhere behind it all, leaking and slipping the information to the press in the right amounts, in the key places to make it effective. It doesn't necessarily need to profit that Faede in anything more than black satisfaction at seeing someone fall from grace. And if you could go back and research it, you'll no doubt find that that Faede was offended in some way by said celebrity or figure of power.

How you accept or refuse things is a careful tightrope walk every time. Do you accept and show that you're gullible and easy to guile? Or do you refuse and show how crude and tactless you are in refusing? Are you polite and grateful, or mean and miserly with your consideration? All things that Ceyggan was watching for, not entirely realizing it himself.

I pulled away from the curb and carefully merged back into traffic on the main road. I headed north, away from downtown and towards the less gentrified length of High Street. A place full of bodegas and blood donation clinics and pawnshops, specialty hobby shops and tiny hole-in-the-wall bars.

Random attacks on random targets by random freaks. Gee, where do we begin finding a pattern here?

I don't have a lot to offer myself, I answered as I narrowly braked and honked at a minivan that cut me off and nearly caused a fender clipping.

They want us on this because they hold us responsible for Spam Tam leaving town. So by extension if the lead-heads are going crazy because Spam's not doing business with them anymore, that means the shit is on our shoulders to take care of it. Seems to me we haven't checked in with our favorite scumbag since last time.

I found myself surprised. *You're right.*

So in theory, he could still be right there where we left him. Could be worth a quick pass-by, to see if he's in. And if so, if he knows anything.

I doubt he's going to be willing to talk to us after last time.

After last time, Soul replied with an ominously flat tone in my forebrain, *he might be more than happy to answer any questions we have.*

14.

Spam Tam's apartment was an immaculate, empty hole.

Unlike some apartment move-outs, where you can see the tracks of dust versus traffic in the carpet, some sun-worn spaces for posters on the walls, generally the ghost of former occupancy everywhere, Spam Tam's former residence was as fresh as if he'd left it under plastic wrap the whole time he'd occupied it.

We killed the last few hours of night by driving to Buckeye Donuts. Body filled up on coffee and crullers to have something to do before dawn peaked out from the skyline and we thought it was late enough that we could hope to rouse someone to let us into Spam's building.

We managed to get a break. There was a sign on the front door of the garden apartment complex, and after about forty-five minutes of waiting the bleary-eyed superintendent arrived with a jangle of keys and a smoking-hot grande-sized cappuccino in his hands.

Since the coffers were a bit better these days, Body didn't try any cute stories or lies about being a prospective new tenant. Just a fifty dollar bill handed, without fanfare, to the man. We were in.

Such as the bribe went, it was a bust investment.

More than just the emptiness of it to Body's eyes, my view of it was even more dank.

Normal air to me is often at least shining…or 'wet,' like glitters off a lake surface. It also is a jacquard-paisley oils-in-water puddle of microscopic living things that are everywhere in the atmosphere. Dust mites, bacteria, what-have-you. Bare minimum, the air should always look like a thin, mostly transparent oil slick of squirming, rippling shapes.

Spam Tam's apartment space was dead. Only once or twice had I ever seen truly *dead* air. It was always capable of leaving me feel a shiver of near-cold sensation, maybe the way salt particles feel right before they start to dissolve in water.

Near the front door and the rear patio doors that led to a little ravine-boxed garden patio area, I could make out where normal air was beginning to seep past the glass and wood barriers. I took it as a sign that whatever sort of cleaning Spam had done to wipe the very atmosphere clear, it was beginning to wear off and normal space was intruding back into the apartment.

The superintendent of the building watched Body for a few minutes after letting us in.

"Nobody wants to rent it," he grumbled, his bulged eyes sweeping back and forth as he took sips from his coffee, keys jingling. "No matter how clean or fresh the paint job. I've had two painters in here. Three cleaning services. Last one didn't even charge, walked out saying there wasn't anything needing done."

"Anyone said why they're not interested?"

A shake of the head. "I've offered all sorts of things. Even first three months free. Nothing."

I couldn't blame anyone for refusing even with reduced rent and the advertised three-months-free special on the door for the end unit.

He asked Body to lock the door after he was done looking, excusing himself with no small amount of visible discomfort.

Body turned around a few times, looking over the same lengths of wall and floor. From empty galley kitchenette across the miniscule living/dining space to the back patio doors.

Where there had once been various card and flea market tables, packed with bottles, gallon jugs and glass phials of every description was that continuing nothing. You practically expected to see a sheen of fresh, sanitary plastic wrapping over every surface, as in a newly-sanitized hotel suite.

Body didn't shiver, but his eyes were wide. *Dead. This place feels unlivable.*

Trust me, it's as dead to my eyes as to yours. What was that line in Beetlejuice? *'It's like a giant ant farm.' Minus the liveliness of ants.*

I almost can't believe he's actually gone.

Really? I recall we wanted him gone. We burned the suggestion into his skin, in fact.

*I know, I know, but...*Body turned again, walking to the bedroom. In the few visits with Spam we'd managed to tolerate, we'd never gone into what we presumed was his personal space. Away from his 'storefront' of stolen fears and terrors kept in those now-gone multitudes of containers in the living room.

A short, shadowy corridor with an access vent to the furnace/air conditioning duct on the right, and on the left a bedroom door, half open.

Stop.

What?

Give me a moment to look first.

More dead air inside the bedroom. More empty space. Even some of those stupid cans of namesake canned mystery meat—bait that he used to coerce the company of many of Columbus' homeless so as to gain the bread-and-butter base of his 'stock product'—would've been a welcome break from the off-whit *sameness* and *flatness* of everything.

What the hell can someone do to make a space like this?

Body followed me in, pushing the door open and standing in the center of the bedroom. Weak light from the ravine behind the building came through the single tiny window as if even sunlight begrudged having to come in. I stayed near to Body, clutched around his midsection. I didn't want to venture out or spread too thin in the bedroom. Not quite vacuum, but maybe this was how air felt in the moment a balloon popped, when the pressure was gone and it was about to explode out.

I have no idea how he could leave it like this, Body remarked, *but I know I don't want to ever be around when it happens. This place feels like the 'after party' of a nuclear blast.*

When Spam left the building, he seriously *left the building.* Body and I went back to the living room. *I wonder if that's not a business tactic. Making sure not to leave any traces of work behind.*

Which leaves us with jack-all. I swirled near the kitchenette entrance. The overhead fluorescents were left on by the superintendent and the cold yellow-sick light provided some basic illumination into the dingy-yet-spartan space. The only air disturbances here were a few bits of natural air sneaking in through the stove vent. *Without Spam as a possible source, we're back to square one for what's going on with the lead-heads.*

Maybe. Maybe not. Body walked to the patio doors, staring out at the ragged, weed-choked ravine past the cracked and dirty concrete patio pad. *Strange, isn't it? I mean, the idea that maybe as bad as someone like Spam Tam is, it was better in some way to have him around where you could find him and check in on him than having him gone in the wind like this.*

There's only so many ways we can interpret this, I replied, staying near the kitchenette lights.

Body continuing staring out the patio doors, frowning. *Enlighten me a little.*

Well...let's start with what we know. Spam Tam has left. But we don't know if that means he's actually quit the business altogether and left town, or relocated somewhere else we don't know about in town, or much of anything else. For all we know he quit, but somehow set this all up before leaving to make our lives miserable one last time. A bit of revenge on our 'human matchstick' act.

Body shook his head. *I don't think the last is the case. He seems to've been gone a while now, since we were last here. The super confirmed that much.*

He was gone less than a week after our warning to him,

yeah. Hell, he probably couldn't stay in town anyway, if he took us seriously enough to stop his work.

His own customer base probably would have a few choice things to say about him suddenly cutting them off, yeah.

I moved away from the kitchenette and hovered near the patio door glass, for a moment almost expecting to see a hot breath-condensation fog against the glass before remembering there was nothing for me to condense against it. *So figure he's truly gone altogether. Made good on our warning to him to quit. We didn't explicitly tell him he had to leave town, but for him that makes sense. No point in hanging around where we could get to him, or any unhappy customers.*

No. That doesn't entirely hold up. If Spam hadn't learned how to deal with pissed-off consumers, he never would've been the best fear bottler in this area. Somebody would've knifed him like a half-assed meth dealer a week into his trade.

Good point. But if he left that quick...this lead-heads thing... it would've started up shortly after he was gone.

Which it did, if Ceyggan's grapevine info and its timeline are to be trusted.

So what does that leave us, though? As I said before: jack-all.

Body shrugged, turning away from the patio doors. *Spam was a possible, not necessarily our only source of info. Although it would be nice to know where exactly he headed off to. Just out of general curiosity.*

All the same...if it's not Spam's absence that's caused this, what else could it be?

Other than Spam, who could we go to about it? Ceyggan was helpful on a few current events, but that's about as far as it goes. And if you say Mr. Q, I swear I'll go to a priest and have you exorcised.

Pfft. As if that would even work. But okay...who else do we know plugged into the weird?

I ghosted along his ankles as we left the apartment complex. Body reached the Vega and paused while opening the driver's door.

We need someone familiar with things like emotion dealing.

Anyone who basically has an ear to the black markets in the Under.

That's a fairly short list for us, considering that they're mostly scum like Spam Tam and we would rather spend time bolted to a theater chair watching 'Mamma Mia!' in marathon loops.

Body got behind the wheel. I hovered above the passenger seat. The phone sounded and there was a moment's frantic scrambling for him to dig it out before it could go to voicemail, only narrowly managed.

"Hello?"

"John?"

The voice was sluggish, packed with wet, slippery mud. Someone sounding like their tongue was tied to a dumbbell. I drew in closer to listen.

"Who is this?"

"You called me, remember?"

"Rod?"

Jesus he sounds like he's been drinking at Mardi Gras for a week straight.

"I got your message. What did you want?"

"I needed...uh...I'm sorry...how are you?"

A long wait. I thought he might've dropped the call.

Then: "How do you *think* I am?"

"I was hoping it was kinda better than that."

"Hope is abundant. My time isn't." Long breath, sizzling over the line. "What do you want?"

Do we even want to ask now?

It's this or ask Loewenstein. You want to spend time talking and explaining things to a day-to-day shrink?

"Can we come see you? Please?"

"Oh hell..." he sounded farther away, as if he'd set the phone down. Then his voice blatted out at us, louder and closer. "Christ, just come by today. Before I think better of it."

"You're still at the house?"

Another long breath. Some wet sound that could've been his tongue licking his lips. "Where else would I go?"

"Fair enough. This afternoon?"

"Whenever. Don't come any other day or I don't think I'll

remember you called."

"Okay." No other words came to mind. No trivialities about work or weather. "Thanks—" He had already hung up.

Well...at least he's willing to see us.

That sounded less like 'willing' and more like 'surrendered.'

Same difference.

Body tossed the phone onto the passenger seat. *You still feel like going out? It's your call at this point. After all it's not like I'm the one he's going to be really listening to.*

Yeah. We need to talk to somebody. I don't think one of Loewenstein's guidance counselor referrals is going to cut it for this. We need someone at least familiar enough with us that we can skip all the awkward preliminaries.

We are seriously overestimating the value of this attempt, you know. It's almost guaranteed.

The phone rang. Body snatched it up to glance at the caller ID.

UNKNOWN.

"Let's see who this is." A blip noise as he accepted the call. "Grand Central Station. What can we do for you?"

"Mr. Flicker?"

"Yes. Who is this?"

"Please return this call at the following number." Breathy recitation. An out-of-county zip code. Without further orders or repeating the number, the call ended.

Body tapped the steering wheel. *Now what the hell is this about?*

No clue. But I'd call that number back.

He dialed. Mistook one of the numbers. *Can you repeat it back? I think I mixed up two of the numbers.*

I recited it for him. On the third ring he got a voicemail message announcing it was the number for King's Sporting Goods.

We groaned simultaneously. The business name gave it away.

Great, I muttered. *The Cut-Up Cowboys.*

I'm now more confused than before. The voicemail blipped to signal it was recording. "I'm returning your call. Whatever you want—"

Click. A live line came on.

"Jerry's Deli Deliveries. You need a catering order?"

"Can we drop the cloak-and-dagger shit? It eats up minutes and my patience. Is that you, Rex?"

"Um." Background grumbles making a decision. "Yes. Yes, sir."

"What do you guys need? Are you guys okay?"

"Can you meet with us for a while, Mr. Flicker?"

You know he's not going to tell you over an open phone connection. Say yes and let's get this train going.

Body rubbed his forehead. "I can meet with you. But not until later today. Maybe this evening. I have another commitment I have to make first. Where?"

"Do you remember that time? With that thing? Second to last in the race?"

Chief Leatherlips.

Ah. "Yeah. I remember."

"Nineteen hundred or so. We'll swing by to see the locusts with you."

Definitely the Chief Leatherlips monument.

The call blipped off.

Why are you the one that's always recalling these needless details?

Wasn't exactly needless when you were asking for the number. I don't know why it is you can't remember anything for shit, but good news is you've got the Phantom Rolodex here to keep you on-task.

Thanks a pantload, Chet.

We'd better get moving.

Oh. Boy. Do we really want to see the Scots Brothers?

We were just talking about who we knew that we could stomach to go see who has their ear to the Under's black markets. The Scots might be that connection we were thinking of without knowing it.

Good point. But whatever it is they want, it can't be as dull as us with no leads on these Believers or the lead-heads and the Faede. Body started the engine. *We owe them one anyway. We'll go see Rod, then the Scots and find out what they want.*

All right. I moved to the back of the car, roving listlessly around old burger wrappers. *But if the Scots offer to show you anything new in their 'collections,' I'm waiting in the car.*

15.

Rod Roscoe is a mentalist. To use a quaint term.

He does not guess your mother-in-law's first name. He does not pass on your dead grandpa's best wishes.

He does not write things on little cards, seal them in envelopes, then proceed to have you open the envelopes and read aloud the written-down answers to question you didn't ask until after the envelopes were sealed, all to audience applause.

Rod can read your mind.

If 'read' is anything approaching a description of what he does.

You can say 'mind-reader.' You can say 'confused.'

You can banter with words like 'telepathy.'

You can frown sympathetically for migraines that last for weeks.

You can think of it like a lame-ass comic book superhero.

You can speak of the greater good possible with such a gift.

You can take all your assumptions about 'reading minds' and how powerful it would make you, and you can pretty much chuck them into the shit-can.

This is Rod's life.

He has three mailing addresses: one nothing more than a post box tacked onto a pole, planted beside the main road going past his land. About a hundred yards from that, along a gravel drive, is a nicely-kept, neatly-trimmed-and-painted house that has the house number on it in small brass numerals.

No one lives in this house. There isn't a stick of furniture inside.

Way back in the woods, at the end of the winding single-lane drive as it continues past the empty house, where there's barely a dirt path discernible by untrained eyes, is the real Roscoe residence.

If you want to contact him, you leave or mail a note to the first box out on the road. There may be all of three or four people who have a phone number for him. Even then, you leave a voicemail the first call or two. Or ten.

A well-trained and long-ago-screened caretaker will come out and pick up the mail. They sort out the junk, forward any bills to his lawyers or accountants to deal with, and take what's left for the pleasant and empty ranch-house.

Roughly once every week or so, a girl who lives in Mount Vernon is brought thirty miles or so to collect this mail and deliver it to the 'main house.'

The girl is Yvonne. She is pretty, if a little wide-faced. Sleepy-eyed but sweet and reliable. And since childhood operating with what the old politically-incorrect called 'retarded' or 'functional retardation.' Yvonne has Down's Syndrome. She often does part-time jobs as part of her Mainstream Program as a greeter at a Wal-Mart near her home.

Her mother drives her. She lets Yvonne out, waiting in the parked Suburban by the sham front house. Yvonne takes what mail is at the ranch and walks it up, alone, to the main house. She puts it in the box and collects a fifty dollar bill left there for her. She is always excited for the fifty dollar bill. And every Christmas, when there's an extra hundred, she is ecstatic enough to want to hug the generous Mr. Roscoe who pays her so much to just collect a few letters every week.

She has hugged Rod once. It was by accident on his part,

when he was impatient for a letter and went out as she arrived, and wasn't paying attention.

The happy embrace left him lying in his driveway, crab-crawling to the house and ultimately to his living room floor with Yvonne's crying and terrified help. He laid there, he told me, for nearly three days. When Yvonne ran, teary-eyed and moaning to her waiting mother, that woman had taken nearly twenty minutes of hushed, desperate convincing as he lay on the couch that she needn't call for paramedics. He gave Yvonne two hundred dollars and reassured them they could make sure the door was locked as they left and otherwise everything was fine.

Still, that one slip-up aside, it's an effective decoy system. Like stringing toy destroyers with twine in a child's bathtub assault convoy. A micro version of the Las Vegas mail drop enjoyed by mail fraudsters for decades.

You leave the note. You hope what you need is important enough to interest him into taking the risks.

If you try to find him, you get a mailbox. If you hang round or track harder, you get an empty ranch house with that empty box. The caretaker doesn't know the ranch owner's names and doesn't care. I hadn't even entirely been sure that the number we had was still a working one until he called back.

With Yvonne, even if you get past her formidable mother, questioning is pointless.

He's always said the need for the extremes is obvious: everything is out to kill him.

And he's absolutely right.

We've known Rod Roscoe a couple of years now. We count ourselves fortunate that he has learned a lesson that most of humanity will hopefully never have to learn for itself. Namely: real mindreading is a nightmare.

Technically, Rod is a 'mimetopath,' not a telepath. The difference, he explained, is that a telepath in stories is a classic mindreader: they pick up clear, distinct thoughts as clean images almost like actual reading of neat, orderly text that doesn't need too much interpretation or context. But the reality of going into another human being's mind is a total chaos of trying to hold two distinct handfuls of smoke: one is your own mind, the other handful is someone else's…and while you're struggling to get a grip on either one, both of them start to slip away from you with inexorable, horrible certainty.

A mimetopath doesn't 'go into' someone's mind, doesn't 'read' anything. It's not a cerebral internet linkup or hacking the human consciousness. It's closer to pure empathy than anything telepathic. He describes it as 'overlapping.' Imagine each mind as one circle in a Venn diagram, and the place where they overlap is the weird eye-shaped shadow where he picks up thoughts and feelings other than his own.

The only difference between a mimetopath and a near-vegetative basket case wearing diapers in an asylum, he also has explained, is a matter of time.

It is not fun. You do not lift your fingertips, press them meaningfully against your temple, wiggle an eyebrow as you glare towards some middle distance, and like Professor X in the X-men comic books read off the phone numbers of that girl at the bar.

Ever ask the obvious question about Superman's X-ray vision? How, if that power were real, all he'd be seeing would not be naked women but walking skeletons and exposed nervous systems? This is the same idea of fantasy crashing into reality. Instead of picking up neat, concrete encyclopaedia entries of the brain, you get it *all*. Everything blown in from the brain with a vein of panic and confusion threaded through. You get the fuzzy dream-logic of disjointed, twisted thoughts, impressions or mental associations making a sort of sense to you, when in reality the other person is a neurotic, idiosyncratic whacko whose illness you're gradually contracting.

You can't read the mind of a killer and get his own brain to turn him in, if his diseased mind doesn't even think he killed anybody. It's like asking color-blind people to paint you a rainbow so you can learn the colors.

The drive up to Delaware's outskirts took the better part of an hour going along Route 23. We took the 315 north to bypass the stop-and-go city street traffic of High Street and rejoined where High Street became the rural 23 just past the outerbelt freeway.

The whole drive up, I did my disembodied pacing in the backseat, moving to and fro amongst the rips in the upholstery, the old food bags and water bottles.

Is this the best approach to this? It's not like he's any sort of licensed therapist or anything.

"You said it yourself," Body answered without looking back, "he's more in tune with who and what we are than your everyday psychiatrist."

Maybe Loewenstein could've explained to them what was up so we wouldn't have to hide or anything. He would've been willing.

"No. This is better."

Better, or simply more expedient?

"Column A and a little of Column B."

That's cute. Is it more like we're just going to see somebody that we figure will be so much more miserable than we are that we'll walk out feeling better about ourselves?

No response. I stayed amongst the litter of the back.

The more I stayed in the backseat of the Vega, stewing and chewing it, the less I wanted to impose upon the man. And not just because it would be most likely a sadistic exercise in self-esteem reconstruction.

When it got down to it, Rod was maybe the only person we could go to. I felt a subtle shudder go through my sense of presence, like an old-fashioned chill of goosebumps, when I considered what lay ahead as soon as I got within broadcast range of him, up there alone in his forest-shrouded house.

****

The door squealed open.

A thin-built man with faintly Asiatic epicanthic lengths to his eyes. A tan-toned skin with a subtle hint of copper in the edges of his face. Black hair thickly curled, close to his skull. He wore black jeans and a black t-shirt. Minimalism in color and design, keeping things as basic as he could compared to the rest of the reality he dealt with.

Hi, Rod.

He touched the bridge of his nose, blinked rapidly a few beats. "Hi."

You okay? Can we come in?

He nodded very slowly. It was like watching someone with recently-suffered head trauma trying to carefully answer an EMT's emergency room questions. Who are you? Where are you? Do you know what year it is? Is it okay if we come in here and the disembodied mind-thing talks to you for a while?

We can leave if this is too much. When I projected the words, I tried to picture them solely as words, like white glowing text from an invisible page in the air between us. I tried to keep it as free of any irrelevant images and memories, any association of thought that would lead to the chaos that most minds caused him this close up.

A shake of his head, his hand still at his nose. "No, no. Just...keep it like that if you can, okay? Just keep it text if you can. Nothing complicated or too fast, as best you can...don't... never mind. Just...come in."

"Are you sure?" Body asked.

"Of course I'm not sure," Rod breathed. "If I wanted to be sure, I'd ask *you* to come in and tell *him* to stay a thousand yards away, playing in the tree branches or something so I didn't hear it all jabbering in my skull. Just...never mind."

"Seriously—" *We don't want to—*

"Stop it. C'mon in." He turned and walked away, heading towards the kitchen along the long central hallway alongside the main staircase. Body closed the door after us and followed.

He sat down at the kitchen table where there was an assortment of pill bottles the likes of which you would only expect to see on the shelves of a fully-stocked pharmacy. Or a drug manufacturer's factory floor.

Body sat down at the chair opposite him and took in the bottles as I had. "You're taking more of this stuff than the last time I saw you."

I glided amongst the labels. *Clonazepam, lorazepam, thorazine, ariprazole...Christ, your breakfast table is like a live survey of the entire Merck manual to prescription drugs.* A pause. *Some of these are antidepressants, but thorazine is an antipsychotic. You've got Percocet, oxycodone, naproxen...and these are* huge, *they're* horse *pills. One of these would be enough to knock out an NFL linebacker for an hour or three.*

Rod plucked up one of the bottles. Without looking to the label, he popped off the lid, shaking out a couple of round, pink pills and swallowing them dry, grimacing at their aftertaste. With a smile he held the bottle out to Body. "Care for one? These are supposed to be non-addictive."

"No thanks. It would be wasted on me anyway."

Rod, man, what are you doing? You were taking a lot of these before, but if anything it looks like you've tripled your prescriptions here...and a lot of this stuff doesn't mix. You've got pain pills and antidepressants and...is this Ambien? This is the size bottle they usually sell bulk aspirin in, Jesus.

"Don't do that!" he snarled.

What?

"*Quit it!* Think *slower,* damn it! Quieter! I can only keep up so fast, okay? Keep it simple, all right?"

Sorry.

"Keep...simple." He heaved a breath.

The point is made. What's up with all this?

"I've gotta sleep sometime." He replaced the cap and put the bottle back with its kin. "I've got blood thinners, blood pressure meds, bronchodilators, acid reducers. There's MMAOI inhibitors, dopamine receptor blockers, seratonin blockers, the whole rainbow of better living through modern medicine."

Body put his hands on the table, tilted his head. "When was the last time you went outside?"

"Nothing out there for me." He sat back and smiled sleepily. "You know why I like *you*, John? Because I can't hear you except when you talk out loud. That is more relaxing than you could ever know. I mean, I can't hear…you. But you, the other one…"

I know.

"Where are you?"

I'm right here. Just over the table, opposite you.

Rod's lips kinked into a frown. "Do you know that you're like listening to someone screaming in one of those anti-echo chambers, the ones with the weird wall formations that totally disrupt all sound, kill it dead? It's like listening to the sounds of someone trapped in a box, screaming into their own throat."

I can appreciate the difficulty.

"No you can't." He dropped his voice like one of the bottles had slipped out of his hand. "It's noise. All of it. At least it only works with people. There's a hummingbird feeder outside my kitchen window, you see that?" He stretched an arm to point at the window above the kitchen sink. We could see the small, red plastic feeder hanging from the eave of the house, swaying in the breeze. "In the mornings there's a pair that come feed. I like seeing that while I'm having cereal. I can't hear or see anything *in* them. Only wings blurring while they dart around. It's lovely."

Body nodded. "I'm sorry I haven't been in touch more."

"Why? You haven't missed much. Oh, it was a little exciting around Christmas. A couple got lost and apparently thought that they could get directions. They tried the decoy house first and when that failed they saw the drive went past that property…came all the way up to my door." He hiccuped. "I could hear them before they got halfway up the porch steps. They were arguing. The woman was hoping to cheat on her husband when they got to their destination, some old classmates of his that she'd slept with before. She also was lying when she told him that he'd got the directions wrong because she didn't want to admit she'd Googled the wrong destination." Another hiccup shook him. "Not that it wasn't a fair trade. He wanted a divorce and was going to ask the same friends if he could stay with them after he announced it to her after dinner that night. He was remembering taking her to prom and thinking about one girl he slept with to cheat on her, how he did it to think about hurting her and didn't expect to actually enjoy it for its own act, and...or was that her thinking that? She wanted to drive and had to go to the bathroom and hated ginger because her father-in-law drank ginger ale and spit little bits of it when he was talking to her and saying awful things about their marriage at their wedding...I can't recall if I could make anything out between the two of them for a minute or two...I didn't answer the door, but stupid me, I left my hall light on. They kept ringing and knocking for a good five minutes before they left. It took about five Percocets to get that to go quiet."

You should put a gate up.

"Tried that." The hand went back up to the nose bridge, rubbing at it with more strength. "It only encouraged kids to come and see what was so important to warrant a gate. Same with putting up anything more than a split-rail fence for appearances. Nobody gives a shit about it if I don't make it look like something to be curious about."

We've had...some problems of our own, lately.

"Do tell."

I tried to project it in a minimum of imagery, though some of the Jennyripper wanted to keep creeping in like rats finding a hole through a fence. The idea of avoiding people. Of anger. Of wanting to hurt people. Unwanted, the image of Spam Tam's twisted, pain-crunched face and an echo of his screaming, his begging, snuck past my control and then it was there, out and into him.

He waved his hands, eyes squeezed shut. "Okay, okay! I get it! Text, *text!*"

Sorry. But...this...

And I forced him with another image.

Body, standing on the sidewalk outside The Nookery.

Those ominous spiraling lines of force drawn in bits of dirt and broken road gravel, all pointing towards his feet. Shreds of paper burning in spontaneous flame, hovering and flittering through the air over Body's outstretched hands.

Rod batted a hand in the air as if dismissing the flits of paper, as if they were actually burning right then and there in the space in front of him. He coughed.

"*Stop it!*"

I drew it back. I tried to picture smooth, unbroken dark. I remembered some old trick, something from a movie when I was a kid watching it on the Friday night local horror show—

"*Village of the Damned*," Rod of course caught and finished the thought I'd barely started. "The schoolteacher. He pictured a brick wall in his head, to stop the children from reading his thoughts behind it. Go ahead, try it. Black void or brick wall or whatever, just…just shut up for a bit…"

"Do you need something?" Body asked. He looked at the counter and sink. "Water or a drink or something?"

A flap of the hand. "No, no. I just…so…this is what you've been through lately?"

It snuck out. Traitor mind. Trina, snarling and leaping. The sounds of books clattering and thudding all around, like a storm of stones wrapped in blankets.

He jerked back as if the vampire girl were actually at his neck, nearly over-toppling from his chair. Body reached out, but his hand was slapped away with a panicked sweep of the arm.

"Don't *touch*!" He caught himself and righted his balance with a stamping of his sneakered feet to the linoleum floor.

His palms slapped to the tabletop, and two of the bottles jump and clattered over to the edge, one rolling and falling to the floor with a hollow popping.

"Just…what do you expect me to do? I have no clue what any of that is, or what to do about your…what, is she your girlfriend?"

No, no. Not exactly. But…someone we saw about this…they suggested—

"See a shrink. A typical response from anyone without a clue."

I thought maybe...you might be able to have some insight on things, an outsider's viewpoint if you were to let me share a little bit—

"You're an idiot."

Excuse me?

"You come to me, the one guy in the known world that can apparently copy over into your mind like it was a cheap hard drive partition, and you expect an *outsider's viewpoint?* What the hell does that even mean, anyway? How can I give you an outsider's viewpoint when the only thing I can do makes me anything *but* an outsider to you? To what's going on in your mind?"

I just—

"No, I'll tell you what you 'just.'" He took a breath and expelled it with a faint whistle, like he'd recently come off a cold and still had fluid in his sinuses. "You *just* wanted to come to me and figured I'd flip through your brain like a rack of travel brochures and point out the one that had the right map to the right tourist trap of your brain, right? You thought like every single other asshole who has ever heard of what I can do but has no comprehension of what it means." His face was an open wound. "I really thought...you, of all the people I've ever come across with this thing...I mean..." A choke that he tried to swallow and failed. It caught something wrong and he hiccupped. It seemed to dispel a little of the gravity; he let out a grin that was equal parts wormwood and honey.

I'm sorry about all this. I am. But we asked for your help because...you have a way of seeing past all the bullshit. You know better than anybody how there are things you can say, can describe, then there's all the other shit, all the layers and nuances and extra material collecting in the skull that nobody else can get out, not with all the hacking and passkey crackers in the world. I needed someone who could look...who could peer in and not just see. You know what I mean.

He nodded.

Body leaned forward. "Please? Only this time."

He paused. It was a long, long hold. He shallowed his breathing so sharply that for a few moments I worried he was suddenly experiencing some sort of stroke or seizure.

As I was about to suggest Body snap his fingers in front of his face, he let out a whoosh of breath.

"Okay. Okay." He stared at his hands in his lap. "This is how it works. I'll be able to...I'll try and relax. Let your mind become part of mine. A copy of it, at any rate. You shouldn't notice any difference on your side. I may seem flipped-out because when I do this...it takes me out of things for a little bit. It's subjective time though. Brain walkabout-time. I may seem utterly catatonic, or I might blink and it's done."

Do you need—

"Shut up a second. I want you to get something clear. I don't control your head. I don't have any command of what's inside there. What I generally home in on when I do this on-purpose is what I call your mental homepage. Your default ground thought."

You mean a base thought I always hold to?

"In a manner of speaking. Most people's minds have some sort of anchor point. A default mental situation, a place or a memory or person, an image or whatever. It's what they fall back on, even when they're not consciously thinking of it or anything else. It changes from time to time as the person changes, but there's almost always something there, something that I fall back to when I'm getting access. That's why I'm not promising anything illuminating or helpful in this. You might have a baseline thought that is important to you on some sub-surface level but is otherwise meaningless to you or me. It could be literally you sitting on your ass in front of your favorite video game one afternoon. Or a looped playback of a top-twenty song Casey Kasem was playing on request when you were thirteen. It isn't always anything really concrete, just strong enough to be your mind's anchor to how it otherwise rotates on its various brain-axis points, okay?"

Okay.

"This isn't some straight Freudian guidebook to touring your skull. Whatever I fall back to, that's all I'm going to look at, and I don't have any expertise in interpreting anything for you. What I see is what you get. And what you get is all that you bring to this, whether you like it or not."

So you're saying this could all be utterly worthless, and if it is it's nobody's fault but mine.

"Exactly."

I've had worse deals.

"As long as you guys understand what this is. You probably *could* get better help from some professional, you know that?"

"A psychologist or psychiatrist isn't who we want to mess with right now," Body replied.

Too many questions and not enough answers, and that's only to sit down on the couch and make the attempt.

"You may still be at less than Square One even with my help, if all you've got in there is a bunch of nothing."

You've made it abundantly clear: this could be a mess o' pottage and a waste of time.

"Yeah."

How do you want—

He started.

****

Books. Shelves of books. The smell of book paper, bindings, old glue and fresh sewn stitching.

Paperbacks. Colors of bright gloss-finish jostled against matte-flat cloth covers and gilt letters.

I blinked.

The whole thing stayed put, not clearing away like the last rags of a dream before you wipe the sleep out of your eyes.

I was standing at The Nookery's cash register. In the cramped cubby space where the old postcard racks slowly revolved with faint unoiled whines.

Windchimes, hanging outside the open front doors, out onto the garden patio. Tables of books marked down. Picked-over dollar-deal paperbacks and children's books and obsolete texts on gardening techniques and macramé patterns. Ethiopian recipe collections crowding for attention next to failed science fiction series hardcovers. Stuff that I bought by the pound from remaindered wholesalers and put out with as much thought as I would the tarps and tent covers to keep off the worst of the sun and rain.

A smell of flowers. Gardenias and ferns, growing wild in the soil pressed between old railroad ties used to give boundaries to the tiled patios of the garden bower that ran alongside the length of The Nookery, separated by a ragged wooden fence from the next door property.

Standing at my cash register. A small speaker mounted to a corner of the cubby played some soft Celtic music, running off the CD stereo system hidden somewhere upstairs.

Spring. Late spring. Warm. Windchimes.

I looked down at my hands. Hands.

Hands.

What the hell?

Looking at the wood grain of the countertop, scratched and mostly covered by a salvaged laminated blotter that had THE NOOKERY in flowing Victorian-styled letters, crimson on white. The bold lettered slogan underneath that: GET LOST!

"John, you want me to re-stock some of those out on the sales tables? Might free up some room to put another end cap out there of the new stuff."

I looked up.

A woman. How old? I couldn't judge. She was lanky, colt-legged and smiling. A long stretch of face and nose but a pretty smile with a slightly crooked overbite, one incisor overlapping its neighbor in a way that was idiosyncratic, interesting. She was looking at me. Right at me. I was here. I was here and she was seeing me and I felt a little dizzy with the weight of it. I could be seen. I was here.

What was the name? She stared at me expectantly. Mandy? Mantha?

"Margery. Yeah. Good idea." I cleared my throat. A throat. A sensation. Pressure…breath…

Windchimes tinkled and almost matched the flute-whistle of the Celtic doodling overhead. "Yeah. Take out the first table and put it in back. We'll donate the mess to the library or literacy program. Get the new Grafton hardcovers out there instead."

She nodded. Chestnut hair done in long Valkyrie braids. A small pin on the lapel of her watercolor-patterned windbreaker, the coat stylized to look like Van Gogh's "Starry Night." The pin was a triangle, point-down, with the bands of the rainbow on it. Superimposed on the rainbow background: two white, lacquered alchemical symbols for female, the circles interlocked and the arrow points parallel, pointing upwards. It clicked against a round tin pin that said "ROCK GRRL" and underneath the windbreaker there was a healthy anatomy featuring a white t-shirt, black text blazoned it reading "DAYMON DAY PARADE '06".

Margery went out the door and started stacking books in her arms. I looked back down at my hands.

"This is why I have mixed feelings." The voice jerked my face back up. Suddenly I was aware of having weight, *mass*, moving with conscious feeling of my flesh, my solidity having to shift, tendons pulling and mass moving...heady sensation, almost drunken.

Rod stood in front of me, head tilted as if listening for something, his eyes fixed on me with a look like you would give to a convenience store worker you pitied for their long hours, even as you still asked for a pack of cigarettes from the highest shelf behind them.

"What?" My voice sounded from the bottom of a well.

His look of puzzled surprise faded. "I've never had this before...with someone with me. Aware. I said you shouldn't notice anything on your side, because you wouldn't be...actively involved in my process. Usually when I do something like this, I'm in here alone." He glanced down at himself, looked at his hands stretching fingers out in front of him. "I make a sort of Xerox copy of the brain and store it temporarily in my own, like cloning a hard drive on my own server. Then I have a certain minimal selective ability to go over its contents until it fades. But this..." he looked around, then back at me. "You're here. I mean, you're actually *here*. You're not a self-image stored with the rest of this, are you?"

I shrugged. The roll of shoulders felt good. "How would I know?"

"You wouldn't. But you're answering me. You're seeing and hearing me. You're not robotically moving through the motions of this memory like she is. So you're here. Different." Another tilt of the head. He walked over to the nearest postcard rack and touched it with a fingertip, making it spin a little faster, a slightly more tormented whine. "Strong baseline memory. Full senses, real people you have feelings towards. This is one of the most complete default mindsets I've ever been in. Maybe as the soul part of you, you're nothing but consciousness, so there's nothing I can duplicate, only interact with. Maybe..." a chuckle "...maybe I didn't copy you, but you simply came inside my head. Bizarre thought, right?"

"Are you all right?"

He shook his head, closed his eyes. Lowered his hand back to his side. "Not sure. I'm never sure if I like it or not. I mean... you...you're *along* with me on this. I don't even entirely know if this is a memory we're both in right now."

"Maybe we should've let your head clear of a few of those painkillers before starting this."

"Maybe you should save the lectures," he snapped, opening his eyes and frowning. "It's usually safer. It usually feels safer, I mean. I have a...it's strange to use the word privacy, but that's what fits best. It's like swiping some files off a desk and being able to run home and read through them on my own, nobody looking over my shoulder as I do it. Is this a memory? I mean, do you have any idea where or when this is to give it some context?"

"I think so." I glanced at Margery's back. "This was...if that was the shirt...this would've been...2007...somewhere early...May? It feels like May, maybe."

"2007? So this would have been—"

"Sometime before it happened, yeah." I looked down at the wooden counter, at the blotter with the store logo, upside-down from my perspective. "This was...we always had open-air sales when the weather turned nice...it was an early spring...I think..."

"Do you want me to leave these Chinese dictionaries out here?" Margery stood at the door, looking at a collection of Pidgin translator guides. She stared at me without any recognition of Rod between us.

I nodded and she went back to work.

"She seems nice," Rod smiled. "Like the pin." He came around the counter to look at the shelf of rare edition hardcovers I kept behind locked glass doors. He tapped the glass. "Do you still have this second edition Lewis Carroll?"

"I think so." I regarded the faded blue cloth spine. "I haven't paid a whole lot of attention to the stock the last few years."

I stared through the glass panels at the old editions. Next to Carroll was a nice WWII-era edition of Thoreau. A black glossy-leather illustrated edition of Edgar Allan Poe poetry with the drawings done by an unidentified author (whose lines nonetheless looked like a primitive Aubrey Beardsley).

"Why a bookstore? Why not a comic book shop or some secondhand clothing store down in the Short North where all the campus kids and young teaching faculty from OSU would shop?"

"I don't know anything about clothes. And the rents along High Street were too high."

"And you don't like that area anyway, do you?"

"I like it fine." I ran a hand along a collection of *Doonesbury* comic strips. "I just prefer here. German Village is quieter. More comfortable."

"Was this place popular?"

A shrug. "I couldn't say."

"What do you mean?"

"I had regular customers. I had some local authors who would come in and moon around, looking for their own books on the shelves and hoping to get a little ego stroking for their work by my knowing who they were. I had a running roster of people who'd come in and out for various hours a week to give me a hand."

"This place looks gigantic. How could you run it without a full team of people?"

"The store is big. The business wasn't." I glanced at a shelf of philosophy treatises. Saint Thomas Aquinas jostling to argue observational ethics with Immanuel Kant's deism and Ayn Rand's stoic empiricism. "As long as someone could stock and walk around vacuuming up a few bits of dust on the floors and keep an eye on the register, and put out or take in the books when the weather turned good or foul, the store pretty much simply was. I was content to let it be itself."

He turned three-quarters about, taking in the windchimes hanging outside the door. A flap of tarp in a breeze that sounded like a flag on a pole.

"What about the Under?"

I didn't reply right away. Underneath the philosophers I had given eccentric sway to a shelf of apparently total random fiction and non-fiction. The memory flicked its flashlight on and hit me behind the eyes: this had been my so-called Sundries Shelf, where I never really kept any track or order but simply put aside any books I was personally reading, such as the long hours sitting at my cubbyhole next to the register on days just like today. Doors open, windchimes, speakers low, breeze plentiful. Lilac afternoons.

"I didn't know about that stuff. Except what most people know: myths and legends and totally made-up nonsense."

"You were a normal?"

"If you like to use such a term, yes." There was one of the paperback copies of E. Annie Proulx's *The Shipping News* I'd read cover-to-cover until they had pages coming loose. Next to that, a fresher copy of Gabriel Garcia Marquez's *100 Years of Solitude*. "I didn't know about it. That's all. I didn't need to know about *any* of it."

"How did it happen?"

Another non-response. I turned and went to the rack of greeting cards near the front door. A draft caught one and knocked it to the floor as I approached. I bent and restored it, feeling that old tug of tendons in my lower calves as I hunched down. A creak in the floorboards underneath me.

There was a whiff of that strange ozone smell, like the threat of a late-afternoon rainstorm. The skies outside seemed clear, but it was a momentarily cold, alien smell.

Water. I remembered water and gasping and only bubbles. Dark and freezing and my hands…awkward knots at my wrists…

"I don't remember. It's never clear to us how it happened."

I remembered dark and the smell of earth, rich fresh-turned soil. An odd smell…chemical…soft fabric tearing in my hands…for a breath of rain-smell it was on me, it was clear as magnifying lens sharpening a sunbeam, a burning camera obscura that—

"What are we doing here?"

I blinked. "What do you mean?" I stood up. I saw one card on the top of the display was backwards and corrected it.

He moved to stand next to me, his voice so close I had a sort of detached *deja vu; is this what it's like when I'm whispering into Body's ear?* "I mean this is *your* memory. I'm basically a librarian looking into a book in your private collection." He waved his hands to indicate the space around us. "Other than speaking to me, you're simply standing in the middle of this moment from your past. What about this time and place is somehow more important than any other that this is where your mind reverts to, the first default setting on your particular brain-amp that I'm listening in on?"

I stepped past him, out to the doorway. The smell of flowers was amplified with a touch of lilacs from over the fence. The neighbor there was an antiques shop that always had huge terra cotta bowls of the flowers out on their rear patio.

"No idea."

"What?"

"No idea at all," I repeated. I smiled and silently watched Margery stack and put books in an open cardboard box at her feet for some minutes.

"This time has to have some significance if this is where your mind goes on first pick."

"I wasn't even thinking of this when you started your whammy on me."

"If this is where you go when there's nowhere better to distract you, it has to mean something." Rod plucked out a book from the shelves and leafed through an Audobon Society collection of Birds of the Pacific Northwest. "Was there any book you *didn't* carry in this place?"

"I wasn't all that picky, other than not carrying any hate literature or crazy tinfoil conspiracy nut stuff. And probably a little of that leaked through in the history section anyway. I don't judge what people read as much as what they do with what they read. Or that they read at all."

Margery was folding the flaps up on the box, hunched down on those long legs in their wrinkled acid-washed gray jeans and the torn cuffs that terminated in a pair of thick-soled sandals. Her toenails were aquamarine with metallic flecks that glinted in the sunbeam that peeked across the rip in the overhead tarp.

"You like her?"

"Did. Not much point, though. But didn't stop me from having her do odd hours at the store whenever she could. It gave her a free expense account for books she liked here."

"I get the impression she probably took more books than she worked off…?"

Another shrug. I always had a tendency for strange depressions and wistful notions. In the case of Margery and other women I'd known like her, it was the old lament about wanting to get into a particular club for the delightful company of some of its members, though I was forever disqualified from even applying at the door. So to speak.

"I could look, at least. And what were a few more books to me, more or less?"

She picked up the box in her hands, straightening and turning around in one smooth motion, jerking when she realized I was standing behind her. "Sorry!"

"It's okay. My fault for woolgathering." I grinned and stepped aside to let her pass.

The cash register space was too tight for that many people. I realized she was going to walk into Rod a split-second too late to say anything.

She passed through him without any effect to her or him,

at once a strange melded man-woman thing and then moving past as if nothing unusual had happened; a real *Christmas Carol* ghost simplicity that I realized with idiotic hindsight should have been obvious to me from the beginning.

He followed me out to the patio, past the tables of books and out where the benches rested, crooked wrought-iron salvage jobs next to a cheap little cast-plaster fountain that featured a little cupidon standing at waist-height, forever pouring out a greenish-looking trickle of water fed from a hose that ran under the flower beds behind it.

"Nice place. Cozy."

"I liked it." I stared at the water trickle, the sunlight glinting off it. "Did you never come to the store?"

"I didn't know you then. Plus, I never really got out much then, either."

"Ah." I reached out and touched the water. Cold. It splashed across my fingertips and made its way into the basin underneath. Almost too much sensation, but I endured it long enough to adjust, to let be just another feeling I could process like so many others. I smelled fern fronds giving out their dewy, secretive smells, green scents on every breath. Flowers. That lilac smell was pervasive enough to almost be annoying. Almost. A wind soughed through the alley and brought a smell of pastry breads baking at the place across the street. Somebody was grilling something in a postage stamp backyard nearby, I could smell the charcoal smoke.

"Is something going to happen soon? Is that what this is about?" Rod stared up at the cloudless sky. The sun was past the tree line, so it couldn't have been earlier than three o' clock. The breeze shifted, stoning the place solid with lilac smell and drowning away the charcoal. The trickle of the water spattered a little as the breeze blew the flow across my fingers to the pavement instead of the basin. I shook my hand free, watching it make little dark spots on the pavement that almost immediately dried away.

"I don't remember. I don't think so."

Almost on reflex, I looked up at the trees, at the phone and power lines that traveled along the back street all the way down to Schiller Park at the far end.

Only a couple of starlings. I caught a flash of carnation red: a proud cardinal, *fwit-fweet*ing and spreading out his wings. A spring ritual. He caught the breeze and flapped off.

No black-oil-smear-shaped things, hunched on the lines or in the tree branches watching me.

I turned around and took in the view of The Nookery front doors. The facade of mismatched buildings that ran alongside down to the streets, the various glazed windows and nailed-shut access doors that followed the down-grade of slopes and steps down to Third Avenue and the front doors of the shop entrance on that street.

Quiet. Nothing ticking or crackling in the dark silences. No postcard racks rotating endlessly even when nobody was touching them. No rooms moving their walls or stairs mischievously deciding to relocate at random.

A car shushed by on the back road. A skitter of leaves noisily sounded after it.

"No. I don't think so."

Rod twitched impatiently. "You wanted my help. You wanted me in here. What's wrong that you need help with?"

I looked at the ground. There. My feet. Huh. My old pair of Chuck Taylors. Had I worn those recently? Did I even still have them somewhere, in one of the trash bags of clothes and belongings I'd grabbed from my old house and—

—my old house. Down the road.

I went back into the store, past the cash register cubby and through one of the side corridors. The Celtic music stopped and the stereo switched to a random selection of some Peruvian flute music, strangely hollow and sounding like cloud-caked mountaintops humming to each other. I went through a room of old travel posters and humorous bumper stickers…through the room that held biographies…Rod was close behind me.

"What is it?"

I didn't reply until I reached the last room, where lawn tending and various home craft books were categorized. This was the rearmost room, the back entrance to the store that opened onto the back street that ran parallel to Third at the front end of the shop.

All the bookshelves and books. Sunlight coming unobstructed through the windows, not soaped over. The hardwood floors were a little dusty but otherwise didn't host any carpets or throw-rugs.

No cot, no desk, no nubbly blue armchair.

Everything as it should be. As it was. As it should be.

As it wasn't ever going to be again.

I leaned against a shelf, my forehead touching the edge of cool, polished wood. The shelf creaked under my weight.

Weight. Hands. Shoes. I hadn't really considered that, either. As natural as it was to be in a memory, you don't ever tend to stop to think at a miracle of being solid, whole, when you never remembered yourself any other way.

I could even smell the book pages yellowing so near my face.

"Is something wrong?"

"No." I breathed. "This is just my old place. In present day, this is where I live. We made a sort of apartment out of this room."

"Big store."

"It's actually several buildings that've been connected together." I fell into the autopilot description I always gave people. "It takes up about half a city block or so."

"You must have been doing pretty well."

"Not really." I grinned to myself. "I recall I was late on a couple of payments on the lease except this place was always in a sort of probate limbo because the realty company that I bought it from went out of business…hasn't yet gone out of business…I paid them already … wait…but…yeah…"

"Hold it together. Don't let this draw you in on yourself."

I looked at him. "What?"

"I told you: you're not the typical way I do this. I don't normally have the baggage of a person actually being consciously with me in this, with a copy of their mind in mine. You're not a copy…this isn't real, John. You and I aren't here, this is a really detailed diorama from your memory. Don't let it get you down. Just try and figure out why we're here at all. Why is this the default place your mind came to, if nothing important happened today or here according to your memory? How does this relate to your current problems?"

I stepped back from the shelves. I looked around.

A faint smell of sun-warmed lilac permeated the room. Must have left a window cracked somewhere. I heard a susurrus of water flowing through one of the pipes.

Nothing weird or shifting or strange. Just an old bookstore. Just me in my Chuck Taylors with my sometime-part-time store employee sorting books in another room. A May afternoon, cool but not cold and lovely. Nothing important at all.

"I don't…" The tension I hadn't realized had been coiled in me relaxed. "I don't…have a clue. Except this…it feels good."

"People usually have a sort of 'default' feeling or memory when it's something important. But there's no major trauma or event here, is there? Is that what this is really about?"

"I don't know. But…maybe. Maybe that's what it is. Maybe…it's because…" I touched the book spines. Collections of composting guides and helpful household cleaning hints. "Maybe I was simply happy. Here. I wasn't rich or famous or had a million friends but…I…I liked this place. Still do. This was…this was a good day. Quiet. There were a lot of them like this. Just…"

"We should go."

"Wait. I just want…I want another minute to sort of…can I just have a second to maybe walk down the road to my place? My old place?"

"We should go." He didn't say it cruelly or harshly, but it was definite and firm.

"It'll only take a couple more minutes, *Christ*, man! I'm only asking for a little leeway here! You want to help me sort through my head, well we're here! Let me have a little Memory Lane stroll here, okay?"

Rod stared at me. He had this way of looking at you so frankly that if you stared back you almost thought he was somehow autistic, like he had gone temporarily catatonic in some sort of fugue. But all he was doing was really looking at you. Even if he couldn't pick up what was in your head, those dark eyes had a way of staring at you so openly and guilelessly. I hated him and those eyes. I wanted to punch him but it would be useless. It might hit, might make me feel better, maybe it would even hurt him in some telepathic way. But who cared? What did any of it matter? Even the lilac smell seemed suddenly canned and artificial and fading.

"How long?" he asked. I barely could make out the words. I didn't *want* to make out the words. "How long do you want to stay here?"

I didn't look at him.

"Forever," I muttered.

"I think I can see why this is your default place. Maybe even what's wrong."

"Great. Help me out, Freud."

"Maybe this is more Carl Jung than Freud, but either way it seems fairly clear."

"Elucidate me, maestro."

He didn't rise to the sarcasm.

"You're unhappy."

"Wow." I snickered, nodding. "Yeah, that's...an amazing deduction. I can't believe I couldn't have simply gotten this from you on the phone and not had to waste your important time solving the mystery of the stolen royal jewels, Mr. Holmes." I sighed. "I'm unhappy. As if it takes a mind-reader and a hallucination of my old job to realize—"

"You want to keep bullshitting yourself while I stand here listening?" The lips moved but otherwise his face remained that same inflexible stare. "I have all afternoon if that's the case, but at some point I'll need to break off to go to the bathroom back in reality." A tilt of his head. "Unless you mind me pissing my pants in the middle of your nostalgia."

I gawped at him. He stared back.

I closed my eyes and laughed.

I breathed in. Laughed out. I rocked on my heels slightly

and laughed. I let my hands dangle at my sides. And laughed.

Finally it tapered off. His only concession was a weak smile back at me.

"I'm sorry." I let my eyes roll to the wood-plank-and-beam ceiling overhead. Dust motes in the air. Another reflexive kick: I was seeing dust motes and a beam of light from the windows. Nothing more. No auras, no microscopic creatures or dead skin cells and weird other-dimensional creeps; no x-rays, cosmic rays or infra-red heat…just looking at dust motes in an unremarkable room that didn't exist.

Before I knew it, I was pushing the door open, stepping out onto the back street. I managed to startle myself at the jangle of a bell mounted to the door before remembering that it had been there when this was still an open store. I left the door hanging open as I stepped to the sidewalk, around the wooden partition and out to the open spaces.

Parked on the sidewalk was a white sedan. I almost walked right into it.

"What the hell?"

"This isn't yours." Rod came from around me, putting a hand to the hood of the car. "It's mine. A '91 Ford Probe."

"What?"

"My first car." The smile rose then flickered away, like watching a wave sine on an oscilloscope that smoothed out as soon as you saw it. "I had to sell it less than six months later. Couldn't focus well enough to drive."

Sitting on top of the car was a tortoiseshell cat that hadn't been there.

Rod stroked it, the cat's eyes closing contentedly as it lifted its nose to the caress, purring with a chuddering staccato from its chest.

"Turtleneck." He glanced at me and then went back to petting the cat. "A cat I had when I was a little kid."

He stroked the cat, and as he stared at its mixed-color fur I looked up the street to see that downtown wasn't where it should be. Instead of the familiar LeVeque Tower and Hyatt building there were more trees and blue sky.

"Bleed-through is already starting," Rod remarked, scratching at the cat's ears. It rolled over with a thump of its tail to show its belly. "This is quicker than usual, but then none of this follows the usual way of things for me. Maybe it's because it's a more intense interaction."

"These things are yours that are meshing into my memory?" He nodded.

I watched him stroking the cat's belly for another minute.

"This was the only pet I had as a kid," he said quietly, bringing his face close to the cat's and nuzzling against its forehead with his lips. "He ran away when I was nine or so."

"I'm sorry," I breathed again. With the laughter and confusion passing me, I felt as though there was nothing left inside to react. "I didn't realize…"

"That you weren't happy?"

I *hmph*ed. "It's funny about that. You can say it over and over again, tell people how miserable you are and think that you've said it pretty plainly enough that it should be obvious to yourself most of all. But I think…I think I've adjusted. I think we've gotten okay with a lot of things…so okay that we kind of forgot about the difference between being mad or bothered about things and what it means to actually be either happy or unhappy."

Rod looked up from petting the cat to take in the store sign overhead, the open door with its dangling bell. "You were happy here? Running this place? Being with a few friends or co-workers? Nothing more complicated or ambitious than that?"

"Yeah."

"Can you regain any of that? Try and restore it?"

I looked at the store sign myself. "No. Thomas Wolfe and all that." He nodded. "And in all truth…there are some parts…"

Trina. Hal. As silly and insane as it all was, knowing people like the Scots Brothers, Justin…if I'd still been a nondescript bookstore proprietor could I have helped any of them?

Would I have given a damn to try?

"I can't say I wouldn't trade it all or that if I had to do it all over I'd stay the same…but…I don't know…I just know that lately I guess…I'm unhappy." I smiled, lopsided and not feeling it. "I remember this place as being the greatest thing on earth for me. Nothing except whatever was the immediate problem to deal with. An order of books that hadn't arrived. Somebody not showing up to work their hours. Some customer trying to swipe a book and put it in their old lady purse like I didn't spot it. Water damage in the basement. The local historic society bitching my gutters weren't painted a 'historically consistent color' to match the neighborhood. Whatever. Not ghosts and vampires and…being something else."

"Things change."

"Yeah. Doesn't that just suck. I can't believe this is all boiled down to…unhappy."

"It's not always that simple, you know. A reason for something can be basic. The problem itself that emerges from it, not necessarily."

"What do I need, doc? A vacation? Airfare to Vegas and a thousand bucks' crazy spending money to blow at a casino? A deep-tissue massage from a tall blonde Nordic goddess?"

"I don't know. But something to consider…" he waved a hand at the cat. "…It wasn't Vegas or a massage that you brought us to, was it?"

It collapsed on me as surely as letting a door slam shut on my hand.

This felt ridiculous.

I felt like a fumbling, ham-handed clown and all of a sudden this whole thing was embarrassing; almost as red-faced to me as getting caught naked in public or having some shameful diary entry read aloud over a loudspeaker at the airport. This was stupid and useless and meaningless. The big secret of why we were miserable was we were *unhappy*? That we wished things were back to the way they were before? Boring and typical and uneventful? That wasn't exactly a hot-shit late-evening headline release. Who *wasn't* in some way past the age of twenty-one in America and not wishing for some return to younger days and easier years? Hell, back in the days when our surroundings had been the real deal, I'd been feeling a little wistful just for the days when I was a kid living with my parents and totally ignorant of how much you had to work to pay bills and keep a roof over your head.

This was…masturbatory and stupid and unhelpful. Loewenstein's well-intentioned suggestions be damned, going to a shrink wasn't going to be any more productive than this… this high-definition-Dolby-surround-sound navel-gazing.

"Get me out of here," I groaned.

****

I was staring down at him, seated at the kitchen table. He was hunched over, various bottles shoved aside where his arms were folded and his head lay on its side against his forearms. He stared up into the vague air where I hovered. All the sense of bodily weight and motion and balance had evaporated without a blink to mark it.

"Done," he grumbled.

What happened?

Soul stayed above, somewhere near the ceiling.

Nothing productive. I'll tell you later.

No, tell me now.

Nothing. It doesn't make any difference. None of this adds up to any useful outcome...

What?

Bits of thought floated down to me, like tugs of a spider web transmitting its primordial Morse code of the trapped fly along the line. I got the sense of the bookstore...a smell of lilacs...Margery?

Jesus I haven't thought of Margery in forever.

I know.

Rod sat up, unfolding his arms and resting against the back of his chair. He looked towards the cold light from the kitchen window, the thin curtains framed around it, the little soap bars on the back of the sink shaped like tropical fish and birds-of-paradise flower blossoms.

"That was novel," he croaked.

That was useless.

He looked at the ceiling. "Not as much as you'd think."

"You were at the bookstore? That was *all*?" The flatness of it, the stale sort of blank, schoolkid's summer-vacation-essay sense of it was more disappointing than I'd realized I was capable of feeling.

He stared at me. I felt I should say something but didn't know what. He preemptively breached the silence.

"Did I ever tell you how I told my parents? What it was I could do? How I found out?"

No.

I shook my head.

"I started having thoughts. Well, okay, any kid hitting twelve or thirteen or so, they'll start to have *those* thoughts. The kind that usually are accompanied with having an erection so rock-hard insistent that you have to stack math textbooks on it just to be able to keep it out of sight."

Ah.

Again I was caught flat-footed and couldn't reply.

"But thing was, I couldn't shut it out. If I was sleeping it was okay…but migraines weren't the half of it. Try concentrating on a television show, on music, on your homework, with random thoughts ramming and jabbering through your skull. It was like standing far apart from a meadow as a storm cloud is flying over it, and you can see the west-east passage of it. Then the cloud notices you, watching it. It immediately maneuvers to blow over you. Suddenly you're in the middle of it where you're the one getting doused and frozen, hit by random bursts of lightning."

"I had to be kept home from school for longer and longer periods. My parents took me to specialists. They were told to go to the specialists' specialists. CAT scans, MRIs…they put me through a couple of spinal taps."

Jesus.

"Doesn't matter. Didn't matter. Nothing. The thoughts kept coming and I kept realizing that these things were exciting to me, interesting. At first. Until I figured out where they were coming from. From somebody else. It stopped being a storm and the clouds split…I was feeling closer to my own thinking...while the other's thoughts and impressions...they were a pressure front butting up against my thinking. Cold and hot pressure waves, meeting and making rain. I *liked* the thoughts, they revealed to me something I discovered before I figured out *how* I was experiencing them."

"But it got terrible. Finally some doctor pitied me enough to simply write a prescription for heavy-duty Valium, Xanax, a mixture of those occasionally with a Percocet. Maybe she was hoping I'd be stupid and teenage-angst-packed and kill myself taking all the bottles at once, I don't know. They certainly thought it occasionally, the doctors. I'd sit in their offices and amidst the lightning and screeching and watery eyes, I know it occurred to them. At least in the back of their heads, where they didn't want to admit there were times they hated the patients, saw their illnesses as weakness and complaining and wheedling. Anything to keep from having to figure out new and exciting ways to explain to my mom and dad that nobody knew what was going on with their son's brain."

He ground the heels of his hands against his eyes, like rubbing the soreness after a hard cry from the sockets. Another heavy exhale, like he was breathing out these things instead of speaking them.

"It was easier to tell my parents I was gay than it was to tell them I could read their minds."

He picked up a random bottle. Shook it with mournful resolve. The clunky rattle seemed to tempt him, but instead of opening and downing its contents he returned it to the table.

"When I say 'easier,' I mean in the sense that it's easier to jump out of a plane with a faulty parachute than it is to jump out without one at all. I still hit the ground pretty hard." A smile. "It doesn't help family relations to come out and then admit a little too much so that your dad realizes that it's his mind you've gotten similar thoughts from. The ones that helped your naïve, teen self realize you were gay in the first place."

I didn't know.

"What, that I was gay or a mind-reader?" His smile went hazy, eyes unfocused. "Don't sweat it. You're not my type. I prefer solid bodies."

I shifted in my seat. "We...I didn't realize you had it that long."

"You know what I really hope for?" All animation left his expression except for the movement of his lips. "You know how you lose things over time? As you get older? Your knees go out, your back gets stiff, it gets harder to keep up the same energy as when you were seventeen and bounding out of bed Saturday mornings? I'm hoping it works like that. Like Alzheimer's or multiple sclerosis. Something in my brain will age with the rest of me and eventually... it'll be quiet. For good." He looked at me with an uncomfortably frank stare. "A guy at the Cleveland Institute once told me he had an idea that what I could do represented an evolutionary step. A big quantum jump forward into what humanity could someday be for everybody."

"That sounds better than nothing."

"Not the way I see it. He pointed out that nature and evolution try a lot of different things. Most of them are failures, dying out before they pass it on to another generation." The stare went cold, only subconscious shifts of the face muscles kept him from resembling a ghastly photo of a corpse, flat and two-dimensional and colorless in front of us. "I'm kind of banking on this being on those natural cul-de-sacs of the big evolutionary tree. Nobody should pass this on to another generation."

"You don't know that," I said. "Nobody knows."

Maybe he's right and you're the future. A future where maybe mind-reading is what we need, a little empathetic chaos in the system. Regain or build some of that mutual understanding we're so lacking in right now.

He shook his head. "You can't force morality and good behavior on people or it's not morality. Having a sense of self, of privacy, of being within yourself, is entirely where empathy, real comprehension and attempt to understand others, comes from. Do I look like I give a damn about any other people because my brain can pick up everybody else's broadcasts, whether I want them or not?"

Not exactly.

"If everybody could read everybody else like I do, and that

was why they were playing good cop all the time, it wouldn't be people being at their best to try and actually be any better than themselves. It would just be everybody being held hostage or invaded by everybody else, held by the pain of it."

Maybe free will isn't all it's cracked up to be.

He looked at the window again. Got up, walked to the sink, eyes never leaving the window.

Is there something out there? A hummingbird?

He looked back at me. Leaned against the edge of the sink.

"I'm not a fortune teller, only a mind-reader. I don't have to be a fortune teller, though, if I can see in the next person's mind what they intend. Maybe a little peace and quiet for once."

Is something wrong?

"Hmph." The smile returned. This one wasn't bitter, but had a nagging, piquant quality. The look of a physician trying to humanely describe the best of two hideous options to a dying patient in a hospital. "The future is what we make of it. Or let it be made for us."

He blinked, looking at me as if noticing I was there for the first time. "Get going. Now. Grab your coat and hat and hit the bricks. I don't have any insights to offer you if you won't try and seek any in yourself."

I'm sorry if we offended—

"You haven't offended me." He straightened, got back to his feet. "Just leave. There's nothing in your head for me that isn't already there for you. I suggest you guys take some time to think things through for yourself and stop looking for anybody else to sort it out for you. Or see a shrink after all."

Do you—

"Go!" He swept his hands out in front of him, rolling the wrists as a drunken man doing a comically over-wrought breaststroke while standing in tiptoe-deep water.

****

I stopped before entirely clearing the front door.

"What's wrong?" I asked. "All of a sudden you're acting like we kicked your dog and took a crap on your dining room table."

"Nothing." His eyes stayed on the floor between our feet. His hand was fisted around the doorknob, pale-knuckled with tension. "I'm getting a major migraine simply from being around you this long and I need to go lie down before I fall down on this porch. Get going. Be on your way to something meaningful. I'm sick. I need to lie down."

We moved away, clearing the door, began to hear the door squealing shut behind us.

"Don't do it."

I turned back. "What?"

"Don't keep acting like you two have to save the world. You're not superheroes. Nobody deputized you."

Like you said: if we were forced to do it, it wouldn't be a very moral choice, would it?

"But you already assume you two don't have a choice."

Not when it matters.

"That's crap." His other hand held a prescription bottle. He brought it up, shook it. No rattle. "Why do you persist in this knockoff morality play of a life? What do you owe any of these people?"

"Nothing, a lot of the time."

"I already know you don't get some sadistic kick out of people owing you favors or in pain. But you're not responsible for the world. You live a single tiny part in it, same as the rest of us." He lowered the bottle to his side. "Where did you sign contracts saying you owe the rest of the world?"

Do you want to keep beating on us about this? Or are you trying to work something out for yourself? We could stand here all day and wait for you if you want.

He didn't yell or reproach.

His voice was hushed. "You can't do it."

What?

"Save everybody. You don't know everything."

I know that taking a bunch of pills isn't any way to help anyone.

"Spare me the sponsor nonsense. It's no better or worse than a lot of other ways out there. People who bury themselves in social media sites, or clubbing or television. Anything that lets them pretend to be anything and anyone else for a while. How many people do you still hang out from high school?"

Not many.

"Why not? Why not keep helping each other relive the greatest years of your life, when you were young and irresponsible and all the rest? Why not help people stay the same and happy forever?"

"Where are you going with all this?" I asked. "Is something else going on? We came here for your help, admittedly not entirely with your blessing. But instead we're getting this flood from you. What's wrong?"

Eyes still down at the ground. A bird chittered its angry diatribe and finished before he spoke again.

"Does it bother you?"

What?

"Not you. You," he looked at me. "Does it bother you that I can read him, but not you?"

"I never thought much about it before. I figured it was one of those aspects of being what we are. Should it bother me?"

"Can't say. I'm not a neuroscientist or anything. But don't you think it's a little odd that I can hear him, interact with him, no substance for any neural paths or signals...but you, the physical, solid body with all that meat in your skull...you're a complete null to me? Ever wonder what Descartes might've made of that?"

"I don't think Descartes has anything useful to say to anyone these days."

The quiet fell between us. Not liking the soured feeling his remarks had created. The experience was like someone flinging a helpless animal into a fighting ring to watch it struggle.

I'm sorry.

"I know. So am I."

Take care of yourself. And if you need anything... please call us if we can help.

He nodded, closing the door without another word.

****

All the way home, the one thing I couldn't help but gnaw on, the proverbial bone, was Rod's blind spot where I was concerned.

He could read Soul. So much so, Soul couldn't be tolerated anywhere near him.

But with me: nothing but dead air, to borrow the radio phrase. Dead air.

So what the hell? Is the body half of a doppelgeist shielded against telepathy?

Or is it more to say that Soul is the only real consciousness that can be read…while I'm little more than brain-meat and chunks of skull, holding together neural patterns as dead as a jigsaw gathering dust? The full picture's there and preserved, but no more lively than its tiny little compartmental pieces? A cardboard portrait of what was once a living, truly thinking mind?

Not a great thought. If it was, in fact, my thought at all.

I think, therefore I am.

Yet apparently…there is more to the definition than even Descartes could sum up.

17.

In more vulgar circles they're referred to as 'the Flying Fuck-Allas.' In more polite rounds they're simply called 'crazy sons of bitches.'

They're the Scots Brothers.

They're human. But in the Under, anyone who is deemed 'just human' and not half-something-or-other, or possessing some weird twitch to their makeup, is a kind of scary in a special category.

The Suicidal Scots. There are things in the Under that would go even more pale at hearing these guys are looking for them.

Rex and Hannibal originally hail from Indiana. They had a grandfather in a senior care home in Noblesville, outside of Indianapolis. As high school seniors, they worked summer jobs as attendants in the senior care home. Jerry Scot was the world to his grandsons. And they were that rare type of person in the postmodern world that believes in paying something back to the people you care about.

Jerry—quite the ladies man in his elder years—had a few 'girlfriends' amongst his care home neighbors. When one of them died, he mourned.

Then another died. Then a third. Jerry talked to the

management of the home about his concerns something other than old age or illness was responsible. The management didn't listen. The old and ill: they die. What of it? Wasn't that ultimately what this place was about, coming to wait and die with a minimum of comfort to send them on their way?

Jerry talked to his grandsons. He was afraid. His grandsons listened.

It took two more deaths and a lot of their free time off-shift staying with Jerry, but the Scots discovered more than the cause of untimely deaths. They discovered in their sudden, slap-in-your-face-with-a-thunderclap way, the Under.

They found a *megacolygium*. Sometimes called a gluttonghast. Sometimes semi-jokingly referred to as a 'hungry, hungry Zippo.'

Try and imagine a dumpy, rotted-pear shape of a guy. Thinning black hair like the sticking-out kind on fly's legs. Squat face, perpetually sad-soft. A guy you don't look twice at on a bus ride, or a long wait in a hospital waiting room. Nobody's idea of intimidating or threatening, maybe creepy at best. You glance at such a person and imagine the guy has a job wearing an easily-drycleaned uniform, a delivery truck driver for a bakery, or hospital laundry service. When you talk to such a person, he's never looking back at you. If he talks back, you may notice he says very little, mostly affirmative grunts and nods.

As unpleasant as the prospect sounds, now picture this person naked. A body that makes you picture wet sand being dribbled out into those ploppy, pie-puddle shapes on the beach. Gumdrops with a pair of broken-off pencil eraser legs, molded in dough flesh with the mottling of mushroom caps.

Where the belly balloons out, now see a massive, wriggling mouth of jagged teeth. Running from under one armpit, around, down, a massive grinning mouth that curves back up to under the other armpit. A mouth of wet, gargling hunger that goes...nowhere. The blackness that sucks up light as you try to stare past the gnashing, mismatched teeth, there's no throat past them. It swallows, chews...but there's no discernible bottom to it. Nothing that corresponds to the visible geometry of the swollen body around it.

That's a gluttonghast. A disjointed, busted-down, bony zipper of a mouth, that chews and swallows away to some nowheresville. A hungry, hungry Zippo. The reason why the eyes never seem to look at you is because they don't work. The head you're staring at or talking to, it's the equivalent of a fleshy ventriloquist's dummy. The grunts and few words it exchanges are the hollow thrown-voice mutterings of the real mouth concealed below.

A megacolygium doesn't do anything as obvious or nice as eating you. It's not a crocodile or tiger that wants basic flesh. What a gluttonghast eats isn't clear. The victims are left looking like a squashed version of themselves. Think of a human being treated like a discarded hotel bed sheet, rumpled and deflated. Very little in the way of blood loss, though the bodies look desiccated. No outright broken bones or burst blood vessels. No animal-teeth bite-marks or bruises. A gluttonghast eats something vital and internal, but not something that apparently will ever show up clearly on an autopsy.

The brothers spent another week of off-shift time, trying to figure out what they were dealing with, trying to get attention to the issue. They quickly realized that management not only didn't care, they were complicit. The gluttonghast worked as a night-shift orderly, perfect cover for its activity. Since they were only part-time day-shift kids, they hadn't met or seen it until they were staying late with Jerry.

The gluttonghast was profiting the facility by letting them continue to file Social Security payout claims for people who were no longer living there. They didn't so much know about the gluttonghast specifically as they didn't care where the extra money they were pocketing originated. The boys knew they were on their own; it didn't take years of movies to tell them that the police wouldn't listen to two kids claiming monsters and corruption at the local senior home.

We've never heard the full story about how they dealt with it or what happened. All we know is the aftermath. By the time they'd dealt with the megacolygium, the senior home was burned down. With Jerry trapped inside, after having saved the boys from smoke inhalation. They were two teenage fugitives from the police, blamed for the arson and the resultant deaths. And Rex was missing his left hand.

If you ask Rex for any details about how he lost the hand in the conflict, he'll look at the stub for a contemplative moment. Then give you a half-grin and answer with "We needed the distraction."

The Suicidal Scots have their fingers on the pulse of a lot of stranger dealings in the Under. A fairly impressive feat that Soul and I can't lay claim to. If you want something taken out (possibly with half the city block around it), these guys are willing to try. They don't get silver swords crafted by ancient dwarves and holy water-filled squirt guns blessed by the Pope. In a pinch, they probably could lay their hands on such things. But they don't generally care to 'get fancy' as they put it.

The Scots buy most of their gear at Home Depot.

If that alone doesn't give you some idea why there are creatures in the Under scared shitless of them, then I don't need to bother with any more hyperbole.

****

The Leatherlips monument is absolutely one of the odder things to see around Columbus. Off the beaten path, away from the traffic that heads towards the Columbus Zoo, in a slightly-affluent suburb of Dublin not far from the ritzy neighborhoods of Wedgewood where my friend Hal operates. If you drive down Riverside Drive and pull off into the city parking lot near the river, you can get out of your car and walk in a leisurely pace to the miniscule fieldstone-laid dock to the Olentangy. Come down the hillside slope that defines most of this park's area until you hit the river. Stop halfway down, turn about-face and look back up-slope...right in the face of a gigantic Native American sphinx blindly staring out at the river.

Limestone slabs, cut in big rectangular semi-brick-shaped

chunks. Laid and mortared at a thirty-degree angle to the slope of the hill so that the whole impression is of a structure thrusting out of the ground towards the river. The slabs are laid down so that over time, as each layer shapes the contours of the whole profile, the whole thing combines to form the head and upper neck of Chief Leatherlips. An off-white, craggy face that looks like it's trying to climb out from the clutch of the earth.

At its highest point from the ground, it's over twelve feet. It shallows as you go back towards where it meets the hill. You can walk up along the back where there's a hidden depression inside the skull. People can stand in this depression, looking over the ridge of the head and see a nicely elevated view of the tree line and the water. A disturbing jigsaw arrangement of stones describing a lipless, somewhat glaring man's sharp-cheekboned face. It's almost as if the face is not really looking at the river so much as trying not to look at everything else around it.

Chief Leatherlips was arguably the Neville Chamberlain of the Wyandot and Shawnee tribes in Ohio back in its frontier days. He advocated treaties with white settlers and cooperated with their intrusions into native land. The name 'Leatherlips' was even given him by white settlers who trusted him to never break any promise he made them. Finally Tecumseh and his buddies got sick of all this concession crap—not to mention that Leatherlips was suspected of witchcraft—and the Chief met his fate via a tomahawk to the skull...somewhere in the vicinity of where his giant stone effigy-head now rests for tourists to photograph.

I got out of the car, leaning against the hood and staring for a while at the monument's left profile.

Man I hope they get here soon. Soul flicked around my shoulders, a hummingbird feeling of tap-the-shoulder, run-to-the-other-shoulder-tap-again, over and over in agitation.

What's your problem? It's quiet enough here. There aren't even any kids running around screaming or bawling their heads.

Maybe you'd feel nervous too if you had seen that monument blink its eyes a minute ago.

I stopped looking at Leatherlips and paid more attention to the glints of the river visible through the tree cover at the foot of the slope.

A few minutes past seven o' clock, only ten minutes since we'd arrived, a beaten-up Ford Explorer painted in shadows of sun-faded red and a couple of replaced passenger-side doors in dented sky-blue pulled up next to the Vega. The windows were partially tinted, an incongruous touch to the rest of the beater. Not tinted enough to be illegal, but noticeable in obscuring a clear view of the driver. Like two-hundred-dollar RayBan sunglasses being worn by a guy in a pizza-stained seventies leisure suit and clown shoes.

A click and whine as the passenger window rolled down. Inside the dim of the interior, a lumpen shape approximating a person sat with both hands on the wheel. I could make out a pair of chunky, large sunglasses underneath the brim of a gimme cap.

A *thwunk* as the car door unlocked.

"Hop in."

I grinned as I got into the seat, closing the door after me. "Is this where you put a bag on my head? Tell me to shut up and not ask any questions?"

The lump in the driver's seat cracked a lopsided smirk. "We have the bag. But it's not like it'd do any good with you two, right?"

Fair enough. Two hands on the wheel confirmed it was Hannibal I was riding with.

Hannibal nodded towards the picnic area near the river. "Can you believe that last time? The crazy trying to get those cross-bred locusts of his out there to breed with the regular locust swarms when they spawned?"

"Was that last summer?" A nod. "Man, that seemed like forever ago. Yeah, thank god locusts are hard to make carnivorous for anything larger than each other."

Though they certainly attempted hard enough to make a snack out of your face.

"I still have one of those egg packages."

"You do?"

"Going to tend it. See what comes out. Maybe he was right."

What Hannibal Scot might find curiosity-piquing about a carnivorous locust cross-breed I didn't feel like asking.

Told you, Soul whispered.

****

Hannibal took us back to 270, and we headed east on the outer belt.

"How's business these days?"

A noncommittal shrug from the driver. "We had a Questing Beast last week in Pataskala."

"Really?"

A nod. "Yeah. It was crazy. It wasn't the genuine article. But it was definitely one of the breed. Thing looked like a greyhound crossed with a Monitor lizard. Had two heads. Dark green and black. If we hadn't had to net it, I would've liked to've seen it race somewhere. Probably could put a cheetah to shame in a hundred-meter dash."

"How do you net something like that?"

"We have an arrangement with a manufacturer. Industrial chain-link. Kind of stuff they make prison fences out of. Not so much a net, really a loose-linked lobster snare, we can drag it with chains for leashes."

"I wasn't remarking on the technique. More the sheer balls."

Another loose-boned shrug. "It's a living."

"What did you do with it?"

"Conservationist in Wyoming. Has a preserve there. They'd already arranged a helicopter pickup, then a cargo plane to piggyback with a military supplies flight out to some base in Casper."

"You do a lot of those?"

"Some. Not a lot of the stuff we get called on are things people exactly want preserved or saved." He left that unexplained.

After a few miles:

Why don't you try asking him why we're currently getting a mystery ride to nowhere?

"What did you need our help with?"

Another mile or two without a reply. Then: "We wondered if you might be able to take a look at something. Give us your opinion on this problem we have."

"What sort of problem?"

Another mile. "I'd really rather show you, Mr. Flicker, instead of trying to explain it now."

"Have you guys gotten anywhere with it on your own?"

Another shrug. "We're...in progress. Why we called on you." A sigh. "The trickiest thing we've learned in this business is to watch out for magical thinking."

"No such thing as magic."

"Magical *thinking*. It's what they mean when people with superstitions or psychic palm reader nonsense go looking and seeing any connection to whatever day to day thing happens in their lives. *'The moon is full on Thursday, same night I got a flat tire, must be the moon that made my tire flat,'* that kind of crap." He coughed, muffling it with a cupped hand. "It can be easy to jump to the quickest conclusion. But you know the Under isn't the land of simplest explanations. The first and easiest explanations get muddled up with people talking about witches and spells and all the other nonexistent crud. There are times when you wish you could go with that, at least it means you can stop thinking at that point, just start acting on it."

"Occam's Razor."

He nodded.

"I know the feeling."

He turned his head. Now I could see better as my eyes had adjusted to the tinged-glass obscurity of the cab. I made out a pair of sharp blue eyes. Glaciers hide that color from the sky so that it won't be scared to loom over them in the Arctic tundra.

"Yeah, maybe you do. I heard about your baddie from a little while ago. The steam thing, they're calling it. The bloodfeeders paid you for that one?"

I shifted in my seat.

These guys have ears everywhere.

"Yeah, we helped out. They asked for a favor."

"Mmm-hmm. Was the favor involving the cute dancer shacking with you after?"

I looked back at the window. "No comment."

He didn't offer any further wisdom, and we didn't have any other useful questions. I continued staring out of the window, Soul resting somewhere around our feet.

****

We got off at the Marysville exit, taking us out into more rural country. People who don't know what Ohio is like assume it's all cow pastures and corn farms. Once a friend from Los Angeles came to visit. When she landed at Port Columbus, her first remark was an amazed "I can't believe it's a *city!*"

The flipside is that Ohio *is* a farm state, so you don't have to go very far from any point in its metropolitan heart to reach grassland and farmhouse county. In fact there are parts of downtown that are still land-grant farms used by Ohio State for animal husbandry and genetics studies.

A few miles from the outer belt and we were passing grain silos and split-rail fencing, holding in milk cows. A few horse pastures and riding stables. I lost track of what roads we turned onto; a few state routes, a county road, probably a service road or farm easement path, based on how the last few lanes were barely two-car-widths graveled passes. I know it's not good to lose track, but I thought it a professional courtesy to the Scots that I wouldn't be able to give their location to anyone else.

Finally we took a long, private driveway amongst high, gone-to-seed cornfields. A closed gate at the end indicated that this was a public-recorded property under probate dispute, next to a battered "Trespassers Will Be Prosecuted" sign. As we drew closer, I saw the battering of the sign involved a few low-caliber rounds of buckshot, like an added visual emphasis for the sign.

Hannibal used a garage door opener and the gate opened

on its own. We crunch-rolled past it with inches to spare, moving along an even narrower path cramped amongst the cornfield rows.

Another minute or so of rolling. Now there were trees growing along the side of the road, interrupting the corn like shadowy playground bullies muscling into the lunch line. Their boughs stretched overhead, weaving together to cut off the weakening daylight. It was like driving through some poetic bower, a leafy arbor reminiscent of a Frost poem. It would've normally seemed gorgeous except that I had no doubts that once we'd passed the gate, I was most likely being watched by at least one security camera mounted on these trees. Or firmly tracked in the crosshairs of a long-range sniper scope.

The Scots know what I am. They know a gunshot, maybe a dozen such shots, wouldn't make any permanent difference. I wasn't looking forward to it if it was going to happen, but I'd take the shots (though recent experience suggested that if one shot hurt as bad as it did, more than that would put me out for a considerably inconvenient and memorable time). Probably in an hour or two, my body would recover and I'd be conscious again. The merits of being a doppelgeist.

But contrary to popular belief, there are degrees of immortality and invulnerability. I already know and have a healthy low-grade running fear of the limits that bore thinking about when heading into unsure territory like this. Being able to heal from any injury doesn't mean the Scots couldn't shoot me, chain me to something, then drop me in about thirty feet of underground darkness to think about my mistake, consider the folly of my ways in a disused culvert or sewage drain for a decade or two. If they were truly feeling ambitious and wanted to kill me, I wouldn't enjoy their trial-and-error efforts. I imagine I could only be burned or crucified or buried alive so many times. Decapitation is most likely not a fun party trick, even if I can reattach my head.

It's funny how, even if you're a dead man walking around, with the ability to recover from seemingly any attack, you nevertheless gain a sizable respect for pain and immobility.

I imagine that long after pain or immobility stopped being a factor, sheer maddening boredom would have its way with me.

We took a dogleg turn amidst the corn and trees, opening into a clearing area that appeared at first to be the graveyard of a couple dozen various truck hulks and rusted pickups. We pulled around one such pile that was five-high with Ford and Chevy remains, revealing a low, long, metal-sided shed. The length of it went back into the thick of the corn. It had a pair of old-fashioned hangar doors, the kind mounted on big sliding tracks rather than barn-door hinges. I wondered if this might not be some long-disused airfield.

Hannibal killed the engine. Rolled down the driver's window halfway. Put two fingers into his mouth and gave a shrill whistle. A quick *bleep-tweet* sounded from somewhere, and the right-side hangar door slid open to reveal a young man built much like an old Amana refrigerator.

He was squared off at the shoulders, defining the same width of his midsection down to his legs, thick-trunked and naturally pushed out when he stood with the feet planted in the soil. He wore a blue Dickies work shirt of washed denim, tucked into a belted pair of Levi's black denim jeans, faded-to-gray patches at the knees. A loose jacket of Army green canvas that seemed to have a dozen pockets on each breast. If the body was a fridge, then his face was a bland cookie jar resting on the top, jug ears under reddish-brown, close-cropped hair. All surrounding a moon face that had no noticeable emotion on it when it wasn't actively speaking or reacting to you.

I think it's that last element—the poker face of implacable calm—that makes the Scots real terrors to their targets. The faces we make really do stick there like your mom joked they would. Make an angry or laughing face enough times, and when you're not actively angry or laughing, the marks of those expressions will still leave their echoes in your skin. But it's a rare face that demonstrates absolutely nothing when it's at rest. The Scots share a flat painting-canvas of necessary features: two eyes, a nose, a mouth, two ears. Neither handsome nor ugly.

When Hannibal and I got out of the truck, I could see both

of them clearly under the crop-cut, peat-colored hair both pairs of those glacier-shadow eyes bookended what authors call a 'Roman' nose. Following the crag of that nose down to the mouths made of thin, pale-pink plastic lips neither turned down nor up. Perfect, dead heartbeat flatlines.

Hannibal gave a nod. Rex mimicked it. Rex stood in the hangar-shed doorway, missing hand tucked away just behind the bulk of his body. He'd been standing that way as if protecting something behind him. Now that he was assured everything was okay, he brought around his arm...all two feet of it.

I stared. "I'm guessing you guys have been watching Raimi movies again."

Rex's shirtsleeve was rolled up to above the elbow. From the joint down, instead of his usual stump that he kept the sleeve pinned shut around, there was a dark brown leather gauntlet arrangement. Some monstrosity of buckles and clamps. At the wrist was a welded steel claw-shape which in turn was welded to the stock of what I took to be a hollow-ended baton. All black metal, about two inches wide at the barrel end that faced me, with ribbed metal near its 'grip' end that was connected to his arm.

"That looks like serious hardware," I nodded at the barrel, jutting at a crooked angle from the elbow, like a cricket-player crooked and ready to swing and cast the first ball towards me.

Rex's face broke the impassive stone. He grinned. Waved the prosthetic in a tight circle. "This thing? Not exactly."

"It's a riot suppressor," Hannibal explained. "Not a gun."

Rex lifted the arm, the whole thing straightening into a salute movement through a clever pulley and tension system somewhere in the clamps and straps at the elbow. "It fires these oversized bean-bag rounds. Gives you a hell of a bruise. But non-lethal."

I would guess with him aiming it, 'non-lethal' would be optional for these kids.

"Just keep it aimed away from me for the time being, all right?"

Rex's grin widened. Then as he lowered the arm and the

tension-straps pulled it into a half-cocked position once more, gave a good-natured frown and used his free hand to start making minute tightening adjustments to the straps. "Thing is, we tried an early version with a real shotgun. The movies aren't as accurate about that."

"What went wrong?"

Hannibal smirked as he walked over to help his brother with a snarl of strap. "Dumbass, here, made the trigger-line too tight. When he tested it, it couldn't fully extend for a straight-arm aim. Nearly blew his own head off getting it right. We figured if we went to a non-lethal load of some kind, we could reduce the risk of 'friendly suicide fire.'" The snarl came loose and the brothers exchanged nods as Rex resumed his own one-handed work.

Rex stepped forward, letting me get a better view of the gadget. Held the arm up, out as if giving that stiff salute again. "The nightstick-arrangement of the bean-bag job makes it a lot easier to handle than a shotgun anyway. You don't have to account for a crooked stock like on a regular gun. The reloading is done at the barrel, like an old musket rifle. You don't have to mess with opening a breech or loading a magazine."

"Great. You mind lowering that thing now? I kind of don't want a bean-bag power-blasted into my skull."

"Oops. Sorry." A bashful smile as he lowered his arm to his side. He reached over with his good hand and did a quick twist-snap motion I didn't entirely see. Then the 'gun arm' was dangling by a couple of leather straps from his fist. "No sweat. C'mon in while Handjob secures the entrance." He jerked his head to indicate I should follow into the hangar-shed.

You asked about the newest toy. That's nice enough. If they start talking about their new 'homemade leather products' hobby, say no thanks and we get the hell out of here.

Settle down.

A snap of old toggle switches went off to my right. The dark space within came alive with overhead lamps, fluorescent tubes, makeshift overhanging lamps that were those dangling bulbs you see used in garages, even old Edison-style incandescents hanging naked from power connections. The whole effect lit the place very well but erratically, blue and yellow, cold and warm dots and pools of light giving the place a harlequin look. A kind of spiderweb-and-county-fair miscellaneous ambience. Pack rat space where the rats were obsessed with collecting light fixtures, amongst other things.

It reinforced the hangar impression now that I looked inside. Standing at the door while Rex closed it behind us, I could see the ceiling was curved, not a flat A-frame job I'd seen outside. Presumably between the external roof and the interior ceiling there was most of the electrical conduit for all the different lights. The corrugated-tin ceiling ran on and on away into darkness at least a good fifty, sixty yards away from us. The whole space we stood in was about fifteen yards wide, with poured-concrete flooring smoothed and shiny with much wear. Grease spots abounded like the confused paw prints of randomly-running giant dogs. A smell of diesel, gasoline, hot solder, cold ozone, and the faintest smell of cornsilk, like old Fritos chips.

There were a dozen makeshift workbenches everywhere, crazy-angled and seemingly placed wherever someone had had a mind to sit down. Half of what looked like a souped-up golf cart lay on its side with a dead dinosaur majesty, electrical guts of wiring and hoses splayed out on the floor next to it. Coils of wire, big wooden-spindled spools of industrial cabling big enough to be dinner tables. Those took up nearly the right half of the whole space. Industrial metal shelving lined the walls, gray gunmetal and pocked with those adjustable-shelf holes, five shelves high. Several rolling hardware drawers as tall as me, shiny firehouse-red and new, glimmering in their spots. There were more hanging cables for mobile electrical sources and dangling surge protectors. Even a motorized block-and-tackle for engines hung overhead, with a track that ran along the center of the curved ceiling. A couple of the worktables had what looked at quick glance like souped-up high school chemistry sets, beakers and burners and pipettes, oh my.

Towards the back were temporary walls, eight foot high

sheetrock nailed to two-by-four stud frames. I could faintly hear the sound of something thrum-thumping in the back, probably a generator. The Scots tended to work off the grid, avoided as much as possible having to establish any false-name billing for utilities. I looked over the shiny-new tools and equipment, pondering briefly how long they may have occupied this space. Or how much of this collection might be abandoned within an hour if they sniffed trouble.

"You want something to drink?" Rex went to a small dorm fridge underneath one of the workbenches. He took out a bottle of Yoo-Hoo as I shook my head. He clasped the bottle in the armpit of his truncated arm, using his good hand to twist off the cap.

Yoo-Hoo. You had to stop and remind yourself that these guys were barely old enough for legal drinking. While he sipped he walked me around the floor.

"We're trying to see if we can get more torque in this go-cart job." He indicated with a tip of the bottle towards the gutted golf cart. "We'd convert it to gas, only we're thinking we don't want this in some of our runs, because of the combustibility factor."

Don't ask what he's talking about. I felt the cool absence as Soul left me to wander on his own amongst the shelves at the far end of the room, weaving amongst the shelves.

Rex began showing—with obvious pride—a converted shotgun that Hannibal had reworked to fire rounds loaded with a powder-clouding payload. The rounds looked like little tranquilizer ampoules and smelled of a weak green-tea-leaf-and-burnt-metal mixture. Rex didn't go into any detail about the composition.

Soul muttered in my head: *Behind you.*

You can be as stealthy as you like. But if the person you're attempting to quietly walk up to is half of a body-and-ghost pair, with eyes not only in the back of their metaphoric head but also the sides, bottom, top and all around, it's a futile gesture. I stepped to the side, half-turning so I could address Hannibal; he took a step back from me as I moved. He hadn't been trying anything dangerous, merely their equivalent of fooling around.

"All quiet on the western front?" I smiled. Hannibal grinned back, mirroring Rex's goofy smile.

"He bored you enough yet?"

Rex lifted the stump of his arm to a ninety-degree angle from his body, pointing it at his brother. "Here's me. Giving you the finger."

A dismissive wave from his brother. He jerked his head towards the back of the floor space, all humor dropped. "C'mon."

Rex fell in behind us as Hannibal took the lead, winding around more workbenches piled with open boxes of electronic components, half-full boxes of shotgun and revolver cartridges, bullet-molding kits and full-automatic conversion kits. One card table was piled with various stuffed animals on one side, and what looked like greasy-gray shiny blocks of plastic explosive on the other.

Really, really *don't want to ask.* Soul fluttered around my stomach, wandering up along my shoulders like an invisible boa constrictor.

We approached the back that was blocked with the wall partitions, going around one then moving to the right. The sheer white walls against fresh lumber, the back-and-forth winding direction, made me think absurdly of a Halloween haunted house layout. Although with the plain white, perhaps it was more like a pretentious gallery exhibit in a museum. We wound around another bend of false wall, and I saw wires and cables tacked up along the exposed studs. On the floor were sporadic piles of sundry supplies, everything from reams of copier paper and toner cartridges to bottled water...and ominous-looking packages of black powder.

Plus cases of Yoo-Hoo.

The *thum-hum* bumping noise was louder. I presumed we were getting nearer to the back of the building. As we came around the last bend, I heard a soft shuffle-hissing.

Around the last false wall revealed a darker area lit by one lone hanging clamp-light. As I stopped and my eyes adjusted, the shuffle-hissing stopped.

If I had a regular heartbeat, that would've stopped too when my eyes saw what was in front of us.

In the back of my skull: *Oh Christ.*

****

My first thought, purely inane, a visual association clicking from synapse to synapse:

Chickens. Chicken coop. Trap. Foxes in the chicken coop.

More fresh, pine-resinous two-by-four studs were used to construct a pair of joined boxes, sided with small-gauge chicken wire. The whole structure was eight feet high, and where the thing met with the corrugated metal rear wall of the shed, heavy-duty steel bolts held it directly to the wall.

It was about eight feet square to each half, the halves sharing an inner wall of chicken wire between them.

In each cell was a lead-head, staring back at us.

I felt a chill quiver of Soul, recoiling back, almost to the top of my head, as if trying to rise out of the entire building.

The one standing nearer to us was a woman. Ageless yet withered in the manner of a piece of flower petal left in a desert. Fruit neglected and discarded out in the woods. I noted how similar lead-heads were to other mundane addicts like long-time meth or heroin users. Similar wasted bodies, tired and bone-haggard faces with mottled, rash-pocked complexions that made you think of spoiled fruit rinds. Blind, gawp-mouthed. The sockets of her eyes made me think of someone having taken fat thumbs and jabbed indentations in the flesh, leaving bruise-dark gaps for eyes that were listlessly, lightlessly staring back. The lips were bloodless. A few more sores around the corners of the mouth, probably vitamin deficiency or zinc loss.

Everywhere that a bone could show had prominence; cheekbones, collarbone, wrists, ankles. The rest was hidden in a dirty blue T-shirt and pair of ragged, hole-worn khakis. She was bare-footed, her feet looking like duo-tone car paint jobs: mud-black soles, cream-white with nasty red rash-spots on top. There was a smear of dried blood on the side of her scrawny neck, under a split-end-tangled mass of filthy auburn hair, nearly dreadlocked with grime. It seemed to hang out of her scalp the way potted ferns succumb to gravity when left to go to pot, glowing over the edge of their soils and flowerpots to dangle and go dusty on the ground.

In the cell farther away, deeper in the shadows, all I could make out was a lankier, broader-shouldered skeleton of murk that restlessly paced a small circle. The space was tight enough to make it look like they were just pirouetting in place.

This close, I could smell the unwashed reek of their bodies. Dirt and sweat, a mix of a darker, sweet-foul smell that wasn't completely garbage...bloody, meaty and going to rot. I swallowed and swallowed again. I tried shutting out input from my nose but my eyes and ears were fully slammed with their presence. I don't have a psychosomatic gag reflex, but some thing you react to in some way or else you risk everything breaking down altogether.

I stepped forward to take a look.

Wait a sec, don't—

Immediately Hannibal swung forward to put himself between me and the cage.

"Don't get too close."

"What the hell, Scot?"

Rex stepped forward and flipped the Yoo-Hoo bottle cap he'd been carrying.

When the bottle cap hit the chicken wire, there was a bright snarl of sparks. A nasty zip-popping noise as the cap rebounded off, hitting the floor.

That would explain the blue-carbon taste that's coming off the wire in waves.

"You have the damned thing *electrified?*" I looked at Hannibal then Rex. Both of them had reverted to those Easter Island faces. "Those are *human beings* you have caged in there! You aren't police officers or doctors! You can't capture living people and keep them holed up in giant bug-zappers!"

"The electricity is as much for them as for us, Mr. Flicker." Rex would look directly back at me. His eyes kept sliding towards the cages. "When we first brought them in, we had the wire up. But the guy back there..."

I looked more carefully. I could make out that darker smudge-shape in the corner cell. Shirtless, bird-chested with a sunken collarbone...it was slanted. Wrong. Broken? As he shuffled in the tiny space, the lead-head was a clearer image. A scabby-scalped, bloody-skinned young black man with a dry, sore-caked mouth. Off to the right side of his concave stomach was an ugly elliptical bruise, as big around as my palm, colored deep plum and fading into lighter shades of purple at its edges.

His hands were nearly gone at the tips of the fingers. The ends were dingy-gray...bone and scabbed meat. Dark clots of where blood had dried, caked to the tips. One of his thumbs... it was hanging at the wrong angle as his arms dangled at his sides. There was some lengths of filthy bandage depending from the wrists...an attempt to try and treat the damage.

"With the shock," Hannibal explained in grim, tight tones, "they stay away from the wire. The floor's smooth so at least they're not digging at that. But the first night...we only had the wire up. The guy kept tearing at it. Messed up his hands. The wire didn't give, but...his fingers...he wouldn't stop."

"I tagged and held him with a taser long enough to try and jerry-rig the current into the wire," Rex continued. His voice was a sadder version of his brother's. "He went down. Only a few seconds, though. I had to hit him again a few more times while Hannibal hooked things up. I tried to bandage... tried to help...it wouldn't take. I couldn't get him to hold still long enough to let me secure the...wrap." He cleared his throat. "With the shock, this way they stay away from the wire. Keeps them from hurting themselves worse."

"Really humanitarian of you," I snapped. "I'm still waiting to hear why you have them in the first place."

"Like we said," Hannibal moved back. "Intel. We had to find out what was going on with these guys, and waiting around for them to attack someone again wasn't exactly the best option."

"This is crap." I practically spat at the cage. "Are they even getting any food in there? How long have you had them?"

"Three days since we brought them here," Hannibal answered.

"They don't eat." Rex still wouldn't look at me. "We tried to feed them, but they either throw the food back at you, or let it drop to the floor and don't even look at it. We stopped after the other day. As for the bathroom…they don't seem to need that anymore, either."

That gave me pause. "What's keeping them going?"

Hannibal stared at me without blinking. "Nothing." He glanced at the cages. "They're just going. Until they can't anymore."

Both figures were staring towards me. The young man's mouth was lolling open, too dry to drool.

Suddenly there was a hard whistling noise in my ears, but no physical sensation to accompany it like dropping air pressure or cold. I clapped my hands to my ears.

I have to get out of here NOW. Soul snarl-hissed past me as a draft that blew through my spine and prickled the hairs on the nape of my neck. He sluiced out to the front of the building, ping-ponging amongst the workbenches.

I could hear the faint rattle of toolboxes being shivered as something passed by them.

18.

I banged against workbenches and toolboxes, feeling that sticky-tape friction when I got too close and partially moved through something solid, tugging away like someone with a sleeve caught in a burr patch.

Body came out front to follow me, the Scots behind him. *What's wrong?*

Sorry, but...those lead-heads...those people...

We've seen lead-heads before. You just exploded like an emotional Roman candle. What is it?

How to explain what they looked like when they had stopped to stare back at us?

I know what Body saw, what they all saw. But beyond that, my own view was...horrid.

To me, each of them looked like they did to the others...but overlaid with that were twisted, ragged forms of the vaguely insectile. Beetle shapes hunched, squirming, multi-limbed with stunted, flailing forms...cellular flagella whipping around helpless and weak...but the shapes were also fluctuating, black-to-gray-and-green, sickly seawater colors. Oil slicks of disease mingled with something rancid. The shapes were fluttering, like fabric that has molded and mildewed, moth-eaten and corroded…beetle-husk-virus shapes made of muslin cloth…

And at the heads, where the human eyes stared out vapidly, something glittered and spat shards of dark that kept rising and falling back in on itself…the image of miniature black holes, the event horizons sucking light at the fringes into…complete nothing. Not the dark-matter calling…this was chewing. Gargling on the living air like hyenas choking on slimed splinters of carrion bone.

I was seeing their *addiction.* The consumption. The wasting, grotesque fatuousness of semi-aware creatures that were riding them. Feeding on their flesh the way they had already slobbered down all of their spirit and awareness.

There are varieties of things in the Under referred to as "clean undead." Usually the bodies of things reanimated by means mechanical or other, but meant to be effectively just meat engines (I know a gal who can run Linux on roadkill). Semi-mobile things manipulated by the direction of some operating consciousness. Nothing to them but the fact that they were once breathing creatures, now reduced to pretty much the chemical and muscle-tissue by-products we all are at the core. Spectrada horses, golemites, things we've never even seen before. "Clean" dead. Unsullied by any sort of diseased motivations running through their chill veins.

But the lead-heads…

The ones that attacked us before, when Spam Tam tried to bully us into working for him…they were ragged but still appeared as functional humans. Sick, on the verge, but human. Fully, vulnerably *human.* Their auras had had a near-smooth blankness that was disturbing but still…sterile.

The things inside the cages of electrified chickenwire had started human, but something inside them had been inverted, torn out, and crushed to nothing. Leaving a vacuum, a living chasm of something greedy, senseless and wet-squirming with hunger and sickness.

A day-to-day drug is straightforward. A chemical of some kind, an opiate or a neuroreceptor trigger. You snort it, shoot it, drink it, eat it, whatever. It pings off whatever sensor in the brain or nerve in the muscle that responds to it. The drug does its thing, the body takes the hit, and it goes on. Some drugs make the body change in ways that feel the hunger for it to encourage repeat exposure. Others are relatively benign, and with time are gone from the body, flushed away with their effects.

But emotion-high addiction—what Spam Tam peddled in various degrees of strength or vintage to his customers—was a different monstrosity entirely.

Emotions and the energies behind them are unique to each person. Stealing them away, provoking them and capturing them, ripping them away from a living being to be fed into the systems of another, alien body…it was more than forcing that person to acclimate to an addiction for more. It was trying to make home in its new host, trying to change it. Think of radiation, pinballing into your genes and warping them, mutating you into something cancerous. But with emotion-bottlers…cells, souls, brains, senses…*everything* warps.

Spam Tam probably watered down his product significantly for his wealthy customers. All the better to keep them healthy and paying for as long as possible. *These* poor things…maybe they were the testers, the beta product folks who got his latest tries at something new that failed.

A drug addicted to itself, taking everything else using it with it. A biochemical, metaspiritual black hole, swallowing and burning and freezing simultaneously.

Leaving these things as waste products. Hissing and Golluming at me with bottomless throats.

Wanting to eat me whole.

Every second that I hovered around Body, looking at them, the only thing I could consciously realize was that the Scots didn't know how badly they'd underestimated what they were dealing with.

If I had stayed back there any longer, the things wrapped around those lead-heads were going to inevitably hunger to such an extreme that electrified chickenwire and stud plank cages weren't deterrent enough. They would've rushed the cages. Clawed, bit, kicked, taken their ragged bloodied fingertips of bone and chewed meat...they would've gone at Body and the brothers with everything they had.

They could've gotten through, too.

Looking at those twisting-rolling things...I don't think shooting either of them point-blank in the skulls would've stopped them at that final depth of their appetite.

The last time I could think of having been anywhere close to that disgusted...that repulsed...

...was Mister Sharkdoll.

Sharkdoll and his floating fishbowl of centi-shrimp-monkey-fish things. His spit-spray of crunched-up creature-pieces at that jogger and her dog.

Some of what I saw and felt bled to Body's thoughts. Though nowhere near the full brunt of it. He leaned against a workbench, absently knocked aside a torque wrench. It clanged to the floor with a bell-ringing on the concrete that faded slowly into a low hum throughout the space.

The Scots stood nearby. Rex with his arms folded, the stump of his lost hand resting on top of his good arm, tapping it slowly against the forearm as if he were keeping time to a musical number. Hannibal leaned against the overturned golf cart, eyes focused on the floor.

Body rubbed his eyes, then rubbed the palms against his jacket as if he'd touched something nasty.

"Okay." He took in a long breath. Gusted it out between his lips. "O-kay."

I can't go back there.

I get it.

Those things are to lead-heads what a werewolf is to a Chihuahua.

He pushed off from the table and paced a few steps past the brothers. He stared off at the corrugated wall so long, I thought he was counting the ridges.

I moved over between him and the wall. His face was as blank as the Scots. *This isn't right.*

No crap, Curly. I fought to keep my self-sense from shivering apart, succumbing to a desire for dissolution away from that memory. *But this isn't a stray cat. We can't let them out, wrong or not. Frankly...I'm questioning if keeping them locked in there is wrong at all.*

How can you condone this?

I don't condone it, anymore than I would necessarily condone murder in self-defense. Reality doesn't need us condoning or condemning anything to still have it be the situation, the facts of how things are.

That's a nice rationalization.

Rationalization is for the rational. Those things aren't. Not anymore.

I don't buy that.

Believe it. Believe me if not your own limited senses. What those things are now...they stopped being living, human beings awhile ago.

What are they, then?

I allowed more images across. The flailing insect-limb reaches...boneless, whipcord things. *Lead-heads. But now I think we have to appreciate there's a whole new depth of sickness possible in that term.*

It's awful but they're still people. They're victims to those things.

As answer, I let a few of the recent memories pulse along our connection. Mister Sharkdoll with his pet creatures...the squirming motion of those beetle-things around their victims. I tried to focus especially on that wiggling, groping sensation that had coated them like a skin-tight wrapping of tumorous second flesh. In particular the sensation of avid, near-mindless urging that had glowered out from those living hole-creatures.

It only took a second or two. He shook his head. *Enough. Good god.*

Yeah. It's like that.

Okay. So they're not exactly hostages in there. But that doesn't put us in any better position.

"Mr. Flicker?" Rex called. Body raised a hand. Rex nodded and went back to tapping out time on his forearm.

So they're a mess. That's not news. We already knew they were practically walking meat anyway. He looked away from the wall, did a turn in place to take in the floor around us. *We're not entirely back to nothing.*

How so?

Let's do what we do best. Make relatively uninformed guesses and hope like hell they're anywhere near the mark. Body put his hand out to rest on the side of the overturned golf cart. Hannibal watched the movement but the brothers continued their silence. *When Spam's guys attacked us, did you see anything like that around either of them?*

No. And I would've remembered that *if I'd seen it.*

All right. So we know that much. There are differences between these and the previous lead-heads we've encountered.

But we don't know what those differences mean. I lazily slalomed along the coils and curls of cable running from the guts of the cart. The spirit equivalent of pacing when you don't have feet.

Fair enough. So...the lead-heads that attacked us basically living people with a heavy bottle-monkey on their backs. Could it be that those things...are what happens when a lead-head is really far-gone?

One of our attackers last time practically cheese-gratered his face using the sidewalk. If these guys are anything farther gone than that, *I don't think a little electrical chickenwire would hold them, do you?*

True. So...maybe these two, with the others going crazy around town...are different in some more fundamental way from the usual lead-heads?

I'm convinced after seeing those things back there. These are not 'standard-issue' addicts for bottle product.

So we're back to the idea that something new is setting them off. It's not as bad as starting over, at least now we seem to be able to establish that something's going on and it's not coincidence.

Magical thinking. I slithered away from the cart, hovering near the curved top of the ceiling, near the block and tackle. *Can't assume connections unless they're right in front of you.*

I'd say those people back there are proof enough for now. You didn't recognize anything from either of them.

No. But...it doesn't make sense.

How so?

The emotion addicts we've seen before...they've been more like slightly-ramped-up versions of everyday drug addicts.

It's not like we go hang out in clubs or anything with a big mess of them every Saturday night to know.

Granted. But still...they go bad. Kill themselves off. Defined by the addiction's toll on them. I always got the impression flavor of...ash? Charcoal?

What are you going on about?

Leavings. Spoor. Burnt remains. Ruins. These things are worse-off than the previous ones. More burnt out, further damaged. Black holes. What was it that Stephen Hawking figured out about black holes? A black hole will eventually fail. It will swallow so much anti-mass that it would destabilize itself. Go back to being something with less density and lose the singularity.

As if the ones that attacked us were still active in some way, while the two back in those cages are what gets left behind when the emotion addictions are done with them?

No. The emotion-addiction creatures are still there. In fact they seem as drained and almost-dead as their lead-heads.

So something else.

Exactly.

The lead-heads aren't snapping because of their addiction—

—the addictions are themselves being victimized. Drained in some fashion. By something else. The insanity, the burst of attacks...that's a by-product.

Body straightened, facing the Scots. *When their rush is done with them, whatever this other thing is, they're left with the hunger...what, mutated?*

As good a word as any for it. What I saw in there couldn't be called any sort of healthy lifeforms or energy. I never saw anything like that before. Not in all the wandering around the city we've done the last few years. Those things were...petty, but also twisted. Almost helpless in their own way. But they'd still bite your fingers off to spite the food you'd hold out to them.

So something's messing with lead-heads around the city—

—and leaving them like this. I came down from the ceiling and took position around Body's shoulders, approximating his line-of-sight to the brothers.

"It's something nasty moving through them," he said, stepping around the cart. "They're not typical lead-heads, allowing whatever you could call 'typical' for these poor bastards. But it's not their addictions. I think…it's looking more like something is using them."

"Joyriding?" Hannibal asked. Body crooked an eyebrow. "Yeah, we know about similar stuff. Like riders. The Witch's Mare, right?"

"I doubt it's witches riding lead-heads around town."

Hannibal shrugged. "Same difference. We dealt with something along those lines a while back. What was it called again?"

"A phantophage," Rex replied. "A *geistelkind* thing. Semi-solid poltergeist that has started using vestigial energies off other spirits to keep itself going, make itself stronger than it normally would be on its own vibes."

"That's definitely a new one on me."

"They don't show up very often except in places where there are more half-spooks and unfinished leavings in the psychic ether than big-time solid, coherent haunters."

"They possess people?"

A shake of Hannibal's head. "Not often. It takes a lot to hold a solid body if it's not your own. They primarily possess other ghosts, burn them from the inside out. Like those South American parasites, the worms that gestate inside snakes then burst out and move on to find a place to lay their eggs. By some accounts they even manage to absorb their memories. Any smaller prey than they are, they latch on like a lamprey. Since the damned things are barely more than shadows themselves, this thing basically sort of pushes into their ecto-skin. It hollows them out and burns through them on its own."

"Christ."

"Not really as bad as it sounds on the surface," Rex opined.

"More like one gnat fighting with slightly-smaller gnat. But yeah, it can turn kind of nasty when some folks have gotten used to their quiet little house spirit, no activity to speak of, then all of a sudden one day your pet ghost starts slamming you into walls and ripping the furniture into flaming kindling because this thing has moved in like a digger wasp."

"They burn out fast, but they can be nasty for all that short time," Hannibal said. "Phantophages are weak in and of themselves. They can't do much without sucking up a half-dozen other poor souls."

I could see Body's eyes go flat for a beat. The barest lilt of air between us whispered a single word:

Jennyripper.

The demon-thing that Body had tricked into temporarily possessing his form a short time ago had definitely not been any sort of weakling proxy-ghost. I could feel the same shiver go through me that he must have been feeling, and I know I had the same thought: *what the hell could we do if there was another damned thing like the 'ripper out there? And how could there ever be another such monster as that?*

"How do you deal with a phantophage?"

"The way we dealt with it was to get it when it hadn't fed in a bit, before it could get to another spirit to suck dry." Rex scratched his shoulder above the gauntlet attachment cuff. "That's the only way you can, as far as we know. Wait it out or hit it while it's weak in mid-feeding. It's vulnerable then. Like waiting for a mosquito to bite and swatting it while it's sucking at your veins."

"How did you manage that?"

"Bait," Hannibal answered. Nothing more.

Body grimaced. "That sounds like a good tidbit to file away for some winter afternoon when there's no good television on. But it still raises the question that if this other thing, this whatever-it-is, is doing something like that, using lead-heads as convenient shells, to what purpose?"

I moved down and spread my presence out along the floor... trying to ignore the nagging sense I still picked up from yards away...

hungry tears in the air, ripping in the very space around them.

"Have you guys figured out anything special about them? Other than they can be staved off with a car battery?"

You're being a little hard on these kids.

Screw this, they're not kids. If they're old enough to be heavily-armed squatters, they're grown enough. That's plastic explosive in piles over there like discarded baseball cards for crying out loud.

They're not doing any of this maliciously, you know that.

Do I?

"We know they still have some minimal response to things," Rex answered. "They acknowledge when you go in there. They respond to the electric shock." He raised his stump an inch from his folded arms. "The guy took a full hit from the beanbag load, right in front of me. And other than jerking from the actual impact, no pain whatsoever. He still tried to rip my head off."

"Where did you encounter them?"

"After we got back from the Questing Beast run a few nights ago," Hannibal replied. "We stopped to do a gas-and-run at one of those truckstops between here and Dayton, I think out near that airfield museum. We were transferring our gear to our next vehicle." He nodded to Rex. "He was stowing gear while I pumped gas and was going to go in to pay off the cashier with the usual 'forget you saw us' money."

Rex picked up. "I closed up the truck and went in after Hannibal to use the john and the showers. I went into the bathroom corridor, heard a bang against the fire exit door, the one that shared the corridor past the men's and women's room doors. I went to check it out. Next thing I know, this guy is on me. I thought he was naked until a few seconds grappling with him I realize he wasn't wearing any shirt."

"Where was the girl?"

"The girl came at me when I heard the hollering," Hannibal said. "I told the counter guy to stay put, and I went back to find out what was happening. I saw what was going on, started to pull the guy off Rex. That's when the girl shows up and comes after me instead."

"We thought it was some kind of highway robbery thing at first." Rex let himself go further slack against the worktable behind him, his arms relaxing to his sides. "It's not like they seemed much different from meth addicts or whatever." He shook his head. "But when I panicked, I jacked the beanbag load right into the guy's stomach. He blew back from the shot but still had his hands clawing at me. Luckily I'd gotten the barrel between us to shoot, so I used it like a crowbar to get some leverage. I got the guy down and twist-tied fairly quick. The girl took both of us to get her under control. I think she might've been a little healthier."

Hannibal nodded. "I had to taser her just to get her down long enough to use my belt to tie her up. Rex had that stray security-tie from the mess we had to use getting the Beast trussed up, lucky there was one left, I'd used mine up. Once we got them down, I got the counter clerk to shut up shop for a few minutes and check that the coast was clear while we got them into the truck."

"When did you figure out it was something other than just drug addicts trying to rob you?"

Hannibal shrugged. "Part of it was their look, how they smelled. Then there were their reactions. Even the hardest addicts, if you hold them long enough for the crap their strung out on to start wearing out, they come down off it. Not these two."

"We were going to call the cops at first. Anonymous tip, leave them at a hospital entrance. But when Hannibal saw what was going on, how they were so nonresponsive, we figured we might have a couple of lead-heads."

"So you brought them *here*? Instead of taking them to the nearest emergency room?"

Hannibal's face made me think of totem pole carvings. "Do you think it would be a good idea to dump two lead-heads, unexplained and unannounced, on an average emergency room? We were at least an hour's drive from any of our friendly locations. This place was the closest where we could control things. If they turned out to be normal addicts, we were going to take them to the nearest ER."

"When we got them in here, we started with them bound to cots. We tried an IV, get them hydrated and calm. Couldn't get near them with a needle. Couldn't try any thorazine or valium. We left them to observe, see what happened. They calmed down pretty much once we had them tied up."

"So what prompted the move from cot to cage?"

"The guy tried to bite me," Rex said. "They calmed down a little bit at a time, it took only about a day, and then they pretty much became what you saw."

"What are you going to do with them?"

Hannibal exchanged a slow look with Rex.

Rex answered in a voice only a hair above whispering. "Bury them."

Body glowered at the brothers. "No way in hell."

"There aren't any places to take them," Hannibal said. He held out his hands in the traditional 'what now?' gesture, more popularly recognized by people with the placid Jesus velvet painting over their television sets, arms out and akimbo, palms up and supplicating.

He's got us there.

Shut up.

"You don't…you guys have *connections*, don't you? When one of you guys gets hurt, don't you have…people? Some place to take them?"

Neither brother spoke.

"You've got to be *kidding* me! If you can't provide anything, take them to an ER then! According to you they'll die soon anyway, might as well not be in cages like animals!"

"ERs are already overtaxed and understaffed," Rex said in that perfectly smooth ice voice. "They're not equipped to handle things like this. These aren't dope addicts, Mr. Flicker. We don't want to be heartless, but we have to be practical. In there, they can only hurt themselves or we wait out whatever's eating away at them. Take them to an ER, dump them on some poor RNs and doctors? What if whatever was running them comes back? If anyone else gets hurt, who will take responsibility? You?"

They looked and sounded deceptively hard; real tough types that terrified so much of the world we interacted with.

But you looked from one face to the other, and if you really listened: these were boys who had been forced to become, not quite men, but something so sad and twisted out-of-true.

Was it fair of us to demand that much more of them? Were we willing to assume that kind of burden?

"We were hoping…that you could tell us something about them that we didn't already know." Hannibal sighed. "We're sorry if we've wasted your time."

"You haven't…believe it or not, this is definitely something I needed." Body picked up a socket wrench and stared at the head. "I was contacted today by one of the Faede."

"Faer folk?" Rex's face brightened with interest. "Do they really look only a few inches high?"

"Depends on the viewer. But they had some of theirs attacked the other night. By a lead-head." He put the socket wrench back in its place. "They wanted me to see if I could find out what it was about. Was it a hit on them specifically, or something else."

Hannibal looked at his brother, then back at Body. "Looks like you can report to them that it wasn't a hit."

"Yeah, but this doesn't help me give them any better answer than that."

"Did they tell you if the lead-head that attacked them was different, like these are?"

"No. I didn't get to talk to the one actually attacked. They indicated that it was a fairly bad attack, that the one who was assaulted…it was bad."

Rex's eyebrows lifted. "I didn't know they could be hurt like that. I thought you had to have cold forged iron, like the legends."

"No. I think they're some kind of anemic, the way we would define human blood with normal iron levels. But their blood isn't like that. I think they avoid iron contact because it would be like…radiation or something. Lead poisoning for them, you know?"

Hannibal nodded. After a few moments of silence, he tilted

his head. "It seems to me that you need to try and talk to the Faede who was attacked, if they expect you to get any better idea about this thing. You can't know if these are related unless you can find out more specifically about the attack they told you about."

"That could be difficult. When I asked to speak to her, the Faede was...cagey about it. Which isn't anything necessarily new about dealing with them."

"If they expect you to help them, they need to help you a little bit when you need it," Rex remarked. "I'd go back and be more persuasive."

Rex's voice went quiet on that last remark. I had an ugly feeling how he and his brother would try to persuade someone they thought might be withholding information they needed.

"I'll go back and ask again. I don't know how far I can push, but you're right. They want me to help, they need to help me a little here."

A phone ringtone interrupted things.

We're getting to be a regular Grand Central Station.

Body answered and I crowded in close to his ear for a listen.

"Hello?"

"Johnny!"

It was Hal, our sometime-employer when Body did his 'side job' for extra funds. "Long time no speak, man! Did you get my messages?"

"Yeah, Hal," Body shifted the phone a little. "Sorry I hadn't gotten back to you yet, I've been pretty busy with some home improvement and what-not—"

"No worries, Johnny, none at all. Look, I called you because she's here in town now, and I promised her I'd do everything I could to get hold of you."

"What? Who are you talking about?"

A cough and a sigh. "Really? I thought you said you got my messages."

"I guess I didn't get them all, or at least I didn't get any in detail."

"Good thing I tried again, then. Sarah Parley contacted me a couple of weeks ago, said she'd be in town and asked to meet you. I mean you *personally*, by *name!* I think she's wanting to do an exclusive shoot with you!"

"The name doesn't ring any bells."

Hal gave another exasperated puff of air. He seems to perpetually think that since Body occasionally does adult films with him that, like him, Body should have a near-encyclopaedic mental catalogue of every porn star, film and production power in the business.

"Sarah Parley, she operates in some movies as Sierra Dunes. Really hot property, only been around about a year and a half or so. Redhead, a little flat-chested but seriously hot. She got nominated last year at the AVN awards for Best Newcomer."

"Okay. She asked for me?"

"Ex-clu-sive-ly, you bet." Eagerness jumped into his voice like a kid hopping into the backseat on the way to the ice cream parlor. "She didn't outright agree to it, but I'm thinking she wanted to check you out and if she likes you, do an exclusive scene or two with you. This could be a serious boost to my West Coast sales against Vivid and the others out there in San Fernando. I made a deal with her folks that if she did a solo shoot for me, I could arrange for you to meet."

"Hal, I don't think this is the best time—"

"Johnny, *c'mon* man." The eagerness died away a notch as a rare earnestness crept into his voice. "I know you've been falling off the scene the last month or so. That's cool, nobody does porn forever and all. But seriously, she *asked* for you. She said she'd seen some of your movies and wanted to meet you specifically, I think it might even be the main reason she's left California to come to Ohio at all."

"Hal, I've got commitments to some people."

"I'm not asking anything that tough, man, c'mon. I've been there to help *you* out when you needed the money, haven't I?"

"That you have," Body admitted. "*Hhhhhh*...look, if I swing out there in a while, would that be all right? To shake hands and say hello? I can't promise any long visits or anything. I really do have serious promises to some other people I have to keep."

The eagerness returned. "Hell yeah, man! You know my

light burns all hours! I don't even need to call her, she's staying as my houseguest while she's in town. She's doing that solo shoot for me tonight in fact! She's gonna be thrilled to finally meet you, I know it!"

"I'm not making any promises beyond swinging by and saying hello, Hal, okay?"

"Sure, that's cool." Another cough. "Man, I'm sorry, not feeling so hot all of a sudden. Been a busy couple of weeks, you know how it is."

"Yeah, I know how it is. I need to grab a ride real quick to my car, then I'll be out your way as soon as possible, is that all right?"

"That's fine. If you have any problems, give me a call. Otherwise I'll see you…say in an hour or so?"

"Fine."

"Thanks again, Johnny. I really appreciate this, won't take more than ten minutes of your time, I swear it."

"All right."

Phone clicked shut, back in the pocket.

"Can you guys give me a ride back to my car? I need to go meet somebody."

Hannibal nodded to Rex. "I'll take him back. You finish up the engine mods on the cart, okay?"

Rex nodded in reply. "Mr. Flicker, we…" He swallowed, glanced at his brother. "We won't do anything with them… until we've talked to you again, okay?"

"Hey, guys, you don't have to ask permission—"

"It's not about permission," Hannibal replied, a little quick. "We don't like this any more than you do, Mr. Flicker. We'll try and keep them safe as long as we can until you come up with something as an alternative." He crossed glances with Rex. "Assuming they *let* us keep them safely."

I floated over the engine block. *I think we just opened your big mouth and got ourselves volunteered for jury duty. At least the foreman position of the job. Shit.*

Great. Another item to add to today's to-do list.

Body pulled out his phone and tossed it to Hannibal.

"Before I leave, take a picture of them for me."

Hannibal looked at the phone as if it were something to be disarmed. "I don't get it."

"I can send the photos to my friend in the police department. Maybe he'd have some luck identifying them. If so, maybe they've got people wondering where they are, people who can take care of them."

Rex gave a sick smile. "That's a good idea. But would your friends in the police department be okay with...how we've accommodated them the last few days?"

"They don't need to know. And if they're not okay, I'll make them okay." Body pinched the bridge of his nose. "I won't presume to tell you guys how to do your thing. But thank you." He released his nose, smiling.

"Welcome." Hannibal clapped his hands. "Okay, then. Let's get rolling."

19.

Hannibal and I didn't talk the whole drive back to the park where the Vega waited dutifully for our return. The silence felt thin and brittle, as if the oxygen had thinned at a great mountain height. Mount Everest propelled us up into a socially rarefied place that didn't allow any words, for fear of one wrong slip of distrust sending everything cascading down to a shattering bottom.

I couldn't judge the Scots brothers. Yet here I was doing exactly that. Worse, I knew it wasn't many layers down in my own moral epidermis that I reached a point where I didn't care.

That was the embarrassing part. Seeing those wasted, shriveled human beings, feeling what I did towards them as a built-in, atavistic loathing…I had to consciously drum up sympathy and righteous anger for their treatment. All the intellectualization in the world could accomplish was to give me a guilt-trip-fueled tantrum that I'd dumped on Rex and Hannibal as if they were any less trapped by the circumstances.

Worse than that lack of control, the sting of acknowledging a basic truth: the Scots were better people than me.

Here I had to make an effort to care, to get angry and argue for their prisoners' humanity. Rex and Hannibal were already able to feel that, unable to shuck responsibility and a sense of moral obligation onto other people the way I could.

The Faede wanted us to track down the source of these attacks because we may or may not have been indirectly responsible for causing them.

The Scots wanted our help because they trusted our opinion and thought we could help them avoid the decision that they otherwise felt compelled to make, taking on the whole burden alone.

Trina wanted us to take care of her and protect her from the pains of the world, even the self-inflicted ones.

Was there a point where people were going to stop wanting us to always be the last resort, the go-to for all their problems that they couldn't or wouldn't bring themselves to solving?

About halfway back, I took a moment to dig the phone out. Hannibal had hastily snapped a couple of shots with the phone's camera, but luckily the track lighting they had suspended all over that compound was so fluorescent-bright that the shots had turned out pretty clear. Too clear, really, when you considered the photo subjects.

I composed a brief text with the photos attached.

> PINNEY: NEED ID ON THESE 2. SICK. NEED
> TO KNOW WHO MIGHT BE LOOKING 4
> THEM. MORE L8R.

Hate using those cutesy number shortcuts, but only way sometimes to keep things brief. I sent it, hoping as I did so that he could find something. But hoping more that he'd try and not be his usual Pinney self and want to bring to bear on me every bit of cop agitation he could have. My relationship with Pinney is on decent terms, considering that I can't really operate as any sort of official—therefore licensed, bonded, trained, certified, insured, vouchsafed, etc.—source of help to the Columbus police department.

Hannibal pulled the truck into the space next to the Vega. It was now full-on dark and the park was about to close. We were the only vehicles there besides a park ranger's brown truck idling in the main driveway, the ranger probably checking the picnic areas one last time.

"I'm sorry if we put too much on you to help us with, Mr. Flicker."

"Quit calling me that. You can call me John."

"Okay." He stared ahead, through the windshield and focused on the streetlamp that made a feeble glow down on the pavement and grassy areas. "We'll figure something out about those folks. And I'm sure you'll figure out what's happening with them around town. Things will work out."

"Yeah." I answered with zero conviction.

He reached into one of his capacious pants pockets and tossed me something. "Take that. Consider it a peace offering."

I look at the small spray canister with the empty keychain-fob attachment where you could clip it to your keys. "What is it? Pepper spray?"

He grinned. "Not exactly. Make sure you only use it if you absolutely need to, and not on any typical mugger, okay?"

"What's in it?"

The grin didn't falter. "Not saying. Something Rex and I dreamed up. Make sure it's pointed at the other person though, and not in a stiff wind, all right?"

"Thanks."

He nodded and I closed the door. I gave a short wave but he didn't see me reciprocate.

Those kids are on the edge. Maybe have been for a while now.

I stood by the driver's side door of the Vega, a hand resting on the roof. Feeling the lingering day's heat in the metal. Looking at the massive profile of Leatherlips as described by the limestone contours of all the stones cut and placed to form it. The Chief seemed to be staring out at the Olentangy River like he was waiting for someone on the other side to cross and join him.

They've handled way worse stuff than we have. On a regular basis.

Yeah, Soul mumbled as he floated over the car roof, *but*

they don't have the luxury of being invulnerable or intangible. They face that stuff every time knowing there's no magical shield or incantation that'll protect them from injury. Or worse. Add in that their faces are probably on a wanted list with every police department in the country and it's amazing they've managed as much as they have.

A lot of people face horrible things without being superhuman. Firemen, police, soldiers over in the Middle East. Everyday people who accidentally see their neighbor beating his wife to death and decide to step in and try and stop it instead of simply relying on calling 911 to do it for them. A kid seeing his dad drop to the ground with a heart attack in their front lawn and administers CPR. The whole world is a cycle of people who know they can and will die but still can't balance that against the life of another person for a given moment.

I opened the car door and got in, started up the engine. Soul slithered into the backseat and nestled near the back window, circling on himself.

Is there really a chance we're going to find out anything useful, or if we do have anything remotely available to us to do about it?

Your prediction's as good as anyone's. I turned onto the main road of Route 23, heading north towards Hal's neighborhood. *But being totally in the dark and unprepared never stopped us before. Why break tradition now?*

****

My sometime-employer/director Hal lives and does most of his video shoots at his McMansion located in Wedgewood Estates, one of the more affluent suburban areas in Dublin. Only a couple of miles up Route 23 are parks, the world-famous Columbus Zoo, and Muirfield golf course. Houses start out at a minimum one to one-and-a-half million dollars, and have barely a dozen feet of lawn between each residence. You don't pay for property in Wedgewood; you pay for the kind of house where you never expect to go outside. Even the ones with the space for a private pool have pool cleaner services that have seen the tiles more than they ever will.

Hal's father made his money in hedge funds and Hal hasn't had to work a day in his life that he didn't feel like it. When the internet made it possible for people to produce adult erotica from anywhere and not be reliant on being in New York or California, Hal decided it would be a fun way to spend his time and money. And a way to definitely piss off his austere, investing-and-conservative-two-piece-suits father.

I parked in the double-wide driveway next to Hal's boxy H2. The Vega gave a huffy *hrrrrhum* before the engine totally cut off. Temperamental as always. If the Vega were a dog I think she'd be constantly raising her leg to the bigger dogs she sometimes has to share a kennel with. Marking territory and dominance for these shiny, showy come-latelies.

Hal was opening the door as I came up the walkway in the glow of the little solar-powered patio lights mounted in the garden spaces alongside the walk.

"Johnny!" Healthy and pink with gym membership good health and a full head of clipped-short, military-neat, ginger-highlighted blonde hair. A handshake that zeroes in on your hand like a friendship-seeking missile. A pair of khakis and a white t-shirt that read I ATE AT JOE'S AND MAN WAS HIS WIFE PISSED in block script all atop a pair of tanned feet wearing Birkenstock sandals. I can't remember an occasion when I've seen him furious or truly put-out by something. He has the usual annoyances over an actress showing up late (or not at all), an actor missing a simple cue or a light stand suddenly popping its bulb. But the annoyance gives way pretty quickly to an enthusiasm for the task of fixing the problem and moving on. There are a damned sight short number of people for whom difficulty defines rather than defeats them, It was this aspect about him that was a great deal why, when I'd first answered his ad on a lark—thinking I wouldn't actually go through with becoming a part-time pornstar—I agreed when he made the first offer.

We did a big bear grab and grip of hands and vigorous

shaking for several seconds before he relinquished his hold. "How've you been, man? I haven't heard hide nor hair of you in *forever.*"

"I think the saying is you haven't *seen* hide nor hair of me in forever."

"Whichever. Whatever. Where you been hiding?" A mocking lift of an eyebrow like Mr. Spock. "You're not working for a competitor, are you?" Hal's hold pulled me into the house as if I'd been harnessed to a pony.

I was infected with grin, letting it spread as a returning smile back at him. "I don't think you even *have* competitors in this town, do you?"

"Pfft. Internet. The whole world is my competitor. C'mon up."

There was new furniture from the last visit. Everything previously had been dark, earthy tones. Blacks and deep chocolate leather couches and loveseats. Fragile-looking glass-topped tables and end tables. Now it was all chunky Missionary-style, blood-red leather upholstery and glowing, hand-polished pine surfaces.

"You redecorated again?"

"Eh. I do it every few months or so. Gets dull seeing the same things for too long, y'know?"

"Sure. What do you do with the old stuff?"

"Let it get hauled away by the Kidney Foundation. Good tax write-off."

I followed him up the stairs to the second-floor landing where there was a more modest pair of suede loveseats and a tiny cut-crystal table between them.

"Hey!" he cupped a hand to his mouth and shouted, "*Sarah!* Whenever you're done, c'mon out! Got someone to introduce you to!"

He waved me to take any seat I liked and turned towards the archway heading into a small but stainless-steel-tidy kitchenette off from the landing. "You want anything to drink?"

"I'm good, thanks." I sat down on the loveseat that faced the master bedroom doors off the landing.

"You been keeping busy with something special?" Hal

clinked ice cubes into a chunky-glass tumbler. Poured out something from the tiny refrigerator on the kitchenette's counter. He flicked his hand towards the sink, tossing off excess drops of moisture, before closing up the fridge and returning to the sitting area. "When I call lately, I get that girl you worked with. What was her name? Trina?"

"Yeah. She's living with me."

"Ha!"

"What's 'ha'?"

"You fell for a co-star." Held up the tumbler. More ice clatter. "To your health. You're going to need it."

If you only knew the half of it. Soul was hovering over the loveseat like a kid hiding behind the couch about to scare their little sister.

"How's that working out for you?"

"Eh." I waggled a hand in the see-saw *comme ci, comme sa* motion.

"Domestic bliss turning into domestic disturbance?"

"No. More like...getting to know your new roommate's habits."

Sure, the snicker from behind me. *You leave towels on the floor. She tries to rip your throat out. I'm sure you'll work out a schedule soon.*

I ignored him. Hal set his drink on the table between us. "It's cool you're with her, though. Honestly. I kind of worried about that one when she shot with us that time. Did she have some issue with it afterwards? I see that every so often with first-timers. They think they can handle having sex on camera but once they're doing it suddenly the light and the camera lens and other people in the room, it chokes them up."

Hal is a true day-to-day guy. By which I mean: he is one of the many people in the world who has no idea there is such a thing as the Under. To me that has always seemed surprising, when you consider how many lamias, succubi and incubi, vampires and such have performed in adult cinema. Then again, how many hamburgers does Wendy's serve in a day? Would a single counter employee necessarily recognize the differences in one sandwich out of the day's batch? Even if that one hamburger happened to have fangs or all-white eyes? I've known a few jaded fast food workers. Trust me on this.

"She was nervous. But no, she was okay with the shoot." I adjusted in my seat for a distracting moment of gathering thoughts. "She had some nagging health and family issues. Her doctors said she's fine, just exhaustion. But they recommended she give up dancing and adult stuff. She's got a good day job now. Doing well."

Hal nodded. "Cool, cool."

A *snap-clatch* noise from behind the master bedroom doors. The bar of light under their edge went black.

"Oh good, for once a performer remembered to turn the lights off when leaving the room," Hal sighed. Gave me a wink as he sipped his drink. "Told you she was total professional all the way. The solo shoot was a real dream."

"I can't stay long."

"Well isn't that the worst news of the night."

The master bedroom doors opened. The room beyond was indeed dark, so as the woman stepped forward I had a disjointed moment of seeing Trina emerging from the bookstore corridor shadows.

Hal tipped his drink towards her, waved the other hand towards me. "John Flicker, Sarah Parley. Sarah, I told you I'd deliver and I have."

Sarah stepped out of the dim and stopped, hands on her hips. One leg cocked slightly at the knee, forward of the other leg held straight. A classic photography model pose.

A nudge taller than average for a woman, almost five-ten and not wearing heels. Dusky skin, a desert sandstone tinge after the last tip of sun has fallen beyond the horizon and you feel the day's heat baked into the rock. A build like a clay model of a gazelle, soft edges but functional. A neck that could've been long enough to seem nearly giraffe-delicate but instead balanced a head that was asymmetrical. One eye slanted on the left, uptilted a millimeter more noticeably than the right. A pert nose that had a bridge proportionate to the long face... it could have been unattractive with any number of subtlest shifts in those features, but on her the whole was organic and persuasive. Light auburn hair the shade of old doll's hair, nylon-perfect and evenly red everywhere. It was cut in a tight swirl of near-curls and ringlets, with a pair of elongated, carefully-spiraled spit-curls coming over each ear and resting below the cheekbones, a fashion touch.

She was standing stark naked in front of us.

Something that people misinterpret about the world of adult filmmaking. They hear that performers often stay naked walking around the set. The average lecher then concludes that all adult erotica production is merely an ongoing orgy that happens to be catered with cameras at-the-ready. Nothing could be further from the truth. The reality is that nudity is par for the course, fairly standard. Same goes for the various latex bondage costumes or lingerie-lace maid uniforms, whatever else are the trappings of a given production fetish. The arousal factor becomes nil pretty quickly when being nude is effectively nothing more than the business dress code, a uniform of sorts. No less attractive, perhaps, on an aesthetic level. But as far as there being some stroll-about sexual extravaganza, it's about as arousing on average as you find the khakis and button-down shirts of the person who works a cubicle next to yours at your job site. Unless khakis are your thing.

Her body was nevertheless sensuously sparse, lean-legged and with only enough muscle tone to make up for a lack of body fat, helping to round out what would have otherwise been sharper, harsher points and edges to the hips, shoulders and knees. Her skin tone complemented the arrangement, and when she moved there was a visible flexing to the muscle groups involved. Somehow her face had escaped this effect, looking softer and more filled-out without becoming out of place.

We've met this woman before.

I rose from my seat, Soul shivering at my belly. *I'm pretty sure we'd remember her.*

"I thought I left you that robe on the chair by the vanity," Hal said.

She cocked an eyebrow at him, then spoke to me: "Yeah. Guess I forgot. Not like anybody here is shocked, though, right?"

She smiled as we approached. Closer, her eyes were a green-favored hazel, like cuts of bernardine stone. Her smile widened as we got closer, and the expression reached her eyes which further enhanced that offset attractiveness of her features.

She extended her hand first as we closed the last few feet. I took her hand into mine.

There's something strange here...

I felt how cool the hand gripping mine was. Even allowing for the humdrum element of nudity in an erotic production setting, I still would have had no outright visceral reaction to her appearance before me. A body like mine is mostly free of autonomous response. Somehow after death and restoration, my body has mostly shunted its old automatic responses to what I picture as a series of mental toggle switches. Flip on: cry. Flip off: nothing. On: erections-on-demand, great for male porn work. Off: pretty much default state, no outward sense of loss for all that.

But I leave my 'main' senses on, the way that people learn toilet-training or muscle memory for playing an instrument. My touch met hers and took in the input.

Near-perfectly room temperature. Near-perfectly the exact same temperature as my own animated flesh. The palms met, fingers tightened gently to hold mine in place.

Her grin glowed at me. "Hey, there, handsome fellows," she spoke *sotto voce*. "Nice to at last meet the not-so-one-and-only John Flicker."

Oh man, Soul gasped. *Oh man. She just said* hello *to me.*
What?
I mean she just said hello to me.

I mirrored his surprise and fought to keep my face politely neutral as she gave my hand one, two, three strong pumps like an old sink faucet well handle.

"I'm glad I found another one like me, finally."

Sarah Parley was a doppelgeist.

20.

Vertigo. A swirling feeling that as soon as it built up to where I thought I'd be swept completely away, it geysered and broke tension, releasing me to feel like I was falling back down. Like having a physical heart again, and feeling it fibrillate.

The air above and around Sarah's head and shoulders showed tiny shifts of molecular movement. The sensation was trying to watch thin car exhaust float away on a summer breeze, the lightest shadow against cloud and blue sky. The normal background radiations moved through this, unchanged.

And yet...the absence of disturbance suggested something definitely there. Like staring at an old stereogram poster, looking into the repeating nonsense pattern to see the real shapes emerge. Here a boat, there a dog by a tree. I had to relax my focus and look again...yes, the air was there...little chunky whirls of nitrogen, oxygen, carbon fillips hovering... radio waves and sparking random bursts coming off the lights around us, Hal's cell phone in his pocket. But that space around her never wavered. A camera lens set to the wrong distance, quietly blurring things enough to ruin resolution.

Is that what *I* looked like?

I hadn't looked into mirrors since becoming a spirit. Well,

there was nothing to see there if I did.

So long...since anyone other than Body could perceive me on my own. Could communicate directly with me.

I had missed that validation, that confirmation of self. It had been long enough that I'd even forgotten... how much that could sting.

You know it's rude to stare.

The teasing voice sounded like it was coming through an old telephone land line. Low crackles and ticks accompanied it. Interference from the normal background? A symptom of the weakness of the connection?

You can hear me?

Of course I can, came the reply. *Two spirits like us can hear each other clear as day. If the other is* listening, *that is.*

I've never spoken. To another spirit like this, I mean. Actually I haven't really spoken to anyone *since I was...*

Ghosted?

Yeah.

Sarah walked closer to Body. As she did so I could see that heat-quiver tighten around her head, a halo of faintly disturbed air. I drew in towards Body and the whole confabulation felt like a crazy football huddle. Sarah was quietly smiling back at Body.

Body stepped a few feet back, resuming his seat while she got comfortable on the opposite loveseat, tucking her feet and legs under her as she curled onto the cushions.

"Hal said you're pretty much his go-to guy for anything."

Body shrugged. "Hal is easy to please."

"I take offense to that compliment," Hal chuckled over the rim of his glass as he drained the rest of the liquor. He hopped up from his seat and returned the glass to the sink of the kitchenette. "I need to go look at some of the playback footage on that shot real quick, Sarah." He nodded towards Body. "Think you can keep him entertained while I engage in boring business?"

Sarah didn't look away from Body. "I'm sure I can keep him occupied."

Hal went into the bedroom, switching lights on and closing

the doors after him.

She smiled at his leaving. "Nice guy."

"Yeah, Hal's a decent fellow."

"He doesn't have a clue, does he?"

"About other stuff and people like us? No, not a clue."

"So I guess we should be a bit circumspect when he's around?"

"Seems a good course to continue so far."

"No need to go chattering about strange dealings like birds on a wire."

Telephone Birds, maybe.

What?

Oh. Right. Sorry.

Sarah-Soul could hear me. This was new...and I was not prepared. In three-odd years since becoming what I am, never able to communicate directly to anyone or anything, and here I was suddenly audible in some fashion. No protection of being the unseen/unheard fly on the wall. The only thing amongst all the werewolves, lamia, vampires, golemites, ghosts and other creatures we'd met that ever heard me was...a less than pleasant experience. Being scream-screeched at by a steam-demon thing is not what I'd count as fully 'communicative' in any two-way sense.

It's okay, the voice said. *You tend to forget thinking of thought as talk these days, right?*

...right.

It's fine. If you think about it like raising your voice...like what it felt like when you raised your voice...you'll find with practice that you can have levels to your thinking, to how you communicate openly or secretly. Assuming of course you want to have secrets from me. A laugh-shudder I felt as much as heard. Like soda pop pouring down a drain inside me, fizzing and gurgling.

I don't understand too well. I don't have a voice.

Neither do I. But remember what it was like to have 'inside' and 'outside' voices, soft and loud?

Kinda. Memory of a kindergarten class. Me, sitting in a circle of other kids, the teacher explaining the principles of 'quiet' versus 'loud.'

Think of it that way. Think of speaking to yourself or to your body as a soft voice, as something you want to keep low and quiet. If you want me to pick something up, though, and be heard, then go to something you visualize as 'loud voice,' as raising it to be heard over a party. Got it?

All I could visualize from that hint was the idea of speaking to someone at a party I'd been to...was it a New Year's Eve get-together? I was trying to pick up a girl and was talking about some self-deprecating secret, something I was sharing to seem charming and vulnerable so as to hopefully get that golden phone number...and the inevitable whole-party-shuts-up-and-the-music-ends-right-at-the-moment-of-my-loudest-speaking hit me, heard across the room.

I got the phone number. But since it felt given more out of pity at that point, I never called it.

Like this? I thought of my voice the way I would have willed my lungs to breathe in before. I pushed the thought out, the 'outside voice' emphasis pictured like blowing huge smoke rings out of my non-mouth.

A wall-mounted lamp beside the master bedroom doors flickered. An overhead chandelier went out, leaving the landing in semi-darkness. Sarah and Body looked up at the change.

"God damn it!" Hal hollered from the other room.

A shaky-quiver response. *Easy there. That thing is loaded. ...sorry.*

Didn't quite catch that one.

This time I modulated it better. Nothing flickered and Hal didn't exclaim over something in the other room busting.

Practice makes perfect.

Why do I feel like we already know you?

Good question: why do *you?*

It was there yet wasn't. When she'd first announced her presence, there was an element of shocking superimposition with the Sarah-body beneath us. Same face, same daring and impertinent features...subtly shifting in a memory that refused to come clear.

I'm guessing it's because my body is probably on about a

dozen box packages for series like 'Girls Who Love Girls' *volume three-thousand-and-whatever. Have you been out west? Maybe to the AVN awards shows?*

I don't think so. No, we haven't been anywhere west. To myself: *I would've remembered meeting you for sure.*

Why thank you.

Damn it. Little voice/big voice, outside/inside voice...

Sarah leaned close to Body, the whole conspiratorial posture feeling silly.

"I needed to find you. Meet with you privately."

"Really?"

Why?

"Because you might be the only person that could understand this or help me."

The chandelier clicked back on. I felt a plume of electrostatics brush past me like a dog passing through the room and rubbing your shins. Body matched Sarah's posture.

"Do you know anything," she whispered, smiles gone, "about something called the Believers in the Second Freedom?"

Oh crap.

And my new fellow-ethereal friend replied right back:

Crap, indeed.

21.

"Maybe we should go downstairs," I waved a hand towards the staircase. The moment popped in my head, and I woke up to the scene as it might have looked to another person. "Oh, uh... can I get your robe for you?"

She laughed and shook her head. She went back in to the bedroom. I heard some words exchanged with Hal and his deep laugh, then she re-emerged with the robe cinched around her, still barefoot.

I followed her downstairs, my thoughts as disorganized as Soul's mutterings in my skull.

I can't believe there's another one. At least another one not trying to kill us or eat me or something.

Calm down. You sound like a squirrel on meth.

He calmed somewhat, though I kept getting little spurts of bleed-through thought-imagery. The sound of a stereo system blaring and then going quiet. Party noise going still. I couldn't grasp it in any context.

We descended to the living room. New furniture from the last time we visited. Everything before had been dark, earthy tones, blacks and deep chocolate leather finishes. Fragile-looking glass-topped end tables and coffee table. Now it was all a chunky, organic Missionary style, blood-red leather upholstering on the two couches and matching recliners. Glowing, hand-polished pine surfaces for the tables.

As I sat down, Sarah took the opposite couch, tucking her feet and legs under her on the cushions, a skittish cat finding her ease at last.

"You've met them?" I asked.

"Not face-to-face, no. The way it started, I got some emails from a fan forum based on me. Crazy messages. Talking about the freedom of my immortal soul and redeeming my flesh on earth. Real pseudo-Biblical kind of nuts."

"Has anyone approached you? Tried to hurt you?"

"No, but—" she froze mid-sentence. "Wait a minute. Do you know what I'm talking about?"

I nodded.

Only too well.

"I had a guy shoot me earlier."

Her face went slack, the mouth an 'o.' "I'm going to assume you're not making a reference to a photography session?"

"If they were doing old-fashioned silver nitrate plate photos, and using silver bullets in place of nitrate? Maybe." I discovered my right hand had come up to rub at the spot on my chest. "Not my favorite new experience to try, I might add."

"How did it happen? Did someone ambush you, try to rob you, what?"

"Nothing so subtle. They guy came up, introduced himself...I thought he was a contractor like the ones I've had doing work on my place lately...and without any warning, he goes and shoots me. Point blank. Son of a bitch was *apologetic* about it. I've had less polite FedEx deliveries."

"Do you know what any of it means? What they want?"

"Not a clue." I watched her visibly take this in. "What made you think I was someone that could help you?"

A mischievous grin. "Oh, a handsome hero-stud like you? I'm sorry...I have a personal disease called Smartass-itis. But no...I mean..." she dropped the smile. "Fact is, they mentioned doppelgeists in some of the emails. When the emails started sounding crazier and crazier, I finally thought maybe you might know something."

"I wasn't aware we were in the phone book."

"You weren't absolutely easy to find. I knew your name from our working...particular circles." She made a little spinning motion with her upraised index finger. "But I didn't know you were like me until my people started to look for a way to deal with these Believers."

Does she seem familiar to you?

The response was barely detectable: *...yes.*

"Is something wrong?" she asked.

I took in a breath. Exhaled it slowly.

"I've wanted...we've tried to find another like us since the beginning. Try and understand ourselves a bit better."

She tilted her head. Folded her arms. Watching. "I'm sorry to disappoint you on that score. I know it sounds selfish why I looked you up—"

"No, it's all right."

"It's just that I've gotten somewhat used to being... sheltered." She leaned back, rocking on the cushion. "I have encrypted email. A webmaster who handles and responds to most of my fan correspondence. I deal only through my booking agency and don't do appearances or feature dancing tours at strip clubs like a lot of other performers do. I keep to myself and like it that way."

"I know the feeling." I folded my arms, crossed my legs, tried to relax back into the plush of Hal's couch. "Did you track down the emails?"

She shrugged. "I tried having my website guy do some digging. But they were disposable addresses from free-site services. Nothing helpful."

"I've never heard of these guys before today. How did you know to come here? Looking for us?"

"When this got bad enough to worry me, I asked around. There's this thing, I don't know if you'd call it a network or a community or something...it's how I keep in touch with the strange stuff—"

"You mean the Under?"

She beamed. "You're not as dumb as you look."

"Gee, thanks."

"Always welcome." A strangely girlish giggle. "Yeah, I did some asking, had some folks look around to see if anyone else was in these nutjobs' line of sight. For a little while there was nothing to go on. Then there was a couple of rumor mill bits going round. About you and how you operate here. The absolutely craziest element of all this was finding out you were another pornstar like me." A grin and sigh. "Do you think that's something we're all supposed to be, somehow? Like working in the sex industry is tied to the rest of it, how we are this way?"

"Doubtful. If it is tied to it, that certainly furthers my belief that there's no intelligence to the universe." She chuckled. "More likely it's the profession that seems to work best for some of us in these circumstances. Decent money, pretty much all off the books, few questions asked. That sort of deal. In an earlier century maybe we would've been simply itinerant workers or circus folk."

"Have you met others like us? No, stupid question. If you had you wouldn't have reacted the way you did just now."

"Not like us, no." I didn't feel like trying to go into the Jennyripper. Maybe never.

"How do you manage the test stuff? For this?"

"What? Oh, yeah. I have some connections in town that handle the bloodwork results I need to stay clear for work."

She nodded. "My agency people handle that stuff for me, too. Monthly bills of clean health so I'm okay to perform and so on."

"So...these guys started sending you threats. You couldn't get anywhere tracking them down. Instead, you tracked me down. Maybe I would've done the same if they'd tried emails first, instead of using me for target practice."

She stretched her legs out, crossed them, folded her arms in a mirror of my posture. "I think somebody has been watching me. I think it's these Believers. I don't have a way to be sure, but...I've seen things. A person that seems to keep being there, but I can never quite nail them down. Or they disappear as I start to really pay attention."

"Been there. Done that."

"I have friends in the Under but they couldn't find out what was going on." She passed fingers through her rings of hair, fingered a lock in a nervous tic. The aggravating sense of familiarity reared up and bit harder, but gave no better clue. Something about that casual flip of the hair, the twisting of the locks around the fingers. "My agency guy Seppeschal, he can usually find out anything with his connections."

"Unusual name."

"He's Faede. And if *they* can't find something out, it usually means it's not there, but still—"

Stop the film.

"Your agency is run by the Faede?"

A frown-smirk hybrid on her lips. "Not the entire thing, but they pretty much handle the entertainment stuff, yeah. Why?"

"Hold on. Trying to think this through."

Don't jump to anything here.

"Did I say something wrong?"

"No, but..."

Magical thinking, remember?

Screw that.

"What is it?"

The Faede are showing up a lot more in the last day or two than I'm comfortable with.

No kidding.

Why are you answering like you're buried in a well full of tissue paper?

A mutter-hiss. The galvanized-fuzz feeling of my arm hairs rising then falling in fast succession as something irritated nerve endings in my skin. He was tight to me, pushing overlap the way you'd feel your legs being pushed at by a nervous dog during a lightning storm.

The other one. Sarah-Soul. She can hear me if I'm not careful with what I say to you or think to myself.

Wow.

Yeah. I'm trying to keep things low. She says if I try and keep my own thoughts relatively quiet she shouldn't be able to hear them. A pause. A sigh in my right earlobe. *But without that precaution, I'm broadcasting everything like Radio Free Europe.*

You don't trust her?

We don't know her. Even though I could swear I've seen her before. Maybe a movie? One of her adult videos?

Hal is always trying to get me as involved and passionate about his 'mature erotica' as he is. But other than doing enough on-camera to get occasional paychecks, neither of us has been in the least interested in the 'movers and shakers' of the porn world. We don't watch any of it except when Hal wants us to look at some newly-shot sequence we just filmed, and that much only out of politeness.

No, we haven't seen her. Pretty sure of that.

Her voice brought us back. "Do you have a problem with Faede?"

"No. At least, no problem that I know of. Around here the most prominent of them is a guy named Ceyggan. Runs a gallery and some other businesses downtown." I leaned my head back against the cushions, looking at the slow-turning ceiling fan several feet overhead. "He's unofficially put me on retainer."

"Interesting. What are you on retainer for, unofficially?"

"So far, nothing. He wanted me to...research for him."

"Research?"

"He's curious about doing porn, amongst other things."

She frowned, then laughed. "Must be an Ohio thing."

"Do you have fear bottlers out in Los Angeles?"

"I need a little more to go on."

I brought my glance down from the ceiling. "Emotional high peddlers. Like drug dealers. Fear peddlers? Anger junkies?"

"Oh. Yeah. They're the 'chic' thing at some parties. I guess the way coke was a party drug back in the eighties."

"Ceyggan's been concerned about some local customers."

"Ah." She was obviously dissatisfied with the remark.

"Sorry to be cagey. I try to be at least a smidge discreet for some friends."

"S'okay. Most of the people I meet, if they have a problem, they do what any other addicts do in Hollywood: tastefully go into rehab and have their publicist tell everybody it's for 'exhaustion.'"

"We're not quite as *chic* as that in the Midwest. But thanks for understanding."

Movies. Something about movies.

"I've seen burnout cases in Los Angeles," she said. She seemed to think better of her pose and brought her legs back up to the couch, tucked her feet against the backs of her thighs. She stared at her hands as they climbed her calves and folded over her knees, resting just below her chin. "Nobody pays a lot of attention to them on Sunset and Vine, you know?"

"Were you in movies before?" I blurted.

She didn't answer for ten seconds or so. She looked up and regarded me with that cat's tilt of head. Like someone deciding whether or not to smile as they open a door on a stranger.

"What makes you ask that?"

"You seem familiar to me."

"I have one of those faces."

Soul swept out from my mouth. *"How did you become a doppelgeist?"*

Jesus, dude!

Sorry, I wanted to ask but I can't quite manage this 'quiet thinking' thing...I was worried it might broadcast. Besides, you were wanting to know too. I could feel it straining at your leash like it was on mine. So now it's out there.

Real slick.

Sarah's eyes widened then narrowed again. Otherwise her whole posture froze, her face composed with all the animation of a mall mannequin.

Finally a tongue licked the bottom lip.

"Rather direct, aren't you boys?"

"Apologies for my idiot other. Although, now that the subject is broached..."

She looked down at her hands again. Something shrank inside her as she spoke. "I don't think it would make very interesting or palatable conversation."

"You can trust me."

"I just met you five minutes ago." She gave a lopsided smirk which immediately softened back into that placid cool. "Sorry. Sorry. I mean...it's not anything glamorous. I can't get all technical about it, I mean I don't understand the real gimmick to how it happened..." She raised her eyes to me. "How did you guys become this way?"

"No clue."

"What?"

"Not a clue. We don't remember how it happened."

"How can you not remember a thing like that?"

I shrugged. "I presume it's one of those aspects. Do you remember?"

Another frown, another cast-down of the eyes. "I didn't exactly have much of a life to get all that excited about the movie version or selling the bestseller rights."

"I'm sorry."

A shaking of the head that caused the rings of red to shiver a second behind the edge-line of the skull, endearing like a slow-motion film in real life. "It's not that it's necessarily a huge thing, it's just...it's actually so petty. The typical girl-runs-from-home, bad-parenting and Daddy-issues package that about a quarter of the Los Angeles County population is made from. Suffice to say, it was a day-glo haze of stupid choices, some drugs, a lot of sex, and a few weeks here and there living in cars or streets or sleeping with someone for a hotel room and a shower."

I said nothing. Any further apologetic gestures would have been insulting. Some people don't want sympathy for what they've gone through. And it's true: some people have been through such hell that they've earned the right to not have people pity them.

"I don't remember the exact details either," she said, reaching down to tap idly at one manicured toenail. I noticed it was a shade of dark blood-cherry that matched her hair. "Probably doing something stupid." She raised an eyebrow and a grinning corner of mouth. "What about you?"

"I ran a bookstore."

"No kids or wife?" I shook my head. "Any girlfriends? Boyfriends? Little of column A, column B?" Another shake of my head. "A dog?"

"Pretty pathetic, isn't it?"

"Compared to some of the things I was willing to try simply to get a bed for a night? A bookstore and no emotional baggage sounds pretty sweet as a deal all around."

"I wouldn't say I was free of emotional baggage."

"No wives or family or other commitments to drag at you? That sounds fantastic. More realistic than paying off student loans or affording a mortgage." She glanced at me. "Do you have a mortgage?"

"Not exactly. I live in the bookstore now that it's closed."

"Must be pretty good not having any mortgage bills and living in a huge bookstore with all the nooks and crannies."

"It has its moments."

"Do you do anything else? Besides porn and ex-bookstore managing?"

"On occasion I try to help people when they have an odd problem or two."

"Like this Ceyggan?" I nodded. "You must have a lot of friends then."

Another shrug. "Friends and acquaintances, they cost nothing and everything."

"I like that."

"Not mine. Gertrude Stein."

"I guess a person who ran a bookstore likes to read then?"

"Yes. I couldn't hack it as a writer, though. Tried in early years. Thought as a teenager that I'd wow the literary world. Write these gritty, true-to-life-and-feelings angst novels. Figured I'd simply start selling the movie rights and bestseller deals, jet-set and be part of the cultural elite."

"How'd that work out for you?"

Soul replied *"I ran a bookstore in Columbus, Ohio."*

She popped a bubbly laugh like decanting an especially fizzy white whine. Recovered with a weak snort and a clap of a manicured hand to her lips. Looked with embarrassed gleam through her fingers at me. "I'm sorry...that's not funny."

"It's funny to me, so no offense taken."

"I guess..."

"What?"

"I thought maybe you might know. The whole deal. What was so special about either of us that this happened."

"Who knows? Maybe if there's a God and I get a backstage pass to the big show someday, I can ask."

"Sounds like in all honesty, you don't know enough about anything really." She saw the look on my face. "No offense."

"None taken."

"So are you making any progress on your research?"

"Not exactly. I've had...a twist or so. But nothing that helps me in this situation. I simply don't have enough to go on to be of any use for what he wants."

"It sounds like you need to maybe talk a little more with your Ceyggan friend."

Oh, definitely. A real pow-wow.

"Yeah." My face felt as fixed as old Leatherlips' stone monument. "In fact, I think that that's the first thing I need to take care of right now, before any of this gets any crazier."

"Really?"

"Certainly. I don't know what we can do about this weird group of Believers or whatever, and maybe that's something that will have to unravel itself while I work on this. But Ceyggan's problem...it doesn't make sense, and I think I let him slide a little too much for the sake of not seeming rude. I should've asked a few more questions or put my foot down harder before agreeing to help with no idea what was the real game."

"Definitely sounds like you need to see your Faede friend and ask those questions."

"Absolutely. And I believe that right now there is a place I can go that'll guarantee I can get Ceyggan's attention without delay."

Soul could see clearly the picture in my mind, shining like a neon billboard.

For a rare once, I am totally agreeing with you.

I let my mouth twist into a sour but determined smile.

"Would you like to come with me as my guest to an art opening?"

She rolled her eyes to the ceiling with a mock grin that spread almost idiot-like across that anything-but-idiot face.

"He asked me, he asked me!" she breathed, rolling her eyes back to me. "Of course. Now that we've found each other, Mr. Flicker, I hope it doesn't sound too creepy to say I have no intention of letting you out of my sight."

****

Sarah went upstairs to get dressed. We waited in the foyer and considered simply running out the door and driving away as hard as I was capable of flooring the gas pedal.

I stood by the door, looking through the cut-crystal glass flourishes, to the dark without.

There is something very wrong about these Believers.

Other than the fact that they've declared open season on me like we're Daffy Duck in a Warner Brothers cartoon? What could possibly be wrong?

If Sarah is being threatened by them, this could be a bigger thing than we thought.

She sounds like she's been through her own kind of hell as it is.

True enough.

Oh, and next time you get a smoking-hot idea about a question to ask, I snapped, *here's a suggestion:* don't.

Hell with it. Soul moved around the foyer, above the weak vestiges of heat that seeped and fell a few inches above the flagstone floor. *Out of the blue another doppelgeist shows up and we have to act like idiotic schoolkids trying to ask a girl to dance at the prom? We don't know her. Hal says she's all right and I can trust that much but Hal doesn't even know what she really is. Or what we are, for that matter.*

She wants our help.

True. But it seems like everyone who needs our help lately needs a lot more than a walk across a busy street with a bag of groceries.

You want to tell her to buzz off?

...no.

She arrived at the foot of the stairs, wearing a single-piece black catsuit with an ostentatiously shining-bright steel zipper from almost crotch to the neck, and a leather jacket in a formal waiter's cut, the kind with the hem at mid-ribcage leaving the lower abdomen exposed. Her boots looked like a chocolate suede and made hushed clocks on the floor. "Shall we?"

I opened the door and bowed. "We shall."

I walked her to the Vega parked in the drive. Sarah stopped to take it in.

"Where did you find *this?* This is like the automotive Ark of the Covenant!"

"It was my mom's. Sort of my inheritance. But it runs great." I jerked a thumb towards the house as Sarah walked around to the passenger side. "Hal okay with his big visiting star leaving with such a dodgy escort?"

"Are you kidding? He's hoping we hit it off and have a huge porn empire or something."

As she got in and I opened the door, I heard a shush of leaves behind me. I turned and could only see a few shivering branches of a high, decorative hedge between Hal's property and his neighbor's. Deer are frequent in this part of the suburbs, and I smiled thinking of what some deer would see if it poked its head and looked in on one of the windows of Hal's ground floor during one of his living room scenes.

"Is Ceyggan going to be okay with me tagging along?"

I started the engine. The Vega throttled and then gasped out. I frowned and turned the key again, pounding on the gas pedal. "C'mon..."

"Maybe it doesn't like me," she tittered.

"No, it's more likely that that Hummer of Hal's parked there has her ticked off." I revved at the engine and it finally turned over, though there was a begrudged edge to the way it turned over and made a haughty cough of the exhaust before smoothing. Thing is, I'd spent a fair decent chunk of Justin's money to have the Vega's engine overhauled. There was probably less than ten percent of her original factory-issue works under the hood...but somehow the '77 still manages to crackle, tick groan and cough when it wants to, as if it's still running on a clapped-out catalytic converter install and a beat-out, ready-to-fray set of belts.

I wouldn't discount that that Ark crack pissed her off a little.

"Really?"

"Really. Don't ask about my car. Even I don't own her." I looked behind me as we backed out. "And don't worry. Ceyggan doesn't have a say in who my guests are. I'm not in the mood for dickering."

"Macho man all the way?"

"I'm so macho, I shit Slim-Jims."

Her laughter lasted us until we got out of Wedgewood and were out on the main highway.

22.

Something soft.

Soft yet coarse...carpet? I looked...

Blinder vision. Edges. Not seeing everything in front of me in a wide panoramic scope...I had edges to what I could see.

Eyes.

Hands and eyes and...I was touching carpet. Looking at strange, crisscrossed beams of uneven diameter...lumpen white-pink-tan—

—legs. My legs. Crossed legs. I was sitting on a carpeted floor.

Somewhere, distantly, I heard synthesizer music, a slow buzz-roll backbeat...

You can look-at the men-nu but you just-can't eat...you can feel the cu-shions but you can't have a seat...

Howard Jones? Eighties hit. "No One is to Blame."

How many years since that was in heavy radio rotation? Or since I'd last heard it at all?

Since...okay, the eighties. Eighty something? I wasn't that good at remembering a specific year for these things.

Carpet. Sunlight. Pale, filtered, but sunlight.

Look up. C'mon, raise your—

...raise...

I swallowed a hard lump sensation. Swallowing.

...raise your head.

A smell of fresh-cut grass. I had hands. I was touching carpet. There was something flashing light in my eyes...reflected sunlight...I was in a dim room with summer heat and the buzz-rattle noise that kept rising and falling...an oscillating fan. I could see more of the room and it was resonating more with memory...I knew this place, this time, this space and feeling...

...and you want her...aaaand she wants you...no one, no-oh one, no one eh-verrr...is to blame...

"Your turn Johnny."

No no no. Oh God no.

Put my hands over my eyes, c'mon, lift them, damn it, lift and put them over your eyes don't turn your head, don't look and see—

My hands didn't listen. They were touching carpet. No, one was on the carpet, the other was resting on my knee. My knee. My flesh-and-blood knee, oh man—

—the other hand now lifted from my knee, reaching forward. Towards the reflecting flash. Something warm and dry, smooth. Curves and a machined twist to it... glass...my eyes were looking. Down. Focusing. A bottle. Pepsi logo. A Pepsi bottle. Empty. Lying on its side.

My eyes were looking up, around. I was sitting cross-legged in a small room, with a couch and some little kids' plastic toys on the floor in one of the corners. The oscillating fan was thrumming and twisting back and forth off to my right. As I shaped this thought, it turned my way and a puff of slightly-less-warm, dank air wafted my way. Stronger cut-grass smells.

There were five kids seated round me in a circle.

No...all the eyes meeting mine were level with me. There were six kids in this circle.

Next to me...

Next to me was my cousin. Mischa.

Jesus, I was looking at Mischa.

Mischa, oh *Christ*, I have *hands* I have *knees* I can feel this glass, the breeze off the fan...I can smell that Strawberry

Shortcake shampoo you used almost every day...I remember...

"C'mon, Johnny, it's your turn," she was flapping her hand at the bottle.

Why did you get in that car? My eyes kept looking at her. She had the same dark black hair that is a trait of all my family. A shaggy cut down to her shoulders, bangs uneven and some sticking up with the hot static electricity of the room.

Why did you get in that car with that idiot boyfriend driving who fell asleep you both fell asleep..,you should've pulled over if you were both tired...the look on my uncle Cole's face when we stood in the room next to the closed casket...I never saw any of the men in my family cry until that day why did you get in the car?

That was...no...that was sometime in the nineties. Sometime...before I graduated high school. Mischa was alive here, seated next to me. Seated and looking impatient. Why was she seated...why were we in a circle...something important... some reason that she had to be the one sitting right next to me, I knew that...what...Christ the cut-grass and strawberry shampoo smells...like bitter syrup...

"Go ahead and spin it," she urged.

She shrugged and nodded at my hand on the bottle. "Hurry up."

I looked from her to the others around us.

A ghetto blaster was sitting on a deckchair somewhere outside. I knew without seeing it that the chair was white with green peppermint-candy vertical stripes on its cushions. The ghetto blaster was on a local station and it was playing Howard Jones but in a moment, as soon as my hand came off the bottle, sending it spinning, the song would end and what was the next one? What was it going to be? God—

"Go ahead." Another voice. The kid across from me. It was...

...no, not you. Not now. Not this.

My hands and that shampoo smell and deckchair strips and the little hairs on my legs...legs...

Annie Spartan sat directly across from me.

That's right. Getting clearer each second. This was an idle

round of Spin the Bottle, something for bored neighborhood kids to play while sitting up in the playroom above the garage at Annie's house. Mischa was sitting next to me. That was important because she was my cousin and cousins couldn't kiss so if she sat next to me the bottle couldn't point to both of us but it...

...Annie was sitting across from me. My traitor fingers flicked, squeezing the thumb to the fingers and letting go, sending the bottle spinning on the carpet. It could only make a partial spin on the carpet but there...of course...it stopped. Stopped with its ends pointing at her and at me.

Music changed. A hard guitar riff *blang*ed from the ghetto blaster.

There is freedom with-innnn...there is freedom with-oooout...try and catch the deluge in a pa-per cup...

Crowded House. "Don't Dream It's Over."

No, not right. Mischa you were so pretty always the one that everybody really thought was going somewhere. You were going to Wright State and going to be an architect you were the one with the top grades the pretty face. They had a closed casket and you were so pretty Mom said you looked so beautiful when you let your hair grow long, why did you have to get in that car?

That hasn't happened. How do I know this? This hurts because I know but it hasn't happened maybe it doesn't have to happen but it does it did I can't stop it but there you are sitting right *there...*

The bottle was lying there as if grinning back at me with malicious joy. *You, I choose you, you knew I'd choose you if I could and I have.* My fingers, my hands...cut-grass-and-sweet-shampoo...I could smell my sweat, my hair was hanging in my eyes...I needed to get it cut why is everything so strong oh Annie it's twenty years or more and I love you still in that teenage, scrapbooked-heart way. So ridiculous but so real and so right now.

Annie was strawberry blonde, a head cloaked in a mass of thick curls like the angels in a Renaissance painting. Freckles that were faded against a constant deep summer tan. She was Mischa's best friend and lived next door to my grandparents in Chillicothe, where we spent a lot of summer vacation days in my teens.

Annie was the tomboy, the one to stay out too late and piss off her mom. Her stepdad was some well-regarded local doctor I never saw, not in person nor in one single family photo in their entire museum of a house. Annie was the one to go run around with the high school boys and ride in their cars out to the woods at night. Or sneak liquor from the kitchen cupboard, the first girl to let a guy touch under her shirt. All those things that fascinate and hypnotize you in those innocently stupid years when hormones outnumber brain cells, the energy of life beginning to really crest on a wave that hasn't yet crashed down into the wreckage reef of adult years.

Of course I was in love with Annie. Sure. Who wouldn't be? Big curious eyes the same Union Army blue as mine. Lips full in a Victorian girl-with-a-secret look. Always willing to smile at you as if you were the joke of all jokes.

Annie Spartan was the girl you want to run with after the moon rose, go riding in the back of the pickup trucks, hair flying in the night wind as you jounced in the open flatbeds. She was something promised in moonlight and early, fumbling experiments in love.

She smiled when the bottle stopped. Already getting to her feet, bending over to take hold of my hand, pulling me up, pulling me along. There was a small restroom added onto the playroom, still little more than studs and drywall with a toilet and sink crammed into the closet-sized space. That was where the 'winners' of a round were supposed to go to kiss as their mutual prize and challenge in this game.

I stood with my butt against the sink. Annie stood in front of me.

No...damn it, I remember this too well, I know what happens.

And she stands there. And stands there.

My eyes are going, not by my control, straight to the ends of my sneakers. I can't look up at her.

In a moment—some moment strung out at the end of this dangling, broken-train-trestle eternity of painfully staring at my shoes when I should be claiming the kiss, my reward from this kid's game—she'll say it.

She'll ask what she always asked in this moment. She'll ask why I just don't do it. Don't I like her?

And I'll keep looking at my shoes and I'll keep my hands balled up into hot fists and I'll murmur out that *Yeah, I like you. I like you too much.*

Love is the right word. But Love is too big, too adult, too ridiculously, insanely big for this little bathroom space. Love is for when you mean it and no kids can truly commit to mean it, no we're just kids. Love is like and like is always love, the euphemisms we hide behind, like dancing between bullets in a firefight.

And she'll ask *Too much for what?*

And I'll say, finally looking into her face under those Botticelli curls, feeling stupid and melodramatic because the words sound like the words only adults in the books I read too many of say, *I like you too much to want to kiss you just because of some game telling us too.*

And she'll look wistful and kind of sad. And she'll lean forward and put her arms around me and hug me. Then that will be that, and we'll leave the bathroom and return to the circle and the game will resume for another ten minutes or so. Mischa will kiss Annie's brother Shawn and then somebody will get called for dinner and the group will dismantle.

I'll never get another chance like this again.

The moment is stretching and my hands...my hands are real and flesh and blood and they're bunched tight as snarls of fishing line at the ends of my arms and she's going to say it it's coming I know it's coming now damn it why didn't I kiss her when I could—

"John?"

The smell of suntan lotion and sunbaked skin so close and cloying. Come on, just say it so I can say my stupid part and get this moment over with dear god—

"This is a daydream, John. Memory. Please calm down."

I open my eyes and look up.

Annie's face shifts. There is a Pepper's Ghost effect, the glass reflection of something else beside her as her own face and light dim, transformative and altering...the hair is losing a little of its curl, turning darker...wine colors invading like weed over the golden-brown shades. Her features rearrange, one eye tilting a little more than the other. The eyes themselves are darkening and going deep with knowing. "John, it's okay. Take a breath." The voice is not Annie's anymore either.

Annie/not-Annie reached out and grasped my upper arms. Arms. Flesh and a pulse and I realized I was hungry, too. Next door at my grandparents' house in the kitchen there'd be a drawer under the bread where the Opera Creme cookies were kept, those amazing chocolate and vanilla cookies with the lemony cream filling...they don't even make those cookies anymore do they? I had saliva...there was saliva forming under my solid tongue and I was hungry and my belly growled at me in confirmation—

"*Snap out of it.* Realize this isn't real."

"Dream?" Opera Creme cookies and suntan lotion and hands touching me, spin the bottle and maybe this time I could finally be a human being, have some spine be a man and kiss the girl, doesn't matter if it was a game you'll never get another—

She shook me by my arms. Gentle but strong. "You're reliving a memory, John."

The blending and bleeding-in of details completed, wiping Annie away altogether. Sarah Parley was talking to me. We were standing as children-high in a cramped bathroom that was hot and unventilated and flush with cut-grass smell but it was me. Me and Sarah Parley staring at each other.

"Memory?" I blinked. My eyes...flutter-flicking shut and open. Physical eyes blinking and shuttering and adjusting and seeing. I was seeing, not simply barraged constantly by light and matter and everything coming at me.

I wanted to lie down and sleep. My stomach voted to eat first.

I haven't slept in over three years.

What would that feel like, to sleep again? Who cared if this was a dream or a memory or a delusion? What could it be like, to lie down and close my eye (real eyes) and dream it all away?

"I wanted to try this with you. I thought it might be easier for us to relate." Sarah shook me again, softer this time. "But you're way, way too deep into this memory. You felt like you were really here again, didn't you?"

An idiotically slow, slow nod. The weight of my neck, the chin bobbing. My head, my skull...hair in my eyes, bangs tickling my forehead...I looked down at my hands...

Not there. Not real. No hands. My forearms trailed away to nothing, like a sugar pastry dissolving into seawater. My wrists went away with them as I watched. My forearms.

My eyes stung. Not real, no. No real eyes, no real tears. They wouldn't weep. I couldn't weep. Not anymore.

"I'm sorry. I'm really sorry." A sigh. "I thought it would be a nice way to do this. I hadn't tried it before...I figured you might deal with me easier if we met on more familiar, old fashioned living terms. I didn't...I didn't know this would..."

"It's okay," I murmured.

Real and flesh. But no. Going, going...none.

The smell of Strawberry Shortcake shampoo and cut grass... Crowded House playing on the ghetto blaster outside ...my grandparents, my parents, my uncles and aunts and cousins all still alive...Mischa sitting in the other room not ten feet away, pretty and smart and breathing. Why couldn't I go out right now and save them? I could try, fight and try to remember the trick of it. That special trick, like how you dream of flying and innately *know* how to do it, you fight the urge to let yourself fall to gravity and suddenly it's there, you're able to *fly*, to jump and not come down after. Same trick, just remember the trick and when you wake up you can bring them all back. There's a simple, simple, dirt-easy secret trick that if you do it right upon waking will bring them all back, save them and they never have to be gone again. Smiling and laughing and loving us...all of them alive again. And I was young and hadn't died either. I wasn't a boring single bookstore owner with no friends or family...I wasn't lost in a crowd of seven billion breathing, loving, screaming, hating, fearing, fighting, forgetting souls squirming and digging and flying around the world.

The day we fly while awake is the day nobody has to ever die again.

"It's okay," I repeated, numb. I looked up. "I just...hands."

She nodded. "Yeah."

Even if you care about nobody or anything and you've never lost anything you gave a shit about, someday you will still lose something you care for. You will lose the one precious thing, the thing that is most precious because it is the one thing you will not even realize has been lost when it goes.

Yourself.

"This seems..." she looked around the bathroom. "You're what? Ten?"

"I think. Maybe thirteen." My own sigh. But not from my mouth. The mouth was gone.

For another of those long stretched-muscle moments—stretched until its tendons were about to tear and it was going to scream itself into nothing—I hated Body. Loathed him. I wished him...not dead. Switched. With me. Let him feel that senseless, bodiless sense of being nothing, less than nothing, less than a breeze and a subtracted flicker from a firefly ghost. For just a moment it was there, but it was so potent. Let him be nothing for a while.

Sarah was gone. So was the bathroom wall in front of me. I could see instead the backyard and the deck beyond it, with the green-striped cushion chairs. The sprinkler was on, making *sput-sput-sput* sounds..rainbows cast across my eyes... not eyes...

It left. I was seeing the street beyond that, cars going by. I turned...sensed a turning...my legs were already gone, hips and body gone...look back into the room, trying to grab a last glance of Mischa, Annie, everyone... don't go...I reached up (can't reach up no hands)—

Snap out of it!

In the backseat of the Vega. Body and Sarah sitting in the front. Me and Sarah-Soul in the back. I hovered near the back window. Away from everything. Huddled. No, not huddled. You had to have a *body* to *huddle* and *hunch*. Can't hunch if you didn't have a *spine*, right?

John!

I wanted to tell her she was using the wrong name. Not John. Not anybody. What did Odysseus call me? Nobody. I'm nobody. Nemo. No-thing.

Trying to get a sense of that communication again. Not lips, not tongue and breath and vocal cords... just think it. Think it and the words are a form, a form into a sensation traveling across... nothing? Air? Invisible telegraph?

I remembered the exercise with Rod. Imagining my words as text, like complex smoke shapes but not so powerful as to blow out the car battery or the headlights like I'd risk with Hal's houselights. Soft...soft...anger but control that...

I'm back. I'm back to here and now. Okay.

A soft susurrant feeling I took as a sort of breath-memory sigh-broadcast from her. *Good. I was worried I'd screwed up and totally lost you in yourself. Somehow letting you sucked into your own bellybutton.*

How did you make that happen?

A feeling of a thrumming shiver that looked/sounded like a semi-translucent, blue-green ripple on a vertical plane, a pond shivering from a cold breeze blowing across it, dissipating as quick as it formed in my thought.

No offense, but as far as consciousness and connectivity goes, you're kind of a gigantic floating cloud of exposed nerves. At least to me. It's not any sort of mind-control if that's what you were thinking. I just...I could get a sense of where in your the mess of you there a more solid point...points...and I gravitated towards one, let it pull me in and expand out. That feeling like little anchors strung around inside you. Christmas light strings, with some lights brighter an65 d others nearly burnt-out. I couldn't...it wasn't like grabbing you and pulling you, you were still yourself, it was more like...uh...

Overlap?

Yeah! A pleasurable bubble of greenish-smoke-flavor-light that dissipated immediately. *You seem to get this whole bodiless sense-potpourri better than I ever did.*

I've been forced to practice. Synaesthesia takes some getting used to.

What's that?

Sensory mixed signals. You know how you see flavors, or taste sounds? That sort of thing. Some human beings have it as a disorder, but for us it seems to be a natural state of not having a body to categorize things in one sense or another. Everything up for grabs to interpret and take in.

I saw a flicker like a whip-curl of motion, ash burning in litmus rapidity, over the other backseat side window. It could just as easily have been light flashing through some motes of dust in the car. Was that where she 'was'?

What's wrong? she asked.

You were there. Don't you have some idea?

There was quiet. No ripples or flashes in the space next to me. When her voice picked up, it was back to that tinny-sounding, old-phone-connection quality, tenuous and fibrous.

I'm sorry. I thought it was a good memory. It felt good to me, at least. You didn't...like it?

It was a pleasant memory. Just...bittersweet, you know? And harder to relive than to remember. I've been through something similar...recently. There's really no getting used to this kind of thing.

I didn't know this person. At all. And she thought she knew me. What sort of life had she had, if one of my most painful memories seemed practically idyllic to her? I fought to keep any broadcast sensation of pity from blooming from me. She said nothing for a while, so I couldn't tell if I'd succeeded while I let my own thoughts calm down.

Sad girl. Sad and sweet and funny lady. I wondered if this is what she'd been like before dying, or if being the soul component of her pairing had changed her the way it's changed me.

But she had reached, seemingly without any effort,

unannounced and without any hint it was happening beforehand, and found one of the strongest childhood anchors in the muck of myself and dredged it out, shiny and polished from the shallows of my memory. Tearing away every bit of dark and holding it out to me like shoving a floodlight in my face.

Former face.

I tried to reach out, surreptitiously looking to see if I could find any sense of 'her' in the space of the car. Seeing if I could picture any hanging cloud of lights, points of gravitation that would be her own memories. Anything that might pull at me, interest me, see if I could comprehend the same frame of reference.

I saw nothing. Felt and tasted nothing. We might be able to hear each other, but somehow where this was concerned we were back to being individual nothings.

Even if there had been something there for me to try...I wasn't sure I wanted to do the same stunt in kind. It was harmless to her, an accident made with the best of intentions. But to me it felt a little too much like breaking into someone's home, rifling through boxes of old love letters, lost photographs, scrapbooks and yearbooks of dead classmates, loved friends.

Too much like thieving.

Too much like letting someone fall asleep behind the wheel, seeing them roll off into the slamming, exploding dark with your loved one grinning and waving a sleepy goodbye from the back window.

23.

There's a hum-and-flutter sensation when Soul is distant from me. I don't feel it while he's at any physical distance, but more when he returns to recognizing a conscious connection and accessing it again. I compare it to if you were using your fingertip in a live circuit to dial a radio station, trying to twist the tip to make a circuit for a particular frequency...then all of a sudden you find the frequency when it blares music in your skull.

The bigger surprise was that I'd *relaxed*. Driving and occasionally saying things to Sarah, who mostly looked out the window or occasionally would nod with a distant, distracted look on her features. I hadn't realized he was 'away' until he was there again.

Hey, I tested, *are you okay? I didn't feel you back there for a bit.*

Don't ask.

Seriously, are you—

Shut the fuck up and don't ask me. I'll tell you if I want to. When I want to. If I want to, okay? Leave me alone a bit.

The burst felt like a physical slap across my face. Attached to it: an impression trailing thin fingers of strawberry bubblegum smell, and a strange-familiar twang of a guitar riff from some old song. Not enough that I could place these things. Something melancholy and young. A context that was mournful but I couldn't clarify any specifics.

I'm sorry.

No reply.

****

We parked in a lot about a block away from the gallery. Owing primarily to the fact that at this hour, with galleries alive with various shows on top of the usual evening traffic, there was no chance of parking on the street anywhere close to whatever given place you were truly intending to end up.

I tried calling Ceyggan's number a half-dozen times, leaving messages each time, trying to secure our admittance to the show. But either he was too busy or didn't have one of his no-doubt-constantly-upgraded phones on him.

Sarah slowed down with me as we approached the short line of people waiting to get into the front entrance. She eyed the line. Noted the black-suited security guys at the front door, silently shaking heads as they turned folks away or waved some other in without so much as a smile of recognition.

"I take it you have a 'plus one' on whatever engraved invitation you've been privileged enough to receive waiting in a pocket somewhere."

"Actually I don't have an invitation at all. I don't think Ceyggan would turn me away, though."

"That presumes you get to talk to him at all in this mess." She frowned. "I doubt that the bull moose up there is going to really accept your statement that we're friends with the owner and wave us in."

I took a better look at one of the 'bull moose.' Nothing stood out. It was near full-dark so he could have been any number of things. *Do you see anything?*

Soul flitted ahead of us. *Nothing unusual. Nice suit.*

So most likely human. Very likely temporarily hired help for the night. No ties to the Under or any clue as to who their bosses were.

I don't have a pile of fake IDs and business cards to sneak me past authority figures. I am not the practiced private investigator in the novels who has a ready talent for coming up with bullshit cover stories.

All I have is a seemingly unchanging body and a ghost that wanders around me like smoke from a birthday candle. That's not much in social situations.

Sarah's hand grasped mine.

"Let's try my way."

She was already tugging me forward towards the bouncer moose.

The bouncer held up a hand as we neared. "Sorry, folks, the gallery isn't open to the public tonight. Private exhibition premiere. I can get you a brochure for when this show goes public next weekend if you like."

Sarah smiled. "We've come to see Ceyggan."

"'Say again'?"

"Mr. Segal," I clarified, giving Sarah a quick bridge-partner glance. Faede hardly use real names for public dealings.

"Do you have an invitation from Mr. Segal?"

Sarah rode with the change smoothly enough. "He said we could come by and we'd be welcome."

The bouncer shook his head. "Sorry, but you have to have a signed invite."

Sarah leaned forward and put a hand on the guy's chest, still smiling wide. "Aw, seriously, Mr. Segal called and said we should ask for him and he'd vouch for us. What's an extra minute to call him and confirm it? Tell him John Flicker and his plus-one is here."

"I'm sorry I can't be of more help. If we call Mr. Segal down here to clear you then we have to do it for everybody, and Mr. Segal is busy handling this evening's event."

This guy is not going to budge. He'll be polite, but he's not going to let us in.

"Seriously?" Sarah frowned. She turned to me. "You agreed to try it my way. Still want to?"

Uhhhh...

She didn't wait for my answer, but looked up at the bouncer. Her fingers on his chest spread out as if she were about to grip the fabric of his shirt.

I felt a small electrical tingle move through the air. Like standing in an open field during a building summer lightning storm, near the only tall tree for miles.

The bouncer shuddered. The pinhead blue light of the Bluetooth hands-free module in his ear winked out. He stepped back, Sarah's hand moved to stay in contact with him.

"I'm sorry...I don't..." He licked his lips. I was shocked to see his eyes well up with fresh tears. He blinked and stared at Sarah like he'd suddenly recognized her. "I'm...do you need...? I can't..."

"You don't look so hot." She turned to look at me and jerked her head slightly towards the guy. I moved forward on the cue, taking one of his arms. He felt like the semi-dead weight of a tottering drunk.

"Hey man," I whispered to him as Sarah took her hand away and followed behind us, "let's get you inside and get some water, okay? You look rough."

The bouncer muttered thanks and let me lead him as docile and shivering as a wet, newborn fawn. I waved a generic 'okay' to the other bouncer who was trapped at his post, unable to leave it unattended while we swept past.

Nobody stopped or argued with us as we went into the gallery, me propelling the bouncer back to what I saw was a table heaped with various glasses and a selection of bottled waters and wines. I snatched up a bottle of spring water, cracked the cap off and thrust it into the guy's groping hands as Sarah pointed to an open chair behind the table. I helped him to the seat and then rejoined her in one of the corners.

Jesus Christ, what did she do to him? Some special five-point exploding heart technique with her fingers?

That probably would've looked messier.

"What does Ceyggan look like?" She made rapid bird tilts of her head trying to take in everyone around us.

"What was that?"

"My human lockpicking trick?" She grinned. "Don't sweat it. Nothing permanently harmful. Call it a static electricity shock. Disorienting but nothing he won't recover from in a few hours."

"That's a remarkably vague answer."

"It's a remarkably vague trick," she retorted, more sharply. "Look I got us in here, okay? That was the major hurdle and we're here. Seriously, look over at the guy, he's drinking that water and he'll be fine."

"I didn't know…we can do that kind of thing?"

"I don't know what you personally can do. I've been able to do it for a while…I found out about it during a shoot when I was dealing with a really unprofessional male performer. Real dick. I didn't mean to. Hey, at least I've gotten some practice with it since then. That first guy got such an unintended hit from me, he ended up quitting the business and I think he helps counsel runaways in a methadone clinic in Santa Monica or something."

"That sounds like more than a love-tap on his heart."

"I don't know what they experience first-hand, all right?" She sounded more irritated by the moment.

"How do you…what activates it? How do you practice controlling the degree of it?"

"How do you whistle? Did anybody teach you how to change your lips to make different notes? You either figure it out or you don't, I don't know how to tell you how to do it."

"I'm sorry. I appreciate you getting us in here, I just…I was curious. I've never done anything like that and it never…it would've never even occurred to me."

She softened. "I picture a sort of plastic bag around them, okay? Like Saran Wrap all over them. And when I reached out and touched him, I pictured…grabbing it. Squeezing. Scrunching the plastic, a tiny bit. It's enough of a shock to the system that the person I do it to gets disoriented, slightly dizzy. One time they passed out. That's it. Nothing that a night's sleep or a strong energy drink couldn't overcome." She started surveying the room again. "Now c'mon, tell me what this Ceyggan looks like or start doing the looking yourself. You said we needed to see this guy and I for one don't intend to pull that stunt a dozen times more tonight trying to flush him out."

I looked around. I could see flicks of some people I thought I recognized. Was that Ceyggan over there, in a corner chatting up a couple of young Goth-hipster types? No, wait. I thought I knew the girl and she looked suspiciously pale-fluttery like another Faede with a half-finished glamour shining overtop—

"The show's great, isn't it?"

The guy had a stubble-grayed skull and a deep spray-on tan that practically made his skin gleam with a burnt umber Crayola tinge. Artfully manscaped black goatee and, somehow, detached ginger sideburns that grew along the sides of his rounded face without a head of hair to root them. A blue denim shirt buttoned with pearl-finished buttons all the way up to the collar and no-brand khaki pants. I thought he looked like a community college English composition instructor after-hours. He held a bottle of local microbrew beer and had a smell of alcohol-base men's body-spray that seemed to be his business card handed out to everybody ahead of him. He was addressing Sarah and acting as though I was another exhibit in the show.

He nodded at a canvas behind her. "I know the girl who painted this one. She really captures the visual idea of homophobia in this one, don't you think?"

Sarah gave him a half-notch of her earlier smile for the bouncer. "Yeah, it's a solid piece."

"Have you been to these before? I could swear I've seen you—"

I leaned into the space between them. "Hey, you haven't seen the owner, have you? Segal?"

A blank stare directed at me. "Sorry, don't know the guy." Back to smiling at Sarah. "Are you by any chance from Grove City? I grew up down there and you look so fam—"

"I'm not from around here, no. Hey, I'm sorry but we're actually here to find someone—"

"Movies!" A snap of fingers. "You're in movies, aren't you?"

"I apologize, I didn't catch your name."

His smile cranked another degree and he put out his hand. "Winston. My friends call me 'Wince.'"

I can believe that.

I made a proprietary touch of my hand on her forearm. "Honey, we said we'd meet with Segal about buying that abstract you liked from the last show."

Winston wasn't slow on the uptake, but a flick of his eyes at my hand on her arm and back to me showed he was quick to see a connection yet persistent enough to ignore or try and slip through it. "You're an art collector?" He turned on the 75-watt smile again. "I envy you, I don't have nearly the kind of income—"

"Wince?" I interjected with a grin of my own, trying to be Mister Friendly, "I apologize for the rudeness but seriously, we're here on a personal matter of some urgency. We're really not here for socializing."

A show of okay-no-problem, hand up and waving. "Oh, yeah, certainly, I understand." He sucked at the bottleneck of the beer as he turned away, made a show of swallowing slow. "Not like I want to interrupt your party or anything."

"Nice dodge," Sarah remarked, eyes roving again.

I smiled. "He said you're in the *movies*."

"Yeah, he looks like the type who probably would recognize a lot of porn stars on the street, when he's not at his computer visiting XHamster or something."

"Don't you want to give him your autograph?"

She regarded me with dry disdain. "You're hilarious. You should do stand-up instead of getting it up."

"I know a friend who does stand-up."

"Make a living at it?"

"He's a detective with the police. But he's pretty good at the comedy."

"Do you have a lot of police friends who moonlight doing stand-up?"

"Just the one, so far."

"Do you see Ceyggan anywhere?"

We tried moving amongst the crowd, steadfastly ignoring

the art so as to avoid getting snagged in any conversation on the works. Even so, we still got tractor-beamed by one of the artists. A rather loud and hectic-speaking woman a good two heads shorter than me with various parti-colored dreadlocks that sprouted from her pale skull like a collection of painted snakes and terminated in these strange beaten-silver baubles and decorative bands, making little clinking noises in a constant background music for her movements.

"I can't understand this mixed-bag appeal of the show," she wheedled. At first I thought she might be someone in the Under because she kept blinking her crow's-feet-framed eyes and exposing a sort of red-and-black-dot ladybug patterning to her irises; after a few blinks and a rub at her slightly-pinked left eye I figured they must be custom contact lenses instead. "I'm a sculptor. Sculpture is a completely different discipline from painting or installation pieces or any other art medium. I can't figure out why Segal wanted these different media together."

Sarah's phone rang. She shrugged a smirking apology and walked away without a word to answer it, leaving me with the tormented *artiste*.

"I guess art is an open field for all kinds of expression," I offered lamely.

"I told him I had more than enough finished pieces that he could simply have done an all-sculpture show with me and maybe one or two other artists. For a juxtaposition of approaches of course." Another scratch-rub at the pinked eye. "It seems to simply ruin the effect for people in my opinion. No offense to the painters here."

I nodded sympathetically. Then I dared the open rudeness of looking around the room while she went on, unperturbed in her warming complaint.

"I love painting, I do it myself, though it's not my principal form of expression." Eye rub, sniff. Sip of a glass of wine that shook in her pigeon hand while her free hand scratched and rubbed. "But how can you really focus on a sculptural piece and give it its proper due, if you've got wall pieces distracting you, demanding attention in a bunch of different formats where you can't stop and take in one. To appreciate it for its three-dimensional depth while the wallpaper is yelling at you, you know?"

"Yes, it's definitely…I can understand distraction."

Christ on pita crackers. This woman could annoy for her country.

Would you please do some floating reconnaissance and try to find Ceyggan in this quagmire of misery before I scream in this woman's face?

Soul swished away from the nape of my neck where he'd been perched parrot-fashion. I sensed him putting distance between us as he moved about the room, checking faces and voices.

"A sculpture has to be taken for all its angles, its multiple possible views. How can you compare that to a painting bolted to the wall, a flat rendering? Sculptural development is where you *truly* see art try and express something about the real world."

"Definitely some validity to that idea."

Sip. Scratch-rub. Sniff. Clink of hair baubles as she shook her head, eye-shadow-darkened eye sockets going wide. "The fact is, I don't think Segal has a lot of faith in any artists in this city, the way he sort of haphazardly just grabs whatever looks shiny."

So said one of the shiny things. Good god, this woman was more self-absorbed than Bounty paper towels.

"Do you do any artwork?"

"No, I'm not an artist, I run a book—"

"Print is so totally dead. There's just no way to engage people only through printed text on the cold page, you know?" I had the measure of her already, conversation-wise. She would only occasionally ask a question because habit had taught her to do so at various intervals so as not to seem like a jabbering idiot. But her questions would only be new doors to knock on so that, if opened by some unfortunate like me, she could push her way past and into the next corridor of the conversation being about her.

God damn *it.* I looked to the closest display column, only a couple of feet high and resting on an aesthetically- disheveled drop cloth on the hardwood floor.

The statue—if you could call it that, and I suppose it technically fulfilled the required Webster's terms for the word—was displayed with a floodlight from the ceiling beam. It was about two feet high and looked to be made of pieces of cardboard cut and pressed into clay or *papier-mâché*…a crude rendering of a cherub, standing in that arched-back posture of a lazy piss-taking. There was a pistol set atop the neck instead of a cute cherubic head, the rendering not quite crude enough that it didn't allow for a small dowel sticking out of the pistol's barrel and a classic red-on-white "BANG!" flag hanging off the dowel.

She saw my look. "You like it? That's one of mine, as it happens." Sip. Scratch. Sniff. "It really represents the idea of violence being thrust upon younger and younger generations with each year, and I think I've managed…"

Oh for fuck's sake, even Andy Warhol would've called bullshit *on this.*

With that moment's self-rationalizing take on modern art, I made an inarticulate yell even as I hauled back one foot and punted into the column's base, sending the statue/art school homework project/whatever-it-was to the ground. *Gooooal!*

It wasn't cardboard. Or at least, if it was, it had been coated in something more substantial. Something heavy like bronze or iron *clung-glang*ed to the floor. The dowel with the "BANG!" flag snapped off at the end of the barrel. Plaster bits and cracks went flying into a spray along the floorboards as the column slammed down beside it.

The woman didn't scream. Her mouth hung open in a completely flabbergasted posture of amazed horror. I almost wanted to pluck the half-finished glass of wine from her hand and quaff it down as a punctuation to the sentence I'd started in destroying her piece.

"Now that I have your undivided attention, ladies and gentlemen," I raised my voice, though the room had gone nearly dead-silent in turning to look at me. I tapped my foot to dismiss a few bits of plaster particle off the toe of my boot. "May I speak with the management of this fine establishment?"

****

An embarrassed woman with a mini walkie-talkie collected us as I noticed 'Wince' closing in to help console the shocked and offended sculptress.

Soul hummed the theme from 'Love Connection' for a few bars while Sarah and I followed the woman with the walkie-talkie to the backroom. Shelves of canvas-wrapped works and pallets of crated sculptures not yet displayed surrounded us. All very neat and tidy, and I wondered how much of this was actual art gallery and the rest clever money laundering front, probably administrated by a Faede legal and PR team not unlike Sarah's Seppeschal out in Los Angeles.

People milled back and forth from the gallery entrance to the back door that was supposed to be, according to its sign, for emergency fire exits only but like most back doors to High Street establishments merely announced by this sign that it was the only way out to a postage stamp of a patio area where you could legally smoke in Columbus. Even a few people blowing water-vapor out of e-cigarettes were heading back there, the stigma translating smoothly to the new technology. Welcome to the future.

A couple of the milling throngs that moved past us to the back eyed me nervously. One guy gave me a nod and smile with a quick 'thumbs-up' gesture. I was already feeling like a neon-bright imbecile standing there with Sarah waiting for Ceyggan, in the meanwhile apparently serving as an all-new live-installation exhibit: *See the Art-Destroying Modern Ape.*

Sarah leaned against a crate and smiled at me. Not saying anything. Only smiling.

"What?"

She shook her head, the smile staying put. "You know how to get a crowd's attention."

"I was getting tired of debating the merits of painting versus sculpture in a postmodern deconstructionist perspective based on hetero-white-male-centric paradigms. And I really couldn't stand that woman sniffling either."

She gave a faint snort. "What, you couldn't find common ground with 'Wince the Wonder Wienie'?"

"The only common ground I wanted to find with these people would've involved the San Andreas fault in earthquake weather."

"Earthquake weather?"

"Cheap literary reference. Never mind. Where the hell is Ceyggan?"

"If he's anything like the gallery guys I know back west, he's probably making a lot of insincere apology-noises to the sculptor whose piece you trashed, and taking a few under-the-table bids for the 'destroyed' piece while he's at it."

"That sounds about his speed."

"Excuse me, sir?"

Your nine o' clock.

He was a thin African-American with a shaved head, skin all gleaming mahogany. A crucifix earring in the left ear glinted gold as he stepped forward, a hand extended as if to shake with mine. He wore a tailored suit accentuated with a pair of fresh-out-of-the-box two-hundred-dollar athletic shoes. For the first second or so, I figured he was another of Ceyggan's flunkies come to fob us off with some excuse or other.

Then hairs on my neck rose.

He looks gray-green and there's something smooth in the air around him you've got to—

"My name is Steve Dwyer, sir. I'm not trying to sell you any—"

My fist was swinging before he'd had a chance to do much more than pull back the jacket flap and let me see the glint off the blade at his belt.

My knuckles made sloppy haymaker contact upside his jaw, socking him into such a meaty nerve point that a nanosecond as our skin touched I wondered if I was hitting him low enough to collapse his trachea or some sort of central nervous shock.

Of course, that glint of light off the knife blade dispelled any notions of polite fighting in favor of brute survival and anger.

I didn't let him fall back or make any recovery from the hit. In total panic-inspired coordination, I leaned forward with his recoil from my hit, grabbed his jacket (hearing a good rip-tear in the sleeves where they met the shoulders as I did so) and jerked him forward, swinging him in an awkward dosey-do dance turn, bringing him around as I spun on the balls of my feet and then turned the push into a shove. The whole sudden shifting of back-and-forth turning him helpless as I turned him over to gravity to do the rest of the work and bowl him to the ground.

It took a moment to realize I was no longer standing, but was kneeling on the guy's hand closest to the fallen knife, holding the other arm out straight with a vise grip, pinning it to the ground. I used my free hand to whack him hard enough across the cheeks that the skin flared dark immediately with the imprint of my open hand, like crude war paint.

He made a *huck* sound, a shocked cough-spitting. A trickle of blood started seeping from one side of his mouth. I gave him a shake for extra measure, bopping the back of his skull against the floor. That seemed to do the trick in getting him to settle.

I shook him again by grabbing his jacket lapel while he rolled his eyes under bruise-dark lids. He winced. Groaned. I felt the tensing of his arms as he tried to raise the one I had pinned in my grip, to try and feel at his head.

"I'm sure if it's bleeding we'll get you a Snoopy Band-Aid." I let go of the jacket flap, kept kneeling onto him.

"What the hell was that?" Sarah had found breath to hiss at me, leaning towards me.

"Call it intuition after a day of being surprised by smiling lunatics walking up to me bearing gifts."

I reached for the knife, careful as I stretched that I didn't lose balance on the knee or grip with my hand to keep him still. It was a matte-black finish, non-reflective. A military-looking model, snub-ended rather than tapered but with wicked, utilitarian serrations along the side opposite the blade edge.

A hush in my ear: *Look at those tiny nicks along the blade. It's hair-thin. That's been freshly sharpened, I bet. There's a tiny concealed buckle-sheath on his belt that it fell out of.*

The buckle sheath was in the waistband of his pants, not quite hidden by the jacket. Even with that giveaway, I felt a cold sliver of doubt slide across my belly wondering if I could've reacted in time if Soul hadn't hollered in my head or I wasn't already on-edge from the shooting earlier. I tossed the knife away, letting it clank-thump against some canistered canvas in a corner, promptly forgetting it.

I didn't look away from him. "He's a Believer." I poked a finger hard into the guy's chest for his attention. "Am I wrong?"

Another *huck* and clearing of throat. His eyes couldn't quite focus despite a sincere try. "Mister...sir...Flicker...you have...we're not..."

"I'll take that as a big yes," I sneered. "It's a shame. You guys are fast making me so paranoid that I pity the next Girl Scout who accidentally knocks on my door with so much as a box of Lorna Doones, for all the beating she's going to risk getting from me as a case of mistaken identity. Who the fuck *are* you people?"

"What the hell?"

"Hi, Ceyggan."

The faer leader had arrived in the backroom, standing at its doorway with a look that probably was the same he would've given if you'd ruined the end of every one of his favorite movies before he had a chance to even check the Rotten Tomatoes website to find out how he should feel about them.

I kept my eyes on Dwyer, but in the corner of my eye I could make out Ceyggan's movement walking over.

"What. The. Hell. John?"

I glanced up. Ceyggan was looking at me, down at Dwyer, then at Sarah, and back at me.

"Keep cool on your heels for five, Faede-to-black," I snapped. I turned back and pointed directly into Dwyer's nose. "I have a few finer points of etiquette to discuss with this asshole. Then I definitely want ten minutes of your time. And it won't be to discuss how much I owe you for that travesty-on-a-pedestal you had on display out there."

Ceyggan's mouth made a token puffer fish gesture of taking in air, about to shape some disgusted or outraged response.

"I'd listen to him right now if I were you," Sarah said

quietly. Ceyggan glanced at her. She gave the barest shake of the head. He wisely deflated and took the advice.

Dwyer's words brought my attention back to him.

"Your soul is damned, Mr. Flicker. The Believers understand your soul's pain and appreciate our moral duty to answer to that pain. To redeem and free it."

I don't like where this is going.

"When the righteous man of flesh and bone died, his immortal soul was meant to be free into the cosmos, to rejoin the integral equilibrium being pursued by all matter and energy in the universe. But it did not choose to take this glorious opportunity." Dwyer turned his head to the side, coughing. A few drops of blood hit the concrete. "Excuse me. But now the Believers are here, to help your soul achieve its emancipation and your body to finally seek its rest."

Oh shit-wow, I really *don't like any of this.*

"Am I actually *hearing* this?" I snarled. "You people believe that my soul is trapped within my body, and that if you manage to, what, kill the body, then the soul gets this great reward?"

"Exactly, sir. We apologize for the understandable fear and protectiveness you no doubt have towards your innate delusion of life, but you must see"

"You people are morons. Do you even know what I am?"

Dwyer's face never broke the seriousness that was like a tax audit. "Do *you* comprehend what you are, sir?"

"I like to think maybe I have a basic understanding, yes."

Soul whisper-buzzed, rolling out from between my lips. *"Speaking on behalf of this particular Soul, I don't feel any need for saving. So you can go back and report to your Boy Scout troop's Order of Batshit that your services are appreciated but not needed. No merit badge for this one."*

Bouncers had accompanied Ceyggan and were now passing him, coming through the doorway and around to help bring Dwyer and me to our feet. I relinquished him to their custody as Ceyggan made a 'follow me' gesture. As Sarah moved to join my side he held a hand out.

"She goes with me, or this has been nothing but a complete

waste of everybody's time," I said.

"I don't know her."

I sighed. Smiled. Smiled at Sarah, then back at Ceyggan. When I spoke, I raised my voice enough to know that any eavesdroppers in the main gallery space were able to hear what I was saying from the backroom.

"Miss Parley let me know an interesting tidbit. That her management out west is Faede. They were the ones that apparently helped her connect with me through her porn movie associates to help her with her problem." I smiled wider at Ceyggan's face turning pink. "Now I think you can appreciate that that's two times in as many days that the Faede are involved in something that keeps coming back to me. Two times too many to necessarily be coincidence."

Ceyggan jutted his head towards me. *"Shut up!"*

I continued, not lowering my tone at all. "I find it interesting how much your folks are involved in so many coast-to-coast dealings like this."

"I have no idea what you're talking about!" he sneered. "Keep it down!"

"Are you still interested in doing porn on the side, Mr. Segal?"

"Shut up!"

I relented to half my former volume, leaning closer to him. "The Faede send her in my direction even as your group hires me to help settle some revenge-attack inquiry about one of yours?"

He flapped his hands at me, darting glances at the bouncers and Dwyer. He waved at the bouncers, the signal that they could take Dwyer away out front, presumably to wait for the police. When he turned to me, he was visibly fighting to keep a measure of calm. "We run a lot of coverage all over the world. You know that. Porn, mainstream, whatever. What's so suspect?"

"Nothing, in and of itself. But when this lady says she's been watched, and I know that I certainly have been, it gets funny. Not ha-ha funny, either. That schmuck you just tossed out for the cops to take is only the latest person to try killing me. Apparently they're the same batch that Sarah thinks are trying to put a hit on her as well. It's a group that's out for doppelgeists on some horseshit holy crusade."

Ceyggan looked to Sarah. His face opened into a blank billboard. "You're a doppelgeist?" She nodded in answer. "I thought you guys were only, like, one in a million or something."

"That's not exactly a low figure," I remarked drily. "But her Faede manager and connections haven't tracked anything useful down about these people. I find that hard to believe."

"What are you talking about?"

"You guys have more connections and more fingers in pies than anyone else I know of. That includes the vampire communities and maybe even the *Spectrada* klatsches. Yet your people can't track anything down on her problem? Meanwhile, you just happen to call me up and demand I help with your issue, even though you have more than enough people and control in this town to do it yourself without bringing an outside amateur like me into it."

"You know why you were tapped for this. I don't see why any of this reflects on me or mine."

"It just seems more and more unlikely that the Faede have suddenly lost all connection to the pulse of things going on."

"We haven't lost anything," he pointed a lacquered-nail finger at me. "Nothing you're saying makes any sense."

"Sure. I could be whistling out of my ass on all of this. But it doesn't feel right no matter what I try and do with it. I've been learning more and more lately that I should listen when I get that feeling. It tends to save me getting stabbed or shot more often."

"If there's some group of crazies after you and your girlfriend here, that's *not* on me." Ceyggan stepped forward. I made the mistake of taking an inhalation, expecting to speak, and there was a watery ripple. He was an inch high and glowing like a sputtering loose wire-lead. Then he was normal again. *Damned pheromone glamour.* "You were asked in about our problem because frankly, the consensus is amongst those that have been approached about it that you are the reason for the problems in the first place. The Faede, the bloodfeeders—"

"Whoa, what?"

What the hell?

Ceyggan grinned, triumphant in the argument at my obvious surprise. "Oh, your buddies amongst the suckfaces didn't bother to clue you in? I called you because Justin didn't want to dirty his hands telling you. Refused to have anything directly to do with you on this. He said, quote," here Ceyggan's voice affected the slow, arrogant tone I knew was Justin's, *"'We appreciate that Flicker's intervention on the fear bottler's work has resulted in a tragically avoidable state of affairs with the local disenfranchised amongst his former customers, and we wish it had been otherwise ourselves, but we have a prior understanding with him and will not act as any sort of proxy for others who are affected to voice their complaints.'"* A gargling laugh in my face. "End of the conversation. For good. That left me and others to deal with you and how you screwed up. And believe me, I'm the nicest one elected to come tap you for it. A few others I won't name thought we should simply go and string you by your balls out over the Scioto where all the school kids could see you dangling in front of the museum on their next field trip!"

Justin wouldn't tell us? This is starting to make a little more sense.

I frowned. That cold sliver sensation was pinging needle tips into my belly like a maverick acupuncturist was practicing on me.

He hosed us. He wouldn't step in directly to tell us about Spam Tam being a problem. So instead he solved it the vampire way. He left us to sink or swim with Trina. No support, no warning. Maybe he even thought Trina might lose it and get us in trouble for it. Give him the perfect excuse to tell us to go pound sand.

It fit way too well not to admit Soul's logic held. The vampire community of Columbus doesn't act overtly. Not their style. They like to be puppeteers, fashion and imagine themselves to be silent partners and unseen string-pullers. This kind of crap intrigue was right in line with Justin.

"Okay...okay." I held up my hands, palms out. "Sorry.

Ceyggan, I didn't know that getting rid of a bottom-feeder like Spam was going to be such a seismic thing to everybody. But what's done is done. I'm taking responsibility for it, I've agreed to help and deal with whatever's going on with the lead-heads—"

"Then stay out of my ass about your own problems, Flicker!"

"Hey!"

Sarah's voice cracked between us as sharp as snapped kindling. We both looked to her.

"I don't care what small town bullshit you guys have between you right now." She pointed at me as she spoke to Ceyggan. "You wanted him to take care of whatever mess this is you think he started, he's trying to do it. Never mind that we're both under some attack by who-knows-how-big a group of religious crackheads, oh no big deal or anything, only getting us shot or even almost stabbed right in your place of business."

Ceyggan didn't reply. Stared at her with his color going another touch of pink.

"He's trying to still deal with your problem. But he doesn't have anything nearly enough to go on to make any headway. The whole reason we came to your pathetic shit-show of an art unveiling—which, by the way, any one of the Frierlich Gallery chains out in San Diego would think was a *garage sale* if you're claiming to be any sort of gallery owner in this hicksville—" Ceyggan winced, "was to try and get anything more about the issue, so maybe he could get anywhere with it. So perhaps you could both stop having a contest to see who can punch each other in the dick the hardest and talk like two people who both have a serious problem in common and a mutual benefit in seeing it resolved. How's that sound?"

Ceyggan and I stared at each other.

He was the first to break down laughing. I followed a microsecond after.

He rubbed his eyes. "Oh, Christ..." he recovered slowly, the laugh tapering off as the last flat bubbles of a left-out can of soda. "Oh man." He stared at her unsmiling. "You are just so *butch.*"

She frowned and folded her arms, but I could tell there was no malice there. "Oh blow me, faery."

"Look..." he took my shoulder in a hand, pulled me closer. "I might...I don't know...there might be things we can try. But, all due respect..." he glanced meaningfully back at Sarah.

"Fine."

I walked back to her. "I'm sorry. Do you mind if the Super Secret Boy's Club president here takes me upstairs for a few minutes so we can privately trade decoder rings?"

She took us both in with her glare. Finally closed her eyes and shook her head. "I know that doppelgeists are supposed to be like the uranium of the Under, the walking atomic bombs... but I don't know if I'm cool splitting up right after..." she waggled a hand towards the floor. There were still the couple of drops of Dwyer's blood drying there.

"Stay here where Ceyggan's people can keep an eye on you for safety, you should be fine. At least safe as anywhere in this place."

I left her and followed Ceyggan back out to the front space, then to the stairs that went up to the loft, going past another couple of barrel-chested bouncers.

He flopped to the cushion throne at the end of the room as soon as the door closed. As he rolled over to a seated position, he made a short bark of pain and then extracted a rolled-up copy of Italian Vogue he'd somehow managed to sit on wrong. Barely a twist of his wrist sent the heavy magazine flying the length of the room. I barely had time to dodge away from its trajectory.

"You already got told the story, Jo-Jo," Ceyggan said, picking the polish off his thumbnail. "I don't know what you think I can do for you. This is your problem, remember?"

"I also remember you giving me a pretty thin story about what happened to begin with. Just enough to make it look important. But you didn't tell me everything you really knew, did you? Faede *never* tell the whole story. You aren't pathologically capable of it. It would be too much like giving something away. But I can't go anywhere on simply 'somebody attacked one of us then ran off,' if you expect me to be of any use. I'm not Sherlock Holmes and this isn't an episode of *CSI*.

I'm not going to come up with tire tread evidence or get out bloodhounds. I need virtually every speck of information you could give me, I don't care if you have to wake your sister Diatha up and get her out here—"

"Diatha's dead."

I heard a hush in my head. Ceyggan's face was a mask made of dirty soapstone. No sign of any laughing or joshing.

"The lead-head killed your sister?"

He nodded. "Tore out her throat. She could've recovered, but it was...bad. We didn't have enough time..." he glanced at me, realizing I was there and listening, and shut his lips with a tightening of the mouth muscles that made frown-lines at the ends of the lips.

I folded my arms and glared down at him. "This is not engendering our sympathy to your problem, Ceyggan. You said *attacked*. You acted like it was no big deal, just a fire under my ass to get me to clean up the mess with Spam Tam being gone. You didn't suggest it was anything that serious."

"So we like to keep our cards close. You already knew that about us." Ceyggan fell back into the cushions, hands going to cover his face.

Are those teeth marks on the edges of his hands? I looked to Soul's prompting and saw what definitely looked like the indentations in that crescent arc familiar turn. Biting his own hands? I didn't know Faede to worry to such distraction.

"Who else was there?"

A whoosh of air between his fingers. "Man, I couldn't tell you everything! It was decided it was enough to go tell you and put it back in your lap."

"What, Justin and this round table of Columbus' local weirdo elite?"

"No! Not anybody else, it was..." a shaking of the head. "Nothing."

"I am already long past tired of this shit habit of your people with holding things back or turning them to suit you. You want my help, you give me some of your own. Your sister is dead. If you give half a damn about finding out the who and why, I need to know everything."

"I truly don't know." The hands flopped away. His arms and legs stretched out, he looked like a magazine model posing on some fake studio clouds made of cotton and silk. His eyes were on the ceiling, roving around with caffeinated rapidity. "I'm sorry. I'm not shitting you here, okay? I don't know who it was I wasn't the one to get any look at who did it. It was over too quick."

"So Diatha was the only person who truly saw the attacker?" Ceyggan nodded.

He's being honest on this much at least. For whatever good that does us at this point. What do we do now?

"If Spam Tam is behind this, he's holed up somewhere tight and close. You wouldn't have come to me if you could simply have your people root him out and deal with him yourselves."

Ceyggan sat up, propped against his hands flat against the floor. Shook his head. "No, not the bottler. As far as that goes, we know he's no longer in town." His head dropped, chin to chest. "She's dead. We couldn't get her there in time and she's gone and there was only a little time, not enough..."

"I'm sorry. Don't torture yourself about it, it wasn't your fault."

"Damned right!" He snarled up with vigorous poison. "You don't know a damned thing about torture or what this like you fucking ghost!" He reached and swiped with the closer arm, missing my leg by a mile and collapsing against the pillows. Gasping. A flailing, half-hearted punch up towards my crotch that I didn't have to move to avoid. Sobbing.

"She's dead and that water bottle killed her and there wasn't *time* she's nearly all gone and you damned well *better* find out who it was, I don't care, call out a bloodhound or CSI or whoever, you find them and deal with this, it's your damned fault..."

I let him cough and sob and bleat for a few minutes more, saying nothing. Past his glamour, those bite marks on the inner edges of his hands, where the webbing of thumb met palm, were darker. Fresh. Hurting. Sallow-faced, puffy-lipped. His hair had lost any chic style and was only an uncombed mess. He made me think pitiably of a kid in their pajamas, lying in the grass and throwing a heartbroken tantrum while their house burns down.

I let him have a few loud, snot-choked breaths. "Should I wait here while you call some dire threats in here to deal with me? Or do you still want me to help?"

"You can't...what good? There wasn't enough of her to matter. Not enough time. Diatha...she wouldn't be any good... they can't...you..." his hands went over his face again, shaking his head and sucking breaths.

"What are you talking about? Not enough time? Diatha?"

From under the muffling hands. "Forget it."

"What? What is it?"

A long, relieved sigh. "There could be...no. Forget it. Fuck me and my mouth. Forget it."

"Is there some way of finding out? Of communicating with Diatha? What is it?"

"She's dead."

"So am I. What are you talking about? Tell me or I walk out of here and I don't care what or who comes to try and string my balls up on the riverfront. Tell me or we're out of here."

"There's...maybe." He looked up at me from where he lay, an upside down view. I wondered if his glamour would make his bruised and tear-streaked face look tragically beautiful to some women and men downstairs.

He sat up. Rubbed hands through his hair. Hunched over, staring at the floor.

"Maybe a way. If you're willing to...man...if you're willing to take a risk."

He's serious.

I know.

"I'm willing to try if you are."

He shook his head. "You might be willing. The *Teaghlach* might not."

The way he said the word, I couldn't mistake the capital 'T' or the subtle royal inflection on the 'gh,' that uniquely Gaelic twist that confused the ear. "Who are the Teaghlach?" Saying it in an approximation of how Ceyggan had uttered the word felt like trying to swallow and talk at the same time.

"I can't...it's not exactly something I can explain in words."

"What? Are they the ruling council or something like that? The Faede godfathers?"

"No. Not exactly."

"Fine. Stay cryptic. Keep the fun intact for your mystery club. But if they can give me anything, the tiniest clue on what happened that I could try and figure this all out, I'm game to try. Can you arrange for me to meet them?"

He shook his head harder. "No, man...I mean...this is funky, all right? We can try. But I'll be honest with you...I can't...it's not anything that's done. I've never seen it done, anyway. Nobody goes and meets the Teaghlach." He pushed himself up to his feet, eyes coming level with mine once more. He sighed, rocking on his feet, looking at the tips of his toes. Biting his lower lip.

"Nobody who's not Faede does this. I don't know if it's even possible. I'd have to go and find out. Make arrangements. See if they're willing to try. The Teaghlach is..." his voice collapsed to a whisper, reverentially terrified. "...I mean, that's God."

"The quote John Lennon: *'God is a concept by which we measure our pain.'* Make whatever the arrangements you can. You have my number, you call when they're ready. How long will it take?"

"I don't..." he passed a hand across his lips. The hand paused, and I saw his mouth quivered near one of those overlapped bruise-bite marks. Then he wiped his lip and dropped the hand to his side. "I'll try. I don't know how long. Maybe an hour or two. Maybe a week. Maybe never."

"I don't have a week or never. This has to get resolved now. Preferably before these Believers get another crack at Sarah and I and we're too busy messing with the lead-heads to see them coming next time. Or before more lead-heads go apeshit and tear up the city worse."

"All right...alright..." he waved his hands in surrender. "I'll try."

I went to the door to the staircase. "You call me when it's on, and where. I'll be there."

"John, man." He didn't turn to see me leave. Kept staring at the floor. His hands working at the pockets of his designer pants like birds struggling to get into a cove before a storm and failing. Fingers scrabbling at the leather. "You could get...I don't know..."

"Killed?"

"No," he shook his head. "Not killed." I felt a very solid tapping of a cold finger in my stomach. The clumsy acupuncturist again, needles all dull. "Killed would be easy. If the Teaghlach will meet with you...you be worse than dead after. You could stop being. All the way. It's not their thing, meeting outsiders. If you want to do this...you gotta accept...if we can even pull off a meeting at all...you might not walk out. You might not be anything. Ever again."

Neither Soul nor I replied, and we tried to not contemplate any literal or metaphysical definitions of that warning as I took the stairs back downstairs.

****

Sarah was finishing a conversation on her phone as I returned to the catering table at the back of the exhibit. It was noticeably less crowded in the gallery now.

"Thanks, yeah, okay." She saw me and smiled. "Okay. Do it." She hung up and returned the phone to her coat pocket as she turned to me. "Was touching base with things back west."

"Anything new to report?"

"Nothing special. Seppeschal hasn't gotten any new bites about the Believers out there." She tilted her face to point the chin back the way I'd come. "Anything useful from your friend?"

"'Useful' is a flexible word right now. Open to interpretation on many levels." I shrugged. "I'm meeting Ceyggan later. Some possible confab that could be productive, I'm not sure yet." I did a partial sweep of the room, at the couple of dwindled huddles who kept trying to not obviously eyeball me as they whispered over their wine. "Either way, I think the gallery hop is done with us for the moment."

With a few hostile glances from Ceyggan's guests my way, and the security guys trying to give us stone faces but clearly relieved we were headed for the exit, we walked outside and back to my car.

I stalled as we reached the Vega. Didn't open the door on her side right away.

"Can I...give you a ride to...are you staying—"

"You're adorable when you're utterly at a loss, you know that?" She touched my cheek. One of those touches you feel a long time after the hand is pulled away. "I can call a cab or bother Hal for a long car drive from the suburbs to pick me up. I have my own arrangements for staying in town. Safer that way, with these crazies out for us. But you need to look into this further."

"Sarah, it's...I can't tell you how amazing it is we've met. Don't get me wrong. But I still have to figure stuff out. Some things aren't making any sense right now—"

"Shut it."

I snapped my mouth shut in commanded silence.

"You're not the only person caught up in this shit-storm, remember? I came looking for you because this stuff has already been in my neck of the woods before it came beating down the trees in yours." She inhaled a breath. "If you need to go do things, talk to people, whatever it is you do, and having me along would cramp that style—"

"It's not—" A hand raised. Back to idiot silence.

"It's cool. I need a break myself. I need to go back to my room. Get a shower. Call folks back in Los Angeles and check in on business. Here." She handed me a business card with a handwritten number on it. No name or other information, only the number in red ink. "Don't go sharing that with your fan club or anything."

I put the card away in a pocket. "I'll call you as soon as I've had a chance to look into some things."

"If you find anything out, or if anybody tries to get you

again, don't wait. Call."

"Promise."

She grabbed the back of my neck with a cool hand and tugged me in before I had a chance to try and sort of slick composure of mouth or face. To anyone watching I must've looked like a classically awkward teenage kid, all wide eyes and high eyebrows as her lips met mine with an audible, moist clash.

She made it fast and it counted. When she let me go she looked back at me with a gremlin-sly grin. All that lingered, other than a sense of contact on my lips, was a weirdly syrup-sweet tint to the air around her, strong enough that I almost had a sense of it trailing away as she pulled back. A perfume unique and tagged to her instantly.

"I have a feeling this is going to be a pattern with you, isn't it, Mr. Flicker? Never enough time to actually hang out with the girl. It always seems like that with the people who matter to us, doesn't it? The interesting and the intriguing folks?"

"William Wordsworth said once that 'the heavens laugh at what makes us weep.'" A poet quote was about all I could manage on the auto-pilot her kiss was putting my brain into.

"So that's me, for all occasions. The never-time girl."

Whoa. 'Never time.' That clicks hard.

What?

"Keep the card close, okay?"

I managed to keep my focus beyond Soul's interruption. "Will do."

We've definitely heard those words from her before. In that tone of voice.

Where?

Movies. Something in movies. But not adult.

I gave a halfhearted wave and smile to Sarah as I pulled away in the Vega with her standing with one of Ceyggan's security guys nearby. The kiss and a smile were sharing my lips as we got back into traffic.

Soul's remarks were ricochets. Now I was mentally rewinding and replaying those words. The internal wire-tapper was crammed back in his tiny corner, all the audio reel-to-reel equipment running at various speeds, backwards and forwards, slowing down, charting phonemes...

Never time.

We've heard her say those words. In some way. The voice bumped and rolled around in the car like an agitated fly. *We've heard her say that. But* where?

We don't even know her any longer than a couple hours ago. In person, no. But those words.

I know. I know.

Driving in silence.

Then: *I have no ideas here. All I can think is, we try the basics now. When all else extraordinary fails, let's give the ordinary a shot.*

****

I returned to The Nookery and found my way to the manager's office. Three filing cabinets nearly filled the tiny storage room that I'd assembled a do-it-yourself desk (and had to hand-cut off the last two inches of its top in order to make it fit). The room was a stair flight's travel up, around and behind the small cubby for the cash register. The postcard racks that never stopped rotating ground and whined harder as I went by, the way cats might beg the returning owner for food.

The office didn't even have room for a proper office chair. I had to use a small four-legged barstool with the legs cut down so that I sat even with the desktop. I tossed my coat on top of the filing cabinets with their conglomeration of old receipts, invoices and obsolete property title info, then powered up the computer.

Another side benefit of Justin's beneficence to us for Trina. A new iMac, 27-inch screen with all the usual trimmings (including a wifi capability that happily piggybacked on the unsecured wifi broadcast of the antiques shop next door; if you're ever in my neighborhood feel free to use it, just look for a broadcast named 'oldjunk4me,' the password is—believe it or not—'12345'...same as an idiot might have as the combination on his luggage).

It booted up quickly and I went to Google Chrome and started searching, using Sarah's name as the basic starting point.

The internet is not as commonly used a tool for me as you would guess. I'm sure at times, telling you these things, you're wondering why I simply don't go online for much of the info that you would easily facilitate via Google or any other search engine.

Good point. But bad assumption. Namely, that the Under works on the internet any more frequently or openly than it has anywhere else.

Sure, there are websites. Wikipedia can have its uses. I've spent hours in curious wandering through link after link on the Encyclopaedia Mythica and similar sites. Mostly though, the internet is as full of rumors, unsubstantiated comments and half-assed opinions regarding Under goings-on as it does with politics, religion, medicine and celebrity nonsense. If you have something very specific to look for, you might have a chance with the 'darknet' and very shady chat-forums. But given the sheer global volume of nonsense out there, aside from a tantalizing bit of reference data or so, getting the street-level dirt on a given person, place or thing means you might as well go out on the street itself.

Her name came up with an IMDB entry, but I already knew about the two movies. No Wikipedia entry. A couple of horror movie afficionado sites that referred to her. On the off-chance, I pulled the card she'd given me out of my pocket and search the number. It was blandly listed as a generic burner phone, no personal details.

It was about all I could have expected, even for someone who'd been in movies. Then I moved on to trying a search for a more hopeless cause: the Believers of the Second Freedom.

Search engine results were numerous with similar names: Believers of Light, Believers in One Word, True Believers (a Marvel Comics fan site). But nothing there of substance.

At my shoulder: *Try using the quotation marks and include* 'doppelgeist.'

Combination search for all keywords. A good suggestion.

I put that in...and came up empty again, this time not even getting any suggested similar links.

I stared at the screen, tapping fingers on the little carpal pad in front of the keyboard. *Anything?*

I blew my hacker wad suggesting that combination search. You come up with something.

Funny.

I watched the clock display in the upper right corner change to five minutes further. Uninspired, I logged into a couple of the free email sites I have addresses with, checking for anything new. Nothing but spam which I deleted or flagged. Logged out.

Watched the clock another three turns.

Do another search for the fan sites for Sarah.

I leaned forward to access the keyboard again. *Why?*

Instead of looking for simple reviews or remarks about the movies, let's try looking for anything personal. Remarks about family, Hollywood gossip, anything like that. In fact, don't do a basic name-only search, let's try the combination keywords again, but this time use 'personal life,' like the Wikipedia articles sometimes have.

Worth a shot. I obeyed the suggestion. Link results came up and I began to scan through.

This time Soul spoke from a space almost at the end of my nose, down near the keyboard, the feeling of someone leaning forward and blocking your view of the screen trying to read it. *There. Click that one.*

Which one? I can't see you pointing with no fingers.

"Horror Hurrahs." *Oy what a name. Click that one.*

Click. "Good god! My eyes! The goggles do nothing!"

Yeah. That is...truly, tragically awful wallpaper for a website. Christ, this guy used an animated gif repeat? What is this, an old Angelfire site from 1999?

What is that, anyway? It looks like...a loaf of bread vomiting?

No, I think that's a skull spitting blood.

The loaf of bread would've been scarier.

The bleeding-line graphic underneath the site title doesn't help much either.

He misspelled 'Blood' right in the title, man...

Shhh. I'm reading.

I followed along myself. Sarah Parley's biographical sketch was, by bits and drabs, offered through a frequently-typo-filled review of her two movies. The two films had also been the only two US-released films by the director, a minor-cult-figure cinematographer named Antony Belascacci. His name was an active link that opened a new tab to a Wikipedia article.

Died in 1988. Heart failure. He was...fifty-six years old? Sheesh, what would that have made Sarah when they married? A child bride?

To each their own, I answered, clicking back to the tab with the "Horror Hurrahs" article.

Hold on...I think...I remember something from that MacWorld *issue we were reading when we bought this...go up to the preferences panel for the browser.*

Why?

Because we can tweak it to reload the page and maybe not have to stare at this god-awful wallpaper animation that's making my nonexistent eyes want to bleed along with them.

I followed his steps, restarted the application which automatically reloaded the most recently-opened tab sites. Now a plain-text version of the site loaded, blessedly free of the eye-nausea graphics.

More mutters from in front of my face as I read. *Married during second movie filming...divorced in '85...some stuff with a stuntman who got injured during filming...*

That's it.

No, wait...go back down again...

What?

There.

The last paragraph made a note of Parley and Belascacci having a child a year into their marriage. But no further mention about the child or anything else other than their divorce. The rest of the paragraph focused on Belascacci's minimal career back in Italy after the two US films flopped.

The voice was behind me, pacing around the other side of

the space. *A kid. Okay. That's...better than nothing. She didn't mention having any kids.*

"Why would she say anything?" I spun around to face the filing cabinets. Stared at the various drawer labels. Some were alphabetic but came from previous owners when I bought them and I couldn't recall if I'd ever actually used them for alphabetically storing anything. The scar-and-dent-marred sea-green one that dominated the other two by a fifth drawer to their poor-cousin four had empty drawer label slots but someone had long ago scrawled Dewey decimal-looking archaic number ranges: 800-4500b, 3400-26(c), the rest were unreadable from when I'd made a half-hearted attempt to clean the mess off with rubbing alcohol.

I would think a kid would be something worth mentioning.

Not necessarily. Maybe the kid was given up for adoption when she became a doppelgeist. Maybe Belascacci had custody and took them back to Italy, they ended up with some relatives out there, end of story.

Maybe.

Why is a kid bothering you so especially?

You know why. For the same reason I know it's bothering you at least a little bit.

True enough. I've never been a parent or married, never even babysat anyone's child. My experience with children was mostly confined to people bringing their kids with them to The Nookery when I ran it. I had a bag of old Halloween mixed candies under the counter that I'd give out to them if their parents allowed it. For the gluten-free, sugar-free, no-artificial-sweeteners-crowd I had a second smaller bag of pure-sugar-cane-sweetened lemon suckers. I dug kids up to a point: screaming, irrational babies with their squeals and hollers and crushed-fruit red faces when they were hungry or hurt set me automatically on-edge. A biological nails-on-chalk-board reaction to the noise, the dumb feeling of non-communicative helplessness I felt around them. Teenagers or near-college I could deal with only if they were halfway intelligent (not always guaranteed with loiterers to a bookstore, some heard from adults that it was a former headshop years back and thought maybe I dealt weed on the side...maybe from a third bag under the counter).

But kids in that formative period...where the smarter ones were precocious and the others were still fine and imaginative, questioning and playful and so maniacally energetic that simply watching them could exhaust me...those were fine. They took the candies and said thanks, most of them, or at least gave wide, missing-tooth grins as they sucked at the treats, most of them barely tall enough for their eyes to see the top of the counter as their parents paid for a purchase. A few would be rotten: grabbing and practically baseball-bat-swinging their arm to make the postcard racks spin harder than a Kansas twister or kick at them to try and knock them over. The worst I'd ask the parents to leave outside. I'd never had to ask anyone to absolutely take their kid and get off the premises.

But no...no friends or family with kids that I regularly interacted with...yet kids struck a good chord with me. The idea of someone having a child but never mentioning it, not even in passing...

I tapped a foot, stared down at the carpet. *The memory thing.*

A verbal nod. *The memory thing. One of our childhood memories. And she was there with me. But she didn't think to mention a kid of her own? Just...it feels off.*

"It's not as if we're the absolute authority on how other people should feel about kids, theirs or anyone's."

True...but it still feels off, right?

I nodded.

You know what I'm thinking?

I leaned back against the edge of the desk. I must have hit something on the keyboard because the Mac gave an indignant bleep that made me jerk upright. "What?"

Guess.

I looked at my watch. *Hrm. Not really that late into the evening yet. No idea how long Ceyggan might take to get on that meeting. I'm not up for guessing.*

We should go to Studio 53, then.

Why?

A shiver around my legs. A bubblegum wrapper tilted on its side on the dashboard. *Studio 53. It's the double-feature night, remember? One of the things we were thinking of going to, to avoid Trina before all the crap hit the turbine?*

Memory gradually opened up circuits, made clicky-clacky relay connections for my brain to catch up. *Oh. Yeah. Why? I don't think now's the time to go see if we can still watch the last half of* 'The Lost Boys.'

Not for the movies, dipstick. The host.

Another relay clicked, like Robby the Robot's ticky-tacky brain-dome connecting thought to thought. *Okay... yeah. So we go see him. About what?*

Let's pretend you are me for five seconds and use that lump in your still-corporeal head. Sarah Parley reminds us of someone, maybe she is that someone. We know those words. We keep coming back to 'movies' in some way, right?

With you so far.

And if it's not porn, then it's movies sometime so far back we can't remember. And where did we see most of the movies in our life before we were old enough to go to the theaters by ourselves?

O-kay. I kind of see where this is going...

I could feel the exasperated sigh in my skull. *I still want to know about her. If she's who we think she might be. Who else around here is a better walking repository of old horror movie junk trivia?*

I signaled to make a left turn. Listened to the signal switch click-click-click as I mulled it over.

Okay. Sure. Yeah. Good point.

Straight as that, our next move was nominated and seconded. We were off to see Fritz the Nite Owl.

24.

If you grew up in central Ohio anytime in the seventies or eighties, you know Fritz the Nite Owl.

If you love jazz music and were up late listening to the local radio stations' late-night shows, you know Fritz the Nite Owl.

If you avidly read Captain Marvel or Superman comics, you know Fritz the Nite Owl.

Fritz Peerenboom is a legend of local television, both via radio and late-night television. Multiple Emmy winner, artist. One of the last of the vanguard of the golden age when local television still had horror movie hosts after the eleven o' clock news broadcasts instead of pre-packaged syndicate infomercials.

WBNS-10TV, the local CBS affiliate for Columbus, was the home of his brand of homegrown hometown television weirdness. Columbus and surrounding towns were graced with his gravelly-scary voice and weirdly rock-and-roll-meets-Lon-Chaney appearance for nearly twenty years, from the mid-seventies to the mid-nineties. He also hosted a radio jazz hour and made appearances at everything from the Ohio State Fair to the Doo-Dah Parade as its Grand Marshall.

Fritz the Nite Owl: possibly one of the most knowledgeable

people alive to tell you virtually any tidbit you want to know about your most obscure dark movies, years before there was any Internet Film Database or Wikipedia to go Google to your heart's content. Joe Bob Briggs and Elvira are great...but to a hometown Columbusite, they don't hold a candle to that Voice of the Night, the man many of us affectionately call "Da Owl."

****

"You seem to have a trust issue where Sarah is concerned."

This happens. You can ask him yourself about the reasons for it. But when we're alone, Body frequently speaks out loud rather than using our 'two-way radio' system. I think he needs to hear his own voice at times. God knows that there's sometimes long enough jags where he hasn't had anyone else for which to use it.

We were almost to the movie theater. *And you don't have your own questions?*

"Yeah. But it seems this Believer thing is a bigger deal right now for both of us. And we don't have any outright reasons not to trust her, do we?"

You didn't think much of that joy buzzer stunt she pulled with the bouncer.

He didn't respond. Another couple of blocks of stop-and-start traffic for the lights.

"You and her counterpart must have a ton of conversation above and beyond our meatsack interactions. Doesn't that help assuage some of that paranoia?"

She's been quiet. Not much more than background noise from her. I wandered the backseat rubbish pile around the floor, contemplative. *I think...I think I embarrassed or scared her or something.*

"What?"

The memory interaction thing. It was...it was rich. Deep. But she did it to us. Like sort of...it's not fair, she didn't know she was doing it. Or didn't know it would be like that. Not sure.

"What?"

I let the image coast across to him without explanation: Wile E. Coyote, painting a fake backdrop of a mountain tunnel, expecting the Roadrunner to go plowing into it...only getting forgetfully excited as the bird passes straight into the illusion and running headlong into the solid rock himself.

"She tricked you with our own memory?"

Not a trick. She...maybe she's more used to that kind of thing than we are. Maybe she thought that was the right way... sort of the non-corporeal-consciousness etiquette when meeting another bodiless entity, you know? It wasn't like Rod...there was no bleed-through. It was pure us, all that moment. It was... hard. But yeah...could this be what it's like between us? Any of us?

"May be." Body grinned stupidly as he shrugged. "She didn't come across as malicious in this, her Body *or* Soul."

So says the guy who just got a major kiss on the lips.

"Is it my fault I lucked out and got the handsome half of this arrangement?"

I'll have you know that I'm considered pretty hunky amongst phantasmal entities myself. Schmuck.

"So her Soul is playing shy or is genuinely bothered by us for some reason. What do you want to do?"

I considered it while swirling around the car floor and getting a little lost in the micropore surface of a styrofoam cup for a few minutes.

I need to apologize when we meet up. She's nice, and it's not like we're going to meet other doppelgeists all that often, are we?

"Who knows? So far it's two for two in about three years. I'm beginning to wonder if we're truly as rare as some folks have made us out to be."

A three-quarters-insane homicidal steam-cloud and a drunken German don't count for much on that tally.

"Agreed."

Although if this is how awkward or staticky it is when two of us meet, maybe it's less about us being rare and more about avoiding unnecessary trouble having two or more of us in close vicinity.

"Get two big enough magnets close together, and it can be bad news for anything in between them, right?"

I didn't answer. More Wile E. Coyote images wandered into my thoughts. These involving big Acme-grade magnets, the red-with-gray-tipped horseshoe cartoon kind. Big lightning bolts of magnetic force shocking the shit out of me between them. Not encouraging.

****

Down in one of the older urban neighborhoods of Columbus, Clintonville is a district of dollhouse shotgun tract houses and old oak growths. The roads here are paved but only just, and many are barely a car-and-a-half-wide from days when you tended to have people park in their driveways and never saw more than one car at a time go down your lane as you mowed your lawn. Along Indian Cola Road (I have no idea where Columbus civil engineers got some of these names) you can find, peeking amongst the houses and oaks, a length of dilapidated-but-hardy businesses. Seamstress stores, a pizza shop...and the glowing marquee board of the renovated drafthouse and movie theater, Studio 53.

We hit Studio 53 every so often to catch a cheap double-feature, maybe have one of the numerous local brewery micro-mixtures. Seven bucks and you could see a couple of first-runs in an intimate, sometimes a little moldy-smelling, popcorn-and-butter-wafting atmosphere. Once a month, this is where Fritz the Nite Owl holds court and runs a new theater-show version of his old WBNS weeknight horror/science fiction movie shows.

I have to hand it to Mike McGraner and his team. They found a local legend who was, in the age of post-infomercial and thousand-channel cable packages, getting something of a short shrift and brought him back to full, vivid life each month with these movie showings. Complete with half-hour interruptions for old commercials found on YouTube and trivia clips with Fritz blue-screened into some scene from that night's movie. Love "Lost Boys"? Then go see when Fritz shows up in the shot as one of the vampires hanging alongside Kiefer off the train trestle beams, the Nite Owl's wry smiling face under those huge dark sunglass lenses remarking with dry wit about some behind-the-scenes movie tidbit. Or see Fritz in a shot from "Friday the 13th" lunging out of a camp shower in place of Jason, then stopping and cracking a gag about the scantily-clad girl in the shot.

This is what made television when I was a kid. Made it something personal and magical. When I heard that the Nite Owl Theater show had started running regularly, we had come to catch a marathon of Corman movies. I'd ended up inadvertently helping deal with a rather ugly issue that had cropped up at Studio 53 that same night, and for that got a good nod of recognition from the Nite Owl himself.

Heroes can disappoint you. Especially if you get to meet them up-close and in-person. You shake their hand and tell them how much you loved such-and-such they did, and they stare at you blankly. Or they get a bitter twist to their face and start going off about the director or their crappy producer. You get to see your heroes as human beings just like yourself...for better or for worse. It's why one of the rarely-acknowledged but truly pleasant gifts you seem to get in life, if you're fortunate, is when a hero or heroine turns out to be every bit the person in the flesh as they ever were in your head and heart.

Fritz is one of my heroes who has not disappointed.

Body parked the Vega a couple of blocks and walked the car-crusted curb down the uneven sidewalk, arriving into the warm incandescent cosseting of Studio 53's marquee board and poster-case lights. A narrow ticket-booth barely wide enough to accommodate the shaven-headed kid sitting behind the glass was where I homed in.

"One for the Nite Owl show." He silently took our five dollar bill and handed back a glossy-printed, not-quite-postcard size printing with the Nite Owl logo—a round moon face split by a pair of owl-horned glasses—on one side, and the calendar of show dates for the summer on the other, and a half-faded hand-stamp of a number ("136") across the logo.

"Hang on to your ticket," the kid called after us before we let the big red swing-doors close after Body.

Wow. I slithered ahead of Body into the lobby/bar. *They have seriously put some money into fixing this place up from last time.*

Gone was the ratty-carpeted, half-lit rumpus room of bar/popcorn machine and old wooden booths, wallpapered in geological layers of yellowed movie posters, one glued overtop another and another, with the glassed-in wall that let bar patrons drink their brew while watching the movie in the theater through the glass (accompanied by buzzy, broken-down speakers that made you feel like an indoor version of an old drive-in movie show).

Now everything was slick, bright, shining beer taps and polished rectangle of bar that took up most of the space. They'd pushed back some walls to open everything up and allow more booth and table seating on the left and right. And the glassed wall was now mostly opaque and had more entrance doors. You couldn't exactly see what was going on in the theater anymore, but it looked liked a lot better soundproofing and effort had gone into making the whole place smooth and profitably homey without making the men's room smell like a urinal cake or the bar area like spoiled beer.

Some nostalgia isn't always the greatest to preserve. I used to not care for the feeling of having my shoes hiss-peel off the sticky floors, or the only chair I could find in the theater being the busted one with a missing armrest, sitting at a half-fallen angle where my butt nearly touched the coke-and-food-strewn floor. It looked like the owners had stepped up their game considerably.

Body approached the ponytailed girl wearing a Neko Case t-shirt behind the counter while I was raptly staring at a gaggle of floating, melting shapes of infrared heat coming off the old-style popcorn popper set up at one corner of the bar. "Is Fritz in?"

She was pouring a beer and keeping an eye on the head of foam. She glanced up, smiled, and told us he was over at one of the restaurant tables, selling merchandise before the show. Body gave her thanks as she went back to measuring out foam-to-liquid ratio with the attention one normally would apply to anesthesiologists tracking a patient about to receive surgery.

On the right-hand end of the room, away from the bar, three of the two-person cafe tables had been scooted together to make a table space approximating a short flea market table. It was covered with 11x17" and 18x24" color posters, all done by a local guy who is part of Mike's crew producing the show for Fritz. The posters all showed the Nite Owl worked into the theme of some movie or other's layout. Fritz next to Gizmo for "Gremlins" or Fritz's head floating in ghostly-Vincent-Price fashion over the original House on Haunted Hill, that sort of material.

Seated at the table were more t-shirted youths and a big guy in a denim button-down, bald with a fringe of chestnut beard—Mike, of course, chatting amiably—and frequently making tiny tic-gesture adjustments to keep the posters lined up and neat as someone bought one or got something autographed. Luckily it was still forty-five minutes to showtime so the crowds were either not yet arrived or already seated in the theater catching the tail end of the earlier double-feature.

There, in the middle of the seated group, a weirdly small lord holding counsel at his grand hall table, was the man.

He was hunched forward at the table, using a silver-tint sharpie marker to sign a poster for one of the kids seated at the fringe of the group. Small-built man, thin as a bundle of cables plastic tie-wrapped together to make a rangy-looking body dressed in a black button-down shirt and a black leather biker's vest. Atop his head he wore a black leather biker's captain hat, complete with silver chain framing the top of the brim. As we approached he straightened, rumbling a joke to the kid at the end that he handed the signed poster to. There was a laugh, and there he was, smiling back. Salt-and-pepper mustache underneath a small beak of nose and those immense, ever-present sunglasses with the small craft-plastic owl's horns poking out from the ends of the frames. His gray hair brushed back, it left a face that was almost entirely swallowed by those ebon pieces of glass, every light in the place finding a spot to reflect off of them. The owl look was more than simply a pair of glasses; Fritz kept his face very stoically composed. An occasional grin-tilt to the corners of the mustachioed mouth, but otherwise he left all the expressiveness to his rolling hum of a voice.

"Hey, there," he noted Body's arrival at the table. "Good to see you."

"Hey, Fritz." Body couldn't fight the kid smile that jerked his mouth wide in a foolish happiness. "It's great seeing you again."

His head moved forward on its stalk neck. "You were the one—" he raised hand to point, snapping his fingers as it hit. "Yeah! You were the gentleman who gave us such a necessary hand that night, weren't you?"

"Yeah." Body's head ducked down against his chest, the smile burning the muscles in his face. "I didn't do much, but I'm glad you remembered."

I floated over the tabletop between them, perusing posters. *Didn't do much except maybe save three-dozen people from being the newest concession stand snack for a chronophobos.*

A nod, the biker's hat making shutter-shadows over the glasses. "You were definitely the man of that hour, if I do say so my humble self."

I looked over the edge of the table as I saw Body's upper legs in movement. *For crying out loud, you're shuffling your feet.*

Shut up. It's only because you're invisible that you're not doing the same and you know it.

No retort to that.

Body at least managed to lift his head up enough to continue speaking half-sensibly. "Yes, uh...listen, I wondered if I could have a moment of your time to ask about something. It's not a big thing, but I thought if you might have a few minutes..."

"Certainly." He leaned over to be heard over the hubbub of the room. "Mike, I'm going to step out for a smoke for a moment with—?" A glance of the lenses at me.

"John Flicker."

"—with Mr. Flicker. You remember him, don't you?"

Mike gave Body a once-over while I hovered overhead. "Yeah." He wasn't frosty, but it wasn't entirely buddy-buddy. Our involvement in 'the night' being referred to hadn't left him feeling all that safely wonderful about what our presence might mean, being here tonight. He gave a nod then went back to talking to others in the group.

We waited patiently while Fritz had the people to his left scoot out so he could maneuver around and away from the table. He swept a gracious hand as he looked up at Body. "Lead the way, my friend."

We went outside to the front street where smokers had planted themselves as close as they could without being actually inside the building and thus in violation of the city-wide smoking ban on businesses. A few milling folks smoking and talking, a couple of kids jumping up and down while their dad bought tickets. The dad pointed Fritz out and he gave a wave and greeting to them as they proceeded into the theater.

Off to the side, outside the aura-fringe of light from one of the poster cases, they stood near a stubby hedge-plant at the property line to the house next door and Fritz lit a cigarette with a casual *click-scritch* of a scratched-up steel Zippo lighter.

"What can I, your humble owl, do for you, John?"

"Nothing major. I wondered if you might remember a movie actress named Sarah Parley."

He *hmmmm*ed with a bass note and gravel finish while taking a long, thoughtful inhale of his cigarette. "Yes," he nodded slowly, exhaling through his nostrils with the casualness of a movie devil, or one of those old cigarette painting-posters you see all done in French and sold at trendy bath-product and housewares shops as decorations. Around him, the air looked like a creased leather coating on an undulating, slow ocean wave seen from above...a slow flag-furl in a weak breeze colored like African violets. Calm, cool, an occasional titter-flash of showtime excitement that proved the guy still loved what he did, thirty-plus years later. "Sarah Parley. Only did two films, not the most memorable of features. The movies were...hrmm...*And the Blood Drips*. Then...*And the Blood Drips Again.*"

And that's bingo. Those weird-ass haunted-house flicks where she played some psychic detective or whatever.

Fritz glanced at the tip of his cigarette. "I believe we showed her on Nite Owl Theater...early eighties, it would have been."

"Pretty sure. I think I watched those as a kid. When you mentioned the titles they rang a bell."

"She was a Columbusite, you know?"

"No."

Okay, another ding on the bell from this one. I kept away from the cigarette smoke plumes and hovered somewhere up in the brick facade of the cornerstones of the theater.

A sage's nod from the Owl as he inhaled and exhaled with easy pace again. "Most definitely. Original name was... let me think..." that funny quirk of the lips giving away a smile without surrendering to forming one. "My computer upstairs," he waved the cigarette towards his biker's cap, "it runs on steam power. Doesn't always return the answers to my queries as quickly as it once did. But...hmmm...yes. Sarah Temple? Sarah Oxford? I'm awful on those little things. But Sarah Parley...an attractive lady. Somewhat classy for those movies, to be truthful. She was from Columbus, yeah. I think we tried to get her to come on the show once or twice, but never managed it."

"I had no idea she was from here. That's pretty... wild."

"Not so wild as you'd think. This is a great town for famous people. Majel Barrett was from here. Gene Roddenberry's wife, the one who played Nurse Chapel on *Star Trek?*"

"Yeah, I remember that."

"As was Beverly D'Angelo, of *National Lampoon* movie fame."

Oh that voice, that cadence and the presentation...he was back into the pattern of the Nite Owl, easily dispensing bit-part homilies about behind-the-scenes and actor/director trivia. I felt as though I was seated back in my dad's overstuffed easy chair again, eight or nine years old with a bag of stale Mike Sell's potato chips in my hands, stuffing my mouth and listening to the voice of the night, practically jumping up and down in the seat for the local heating-and-cooling and siding company ads to be over already so Fritz and the movie would come back on. "Columbus is a great place to be famous. Assuming of course that you leave Columbus first." Another puff of the cigarette. "Come across any bootleg DVD or Blu-ray copies? Doing a research project for a school assignment?"

Better not bother with trying to explain. Keep it simple and plausible.

"Nothing like that. I was thinking of looking her up. Maybe, I don't know, writing a fan letter. I liked those movies."

"They had a charm. The director was known primarily for doing art-house shorts in Italy and France. He never worked in an American release again after the second movie."

"That's what I understood."

He held the cigarette at his side. Some of the smile left his voice. "This wouldn't be something like...what happened?"

"No. Oh, no. Nothing like that."

Liar.

Shut up.

"Old fans die hard, don't they?" The grin returned to his tone as he inhaled more smoke.

"No argument there."

"I was always a fan of Rod Serling, myself. Still am, despite...what happened. That night."

"I understand. I'm still a fan, too. If it's any consolation, I'm pretty sure that wasn't Rod Serling."

A thoughtful nod. Then, in a flush of smoke wisps: "Sure looked a dead-ringer for him, though."

"That's sort of the nature of those things. It was definitely his appearance, but I feel confident in saying the real Serling wouldn't have tried consuming a theater full of innocent people."

"Mmmm. Did one of Parley's movies come up on cable somewhere? I'd love to see one of those again, now that we mention them."

"No. I came across some random reference to the movies on the internet."

Puff. Nod. Those lenses were uncomfortably dark now that we were away from the bright lights of the theater interior. Out here they reminded me of how much the Nite Owl had been quite terrifying on his show when he turned on the fright-juice. That dark, low voice could speak of menacing things and shadows with the same casualness that a MoviePhone line would recite showtimes and admission prices. It was a voice that had narrated some of my tossing and turning nightmares as a kid, not just bouncing in the old man's chair and flinging potato chip crumbs everywhere while watching a Superman movie or some cheapie horror flick. When he'd played the first *Tales from the Crypt* movie or a werewolf film, or did one of his patented blue-screen transformation bits where an actor's face on a poster or screenshot would slowly dissolve into the face of the Nite Owl as it spoke to you through your television set... it could be chilly in a way that dry ice only aspires to, hearing that voice rumble about giggling things in the dark about to grab you by an ankle, drag you away to the kinds of places that the late night movies only suggested with bad special effects and gory titles.

Everything Under was in his voice, even if Fritz himself wasn't amongst the Under in the usual manner. I realized that he had been a sort of subconscious narrator for some of my fears of late. When I thought of truly gruesome possibilities that await some hapless folks in the dark undersides of my hometown, I inevitably was hearing this voice before me, calmly describing the rend and chew of a hunter in the dark.

"Do you know if she ever came back to Columbus? After the movies?"

"Not that I recall hearing about, no. The movies were a couple years old when we managed to get rights to broadcast them on the show. My stage director tried to get in touch with her but this was way before any internet to make it easier. We tried through, I believe it was the distribution company, who got us in touch with the production company that funded the films...but there was never any results from that. Eventually my stage director wrote it off and we figured it was just a shame we couldn't contact her. I didn't have others on-screen with me very often." A chuckle. "Not amongst the living, at least."

Body smiled back, some cheer returning despite the ominous voice-association that had shivered my brain a moment before. "She seemed like a good actress in those."

"The film had a surprisingly good group with it." Another didactic pause. "There was a big trend in the late seventies, early eighties for low-budget horror movies. *Friday the 13th* and *Halloween* had demonstrated that a movie with a tiny budget and no known stars could, with the proper marketing, rake in big bucks for small box office capital. Unfortunately, slasher movies seemed to dominate that success, as anything else in sci-fi or horror with a less-than-stellar budget to invest in effects and makeup never came off as more than campy, formulaic writing and bad acting. Have you ever seen *Trick or Treat,* the original movie by that name starring *Family Ties'* Marc "Skippy" Price?" Body shook his head. "A rock-and-roll haunted possession story. It is wonderfully awful in its total, straight-faced, unapologetically poor premise and absurd production values. A fine example of filmmaking taken to a completely unmarketable ending."

More customers were coming down the sidewalk towards the theater. A few waved and cheered as they spotted Fritz, who genially raised the cigarette-holding hand to wave at them. There was a short line beginning to form at the ticket booth.

"I should let you get back to things."

"Coming in for the show?"

"I can't, I wish I could more than anything."

"You could sit with me and Mike and our merry band. Best seats in the house."

Oh wow.

Damn it. There was a beat where I was sorely tempted to say to hell with Ceyggan and Sarah and everything else and tell Body to go with it. Watch a movie with a childhood movie hero, what the hell? Sit and blow a couple hours of mindlessness in the fun of a chiller-thriller feature at midnight. Listening to the heavy tones of his jokes and chiding trivia up on the screen like I had every Friday night as a child.

But the voice was also there in the dark, where the light from a flickering movie screen couldn't reach in my head. Fritz's voice laid over a grumble-guttural, throaty sound that I associated with gnawing things and childhoods spent racing past the dark basement staircase whenever I had to pass it to get to the kitchen in my childhood townhome.

The things like we were responsible for dealing with nowadays, for better or worse. And if somebody ended up getting hurt while we were idling away two selfish hours sitting and smiling next to Fritz the Nite Owl in a darkened theater... maybe someone like Trina, hurting and screaming for help while I was off watching an eighties horror flick for the cheap fun of it all...yeah, that wasn't going to work so hot for me.

"I'm strongly tempted, but I have other obligations to meet."

"Well it's good you at least could make time to follow up on an old bit of fan-fun, isn't it?"

I couldn't read behind those black lenses if he was being sarcastic or not. The voice for once gave no indication of any sardonic edge or flat affect to what he meant. And the air around him was so calm, he could've been a five-foot real owl, perched and blinking down at the meadow mice below. Body took the safe middle route and only nodded in response.

"Next month, first Saturday, we'll be playing *Alien*. Perhaps you'll grant us the pleasure of your company and come out to see it?"

"I will pencil it in."

"Use permanent marker. Much more easy to read." He dropped the butt to the sidewalk and stubbed it out with a loafered foot. The lenses swung back up to regard me with beetle curiosity. "Next time you come out though...if I may make a humble request, as one Nite Owl to another in the dark with the other fourteen viewers?" Body shrugged, smiling acquiescently. "Just be sure not to bring Rod Serling as your guest to the show."

With that he walked back into the theater amidst more patron cheers and the noise of the interior welcoming through the bright red doors.

Body stared up at the marquee for a minute, at the night sky with the purling of clouds jostling across the stars, weaving in and out of each other. I watched the waves of heat coming off the bulbs, looking like spring-coils of hot red-orange disappearing into the moist air of night.

Cool dude.

"Yeah," Body breathed. A breeze randomly disturbed some bushes near the alley that ran between the theater and the old duplex next door.

I could stay here and catch the show. Tell you all about it later. Nice try, assclown. Get in the car and let's go.

****

The phone rang as we got back to the Vega. Body glanced at the caller ID. *It's Pinney.*

Good. Maybe he's got something.

"Hey, Detective."

"You are in a shitload of trouble."

What the hell?

"I need a little clarification on that."

"Okay." A breath. A huff. A cough to clear the throat. "Here's clarification for you: about ten minutes ago, a report came in about a dead body being discovered. Female."

I thought immediately of Sarah Parley. I know Body did as well. I saw his free hand creep into the pocket where he'd earlier put her card.

"Yes?" he croaked.

"And the body in question was found at the back door of your bookstore. Does that clarify things for you any?"

Oh damn.

"Have…is there…have you identified her?"

"Not yet. There was no ID on the body and there's…it's

not good. You need to seriously come down here and it needs to look like everything's fine and dandy as far as you know." A pause. "Do you know anything about this, John? Seriously. Not that I think you would have—"

"No, Detective. I don't know anything about it. But I would like to know a good deal more. Are you handling the scene?"

"No. Bill Hartsleg is the guy put on this. But I can be down there in…about five minutes. What about you? Are you nearby?"

"Yeah. I should be able to get down there to meet you."

"Good." Another pause. "And if it were me getting this call right now, man, my suggestion would be that you make sure you have a speed dial to a good lawyer friend ready to go."

25.

The photo was a digital camera print-out. I recognized the little metadata time-date stamp in the upper right-hand corner. I knew the pavement and the bottom edge of the fence in the shot: the little semi-fenced-in alcove that wrapped around The Nookery's rear entrance, the door I used the most frequently to go directly into my little apartment in the rearmost book room.

What caused my reaction was that the body that took up the majority of the field of view of the shot was also recognizable.

We have to call the Scots Brothers as soon as we can get out of here.

The woman lying on the concrete wasn't much different than when I'd seen her alive.

In the back of my mind I heard chickenwire sparking.

I wondered if, had I been standing over her instead of seeing this through a photograph, if that furious dark hole-thing that had enveloped her was still lingering or if it had died or abandoned her completely, moving on to some other feeding when her life finally quit.

What happened to the other one?

I looked away from the photo. *The bigger question: why the hell did the Scots Brothers dump her on* our *property?*

We can be sure to ask that the next time we have a discussion with them. Very soon.

"Mr. Flicker," Hartsleg was asking with a slow, measured cadence that I recognized from Pinney's technique. Speak slowly and weight the response to every sentence as you go. See if you can catch the interrogated subject off-guard with anything before they could muster a defensive lie. "You know this woman?"

"I've seen her before, yes." I avoided looking at the photo, tried instead to focus on the ballpoint pen sitting by the papers on the other side of the table. "She's...I think she's homeless. I've seen her a few times in the neighborhood. Asking for change. I gave her a few dollars before. I didn't know her name or anything personal."

"Are you sure?"

I nodded, and pulled my eyes up to meet his. Hoped he didn't see anything that looked more than nervous and uncomfortable in them. "Yeah. I genuinely didn't know her, though the face is familiar. One of those people you see a few times enough to recognize their face, that's all."

"Do you have any idea how she could have ended up behind your store?"

"I don't. I'm sorry. Did someone...I mean..."

"We can't go into details of an active investigation with you, sir."

"Who discovered her? Was it one of my neighbors?"

"It was anonymously called in by a motorist who saw her as they drove by. Do you know of any relationship between any of your neighbors and this woman?"

I shook my head. "If you asked around, maybe one of them knew her name, gave her a few dollars like I did. Maybe one of the bakeries or restaurants gave her something to eat. I genuinely would not know, but it's possible. German Village has always had a sort of on-off situation with the homeless in the area, you know?" He nodded.

I waited for him to finish and things to wind up. I didn't know her, my recognition of her was minimal and perfectly plausible. I felt a desire to get up and go running to the outside where I could safely use my phone to call the Scots. I held it in check, but it was a narrow thing.

Instead, he looked down at the papers. Moved the ballpoint aside a few unnecessary inches while he sifted through the thin folder contents.

"Do you recognize this?" He brought out another digital print-out.

This was a dull forest green, chipped box cutter. You see a million of them in toolboxes and drawers anywhere that people have to regularly open packages or cartons or cut away shipping packaging. My last name was written in smeary white-out along it. Next to it in the shot was a pocket ruler, showing it was about seven inches in length, the stubby triangle of blade extended.

The blade was dark in the picture. I didn't look hard.

"Yes. That's a box cutter of mine. I used it for opening boxes of new stock when they'd come to the store."

"Do you have any idea of how this object was found at the same scene as the body?"

"No."

Not good.

I can't even remember the last time I used that thing. I thought I had it…somewhere—

"Mr. Flicker I do want to remind you that you're welcome to contact your legal representation or request a court-appointed attorney at any time during these proceedings."

"I don't have a regular lawyer. And I don't see why I'd need one. I didn't have anything to do with this, other than the woman being found at the store." I tapped the photo of the box cutter. "I may have lost this or it might have simply been picked up by someone else around the property, but I didn't kill this woman."

"You no longer actively maintain the storefront, do you?"

"No. I haven't been open for business in a little over three years."

"Why do you maintain the property then?"

"It's inexpensive and I consolidated my holdings a while ago to simplify my personal and business finances. I'm not closed forever, only for some major renovations. It's an old building."

A nod. He tucked away the photos. "You've had recent work done to the property in fact?"

"Yes." I gave him the name of the construction company and he wrote it down.

"Do you know of anyone amongst these contractors who might have had any interaction with this woman or any reason to harm her?"

"No."

"Have any contractors asked you for a box cutter or any other tools around your property?"

"They bring their own tools. I've mostly been simply in and out of the place while they work, haven't had much interaction except with their boss."

"What is the nature of their renovations to your property, if I may ask?"

"Nothing major. I decided to try and make some improvements to the interior. Open up some of the smaller spaces, remove the unnecessary wall partitions to make better use of the space when I re-open."

"You've had plans filed for some reworking of the water and sewage lines as part of the work."

Christ. How much had this guy looked into us before I'd gotten here? He wouldn't have gotten this from Pinney or Trina, and I could think of nobody else that would've told him. Had he contacted the contractor? What had they told him? That I had a young girl living with me who wanted a whole new bathroom suite put in?

"Yes. I'm having a better bathroom facility put in. Not just for customers but so I can use it after-hours. Shower and bath, bigger vanity counter, that sort of thing."

"Are you zoned for semi-residential use of that property?"

"The Village codes allow for a semi-residential use of that property so long as I don't significantly alter the exterior appearance of the buildings without prior approval by the local historical board or city office." I'd checked that out a long time ago, when I'd first decided to relocate to the store and cut my ties to my old house or anything else that might draw too much attention to the fact that I was no longer amongst the breathing.

"I noticed when you were providing your identification at intake that you haven't renewed your driver's license in a few years."

"Don't drive enough to warrant it."

"You also haven't renewed your tags in the same amount of time."

"I've been lax. Like I said, I've never been a big driver on any regular basis."

"But you still have an active proof of insurance card."

Thank god at least for some things. As long as nobody busted me for driving without a license or active tags, I was coasting but okay. And for the periodic glance of a police officer looking at my license plates, I would 'borrow' the tag stickers off a neighbor's car (not good neighborly behavior on my part, but you rationalize that sometimes little evils help avoid bigger headaches).

But proof of insurance is one of those things that the State of Ohio wants to occasionally check up on and make sure you're still a good, responsible fellow motoring citizen. Luckily insurance companies all let you make your payments and renewals online so it was minimal risk for me to occasionally log in and keep those up so that I could respond to the couple of 'friendly notices' that the BMV sent me, asking to send in proof of active insurance coverage.

"I don't drive often enough to maintain much regarding a vehicle, but I want to make sure if I drive anyone else's vehicle or decide to go for a day-trip somewhere that I've got my insurance taken care of, in case anything happens."

He nodded. Another print-out. "You own a 1977 Chevy Vega, correct?"

"Yes. I inherited it from my mother when she passed away."

"You own no other vehicles?" I shook my head. "I didn't see the Vega parked anywhere in the vicinity of your store when I was at the scene. You weren't driving it illegally anywhere, were you?"

"I park the Vega in a friend's garage, since I don't have a garage space here and she doesn't need to use hers."

Another nod. "Who would this friend be?" I gave Gene's name and address and hoped he didn't go pestering her about my car-park arrangement. Gene was a retired schoolteacher who was tough enough that she didn't care that people misspelled her name as a man's spelling and liked it enough that she kept it that way. She wouldn't lie for me, and there wasn't anything to lie about—I no longer lived in the other half of the converted Victorian duplex down the street that she occupied, but I did still take out her trash and recyclables bins every week, and she let me use the garage at the back of the property because she didn't own a car of her own.

But if he started asking about my no longer living there, or if she'd noticed me taking the car out in recent times when he knew I didn't have it properly tagged or a license to drive it…I was probably only looking at some minor fines if it came down to an issue of driving with an expired license, but under these circumstances I didn't want someone like Hartsleg looking too severely into my day-to-day existence.

Yet I didn't dare lie on anything or get too cute with explanations. Clearly the contractor and car stuff meant Hartsleg had been doing some checking on me once my name came up in association with this case, and he was a conscientious man, giving more than plain due diligence to his work.

"You said you were visiting an associate when this happened."

"Yes."

"Would this have been the incident at the Segal-Shore gallery on High Street?"

Crap.

"There was a misunderstanding over that. I was there to meet with Mr. Segal and got into a minor fight with someone at the show."

"Was it over the damaged sculpture?"

Easy.

"No. Well, it might have been. I couldn't say."

"You couldn't say why you got into a fight with someone?"

"Not in this case, no. The guy attacked me, sir. I didn't start it. He didn't say why he did it. It could've been he was a friend of the artist and was mad about my falling into the sculpture."

"You fell onto the sculpture?"

"I was an idiot. I was actually talking to the sculptor herself and we were talking about various forms of art medium. Sculpture, painting, interpretive dance. And on that last one, I made an ass of myself, doing this little skip-and-kick number as a parody of a recent performance I'd seen. I accidentally fell into the sculpture there."

"Doing an interpretive dance?"

You are completely on your own on this one.

"A parody of one. Like I said, I was being an ass." I shrugged. "There was an open bar."

"And this man attacked you because of this?"

"He didn't say why he attacked me. After the accident I waited to speak to Mr. Segal. I wanted to try and smooth things over, make any restitution required for the damages, that sort of thing. While I was waiting for him, this guy attacked me. Maybe I wasn't the only one making an ass of myself."

Another of those infuriating nods. "Did you know the man who attacked you?"

"No. If I'd known him, maybe I'd've known why he did it in the first place."

"Did Mr. Segal know him?"

"I don't know. He was at an invitation-only event, so most likely."

"The man who attacked you didn't file any charges."

"We didn't have any real animosity or anything."

"He also refused to give any information on why he did it."

"Maybe he was embarrassed or had some reasons of his own."

"Are you a supporter of the arts or a personal friend of Mr. Segal's?"

"Friend."

"But you didn't have an invitation."

Just where the hell did this guy get all this so quickly?

"Detective, I have to ask: what does any of this have to do

with this poor woman being found dead near my store?"

"I don't know, to be frank." He closed the folder and clasped his hands together on the tabletop. "But when I come across a body on a property, and that same property owner's name comes up in association with a minor altercation reported at a downtown gallery in the same night, not to mention a few irregularities in the recent background of said same individual when it comes to things like having an up-to-date driver's license or vehicle registration. Not to mention keeping residence in a storefront that has not been open for over three years. Doesn't that at least sound to *you* like something that might be related?"

"I could see those things seeming to be odd coincidences. But coincidences *do* happen. Especially if you consider that I was at one location for one incident and the other had nothing to do with me in another part of town at the time."

"Did Mr. Segal seek restitution for the damages?"

Curveball questions. Derailment tactics. Even knowing Pinney and about a thousand hours logged in having watched police thrillers as a kid, I appreciated how they worked. You couldn't prepare for them. That was the point. And having no idea to what level of detail he'd done his homework, I couldn't risk embellishing anything. Anything he didn't already know, he could presumably check out based on what I gave him now.

Assume they know Dwyer's name then from the record. They must've gotten a report of the incident and your name from Ceyggan or whoever at his gallery handled calling the cops and having Dwyer hauled off. But if Dwyer didn't tell them anything, we can keep stupid on it. But the box cutter seems flimsy. Not great, but flimsy.

"Something you want to tell me?"

I shook my head. "No, sir. I was just thinking that all this seems strange but not impossible. Like I told you, the woman was around the store a few times in the past. I had to ask her once to leave the patio area because a customer complained about her panhandling him. But that was all. I didn't call the police on her or think it was necessary." A different angle opened to me. "Have you identified her? Does she have any friends or family that can…look after her? I mean…as far as arrangements or anything?"

"We have made an identification. But if you don't know her, then I really can't discuss it in detail, Mr. Flicker."

"You can call me John."

"All right. John. Thank you." He rolled the ballpoint pen an inch, then back. Forward. Flattened his hand over it. "Do you typically manage to keep your stories straight like this?"

"It's not a story." I let an edge creep into my voice, the right measure of annoyed-citizen. "I haven't done anything, sir. I appreciate you found this woman's body near my store and that there was an earlier issue involving me at the gallery tonight. But other than those things, I don't see why I'm sitting here going over a few instances of my being forgetful or lazy about my driver's license renewal or the fact that I got a little drunk and over-excited at the gallery show."

"Who was the woman with you at the gallery, John?"

"I think that's enough questions for now if you're not charging me." I resisted the temptation to fold my arms and instead forced my hands to casually rest on the table, matching his posture. I didn't look away from his stare. "I still don't see a need to call a lawyer, but do you have any real evidence that I'm involved in this murder?"

"Your fingerprints that you provided matched those on the box cutter."

"Of course they would. I freely admit that it's mine. I've had it for years. As to how it got there with the body, I don't know." That part was still bothering me, finding it with the body. Even though I don't leave fingerprints now, I didn't have any issue with that aspect; my fingerprints are still all over practically every inch of the store and its contents. "In the photo…just now…I didn't see anything that suggested there was even any cuts on her body. Was the box cutter used?"

"I can't go into the details of that."

"I'm getting a little tired of being the one providing all the details to *your* questions and curiosity. With all due respect."

"Do you engage in any recreational drug use?"

"What? No. I tried a little pot in college, that was all."

"Not even the occasional use of maybe some painkillers? Occasional migraine, maybe a friend gives you some old oxycodone they have in their medicine cabinet or something?"

"No. Why?"

"I suppose it would be too much to hope that if you've been this forthcoming so far, that you'd honestly answer that question?"

"I don't have anything to cover up or lie about here. I don't use drugs."

"But occasionally indulge in a little too much to drink?"

"Who hasn't once or twice? We all make mistakes."

"The sculpture was estimated by the gallery for the insurance bond over the exhibit at about thirty-five hundred dollars."

Highway freaking robbery, Soul snickered.

"But you weren't held culpable for any damages by the artist or the gallery?"

"I believe Mr. Segal remarked on it being insured already. He didn't ask me to make any payment on it. And I didn't see the sculptor after that."

"Sounds like you were very lucky. I'm not all that up on the art scene, but my general assumption was 'you break it, you buy it.'"

"I'm not all that up on the scene either. Maybe things are different from what a layperson would assume."

"May be."

"Do you have any more relevant questions for me, sir?"

He lifted his hand off the pen, plucked it up and jotted down something inside the inner sleeve of the folder. Looked over a sheet of paper again with very deliberate and slow consideration. Finally: "Not at this time." From his belly came a bleating tone. He reached down and plucked up a phone. Glanced at the screen, then at me. Put the phone away and collected his folder as he stood up.

I started to rise with him, but he held a hand out. "Please stay here, sir. There is another officer that wants to speak with you."

"About what?"

"Perhaps another of those coincidences. Please stay seated. Would you like anything to drink?"

"No, thank you." He left without further explanation.

I sat there and stewed for a little while. I relented enough to fold my arms and tuck my chin against my chest.

He's talking to another guy behind the glass.

I didn't move. *What about?*

One second. A shift as faint as the air conditioning blowing from the vent overhead.

I waited.

A minute passed.

The whisper came in my left ear: *Talking about you. And about some 'related issue.' There's some discussion about case overlap, I don't know the terms here.*

Anything distinct?

No. Whatever it is, I don't think we're going to like it. Something about cooperation in investigations.

Who's the other guy?

At a guess? Another detective. He's not uniform and I didn't see him in the building when we came in, so couldn't tell you if he's another CPD guy or what.

Never mind, then. We'll find out when we find out.

I don't like any of this situation.

What's to like? I'm sitting in a police questioning room while there's a woman in the morgue who was found at the bookstore, and before that we know she was kept prisoner by the Scots Brothers in a partially-electrified chickenwire cage with another lead-head who is unaccounted for at this time. And to top it off, they find my box cutter near the body and already had a report on file from that Dwyer crackpot about attacking me at the gallery. Am I missing anything?

Yeah. Get your tags renewed.

You're fucking hilarious.

I try, I try.

Try harder.

The door opened and admitted another rack-suited figure. This one was sporting a pepper-gray buzzcut about a size too small for his double-chinned moon face. He looked like he'd gone through some bout of bad illness, because his cheekbones and eye sockets showed a bagged look that wasn't just being overweight. Underneath the dark blue blazer and khakis he had a bunch of pens overburdening his shirt's breast pocket and a faint jingle of change or keys in his pants pockets. He carried his own folder, though unlike the CPD file this one was a dark manila-orange color and had black text printed across it with lots of various hand-jotted notes in the pre-printed rule lines.

"John Flicker?" I didn't rise or offer my hand this time. He opened his folder on the table before him. Clicked a pen into action. I nodded and he checked something off on a form in the folder. He had on rimless bifocals and made me think of the guy who sold me my first used car when I was sixteen. "I'm Deputy Van Gibbins. Delaware County Sheriff's office."

Delaware? What could that *be about?*

I felt a queer drop in my stomach. "Hello, Detective Gibbins. What can I help you with?"

He sat down with a gusty sigh, as if settling into a porch rocker on a summer afternoon with nothing more pressing to talk about than how late the paper boy was delivering the weekend coupon flyers lately.

"I need to question you in connection with the murder of a Mr. Rod Roscoe."

Then the quiver in my stomach became a complete seismic break.

26.

I stopped flittering and moving about and looked at Gibbins with sharp note of the orderly, soft wave-shapes that tasted like fresh coffee and furniture polish coming off him.

He's completely serious about this. It's not a trick or a new questioning tactic.

Body dropped his head, eyes wide and staring at the table.

Barely a whisper: "When?"

"Mr. Roscoe's home was fitted with a security system that included a 'panic button' option. Most of the rooms in the house were wired up so that in the event of an emergency the security company would be alerted, and they would call the police as first-responders."

He looked at the sheets in his folder to refresh. "At 2:43 yesterday afternoon, the security company received an alert from the system. The kitchen button had been activated. Police arrived to discover the house forced into and Mr. Roscoe was dead on the kitchen floor."

I thought about a cat sitting on top of a car, purring. I felt a sensation like someone putting a hand against my chest and shoving. Hard. But it had no body to absorb it, so the sensation rippled across me and seemed to find places to keep bouncing back and forth. Painfully.

We need to get out of here. As soon as possible. Whatever you have to say, or do, whatever, we need to get out of here and find out what the hell has happened in the last several hours. We need to call the Scots, we need to find out—

Shut up. I can't think straight with you hollering and bounding around and this guy is going to see something's up.

I fought it down and got quiet.

Body pursed his lips. "What evidence do you have to involve me?"

"When you were processed through intake here," Gibbins opened the manila folder and began to arrange papers inside, "you were digitally filed into the investigation records as standard procedure. Your name and information went through a standard filter of outstanding warrants, person of interest notices, kidnapping and child endangerment alerts, all that sort of mess. Detective Hartsleg has probably already explained that part to you."

That explains at least where he got all the cute registration trivia.

Gibbins continued. "Oddly enough, all things being... what's the word? When things seem to oddly go together at the right time?"

"Serendipity?" Body volunteered.

Gibbins nodded. "Exactly. All things being equal, we were lucky. You were getting processed in Columbus for this mess at your bookstore and the information screen rang a bell up in Delaware."

"May I ask a question, detective?"

Gibbins nodded, not looking up from his folder.

"Does it make sense to you? The idea that I would kill a woman and leave her body literally at my own back door, as well as within the same twenty-four-hour period run to Delaware to kill a man and leave him in his own home, with my name and incriminating evidence all over the place?"

Gibbins stopped shuffling papers. He looked up at Body and blinked those wet egg eyes at him slowly, like footage of a praying mantis cleaning its compound eyes with its forelegs.

"When I was in uniform, about two years into my work, I had a domestic call. A mother who was calling 911 for help because her son and his girlfriend were fighting in her basement about something and it was sounding more violent by the minute. A neighbor even called in on their own while my partner and I were en route."

"The property had a short arm's-long list of previous complaints. Noise, disturbance, but also suspicion of being a dealing point for methamphetamine and marijuana. No big kingpin lair or anything. Just another average Midwest dump neighborhood on the west side, little tract houses run to junk and a lot of people on pensions and disability blowing money on wheel rims and drugs."

Gibbins' delivery was as rote and squared at the corners as an old school anchorman delivering the next week's forecast and last night's sports scores.

"We were almost there when the 911 operator relayed through dispatch that contact had been lost with the mother, who had stayed on the phone with the operator up to that point. We put a little extra gas on and got there within a minute. When we got there, the mother and the girlfriend were dead. The girlfriend had already been dead a little longer than the mother. You know what he was doing when we went down to the basement?" Body shook his head. "He was sitting and smoking a pipe. Not anything illicit, though we found yards of enough illegal stuff on his coffee table and in the drawers of the kitchen for that not to matter. He was smoking his father's old cherrywood pipe with this sort of high-grade sweet tobacco, real quality stuff I guess was left over from before his dad died. He had his feet propped up on the table in front of the couch like there wasn't a thing wrong in the world."

"Underneath his legs was his girlfriend. He had one of his dad's old souvenirs. A Korea-era machete with a flat end, like a steel bar sharpened on one edge. Something his grandfather had brought back from the war there. He'd simply whacked her across the stomach and chest a few times before she went down and stayed down."

"His mother was on the stairs. The phone cord was broken, it was one of those classic twenty-footer jobs that went all the way back to the wall phone in the kitchen. But she still had the receiver in her hand. Her, he hit in the head. If things weren't bad enough like some piss-poor television drama, there was a prescription pill bottle in her name, empty on the floor. He'd taken a mess of her heart meds thinking he'd get a buzz off them. But heart meds and meth don't mix too well. Some psychotic overload."

"There he was. Didn't give us a bit of trouble. My heart was pounding probably twice as hard as his was by then. I felt like I sweat a gallon of water in the time it took to get in there, assess things, finally collar and bring him up to the cruiser. He didn't argue. Didn't even speak. Nodded and smiled at us as we came in hollering. Didn't even lose his mouth grip on the pipe stem while we pushed him down and got him handcuffed. At some point in the kitchen when we were getting him through the door I couldn't stand it and I slapped the pipe out of his mouth. He just smiled and nodded. My partner apologized to him. It was that surreal. That impossible."

He stopped and blinked the soaked eyes once more.

"I'm sorry to hear that," Body answered blandly.

"I tell you that because Ron Pinney vouches for you. Says you've been a help to him on a few things and that you always shoot straight by him."

"I try to."

"Hartsleg doesn't know you, but the read he had on you suggests you're a big pain-in-the-ass but not coming off as a killer."

"Glad I made a good impression."

He nodded. "But that guy's mom would've vouched for him, too. Even when she was on the phone with 911, she insisted she wanted the police to only come over to break things up, to get things settled between her son and his girlfriend. She wouldn't have pressed charges if he'd had a gun to her head when we arrived. And then there was the mess of drugs found at the scene."

The bottles. He's talking about the bottles in the kitchen.

"You found a lot of prescription drugs at Rod's house."

He made an exaggerated gesture of pointing at me, the *ah-ha!* motion. "Hole in one. So far, every one of them check out as legitimately prescribed to him. We're still waiting for confirmation from a couple of doctors' offices, but I suspect they'll all check out. But the amounts missing from most of them, considering how many had been recently refilled, suggests that he couldn't have been taking them all himself."

You can't tell this guy. He's in the day-to-day. He doesn't know anything to get this. You tell him the truth and you'll be locked up at least another month waiting for indictment.

No shit, Serpico.

"Are you thinking Rod was selling some of his prescription meds?"

"That is a line of thought, yes."

"And you figure that I was a customer, and maybe something went wrong or I tried to take a bigger helping than I was paying for and things got out of hand?"

"Another line of thought."

Body stretched out his arm. "Test me."

What? What the hell are you suggesting?

He continued, heedless of my hollering. "Take a sample of my blood and run it through whatever tests you have to." He drew back his arm. "Need a piss sample instead? Give me that cup and I'll do it right here, right in front of you if you want to be sure."

Gibbins wasn't fazed. "You may not have taken anything. You may not be using at all."

"Perhaps I was an angry competitor or a retailer for Rod, and we got into a heated negotiation?"

"That is an alternative to the line of thought."

"Detective, with all due respect, I'm not seeing this. I'm sorry about that mother and her son and all. I realize things like that happen and that when drugs or booze are involved all sorts of expectations go out the window. But you seem to be wanting to have your cake and eat it, too."

He shut the folder and stared back, polite and curious. "Go on."

"The presumption is either that drugs were involved because I took them or because I dealt them. But if I took them, you're telling me they could have made me so crazy that I went bonkers, killed Rod and presumably this woman, and was so further distorted on their influence I didn't think twice about trying to properly dispose of the evidence. On the other side, if you take my blood or urine which I'm perfectly willing to submit and find no physical evidence that I'm using, you can fall back on the presumption that I'm clean, sober, and a drug dealer who killed Rod for some professional dispute. Yet if I'm clean and sober and that self-interested, why would I have not had presence of mind to make at least some nominal attempt to cover things up? They're mutually exclusive. I'm either too drugged and out of my mind or I'm too sane and clear-headed. The total facts don't fit either way."

Gibbins regarded Body a few more beats where all I heard was the tick of the wall clock. "You have a good eye for inconsistencies."

"Don't tell that to any of my friends."

He re-opened the folder and regarded something inside. "Not that you have many of those, do you? At least, you seem to definitely go for quality and not quantity. Ron says you're strange and not always forthcoming but you haven't lied to him or shirked giving a hand. Even when it's not entirely wanted or needed."

"Call me an over-eager good citizen."

"What I consider you is suspect." Gibbins was no longer a blinking owl-bear figure. His lips were tight and there was a color in his features that wasn't entirely from wearing a jacket indoors. "Your clever logic notwithstanding, there actually is such a thing as stupidity in criminals. People have been perfectly level-headed and still done remarkably idiotic things when confronted with the scene of their crime."

"You would know better than I would," Body allowed, "but wouldn't I also potentially be protesting, screaming, demanding a lawyer, talking about my rights or your badge or whatever? I'm trying to be cooperative, sir, but I also didn't have anything to do with these deaths. Rod was a friend. Not the closest friend, but no one I would ever see any reason to do anything to him. So I'm basically waiting for your questions and sitting here, trying to be patient and wait it all out to see what happens."

"I don't know you," Gibbins answered. "You may have some friends here and there who would swear on a Bible that you're a boy scout, but nobody really buys character witnesses anymore. And if think you're not involved in something because you didn't personally kill anyone, you certainly never attended any law classes in college, did you?"

"I didn't graduate college."

"So more the pity. But in police work, especially homicide, when a body is found on someone's property, and another body is found less than twenty-four hours with that same person's fingerprints and other evidence of their presence as well, we don't consider that the mother of coincidences. We consider it an argument that they're involved in some way."

I shrugged. "I can't help you there. I didn't know the woman and Rod was a friend I visited recently."

"Any particular reason why?"

"We were friends. But I hadn't seen him in over a year. He kept to himself a lot."

Gibbins nodded. "Three mail drops. We already spoke to the girl's mother, the one who brings his mail in every week. Nothing there. The mother and the girl were at the doctor's, as a matter of fact. Two hours while the mother had a cast put on a foot she broke on the steps to the backyard this morning. Guy lived in a big house, no roommates or spouses that we can find, basically keeping the world a good five hundred yards minimum from him. Big house, paid for outright, a trust set up with a law firm in Dayton to pay the taxes and utilities like clockwork. Neat and tidy, except for the kitchen having a table that looked like a Pfizer R&D lab trash bin was emptied out on it."

"Rod had a neurological disorder. It caused him a great deal of pain. He took those pills, in extraordinary amounts. I even remarked that I wished he'd cut down or stop altogether when I visited."

"Over-eager good citizen again?" Body shrugged. "Mr. Flicker, you understand we can hold you for twenty-four hours simply to have you available for further questioning and perhaps fill out an affidavit for your account of your visit with Rod Roscoe, right? You're at least up on all your television cop dramas enough to know that is true, correct? I know Hartsleg reminded you of your right to have an attorney present and you've so far waived that."

"Yes."

I felt a slick of cold run over me. *We can't afford to have you in a cell for the next day. Those Believers could try for Sarah again, or Mister Sharkdoll might try.*

Calm down. We need to see where he's going with this.

"Are you sure you don't wish to consult with legal representation? Or perhaps amend your testimony to better account for these things we've discussed?"

"I can't tell you any other story than what I've already told you. It's the truth."

"Somehow I feel that Pinney had you pat: you're telling me the truth. I could decide to play TV detective and drag an old polygraph kit from the basement or get our guy at TechTruth LLC to come in here with the fancy digital galvanic response readers and get you all strapped in and you'd read stone-cold true the whole way. For as long as you stuck to the questions you've answered. But it's not the whole truth, is it?"

Gibbins was a day-to-day person. No superhuman powers or second-voice consciousness floating around his head. But he was intimidating all the same. Like Pinney and a few others we'd met, he had obviously gotten into law enforcement because he not only believed in a little peace and order, but because he had a genuine rapport with people that allowed him to read their reactions as clearly as doing a Google search for movie times, right down to the ticket prices and the theaters-by-zip-code. Details did not escape him often.

"If I seem like I'm hiding anything," Body spoke carefully, "I apologize. The truth is…Rod and I…had a private relationship. One that I don't feel at liberty to…disclose a lot about."

Gibbins regarded Body with another blink. "Were you and Rod Roscoe intimate?"

"I'd rather not say."

What the hell are you talking about?

Calm down.

"You are not obliged to tell me of course," Gibbins sighed. "You *are* protected in your private life. You may keep such intimacy to yourself, I can't compel you to give any details." A flick of eyebrow. "Nor am I inclined to want to hear them."

He doesn't like it. I can't believe you're pulling this.

A lot of people aren't openly homophobic but they still don't want to hear or think about people who are gay or their relationships. If it makes him not look too closely at some of this, so much the better.

"Nor do I think they would be germane to this issue," Gibbins continued. "At this time, I do not believe we have need to hold—"

A rapid knock on the interrogation room door. Gibbins hardly had time to turn his head to reply when the door opened.

And, like any classic joke set-up line, in walked a fairy in a pinstripe suit.

****

I saw Body close his eyes and let them roll under the lids a full spin before opening them to take in the new arrival.

He was tall and thin-built. His suit had the kind of neat and tailored lines that, combined with his build, made you think the suit had almost been cut and sewn around him. It didn't look like there was an inch of fabric to spare to let him do anything but stand and walk, no sitting or bending possible. The suit was an expensively smooth-looking navy material with faint white pinstripes. Underneath it he wore a matching waistcoat with a small gold fob-chain poking out of the watch pocket and connecting to the waistcoat by a glittering decorative fob-latch. The whole thing was clashingly off-set by a salmon-pink button-down shirt underneath, with no tie and the top collar unbuttoned. His footsteps had the confident clocking noise of thick wooden heels on well-made leather shoes.

He walked in with one hand free and swinging, the other in a pants pocket. He wasn't walking into a police interrogation office, that posture said. He was strolling through a museum gallery and had been looking for the men's room.

The face above the salmon shirt was a windburnt face, all grins and fluffed blonde hair. Eyes that really squeezed with his smile. He didn't give Gibbins a chance to put up his guard but walked straight to him and before the door's hissing piston had shut the room up again he had his hand out and Gibbins was bewildered, reaching out automatically to have his hand pumped with enthusiastic rapidity.

The air around him had a confusing motley of what looked like chess board shapes melting and flowing, reforming further down into a new board, then the squares scattering and fluttering as startled birds. They were blue and gold and then shivered out of sight, only to start up again a second later. There was a taste of quality vodka mixed with the smell of steak and high-gloss sour car wax sputtering around him.

"Anthony Dario, Detective." A voice that matched his presence. Relaxed, unhurried. He released Gibbins' hand. "I'm Mr. Flicker's attorney. Sorry I didn't get here sooner. John's bad about giving me a heads-up whenever he's helping the police."

Gibbins had started to rally back. "He's not exactly helping us, Mr. Dario."

"I know, I know," Annan waved a hand. "He's just an amateur, a busybody type. That's why I'm here, to smooth over any misunderstandings and help him properly answer for any interference he's caused. Did he cause a disturbance or interfere with an investigation?"

"Mr. Flicker has not been charged with anything."

The smile dropped. He looked like an enormous shocked kid, the one who runs down the stairs at Christmas to find the tree gone and no decorations up on the fireplace. "What? I'm sorry. I was led to believe there was some problem here, that's what John was here for."

"Mr. Flicker is being questioned in relation to some recent discoveries, one of which was on his property—"

"Oh, yes, yes." Dario pulled out a smartphone and made little clicking ticks at its surface with his thumb. "The woman whose body was discovered on the sidewalk, correct? Awful thing. Unfortunately, I'm afraid the police may have acted hastily in having my client here on such grounds."

"Grounds? He owns the property the woman's body was found on—"

"Actually, he doesn't." The smile came back, sunny and as certain as a cloudless sky. "The body as I have determined, was actually found on the sidewalk, which is city property."

"Right outside his store!"

"Coincidence is not evidence, Detective. I'm sorry to disappoint you, but Mr. Flicker had no association with the woman and there are at least three other businesses established in relatively short distance of the body's discovery on city property. Have you detained the other property holders?"

Gibbins breathed. "No, however—"

"Then Mr. Flicker has been more than helpful coming in to answer your questions, despite that rather tentative association the police have drawn. With all good intention, I'm sure. We all want a murderer to be caught and secure the community—"

"Do you know this man?"

Gibbins snapped this at Body. Body's eyes flicked at Dario, then Gibbins.

"He's my attorney."

"From what firm?"

"Detective," Dario interjected, "I've come to assist Mr. Flicker and make sure he's given his due—"

"He'll get whatever he's due," Gibbins cut back. "There is also the matter of a homicide in my jurisdiction—"

"I apologize! I'd wholly forgotten that aspect of it!" The grin widened and it was a positively reptilian amusement. "We don't have a member of the Columbus Police Department present at this interrogation as required! I'm glad I caught this before things got too out of hand and affected the validity of your investigation!"

Gibbins' face had been in turns surprised and then sour. Now it went past sour and curdled, the wet eyes looking pink-rimmed.

"Mr. Flicker was informed of his rights and—"

"Yet hasn't been charged with anything and is only here to assist as much as he is capable, having had nothing to do with the actual crimes."

Gibbins' face had pinked to match his eyes. Body looked back at him, so he was pinned between Dario's open stare and Body's.

"I will notify the officers of Mr. Flicker's release and contact information," he spoke as with teeth wired together. "And permit you time with your client."

Dario nodded with warm concession and even opened the door for Gibbins as the latter stormed out wordlessly. I watched the air shapes playing their little melt-and-meld games as the lawyer sat down in the vacated seat.

"Nice work," Body remarked.

"You won't think it's so nice if you see my bill." The attorney put the smartphone down on the table between them. "If Gibbins checks too thoroughly with the Columbus police about exactly where on the sidewalk they found the body, it could be trickier. But for now they've goofed a little too many ways to get away clean on it. They offered you legal counsel?"

"Yes."

"But never once mentioned a charge?"

"Suspicion of murder, maybe some nonsense about drugs. The only thing they really have me pinned on would be out-of-date tags on my car or an expired driver's license."

"They were planning on doing a standard fishing tank hold. Putting you in and using every minute of the 24 hour window to make their case solid. I don't know what Delaware's attitude is on this, but if Gibbins is any indication I'd say it wasn't good."

"I didn't do anything to anyone."

"It wouldn't matter to me if you did. I'm not here to be a priest or bartender. I've already got people processing your release. Since nobody wants to say you're charged or an actual out-and-out suspect, seeing as how they don't have anything more than circumstantial evidence for now, they're not considering it a bail issue and you'll be released on your own recognizance. They'll want you to stay in the city limits and notify them of any travel plans. They'll either have something more substantive and bring you in or hope that you don't say another word if they go on another suspect."

"Who sent you?"

"No one of consequence to this matter." No hesitation. He proceeded to open documents and review things on the screen.

He's not a day-to-day.

What does he look like?

Living. I peered at the space around him, moved around and to his back. Those melt-and-reform shapes were faded as he focused on the phone screen. Instead I saw a familiar sort of wave form...a kind of slow cosine flowing... wanting to turn the air around him into something else...

He's a Faede.

"Did Ceyggan send you?"

He gave Body a stock-still glance. "Ask me no questions I tell you no restraining orders," he grinned.

"Is Anthony the real name? It's not, is it?"

"Between you, me and the wall, it's Annan. You *do* get around a bit, don't you?"

"I don't like being obliged to people more than I can help."

He put the smartphone down. "Then you're operating on a really stupid, not to mention irresponsible, basis."

Body's eyebrows rose.

"Look, I know about you. Don't ask how, just trust that I do." Dario leaned forward, elbows on the table. "I know deep down you've got this hero mentality, this romance novel crap about woe-is-me, only-I-should-pay-for-my-sins kind of loner nonsense. And don't get me wrong," he held up a hand, "I'm sure it does wonders with the women. But you don't live in a monastery out in Iowa. You're in a major metropolitan city, part of a much larger community than yourself and your little bookstore. You have agreed to help some rather big players in that community. You're going to get help whether you like it, or want it, or not. And that's because it's not always about what you like or want. Mostly it's about what you need. People have a stake in how you're working this. Can you wave your hands and have that door open and let you out?"

He paused for an answer.

Body shook his head. "No, of course not."

"Well there you are. I, as a matter of fact, can do that. And I'm doing it now. So accept the help and get back on your romantic hero way."

"What do I owe you?"

He rolled his eyes. "Look at me. Hell, look at this phone. Do you think you're the one getting my bill?"

"I'd rather spend twenty years paying you back than whatever Ceyggan or whomever is paying you will want from me in trade."

His eyes narrowed. I could see that past the salon tan and hair treatments, there was a pallor, a kind of dull flint that sparked around him. A *glamour* that was not just the usual Faede genetics at work, but a genuine ability to deal with people and negotiate. I thought back to the weird melting-checkerboard shapes and wondered if that related in some way to his organization and focus, impressing itself on the very air around him.

"Would you really do that? Take that on yourself to avoid owing someone? Even for helping, offered free and clear?"

"There's no such thing as 'free and clear.' I've learned that the hard way. More than once."

"There really is no expectation to trade or any *quid pro quo* here."

"There never *is* any expectation. But it tends to come up eventually, all the same."

He regarded Body for a long look, then uncorked the bottle of sunny smile again. "I don't think I'd like you for very long. But you're stupid and stubborn in the right ways, at least." He went back to his smartphone. "I've taken care of the paperwork. Nothing to sign or anything. And in about a week they won't know you were ever even in here. On paper, at least." The smartphone chimed. "Okay, next case. Another delinquent, another dollar."

Body and Dario rose together. Before the attorney could leave, Body put out his hand.

Dario glanced at it, not smiling. Then accepted it with a healthy shake.

"Keep your nose clean. And if you have any other dirty appendages, keep them to yourself." The phone chimed again, this time more insistent. He answered it and left the room.

****

Body signed off on his release. Dario's assistant, a lime-lipsticked girl with cat's-eye frames in black plastic and emeralds, handed him her card with Dario's personal cell number scribbled on the back of the impressive black-embossed-and-gilt logo thirty-pound linen card. Body put it away with other recently-acquired business cards: the contractor's, Jennifer Yu's...

We're starting to really collect a better class of paper junk, aren't we?

Body didn't leave via the front lobby, though. He turned to the precinct building main offices and administrative services.

I flew along with him to the elevators, then down the corridors. *What are you doing?*

We just wasted a bunch of time being treated like Mark David Chapman or an Al Qaeda suicide bomber...I'd just like to hopefully find out a little more about what the fuck this is all about.

He steered us to Pinney's cubicle on the main Homicide Investigations section of the officers' floor. Pinney had his coat around the back of his office chair, shirtsleeves on a yellow office shirt rolled up to his elbows. His chocolate face was screwed up in concentration at his computer screen displaying emails. The desktop looked like he had been trying to bankrupt the copier room of every piece of spare copier paper they could give him to print anything or at least use as half-torn scribble-and-doodle sheets.

Body hadn't said anything at our approach. But as he leaned against the outer cubicle wall and gave it a faint creak Pinney dropped the pencil he'd been holding between his lips, letting it clatter to the desk. "Whatever you want, Flicker, I'm way too knee-deep in this to bother. Call me in a couple of hours. Better, a couple of days."

"Ron, I could really use some help here. I need to know what happened to Rod Roscoe."

He spun around in his seat, looking up at me with the same look he would gave when he thought someone was cheating at a card game. A flapping of his hands at the empty chair in the corner of his cubicle opposite his was my invitation to take the seat.

"I dislike sneaking around on official investigations to which I am not an official investigating party, sir."

"I don't want you to get in trouble, but I need to know what happened to him. I need to know who was involved and if there's any better evidence than the nonsense that those guys had me in here based on."

"Hartsleg already is giving me the stink-eye when we talk. Things I'm so much in your corner that I'm practically holding the spit-bucket. And Gibbins isn't much different, though I haven't worked with him before so it's more mutual-cop professional courtesy attitude from him. I tried to do what I could to seem detached from this, only vouching for you as far as I could with respect to the help you've been on past cases, but I couldn't risk making a bigger stink about things and seeming to be in cahoots or whatever."

"Cahoots?"

"Or whatever. But giving you case details, if you're not involved in this—"

"I'm involved, man. No doubt on that. But I'm not the killer."

Pinney pulled out his phone from his pants pocket. Clicked it on, finger-swiped a couple of screens. Then he held out the phone, screen towards Body.

I could see the photo. It was dark, somewhat blurry, but still clear enough: the picture of the lead-head woman that was taken at the Scots compound.

"I almost can't think to ask how you sent me a photo of the same woman who was found dead later on your front door."

We have got *to call the Scots.*

No. The response was as firm as fresh-hardened concrete between us. *First we settle some of this with Pinney.*

Pinney pressed the case. "Do you know where the other one is? This young man?"

"I wish I had a better answer for you other than 'I don't know.'"

Pinney stared at Body, then returned the phone to his pocket with slow, deliberate care.

"I don't like you being involved yet somehow not responsible. Seems like that's the only way you and I end up meeting like this. With you, deep in the shit but somehow utterly not-to-blame. You know how often we see real criminals in here that try to argue the same thing? Maybe I should simply let Hartsleg and Gibbins do their little dances and have you for an overnight slumber-party in a holding cell."

"I didn't kill anyone. But the body was found at my place. Rod...I had just visited him a few hours before somebody killed him. You have to give me that much, that I'm involved but it's not looking like I did any murders."

"I've never seen you as a murderer type, no. But you certainly do a fine dance with the edge of what's right, don't you? You'd be a real son of a bitch if it had to suit the moment for you, wouldn't you?"

"Please. Rod Roscoe. Did Delaware not let you have any information when Gibbins showed up and wanted time in the room with me?"

"Gibbins is already bitching because he's gotten some unusual phone calls and emails his way."

"Unusual how?"

"Corporate lawyers. He wouldn't give names, but he said one was a major international bank and brokerage house. A couple of big-dollar tech firms from San Francisco. Even a company that runs the casino, the new one west of downtown. You wouldn't have any idea about why these company lawyers and security heads are bugging Gibbins about a murdered shut-in doped on painkillers, would you?"

"If I had to speculate, and if I had to try and put it in layman's terms—"

"Oh, please feel free. We layman are such idiots after all."

"I didn't mean it like that."

Go easy. He's edgy and he tastes like burning rubber right now. Really pushed to his patience here.

"Rod got stipends from various companies. He was a consultant."

"For corporate law and security?"

"In a manner of speaking. You know those urban legends, about guys with perfect systems for beating the casinos and how casino owners pay them to stay away from their business?" Pinney nodded. "Rod was a kind of version of that. He was paid money from one company or another in regular installments so as to not use his skills against them or their investments."

"Do you think it was one of these who might've had him killed? Decided it was cheaper to take him out of the picture than to keep paying?"

"Not sure. That was how we met in the first place. That casino you mentioned from near downtown? When it was going to open, Rod approached the principals there. Made his pitch. They decided to call in some negotiators from Youngstown, if you know what I mean."

"Hired help?"

Body nodded. "He hadn't expected anyone to get violent. It never happened before. Big-ticket companies find it much cheaper to pay things off than deal with lawsuits or...bigger risks they can't take to court. A friend of a friend got him in touch with me. He wanted help dealing with the Youngstown folks."

"Mob?"

"Let's say a family-oriented company."

"Why did he get referred to you specifically?"

"He'd heard I was someone who wouldn't be scared of dealing with these folks."

"How did that go?"

"I wasn't scared of them, if that's what you mean. They tried to negotiate things a little less in his favor. I managed to give their hired negotiators a reason to reconsider and take the message back to their corporate masters. They ultimately chose to go with Rod's proposal."

"So these lawyers and security people—"

"Are probably calling and emailing Gibbins because they want to try and find out if any documentation was left behind. If Rod left any records of what he had on them that they can nip in the bud. Maybe they were worried he had some kind of 'deadman's switch' set up. The usual threat. 'Anything happens to me and the stuff you wanted me to sit on gets sent to the Dispatch with a bow on it.'"

"Did he have anything like that set up?"

"I wouldn't know. I didn't know the deeper details of how he made his money or managed things. You would probably need to contact his lawyer to find out. I think the lawyers handled everything for him. He wasn't exactly on-the-ball with a lot of day-to-day details, given his condition."

"About that. What was his condition, exactly?"

"Neurological. It caused him a lot of pain. That's all I could tell you."

"All you *could*, or all you *will*?"

"Either way."

He stared at Body for a moment. The air around him was softening, losing the burnt-rubber taste-smell and becoming a more default warm-pine-floor-and-cup-of-coffee aura that he typically carried with him when he was on the clock.

"I realize you operate in circles that aren't quite in-the-norm, but why do I get the distinct hunch that Roscoe had some arrangement that the companies wouldn't traditionally call a 'consulting' gig, and that you know all about it?"

"The old kid's rhyme, man. 'Ask me no questions, I'll tell you no lies.'"

Pinney called up a login screen on his computer, did his dance of fingertips clacking on keyboard keys to access case file displays, called up the appropriate summary screen.

"Gibbins already questioned you on the main time and facts of the thing. Otherwise it seems like simply a fairly brutal home invasion thing."

"How was he killed?"

"Still waiting on autopsy report. But the preliminary assessment showed no death by trauma or gross injury. All the damage done to him was post-mortem, thank god."

"Damage?"

"Broken legs. Broken ribs. About half the neck ground to dust. Somebody killed him in some way we don't yet know, maybe strangulation or he suffered some heart failure from all the pills. But once he was dead, they definitely worked him over. Treated his body like it was a   soccer ball and they were kicking goals on every shot."

God damn *it. We could've* done *something.* I floated over the desk, feeling the hum and slither of electrical signals and internet data packets sliding back and forth from the computer on the desk. The overhead ventilation ducts rattled and the smoke-and-oil-in-water blooms of different temperature fronts blew through and around me as I took it all in. *Damn it, we should've known somebody could be following us, even out there. We should've been more careful about all this.*

Body bent over his legs, elbows on his knees, hands dangling between his thighs, looking at the dirty linoleum.

"Jesus."

"He was missing some of his teeth," Pinney read. "Early assumption is he swallowed some of them, but we don't yet have the full autopsy to confirm It was difficult to tell because his teeth were mixed with pills. A lot of pills. The initial assessment is at least four or five heavy prescriptions were chewed and in his system from his mouth to his stomach."

Body rubbed his eyes.

Jesus, I can't believe this is happening. I moved around the room, staying close to the area of the desk but not wanting to stay in one place. If I kept moving, maybe I could somewhat avoid any of this being entirely real.

"Nothing appears to have been taken from the scene, though there were so many prescription bottles all over the place that it will take some time in checking everything out with his physicians and pharmacies to be sure there isn't a bottle of pills gone."

"But Gibbins already knows it's not about pills anyway, right? Because if it was about pills and drugs, the place would've been cleaned out. You could've just tipped the kitchen table over into a pillowcase and had a year's black market goods right there to sell and run off with."

"What is this?" Pinney's voice had gone from report-reader to something bland but tinged with up-tilts of unease at the ends of the sentences. "A couple of months ago, you're running around the city while everybody else is going crazy. I come out to help you, and meet up with people even more weird than you are that you're gallivanting with...then nearly get killed fighting some sort of...I don't know what. I spent two weeks on medical leave trying to figure out a clear memory of what even had smacked into us. A tornado crossed with a pissed-off brewery machine?"

"Close enough assessment, I'd say."

"I told you that I don't like having my chain yanked, even when people doing the yanking think they're doing it to pull me out of the line of fire. Is this something that's going to blow up in my face again?" He was tapping his leg, and I saw it was the same one that had taken a rough twist when the Jennyripper had attacked us at the Stained Glass Brewery.

"I don't know."

"Are people after you?"

"Why do you ask?"

"Well, to start with: I don't buy this Dwyer's report at all. He said nothing, denied nothing, confirmed nothing. Had some lawyer pay his bail and left." Pinney regarded the photocopies on his desk. "You at an art gallery for one thing. I wouldn't it put it past you to have a normal nightlife. But you show up at a gallery, vandalize a piece of work on display, get attacked by a totally random stranger before everything gets hushed by the owner? Are you and Segal in on something together? Something that Dwyer might've stumbled upon?"

"I'm helping Segal out with something, but we're not technically working together. And no, I think I can safely say that Dwyer's attack was one of opportunity, not related to that."

"Really? So how did this guy know you'd happen to be at this gallery show?"

"I couldn't guess."

"You don't go to any efforts to hide yourself. I know you think you're probably a real cloak-and-dagger type at times, but you're not."

Pinney opened the right-hand bottom drawer of his desk and reached into a tabbed folder that hung amongst the packed assortment. Withdrew a much-folded-and-re-folded piece of paper, flattened it out carefully on the desktop. Turned it so Body could see it.

"I need to know something, John Flicker."

As I made out what it was, a sensation of chill met up with a warm front of weird affection, almost like nostalgia for a much-loved hangnail.

Time to start thinking of cute answers again.

It was a photocopy from the Franklin County Department of Health and Human Statistics. I knew it even though before now we'd never seen this particular document before.

"Are you the same John Flicker listed here?" Pinney tapped the entry for NAME. "The one who, according to this, died on this date?" Another tap, at the DATE OF DEATH entry field.

I stared at the photocopy. I could tell it wasn't an officially-released copy, because it lacked the faint imprint of a notary stamp into the paper.

"Where did you get this?" Body asked.

Pinney stared as though he was still waiting for an answer rather than the question given as response. "You'd be surprised how much trouble I had to go through to get this." Pinney sat back in his chair. "I had done some minor checking on you before, when we first met. Nothing major. Your local business license. Lapsed, but nothing in the Better Business Bureau, no lawsuits against you. No outstanding tickets or warrants. A couple of parking tickets, but they'd been paid a while ago. Almost about to drop out of the system, in fact. But with the recent goings-on…I thought it would be a better idea to find out exactly what the hell I've been dealing with."

"Don't you mean 'who' you've been dealing with?"

He neither smiled nor frowned. Merely continued staring down at the paper between them. "This is public record. Or at least, birth and death are supposed to be public records. Even available online. Most folks, I get on the phone and call the county office up, the one down there on the riverfront, and ask for the stats they have. With this, though, I couldn't find an active entry. They dug around and found nothing. So I escalated my request." He folded his arms over his chest. "That's when it got very intriguing. I was told that I had to file a formal warrant request, as if this were part of an investigation. You normally only need that kind of thing for credit card or bank or phone records." A shaking of his head, the brow furrowing with a kind of bemused interest. "I went ahead and put a request in. Rejected. Three times. Since you weren't part of an active investigation under my assignments, I couldn't get it done. Then when this monster thing hit, and I was put on temporary medical leave, I was able to convince someone to put a request in for me as related to your being there during the attack. That got me another step or two in. But then the request was rejected. Again. Due to the investigation being found 'resolved with no further remark' on the files. That is when a case is considered either solved or so cold or so indeterminate that we can't pursue a suspect even if we figure they're guilty for lack of acceptable evidence."

He looked up at the paper, then at Body. Body didn't give him any response or reaction. Merely stared back.

The warm-wood-and-coffee senses were cleared away.

Now something that surrounded him was...brighter? Thinner? It was like...laundry dryer heat, mixed with sandalwood? What the hell?

Was this the sensation of someone steeped in...what? Honesty? Integrity? Clearing the air, in a literal and metaphoric sense simultaneously?

I have no clue where any of this is going except maybe straight down to hell in a hand basket for us.

He rocked in his chair with a groan of springs. "So I tried another tack. Not one I like, but I went down to the office myself and intimated that maybe I was doing some under-the-table investigating. Nothing official like an Internal Affairs arrangement. Just something that might involve murderers using old, deceased identities to avoid pursuit by law enforcement. Maybe I suggested that someone in the office had anonymously tipped me that someone in Health and Human Statistics was selling information to establish identities for said purpose. They got nervous on that one. But not so nervous to call my supervising officer. But when they looked, what did they find? No entry. Not denied, not blocked, not special-request-only. But gone. It had been taken out of records a while ago, by a master entry ID that didn't leave a log record."

Looking at Pinney's broad, impassive features as he recounted these details, I was feeling very unhappy at the prospect of us being at the receiving end of this scrutiny. And I could easily imagine how it must've felt to the poor clerk or administrator that he'd turned this particular charm upon.

"That had me stumped. But the oh-so-helpful records clerk mentioned that all the new digital files are required by state law to have backups. A new term I learned: 'geographic mirroring.' You know that?" Body shook his head. "It means that when there's a digital archive of something, they're required to have it automatically and regularly back up everything to another server located in a different area, usually a whole other state, so that they're not both victim to the same kind of earthquakes, power outages or whatever-else might hit a given area."

A tilt of his head, the bemusement becoming a ponderous thoughtfulness. "So the clerk contacted the IT people who handle the state archive backups. It wasn't easy and it took another couple of weeks' waiting to work it out while I had to go back to my official pile of work to clear. But finally, they have a print-out made and faxed to the clerk, who then called me and I went and picked it up so it wouldn't show up in the precinct email or fax records."

"You're a thorough investigator."

"No, I wasn't." He sat up with a squeal of his chair, leaning in close. "If I'd been thorough, I would've done all this before I so much as spoke to you after our *first* meeting. And after that, we didn't deal with each other that often, but when we did I found you tended to be the go-to guy that had a line on the weirder stuff in this town…the strange stuff that otherwise never gets a solution or lead anywhere. I *should* have officially filed a report of inquiry on you. I *should* have done this digging before. Now are you this same man, or are you somebody masquerading as him and hiding out in his old store?" The look he gave made it clear: give an answer, one way or another, but no jokes and no prevaricating.

Body looked from him to the paper.

He already knows enough. This isn't going to exactly blow his mind anymore than we've already done it up until now. We owe the guy.

Body sighed. *Yeah but he's also dedicated. If I tell him… what if he decides that's one thing too many? What if he does put this in official record and start digging at it? We can't afford to have all this get out in the open.*

I drew in close to his side, speaking into his ear. *Never mind it getting out in the open…have you considered what could happen to Pinney if he does pursue this, if we refuse and he goes barreling after us through official channels? What do you think* Justin *or* Ceyggan *or* Mr. Q *or any of the others in this town with a vested interest in us will consider the only viable solution to his prying? Maybe they'll call on some Youngstown assistance of their own.*

"No. I am not someone else masquerading as John Flicker." Body reached over and picked up the paper, looking at the bold-print statistics entered into the various fields. Height, weight, eye and hair color...

"You are the same John Flicker as is recorded being dead on this paper?"

"Again: yes."

"I'm already regretting a lot of things, so I guess I'm all-in. I'm not going to ask the how's and why's...I probably wouldn't grasp half of it anyway."

"I don't have a lot to offer on that subject regardless."

"How about I stick to practical matters: what are you?"

"I'm not being flippant when I say that I genuinely wish I knew."

"Try a guess."

"Have you ever heard the term 'doppelgeist'?" He shook his head. "It's trash German wordage. It means literally 'double-ghost.' It's someone who has died and somehow come back, but as two separate beings. One is a physical, tangible body. The other is an invisible, inaudible spirit component." Body tapped the piece of paper with his free hand, making a rattle as it shook in his grip. "Both of them have the exact same memories, feelings and everything originating from the person who died. But they operate as separate independent beings after becoming a doppelgeist. And that is where any official or reliable knowledge about this stops." Body put the paper back down on the desk. It held about as much interest for us as looking at a greeting card for a stranger's birthday.

"This is what you've been since...this?" Pinney pointed to the print-out. Body nodded. He rubbed a hand across his mouth. "Are you like those others? That woman that was with us at the brewery?"

"Dhara? No. She's a vampire. There are all sorts of different types of person in my circles. I happen to be a doppelgeist."

"I'm not sure I'm in a suspension of disbelief to yet accept there are even such things as 'vampires.'"

"As they say in science, the great thing is it doesn't need

your belief to be true."

"Who else is like you?"

Body almost wanted to say Sarah's name, but kept the instinct clapped shut in a small mental box as soon as it tried to peek out.

"Nobody that I know of. Doppelgeists are kind of rare, even for the Under."

"You said that you operate as two distinct beings—"

"And that's where I come in to the picture," I sigh-thrummed through Body's throat and out of his mouth.

Pinney startled, his head snapping back on his neck as if avoiding a narrowly-missed swing of an axe at his face. A hand slapped down on the desk, ruffling the papers. The air around him had soap-bubble pops of calm as he tried to regain his control from the reaction.

"Christ!"

"Sorry. That tends to happen the first time anyone hears me."

"If you're both John Flicker, how do I refer to you? Either of you?"

"For convenience, you can refer to me as simply 'John,'" Body replied. A flap of his hands. "As for my other, we use the term 'Soul.' Or 'Body' and 'Soul' to differentiate whenever it's needed."

"Which of you is the real Flicker?"

"Neither. And both. John Flicker is dead, like the paper says." Pinney's eyes widened but I softened my voice as best I could manage, and even with the bizarrely metallic-thrum echo-chamber aspect to his speech, with familiarity there was visibly an amount of acclimation already taking place. *"Both of us are basically John Flicker, but…it gets complicated."*

"I'll bet."

"I'm going to lay this all out on the table for you," Body continued. "Dead men don't have a lot of legal status. I can't go get my license renewed or go to the hospital or basically anything if it requires my showing up in public for any medical tests, or anything that could involve too many legal entanglements of checking my identity. That's why we've lived in The Nookery since this started: the store is in such a state of legal limbo that we can maintain the property and simply pay the few bills related to it without having to answer a lot of questions. But with our old house, my landlord runs a five-year credit check every time I'd go to renew the lease, and I couldn't be sure that something wouldn't come up that raised any flags with him. Or if I tried to move anywhere else. Plus when this started I came to realize…I didn't really need a lot. So why pay two rents? So I closed the shop and started living in that back room that I fixed up like an apartment."

"So how did you hack the Health and Human Statistics computers?"

"I didn't. I can't. I wouldn't have the faintest idea where to start. Until a few weeks ago my computer was a six-year-old iMac and I can barely set up my email without the program's help walking me through it. This…I didn't know about this thing."

"But you don't strike me as all that surprised."

Body shrugged. "Those people you already know about? The ones that have an interest in me when I'm working on something? I would guess that they're responsible for helping cover my trail. Looks like one of their experts missed this, though."

"No doubt. Is this why you do the 'side jobs'?"

"Yeah. The porn stuff. Not all the time. But I found out that it was the only way I could not have to get an official day-job sort of entanglement, same problem these days as licenses and rental agreements. I'd get screened or reported to the IRS on some W-2 and get into too many situations where people might start wondering how a dead guy is still paying to Social Security. I saw an ad, answered it, and it's been handy for occasionally picking up extra money with no questions."

Pinney stared at Body with a newfound curiosity. As if meeting a man who had recently lost a limb and he had the natural overflow of curiosity, the questions of adaptation and adjustment. "How do you know you're dead? I mean, I'm not nitpicking your certainty, but how…I mean what if this is some delusion, or you're throwing your voice with some sound-mixer gadget in your pocket?"

Body pulled out his pocketknife and snapped open the

main blade. In his head, I could weakly see pictured light switches. Shutting down. Power off, lights out.

Before Pinney could protest, Body put his free hand, palm-up, onto the desk, and drew the blade deep across the palm. A dark welling of blood sprung up with an eerie sponge-cake rising motion along the wound.

"What the hell!" Pinney snatched at one of his drawer handles, probably to get tissue or something.

"Wait."

The detective stopped pawing at the handle and looked at the hand.

The blood rose...pooled...and stopped. One stray drop managed to leak away but was so shallow it died away to a streak of red along the middle finger.

The cut was already closing, the blood dropping in like time-reverse film.

Pinney didn't blink, his eyes were fixed on the phenomenon. After a minute of silent watching, the cut reverted to barely a red ink-line along the palm. As Body flexed the fingers to show everything recovered, the red line faded and there were no other lines on his palm other than the old fortune-teller ones. He withdrew his hand, closing the knife and returning it to a pocket.

"How can you do that?"

"Another mystery I can't answer. But this body seems capable of healing from virtually any injury."

He pulled his hand back.

"I am no longer a living human being the way John Flicker was born and how everybody else is." His recitation was static, his eyes never flinching from Pinney's. "I don't need to breathe, eat, sleep...I don't shed skin cells or leave any sort of fingerprint oils. No scent, as far as dogs and other animals have reacted that I can tell. I don't have a heartbeat or anything else. Though I can fake those things. I can will my body to breathe, my heart to beat, the body temperature to go to normal or whatever."

"I guess I wondered how it was a regular guy like you could be caught up in the crazy stuff you deal with and still be walking around."

"Walking around, yes. All the other stuff? Not so much."

The phone in Body's pocket rang. "Sorry."

Pinney kept quiet as Body answered the phone and I pulled in close.

"It's me." *Ceyggan.* "It's time. The Teaghlach have agreed and you have to get here now if it's going to happen."

"Right now?"

"Yes. If you're going to do this, you've got maybe twenty minutes to get your ass out here."

"O-okay."

Body grabbed a pen off of Pinney's desk. With no better inspiration for a surface to write on, he flipped the photocopied death certificate over and used the back to jot down Ceyggan's hurried instructions. As soon as Ceyggan heard him confirm he'd written them down, the line went dead.

Pinney watched the entire exchange. When Body returned the phone to his pockets, he leaned back in his chair again. "People to meet, places to be?"

"I'm sorry I can't stay to try and clear this up any better for you."

"I'm still sort of digesting the idea that I've been getting help from a dead man these last few years."

"Trust me," Body stood up, "it's far less to take in than *being* that dead man for the last few years."

"Is this latest thing you're running off to, is it part of all this? Is it tied to the Roscoe murder or this girl's body?"

"I don't know. It might."

"Is this going to be a situation where I end up having to arrest you? As if maybe I shouldn't already be doing so?"

"If you have to arrest me, go ahead." Body stood still, staring Pinney down. The detective's brown eyes looked back with that hard look he gave when he wasn't sure if he should be angry or put off, and was instead achieving a measure of both.

Finally he shook his head. "Go. I need to think about things for a bit. Maybe even re-evaluate my professional associations."

"For my two cents, I've appreciated our working relationship.

No hard feelings if this is all too much to deal with."

"Too much? Almost getting killed by some screaming banshee-monster in the Brewery District, *that* was too much. By comparison, dead men and vampires are getting downright dull around this town."

I couldn't read anything off Pinney to tell if he was making a joke or some sort of resigned end of it. Either way, we couldn't hang around any longer to sort it out. He didn't even comment when Body folded the directions, with the death certificate copy printed on the front, and took them with us.

27.

I followed Ceyggan's directions to an address on the far east side of town. I was almost to Pataskala, pretty well outside of downtown limits, and starting to wonder how much farther along Broad Street I was going to be driving when I saw the tiny service road that I was looking for and took the right he'd instructed.

Another good half-mile brought me to a strip-mall-like cluster of office building suites and a golf pro shop…and then behind these, away from the main road, a personal storage rental business that was my destination.

The Vega's engine started to play choppy and I thought it was going to die before I had a chance to park it.

"Not exactly lit for business, is it?" The place was dim to the point of being lost in the night against the city sky backdrop, save for a couple of low-yield copper-tinted arc-sodiums that probably had been installed back when Nixon was lying to the press.

To you with the meat-eyes, sure, Soul replied in a nervous sigh. *But this place is broadcasting something like the baby that gamma rays would have if they humped cosmic radiation.*

What is it?

Let me see…I'll check my handy Guidebook to Strange Invisible Emanations. *I don't* know! *Maybe it's an illegal Time-*

Warner Cable bootlegging operation somewhere here, who could tell? It's even pushing back against me a little... can't you feel that?

I could, now that he brought it up. I wondered briefly if this feeling—similar to the sort of drifting-breeze feeling I get sometimes with Soul's movements close to me—was how it might feel if you strayed too close to some massive magnetic field powerful enough to start tickling the iron in your blood. But then realized it was far too subtle for that. And unlike Soul's furtive blips across my physical radar, this was directed. It moved towards us, the Vega making a few extra clickings and shudders before shutting off into its uneasy sleep. As I started to walk towards the last block of dayglo-orange-doored storage lots, the tide of the sensation shifted and started to tug/push slightly right-forward-to-back-left of me. West to east, in a very ragged way.

Remember the river in Oz? The one that the Scarecrow and everybody tried to ride to the Tin Woodman's castle?

Yeah, I nodded. *The one that would randomly decide to switch directions and start going back up-hill whenever it felt like it.*

Except I don't see any handy trees to grab and hold onto if this thing starts to get really pushy, do you?

I consulted the piece of old receipt paper I'd scribbled the information onto. *Row E. Unit 2112. Two more rows down from this one.*

I squinted my way along and Soul had to tell me when to stop because the paint for the numbers on the units was so old that much of it had faded or flaked away to near-unreadability. I saw padlocks heavily furred with rust. *How long have some of these units been rented? And when was the last time anyone visited their storage unit in these rows?*

Soul moved along the corrugated-metal doors. *This isn't even a Yale or Kryptonite lock...what is this? Armbruster Steel? Does that company even exist anymore, you think?*

The sign wasn't kidding about 'long-term storage available.' I wonder...

I could sense the distance widening the way you'd have a

sense of a car behind you backing away slowly. I frowned. *Hey don't do that, man, it's not cool—*

I just thought I'd have a look to see what's worth keeping here so I—this one is empty!

A shift in that tether-thread between us.

So's this one next to it!

So they're empty. I looked around, fully expecting in this ideal Murphy's Law moment to have some flashlight-wielding security blast at us with their ten-D-cell Magnum. *Leave it alone, man, maybe they're unrented spaces. Stay out of other peoples' stuff.*

The whole row is empty! Not a single one of these in use!

Astounding. You should go join those jackasses on that TV show about storage auction bidding. You could clean up.

He didn't hesitate or reply to the insult. *The next row is empty too! How much you bet me the entire place is totally cleared out? They can't all be empty at the same time, can they?*

They can if this is a sucky storage rental place. Look around, we're not exactly in the thick of the city. Most people probably don't even know this place is here, if they only have business with one of the businesses down the road getting their golf clubs polished or something.

Exactly. Most people would go by and even if they came out for some business this far, they'd never notice this place. Except for the occasional drug dealer looking for an inconspicuous drop site or something.

So the place is empty. Could also be out of business.

No, it's not. That lightboard underneath their sign is up and running and in working order. It showed the current time and temperature. If they're out of business, somebody's still paying for power. And those light poles are still working. But this entire place is empty.

And I didn't like standing there amidst the rows of said empty storage units. A giant stage. That was the feeling, with the cracked pavement and weeds sticking out of the cracks, the rusted padlocks and flaking paint…flickering light posts…the whole thing had a silly feeling if I stopped and considered it.

But enter into the equation the wafting motion that underlay every nerve ending around the site and the silly evaporated.

In the Under some things live or die by appearances. It made sense that if we were engaging in some clandestine meeting with Ceyggan's head people that it would be somewhere out of the way where they could be assured of privacy. Or an advantage.

After all: a stage isn't a stage, unless there's an audience somewhere watching you perform.

"You're here."

I nearly jumped at the sound of Ceyggan's voice so close without warning. Turning around, I saw he was looking out at me from one of the cinderblock wall sections between storage unit doors.

Walking over, it became clear he was leaning out from behind a tall, narrow panel flush with the wall, artfully weathered and surfaced to match the rest of the cinderblock but in fact moving aside into a recess reminiscent of hanging-track closet doors or shower stalls. As I joined him and he slid it shut, though, there was a solid *cluh-thunk* that told me it was not pasteboard or plywood. A rapid series of mouse-small clicks around the frame of it told me that automatic bolts had socked into place.

We stood in a narrow darkened space, lined with cinderblock wall and lit from the staircase immediately in front of us. There was a gleam to the walls picked up in the light. Soul sighed ahead of us. *This place is definitely not run-down this way.*

I followed Ceyggan—who was remarkably not bouncing and talking a mile a minute about new music or porn—to a basement space floored in shiny concrete and ceilinged with end-to-end fluorescent bars. This lower chamber resembled the upper rows of storage spaces, with the exception that it was about a third of the length of those above, and the doors here were all sporting either keyless entry numeric pads or, in the case of the last couple towards the far end from us, what looked like little panels of glass about two inches square, set above the handles of the pull-tab doors and glowing with refracted ruby light.

I pointed. "Are those biometric scanners?"

He nodded.

If they're protecting the stuff in these units this heavily, I'm not going to go looking to see what's in them.

Good policy.

At the far end of all the shiny surfaces and laser readers was a single steel door, the frame of which was blistered with large bolt-heads, matte black with some sort of rubber-looking finish. The door was of a matching lightless black tone.

There's no handle.

Nor were there any high-tech scanners or keypads. It was hard to entirely tell it was even a door for lack of any visible hinges or supports. Only the fact that it was set at ground level, dead-center of that wall and seemed to have the traditional dimensions of a door even suggested it had any function as such.

"I take it we have a choice between Door Number One and Door Nothing Else?"

Another nod.

"Is this all under penalty of death or something?"

Under the fluorescent lights anybody can look bad, yet without his glamor to cover it up, Ceyggan's features looked as if someone had made them entirely out of mortician's putty. A yellow shift to the normal health of his face, and there was something that I thought might be the pinkish-indigo equivalent of bruising for a Faede's eyes. I could make out a pimple along his jawline.

"The Teaghlach agreed to this, but there's…it's not clear what that may mean."

"Are we meeting them or not?"

"It's…you'll see in a minute. Maybe." He shook his head, frowning. "I can't clear it up much better than that. They've agreed to let you come to them. Whether or not they'll respond, or if this is a meeting to try and help or…I don't know…it's not…" All words failed at that point, and his eyes merely regarded me with a bewildered lost look.

"Are we going in there for a discussion or to be eaten or

something?" The tidal pull was stronger down here, but there was still no visible sign of it. If it had been something making the hairs on my body move, or electrify, or the phone in my pocket suddenly died…anything concrete and clear to look at, point to, say that happened, I could've felt somewhat relieved, at least knowing the world around me acknowledged the influence. But the maddening sensation seemed to be just for Soul and me. And while it was pulsing harder, it was still washing and waning back and forth…and the direction was now much clearer, definitely a line straight out from that odd door.

"When you go in there, stay in the light."

"Okay."

"This isn't optional. You stay in the light or they might think you're trying something. Don't put them on the defensive."

"I understand."

"Shut up and listen, don't 'understand,'" Ceyggan snapped. I stared back at him. "I'm sorry, sorry…you have no idea."

"Just tell me the rules. If things go wrong none of this is your fault."

"You can't make that sort of promise," he barked, but there was no bite in it this time. He wiped his forehead, his cheeks. His eyes were fluctuating and rolling around like a bird with cats lined around its tree. "Stay in the light. No sudden moves. Speak when you're spoken to." He expelled a heavy breath. "And it's going to hurt."

"What?"

"You'll…you'll see. I hope. Just be ready, okay? Like when you take a deep breath and hold it before the doctor puts the needle in, you know what I mean? You need to expect that it can hurt. Try not to let it surprise you or make you panic."

"Hurt like how? How much?"

He shook his head. "I have no idea. But they…the Teaghlach said it could hurt. You aren't Faede, so there's no…what's the word? Like when you can easily talk to someone their way, in their own time?"

"A rapport?"

"Yeah. A rapport. You don't have a rapport with them, at

least not yet." Another loud breath. "They wouldn't even agree to try this except that the situation is bad. Plus you...never mind. We're wasting time with this."

"Plus I'm nobody, right? I don't matter in any significant way if things go really wrong and splatter me across the state?"

"It's not like that at—"

"Relax. I'm assuming this risk, so if it fails then I'm the proverbial ass, not you."

Ceyggan tilted his head to indicate the door and walked ahead of us. I felt Soul stay low to the ground near my shins, not circling or rushing ahead but staying close.

I like this about as much as I like the idea of trying to pass through a sewage pipe filled with slaughterhouse leavings.

Settle down. I'm sure we'll have plenty of reasons to panic soon enough.

As we got close to the door, there was a sharp expulsion of air somewhere, hissing like a garden hose on high. I felt a blush of air waft against my face, smelling of...nothing clear. Cinnamon? Old, spoiled fruit like peaches left in a cellar? Sweet but dark. I took a shallow sniff and immediately was hit with a rash of fast associations: tzatziki sauce, bitter and creamy on Greek salads...sprigs of mint and garlic mustard weed crushed in your nostrils...an unpleasant under-aroma of meaty, bloody smells of unwashed things hanging on hooks...

He stopped at the door and turned to me. "Please don't do this, man. I'll try and help you out whatever way I can. But not this, okay? This isn't some crazy from the bayou this time. I was a complete fucking idiot to even suggest this in the first place, I shouldn't've said anything."

He's not lying or full of shit. There's a refrigerator stink coming off him like high school kids in a Halloween haunted house. He's jacked on whatever the Faede have for adrenaline.

For the first time since we'd met him, this prince of the Faede was sweating and showing real terror. Not for himself, but a sincere dread on my behalf if I continued on this path. He wasn't fishing for weaknesses or advantages, not trying to get some circumstantial upper hand on me. He flat-out didn't want me to go through that door.

I shook my head. "I appreciate the warning. But I can't turn away at this point."

"I can't…I can't help you past this point, you know that. The Teaghlach won't even let me stay in the room when you start… when the conversation begins. There's still a chance to say no to this and we walk out. I'll eat some shit for it and have…have apologies to make. But not like this. Not if you go in."

"I understand. Open the door."

He turned and put his hands on the door. Held them there for several seconds, his head tilted to the side as if listening for some cue.

I was about to ask what were we waiting on when he nodded at the door and stepped back, moving behind me.

Another smaller plume-hiss of air, and the door moved forward. Not hinged and opening along one side, but the entire thing coming forward, like a file cabinet drawer. As we moved aside to let it fully open, its passage revealed that at each corner, top and bottom, was a grease-covered, shiny steel piston affair. This was where the hissing came from until it stopped a few feet out from its frame, the piston shafts going back into utter darkness.

I looked at Ceyggan. He nodded forward, indicating the darkness.

I didn't move. "This is all really cool Mission Impossible prop work and everything, but are we going to do this? Is this really what we're playing at, this big-dark-chamber-and-secretive-society nonsense like I'm meeting a Secret Pope or something?"

Ceyggan's eyes widened. "Don't…"

"Relax. I'm trying to keep this as friendly as possible, that's all."

"Do you remember how we met?"

"Yeah."

"You were dealing with that, what was it? The collections guy?"

"Fredericks. The guy from Louisiana who called himself a vampire hunter. He nearly got away from the club if you hadn't tripped him up."

"And he would've cut my head off a second later if you hadn't clotheslined him to the floor."

"I'm not up for trips down Memory Lane."

"I'm really sorry, my friend." He wouldn't look at me, only peer into the dark beyond the open doorway. "I'm sorry and hope you walk out of there when it's done."

"Thanks."

I turned back to the darkness.

Not welcoming. Not warm or humid, but a sense of something inside…even as I couldn't get any sense of dimension beyond the doorframe.

Maybe we should take him up on the offer, Soul whispered in my head. *He's terrified and I can't say we're far behind him. We need to regroup on this, maybe this is overkill just to find out—*

<forward/NOW/enter/come/IMMEDIATE>

I was forced a step back, clapping a hand to my forehead as if someone had rapped at it with a toy tack hammer, the little genuine kinds with real cedar handles and steel hammerheads.

There was a sudden explosive ping over my left eye and the one word that crackled across my few connecting thoughts for a moment was *stroke stroke stroke having stroke this is what stroke feels like.*

It was a voice. Maybe it's how planets talk to each other when they pass each other's orbits in the perpetual night.

I could feel movement around us, shifting back and forth more rapidly in time with it…but though it was a voice, it wasn't words.

I can't go in there. The tether to Soul shook and vibrated between my temples as he was struggling to stay near me, not to bolt and fly straight up, through the stone and soil and whatever else merely to get to the sky, the open air, away from this place.

The pain subsided immediately. I lowered my hand, expecting to open that eye and see some red film from burst blood vessels. I blinked and found both eyes clear.

I looked at Ceyggan, who simply stared back at me, eyes

still wide. I didn't have to guess that he'd picked it up too.

"Go in," he whispered breathlessly. His chest rose and fell with the rapid depth of someone caught in a deep nightmare, unable to wake.

"I can't do it."

He didn't shake his head, but the way his lips tightened and made faint wrinkles in the skin around his mouth, the gesture was clear. "It's too late. They've spoken. They've acknowledged you're here. There's no more offers I can make to take you out of here until it's done, now."

"No, Ceyggan, seriously, if that was simply a hello from this...I can't—"

The voice was dead and merciless with utter surrender. He closed his eyes. Maybe it was more polite than him turning around and putting his back to me.

"Do it before they ask you again. They will, if you wait too long. They'll demand. Louder."

Cold that sank down into the nerves from my balls up to my spine. The dreadful anticipation that made me think when a man is kicked in the nuts and has a few milliseconds to ponder what's coming before the sensation of cramping agony actually manages to rocket up to the brainstem and start really pounding its stakes home. I wanted to protest more, turn around and leave, but I knew that voice-wave could reach me well before I could even reach the bottom stair.

Fear can motivate you to run away from pain. Greater fear of an even greater pain can be a better motivator to stay where you are. Or step forward.

I felt Soul lag behind as I began to move around the door, stepping over one of the piston shafts to enter.

<all/whole/COMPLETE/you>

Another slam into that meaty place over my eyes. I didn't raise my hand this time, but winced and gasped. I put a hand out to the doorframe and wavered.

I think that means both of us have to go.

Tough titty. That thing felt like getting—

Hit in the head with a hammer. I know! *I feel it too. Get your ethereal ass in here with me, we're going in together or not at all. And if it hurts you as much as it does me, neither one of us is making it out of here except through this door, apparently.*

There has got to be another way—

It's too late for that. On that much I believe him. You know that, too. We're stalling, that's all.

Hell no I'm not stalling, I want to run out of here and not look back, period.

We agreed—

<FORWARD/IN/before/PRESENT/NOW>

The 'NOW' of that had the added fillip of another pulse-tap against us, one that felt like it had a tapered icepick tip to it compared to the dull thunk of the previous summons.

The hiss-roar of air re-pressurizing and the door pistoning shut behind us decided the matter very quickly, and as the dark slammed down onto us I felt the severity of it all sink in.

We had been offered to meet with the elder order of the Faede. The big Powers That Be amongst that eldritch group. We had accepted the offer, and even against the advice and pleading of the same person who had mistakenly made this offer, we had held onto our stupid hero-image idea of how to resolve all this for everyone. We had so miscalculated the scale of our own importance or value in all this. Now there was the dark ahead and the ringing-thumping of its after-echoes vibrating through my skull and Soul at the same time.

I'm sorry and I hope you walk out of there when it's done.

It became chokingly clear he hadn't voiced a wish that I'd be able to *at least* walk if I ever left this chamber.

****

Soul stayed around my shoulders. *He said stay in the light, where is any—*

A snap-crack of some circuit being made, like someone near had flipped an old-fashioned mousetrap switch, and a sputter of electricity declared 'let there be light.'

A pool of light, an ellipse of spotlight about five feet

around, appeared ahead of us. It came from a light mounted somewhere in the ceiling, but looking up I couldn't make out a clear source. It seemed to form a cone that kept going up, and up, and disappearing into some sort of smoke clouds drifting up there.

We didn't come this far down the stairs. We can't be this far underground.

Soul stayed around my chest, swirled at my neck. *If we're even anywhere that could be called* underground, *any longer.*

A drip of water echoed.

I stepped forward into the circle of light, my hands out and hanging at my sides.

No sudden movements, no threatening-seeming motions.

Another drip of water, followed by two others in staccato haste. A puddle somewhere, echoing weakly in the massive chamber.

The dripping sound became more frequent, as if someone were twisting a spigot handle and letting more water flow, but where…

…I realized it wasn't water dripping in some dank corner. It went from staccato to an insectile humming that rose, quavered.

A shiver in the air around my neck, a scarf made of icicle chips that was Soul tightening around me. *Oh god, the air is like piles of brick, but bricks made of dry ice and deep space radio echoes…I can't see more than a few feet ahead of us…are you* hearing *me? I can't see ahead in this!*

My eardrums felt leaden. My jawbone seemed to gain ten pounds. The back of my skull suddenly was made of some sort of warming, inert metal that was making it harder to hold my head up on the champagne flute of my neck.

It's not talking to us, it's/they're talking in us, through us, around us…oh shit I feel like I'm a box of paper clips shoved into a paper jogger…

<hhhhhh>

Not a sound and not a thought. An impression that was the vibration of the air around me, bone conduction through my skull but also somehow memories being gleaned and culled quickly from my back-brain.

\<her-hell-whuh-ttt-sss\>

Think of sounds of letters and words like the audio equivalent of a hostage ransom note, those movie notes where the letters and numbers are each cut out of different magazines and newspapers to make a random hodge-podge of fonts forming the final message. I could hear echoes of my friends, family, old classmates. A susurrus blender-whirl of movie stars and favorite television character catchphrases. All of them being ransacked and hastily composed into phrases.

\<hhhhulll\>

If this is all it's going to say we're gonna be here for twenty years before we've finished a 'hello.' Or we're going to explode.

My eardrums popped.

\<hhhellooo…ghost-thing-PERSONNNnn-man-beast\>

"Hello?" My voice sounded tiny, pressed through a phonograph needle and relayed through a rusted copper wire.

\<ffff\>

\<fam…family-gather/COLLECTION here\>

The Teaghlach announced their arrival. I blinked furiously for a few seconds, and as my eyes adjusted a little further to the darkness around the cone of light, I began to get the weakest glimpses of our host.

28.

The Teaghlach voice was this amalgam that somewhere in the mess of sound and white-noise achieved a bizarre synergy. It became a voice that you would think you'd hear if you could ever strike up a conversation with an abstract of some feeling, like the embodiment of how people lay in bed at night and start to slowly panic when they think of the inevitability of dying. A voice-sensation that to me had added flavors.

Woodsmoke and burning oil, bonemeal blowing in a sulfur wind off a desert dune baked in a heat wave.

They spoke to us in shades of blue and the black of aged blacktop pavement. Heavy traffic, long use, cracked and broken voices that were trying to swallow a tablespoon of raw cinnamon and choking, gasping to ingest each syllable. Broken shards of old daggers buried in graves of long-gone fighters in wars nobody had names for anymore.

Dagger-shards…and the teeth of great beasts that had fossilized well before my kind had evolved from the lowliest of basic mammal forms after the last great extinction.

In the dim, I heard/felt a shift of something that made me think of massive cranes. Earthmovers with tires wider than a man's height. Mountains shaped to curve like the hinged hind leg of a gazelle or tiger. As it moved, air was pushed away in slow, lazy clouds.

The far end of the room opposite the way we'd entered, I could tell there was something there where before there'd only been shadows and space and dust. Being this limited was new, though my recent memory-jaunts helped buffer me better than if I'd been raw and new to it. I could treat my vision more as if it were the old, physical me looking through the kind of limited eyes Body had.

Something was out there. Filling the space and making me crazily think of Indian pueblos made of shifting sand and fleshy, low grass hills like burial mounds in ancient Celtic lands. Shifts and twists…kraken motions, jellyfish tentacles the length of tapered bridge cables swaying, swaying in the dim. Tasting and testing every sensation. I tried to ignore that some of the tentacles were twitching and twisting and pressing like play-doh to lengthen towards us, towards the pathetic little dime-window of light we were keeping to.

You are different, <ghost-man-thing.>

That was the closest thought that could frame around what it actually said, when my mind attempted to decipher the mix of tastes and sounds and phantom sensations moving through us into a coherent set of something as simple as English, sentences, understandable communication. Some sound/force/tastes it emitted simply didn't use syllables or phonemes, not even pheromones or vibrations to completely express themselves. There was an unnerving sense of *extra* and *more* to its speech, so much that every so often when it lapsed away from comprehensive words, we only got those impression-jumbles.

Even used to the ephemeral as I was as a Soul, it made me feel almost solid again, trying to listen to the wind talk and the sky grumble as the earth was making up its mind whether or not to quake and swallow us whole.

It is not where you want to be, or how you want to feel, when talking to things in the dark.

<Disturbed-bothered-angry-sad> *we are. One of our*

<larva-young/pride/JOY-legacy> *is broken from us now.*

"I'm sorry for that." Body bowed his head.

Why are you here <spirit-strange/smoke-man/ DOUBLETHING>? *You do not* <mourn-miss/desire/REVENGE> *for us. You were* <summoned-sent-dispatched/invited/ DEMANDED> *to find the source of this pain and its* <motive/ REASON/why-because>.

Aching…I felt trapped, bottled inside those word ideas…I saw myself as being some sort of transparent sweater, and they were unraveling, unknitting me and pulling the thread of me away, to re-weave me into something else, something simpler and more brutal and it hurt so much it was all I could to stay in place, to not panic and try to flee. To stay around Body's form and try to use it like a sort of makeshift anchor, a point of reference to remember why we were here and what this all meant.

"I am sorry to come when you are in pain and loss." Body spoke slowly, measuring the words carefully. There was a shiver in him that I could mirror in my own incorporeal way: listening to these things speak was like willingly diving over and over into a swimming pool filled with old blacksmith anvils and barbed wire remnants. "But I am trying to find out what happened, both to Diatha and to others I know who have been hurt recently."

We do not follow the comings and goings of <humanity-under-all/DAYLIGHT/living-small>.

"I was led to believe…you might have a way of obtaining what Diatha experienced. Before her loss. And share with me. So we could help."

In the cold beyond the small pool of light around Body, the air shuddered harder. There was something I could only make out as a lithe, frightfully graceful flutter of a wing-leg-claw shape the size and length of a 747's wing, but curled inwards like a sickle. A baby-bird's massive wing in the horn and ivory of a saber-tooth tusk, and the space around it was actively pulling away, shivering back from its motion.

<Diatha/child-being/SELF-MORE/out-within-family>

The air around Body became a stone mass, the shapes

of normal activity slowing, hardening. It went from a feeling of activity to a sullen, concrete weight. Something, or some things, were suddenly looking at us very, very hard.

There were several seconds that might have been anger, shock or simple deliberation.

...you want us to <violate-rob-implode/PLUNDER> *our own* <young-gone-bright/LOST-TO-DARK/loved> *for what they felt in their final moments?*

The air got more still, and in the black space ahead of us, I picked up a larger mass than before, rolling with a slow, sickening tidal motion. It was the feeling/sight of something swallowing in its own belly, vomiting out its mass into a sort of sea-cucumber wetness, shiny and glinting in the dim. The bulk of motion suggested an entire beachline of shore at high tide, falling and tumbling on itself. Like watching masses of stormcloud mating with maggots.

There was a low hissing, scraping on the stone floor. What sounded like a wind tunnel purring through a gelatin-filled firehose sucked and exhaled around us.

It faded a little, down to an arrhythmic jackhammer wrapped in felt.

You ask much, <man-shade/DREAMER-COPY>.

Body's ear showed a faint trickle of blood beginning to seep down to his collar. I was feeling the effects in my own way, the vibration/burning/churning sense of the things' speech pushing and tearing at my sense of self every moment.

"I know," he nodded.

You ask to be part of something much <greater-larger-/BRIGHTER/wider-higher/OLDER-burning> *than yourself. This has never been done with anyone* <not us/OUTSIDE/unworthy-unborn/DEAD-not/un-belonging>.

Another roll-twist in the dim, and this time it was bulbous, hints of spikes and glistening scale, rolling and smoothing out to become a gigantic...eye? Bulb? Like the pitch onyx glare of a pitiless, giant crab taking us in. The suck-and-sloth breathing went loud again. Body shuddered and blinked.

We are in serious *trouble here.*

He grimaced. *No kidding.*

Minutes clunked and tocked past. Body swayed on his feet while I kept fighting an urge to let myself be blown apart like so much dandelion fluff, silver wisps into the breeze of our host's massive presence. All the time, the shadows kept mutating and reforming into nightmare suggestions, things from where ocean fish are afraid to go, and cave things deliberately go blind to avoid ever laying eyes on. Curls and slithers of meat crackling into bone shards that became crowns around heads of immense mouths, eyeless and gnawing on their own lips until they would sudden splash, as liquid as water, to cascade back down into the roiling flesh.

If it hadn't been so electric around us, I would almost have though this was the equivalent of what a shapeless, amorphous god-mass does when it's alone and bored: taking 'playing with itself' to a new dimension.

It's deciding how it wants to crush you and make a paste.

That sounds like an optimistic scenario.

The chudder-rattle of breathing slowed.

Suddenly there was a crushing blow, like being slapped upside the head by a cyclone's debris, a stray length of tree trunk borne by the wind.

Body collapsed to his hands and knees. The blood trickling out of his ears pulsed, grew thicker. His nose began bleeding from both nostrils. He kept his eyes clenched shut.

I could hardly keep myself moving, keep my sense of self intact…I was crushed against the floor with him, feeling inexorably pulled towards the ground like iron fillings above a massive electromagnet.

Images and sensations ramped up to concert-level noise, then went further. This was more than the Wall of Sound, a megalithic blast of ideas and suggestions…

…deep in the dark and the cool, soft waters, the slime and soils of the primordial…shapes…the tentative feel of membrane walls, feeling out the environment.

Too much noise. Too much tearing apart into new cells, new structures. Adapting, evolving, too stressful and too untrustworthy. To break apart, to form larger and form numbers, too risky. Cancers and tumors and evolution of competing cells, clusters fighting to be supreme in the tidal pools...so much noise. No bones, no claws, no fur, no spine no nerves...light and lightning.

More. My brain was pitifully trying to collate, collapse, categorize...

There was some other things hinted at but I couldn't even begin to absorb them in any great detail or depth. Something about quantum shifts...about partial dissolution into some sort of sixteen-dimensional space; a tesseract mind that was never entirely focused in our three-dimensional perception, and bypassed Time altogether to exist in a safe sort of pseudo-state of matter that never fully accepted depth or mass or volume, could only be expressed in exponents of dream and algebraic equations of eons of pain and love and loss and so much there...so much...

So easy to get lost here.

This was a living pile of superstring reality, a membrane in the brane universe fractures that had lived not quite on Earth and never quite in Time...we could see a future here if we stayed longer, let it swallow us and put us in a special place amongst the Oneness...

*..no...*Body's gasp in my thoughts that I mirrored. *No... keep us to us...they're not us...*

...remember Annie hugging us in the room above her parents' garage. Remember Dad making pizzas and Napoleon frowning no that last isn't us. Hold onto us...damn it, hold on to us...remember that girl we took to prom, remember when mom died...keep it to us, they can't have us.

Why would you risk this <boon-request-demand-taking>?

Body opened his eyes, looking at the floor. The whites of his eyes were a rich pink, oxygenated and throbbing. "I'm just...I'm trying to find out what happened. To try...and make it...right."

...swallowing oh yes become part no longer be apart come in, swallow and be taken, the tides are so soft and cool and forever you can taste the flavor of the big bang from the corner of the

haunted house that is god's empty mansion and this is but one room of many dimensions/mansions oh god get out of there—

A crack exploded through the concrete floor between Body's outstretched hands. Concrete dust plumed up and through me, settling on Body's back and shoulders. He crushed his eyes shut.

No no back off of us, do not take us we don't want remember keep us to us they can't have US GOD DAMN IT—

A chip of concrete flew up and immediately was pulverized in mid-air, the dust flowing away from us, out of the light and in little loops and whirls.

A sense of being jerked away from the light. A feeling that was silence and calm so noisy and loud after the cacophony that the Teaghlach had shoved into our throats.

The thing hadn't expected this. The floor cracking, the crack went from us all the way into the darkness...but the crack was more: it was a breach in more...sixth-dimensional possibilities. Somewhere in some far part of never and might-be, the Teaghlach had just gotten punched in their figurative head by our reflex response.

A sigh. The tidal pressure relaxed and Body could raise himself off his hands into a hunched position, knees to the floor as he kneeled.

Shocked quiet. A few shifts, uncomfortable and making the air tastes-feel like the smoke off a burning tire factory.

We are <apologize-sorry-sad/ANGRY/hello/GO-AWAY-SCARED>.

That last was the clinch. *Scared.*

You are <curious/HUNGRY/selfish-gleeful-sick>?

"If I understand you...no." A swallow. Another bubble of fluid, now yellowish-clear, coming from the ears. And Body was starting to buckle at the small of his back as the pressure kept waxing and waning in odd spurts. "We are not wanting this for...some gratification. We want to...genuinely know what...happened to...try and stop it from happening...again."

More sigh and hiss noises. Considering? Contemplating?

This has never been done <other-time/BEFORE-

wayback-old>.

But more than what they just said, I felt an underlying untruth, a half-tale they weren't finishing.

"I understand."

No, you cannot. What you are asking is a <sharing-breaking-melting-fusing-swallowing> thing.

That half-truth...I could only sense it in my mind's eye... sadness. Sadness and a night sky. No, was that really a night sky? The stars were too beautiful, too bright and ochre-tinged and everything was swirling, breaking apart but rejoining an organic whole...

...the stars in a night's sky and pain and there was the briefest touch. A tinge of regret, a bittersweet taste of something so heartbreaking. Bright colors and shapes. *Why could not the world be all this in a night?*

Something broke my heart even though I don't have one.

We can't fight that forever, I hissed to Body. *There's no way. If we try to go any further into something like that, it'll eat us up and we'll be lost in there, screaming and forever. No way can we keep this up, we need to get out.*

"I believe...I have to risk it."

Another long pause, more slowing-and-quickening breaths of steam and breeze from the darkness.

Then: *Why?*

Body frowned. His brows tightened. His whole face looked like a fist was pinching it shut. Then it relaxed, smoothed out.

"Because I need to...do whatever it takes to...try and make things right. I can't...leave it to others...to do it."

The motions and movements and noise of it all suddenly went dead.

The air itself felt as though it was sucked in and held.

A low exchange of motions. Trying to take them all in was like trying to watch icebergs shudder and dance in a slow waltz while making love lying flat on the ground between bus-sized masses of half-melting taffy. It filled all peripheral vision and threatened to overwhelm any miniscule remaining sense of scale and relative proportions. I saw that Body's eyes stayed firmly pointed down at the floor.

The air suddenly whoosh-relaxed. A wave broke and was receding away from us. The shapes in the dark became more still, relaxed, looking more like towers of dim pillows and mattresses shifting in the dim. I wished I could sigh in relief as I felt the crush against us lift. It was like being in an oven and then being thrust out into cool winter air atop a mountain. Almost painfully refreshing.

Quietly, hushed: *We will...try,* <ghost/MAN/knight>.

He blinked at that. *Knight?*

I guess we've been knighted.

Body shook his head. *I don't feel so armored.* He wiped some of the clear fluid off the side of his neck and stared at the mark on his fingertips. *I think they actually might've caused a small hemorrhage in my cerebellum.*

I feel like I am a hemorrhage.

<you must rest/sleep/die/CALM> *now.*

"I'm fine," Body replied, but then something pushed hard from the Teaghlach, something that was like feeling a giant sweep...an arc motion as of a massive pendulum...or an arm, with an endless-fingered hand at its terminus, casually moving out across space and catching us with no more consequence than it pushed out planets in their orbits.

I have been in the presence of big things before. The Dragon, the Stone God...there are things that move in the tides of the world and they do not swim the ocean. They are the very bedrock that tolerates the ocean's presence above them. And every so often, something like that shivers in its rest, notices a stray bit of sun that has somehow lost its way and managed to reach those depths against all physics telling us it is impossible.

And as those great things simply blink in very mild surprise and curiosity, that beam is swallowed in a pupil the scale of worlds, and is lost in the black hole of whatever regards the universe through such an eye, and dreams under such a blanket as the entirety of the sea.

Then the great things go back to sleep another epoch or two. We hope.

The sweep blew us both back towards the door, pushing me to a limit of self-sense that I hadn't felt since almost being burnt-eaten by the steam-cancer mass of the Jennyripper not-too-long ago. It was all I could do to maintain a sense of presence and cohesion as Body simply was flung back in a clumsy backwards toss that degenerated into a bone-rattling reverse somersault, clump-thumping to a stop a few feet from the door.

<come/CLAIM/collect/restore>

The last echoed and shifted, dying away in the dark as the door cracked open and admitted a bright rectangle of light framing a familiar man-shape.

"John?" Ceyggan came forward in a crouch, the way someone might enter a room where they have heard a heated argument and the sound of flying, breaking valuables striking the walls. I was fluttering, feeling like a pile of raked leaves that has just been kicked a-scatter by a rambunctious bunch of schoolkids and trying to reassemble myself from the broken whole. Ceyggan kneeled down and put a hand to Body's shoulder. "John?"

A low moan. A very slow shake of the head. Body looked up, blinking and gasping. There were fresh gouts of blood coming down his lip from his nostrils, and a shiny snail trail of ichor coming out of each ear. He couldn't reply in any meaningful way but simply shook his head a few more times and didn't offer any token assistance of his dead weight as Ceyggan got hands underneath him and started to maneuver him into a position where he could help him to attain shaky legs and leave.

As I wafted behind them, there was a last long exhalation from beyond the line of shadow.

Or maybe it wasn't a breath, but rather the blinking of a long, slow, dark eye under the ocean. Taking in the rays of light from the room beyond before going back to a glacial sleep.

29.

A hand touched me lightly on the arm. I almost jumped out of my own skin.

Ceyggan was staring into my eyes, standing outside the pool of light around me. His skin had a waxy sheen of what I took for sweat, only it was a solid layer evenly across his visible skin rather than in clumps or blots. His lips were pressed so tightly as to suggest they were gone altogether, leaving only a faint line to mark his mouth.

He tugged gently but insistently. I staggered back to my feet, tested my legs with a hesitant first step, found the second and third vastly easier...finally I followed him into the light, away from the congregation of flesh that was the Teaghlach and back out to the cool air of the outside waiting chamber.

Ceyggan's arm under mine, his hand on my back. My tongue, thick and wallowing in spit as I mumbled.

"Ff...fff...*f-fairies, get thee hence. I have...I have foresworn his bed and..c-company.*"

"Oh you're hilarious," Ceyggan frowned at me. "Assclown."

The storage unit fluorescent bars seemed to strobe in interminable and sporadic lengths. It took a few blinks to realize they only flickered in quick little spurts but my perceptions of them upon first emergence from the chamber had been immensely dulled, like playing a classic 75RPM album at 16RPM on an old turntable and making even Alvin and the Chipmunks sound like stoned barbershop quartet bass singers.

Everything was pure sensation in recovery. He supported me for as many steps as I could manage, only about half a dozen before my knees forgot how to work and I was slumped against the wall, the cold floor seeping up through the fabric of my pants and making me feel I was slowly melding into the glossy-finished concrete.

Ceyggan looked down at me, his expression pure poker face. After I had breathed in and out a few minutes, trying to recoup some calming effect from the exercise, he slowly lowered himself to his haunches. The leather pants made tiny creaks as he rocked up on the balls of his feet.

He fished in one of the pockets of the zippered shirt and came up with a wad of tissue, held it out to me without meeting my eyes. "Here. You've got…uh…"

"Thanks." I worked up a little spit to dab the tissue against my tongue, then made an effort to swab off the dried blood from my ear canals. I unwadded and re-balled the scarlet-streaked paper to then make a nominal effort at clearing the same mess from my nostrils where it had crusted against my upper lip.

"You don't look so good."

"The old saying, I believe, is: you should take a look at the other guy."

"Are they hurt?" The urgent brightness of his voice made me forget my futile clean-up and look at him.

"No, it's all right. As far as anyone like me would be able to tell, I don't think I could've hurt that…I mean, I don't think I could've done any damage if I tried."

He didn't completely relax. "I wasn't sure you were coming out. I thought I'd done something incredibly stupid. Which is not altogether unheard of for me."

"You *did* do something incredibly stupid," I went back to trying to wipe blood off my face. "But then I took the ball and carried down to the end zone of stupid for you."

He passed a critical eye over my features. "It doesn't look like you're still bleeding."

"I can call my showbiz agent and tell him thank god, I can do commercials again." I crumpled up the tissue and was about to be the responsible adult and put it in a pocket…but then somehow I looked at the gleaming polished concrete and thought *Screw it* and tossed it away from me to bounce and settle in one of the corners. Ceyggan didn't reproach me for the deliberate carelessness. Looking around, I imagined that someone was going to be coming within the day to clean up any mess, buff the floors again, erase any signs of the slightest dirt or intrusion on this holy-of-holy antechambers underneath the U-STOR-WORLD.

I felt Soul move along the wall behind me, feeling along the corrugated edges of the dayglo-orange storage locker doors. *That…I feel like I've been inverted or something. Like having your skin pulled off, flipped like a sock in the laundry, and shoved back down onto me, wrong-end up.*

I want to lie down.

You're already *sitting down.*

I wish the ground was lower so I could be down that much further.

I thought your head was going to pop like a dandelion off its stem.

Frankly I think I might've felt more relieved of this if it had. I pulled my knees up against my stomach, put my forearms on top of my kneecaps. I stared out at Ceyggan overtop this child's primitive wall.

"What *is* that? The Teaghlach? What did I really do in there?"

Did we do anything?

Ceyggan stared back at me but didn't immediately reply.

"What did it feel like? What do *you* think it was?"

"I couldn't…I don't have words to nearly get close enough." I rested my forehead against my forearms. "It was…big. Bigger than big in some ways. But I felt like…like it was…this is crazy…like it was shaking my hand somehow. Not physically, but somehow…the whole sensation was…it was as if I was being introduced, but there was only its presence there…"

Ceyggan nodded. "You met the tautarch of the Faede. Nobody else can get you more into the family than that."

"I don't know that word."

"Tautarch? It's sort of a portmanteau. You know math?"

"Only enough to figure out the tip on a restaurant bill."

Not that we go eating out much these days.

I wish I hadn't brought up anything related to food. My innards felt loose, as if someone had poured a gelatin mold of my internal organs and they were currently sitting in half-congealed preservative.

It sounds almost like a good deal on paper, not reflexively getting sick or throwing up or anything. Like you'd have a non-stop booze orgy and never worry about so much as a headache the next day. But remember that all functions, even getting sick, have a purpose. Without anything in me to purge, all I could do was feel generally awful. And since it didn't entirely come from any physical reason, I couldn't 'wish it away' like I could more brutal injuries or sensations.

More creaking of leather as Ceyggan let his weight shift back to his palms, did a little twist to bring his legs around and under him. He positioned himself into the Indian cross-legged position so familiar to all schoolkids, his polished shoe tips pointing at my feet.

"Tautology. It's an aspect of logic. Propositional logic, when you break stuff down to better understand the structure and figure out if it's gold or bullshit. A tautological statement. The single that is true in every lesser expression no matter how you move the factors around. You've seen simple examples in algebra, you know: if A plus B equals C, then B plus A *also* equals C, or A equals C minus B, so on. Basically, no matter how you re-write the equation, as long as all the internal parts don't change in their inherent qualities, then the essential relationships between them aren't changed in any way simply because you've rearranged the appearance of the whole."

"No offense, but I didn't take you for a real high-logic and studies type."

He smiled. "None taken. Asshole."

"So disinvite me from your next rave party as penance."

"Sure thing. Yeah, I didn't go to school. Not day-to-day school or anything. I don't think I even cracked open a book. Only menus and magazines."

"Where did you get the info?"

His smile faltered, but he shrugged and gave the appearance of indifference. "You pick it up. We're sort of word-of-mouth taught in the Faede. Not much need for formal education. Some of us go further out, get real schooling and do the diploma-and-gowns thing. Usually if they're told they need to do it because they'll have some specialized role for the families."

"The Teaghlach? It's what…it's who assigns the roles?"

"Yyee-ahh. That's a way of looking at it." He scratched at the stylish stubble on the cheeks. "You're…that's different. There haven't been many people to try what you just did, let alone come walking out of the room afterwards."

"How many?"

"How many tried or how many walked out?"

"Tried? Maybe a few dozen over…years."

"Walked out?"

"Hard to say."

This is not a promising line of questioning.

"Hard to say as in you don't know or hard to say because you don't want to tell me it's an appallingly smaller number than 'a few dozen'?"

"Pick whichever one won't make you ball up in the corner and crap yourself."

"Either way I've already gone past ruining this pair of pants, so level with me."

"Maybe…two."

"*Maybe* two? You don't have that figure nailed down to any certainty?"

"Certainty is hard to come by when your definition of 'surviving' something could be different from mine."

"Try simply 'walking and breathing without help ever again.'"

"Definitely one, then."

"Not counting me?"

"Somewhere between one and zero, in that case."

"How old is the Teaghlach? I couldn't get a read on it."

"Look, I can't really go into this, all right?" His shoulders twitched, hunched up. He looked as though some schoolmaster was striking a ruler across his back. "You'll…there's two basic ways this could go now."

"I'm listening."

"The first way is simple: you don't make it in for a meeting. In which case, probably shouldn't be of any value to you to know all this anyway. And if you're approved to go back in for a real conference—"

Soul blurted out of me: *"That was only the* preliminary?"

I recovered my own lips. "You're shitting me."

He shook his head, a big hangdog look of apology on the magazine model features.

"If I could raise my arms any higher than my knees right now, I would knock you even harder on your ass than you're already sitting on it, Ceyggan."

He held out his hands. "I told you this wasn't the best choice for how to proceed, but it's the only way if you want to find out what Diatha knew, if anything at all. Did you really think the Teaghlach, the basis for our entire existence in the Faede, was going to let you simply walk in and have a coffee chat with them without some sort of vetting beforehand?"

"I thought *you* had vetted me. You made such a deal about having to vouch for me to even get me into this."

"That was to get the Teaghlach to be willing to take the risk. Dude, I told you only a few dozen have tried, and we're talking over…a long span of time in this. Just to let you in their presence, to know they even exist or where they are in this vicinity? That's a huge risk without even discovering that your head could explode the second they came in contact with you."

Even my sour frown felt exhausted on the muscles of my face. "So do I pass the initiation? Am I in the frat, Brother Ceyggan?"

"I don't know for sure, not yet. The Teaghlach will decide."

He peered at me in closer inspection. "Did you get any impression from it? From contact in it?"

I shook my head. "I couldn't put it all into clear terms…do you think we passed?"

"If you didn't, I think I would have been dragging you out there and calling someone to help me find a place out in Sharon Woods to bury your remains."

I rubbed my temples with my fingertips. The mental nausea was fading fast. But it was fast having the space re-filled by the dread of anticipation. Only the opening interview…I hadn't felt this tense even when waiting for a callback interview for a day job when I first dropped out of school…oh Christ, would I need a tie and dress pants…?

"I didn't get all that much from it. I felt like it was…that handshake sensation. Holding back."

"You got the right idea, then."

"I don't think either of us could take a heavier interaction than what we just went through."

He was quiet for a minute. He locked his fingers against the nape of his neck and expelled a whoosh of air.

"I want to tell you that the Teaghlach wouldn't consider you if you couldn't handle it. Maybe they'll say no when they've really worked it through and you're out of the woods. But man…I won't lie to you…" his eyes looked like a dog not sure if someone was going to pet or pummel it, "…if they agree and you are willing to go back into this…it's going to be at least as bad as now. Most likely worse."

"Why did I agree to any of this?"

The smile was like unsugared coffee on those movie-bland features. "I'd say it's because you've gotten too big a reputation for being too big a pushover." The smile went hollow. "And because in this situation, not to be a dick or anything, but you *did* get rid of Spam Tam."

"Are you suggesting this town isn't better off with him gone?"

Ceyggan held out his hands, shaking his head. "I'm not defending the guy. Like I told you, we don't use his stuff, no thrill there. But…the devil you know, right?"

"This isn't the lesser of two evils here. Spam is unrepentant bottom-feeding at its worst. I consider him in pretty much the same league as child pornographers and people who run dog-fights."

"A bit harsh for a drug dealer."

"He's not a drug dealer. He likes people to equate him with that, because for the most part drugs can only hurt the person using them. He wants you to think of him as little stranger than a pot or meth dealer. Hell maybe he has some pathetic *Breaking Bad* self-image of himself as a great anti-hero dealer. All the rest of a drugs' effect on people around the user is peripheral. But Spam is a fear bottler. An emotional high-peddler. And his product comes directly off the exploitation of other peoples' pain. And as far as the effect of his users on those around them…" I thought about the Scots Brothers little holding cell, at the gored-clean feed-things attached to the two lead-heads, and couldn't help but close my eyes and try to clear the thought from my mind, "…it's crap to think that there's no serious collateral damage that's simply 'peripheral.' If someone uses his product, that's pretty much a guarantee they're inevitably going to be a liability to everyone around them."

"I didn't say he was necessarily preferable by my comment. I mean: do you think he's ever going to change?"

"Spam Tam couldn't change unless you set him on fire."

A twist of chuckling in my ear canal: *I seem to recall us doing exactly that.*

"So allowing that he's always going to be a problem, and allowing that what he does is by all accounts not recognized as a crime by the day-to-day world…do you like the idea of him now out there somewhere, unknown and unaccounted for? Or was it maybe better when you knew where he was and some idea of what he was up to?"

I shook my head. "I'm not debating this with you. I'd rather he completely stop altogether. And apparently nobody—not the vampires, not the Faede, nor any others in this town—felt any willingness to take a stand and stop him."

Ceyggan stared back at me. The puppy looked as though

he'd gotten the slap across the muzzle he'd feared. But his eyes seemed to go shades darker.

"It's not anyone's job to police the Under, Flicker. Not even yours, Mr. Vaunted Doppelgeist. We have police, fire departments, tax agencies…there are things that the day-to-day can try and have a firm grasp on. But you know as well as I do, maybe better than most, that the Under doesn't play by those same rules. If it can be said to *have* any rules. We all do what we can to mind our own house, and that's as far as anyone wants to push it." He leaned forward, putting his face close to my knees, close enough to feel the breath of his words. "The minute any group decides they know what's good for everybody else and starts trying to push that crap around, would you like to venture a guess what will end up happening?"

"I think history has provided sufficient examples that I could venture a guess."

A slow nod. "Good. Then I believe the point is made." He rolled his head around on his neck, popped a shoulder. "You should already be familiar with this, given your latest girlfriend."

"Trina isn't a threat—"

"No. The other one. The one that was with you at the gallery show."

"Don't give me any shit about Sarah. She's…cool. She's okay."

"Okay?" A chuckle, a shake of the head. "Christ, man, she deals with Seppeschal, one of the L.A. people. They're the only reason I don't really ever make the jump to trying porn, even for fun."

"What are you talking about?"

"Seppeschal is *Brokerage*, man. *The* Brokerage."

"Yeah, he's her manager out there. I knew that."

"No, no, you're such an idiot. You don't know the Brokerage?" Another chuckle. "Of course not, or why would I be asking?"

"Ceyggan, pretend I'm a village idiot and explain it in short words with big pictures." *Before I punch you in the friggin' throat* was the unspoken end of that statement.

"The Brokerage. They're like…the ultimate management

firm. Not William Morris, not The Firm, not Belago-Saber or any of the names you hear about in Hollywood parties and restaurants. Nobody knows the Brokerage unless they're doing business with them. And to do business with them, you have to be serious money and power. We're talking people who never make it to the Forbes list or the People Magazine 'top 100 movers and shakers of showbiz' bullshit. They're people you've never heard of but they have heard of you. Assuming you matter enough to know about. And they're dark. Dark shit."

"In the Under?"

He nodded. "The Brokerage makes this town's vampire community look positively PTA material, at least in L.A. and thereabouts. You want to be famous? They don't deal in penny-ante shit like fame. They don't sell marketing deals and public relations control. That's for the companies and people you know. The Brokerage deals in dark, nasty business. And not even low-key evil like assassinations or scandal-framing. Most Faede accept that much as part of the fun, you know us." I gave a shrug to his semi-apologetic smirk on this observation. "But the Brokerage...they do the scary things that the crazy-rich like to do just because they can. You want to sample a conversion? Be half-made into something? They can do it. Buy a night of watching murders live and performed on your living room carpet without so much as a blood drop on your white Persian carpet the next morning? Done. You have enough money and pull, they are the ones that get you anything and everything and make it seem after like nothing ever happened. If your lady-friend is run by Seppeschal, believe me, two things are clear up-front. One: he is not the one working for her. And two: he is not managing anything to do with such small potatoes as porn stars." He tilted his head, pursed his lips. "Maybe if she's some sort of seriously out-there escort. A kink type for people who want things normally not allowed on the whole 'up-and-legal' scale of kinky."

A distinct possibility, the whisper in my ear. *Considering what sort of punishment her body can probably take, if you're any example.*

"Seppeschal is dark Faede. What we sometimes call 'caste-off.' We deal with those types only when we bare-minimum, last-resort, absolutely-have-to. Usually if something threatens many of the families together. The last time I came across his name, it was associated with shit you wouldn't want to read about in a Stephen King novel. Body-snatchers for spirit-trade. Spectrada negotiations. Zombie-for-hire production. Fucking zombies, can you imagine anybody wanting to hire those things made? On *purpose*? Pfft. Spam Tam? You think he was awful? He wasn't even a small fish in a small pond. He was *protozoa* next to this stuff. Are you getting the gist here, man?"

"I get it. And you're still not delivering anything that is truly news. Sarah has dealt with some bad shit, and there are people after her same as after me right now. Seppeschal sounds like maybe the kind of fight-fire-with-a-flamethrower attitude that might be keeping her safe out there."

He frowned and shook his head. "Whatever. Can't force the horse to drink, no matter if you shove his freaking head into the lake...just watch it. She asks you to meet with her manager, I suggest you take that flamethrower."

"Thanks for the two bits."

"De nada."

"But one point I'd like to interject before dropping the subject. Not a have-the-last-word thing, mind you, but simply a Devil's advocate sort of proposition."

Ceyggan waited a beat before giving a nod of assent, and a go-on wave of his hands.

"What happens when something or someone gets bad enough out there that it's *all* your asses on the line? I'm not talking about anybody playing dictator or Polyanna arbiter of moral good or etiquette or whatever...but flat-out simple mutual survival? What happens when it gets out that something bad happens and maybe it was something that grew out of a simply stupid little nothing originally? Something that could've been stopped before it got that bad, if only one of you had decided to step up and take the risk of being called the buzzkill at the party?"

He looked down at his lap. Scratched at his stubble.

"Then we deal with it." His whisper barely registered even across the short distance. "But nobody can tell the future to say that some little spit like Spam Tam could ever be that kind of risk."

"Everybody says that. Before it happens." I rested my head back against the wall. "I'm no archivist and lord knows there's no grand library of the Under…but can you look me in the eye and say there's never been any seriously huge, dangerous shit threatening more than one little community in the Under?"

Ceyggan nodded. "But never…it's big stuff. You know that. It's not like Hitler, getting huge and dangerous and sweeping Europe. Big stuff tends to come from big."

"Hitler was a half-assed housepainter. Nothing is born full-grown. Not really."

Ceyggan didn't offer any further argument. But I didn't feel as though there'd been any sort of resolution or clear win on the issue.

After all: you don't feel thrilled when the argument you win is that essentially the nature of evil in the world is a really crap and futile sensation of helplessness against it.

****

While Ceyggan was helping me out to the car and getting me bundled into the driver's seat, the phone went off. He expertly dug it out of the right pocket on first hearing and put it in my hand without a word, just walked away back to the storage unit entrance and disappeared within.

"Hello?"

"Who did you tell, you son of a bitch?"

30.

I knew the voice immediately as it resonated from the phone's tiny speaker.

Hannibal Scot.

"Christ, Hannibal, what happened out there?"

"Who did you tell?" His voice was so implacable that I couldn't help but conjure the image of his expressionless face in my thoughts. I wondered where he was calling from...and if it was while watching us right there.

"Nobody. I told nobody."

"How exactly am I supposed to believe that?"

"I don't know. But if you didn't believe it, why would you even ask me the question?"

Moments. A breath.

"Hannibal? What happened? Are you and Rex okay?"

"Someone was out there. They knew where we were. You're the only person who has been out to that location."

"You drove me out there yourself. I didn't memorize or even try to pay attention. I expressly avoided that so nobody could get it from me."

"We both know you don't have to exactly rely on maps and memory."

"I didn't give you away either, Scot," I snapped from Body's mouth. *"Don't start throwing accusations. We could've been followed."*

"We *were* followed. Or more like, you were followed." Another breath. "Why didn't you tell us you were being followed? We could've taken additional precautions."

"I didn't...we didn't know."

Bullshit. Are we going to make this worse by continuing to lie to people we trust?

"We could've taken precautions."

"Where's Rex? Are you guys safe?"

"They came at us while I was taking you back. That girl... they were..."

"What happened?"

"I got back and Rex was...holding them off. Sort of. They killed one of the lead-heads."

"They killed them both."

Another breath. "What?"

"Whoever it was that attacked you guys, they left the girl dead at my store. I just spent a few hours as a guest of the Columbus city police department." No response. "Hannibal, *is Rex okay?"*

"He'll live. He said...I managed to get him to a friendly place. I'll have to go back in a day or so and see if we can salvage anything. Site's compromised for good."

"Who was it that attacked? Who did this?"

"No idea. It was...it was two. I think. Maybe three. It was hard to tell. There was...interference."

"Start at the beginning."

"I got back and the gate was run over. There was a truck parked by the compound. Whoever it was, they must've not known that running down the gate would set off alarms. Or they didn't care."

"I don't get why they bothered attacking you if they were following us."

"They'd gotten the lead-heads free of the cells. Rex was shooting but I found him...wounded. Bad slashes. Lacerations on his body. A few inches too high and they would've had his throat."

Oh shit. "Who was it?"

"I only saw shadows. Somebody. A guy. Pale and weird... but I couldn't get a look."

Shadows. Shadows and hard to see.

Mister Sharkdoll.

"But the girl...she was the bad one."

"The lead-head?"

"No, the other one...one of the attackers. She was...it was small but she...black. Black and white. I couldn't keep my eyes on things. I was trying to cover our back and get Rex to the car. They just...they just *came in* and did what they wanted, Flicker. All that hiding and security and it didn't make a difference to those two. Three."

"Three?"

"I was getting Rex to our panic space. I heard the car outside. Their truck. I heard it. It started but they were still inside, trying to get at us. Yeah...I think three...someone outside with the truck, someone I didn't see when I was running in."

"Did they take anything? Say anything?"

"No. No talking. That pale one...the taller one...he seemed to keep...whistling? It was like he was whistling but maybe it was a dog whistle or something. I couldn't...I couldn't hear..."

No. No no no, not you guys too. "Hannibal, did he ever do it directly at you?"

"What?"

"The whistling thing. He looked like he was whistling?"

"Yeah."

"Did he do it towards you?"

"Once or twice he tried. I was shooting. He was moving...Christ, he could move...I don't think he...was he trying something?"

"Yes. But I don't know if he managed to do it, if you kept him busy."

Monkey-centi-shrimp monsters. Sharkdoll's nasty familiar-whatevers. God, if any of those had managed to latch onto either of the Scots brothers...

"Rex is sleeping right now. Doped." A dry click that might've been Hannibal swallowing. "I had to use up a whole case of bandaging and suture packs to get him stable."

"Are you safe?"

"We're...at a friendly place. I'm tired. I need some rest too, but I have to...I have to wait for our relief to show up. I couldn't call you until I'd secured a line and had things...settled."

"Do you need our—"

"No." His voice sharpened, awake again. "No. No offense, Mr. Flicker, but..."

"I get it. We've done enough damage." I felt a cold sinking run through me. Ashamed and embarrassed.

"No, sir. I don't...I'm sorry I accused. You didn't do this. But if they were following you...it might not be safe."

For anyone around us, you mean.

"I get it. Please find a way to let me know how Rex and you are, okay?"

"Yes, sir."

"I said you could call me John."

"Yes, sir."

Damn it.

"Hannibal, they took the girl from you and left her dead at my door. That had to be quick, because from when I left you it was only...a few hours' time, at most. If these people have been following...me...then I don't know how many they might have with them."

The Believers? Could it have been them after all?

"I understand. I have to go and check on Rex."

"Is he really all right?"

"I don't know. He's stable. For whatever that means. I want to watch him and make sure he gets...through it."

"I'm sorry. For what that's worth, I'm sorry."

"So am I, sir."

The call ended. Probably by whatever pre-determined time Hannibal had figured he could safely call and not risk a trace of the connection.

Could it be the Believers? I repeated. *Is this something they could have pulled off?*

The two Believers we've met are human. Sharkdoll is definitely not. Maybe this other that was with him, too. And why would the Believers want to frame us? They want me dead and you off to Nirvana or wherever. What good would framing me for murder—and not very convincingly, either—do for that goal?

Body sat in the driver's seat, staring out the window at the storage building's lightboard. It clicked over a couple of minutes. Changed a degree in the temperature reading.

Something is having these things follow us. And for some reason decided to mess with the Scots to get to the leads.

But why kill one and take the other?

Your guess and mine, man. None of this is making the slightest sense.

Maybe it's something to do with Sarah.

What?

I hovered around the dashboard. *The Believers are after us both. We already know things are run a bit different out where she hails from.*

Okay.

I floated near the rearview mirror...for a moment almost expecting to see a face in it. *So maybe the Believers out there are a bit on the stranger side. The not-quite-human side. Maybe they're not following us so much as ganging up to watch both of us.*

Which means it's time to perhaps regroup with Sarah and compare whatever notes we have.

****

I made the suggestion that we would probably be better served driving somewhere else before using the cell phone again, so as to not further risk anything that could be construed by the Teaghlach as compromising their space. He left Pataskala, returning to 270 and taking the belt north towards Westerville. He got off at the Easton shopping area and picked a random parking space amongst the various Colonial-styled shops and store parking spaces.

It was already becoming dawn. Had we already been at this

nearly two days? Had the mess with Trina only been the other night? Where had the hours gone? What was all this?

Body managed to reach her after a couple of rings of the number on the card she'd left us.

"Sorry, was cleaning myself up just now. Felt kind of grimed-out after our recent expeditions." Laughter in the breaths between sentences. "Anything new to report?"

"I just spent a few hours as a guest of the local police department. Accused of murdering two people."

"What?"

He filled her in on the basic events, leaving out the last conversation with Pinney. "It basically boils down to: we think...these Believers could be doing this."

"Why?"

"No idea. It could be coincidence. But I think it's a possibility that the ones who've been after you and the ones after me are ganged together. Sharing resources. If they're all part of the same cuckoo club, it makes sense."

"But framing you for murder doesn't—"

"Doesn't fit, I agree. But I don't know enough to think otherwise yet. Some friends of mine were attacked. Badly."

"Are...they okay?"

"Yeah. They're okay. They're safe. But they indicated that someone...some people...probably the ones who've been watching my place...did the attacking. They're the ones who got the girl away from them. The one that was found dead at my place."

"This...is a lot to take in."

"I was thinking we should meet. Or at least, if you're okay—"

"No, I agree. We need...we've got to stay close. This is getting insane. Or more insane."

"I can meet you wherever you want."

"I can come get you."

"No, it's all right. Hal loaned me one of his cars for while I'm in town. Just tell me where and when."

"There's a place in the campus area on High Street. It's a sort of coffee shop after-hours place, kind of a bohemian-wannabe place. It's called Night Shots. They should be open."

"I'll find it. Be careful."

"Lately, 'careful' hasn't entirely been an option."

****

The Vega wouldn't start.

Body thumped the heel of a hand against the steering wheel. "C'mon. *Not* cool."

I moved across the dashboard...briefly tugging through the glass of the windshield. I followed along the seam of the hood where it was hinged against the cab of the car. I was able to use the opening to move, shift, compress down and through so I could avoid having to move through any solid matter too directly.

The engine still had faint cloud-puffs of residual heat. I could move along some of the cables from the battery, tracing faint lines of chemical energy paths that glimmered yellow-white, like sunlight captured in a faded Polaroid. Moving around...

...I can't make out any outright interruptions. I pulled back, away from the fan belts and starter which could disturb me. *Try again.*

Body churned the key in the ignition socket. The starter gave bright spark-spits of energy. It traveled. Gasoline combusted. Fuel fumes whicked and snapped and there was a sense of compression, of action moving...then inexplicably going still.

It's starting. It's just...not starting.

I moved along the exhaust pipe...no blockage...I'm no auto expert. *I think she's...being judgmental.*

I returned through the back glass to hear Body hum-growling slowly to himself. Tapping fingers on the steering wheel.

Something's wrong but not that I can see.

"What is it?" Body asked aloud. He glanced across the dashboard. "Are you demanding we get you detailed? A new air freshener for your mirror? *What?*"

He tried the key again. The Vega shivered, then like a horse given enough of a kick with the heels of a rider's boots, chug-ground to life.

Last time it did that was when we parked at a White Castle's. I took in the surroundings. *This is Easton Mall. We've been here before. What's bothering her now?* Apple *stores? That* Au Bon Pain *restaurant?*

"Who knows?" He began backing out of the parking space, eyeballing the car that was parked behind us. I watched the exhaust fumes out of the back, felt the hum-growl of the Vega's motor as electricity gulped from the alternator to the battery, piston energy turned from potential to kinetic, and two tons or so of metal, rubber and other materials became animate in its limited but useful way. For a moment, it occurred to me in seeing the glow-twitch of energies moving how there wasn't a lot of outright difference...between the Vega operating and a tree, processing sunlight. Or a living creature, feeding and metabolically processing energy.

The picture of the Vega, though, simultaneously running along at highway speeds as we got to the 670 connection that would let us cross-cut into the downtown area, dropping its exhaust-fume waste like a cow casually crapping as it walked along a pasture, had me chuckling hard enough that eventually Body had to ask what the hell was so damned funny.

****

Night Shots was pretty much a dive coffee bar, a species of place that only Ohio State's campus area could allow to survive against the onslaught of Starbuck's and Cup O' Joe franchises. It took up the bottom floor of a sunken two-storey structure. Upstairs was a stainless-steel-and-bamboo-styled sushi place only open for daylight customers. Take a few steps down to the patio and front entrance of Night Shots, though, and you found a place that had all the feel of a punk bar basement. Mismatched chairs. Chess sets free to use but missing pieces. A TV mounted up in one corner but never turned on. Speakers mounted piecemeal and playing nothing but local music (the hand-lettered sign taped up underneath the speaker by the restroom entrance declared 'Don't Like the Music? Start Your Own Band.').

Body bought a pair of coffees. Straight black, no cream or sugar or Italian embellishments. Found a corner seat where a duct-tape-upholstered booth faced an armchair that was a brown, more scuffed-up cousin of my nubbly blue chair back at The Nookery. Body took the booth seat with its back to the wall so I could watch the entrance.

A few students with laptops. One bedraggled-looking ancient guy in mismatched sweatpants and jacket who was probably one of the homeless that often used the open-all-night aspect to try and have a place to doze until the management asked them to leave. Piano jazz—something originally in a Duke Ellington vein—playing on the speakers.

I kept circling by the overhead vents. Watching curls of coffee-smoke and a fine dusty sheen of cooking-smells traveled from the kitchen to the natural vacuum of the door every time someone opened it to enter or exit. A couple more students, late-night refugees from some nearby campus bar scene, came in and loudly joked and made a bunch of mixed-up coffee orders to the overworked barista by the counter while I watched the room.

I am not cool with this. We should be back at The Nookery. Or trying to find the Scots brothers and help, see if Rex is okay.

Rex is okay if his brother says he is. Body picked up the coffee, mimicked taking a sip. That was always an awkward sign: when he didn't feel like going through the motions of actually eating or drinking, even for appearances. The coffee bled heat energy into the paper, then the air and tabletop around it. Everything trying to seek balance, even distribution. *He made it clear that we're not wanted, helpful or otherwise.*

We didn't even consider that we were being followed. I saw that guy and I knew we were being watched and we totally let it slide with all this other crap.

All that other crap, as you refer to it, was a bit on the

distracting side. We can't live like we're constantly under siege.

Really? I moved down to above the coffee, letting the waves of its warmth pass through me. *Then it occurs to me that maybe we got into the wrong game. There are people out there that don't like us. And living like we're still Joe Nobody in an old bookstore is a delusion. There are people out there who would like to see you and I at the bottom of the river. Or worse.*

Body frowned at the tabletop. *Bottom of the river. That's a low blow, asshole.*

Whatever it takes to get you to appreciate the situation.

You think I don't? I'm the one who took a bullet the other day, remember?

And immediately shrugged it off. I wafted close to his ear, snug to a shoulder. *I know you. Remember that, too. I know it hurt. I know it was scary as shit. And that's okay. I know that. I was scared for you. It's not about being vulnerable. It's about not appreciating what we've done the last few years.*

And what is that?

We've stepped up into new leagues. Maybe more than we can ever expect to be capable of handling. I mean, what are we at the end of it all, when you break it down?

Tell me.

We're a couple of circus acts. You're the Invincible Man and I'm the Amazing Mentalist Act. You can have all the swords shoved through you, and I can whisper the contents of the audience's pockets while you wear a turban and waggled your fingers mystically.

Probably could make better than porn money doing that.

Ha. We've started to see gods. *Monsters bigger than we imagined were real. We acted like we were so blasé cool about it, like meeting vampires and ghosts meant we were so metropolitan about this whole Under that we've become part of. But it's obvious that deep down where it matters, we're still like the day-to-day people.*

How so?

We still want things to be explicable and clear and have purposes and connections so that we have a chance at grasping.

We want to believe that we matter enough that the rest of the world will make sense for us.

I think we've grown a bit from that.

Maybe. But remember how you felt? After the Jennyripper? Wanting the world to know about it? Wanting some acknowledgment of the danger, the risk it was for us? I saw that thing. The Stone God. It didn't give a shit for us. For the human race. All it cared about was slapping the 'snooze' button on Eternity and going back to napping in the sediment. We're tickling the noses of some big lions, man, and we don't even properly know which way is the escape hatch from their cage.

Sarah arrived before I got any reply. She was dressed in the same black leather coat she'd worn to the gallery, but her pants were a skin-tight aquamarine pair of denims with bright copper rivets. She smiled and pointed at the second coffee cooling on the table. "For me?"

Body nodded, waved a hand towards the opposing seat. She plumped down onto the cushions with a faint squeal of springs in its puffed mass.

"You look like a stray cat came along and pissed in your coffee." She tugged off the shapeless beret-styled hat she'd had on, letting those ruby curls flip free. Shook her head to loosen the locks.

"Just...thinking."

"I find that never makes me happy."

How do you do it?

No answer.

"I didn't know what kind of coffee you liked. Or even if you liked coffee, come to think of it."

"It's okay." She lifted the cup for a sniff. Took a sip. Put it back down. "It's all the same to me, these days."

I moved across the space, borrowing the hollows of Body's throat. *"Have I done something to piss you off?"*

She blinked, hand around the cup. Made a quick glance behind her at the rest of the room where everything else continued on, not noticing the goings-on in our corner. "What?"

"Your other. She's not answering me. Have I done

something wrong?"

Sarah looked down at her coffee. Swallowed.

"It's not easy. Not all of it. Meeting another one of us. I didn't even know until recently there even could be another doppelgeist."

"I'm sorry. I don't mean to be pushy."

"It's not you. It's us. And...the memory thing...when she was trying to connect—"

"That was on me, not her."

"I know. But it was still...jarring. To have you react that badly to it."

"I apologize."

"Just let her have her own time on this, okay?"

She started to lift the cup for another sip, something to do so as to not look at us.

"Can I show you something? Something about us?"

Sarah looked over the rim of her coffee. Put it down on the table slowly. Kept her hand wrapped around the cup while staring at it.

"Why don't you tell me instead?"

"But I could show you, I could try sharing like we did before—"

"That didn't work out so well for either of us. I don't want to try it again until we're more comfortable with each other."

"I could—"

"There are things about me I'm not ready to share with you yet, okay?" Her eyes were shiny-bright and glistening. "Look...I know you're all excited. So am I." A weak smile, unbalanced and not pretty. "I'm sorry...I'm sorry." An inhalation that was long and wheezy. "I can't...I'm not proud of everything I've done in my life, all right? And there are times...there are things that I have in my memories that aren't as sweet as...playing spin-the-bottle with my first crush, okay?"

"I'm sorry."

"It's all right...but...John, this is truly awesome. But we can't run into this like idiots. I'm still learning things about what...about what we are. Same as you. You were surprised by that trick I pulled at the gallery? Well, I was frankly just as surprised at your reaction to the memory-share. And I didn't choose the memory, it was simply a strong light inside your thinking when I encountered it." She went back to staring into the distance within the coffee cup. "You don't know the kinds of things that are strong memories for me. You don't want to know right now, believe me. What you could accidentally tap and bring back to life for me, out of *my* head...no."

Body reached across the table and touched his fingertips ever-so-lightly on the backs of her hands. "You don't have to do anything you don't want to with me."

"Or me," I whistled. *"Ever."*

She nodded. "Thanks...thank you. I'm sorry to sound so melodramatic—"

"It's a trigger for you."

"You sound like a rape counselor."

"I have...we've heard some of the terminology, yeah."

She wiped at her eyes. Cleared her throat. "Ah-uh! Never mind me...I get stupid like this. Sometimes Seppeschal is so pissed, I can go weeks without being willing to take on a job, I get so...I get hit with something that sets it all off and then I can't think straight until it just...goes away."

"I understand."

She smiled, brighter and prettier if still with a tinge of brittle hurt. "Yeah. You probably do. So...what did you want to...share?"

"There was something that I only touched on recently...it got clearer after some of these new...memoryscapes? Braincaves? I don't know what cute euphemism to use for them. But it was something that happened..during that same summer, I think. The one that you were there for...the other moment."

"Okay."

"I played a lot with Mischa and Annie and the other kids when I was down there in Chillicothe. That was my whole summer some years. You picked up on that much already. But I also had time alone. My grandfather still was working then. My grandmother would get tired, there were years when she had to go back for...chemotherapy...and she'd get tired having a couple

of teenage kids running around. Mischa would go to cheerleader camp or something. Annie had summer school. Point is, there were times when I was left to fend for myself."

"A vacation-season latchkey kid?"

"You could say that. Chillicothe wasn't exactly a danger zone of kidnappers and child slavers lurking around the corners. Where my grandparents lived was at the top of the one of the big hill communities that are the crown around the valley that is downtown Chillicothe. Somewhat posh upper-middle-class, though I didn't think that at the time."

"The Hess family, they owned pretty much that hill. Sometimes I heard it referred to as Hess Hill. The Hess couple, they had their own home across a wide, undeveloped meadow from the end of the street where my grandparents' and Annie's house was. A nice older couple, no children. There was one afternoon where I came across their house, out there in the middle of the high grass and old oak trees and such...it was like... finding an English manor in the middle of the forest. Something you would dream about. Their house wasn't huge, but it was still fairly big. It had four floors. I'd never been in a house with that many floors. Mrs. Hess showed me this big hammock-looking net that was suspended from the top floor railings...it hung across the space in the middle of the wraparound staircase that went down all the floors to ground level."

"A net?"

"She told me it was an old invention intended for catching any kids who played too wild and somehow fell from the upper floors."

"Wow."

"I thought that at the time, too. Maybe it was a lie, though I can't think now of any other reason why an old house like that would've had such a thing. The ground floor had those black-and-white checker floors, each square like two feet wide. To this day, somehow I associate black-and-white checker-tile floors with big, fancy houses and expensive estates. Crazy, right?"

"I think the same thing of Louis the Sixteenth furniture,

with all those gilt frames and curls."

"You got it. Mrs. Hess liked giving tours to neighbors of their house, all the neat touches like that net. They had the tidiest garden and hedges, eight-foot hedges. Even yew trees. I didn't know back then that English yew is virtually nonexistent in this country."

"So Mrs. Hess told me after that tour that anytime I wanted, I could feel free to wander their property. Which meant effectively half the top of that hill where they hadn't sold any land for further developing of houses, the way the part of the hill with my grandparents house had been sold. When I was left alone on those vacations, I'd go wandering."

"This summer that I'm talking about...I went out to their lands. I didn't go to their house. I found this narrow track in the high weeds, past these immense piles of bricks that were...they made me think of Indian burial mounds. They were at least ten, twelve feet high. You could climb them, if you were willing to risk getting scratched and tumbling onto your ass on a bunch of bricks."

"Ouch."

"I think they were leftovers of some of the houses built elsewhere on the hill. I went past those, across the meadows. Into this heavy, heavy-thick stand of pine and oak trees. I mean it was so thick, a couple of times I couldn't follow the track without going sideways and stretching across a space between two trunks."

"It was dark there. The trees were so close together, and their tops were such thick cover, that even though this was...four o' clock in the afternoon? Five? I recall the sunlight was already starting to slant diagonal and not down, so it must've been more like six or seven now that I think on it...but I was in this small copse amongst these thick-bunched trees. Pine needles carpeting everything, pine cones here and there. Fallen chunks of oak trees. I couldn't even make out any birdsong or animals, though there had to have been animals living there, it was so quiet and nobody must have come through there very often."

"There was light ahead. Couldn't have been more than... fifty, maybe seventy feet into this grove. I felt as though I was walking through...a painting. A Currier & Ives print...some

English countryside. In my head I could hear classical music that I always associate with those moments. Pastoral. Pachelbel's Canon in D Minor, *that sort of music."*

"When I reached the clearing at the center, I stopped because it looked like someone had painted the ground in this wide, ragged space about thirty feet around."

"Painted the ground?"

"It was ice. Ice and a rime of snow where it met the unfrozen ground."

"What?"

"What tiny bit of light reached through the tree cover overhead was getting reflected off the ice in this clearing. I couldn't believe it, but the chill that I'd thought was simply it being so dark and sheltered from the summer heat—this had to have been June, July when this happened—and not anything extraordinary."

"But I was alone. Standing at the edge of this...it wasn't a pond. I pushed a toe at it, cracked the ice...to prove it was real. Like pinching yourself. It cracked and there was water there, soaking the tip of my sneaker. It was there and all I could think at the moment was that somehow, this patch of frozen water...some sort of holdover of a rain puddle or something that might've frozen back in January or February...that it had been unbelievably preserved. Kept close and safe and protected by the tree cover being so ridiculously dense."

"I mean, how else would you have explained it? I could even see a wisp of my breath and started to shiver. I could see that where it met the soil, there was a tiny sliver of true snow powder, but that was thin and dirty. There were no visible animal tracks or anything, but I had to believe deer or squirrels or at least birds were around. Here it was. I was standing in front of the kind of thing you figure could only exist in books or movies where there's such a thing as magic and wizards and other nonsense. I saw winter, hiding from a summer world. And it was real."

"Maybe there was some other reason."

"What reason? An ice truck had an extra delivery they could make and dumped it there? It wouldn't have explained why the water was frozen, rather than a pile of melting ice

settled, embedded into the ground the way it would have been during winter. And besides, who could have made such a massive unloading, with the trees so heavy until you reached the clearing? I couldn't have walked my bike there through those trees, let alone any indication a truck or anything else could've hauled something there."

"Did you tell anybody? Go and bring anyone back?"

"No. That was…I can't truly remember why not. I remember there were reasons. Mischa was crazy with her cheerleader camp sessions, like I said. I think Grandpa worked late and he was the only one then I could think to tell, or try to bring and show him."

"I think part of it, though…part of it was wanting to have that be mine. If I brought someone else back the next day, I felt like it was a guarantee that all I'd do is drag somebody through scratching branches and dirt to come see a big patch of black, thawed dirt and nothing left. Or they'd see it, but they'd have some boring and awful explanation that would ruin it all, make it all rational and neat and explained away."

"I didn't keep it secret to own it. I knew I didn't own it. If there was such a thing as owning a pocket of winter, it was the Hess couple's property. But it was…it felt special. It felt very unique and as if my being there alone and seeing it was almost as responsible for it being there as any freak weather explanation or vectors of temperature and humidity meeting to put it there to be found."

"I didn't want to keep it secret. It just felt like it already was. It was dark and lovely there, and it was like the air was thick enough to defeat anything more loud than breathing heavy. No animal noises, no cars or people. Not even the sounds of summer. The rest of the world was warm but here was this final, tiny scrap of something that didn't belong, struggling to keep itself beautiful in the quiet corners of this place. Maybe the trees were accomplices, trying to keep it there and tucked away. I know it sounds silly and all. Sometimes I convinced myself in years since that I had to have completely misunderstood or seen something and interpreted it wrong. For all I know, somebody did paint the ground or spray something wrong and I mis-read it."

"You don't really think that, though, do you?"

"No. I still feel sure of what I saw. I hadn't thought of it in years, but recently...when it came back to me, when I was able to take a moment's recollection, to seek it out and find it and remember what it was...I don't have any of those intervening doubts. It's a straight sense of absolute memory. I saw a frozen space amongst a deep thicket of trees, in the middle of a hot Ohio winter, when I was a kid. It was impossible but it was also lovely and it was there."

Inside, a whisper from Body. *I can't believe we ever forgot that. That was...the hidden winter pond. Yeah. You nailed it.*

I started getting traces of it the other night, before that Jennifer counselor showed up. I had a moment alone and somehow...I don't know how, but everything seemed to make it all go back to that for me.

And between us, not needing outright articulation, was the quivering feeling, the pass-a-charge-through-a-wire assuredness of something else to that lost moment:

That was one of the only times when, before the last few years of our dual existence, we had for a heartbeat or two believed there were fantastic things beyond our day-to-day lives. Maybe not magic...but we believed in something far larger, darker and more lovely than what humdrum and mundane had to offer us. Not to keep or abuse or hoard, but just to be.

That was the first time we had encountered the Under.

Maybe not anything as dramatic as a vampire or a demigod. But it was the Under all the same. It was still something hidden away, maybe something few if any other people could have experienced in that moment.

It was still something that you can't simply go look up online or order from a catalogue or explain with an acute thesis essay. It was there. It was Pachelbel's Canon trapped in summer ice and winter trees defying the sun and the wind and the warm.

I've only ached for that the one time. Every other time I felt a pang, it was for a woman or a place or a family or friend now gone. That was the only meeting of a perfect place, time and oddity—the kind only now encountered with my eyes-open-blunt-adulthood experience of the Under, that I could consciously ache after and wish were still here.

No memory reenactment or delusion was going to happen for that place. Nothing less would ever fool me. Somehow that… seemed relevant now. In all the confusion of memory and new experiences, what was real and what was wish-fulfillment, what was lie and what was unknown…winter-in-summer was a lodestone point that perhaps could draw me to it and keep things safe…grounded.

"Did it mean anything to you in particular?" Sarah interrupted the reverie.

"It was…wonderful. A real mystery that didn't need solving, only experiencing. That was the first and only time I can think that I had a bit of that veil lifted and saw there truly were great things that weren't all myth and falsehood to the world. Even years before we discovered there was the Under and everything else."

It was the only thing that could ever hope to counter jellyfish nightmares that made the oceans dark and forbidding.

A faint, weak whisper in the air between us.

Wish I could've seen it with you.

I felt a smile flutter through me, hearing that un-voice at last. *You would've liked it, I think.*

The cell phone went off. *Fish heads, fish heads—*

"Hello?"

"You've done it." *Ceyggan.*

"They're willing to meet with us? For real?"

"For real. You need to get back here now. They agreed, but you…it'll take some doing."

"Whatever. I can be out there shortly."

Ceyggan grunted some affirmation and hung up.

"Is this another occasion where you apologize and run off for more derring-do?"

"I'm really, really sorry. But Ceyggan has arranged something…it might make the difference in figuring this out."

She tilted her head. Made a pout of her lips. With those tight, red curls framing her face she looked like a flapper girl in some old poster from the Roaring Twenties. An F. Scott Fitzgerald girl, sitting in a flivver and waiting to go racing off to the nearest speakeasy.

"Never-time as always, right?"

"It's that or I could cancel. I'm sure I could cancel."

"Rr-iight." She smirked. "You cancel on a Faede prince. And then you would, what? Show up on milk cartons in a few days?"

"If I was lucky."

"Go. Go meet with this guy. Find out whatever you can." Her hands came out to touch Body's, this time her fingers brushing the knuckles of his. "Be careful and be wary. Don't trust anybody if you've got these Believers coming at you like this. There's no telling what is the endgame here, with these kinds of crazies."

"Are you sure you're safe, driving around town and being by yourself? Hal can't help you with this, he's day-to-day, and I'd just as soon he be left that way if possible."

"No. I don't think anybody even knows I'm out here except maybe Seppeschal and you. I made arrangements to come out here incognito."

"People trying to be incognito have a way of getting discovered lately, when we're with them."

"Don't worry. I made it this far, I think I can make it okay a while longer."

"Stay safe. I will meet with Ceyggan for this...appointment."

"And call me after?"

"Assuming I still exist after, sure." Body got up, collecting his cup of untouched coffee. "If you don't hear from us in a while, start looking at milk cartons."

31.

Ceyggan led us down the hidden staircase again, to the black door at the end of the chamber.

The door didn't open.

"Okay." He stopped a few inches from the door. Placed his hands against the ebon surface. Leaned his head forward to touch his forehead to it. "O...kay." There was no sound, no motion.

That wave-wash feeling is thicker, but lower, Soul whispered. *It's like smoke finding the lowest point or something...a chemical fog...*

Ceyggan cried out. Staggered back from the door. I moved forward to grab him but he battered away my reach. Instead he let the wall to the right of the door catch him, between two of those biometrically-secured storage doors. He sank against the wall while regarding me with wide, blue-white eyes.

"You have *really* done it, Flicker."

"What did I do wrong?"

He shook his head, grimacing. "It's not what you did wrong, it's what you did right. You...*impressed* them."

"O-kay...I guess I'm not tracking."

"It would've been better if you had pissed them off. Or just not gotten their attention either way." Ceyggan kept shaking his head. "The worst they would've done is...sure, pretty bad, but it would've been *all* they could do. They would've sent you off and that'd be it. But you...they *like* you now. They want to try and help you. And that means you're going to be taken into part of their Bond."

"That's what I wanted."

"You don't have a *clue* what you wanted," he moaned. "They're going to let you into their Bond, and I don't know anybody that has ever done that. Not anyone who wasn't Faede. You don't join the Bond until you join *them*. This isn't a handshake and you walk away."

"I already figured this wasn't going to be any walk through the park or anything, Ceyggan. I've had rough connections with other beings before—"

"No you haven't." Ceyggan's eyes were fearful to the level of near-pure animal adrenaline. His glance quivered like trying to balance a toy ball on the tip of a sharpened pencil. He wiped a slick hand against his mouth. "You've done *nothing*." He straightened up and pushed effortlessly from the wall to stand inches away from me, peering into my eyes. "They're going to try and bring you into their Bond, but even the Teaghlach don't know what that entirely means." He looked at a Bulgari watch that glittered at his wrist. "They're going to need to...there's things that need to be done before you can try this. Wait here." He walked out.

He was terrified, and I appreciated that terror. But at the same time...I thought of Mister Sharkdoll and whoever his friends were watching me. The sterility of Spam Tam's apartment.

And I thought of paper, shredding in mid-air and burning away simply at the thought of it.

Perhaps the Faede had more to fear from bonding with me than the other way around.

****

An hour passed. Ceyggan would leave and return at random intervals while I sat on the floor, back against a wall, legs crossed. Sometimes he would put his hands and head to the black door. Sometimes he would ask if I needed anything, food or drink or whatever. I'd shake my head and he'd go off again. I stayed seated against the wall. Trying to clear my head of the previous 'conversation' and its echoes in my brain.

The familiar sigh near my ear. *This could wipe us both out.*

I kept my eyes closed. *Yeah. We've taken risks before.*

Not like this. Ceyggan is looking edgier every time he comes back. That…the Teaghlach…I didn't expect anything like that.

We were expecting some sort of super-fairy, right? It wouldn't be the first time we'd been surprised by the reality behind a myth.

It was more than a surprise and you know it. I felt like…I've never felt anything like that. Even when we've faced down some true monsters. They didn't have presence *like that. They could kill us without even meaning to, if they overpower us both with the sheer bulk of what they are, and you want to try and connect with it? Maybe get swallowed up by it?*

I couldn't argue. The sense of simple communication, of the feeling of an ocean trying to bottleneck its way through a tiny reef in simplifying and shrinking their way of expression into our human frame of reference, had left a mark on my thinking. No matter what I tried to conjure up or think about, behind my eyeballs was a feel, a memory of deep-ocean pressures and a scraping, velvety friction feeling that wouldn't clear up.

I couldn't move when they were really ramped up towards us. Me, the one with nothing to 'hold down' to begin with, I couldn't move. Can you dig this? We're asking for an audience with something that shares virtually no point of similarity with anything you or I know.

We'll adapt. We'll have to. Or we cease to be.

Is all this worth the risk?

If we don't try, who else out there can?

No further debate came from him after that. I could sense

him pacing the room, swirling from corner to corner and skidding along the floorboards. Ceyggan returned twice more, always going from the entry to the rear door and the storage beyond. Another hour went by like this.

I lost track of time, with no windows or any other indicators of the world outside. I couldn't fall asleep or nap, but I stayed with my eyes closed and my head back at rest against the wall, trying to calm myself. Trying to keep the issue as abstract, as distant, as I could.

When I was about ten, Mischa and I were taken to the Circleville Pumpkin Festival, about a half-hour south of Columbus and an annual event of some local note. To more 'sophisticated' types I'm sure it would have been seen as a truly rinky-dink county fair deal. A few shaky rides, booths selling junk and food, all of it culminating in a pumpkin contest.

We got ride tickets for the haunted house ride, but the line was a little long. And the whole time we were standing there, I stared at the grotesque paintings on the sides of the trailer that housed the ride, and my mind pictured all these horrible things that were waiting within. I couldn't describe any specific details, but for some reason a greater and greater mounting panic was filling my chest and making me sweat and clutch my ticket until it was almost wiped clean of ink. Finally Mischa got sick of it and yelled out for my dad to come and get me while she rode the ride alone. I was grateful to leave the line, I was so panicked at the idea of all the deadly terrors I was sure were inside.

When my dad offered to ride it with me a little while later, I relented only because it was my father and not my cousin. An adult was an assumption of responsibility, a naive guarantee of safety.

The ride was pathetic. A rickety car that kept jerking and starting as the track would cycle along some bicycle chain attached to a motor. Sunlight leaked in through every poorly-matched seam and joint in the walls. The track was all one big exposed trailer space, not even partitions to hide or surprise you as you rounded bends in the track. A few plastic skulls painted with day-glo colors, some loud buzzers and noisemakers and flashing strobes. A string of rattling soup cans attached to a plastic skeleton. A werewolf mask bobbing on a mannequin torso. Then we were out and it was done and I was humiliated.

But it gave me one of my earliest lessons that I can remember as clearly feeling like one of the initiations into the adult world: there is rarely anything as scary as what you can dream up in your own mind and horrify yourself picturing to the point of shock.

I kept trying to repeat this mantra in my mind. *Nothing as scary as what you're imagining, the reality is mundane, maybe even disappointing. Relax, relax. Nothing as scary as what's in your mind.*

Ceyggan tapped my shoulder. I opened my eyes.

He looked down at me, his expression neutral for the first time since we'd started waiting.

"It's time."

Nothing as scary as what's in our mind, Soul repeated for me. I felt him collect around my shoulders, peering in parallel with my eyes out at the world. *Nothing as scary as what's in our mind…and maybe what's waiting for us in the next room.*

32.

This time as we passed the threshold into the Teaghlach's presence, the pool of light was already on and waiting for Body to step into its influence.

I stayed close to him, using the light's perimeter as my own guide for where I would not stray. Out there in the dark, the same insect clicks and clacks, snaps of fleshy curtains that were neither wings nor gills, but some sort of bellows membrane like a lung made of inflated swim bladders, fish meant to glide in the open sky...darker meat-tough stringy things with stinger-tips and eyes clicking their lids closed like mouths of sharp teeth...

I was grateful that whatever its influence on the atmosphere was, it blocked my ability to peer past and see more than the faintest infra-red heat suggestions of shapes.

A slow sibilance rolled out towards us from the dark.

There is a <first/BEGIN/introduction/ UNDERSTANDING> *to be reached between us,* <ghost-man/DOUBLE/spirit-thing/ leaving>.

"Okay." Body was trying to keep his eyes to the floor, and I followed that lead, directing my own gaze to the terminator line where light sharply dropped to dark. I tried to think of this as the line where we were safe, the way old fraud mystics would claim you could draw pentagrams and circles of protection when conjuring the Devil.

We must <show/share/ENTER/resolve> *some information to you. Through you. You need to* <listen/FEEL/touch/TASTE-SEE/ENGORGE> *some of the* <we/US/OUR-KEPT/memory/SELF> *before we can initiate any attempt to* <bond/BECOME/ENTER/SHARE/keep/CARE>.

"All right."

I tensed. With no muscles or tendons, all I could do was engage a feeling of self tightening, drawing in, building up a feeling of pressure like holding your breath and trying to reach as far down to the bottom of the diving pool as you can before your lungs begin to punch at your esophagus, trying to buoy you back to the open air.

Watch the terminator line. Follow the curve of the light against the dark. Watch it and—

We were looking at the earth. I was staring at the terminator line where the edge of full night was creeping on daylight.

No, not Earth. *Wait, is it...that looks like South America... but it's all wrong, it's...that looks like—*

Asia. But Asia all cramped with Russia, and there's no Pacific Island chain...wait...this is...

Pangaea. We're looking—

—not Pangaea. After. What was it called?

Gondwana. We're looking at Gondwana and Laurasia. The supercontinents after Pangaea broke up—

—but that was...are we looking at 180 million years ago? *Holy Christ, that would mean that whole basin there—*

—we think it's the southern Pacific, it's the Tethys right now...the massive shallow saltwater sea basin—

You are seeing <long/away/PRE-TIME/no-new/AGO>.

Yes. We...are realizing that.

The terminator of dark crept from the right towards the left. We were seeing the shapes of continents that were gone before even the most basic upright mammal started to look around at a height above its shoulders slumped to the ground.

I started to feel a very real and very solid fear petrify in the middle of me, and send calcifying stem-branches of its hardening, artery-clogging sensation across my sense of self.

What were we being shown, exactly? A scrapbook of prehistory?

What the hell was the Teaghlach? What did we agree to enter into here?

The Earth blinked out. Leaving us with nothing, not even the pool of light from earlier. Utter dark flooded in to take light's place. I felt disjointed, broken away from any sense of gravity or direction.

<smaller/TINY/easier> *it became to* <survive/continue/GO/forward>. *But we could not do this. Incapable of surviving* <smaller/weaker/WORSE>. *But the world was not* <good/FAVORABLE/desired/supportive> *of our state.*

We heard the faintest sounds of distant explosions. Things that roared with bestial freedom, the terror of things in the night that had never had eyes to make out the sun or stars.

Moons shattered. Great heat. Air that we could not <breathe/RESPIRATE/process/burn/EXPEL> *filled the space. Great bubbling. Noises and cries in the daylight that* <burned/DESTROYED/finished/COMPLETED>.

It was around for the last great extinction. The Permian? Wasn't that the one that killed like ninety-five percent of everything?

Body's reply, the only sensation of distance or proximity in this surround-sense nightmare of black. *I think so. But this...it existed in some way. Managed to survive it. What the hell was this thing? Is it? Are we dealing with some sort of dinosaur? Some giant amoeba that survived and just kept growing bigger instead of dividing or evolving?*

<ALL/NONE/some/RIGHT-WRONG>

It heard you.

<HEAR/PERCEIVE/pickup/receive> *all in this connection,* <man-shadow/THING-FLESH>. *We have no words for what we are, or were in this time. You may find words yourself. We find them* <limited/TRAP/CAGE-THOUGHT> *to try.*

We found this way. The way to <split/spawn/DISFIGURE/disguise>. *To become* <MORE-LESS/OTHERS/smaller> *in a way that did not compromise the entirety.*

I couldn't keep myself shut, I found myself asking with sheer fear-fueled curiosity, knowing somehow an answer could blow us all up but needing to have some grasp. *Wait...are you saying you* evolved *into this?*

<EVOLVED/grew/expanded/UNDERSTOOD/learned/experimented/DIED>. *Yes. We were able to find the way of both ways, compromise to the larger whole that served through the smaller spawn.*

Light crept back and now we were at some perspective approximating ground level. Body stood on a stone slab a mile wide, half a mile above any discernible ocean level. Air was thin and a sense of brushfire heat, of foreign gases that didn't condense so much as congeal, thick and syrupy in the lungs. I could see a landscape that was sere and clay-baked. Ferns the diameter of small ships, spreading out brittle fronds beneath a sky of white sun and bluish-green methane sky in huddled patches thirty feet wide but surrounded by powdered bone and crushed quartzite.

Nothing constant. Even as I was registering this vision the skies were changing. Time flowing...maddeningly reminiscent of watching George Pal's Time Traveler sitting in his Time Machine, watching the rapid-fire shutterclick of sun-moon-sun-moon fly by. Nights were hot and the oceans cooked. Oxygen so plentiful...I almost wanted to take a breath but I sensed the pain. Like trying to breathe pure fuel, burning and roaring through the cells...

Beneath us the rock collapsed, was sanded away by wind and turns of storms made of water and condensed liquid methane...carbon dioxide bubbled in the air and the heat took turns with a cold so shocking it burned even as I tried to let it pass through me.

Body was screaming.

I saw a flash of sunlight for a millisecond on his face and he was purple-faced, gasping. Blood clotted at his nostrils, at the corners of his mouth. His eyes were yellowed around the corneas. Then the dark. And a gasp, sobbing in air. Gases burning.

He didn't need to breathe...just the sheer toxicity of this

vision, this echo of the Teaghlach's recall it was sharing, had been enough to burn, to saturate and poison the surface cells.

...the Teaghlach was sharing some of itself. From the beginning. An understanding.

Are you okay?

The hesitant reply cough-thought back to me:

...that was an illusion...of...acid rain in my...lungs...fuck you with your...'okay.'

This is what we are. This is I am, the great <SINGLE/all/whole/GESTALT/everything>. We lost much ground with the <FALLING/crashing>, but by then the process of loss was already begun. The torment of the last was only the final stroke in a long painting of our pain across the world.

Body responded with more strength. *The falling?*

The great blast. The landing, crashing fury. It boiled air. The many small and great were <ended/KILLED/obliterated/RENDERED/REDUCED>.

Holy shit. Holy holy shit. *It's the falling. The crash it's talking about...oh crap, it's not a dinosaur it's nothing that* young.

The Teaghlach rolled on as if we weren't even there. *So much would have still <survived/GROWN/thrived> but for so many other wrongs. The air was wrong, the water wrong. The trees that buried released the toxins. We could not breathe, we could not change. The great tried to become the small but were not in time. The falling struck and so much was lost. We could not <endure/SURVIVE/IMAGINE/tolerate> another loss. The heat from the earth, blasting into the air. The clouds. The dark. The <pain/AGONY/SUFFOCATION> was immense.*

The others...the other creatures...they died out or hid from the danger? Waited it out?

I felt an affirmative, almost a smile.

You <perceive/SEE/INTUIT/arrive-at> correctly. We have been long, but we are not <ALL/eternal/EVERYTHING>. We are <FAMILY/host/sire-dam/KWA>.

More light, like a magician lifting his hand to reveal the trick, the hole card exposed. An awful trick. I could see the corpses, bloating in the dimmed sun. I saw ash, white as snow, falling in holocaustic drifts that piled high as hills over the bones. I saw the small, furry things that had evolved downwards, down into the safety of the caverns and burrows.

I saw nights where the ocean bubbled with carbon dioxide heat, methane gas bursts. Hydrogens and sulfides burning like swathes of rope made of plasma where the oceans steamed to trenches.

I saw the plants die away and return. Tides of fish corpses, rotted and slapping the tidal pools and shores in silver-mackerel scales of coastal waste, countries-long...everything going forward...the air, cooling...

When it next spoke, it sounded...hesitant. Almost hushed.

...but something...<BROKEN/not-whole/SHIFT/loss-space>

The falling. The cataclysmic destruction. The sheer concussion and shock of it striking...the Teaghlach conveyed that feeling again.

The <not-all/HERE AND THERE/ALLSPACE/sidereal> sense. *Not entirely...solid. Not altogether here.*

Not words...sensation...feelings folded in on me. I felt as though we were at the center of some immense sheet of paper, going off endless in any direction...but impossibly, the paper was folding in...turning...an origami that was like trying to perceive a headache, like trying to taste sadness, sucking on tin foil and chewing on dirty pennies.

The feelings curled...and now the paper's infinite edges were somehow meeting, so far away that they seemed to be one and the same surface...a Möebius of feeling...

They existed in something left of field to the solid, outside of three-dimensional comprehensive space.

I felt like a Flatlander, trying to see Lord Sphere as a whole but only perceiving the size-shifting series of concentric, flat circles.

Something about the Teaghlach was immense, but also tiny. But not the way that the Faede's glamour confused peoples' sense of scale. The Teaghlach was...like the camel that could get through the eye of the needle...the needle immense, the camel microscopic...space and relations vacillating. Compressed in 'sidereal' space. Loss-space. Shunted there and partially trapped...like setting off dynamite in a fox hole and seeing the animals stuck halfway in and halfway out of the holes. What was that? Some way of expressing space like a fanned hand of playing cards. Each coordinate a different suit, with the shuffling of the deck as an expression of changing location, space and dimensional volumes...so beyond me, so beyond math or explanation. I thought of the Teaghlach briefly as a mass, an amorphous shapelessness that...stacked itself...folded in and stretched into three-dimensional existence only as a by-product of sheer *being*. Trapped in extrusions into our space and time like...

<what/WHO> *is Winnie the Pooh?*

I tried to emit dismissal. *Not important.* Ephemeral associations. In the drift of meeting minds, it was difficult to differentiate what was coming or going, transmitting or receiving.

There is <growth/TIME/ever-more/so-MUCH> *that we cannot commit this to you. But you must know this to* <comprehend/BOND/see/FEEL/KNOW> *some measure of what you proposed. Can you* <imagine/PRESUME/accept>?

Body's response was so low I almost couldn't perceive it. *They want to know if we can handle what they're going to show.*

How are we supposed to conceivably answer that?

A pause. Out in the black. Clicks and hums. Something that cracked as loud as a mastodon's jawbone...it might have *been* a mastodon's jawbone.

I think the answer is irrelevant. We're here. It's too late to try backing out.

Do you <accept/ENCOURAGE/relent>?

Yes/yes.

In the worming darkness, I made out forms that were like charcoal against space. Barely discernible darkness against deeper dark. Not hands and not tentacles...I thought of tree branches made of rubber, of octopus arms that ended in hairy spider-leg talons.

The repulsion was immediate and felt like having a dry-ice blade shoved through my head.

I wanted to scream, twist away, not let them touch me. But

there was nowhere to twist to, we were nowhere and nothing in this head space.

The contact was shockingly contrasted against what I'd been fearing. Soft as rose petals, old women's skin, the daffodil touch of air from a summer breeze. I felt flooded with the smells of earth, dry leaves, a spice of aged wood and the must of dank fungal growths under logs in a deep forest. Squealing. A feeling of being stretched, impossibly extended and crushed and pulled, a taffy spirit in a grinding spin of sensation.

The <birth/SPAWN/separating/BEGINNING/assignation>.

Cries. Shards of light flickered, and I read these as eyes batting open and closed rapidly.

I saw a field of green, impossible flowers. Other faces, planets hovering over the stunted horizon, tree trunks of bodies. Others, hands reaching down to free us...a sense of more stretching...arms being pulled upon, pulling us up, up and *welcome, welcome Diatha sister-cousin-new-one.*

Welcome, lovely. This is life. You are no longer of the <whole/gestalt/BEING/ENTIRE/one>, *you are now part of* <family/ALL/ELSE>.

Birth? Spawning? Some form of welcome, of release from the great mass and now a singular identity...a blur of light, of breaking glass pieces of days and thoughts. It was swept out before I could process it.

Body: *I feel like I'm going to be sick.*

There's nowhere to be sick into.

I'll find a way.

Hold it. We have to keep steady here.

Whispers in a hallway. The dark continued, but now there were barks and raps of sounds around us. Like sitting in a surround-sound theater in zero gravity. Floating and hearing snatches of song—was that Gaelic? Akkadian?—old mutterings of love and lust...a scream...a declaration of hatred.

A softer, feminine voice. Beseeching. Pained.

Robeyn. Robeyn, never-good, why are you refusing?

Gruff, responding with a voice that was silk buried under rock. *You would refuse too, if you knew what it would mean.*

But we can't. You can't. It is part of all—

The conversation snatched away; you could feel a tendril of something almost literally reaching out, grabbing hold of the vibrating string of that memory conversation and snap it away from us. But a persistent echo-ghost seemed to eagerly linger before dissipating. *Robeyn never-good. Robeyn...*

...blat of trumpets. Jazz music? The taste of fizzing, lemony...something bitter and bright and sparkling down our throats...songs of a war...

This is <NOISE/distraction/EPHEMERA/irrelevant> *our apologies we must* <TAKE/ABSORB/have/handle/CARE/keep> *what little we have. Here...here then...*

...light forming. Wandering in, like latecomers to a theater show. Tendrils of light coming from outside our frame of view, coming forward... merging... knotting... forming a scene of jagged angles.

Weight. Gravity. I felt something pressing against my right cheek. Hard and gritty-grimy... asphalt?

Pavement. A piece of bubblegum against my cheek.

I could smell sun-hot pavement. Garbage. Car exhaust. A car horn honked a million miles away.

I was lying on pavement. Looking up and away at an alley.

Another face, another moon in the heavens staring down.

I was looking at the lead-head woman. No way to mistake the grubby-faced pale blob with the bruise hollows.

Cries. Someone yelling. Ceyggan's voice.

The lead-head turned away. Stumbling, walking drunkenly in a zig-zag as if invisible objects were ricocheting her. A squeal-grunt of tires. At the end of the alley was a truck clunking to a stop.

More yelling.

Pain.

It had finally caught up. It caused everything to break up and shake, like attempting to watch a film run through an old-fashioned spool projector, mounted to some shaky wheelchair and shoved across a gravel road. Shaking, juddering. Pain flashed silver-hot across my throat. There was a desire to swallow but it kept hitting a sharp spike when she tried.

Scared. There was so much terror wrapped up in the pain that it was hard to focus and remember that this wasn't us, this wasn't now.

I felt Body hardening against it more effectively than I could. *Switches.*

He was speaking to me.

Switches. Think of them as switches in a stranger's bathroom where you're a guest. Flip the lights off. Turn off the fan. Don't let it all blow you away.

I could handle the distant past, the acid sky and the explosions of earth. Here, he could handle the intimate pain of a torn throat, a pebble lodged in the small of the back where this girl was lying helpless on the pavement as the lead-head stumbled off.

I fought past the metallic burning and pictured them. In my head they were cheap, plastic-covered switchplates. Off-white and chipped, against a robin's egg wall. The lights were on and bright and burning, but I saw a hand flip them down. With the dark, the colors disappeared, even the switch went away. The pain stopped screaming.

Did the Teaghlach know this was our capability? That each of us would be some sort of anchor to the other getting through the whole experience? Was that why it had agreed to this?

That is definitely the girl from the Scots compound.

I had to try and stare at the dirty feet, the ragged edges of her pants legs. More yelling. There was an ugly gurgle-chuckle that sounded below...away...like air escaping the wrong way...

The truck. I don't know that truck, but—

The passenger door that faced us swung open.

Shadows skittered out of the door and fell, scrambling and wisping into nothing like mice loosed from the gangplank of a sinking cruise ship.

Shadows dissolving from the cover of the cab.

A hand reached out. A face leaned forward into the sunlight.

Plastic white doll face. Black eyes. I couldn't see them—because Diatha hadn't seen them—but I could almost sense the swimming, squirming monstrosity that I knew had to be bowled around that head.

Mister Sharkdoll.

The lead-head was about halfway to him, as if all notion of the attack was forgotten. A child distracted from something shiny.

She hesitated. Stopped. Swayed.

And Mister Sharkdoll frowned. Lowered his outstretched hand a few inches. His mouth was twisting...the lips distending...and the half-seen growths around him went more furious...he was chewing.

Instead of pursing his lips, he let a corner of his mouth crack, like a cartoon gangster muttering out of a side of his mouth. The cheeks puffed, expelling...

I couldn't see it strike. But a second after, the lead-head jerked. Her shoulders rolled. There was a high-pitched whimpering not unlike the dog from before.

She lurched forward. In a moment she closed the distance to reach out to that cold corpse hand, letting herself be drag-jerked into the truck's interior as a stringless puppet.

More yelling. I felt hands touching me, distant and faint.

The voice intruding in my head as the light began dimming.

Robeyn. Robeyn not-good. Ill tempter. Why won't you come back?

You wouldn't go back if you understood what you give up. Who *you give up.*

The pain was trying to shove in on my thoughts again.

Sharkdoll is the passenger. Sharkdoll attacked the Scots.

I rallied enough control to respond. *They already had her. Why did she end up attacking the Scots? Why didn't they still have her?*

A telepathic grumbling from Body. *More than that...if she was so important to get back like this, why lose her at all to have to go and mount some commando attack to get her back from the brothers?*

No sense. No sense at all.

I tried to peer harder at the truck, to see if I could make out a driver. It was useless. It was the trap, that disorienting feeling like when you watch someone else playing a first-person video game, or sitting passenger in a car. I kept wanting to turn, to look at more things, to get bearings. But Diatha hadn't moved, so I couldn't make her. All the instincts were hers, we were as trapped as men sitting together in a sinking diving bell, watching the depths piled up above as the darkness from below reached up to take us into its cupped grasp.

The feelings were of more than pain and fear. The feelings were of...something despairing...regret. Guilty? Yes. Like a child doing something it was told not to do. Disobedient guilt.

A flutter of trash to the right of my dwindling vision distracted. Pretty movements in a breeze.

Robeyn.

Pain.

A new moon eclipsed the sky. Ceyggan.

He may have said a name as his lips moved, his hands were reaching down towards us. Towards her. Maybe her name.

Everything curtained back to blackness.

A hush. A feeling of assembly. Of shapes in the black, gathering together. Faint water drips. A clicking. The sound of a distant summer locust (carnivorous?) shivering in the dusk.

That is <all/LEFT/little> *to give. Do you* <see/comprehend/ FEEL/grasp/KNOW>? *why we wish this thing found? To know the reason? The person?*

Yes/yes.

Another pause. The thrum and chittering became more agitated even as its volume lowered.

Not a good feeling. It was the sense of how a dog's happy bark could drop volume to a warning growl.

You are not <enlightened/HELPED/educated/INFORMED> *by these things?*

We are, Body quickly replied. *But what it tells us leads to more questions.*

A longer pause. Out there in that ebony space I felt...a taste of winter cold. Gathering. I think maybe it's the sensation a longshore fishing crew or lobstering ship gets, when they look out at the horizon of ocean and see the big swells rolling forward. The kind with Titanic-sized troughs in their valleys, ready to swallow them into the brine-dark folds. The tidal wash that I'd experienced in the outer chamber now was less directional...it was now a sensation as if I was Moses and suddenly the trick to keeping those massive walls of the Red Sea away...the hushed moment before the water was reminded by gravity that it had every right to be where we were, rushing in to crush us.

We are not in good territory here.

I know, he answered.

Perhaps...there is not enough of the <bond/CONNECT/SHARE/strong-force> *for this to be of use.*

New light pierced the darkness in front of me. This was tined and jagged, lightning bolts colored in rainbow oily tints. Again, a flash of the terminator of earth. Another slash of light that smelled of sulfur and which I instinctively knew was musket-fire. A pounding that was tribal and tympanic, stretched deer-hides over hollowed tree trunks. The lightning flashes of color faded away, leaving sparkles that were old constellations, unnamed formations of the stars overhead that no longer were visible in modern times.

What was this? More voices. Feelings like hands touching skin. Rubbing my head. Stroking cheeks. Touching my groin, my toes. Laughter. Screaming that choked off too-fast. More silver-hot pain, needles that widening into chasms of blunt force, assailing me from everywhere.

Perhaps there needs to be <BOND/FORM/stronger>

Body and I resonated the same realization:

They're trying to take us in. To enfold. The Bonding.

I recalled Ceyggan's worried, sickly features. *You may not even* be, *anymore, if you try this.*

In the midst of the dark, when the stars wheeled and the lightning tines of color started cutting in faster and faster...there was the center. The vortex point. In that core there was a feeling of ground zero. Solid. Implacable walls of something existing. Twisted and forced out-of-true by space/time but no less real and invincibly there, inescapably porous to everything...

...I was smiling at a boy, *oh he was gorgeous, look at that black hair and the lips that tasted of apricots but were colored like plums, white skin at my hands...no...*

Ache. An ache of something being over. Over and done, so many times. I should have kissed Annie. So many completions, endings. Bleeding away like life on the pavement...

You wouldn't, if you knew what it meant. What you would lose. Who you would lose.

Robeyn. Robeyn not-good, never-good. Who was that?

I smelled rotting flesh.

I heard someone hollering and clanging a war-bell, a call to arms in the late nights.

We were ambushed by a feeling of magnetism... inevitable, inexorable pulling down...down and inwards...the sense of being shoved small, compressed as a tablet of sugar...sugar about to be stirred into a massive ocean...

...no...Body was fighting, and I mirrored his sense of panicked resistance. *No...no...*

<STRUGGLE/resist/FIGHT> *is not necessary. Bonding will make us* <one/ALL/everything/COMPLETE/SHARED> *and you will better to enjoin with what we* <KNOW/FEEL/sense/ REMEMBER/ARE>.

No, we are not here to Bond. We have seen what you had to offer. We have to go.

<STRUGGLE/resist> *not necessary. Or desired. Relax your* <SELF/being/ENTITY> *and stop being* <GHOST-DOUBLE/ SHADOW/copy-man/thing-flesh> *cut off from the* <rest/ ENTIRE/whole>.

We are our own being. We are not Faede. It would not help you to do this.

Irrelevant. The hiss and scuttle in the dim, the dark between those rolling stars, was coming closer...the sense of the parted ocean waters were beginning to reach us, the spray of the foam of dark and gravity was licking at me.

I couldn't remember the name of my first dog.

My high school was a mascot with no context, no school colors.

No. I didn't *have* a dog.

No, you are not...thank you but no, we cannot be part of this.

<permission/CONSENT/willing> *not a factor.*
It is to us!
Your being is not a factor for consent.

The swirling draw-down...I could taste hot meat, unidentifiable and gamey-exotic. Smell flower petals in rain. The loam of freshly-turned earth. Gravesite or farmlands, I couldn't tell.

And that face that kept coming up. Different times, different cries, but always the same eyes, the same rock-under-silk: *you wouldn't if you knew what you have to give up.* Who *you're giving up.*

Robeyn not-good. I wanted to yell for this Robeyn whoever to help, but these were memories...absorbing, cloying memories like being drowned in wine- and urine-soaked blankets, sheets made of skin and leather and leaves...the Teaghlach was so *much*, so much and it was as if we were fighting with a thousand cluttered attics and cellars filled with disorganized, mismatched centuries. Nothing catalogued or neatly arranged...

...was this what Rod experienced in dealing with human minds? Was this overlap? Trying to find sense in a chaos of so many...so long...what the hell was this? We were drowning in something so old and massive yet it all seemed so stressed... pulling in so many simultaneous directions...what was this feeling of crushing and tugging...?

No. No, you can't...you can't have me. We're not up for grabs. This isn't a Bonding, this is a Sharing. *We walk away. You let us go. We didn't—*

This is not <dispute/ARGUMENT/negotiation/tantrum> *you are to be* <part/all/whole/of us>.

That's not how this is going to work.

I was sitting in Annie Spartan's garage playroom. I smelled strawberry shampoo. Sun-warm carpet and the smells of cut grass...no...*nnnnno...you can't...*

...I saw a grinning face, grinning so wide it seemed the smile was wider than the head supporting it. Just a Cheshire smile, and a name fluttering in the smell of cut grass. *Robeyn,*

Robeyn, how impudent you have been, such a good fellow to dance before the mortals, show them a trick or two then return... come back...

...Robeyn—or whoever it was—dissolved into Annie's face, frowning at me because I couldn't...wouldn't...kiss her...

...Dad, frowning at me. But Dad's face was stretching, looking down at me where I was floating, flailing in cold March water between the boat and the dock...I was dissolving away into the water and Dad's face was the full moon above me, a bloated harvest moon of disappointment and it was filling the sky, the water seemed to be bearing me up, helpless to meet it, horizon kissing horizon and everything...

...everything...cold...

...no...

<bond/join/part/be/are/come>

...no...something...cold. Cold water and cold breath.

I felt a grip slipping somewhere, and heard Body screaming again, but it was my scream as well and it seemed to warble, fail as a speaker going dead...

...Dad, frowning. A kiss from the moon. I was shivering... shivering but it wasn't winter, it was—

—summer—

...winter in summer...a lovely impossible...the lovely impossible...yes...

break <away/apart/fly/come/fall/with us>, <bond/be/part>—

—no—

...*you* <will/are/have>—

—winter in summer. I was standing in front of a wide pond of frozen water, ice in the middle of a summer thicket of trees. And it wasn't daylit, it was night. It was night, and overhead, in the tiny clearing amongst the tree cover the moon was huge. The moon wanted to fill the sky. Not Dad, not Annie.

No—

—the man in the moon was smiling and opening its mouth and swallowing the sky and it seemed as though I would fall up, up into the hole of the sky—

...no, leave me alone, leave us alone, this wasn't the trade...

No <trade/exchange> *possible, you are to be* <part/whole/ dissolve/eat/swallow>.

...no...

My feet, planted in the dirt. The ice pond, lovely and dark and forever kept secret amongst the trees. No animal song, so quiet...the man in the moon was trying to swallow it all but how could they? How could they take any of this, grounded to me and me alone, winter defying the summer of the rot and the breakdown and the humid, swallowing everything...no...

I could stand on this ground.

No. This was something special and real, and nobody else saw it. You can't have this.

In my sense of self...hands. Flailing. Helpless. Groping.

And finding other hands. Another grip of minds. Body, reaching across and finding me as I found him.

Clutched. Interwoven.

I had forgotten.

I hadn't.

The ice in summer.

We looked up at that moon, that bloated and expanding, swallowing hole-shape in the sky. A light that was pale yellow-white, the waxing illumination of dying in harvest fall...no.

No.

Our mouths opened. Our voice reached out.

Imagine smoke rings, expanding. Imagine text in the shape of your thoughts.

But imagine them loud. Wide as the sky. Hard as the ice. Cold as the space that was still greater than the growing moon. An eclipse against a supernova.

Fire and smoke and the defiance of panic.

It flew out, seemed to stall, and caught a second breath.

The sky shattered.

We thought of the moment of that old silent film, the Lumière brothers and their journey to the moon. The primitive bullet rocket piercing the eye of the Man in the Moon. No longer grinning but weeping thick, milky gobbets of ruined lunar flesh.

The moon buckled. Winced, its face pinching into that hole, dissolving and breaking away. Pulling back its shards and shattered limbs from our mind.

<STOP/END/CONCLUDE/not/NO-BOND/NO-SHARE>

Get away from us.

We are only trying—

Get away. A child-me, standing with fists clutched at my side. The darkness of the trees as silhouettes against the blue-purple night. Breath fogging. Smoke ring dreams.

Hands tightly twined and muscles tensed as if galvanized, electrocuted.

Go away. Leave us alone.

Child's voice. The way a baby's lungs can scream, can screech at a pitch no adult can make. And no ear can stand.

The moon tried to recover, a small sparkle-flicker of stars against the dark, attempting to re-form their constellations, their will into shapes imposed against our own small space. The precious pond of winter against a burning rocket summer of their collective desire...

We only—

Or we will break you as we break the sky.

The sky swallowed the moon. And we broke the sky. It shattered as bone china shot from a cannon at a steel wall. Pulverized and misting.

The pool of light returned.

Body was on his knees. And I was hovering over his head, looking down on his quaking shoulders and the crown of his skull.

I was shaking as well. I felt as though I had gotten off a roller coaster and all the vibrations were still rummaging for places amongst my former innards.

No. No.

Out there in the dark of the chamber, the hiss-clattering had died away.

Only silence. A terrified silence.

And the stone floor around Body was cracked in a mosaic of lines.

Spiral lines. Spiraling out like lightning blurred in a

kaleidoscope lens, trapped and traced, its lines copied by hammer and chisel into the rock ground.

A sigh of dust, stone dust, settling around us.

Like fogging breath over a frozen pond.

And from the dark. A sound.

An actual sound.

"...go."

I had to take it in and hear the faint clink of metal-on-metal, a sound like a dropped nickel on the floor, to look and see that one of the largest spiral arms had zagged back to the chamber door behind us. It hung on twisted pistons and hydraulic vapor was pumping out in short, weakening bleats of air. Light skewed in through the diagonal crack where it had come off its mounting.

Beyond, I saw the gray silhouette of Ceyggan, peering in.

"Go."

Not trying to talk to us in its mind-voice. Reduced to shaping lips and throat and lungs, solely to make the sound. The base, primitive word and noise.

So as not to risk touching us again, in that dark frozen place down below the broken moon.

Body stood up slowly. Brushed off dust from his knees. Looked out at the darkness with a blank face.

A breath.

"We'll see ourselves out, then."

****

Ceyggan backed away as Body strained and shoved the broken door panel far enough to a side that he could squeeze past it to the outer corridor. He stood several feet off as Body regained his footing, nearly tripping over the edge of the door but recovering in a faint swirl-haze of chilled hydraulic mist.

"What did you do?"

Body stared back at Ceyggan.

"What did you do?" he asked again. But his voice cracked. He swallowed.

Body took a step forward.

Ceyggan took two back. His hands were open, in front of him, the posture of a man confronted by a stray dog snarling.

"You don't want me to tell you that, do you?"

Ceyggan didn't answer.

Body shrugged. Dust shifted off the shoulders of his coat. I stayed down low amongst the curls and drifts of dissipating mist. "I couldn't honestly tell you if I tried."

"Is it..."

"I don't know. I don't think it does, either. Maybe when it figures it out, it'll tell you itself. But we're out of here."

He risked stepping between Body and the staircase, hands still spread out in front of him.

"Did you...was there anything—"

"I don't know. I wasn't bullshitting. Maybe it's something. Right now I. Don't. Know." Body nodded towards the stairs. "We're going, Ceyggan. Call a service to fix your door. But we're done here."

He seemed about to ask something further—

"...*go*."

It rolled from the cracked doorway, as ephemeral and evaporative as the mist. Ceyggan's glance flicked to over Body's shoulder and in that gap Body pushed past and reached the staircase.

****

The phone went off as Body started the car.

How is it that phone never seems to get broken into a million pieces when all around us does?

Body frowned and shrugged as he brought the phone to his ear.

"Hello."

"Don't take this as a sign that I'm as-yet entirely clear on what we're doing together in this situation."

"I will assume nothing, Detective."

Pinney sounded sleepless and I could almost hear a rasp

that could've been an unshaved cheek against the receiver of the phone.

"We have identification on the woman." A flap of paper in the background. "Hope Cambridge. Worked primarily temp jobs. Secretarial, receptionist sort of positions. Nothing remarkable in any way other than that she hadn't reported for her last couple of assignments. No close friends or family to report when she went AWOL. There is the gap between that and when she was discovered at your door."

"The name means nothing. I don't have an idea why she would have been left there except to frame me somehow."

"Maybe this Dwyer? Someone working with him?"

"No. I don't think they'd be trying to frame me. It wouldn't suit their purpose."

Kill you, sure. Frame you? No.

"Have the police been to her home?"

"No. Given the state of her...and the nature of her discovery... we are slating that part of the investigation for the morning." A puff of air. "You're going to ask me for information so you can go do something highly illegal and stupid, aren't you?"

"You really know me better than you think, good sir."

"It's too late and I'm too out of it for banter. You want the address, I want a promise that you're not going to do anything to compromise a potential investigation site."

"I promise I will not cause any harm or interference to your investigation."

"You're being semantic, aren't you? Something is going to happen or you're going to get the bright idea to do something and then later you'll have a cute response about how it wasn't you that really did the harm, or how whatever you did wasn't *technically* interference, or some other splitting-hairs bullshit."

"I promise that that is not my intent."

"I will give you the address if the next promise is no more promises."

"I don't think I can make that kind of commitment."

A whispered *son of a bitch*. "Okay. Fine. If I said no you'll have some other way of finding out anyway, it might as well be from me and not risk you causing some other riot downtown again."

"I didn't cause that—"

"Shut up. I'm speaking generally."

He recited the address. Body thanked him, for which there was merely a grunted resignation and the call ended.

For the first time in a while, Body thought, *I am considering just going home, pulling a blanket over my head, and pretending to sleep while the rest of the world makes up its own damned mind on all of this.*

I whispered from the back glass, looking up at the stars and feeling a little relieved that these refused to move. *And yet there is an as-yet-untouched place we can go check and see if it gives us any clue as to what the hell all this that we've been experiencing the last thirty hours or so could mean.*

I don't care.

You also don't sleep.

I recall Trina remarking that people who never sleep go crazy. That ship sailed.

You're not going to leave me alone about this.

I pulled my gaze from the stars. *I don't have to pester you. I want something to think about other than what we just went through. And so do you.*

I hate you.

Technically that's self-loathing. Not healthy.

He put the Vega into drive, and the car seemed to emit a relieved shake of its frame as he began to back it out of the storage space parking lot.

Fine. Let's go play boy detective.

33.

Hope Cambridge had lived in one of those multi-layered, Colonial-façade type of apartment complexes, all jet-black shutters against stark, hospital-white sidings. The kind with scatterings of townhomes and garden single-floor flats, all facing artificial miniature duck ponds with curvy, graceful and tasteful walking paths amongst the cattails waving in the breeze.

I'm sure such places are nice. But somehow I have always had the impression, as I'm driving by them, that they were one of life's great waiting room areas: built not to accommodate any real roots-putting or building-up of a life, but more to putter through a year or two's distractions of work or school until the Next Big Thing comes along to sweep a person out of state, following a job or a lover.

The cattails were so neat and green, I was pretty sure they were regularly re-planted so as to never wither or rot in the shallows of the tasteful, graceful duck ponds. As I pulled into the main drive that tree-branched out into the smaller service and apartment parking lanes, I passed a whitewashed wooden sign done in that Williamsburg Blackletter style, proclaiming I was entering Sheffield Forest Estates, with the lesser slogan line telling me this was Condominium Living for the Next Millennium.

In all truth, I wondered if they meant this was Condominium Living the way it would be in the new Millennium...or if it was a punitive sentencing from a court of culture: you are hereby sentenced to Condominium Living. For the Next Millennium.

I was fortunate that while it wanted to present itself as an upscale complex, Sheffield Forest was not so upscale as to be a gated community. Next millennium or not, gated systems are expensive and tend to open you up to liability when they inevitably have their failings. A friend of mine in Las Vegas had been proud to tell me during one of her visits back to Columbus that she lived in a gated community. The next visit home a few months later, she was complaining how the 'gated security' wouldn't even keep out the local ice cream vendor who kept coming in on a borrowed code and parking his truck behind her car, blocking her in before she'd leave for work each day. A security gate had its weaknesses for even a relative dope like me to exploit; nonetheless I was glad for the lack of yet another obstacle to deal with.

However I discovered very quickly that what the owners had lacked in generosity towards a gate budget, the planners of the property had made up in confusing, twisting, nonsensical interior arrangement. Since apartment complexes are rarely a part of the overall municipal street scheme, it is very difficult, once you get to the overall street address of the complex, to be able to clearly track down where the hell in all the mess of Lanes, Brooks, Curves, Circles and Courts is your target.

I tried a brief period delivering pizza after high school, and it was always the addresses in the newly-built condo areas that made me groan. It's all very well to be told someone lived at '1234 Merry Morning Drive,' but you'd arrive at a layout that looked like one of the lost scribbling of Daedalus when he was sousing out the Labyrinth at Minos, and just know you weren't going to get that pizza there in any decent time to expect a tip.

Hope's unit was designated Unit D, in the 3400 block of Glacial Path. I had missed the turn twice before finding Glacial Path (off of Firelight Lake Road), then somehow couldn't find the 3400 block. All the four-storey towers looked alike, all the parking lot areas were fat oases of freshly-painted, freshly-tarred mid-level compact models in black, red and silver (or if you were really daring, light champagne). I passed the 1100s, the 1300s, though I had the order and direction down, then after 1500 came 2200, and I was lost again.

Apparently the order broke up at the tiny creek that had been put in (probably for drainage) between the 1500 and 2200. Why a creek would qualify as a block of 700 digit spaces in the order was beyond me. But once I saw that it had broken at the creek and that the order had switched from even numbers right to left after the tiny crossing bridge, I was able to finally find Hope's block.

Each tower was a set of single-floor, two-bedroom apartments with internal-facing front doors and mail boxes. A and B were ground floor, with switchback staircases at the far end of the internal hallway taking you up to C and D, with E and F, G and H finishing up the arrangement.

After I parked and walked past the tasteful and graceful myrtle trees flanking the entrance, I had A to my left, B to my right, switching back on the next floor, so that going up the staircase meant C was on top of A, and D on top of B.

The internal corridor was so shadowy it was several degrees cooler than the day outside. A faint echo from the poured-concrete flooring and walls. Above each mailbox was a brass-finished sconce lantern, most of them turned off for the daytime.

Unfortunately I'd been expecting to deal with a fairly standard lock. What I confronted as I stood at Hope Cambridge's door was Sheffield Estates' further answer to semi-upscale condo living: a numeric keypad.

Crap.

Soul swirled forward, I sensed the mild weight leave my chest and shoulders as he invisibly hovered at the keypad.

Huh. Funky.

Can you make out anything?

Well...lean in. Look at the keys.

I saw what he meant right away, and felt a fool I hadn't thought of it right off. The most commonly-tapped keys were missing bits where they had suffered repeated tapping.

4...1...2...and the pound symbol. Each one had slight thinning of the black type on the white soft plastic, and the pound was almost half-rubbed away completely.

Great. I straightened up, frowning. *But does that mean it's a three-digit code, or four digits and one of these is repeated? Or it could be five, six or whatever anyway, if any of these are repeated. Not much help. Assuming it's simply a four-digit code... what's the old math formula for permutations? Four times three times two times one? So...twenty-four possible combinations?*

No, you've got your math totally wrong. The formula for the number of possible 4-digit codes, if you have all the numbers from zero to nine to choose from, is seven hundred and fifteen possible combinations.

Terrific. And here I was giving up hope with only twenty-four. We can't sit here tapping away for hours making guesses.

Ah, I beg to differ, good sir. A sigh of air around my ears. *Your eyes can only see the physical wear on the numbers most frequently used...but I can see a little more than that. To me, I can see...hrm...trails? No. Smears, more like.*

Get to the point, Poindexter.

Well, the smears...they have different...what would fit best? Thicknesses? Brightness levels? It's not quite either or neither on that. But it boils down to: I can see a pathway here, and if I'm reading it right...assuming the thinnest/darkest lengths of the smear-trails are the oldest...then I think it...hrm...

So what does it look like?

The 4 is overlapped. A dim/thin but then a blot that's...hot? Hot-bright?

I really wish you could stick to simple descriptions.

Descriptions assume a mutual frame of reference, jackhole. If you forgot, I don't exactly operate in the five senses these days.

Fair enough. Okay... I leaned down again and gave a solid peering at the keypad, as if I could see the same 'smear-trails' that Soul was describing. *You say the '4' key has an overlap, the weakest and the strongest. So if you're interpreting things right, that suggests it's the first and the last number of the sequence. Do you see any other overlaps?*

No.

So the '1' and the '2' only get used once. Can I presume the smears suggest a sort of path from one key to the next?

Yeah. From the 4 there's a line cuts over to the '2,' then from the '2' to the '1.' Then there's a blotchy spot on the pound symbol, only slightly brighter/thicker than the one over the '4.'

I reached out and tapped 4-2-1-4. After a second's hesitation where I pulled my hand back an inch, I then plunked on the pound sign.

A faint *bleet*, and the solid *ch-chunk*-clack! of a door bolt releasing. A turn of the handle and we were in Hope Cambridge's apartment.

Damn, I'm good.

****

We are not detectives. I know sometimes talking about these things we've gotten involved in, it seems like we're playing at the kind of half-assed amateur sleuth work like makes up the worst, most boring 'garden club miss' detective novels that have flooded the earth ever since Agatha Christie croaked. But I'm no more Sherlock Holmes than your average garbage truck driver.

Before opening the bookstore, when I still had a series of various day jobs to pay the bills and save up towards my entrepreneurial dream, I had minor aspirations of being a writer. I imagine that's the only curiosity-bone in my system that explains what we do now. An inclination to want to make up a story, a tale to fit between ideas. Only in what we do now, I'm trying to make up stories to fit between facts, and hope that the story is the right one.

Hope Cambridge appeared to have been a pretty much ordinary human being. Her apartment was done in a pale pastel pink, with a beige carpet running wall-to-wall. All of her furniture was that assemble-it-yourself variety, photocopied wood veneers over cheap particle board held with plastic dowels and those strange European-invented turned-and-tightened screws. The one good piece of quality furniture was her couch: a huge, poofy number of black leather squeezed against a shin-banging coffee table, all pressed claustrophobically against a fern-draped entertainment center with a respectable large flatscreen TV.

What are we even doing here, really?

Looking for something. Anything.

She was a lead-head. A burn-out case. Whatever life she might've had before she got hooked onto emotion-peddling, she left it behind completely.

No. I don't buy that. Spam Tam and others like him don't do business just burning out customer after customer. People do it for a while and either quit or die off, but they can do it for a while and maintain. Any addict can maintain during that illusion period where they think it's under control.

Fair enough point. But what does that mean for us here?

I don't know. But she was dead on our doorstep and nobody else so far has shown up as a corpse special delivery. I want to know if there was something different about her.

Like how she managed to get away from the Scots brothers and somehow make it to our home?

Exactly. She wasn't in any shape to go hotwiring a car and joyriding all the way back to downtown.

Somebody left her there.

You got it.

The bathroom was equally unremarkable, though it gave more sign of having been lived in. Some soap scum on the bottom of the sink basin. A used lady's razor sitting by the faucet.

Old tricks picked up from reading books. I squeezed the towels hanging on the rack by the bathtub, over the toilet's back tank. Dry. Risk taking a sniff. Very, very faint smell like mildew, but old.

Bathtub. Dry...until I ran a fingertip around the drain.

Water. It hadn't been used in a little while, but at least in the last…what, half a day or so? Maybe less?

And a persistent smell, very weak. Coming off the shampoo bottle when I checked the couple of squeezable bottles resting in the little in-set shower stall shelf. Strawberry mousse perfume shampoo. For treating colored hair, the label read.

It's a good bet she didn't shower up then put on the same dirty clothes between getting away from the Scots and being left at our doorstep.

I turned out the bathroom light.

In the bedroom, the first thing I found was a towel on the floor by the doorway. Damp. Smelling of soap and shampoo, a match for the bathroom bottle. I picked it up, sniffed to be sure, dropped it back in place. A glance around the bedroom suggested it hadn't been slept in recently, even if someone had dropped a towel instead of hanging it back up in the bathroom.

It's a dead space.

I stopped looking around. *What? Like Spam Tam's apartment was?*

Not the same. That was so wiped clean it almost hurt. Like spiritual bleach. This place hasn't been cleaned so much as…nothing useful left behind. There's disturbance that's only just settling, the usual motion interruptions. Someone moving about…but no sense of anything else. Nothing like the keypad outside or some of the little trace leavings that I think were Hope's. This room…it feels and looks and tastes like watching something on television. I can see it, but it has no impression of realness to it.

*You know…*I turned on a heel, looking around the bedroom. *There is something wrong here.*

How so?

I took in the bedroom as a whole. Bed sheets nominally pulled up to the pillows, the sort of working-person's hasty half-assed making of the bed, rumpled but not suggesting recently slept in. A few tissues in the trash can by the bed. Some books left on the bedside table.

Not a neat freak. Something…

What is it?

I went back to the closet, this time not bothering to look at the clothes, but sweeping them aside and looking at the floor.

A shoe rack that held a few pairs of high-heeled pumps. Some sneakers. A pair of paint-splattered flip-flops.

Someone else was here and used the place. But I couldn't tell if any clothes have been taken.

More dead space. Movement without energy.

Okay...

I went through the shoes, picking each one up and shaking it. Tipping it so the mouth was upside-down. Nothing in them.

Without pause, I went back out to the kitchen. The trash can still had a half-full liner with some dried tuna cans, a cereal box. Some cheese slice wrappers.

The drawers had nothing but cutlery and some odd junk drawer contents of batteries and coupons. The cupboards displayed nothing out of the ordinary either.

No containers.

What are you talking about?

Spam Tam. His apartment. Remember? Dozens of all those bottles and jugs and cartons.

Yeah, he was a dealer. A drug pusher. That was his stock.

But none here.

Wait...you're thinking that she—

She was a lead-head. An addict. Even if she was maintaining for a while, she was using it. And this trash and the bedroom prove she wasn't some sort of OCD neat-freak. So where is a container? Even one container that housed any emotion-drainage? A drug addict, especially one that far-gone, would have left some sign of her addiction's toll on her, if she was that over the top with it by now.

We don't know that this mess, any of it is hers. It could be whoever left that towel and used the shower.

But didn't use the sink? Ate and has been living here but no mark of anyone else like a roommate? It's a one-bedroom apartment besides.

You think this is her apartment but something else going on besides being a lead-head?

There'd be at least some discarded container, something to indicate she was using.

She might not have done it at home.

Could be. But think about the girl we saw at the Scots. Did she seem to have it together enough anymore to care where she fixed herself up?

So she was using. But she hasn't been home in a while. And while she's gone, someone else apparently used her apartment. And…you're thinking that whomever knew her apartment was available to make short-term use of, a quick shower or place to change clothes…had something to do with her being found at our place. Maybe something to do with her attacking Diatha.

Yes. That's my thinking exactly.

And then the image popped up clear as day:

Shaking that Believer on the floor at Ceyggan's gallery. The little glass vial that had dropped out of one of the jacket pockets. The vial that had looked empty at a glance.

Do you think the Believers are addicts too?

Maybe. Don't know enough.

But if Hope was a lead-head, an emotions-addict…this place doesn't look nearly trashed enough, either. I don't know if it's like traditional drug addiction, but wouldn't she have…I don't know, sold her television? Sold off a bunch of clothes? Maybe not had money for those groceries we saw in the kitchen?

That's assuming that it's always money that guys like Spam Tam take for their product.

A faint shudder in my mind at that prospect. *Okay, so this apartment doesn't scream 'drug addict,' yet Hope Cambridge was most definitely a lead-head, at least when she attacked the Scots brothers. That doesn't really tally with anything else going on right now, does it?*

It does if Spam Tam is still the one causing the trouble with the lead-heads around town, yeah. So far he's the one thing that is really popping up as a common factor in all this, even if it looks like he really left town. But we don't even know if he was the one she got her product from.

You know better than that, I retorted, frowning. *If it was anywhere in Columbus, it was bought from him.*

True. A whisper of air near the bedroom door. *Hey, if she was using at all, is it possible she had a record somewhere? Maybe just a notebook or address book where she'd have left a number, a note or something?*

*Worth looking. I think I saw a phone charger cord in her bedroom...Pinney didn't mention any phone found on her... maybe the phone is somewhere...*I went back into the bedroom and this time aimed for the plastic-finished vanity against the far wall.

As I came around the bed to approach it, I saw the framed photo lying on the floor, a scatter of glass around it on the carpet.

One element out of place. That was all it took for that edge of trespasser's nerves to ramp up to paranoia.

Not good. I went and picked up the photo, bits of glass tinkling and falling away as I looked at it.

Soul, at my shoulder:

Oh...well...

Yeah, I said, staring at the color print. *That seems to bring something out of the dark doesn't it?*

Trouble is...what does it actually mean?

I started to turn the frame over, looking for the little catches where I could free the photo from the frame. I didn't know if I wanted to look closer at it or take it out of the frame to keep or whatever. As I'd gotten it free of the broken frame—

MOVE—

Whatever the outcome would've been to my reaching for the picture became meaningless as something slammed into my lower back with enough force to drop me, crashing, into the vanity and shaking my head for the spots that it brought up, like black morning glories flourishing in the bright dawn cascade behind my eyes.

Teakettle noises. I shook my head back and forth with the rapid, bruised hurry of a wet dog.

"GET THE HELL AWAY FROM ME!" The vibration-sense of my mouth as Soul yelled through my throat. I panicked. Swung an arm out while my other hand went to the small of

my back which felt as though someone had played hob with an aluminum baseball bat and used me like Ty Cobb using a practice oak-handle to get a few easy home-run hits in before the game started.

More teakettle sounds, in movement. I spun around to see, but as I did there was a crunch-spatter din of glassy clay pottery noises. The lamp was smashed from the bedside table, and before the room went too dark I caught a blink of pale fish-white flashing out the bedroom door.

The pain in my back was receding with all due protest. I didn't know what had hit me so hard, but then I felt a flapping of fabric...rends in the cloth. Tears where something had slashed with a razor or knife...and there was a sticky wetness running down the back of my pants. Something so sharp and fine and fast, all I'd felt was the blunt force of the blow behind it, not the slice-slither of the cuts.

There was a crack and *thwam* of the front door being hurled open. I wavered on my feet.

Ah damn it, Pinney was right, he's going to—

Get moving!

I don't know if I can take...a step...without falling on my face. What the hell was that?

It moved too fast for me to pick up. It came in...I was looking at the picture, same as you. But...it hit and it looked like...some small wolf-thing? White and hair flying...I don't...Jesus, are those cuts in your back?

I don't know...I found movement still possible, down below my knees, as if all motivation to move had fled down there to hide from the bottom of my spine. I shoved the fist of balled-up photo paper into a coat pocket so as to free my hand to use as an emergency grappling hook, latching onto any semi-sturdy surface to sustain me. I let my weight throw me forward and somehow managed to time one lurching, croggled-and-shaking-ankle step after another, out the bedroom down and then out the apartment door.

As I reached the open apartment door (with a skitter of dust and broken plaster bits where the door had been flung so hard the doorknob had partially embedded into the wall), I heard a bright scream from outside.

It overlapped near-immediately with another.

****

I found my way to the corridor outside, eyes roving back and forth along its length—

Three o' clock, the staircase.

I moved to the direction, and there at the opening of the corridor was a man kneeling, kneeling before a woman on the ground. The woman was making the higher screaming noise, warbling out with broken, staticky huffs of air between contralto agonized sound. She was wearing some sort of sleeveless top, and her right shoulder was freely bleeding from finger-wide gashes that went from the knob of her shoulder almost halfway down the bicep. She jerked like a landed fish, eyes locked down at the wound.

The man kneeling beside her had his hands clutched at his stomach. A sheet of darkness was coating the lower belly beneath his held-tight hands, black drops forming and falling from the crotch of his jeans to the ground between his knees.

I moved to the couple, kneeling next to the woman in a mirror of the other man's position opposite me. I put a hand against the woman's collarbone, pressing as gently as I could. "Stay down, lie down." Still screaming, bucking. Eyes went from the wound up to my face. She was a dirty blonde with a shaggy haircut, something from an eighties rock band video only missing the three-inch gold-hoop earrings to go with it. Her eyes were white around a startling robin's egg blue, and every tendon and urge in her facial muscles was bulging, taut as wire while my hand struggled to keep her still.

With my free hand I dug around in a coat pocket and found one of my handkerchiefs. Held it by a corner, snapped the wrist to extend it out. Lifted my hand to grasp the opposite corner with the other hand. Stretched it as much as the cotton weave would allow and gave it a rough half-fold into a long triangle. Put the fattest wedge of the triangle down against the gashes in the wound, where it immediately soaked it shiny-wet with crimson. Drew the corners down, one over the shoulder, the other end shoved down into her armpit. Tugged, let go long enough to take one hand away, go under her arm, recover that corner and then draw them together. The handkerchief wasn't long enough to reach all the way or I would've tied it into a tight knot. Instead she was going to have to work with me a moment, if she could stop screaming.

"Miss, can you...please...I need you to...miss? Please..."

The guy had stopped hollering and broken down into snorting, gutted snot-filled moaning and grunting. He wouldn't look down, his hands kept clutched and releasing, covered in bright red liquid gloves. He rocked on his knees.

This isn't any good if she doesn't shut up.

"Have you seen that new YouTube video about Grumpy Cat?" I yelled into the woman's face.

She stopped yelling, her mouth hanging open with hoarse gasps and her eyes still wide, but now questioning and confused.

"Fuck?"

I wasn't aware that could be used as a question. Wow, it truly is the universal word.

"The new video, you know, where Grumpy Cat is wearing a tuxedo?"

"What the hell is wrong with you?" She screeched into my face.

"Never mind. Can you try and keep this tucked under your armpit? Can you bring that hand..." I gently tugged her right hand over her chest and placed it over the soaked cloth. "Yeah. Keep pressure there. It's not perfect but it can help."

"Mountain lion."

I looked up at the voice. The man was looking back at me. His hands were still clenched against his midsection, and capillary action had wicked blood up the fabric of his shirt into a tie-dye forest of bloody trees on the front of his lemon-yellow polo shirt. He was as pale as a freshly-laundered linen napkin and shivering.

"Oh man..." I swallowed. "Okay...uh..um...can you just...

keep your hands there?"

Yeah it's better...whatever is wrong with him...however bad those cuts are...you can't pull his hands away. His hands need to stay.

"I didn't know mountain lions were in Columbus." He spoke in a husky, fluttering voice.

A motion over the man's shoulder caught me. I looked past him as he moaned about mountain lions in the city.

Those decorative bushes with the sickly hydrangea blossoms near the parking spaces.

I see movement disturbances in the bushes.

"So do I."

"What?" the woman was squeezing her hand and the handkerchief squished.

"I'm sorry, I was...talking to myself. I'll..."

"Mountain lion," the man murmured to his own belly, his gripping hands.

You need to move or whatever that is will move for you.

I pushed off my knees, stagger-running and getting to the bushes as the moving something rabbited. I saw a flicker of bright off to my right, heading from the parking area to a small alley space between two apartment blocs.

I reached the corner and felt a whoosh of presence ahead of me.

Dead end. It's blocked off for garbage dumpsters. Dead end, get over here before it back-tracks—

I got the corner as motion detectors were tripped ahead of me and blue-white brilliance filled the small bricked alley space.

Captured in the light, as pinned in its place as a butterfly in a killing jar. But nowhere near as hideously lovely.

****

It was a girl.

Her face had a bulbous, egg-turned-on-its-small-end look. Milky-skinned, vein-riddled like a chunk of marble. Underneath the hydrocephalic bulb of forehead peered out a pair of wide-set, vacuous eyes that looked like two pieces of freshly-wet tar punched into her face where eyes should be, a child's scrawled idea of a snowman face. Almost nonexistent nose, barely two token nostril-holes with piggish up-tilt to them.

The mouth was a wide, fish-flapping affair with an underbite that hung open and showed a small pencil eraser stub of tongue past the slick-wet sheen of the bottom lip, with small jowls that hung to the sides of her oblong face. All of this seemed to dangle on a curve of neck...the whole impression I had was of one of those gruesome invertebrates that live in the unlit depths of the ocean. Like anglerfish, carrying their little phosphorescent balls of bait-light in front of them to trick the helpless fish into their maws...looking at this girl was a way of making your *eyes* want to shudder.

She was taller than me by a few inches, but the gangly build seemed to cancel this out and make her more frail, like a pipe-cleaner mannequin.

She wore a flimsy-looking shift of stained and tattered coarse fabric, some sort of burlap or roughspun cotton. The straps came over her knob shoulders and displayed a nonexistent bosom with a collarbone so pronounced it almost seemed to collapse back on the hollow of throat, the delicacy of a kite's cross-bars. She hunched, her arms kinked at the elbows and the hands dangling from the wrists with a boneless grace, giving her whole body the look of something constantly being caught in the light and shocked into stillness. Rats and roaches and deer, gawking at bright light splashing onto them. Raw, pale flesh formed into two ragdoll sticks that served as legs, with token snaps of sharp, harsh joints for ankles into the feet.

The feet were jet black, and so flat as to seem as if she were standing on two millimeter-thin plates of metal welded to the ground rather than free-standing and supporting her weight. Like a fish standing on the flaps of its tail.

Black and white. Girl. Hannibal.

The girl-thing. Black and white.

As her eyes focused on me, the mouth tightened and a low hiss emanated from it. The hands jerked up like a marionette's on the loose wrists, a patter of fresh, wet drops from their tips as she moved, and I could see them as the long, tapered-end talon-things that they were. They weren't as dark as her feet, but they had a mottled skin that was like a rotting lizard's scaly hide. Palms out, the tapered ends stretched and I heard knuckles crackling, sharp as spring ice thawing. Each end didn't look like a nail so much as a fused single digit, finger and chitinous nail in a single icepick tip, five to a hand like a clutch of thick darning needles flexing towards me.

I put my own hands in my pockets with as much feigned casualness as I could manage. I rocked a little on the balls of my feet, like a theatrical colonel in some Army farce nonchalantly looking at a line of troops. "Well then…" I pursed my lips. "I guess this is kind of awkward."

She didn't reply.

She blurred.

I was unfortunately on the back-tilt of my heels when I got blasted by a sour-smelling flicker of burlap and maggoty skin moving by me at unbelievable speed.

When Trina attacked me, I'd at least detected the arc of motion coming at me. This girl moved like she was popping in and out of space, one moment standing there and the next right on top of me.

It took me further off-balance than it should've, and I was sprawling back, one hand coming out of a pocket to try and pinwheel to halt the fall that was going to happen anyway.

Luckily I had presence of mind to keep my right hand in its pocket even in the midst of the fall. It allowed me to pull out the canister I'd been trying to more subtly tug out before this insane-looking speedster had bolted for me.

If only Hannibal knew who it was I'd get to use this gift of his on. Maybe we'd get a chance to tell him someday, if he ever let us see his face again.

Most of the Under of course is as grounded as anything else in the physical and biological laws you or I understand in the day-to-day world. Acids burn, knives cut, bullets painfully ventilate, and so on. Creatures have to often eat, breathe, sleep, or some versions thereof to keep going. Even some of the stranger things amongst the Under that don't need to eat, sleep or breathe still succumb to the laws of gravity or momentum like any other motion through three-dimensional space with us more banal creatures.

Rex and Hannibal obviously figured that as uniquely situated as I was, I might be able to use something a little stronger than mace or pepper spray, stuff that they couldn't use themselves without risking serious personal harm if it got away from them...much like Rex's riot-suppressor beanbag gun.

My guess is, it started out as a capsacin mixture much like typical, legally-produced pepper spray; same kind carried by any college coed on a dark night. But the Scots had cracked that formula and added in a varied voodoo mixture I never wanted the recipe for making.

There was a metallic-flake mixture of industrial gold powder and silver nitrate, plus something that was way, way heavier than pepper spray or old-fashioned mace. I guess they wanted to be prepared if they were attacked by vampires from a Bram Stoker novel or Cybermen from "Doctor Who."

I was glad I didn't have to breathe and could suppress pain response as I snagged it out of my pocket, using my thumb to first snap off the red plastic safety tab then mash down on the nozzle button.

I slitted my eyes and finished falling onto my back as the cloud of contents sizzled out into the air where I'd been.

The Scots must've also jacked up the pressure in such a small canister, because it emptied in only a two-second span and the fog of material—faintly grayish-pink as it hovered in the air—had that glitter-spray coat of gold and silver to it. Confetti from hell.

The blur girl had mis-timed with its second strafe-run trying to pounce on me as I went down. There was a sense of weight, a heavier stench of sweat-rot-blood over me, a shadow of her moving overhead, but then she was stopped and no longer as blurry as she collided with the cloud.

I heard another hiss-gurgle turned almost immediately

into a screech-coughing that degenerated into a horrid wet slap-cough-retching. She was jerking back and forth, those talons scrabbling at her own throat, face pinched shut as those fish lips *ploosh*ed out in a sort of kissing-vomiting plosive of hacking. She doubled over with heavier gasp-squeal-whumps of wretched twisting, turning and staggering off from me as I sat up.

Some of the glitter-mess settled on my shoulders and hair, and my eyes immediately started to get cloudy. I couldn't feel whatever pain I was normally supposed to respond with, but my eyes were clearly reacting with serious tear-duct activity. Not crying, but I could see things getting slight light-haloes as my eyes were getting moistened and irritated by this mystery spray. I grimaced, rubbed the eyes hard with my free hand, and tried to focus on letting them stay open and dry as I got back on my feet. I held the spent canister out in front of me to give the impression it could still offer more where that came from.

Her face was still that cheesy-pale pallor, but there were pimple spots of dark red strawberry-blossoming on her cheeks and forehead. Her chin had a rash-streak of the same that visibly widened. Filmy streaks of the cloud had torn away and stayed with her as she'd stumbled back, but even as those thinned and fell away like cobwebs, I could see that whatever was in the Scot Special Blend was corrosive.

I glanced at my free hand and saw similar spots of burning, red skin that immediately closed up like tiny mouths sealing shut as I healed from the damage. Probably spots were opening up on my face and neck but I didn't have to worry about them. Unlike Miss Snarl, who had her eyes squinched so tightly shut I almost thought they were going to collapse back into her skull, which wouldn't have taken much to begin with.

The gray-red-glitter faded away and settled to the ground like recent rainfall. I took a step forward, trusting that her bare feet might look nasty but be at least slightly more vulnerable to the fallout on the ground than me in my Doc Martens knock-off. She was still hacking and gargling away, the burns on her face no longer growing though some of them on her forehead and cheeks had merged into nastier birthmark-looking patches. There were similar streaks of damage along her shoulders and breastbone, and her claw hands were red from seepage at her throat where she'd frantically scratched it bloody.

I glanced down at the canister, but it was just smooth black plastic. No labeling or warnings.

Some of that passed through me. It tastes-looks like sour milk and gasoline, it's glitter with a side of napalm.

Trust the Scots to want to 'surprise' me.

Looking at the twisting lines of boil-burns on this girl-thing's skin, I made a mental memo to ask the Scots for a more thorough FDA accounting of their gift packages.

Her eyes squinted open and the hate-glitter glowered at me with killing intensity, but she didn't pull any blur tricks. She stayed hunched over, shivering. There were brown-edged-into black pocks forming in the top and straps of her clothing, and a flicker of the glitter caught in the crude fabric.

Christ, what was *in* this stuff?

I gritted my teeth and took another step towards her. "I don't want to do that again, so don't *you* do *that* again either, okay?" She continued to glare at me. "*Okay*?" No answer. "Fuck it. Fine." I waggled the canister in front of her. "I've got the *burn-burn*, so you stay right there, *kay-kay*?"

She didn't speak, but her response was to narrow her already-slitted eyes further and give a gravel-studded purr-growl, idly scratching at her throat where it still burned.

"I'll take that as a loose agreement. Who the hell are you?"

She padded back and forth from the left foot to the right, making these nervous *plap-plap* noises that further reinforced that fish-tail sensation looking at those black limbs. The arm that wasn't scratching her throat came up and tucked against the crook of the other. Her face was more open, less challenging and more animal-scared. A shiver visibly shook her frame. She darted looks to her right and left, but the alley was narrow enough that she was going to have to make a pass at me again to get out. If she'd been thinking at all, she might've tried to go past me when she'd knocked me down, but clearly she had perceived me as easy prey before I pulled out the canister of burning hell.

"Since you don't seem inclined to answer me with anything more than a nod or a growl, we'll work with that." She focused on me, one eye puffed around the socket and showing a deepening purple-red color like a bruise near to bursting the surface. "I'm sorry that it hurts so much. I really am. I didn't…I didn't know it would do that, I really didn't. But you came at me…why did you come at me?"

The lips twisted like earthworms coming out in a fresh rainfall, but no reply.

"Can you talk?"

More twisting of the mouth, tiny nicotine-yellow pearls of teeth biting at the bottom lip.

"Did someone send you after me?"

A dart of eyes past me. Left, right. A bird twitch of the head looking behind her at the alley wall. Back at me.

"Cousin Nightsock does not speak, I'm afraid. But I'll happily answer your questions, for what worth such answers may have."

The voice was shockingly close and yet I couldn't make out its direction. The girl's lips froze, her whole body going into a freeze of anticipation. One corner of the mouth kinked in what I took for an ugly breed of smile.

Soul was near my left ear. *I can't see anything nearby. He can't be hiding behind anything, there's nothing here, not even a dumpster.*

"I take it you have never encountered a child of the *wildeweird* before, good sir?"

"No, I haven't had the pleasure." I figured people that were talking were people who weren't yet attacking.

I risked breaking eye contact with the girl to glance around me quickly. Still no way to tell where the voice was coming from. Soul broke away and hovered higher, above my head and floating upwards. *I can see the usual air disturbances but… nothing clear. It's almost like…oh shit…*

"But then, you're a relative novice in the things of the

Under, aren't you?"

"Aren't we all a novice at some point?"

"Too true, too true." A breath. "Sadly, I don't think you're going to get the opportunity to ever rise above such a status."

Wait. He's talking to us. We're hearing him, right?

Right.

So if nothing else, even if he doesn't give off body heat or anything else, he's making a sound. Can you see if there's any movement when he talks, the air transmitting the sound of his voice?

Good call.

"You seem rather pessimistic about my odds. Are you the one who's been watching my store?"

A pause. During which I got the distinct impression I had broached something, an uncomfortable point of pride or sensitivity.

"What? Not used to people finding out you're there?"

"You point out a rather disturbing failure, that's all." The voice was cooler. "They were not supposed to be detected by anyone, least of all the subject of their surveillance."

To your right and behind you. Your five o' clock.

I turned to a midway point between that direction and still facing the girl. "Sorry to disappoint you. Hopefully your monthly performance review will go easy on you and you'll still get that bonus the boss promised."

A faint chuckle. "The propensity for poor humor. I do love that in human beings."

"Why don't you come out, let me meet you? You sound awfully sure of things so why not?"

"And I imagine that in your usual supreme overconfidence this is another way to try and prolong things, gather intelligence, perhaps find a weakness." Another watery chuckle, like the sound of a coffee percolator beginning to brew. "But why not? It's not every day that anyone asks to meet us directly. Or gets a chance to live long enough to acknowledge doing so."

When Soul had given me an indicator, somehow the added focus made it easier to hone in on the source of the voice. As the owner of the voice manifested before me, there was no doubt and even less pleasure in the confirmation.

But when I turned, the girl twisted. Bucked like a fish on a boat deck.

The feeling was so muscular, so impossibly hard, I would've sworn moving like that, resisting would've broken something inside her. Maybe it did and she didn't feel it or care.

Something slammed me again. But harder. And not in my back. My skull was smashed as solidly as if I'd lain down in traffic and let a COTA bus run over my skull and pulp my thinking into so much pig-trough leavings.

It went dark. But not painlessly.

34.

I stood at a shoreline.

I looked down. Legs. Hands. The familiarity was quicker now. It was as if I'd played a musical instrument years ago and fallen out of practice, but memory and old habits were quickly reasserting themselves.

I tried a breath. Found that habit easy to keep up. Crucial, in fact. The air was cold but the grounds were clear, brown... no snow even though I had a jacket on.

Tested the neck, the eyes. I could move. The sky overhead was barely marked with only a handful of streak-stretched cloud, otherwise it was early twilight, the sky beginning to turn from blue to indigo. I could hear a throaty ululation from far off...a loon. It seemed to get an answer, because a second later the uglier *quack-squawk* of a duck responded from another direction.

I looked down; saw I was standing on concrete wall stretching out from the shoreline, out into the water. The waterline made faint, rolling lap noises below me.

Set into the top of the concrete about every ten feet all the way out to its end, and set all around the upper edge of it, were dull steel cleats.

Smell of soil and river water. No salt sharpness like the ocean, but a flatter smell. As a kid I called it "earthworm" smell. Overlaid on that: the somewhat sterile bite-smell of Midwestern late-winter cold. Like an exotic, refined metal filament held under your nose.

The water was dark brown-green with a faint scum of green-white algae foam where it pooled amongst the weeds and rocks of the gritty shallows. The shore was humped like a sere brown narwhal's back with the concrete dock jutting out into the water as the narwhal's rectangular, gray horn.

Bright yellow, a day-glo flash in my hands in front of me. Nylon utility rope. Less than a half-inch in diameter but the braided line was strong. A fifty-foot coil of it at my feet, a length of it trailing up and wrapped several times around my right hand. The line of it went taut from my hand down to… the water…

Some things imprint on your memory with simple shape and pattern recognition. As the years pile up and demand you drop all the other sensory data in favor of new priorities and shinier objects in the back-closet of your thoughts, you simplify memories into a kind of child's toy. Those colorful thick-cardboard distractions they give toddlers where a scene of a zoo or a barn is displayed, with chunky cut-outs of the scene. And the child is expected to pick up the corresponding pieces, with their little plastic pushpin handles, and find where does the cow line up with his cut-out silhouette, where does the horse go.

In the water at the end of the yellow rope was my dad's bass boat. A big Johnson model with a fat Evinrude motor bobbing along at its rear. A twenty-seven-foot length of fiberglass hull with black-with-mica-flecks finish and red racing stripes down its sides.

The sight of it clicked with a faint—but detectable, definitely detectable—ache of shape recognition. The big cut-out fitting home.

Dad sold this boat. Trying to keep up house payments. About…what, two years before he died? Mom was already gone. I couldn't remember just when that had to have been. The only evidence I had was on a rare visit to see him, try to talk and make some sort of peace however temporarily, and the boat hadn't been in its usual place in the driveway in front of the garage at his house, covered in its custom black canvas cover with the Johnson logo on it.

Here it was. Bobbing up and down in the water at my feet.

That was my job. Going out with my dad to fish at one of the local lakes or ponds or…wait, yes, this was Alum Creek, I recognized the sandy shorelines now…keep the boat next to the dock while Dad went and got the trailer to come and collect the boat from the water.

"I'm heading up for the truck!"

I snapped my head to the sound.

He was halfway up the grade heading for the parking lot that was at the crest of the embankment.

Heavyset man, a hair over six feet tall and with a sort of gone-to-seed defensive lineman build, heavy in the round shoulders. Chestnut hair with blonde streaks from long hours outdoors in the sun, the hair down to his shoulders and swept back. Skin that was always at least pink from those same hours under unfiltered sun. From here I could only see the back of him, in bleached-out ratty jeans and leather moccasins worn until they were practically beige-white from all the scuffing of the leather. A rainbow-colored tie-dyed long-sleeved sweatshirt.

I stared at him walking away, a wave of his arm to me as he was going away, leaving me with the Big Job, keeping the boat to the dock.

I wanted to yell something. More, I wanted to drop the rope and run. But I stood. And stared.

There is the cliché that seeing a parent who has passed away is difficult. Very much another of those 'Christmas Carol' moments where Scrooge gets all choked-up and sentimentally wet-eyed and regret-stricken.

Important thing to remember: clichés are only clichés because they happen so often.

Hard to hold on to the idea that this was memory. This had

happened. This wasn't some magical way to fix things. Even if it was, fix what? Thirteen-or-fourteen-year-old me wouldn't have those problems, years down the line. What could I say?

And watching Dad walk off, I didn't notice immediately another boat that had been speeding down to a dock further down the reservoir's length, traveling too fast and too close to the shoreline and sending a hard wake clumping down to the dock and passing with those odd, random quirks of fluid harmonics the wake wave passed between the boat and the dock, and split, causing the water to rise in such a way between the two that now the boat was being pushed away from the dock.

The rope tightened around my hand immediately, cutting off circulation to my fingers. I unwound and released it, at the same time putting out one wobbling foot to tap at the railing of the boat, managing to get my sneaker down onto the deck carpeting.

I almost fell right then. The boat treacherously dipped and shifted under my weight.

"*Shit!*"

Wait, what? I hadn't spoken!

No, the sound came from me, I knew my own voice..what?

No...I said that when this was happening. Of course. Like a dream, I had a little allowance, slight movements I could make within reason, within the plausibility of the moment... but like a memory, I was also more restrained to replay out things as they'd happened.

If the memories I was visiting were sharper or more recent... would I be even more trapped to what exactly I remembered doing or saying or...even thinking? God...all of a sudden it was a cloying, suffocating sensation...like being one of the people in Vonnegut's novel *Timequake*, forced to relive the actions of an entire decade all over again, their consciousness trapped inside bodies still moving through all the exact same motions as before, helpless to change anything but having to still suffer and experience it all again down to the most minute detail.

This was going to take some serious adjustment, this live-or-instant-replay ability I'd discovered. This wasn't a time machine, however poetically I might call it at times. This was a scrapbook, a music box that played the same music over and over even with slight variations in the humidity of the box or the wear-and-tear on the wood…and if I forgot that or lost sight of myself in this place…could I be lost for good, replaying things without even the benefit of knowing it?

I could appreciate why Rod had warned me about being inside my own mind for too long. There were good memories back here as well as bad, and in many ways a good place to want to revisit was far more insidious than any evil I wanted to avoid recalling.

I hadn't put my foot squarely down. Which meant the boat also drifted away a little faster, propelled now by my added energy.

I doubled over, snatching for the edge of the boat like I had with my foot. My hand managed to snag a chrome-shiny cleat.

Immediately, I saw the idiotically comic trap I'd put myself into. And with that, the placement of this particular memory snapped home, the last of the moo-cows and neigh-horses in the child's cardboard barn cut-outs needing to be lined up.

I tried to haul back my arm and leg, already knowing it would be futile. My center of gravity was almost perfectly between my limbs on the boat and those still on the dock. I couldn't stop the boat, and I didn't have enough weight compared to its free-float on the water to draw it back in…all I could do was mildly retard its leaving…and I was still clinging to the edge of it while it was inevitably pulling me further and further from the dock…and my remaining hold to the ground.

I knew what was going to happen and I knew I should let go. I also knew that this was thirteen-or-fourteen-year-old me. And thirteen-or-fourteen-year-old me had thought this was a deadly serious affair.

The boat was important to Dad. He loved and tended it as any collector or connoisseur tended to the best of their collections, the same as any antiques car collector or furniture restoration expert. It got wiped down of water after every ride—other boaters often let the water stay on the hull after taking it out of the water, letting it get milky with collected mineral salts. Other boaters would ding and scratch their trailer's taillight mounts against the boat's edges, not minding the ever-increasing number of marks and notches into the finish; Dad was scrupulous about getting the trailer lined up so perfectly that all he had to do once it was align was pretty much take his foot off the brake and let the truck and trailer coast back, smoothly skirting under the hull and letting the boat practically ride itself up onto the trailer's skids.

My job was simple but basically crucial: keep the boat to the dock until he got back. And he wasn't back yet.

The boat drifted...already I was feeling the strain throb through my calves and my back, my shoulders aching...the water kept lapping away with the same mindless regularity underneath me, only now there was a boy-shaped starfish shadow over the obscure water. And the heavy earthworm-water smell wafting up at me only a half-foot or so below.

"Shit!" This time I didn't fight history's urge to replay the sentiment. Had I been this obsessed with cursing when nobody was around to correct me? Yeah, of course I had. Every kid with parents who teach them right from wrong conduct gets to enjoy the brief freedoms when they start to test their adulthood with that tiny victory: the right to say 'shit,' 'fuck' and whatever else occurs to you without your parents being able to do much more than frown or shake their head...or as in my dad's case, laugh at the joke.

The boat kept drifting. Now the rope fell into the water, bowing down far enough between the coil on the dock and the cleat to make a dark shadow-line across the boy-shadow's legs...crap...I was fast losing my balance and now I wasn't just hunched over my arms and legs, I was pulled far enough out that pretty soon I was going to look like a kid re-enacting a massive jumping-jack while lying face-down...one of my knuckles popped like a walnut shell.

Somewhere far away was the sound of a truck engine starting. The grind and pop of gravel and bits of broken glass on the pavement as its heavy-gauge tires rolled. Then a *scritch-grind* of brakes applied.

Padding of footsteps running. "JOHNNY! JUST LET IT GO!"

I managed to raise my head, even though my arms were strained enough that this was like trying to look straight up at the sky while carrying fifty-pound dumbbells in your hands. Dad was at the beginning of the dock coming towards me. But the dock was fifty, a hundred yards…a thousand…he wasn't going to get to me in time to be of any help…

I looked down at the water, knowing what was coming. And achieved a disorienting symmetry of thought with my thirteen-or-fourteen-year-old self: oh Christ to hell with it, I can't do anything else.

I let go my grip of the boat and let my knees gratefully buckle, already feeling them thank me with fatigue as I succumbed to gravity and *splah-thwosh*ed into the reservoir water.

I wasn't at risk of drowning. Not only could I swim and dog-paddle fine, but the water couldn't have been more than five feet deep and I tapped a toe against the bottom as I initially thrashed and recovered myself in the second after hitting the water. I didn't actually have any fear at all. Only the worry I let the boat go. The boat will float away and we won't be able to recover it and maybe Dad will have to call the park services to come out with *their* boat to drag it back and fine him or charge him a fee or something and I'm all wet and man this water is cold…

I heard Dad hollering at me, just my name twice, three times. I brought my head out of the water, scowling and paddling. Coughed. My clothes were now bonded to me like a potato skin.

"S-sorry, I—"

"Why didn't you let it go or just hold the rope?" A wide face with a brown-and-blonde beard to go with his hair. Blue eyes under almost-white eyebrows. I inherited his pug-ball-tipped nose and wide smile.

That look. Another one of those shape-recognition clicks, but this one felt more like a dull break inside my stomach and throat. The dismayed look that seemed to convey every prior disappointment before this one, with the latest simply added to the pile of broken and dissassembled things I'd done to not be worth respect.

"You could've let it go," he said more calmly. He waved his arm towards the shallow of the dock where the ramp came up out of the water. "Hurry and get to the ramp, get out of the water."

"I'm okay, I'll get there—"

"Hurry!" A bit of panic emerged in his voice. "It's March, that water can't be more than a few degrees above freezing, get out or you'll go into shock."

I paddled until my feet found better footing and I walked up to the open air.

Now I appreciated the reality of it being March and I was soaking wet with river-water. As it hit, something bypassed goose pimples and went straight to hard, wind-up-novelty-toy chattering that rattled my skull and made everything in my vision shake as if I were sitting in a paint-mixer. My nerve endings were alive with a cold feeling that was almost thick, like someone had hollowed out my circulatory system and poured ice-cold 2% milk in place of blood. I instinctively bent over, hands on knees, chattering and clicking.

"You need to get those clothes off."

I stood up. "What?"

"You can't stay in wet clothes. Get your clothes off and get in the car. The heater's already on."

"I-I-I-bbbb-b-b-b…ff-fi-fif-ff*fine*-nun-nuh…" My tongue narrowly avoided a nasty bite from my front teeth on the last slippery syllables. I wiped away water that kept coming down into my eyes from my hair.

"Get in the truck." The dismayed look shifted quickly into the no-nonsense look, the one that even with my adult mind temporarily housed over my thirteen-or-fourteen-year-old one made me inwardly flinch. I chatter-stumbled to the passenger side of the blocky metallic-sky-blue Ford pickup and opened the door.

The humiliation might have been memory but this was all fairly fresh with strong ink on the page, so my reading was still sharp. I hated the feeling as if a million people were watching me as I took off my clothes, wadding them together and shoving them into the space underneath the glove compartment. There were no other people in sight other than Dad and me in the whole park area or dock site, but as I got down to my sopping underwear (leaving those on because no amount of hypothermia was going to extort thirteen-or-fourteen-year-old me into getting naked out in the open) I had a burst of speed to get into the seat and jerk the door shut behind me with a slam.

Dad got into the driver's side seat. Kept his head and arm sticking out of the window all while using his other to steer the truck and trailer in reverse, lining it up to submerge the trailer and reclaim the boat. "Looks like a wake caught it," he remarked blandly. "Counter-wave caught, though. It's actually staying in place." Faint *hmph* to this as he steered.

I said nothing. At first because the air blowing off the heater caught the water still on my skin and even hot, breeze was breeze and my chattering went up an impossible notch. My tongue was too tired to keep up the dodge and finally got a nasty clip from my incisor, leaving the right fat and throbbing. After the heat from the vents started drying me and I recovered from the chattering, downgrading it to merely palsied shakes that wracked my shoulders and spine every few seconds.

When I could see the line of the dock over his shoulder through the window frame, he put the truck in park and got out.

I stared out the windshield while he started up the boat's engine, ran it up onto the trailer's skids and then the click-click-clack of the trailer's hitch as he brought it up the last few inches and secured it to the mount. Staring out at bland concrete parking lot and park treeline. One lonely streetlamp that as I watched achieved sufficient darkness that the sensor noticed and it sputtered on with blue-white glare.

Miserable. The cold wasn't half of it. That was merely discomfort. The misery was my throat feeling raw and my skin pimpled with embarrassment of sitting in wet underwear leaving a puddle on the couch cab seat. Air blowing on me in a hairdryer roar while I called myself an idiot and muttered 'shit' a couple more times.

Dad climbed back in and there wasn't any conversation while he got the truck and trailer pulled up from the ramp, hearing the loud swash-splatter of water as the boat's mass lifted free of the dock and we left the park, getting out towards the freeway and back home.

"Why didn't you just let the boat go?"

I shrugged.

"Even if it'd floated off, there was the rope."

"I couldn't hold it. I-it started to pull and I tugged but the wake was t-too strong."

"So why did you do that stunt with the wishbone act?"

Another shrug, half-shiver thrown in with it. "I d-didn't want to l-let the boat get away."

"You could've frozen to death or gone into shock falling in." He finished with an uncertain and incomplete thought. "It's March."

"S-sorry."

March. His repeating it had another tumbler fall into place. I couldn't yet feel out the shape of an exact year, but I knew what day it had to be.

My birthday. I had pestered Dad to take me out for a ride in the boat for my birthday. The fish weren't yet spawning worth a damn to try really fishing and I'd spent most of the zooming, roaring ride thumping up and down and thinking my body at any moment would be violently flung out into the water… eyes streaming so hard with tears that I couldn't see more than blurry suggestions of the waterline and trees going by. This was my birthday gift I'd asked for myself on top of whatever else they wrapped up and had waiting for me at home.

Mom would be there. Making a German chocolate cake with coconut icing which was my annual request as well.

My birthday and thirteen-or-fourteen-or-maybe-now-fifteen-year-old me in my underwear feeling small and ridiculous next to my dad, who would periodically chuckle and shake his head over some aspect of it all as we went home.

I didn't want the boat to drift away because you cared so damned much about it, my adult mind was trying to rally against childhood sensations. *I didn't want the boat to drift off because I was scared it would get away and we'd lose it or I'd get in trouble and get the belt or because I like the boat too and know how much you care about it.*

Another shake of his head, but now he was smiling. "Won't do that again, will you?" I shook my head. And adult-me could attest this was, in fact, something I had learned never to repeat.

We were laughing without realizing it was happening. It started with me and ended with a sudden burp of river-silt water flavor. That set off Dad. And when he ruffled my hair, I remembered that along with that look of disappointment while he stood on the docks looking down on me, his voice had been definitely one of worry. And not for the boat.

I turned and smiled at him.

And my adult self was sitting in a chair next to me instead of Dad at the wheel of the truck.

My memory was still laughing. I was caught for that moment, laughing like a cartoon imbecile while goggling inside at the sight of myself sitting on a chair in place of the cab seat next to me.

No...my arms were behind my back and bound with tape...and I looked to be shaking my head, eyes closed...

...what...

The voice, but no movement of my lips.

No, not me, this wasn't the lake or the car or Dad...it was Body but where were we and what—

35.

I opened my eyes and at first couldn't tell that I had.

What slowly woke me from unconsciousness was a faint dripping sound. Water or something like it, plapping onto stone in a hollow wind chamber. It was far away but still distinct, trailing its echo to my ears like a ragged tail.

Don't move or make a sound.

I immediately made my eyelids twitch, rolled my eyes a little, and let the lids close once more.

What is it?

She's about twenty feet away, crouched like a bullfrog on the floor, and watching you as sure as a hawk. I don't know if she can actually see you in the dark, but she certainly acts like she can. And she hasn't tripped on anything or bumped into any of the mess in this place yet.

My mental librarian looked over the recently 'checked out' section of memory and was able to swiftly pull up the catalog entry for 'she.' That fish-faced, black-footed girl-thing that fought like such a bottled hurricane of claws and toes.

Where am I?

One of those industrial warehouse wrecks off 670, almost out to the sticks. Looks like a place for people to toss whatever junk they couldn't have hauled away or sell on Craigslist. A sigh of air around my ankles, then moving behind my head. *I thought they'd have some issue with transporting you, but then I saw her pick you up like you weighed nothing and slop you into the trunk as easy as a sack of cat food.*

Did you see which way we came?

No answer.

What?

A blurt of cool, moving around my ankles.

I know you. I know when you don't want to answer a question. What's wrong?

I...I got lost.

Lost?

That bit? That memory bit?

Bits and pieces filtered through our connection.

Dad and the boat. The dock. The cold.

Christ. How does she do that?

I don't know. I don't think...she wasn't...it wasn't the same this time. I don't think she was actually...there. This time.

What?

She didn't show up. This was...it felt richer. Heavier.

You think you did it to yourself?

She said it was something we could do. Soul-halves, I mean. Go back into ourselves, our own memory. I guess if I'm nothing but consciousness, going into my own memory is...a bit more heady a trick than I realized. When you got knocked out there was that moment—

Yeah. I know. I'm sorry. It felt so similar...

I know. I get it. But that's what happened, okay? I didn't even realize what was going on until you started to recover and it helped me pull out of it. But yeah. I got lost in there a bit. Going to have to watch out for that in the future.

So that girl-creature is in front of me, watching me? You say she carried me to their vehicle?

That was what I saw when we got here and I recovered enough to be aware again, yeah. I was obviously out of commission when we first got sapped, but I gather if she carried you out she probably put you in.

That doesn't make sense. If she was that strong, there's no way *I could've subdued her.*

Maybe you really need to put 'ask the Scots brothers what the hell is in their voodoo pepper spray' *on your higher priorities list after this. Once her face cleared up, she certainly didn't seem to have any trouble hauling you around like a fireman with a sack of kittens.*

If there was an 'after this' to make notes. I noticed that I had tensed my shoulders. I made myself relax as gently and undetectably as I could hope to. As my arms lowered, I felt them immediately tighten with the resistance of the binding around my wrists. I let my left hand pull a little more, just a test. I was rewarded with a faint rubbery grind. Duct tape. A few stray wrist hairs pulled free with that familiar band-aid tingle.

Don't move too much. Her fingers twitched. She might see.

I can't simply sit here.

I suggest you get really used to the idea really quick. Her face is still bruised, and the color-feel coming off her is sheer murder. She looks like she'd truly enjoy a chance to gut you with her nails if you give her half an excuse.

Who knocked me out?

A beat. Soul's voice sounded smaller:

I didn't quite see. But before you and I both shared a big Bye-Bye together, I think…I felt-saw that same squirmy nastiness…I think it was Mister Sharkdoll.

That's…not good.

No kidding.

We didn't exchange anything else for a while. I don't know how long it was, as I sat there fighting every instinctive desire to move, to try and squirm and twist myself free or at least into a more advantageous position. My only saving grace was I could will myself to go dead in the nerves, so if there was any discomfort or damage from being bound so firmly, arms against my lower back with the back of the chair wedged in the middle, I didn't suffer it.

In the dark, with nothing else to do or focus on, I became

more aware of the surrounding ambience. A weak smell of stagnant water, rotten and garbagey. The water drip waxed and waned, like a spill of milk finally petering out. But then other sounds became apparent. The occasional crick or faint echoey crack of some overhead beam. A bird angrily *fweet-fweet*ing for what seemed like interminable lengths of time, furious at some unseen intruder on its turf.

And breathing. Ragged, shuddery breathing that occasionally stuttered with a faint hiccup or a sigh of air like the aftermath of a belch. The fish-girl's breathing in the dark; an animal pant that I had little doubt was a symptom of that barely-checked fury Soul saw.

How long would she be willing to sit there, waiting in the dark with me, the vestiges of the burning and scraping on her face still clinging to the nerve endings, taunting her to act?

In the course of time the other noises filtered out. All I had in the obscurity of my immediate world was her breathing.

In out. In out. Hiccup. Sigh-hiss. In out.

I considered willing my heart to beat, to let my lungs start putting out weak breath. Anything to generate some counter-wave to that staccato hiss-wheeze coming at me from the dim. I wanted to open my eyes, let them try and make out any shapes, any signs of help or escape, but I kept Soul's admonition in my forethought, kept my eyes closed and let my body's natural inclination to be an inanimate object take over. For all that anyone would have been able to detect, there was simply a corpse bound up and left to cool in a chair. I hoped.

In out. In out. Hiccup. Faint moan-turned-groan. A clatter. Was she playing with something? I thought absurdly of dropping dice. Not rolling, but simply plucking a die up, holding it between two of those spindly talon-fingers, and letting it go, letting gravity clack it to the ground.

Clack. Repeat. In out. Hiss. *Clack*. *Clack*. In out. *Clack*. Hiccup. Sigh-hiss.

More than ever, I wished I could sleep again.

****

Soul left after some time to try and scout more information about our surroundings. I received faint reports from him along that mental tether we share, a sort of psychic tin-cans-and-string with one terminal in my head and the other floating along wherever he goes.

The warehouse was indeed a run-down former factory space, one of many that dot the landscape as you leave Columbus in any direction and before you hit out-and-out cornfields and farms. We were on the east side of town, in the vicinity of the 670 bypass but not actually outside of the 270 freeway outerbelt. I couldn't hear any traffic, which suggested we were far enough away to not expect any regular traffic to spot any strange goings-on. We were pretty well isolated, Soul confirmed. There was little more than high weed and rank grass around the building, with a dirt-and-gravel drive going a good quarter-mile back to the nearest paved service road. No trees or heavy cover, but no neighbors in sight either.

In out. Hiccup. *Clack*. In out. *Clack*.

I tried a flutter of my eyelids again, let the orbs rotate noticeably in their sockets. Made a little shift in my left shoulder. All to suggest I could be surfacing from unconsciousness.

Clack.

Breathing stopped.

Waiting.

I stopped fluttering my eyelids.

Then that smell again. Rotten fish and cinnamon. The barest sensation of body heat registered in the air a few feet from me. I kept my eyes closed but had to resist squeezing them shut. Play dead. My best trick.

Very, very weak: sigh hiss.

A long hold.

Then: *hiccup.*

The heat signature dissipated. A few moments later, distant again: clack.

Clack. In out. Hiccup. *Clack*.

There's a truck coming. Soul's voice floated down with him from above.

What time is it?

No idea. There's no clock or display anywhere in the area. It's still night though.

When it pulled up near the building, I heard the rev of its acceleration the last few yards and the tired chunk-chuck as someone killed the engine.

Chuff-scrutch noises. Feet on gravel. High, unoiled screech-squeal of a door opening…clatter of panels, so something like a garage door or warehouse docking entrance.

Scraping, punt-drag sounds: steps on the concrete floor. A pause. Then a snap-clack, the sharp plastic note of a switch being cast, and my eyelids bloomed red with the lights.

I took the risk to flutter my eyelids again, this time letting my eyes peel open with a groggy, slow regard. I blinked to adjust to the light.

My chair and my fish-girl warden were in a semi-circular clearing amongst various-sized mounds of trash; discarded furniture, old toys and bicycles. Mystery cardboard boxes full of paper and old receipts, books and water-bloated magazines. Dark puddles of different sizes glittered on the gritty floor. The ceiling was a good thirty feet above us, it looked like rust-speckled corrugated tin supported by thin iron beams, furry with dangles of ivy and old, petrified birds' nests from any number of long mating seasons past. You could see the active dust and grime in the air billowing around with every draft or disturbance.

The padding shuffle of feet, with a clocking noise that was familiar…I was trying to place it when around the high mound in front of me emerged the source.

A satyr or troll. Wearing an ugly-bland Hawaiian shirt. Dirty cargo shorts that stopped just above doorknob knees. And flip-flop sandals; the clop-clopping I heard with every step. His head too big for his scrawny body. Not tall, probably barely registering above five-one, five-two. A bald head spotted with moles and odd pimples and warts like an inverted planetarium. All of his upper body had a lopsided, vulpine quality. Ears that terminated in suggestions of points like oversized pimples on the cartilage. Unkempt eyebrows that skewed out a good inch from his prognathic forehead. Thick-lensed, tape-patched chunky-squared glasses that magnified blinking black eyes reminiscent of a patchwork stuffed animal behind soda-bottle glass. A petulant, flap-lipped mouth that had a default frown, punctuated with a snarled little comma of black hair in one of those pretentious-looking soul-patch cuts, as if he wanted to seem cool but didn't have the spine to commit to anything as 'risky' as an actual beard or mustache to justify the growth.

His head hung on the neck with that same continuing vulture theme, the crooked posture hunched and a pot belly ruining the lines of the sweat-stained Hawaiian, dark underarm circles marring the beige-and-gray pattern of surfboards and palm trees. Not real Hawaiian. One of those 'trendy' dull knock-offs sold in golf pro shops and middle-to-senior-age-demographic-serving clothing stores in malls, a kind of AARP-meets-Banana-Republic look. The cargo pants had a lot of loose change which was obvious because his leg motions kept them tinkling and jangling every second. As he stopped in front of me, crossing his arms, even standing he had to keep impatiently twitching one or both of the legs.

And the legs had two knees. Each. The doorknobs under the hem of the cargo shorts twisted the legs back at a painful-looking angle, only to meet small, knobbier secondary knees that crooked the leg back into the original direction to terminate in hard-callused, horny-nailed bare feet with black hair on the knuckles and a tattered pair of bubblegum-bright plastic flip-flops. The jangle-jangle of change seemed to try and counterpoint a broken rhythm with the dull tuck-tuck noise of his flip-flops tapping the floor. The arms that emerged from the shirtsleeves were stick-scrawny and didn't look strong enough to bear the weight of an empty envelope.

He looked dangerously ludicrous. The kind of person that I'd come across back when I still had to work office day-jobs before I started my own business; you encounter them frequently in middle-management or what I called a "simper buffer," an ass-kiss level that never really got any true power or responsibility of their own. Just what they gained by proxy of whatever higher-up in the ladder they managed to brown-nose enough with to get a small dog-bed corner of their notice. But dangerous in the sense that they squeezed every bit of pseudo-authority they could from it, and would back-stab you in a heartbeat to cover up their own incompetence on any job. A gnomish goat-thing with a face of a simpering bureaucrat and the clothing choice of a retiree in a broken-down Florida senior's community.

I've seen one or two satyrs. He wasn't a true one—no horn growths on the forehead, the ears tipped but not nearly pointed enough—but maybe he was some distant offshoot. But those were true human feet—well, barely—at the ends of those double-joint legs, not hooves.

Overall, this stumpish man-creature didn't engender a lot of faith in me that he was going to be anyone I wanted to talk to. Even if I hadn't been knocked out, dragged here and taped down to a chair.

He smiled. To be more accurate: his mouth twisted and like a pitcher of flat beer it poured out a grease-slick of a grin, revealing cigarette-yellowed too-small teeth and spotty gums.

"Well hello there!" A grating whine-wheeze. If you took a kid's wind-up talking toy and left it to rust a weekend in an old community kiddie pool, then indiscriminately sprayed it with WD-40 and overwound its key to let it squeak-grind out its pre-designed tinny little phrases, it would have been this guy's voice trying to finger-crawl into my ears. An earwig voice. "Sorry we couldn't have accommodated you in a more friendly setting, good sir." Dear god, was he giving the most contrived and poorly-faked…was that actually an attempt at some sort of mawkish English butler's accent? "But time and circumstances didn't permit us much better options for you. Are you sitting comfortably?" The wind-up doll chuckle-burped at its own joke.

I simply stared, waiting for there to be a point. But when I started to get too comfortable with simply disliking him, I saw a flicker and a face peer out from behind the dollar-store satyr: the fish-girl. Glowering at me so hard I was wondering why it hadn't practically glowed in the dark at me earlier. There was a nasty blistered-red swatch of skin around her eyes and nostrils, and she gave a loud, hard snort of snot sucking back as she locked eyes with me. A hard, drawn-out hiss emitted from between her rubber lips.

The satyr-thing let his smile slime Muppet-wide and waved a hand pettishly at her. "Now, now, Nightsock, don't be rude to our guest."

"Nightsock?"

He glanced back at me, goggle-blinking with momentary surprise that I'd spoken. The grin recovered quickly. "Yes. She's our dear Cousin Nightsock, owing to her rather unusual and dexterous little toes."

"And who are you then? Uncle Goggles?"

His face blanched, all animation dropped like a heavy stage curtain. A cold and definite hatred. Pretty much as I'd characterized him on sight, he really was like those mid-level sycophant types I'd dealt with in the past. Namely, he had only the most vague sense of humor and it suffered nothing he considered even remotely an insult on himself.

He made a faint sputter, lips pursing like he'd gotten stuck on a lump in a straw he was drawing on. The smile returned at half-power.

"Funny. You don't seem to appreciate the full depth of your situation, if you're making jokes." Now the voice was the schoolteacher talking down to the kindergartener. He even gave a shake of that swollen skull like he was disappointed in my behavior.

"I tend to make jokes to break the ice with kidnappers holding me in a warehouse."

"We didn't mean to inconvenience you." A wag of the head, more schoolteacher ooze. "You apparently gave quite the scrap to our little Nightsock." A hiss-giggle that turned into a broken-glass titter behind him. "She says you were quite naughty with your toy."

"She was quite naughty with her claws of death."

He bowed his head and closed his eyes. His wart-mottled skin went from its sour yellow to a sunburnt shade of pink, not quite a match for his flip-flop bands. A faint shudder showed in his shoulders. For a beat, he seemed to...shimmer. Heat-mirage flickers. Was that what he'd done in the alley? Hide himself, in some way like his fellow strange-oid could, Mister Sharkdoll and his scared shadow-trails?

"You are testing my patience, young man."

"You've utterly failed mine, goat."

That was the last turn allowed in his book. With a clumsy lunge, those double-kneed legs wobbled him over and with a surprising speed one of the folded arms undid itself from its chicken-bone tangle and swung out, catching me with a hard *thock!* noise. I rocked to the left, one leg of the chair rising with me before clattering back to the floor.

I'd left my nerves numb for my hands bound behind my back, so his blow made as much difference as someone sneezing in the next room. My body reacted to the impact, but otherwise he could whale away all night and I wouldn't have any problem.

In out. Pant. *Clack.*

Seriously, man, pissing him off is one thing, but...

I shook my head as if clearing it from the aftermath of the blow. But I got his gist. This goat-schmuck was one thing to antagonize. Cousin Nightsock, though, was a different story. If he let her loose on me, she wouldn't simply give me some slaps. She'd use claws and teeth. And she'd dig deep. Things I might miss or not enjoy, numb corpse or not.

"An apology is traditionally the best way to settle things, young man."

I decided to compromise. I said nothing, neither apology or provocation. Simply stared at him, mouth closed and eyes open and expressionless.

He stared back, and after several long breaths pluming out of his nostrils, shook his head with that same disappointed teacher air as before. He turned to the crouching girl behind him and made a waving gesture. She nodded and disappeared so fast I only saw a faint flash of her ragged clothing.

"While Nightsock is on that little errand, let me perhaps try and make the position a bit clearer for your comprehension." That fake accent, trying to clip the ends of his syllables with crispness, was ruined in its pitiful effect by a lisp that slithered at the ends of his words. He was trying for some kind of Noel Coward and instead came off sounding like a Rowan Atkinson parody.

Another flash and clunk. A fold-out chair was beside him, Nightsock's fingers wrapped around its back as she shoved it forward. He beamed a smile at her, even patted her on the head in a grotesquely paternal fashion. She slid back from him as he took the seat, disappearing amongst the mounds of trash. I heard the faintest *clack-clack* as she did her maddening little dice-rolls again.

He nearly fell because one of the legs was a smidge uneven from the rest and it *chuh-chunked!* under him. His queer legs flailed out and barely stopped him, but for a moment he was splayed out like some Hawaiian-shirted hairy starfish, shivering and sweat-bubbling.

I must have been smirking without realizing it when he looked at me and those black bead-eyes blinked rapidly, the pink going a shade darker as he corrected himself. "You find a lot of things inappropriately amusing, Mr. Flicker."

"Call it a shortcoming."

"I call it rude and that's all there is to it." He sat back in a posture that almost emulated a traditional relaxed sit-back business pose, minus that he couldn't cross his legs to play with the crease in his nonexistent pants leg. He looked at the fingernails on one knobby hand to deliberately make a show of not looking at me. "Do you have some conception of where you are, situation-wise?"

"Not really. Feel free to enlighten me."

"I am Dusk. Pelatiah Dusk. Pelatiah is old Hebrew, did you know? It means 'God delivers.'"

"Thanks for the etymology lesson."

"You are to be delivered as well."

"What is all this about? You watch my store, report on my

actions, attack me, and now this little diatribe about Hebrew names and family titles that sound like a bunch of inbred farmhands in a Virginia mountain hollow."

A hiss from the girl.

"Cousin Nightsock does not appreciate your blend of humor," Dusk spoke flatly. "And I am reaching the end of my own reservoirs of appreciation as well."

"I can save you a lot of driving time and wasted gas. Tell me who hired you and I'll go see them myself."

A smile of mock resignation. "I'm afraid such directness is not permitted. We still must retain a bit of subtlety."

"You may refer to me as Brother Dusk."

"Oh, may I?"

Another dead stare at me, fingernails forgotten. He swatted at some unseen dust or hair on one knee and recovered. "My family and I have an interest in your recent goings-on, as you are no doubt now aware."

"Family? Nightsock and…who's your other cousin? Larry, Moe or Curly? Or is he Zeppo?"

"I believe you refer to Nephew Soursmile."

Soursmile. That name clicked for me and the faint images I'd gotten from Soul. Not Mister Sharkdoll. Somehow, as I recalled the look of that squirm-ball hovering around his plasticine face…Soursmile. I thought of the dog, whining then howling from the torment of those insect-shrimp things spraying across the air…yeah. It fit.

"Are you really all family, or is that just another of your affectations like bad shirt patterns and silly girl's flip-flops?"

Thwock! That time he gave me a pretty good socking, this time to my right. Hard enough to actually make me double over when I recovered, stomach pressing against thighs before I recoiled from its momentum. But before I could straighten, I'd been knocked too far and a comb, some coins and a rolled-up tissue. The change rang like tiny zinc bells on the concrete, the comb making a fast plastic rat-a-tat before settling next to them.

There was a noisy squall of bird-sound overhead. The *fweet-fweet*ing died out and there was a sound of light wings, flapping against the draft. The noise was disturbing some roosting bird in the beams over us.

He hunched over and leaned into me. His breath was rancid, full of garlic and that bland rotted-oat smell I associated with the clouds around the microbreweries in German Village, the waste-water that stank around the huge Budweiser complex in the north end of town. The teeth were thrown in even harsher corn-kernel relief, spittle roping between his gums. At first he didn't even have any words. Just a gurgling, inarticulate species of keening that came out as his tiny eyes practically glowed behind the myopic glasses.

"Do you ever shut up in the face of your superiors?" he snarled. "From what I have learned of you recently, I would have thought you would have long since learned your place in the arrangement of the world and come to appreciate when you are in the presence of those higher in station!"

Who talks like this? It's like he learned all his dialogue watching old PBS episodes of "Masterpiece Theater."

"I always show respect in the face of my superiors." I kept my face composed even though what I wanted to do was lean as far away from that gangly troll-face as the chair and duct tape would allow me. "And when they get here, I'll be sure to mind my p's and q's."

His face finally crossed into beetroot territory. A childish part of me that has always reveled in defiance and annoying people to get them at their worst was enjoying this, even as a rational angle of me was quivering and humming like a musical saw at the risks being taken. If he called back Nightsock to let her have-play at me…

…but he didn't. Clear thought didn't even seem to occur to him. He leaned in another inch, trying to somehow make his tiny stature count for all the looming quality he could muster while I was in the chair.

And that was when he got close enough.

I closed my eyes, imagined the idea of a cobra…leaned my head back a little, as if I was succumbing and trying to pull away from him. There was almost a glint of satisfaction birthing in his eyes at this, but I didn't see if it stuck around when I closed my eyes and reversed my action with violent, hard thrust for all my neck, shoulders and skull were worth. I drove my head, forehead first, into his face, with my mental aim striving for that crooked beak nose and the little grimy septum divot underneath it.

I hit dead-on, by the muffled *ka-chrunk* noise and a following snap-clatter on the ground, like stepping on baby birds trapped under a dishtowel on the sidewalk. I opened my eyes just in time.

He sucked back a ropy gagging sound and staggered back, double-knees all a-wobble as he collapsed into the fold-out chair, one hand scrabbling for the back of the chair and stability, the other clamped against his face.

His glasses, the bridge broken and a ribbon of loose tape dangling from one arm, lay on the floor between us. The lenses hadn't broken—they were that kind of cheap-yet-durable plastic that you make little kids' eyeglasses out of—but one half had landed in one of those small puddles of water-or-something-nastier that dotted the floor around the place.

Score! Even Soul couldn't deny a bit of sadistic glee on this count.

Between dirty fingers blood was flowing in a pretty healthy gout. No arterial spray or dramatic rivers. But a steady drop-stream occasionally interrupted by big blood-smeary bubbles as he tried to exhale or blow out a clot and only managed to pop a small scatter of droplets all down his shirt front and into his hand.

Exposed, looking over his fingers at me, wide and unprotected, his eyes were a horror.

Instead of the slightly ovoid-and-tapered-sides shape of human eyes, his were disturbingly perfect and round, like the stalk-bases of crab's eyes. What I had taken for normal eyelids blinking in angry agitation were actually a weird pair of palm-frond-like flagella above and below each of the bulging, all-black-shiny protrusions. These flapped open and shut wildly around the black ball of the eye like an approximation of eyelids. But there was a faint, orchestrated delay so that instead of looking like an eyelid, all closing of a piece over the eye, there was a little wave-shuffle that revealed to even the most casual observer that it was in fact a dozen little extrusions each moving with its own tiny muscle-group...more like watching spiny, multi-jointed little fingers each clasp shut to make a half-fist around the eye in its palm. The whole thing was raw-looking, wet like he'd been crying, but instead of clean and clear saline there was a faintly yellowish-white residue caked at the base of each eye. And the more-furious action of the clutched finger-cilia was squeezing more of it like pus through the spaces between each mini-finger. His eyes were like watching blackheads being playfully squeezed in rapid, hummingbird time over and over.

I let my own eyes drop, trying instead to focus on a point somewhere around the middle knuckle of his middle finger, above where his upper lip had to be.

He was shaking his head, and those caterpillar eyebrows waggled...and some of the longer ones swayed slower than the rest, like antennae or sea anemone fronds in a tidal sway. He wasn't a satyr or a faun...more like some kind of weird coral-reef conglomeration of all the things you like the least about the biology of oceanic life.

Soursmile...Nightsock...and this, their apparent leader, Brother Dusk. Who the hell were these people? No, *what* were these people?

Slurping. Sucking. I simply stared at the middle finger knuckle. A long, honking snort of fluid. Another spit-spray. He lowered his hand to examine the damage, staring down at whatever clotted mess was in his palm. His blood was dark and drying quickly, already within a few minutes a crust around his mouth, making a nasty sort of painted-on goatee that terminated in that stupid little soul-patch of grotty hair.

He started to say something...he stopped, a faint 'awp' popping from his lips. Mouth agape, I saw a tapered, purplish tongue lick out and test his upper teeth. One of those corn kernels very visibly wiggled. He winced to test its looseness.

Saliva wallowed in the pits of his cheeks and he spit, a mix of blood and spit that fizzed a little as it hit the floor near his glasses.

I kept looking at the spot above his lip, below his nose. Anything but those frond-waving, blind-grasping eye-things.

The only sound between us was his breathing. It had died down to the shuddery pant-suck-sob of a kid who has just gotten spanked, slowly recovering his wits and getting control of his crying. Every so often there was a crackle sound as his mouth would move and break some of the blood-crust around the lips.

"…you…you…"

I tilted my head, as if I were taking in an interesting painting at the museum. "Me. Yes."

"…don't you…*ever*…"

"If you need it," I stretched my leg out and toed the tissue ball on the floor in his direction, "feel free to use that. I can't remember what I used it for, but I'm sure it's cleaner than your hands at any rate."

His hands dropped to his sides. The horrorshow eye-stalk-holes clasped and unclasped at me.

The hands curled into clawed shapes, the way etchings of eagles on coins grasp the sheaves of arrows and wheat. His mouth, painfully loosened teeth or no, opened in a feral leer. The eye-things actually clicked and chittered as they moved faster. His double knees started shaking as if in the grip of a seizure. The bloodied Hawaiian shirt saw an explosive bloom of more sweat widening the circles at the neck and armpits.

As he threw his weight forward, about to come full locomotive at me, there was another flash of dull non-color, of motion and a faint pepper smell.

Nightsock stood between us.

She was smaller than even this dwarvish monster, looking somehow dainty in front of him. She had one scabrous hand out, its dirty grayed fingers stretched out and pressed against Brother's chest, right in the biggest bloodstain. His weight was enough that she was pushed back and had to back a step before her feet were planted enough to stop him, like some cartoon of a matador stopping a bull with one hand outstretched.

His momentum checked, Brother made a gargled snarl at her…then something clicked and his face, his whole body lost all that energy like watching an old fuse blow and go dark.

The fingers released and went slack. The posture drew back into a stand rather than a lunge. His eye-stalk-holes slowed and seemed calmer. He took a long, softened breath that would have been peaceful if not for the punchline that at the end it hit a snot-whork honking noise.

She stared into his eyes, the tableau utterly still. Her eyes into his eye-holes.

Slowly, she turned away from him and bent down. As she picked up the halves of his glasses, she glanced at me.

Empty. Utter nothing in those vapid eyes.

Clack.

She tore the little strip of loose tape and fiddled with the bridge, using the tape to give them a crude mend. Then slow she held them in both hands and delicately rose on tip-toes to place them back onto Brother's face.

The gesture had an alien yet endearing quality. I thought of when you watch mating dances amongst strange and colorful Amazon River insects, a sense of something calmly familiar but being shared between two utter grotesques.

Another long, shaky breath from Dusk.

"Thank you, my dear cousin." He tried to smile but stopped halfway, wincing at the tooth.

She nodded. And stared at him.

Finally he tilted his head and gave another mock-sigh. "Oh, all right. I suppose you have earned one, then. But only one. Go ahead."

A hiss-sizzle, a cat with hot grease in its mouth, was all I heard.

I was lying on my side and one of my eyes didn't work. Air bellowed out of my mouth like a cold draft. My cheek was against something wet.

My left eye was dark. Something cold and wet was falling across my nostrils.

I shook my head. My left eye wasn't closed. More wet. Dark drops on the concrete under me. Not water.

When I fell, my body had jerked so hard and fast, my arms had broken the frayed duct tape holding them. My right was pinned under me, my left dead against my side, flopping forward like a broken wing.

Oh man...

What?

*You...you've got to...I don't know...*the sensation of Soul near me went hollow, as if a wind had blown and opened a space amongst tree branches for a brief, tunneling moment.

I found movement in my left hand. I was able to make it come up, groggy as a punch-drunk fighter but grudgingly obeying me. I brought the fingers up to my neck, feeling more cold-wet there...blood...nothing surprising there...

My fingers probed...probably a broken cheekbone...my nose felt too large and lopsided...my fingers brought back news that blood was usually thinner, even if my own tended to be cold...this was viscous...a jellied touch...

...my left eye was gone.

No no no...no...

There was a moan coming from some wind down from the rooftop. No, it wasn't, that moan was from me. It simply sounded too hollow, too empty and agonized, for me to recognize as I used my right hand to grunt and shove myself up to a doll's sitting position, legs out in front of me, idiot mouth hanging open as my hands went to my face, feeling the new absence where I'd had sight not a second ago.

Calm down, man, calm—

I screamed, drowning out even the voice in my head. My right eye's vision was fuzzy and my eardrums crackled as my voice hit the high register of a terrified roar. My right eye blinked. Something wet there, but it was tears. Blood in my mouth.

I panicked, and it overrode all control. It overrode the old-fashioned toggle switches I picture in my mind when I shut sensations down.

In a brilliant supernova I *felt* my eye was gone.

I felt my hands *throb*, screaming, realized they were dark with blood that had settled. My shoulder blades and joints were in a knifing hot agony that was only overtaken by the king of all the pain, the silver-cold screech and papercut-hot exquisite shock that was the dark cavity cutting my three-d vision and depth perception down to nothing. As I screamed it seemed as if having my left eye gone meant somehow a whole left of my head, of myself was gone with it. I could perceive on that side anything except dark that roared out of its cavern in my head like a steel bear, claws a foot long each and tearing, jagged sweeps through my nerve endings.

I shivered and shook. My left hand stayed against my cheek, my eye socket, my entire head was on fire, burning with dry ice flares like a lighthouse in the middle of the Arctic wastes, calling home the ships of every other part of me that was in some degree of discomfort.

Chitter-hiss. Hiss. *Huck-huck.*

I looked up and my right eye blinked away some of the fuzz and as it cleared I saw Brother Dusk, looking down with a fatuous grin of satisfaction. His own pains were clearly forgot as he viewed Cousin Nightsock's work. Her own features were still blank, empty and smooth as a soap carving with two shoe-polish-dark holes for eyes looking out at me.

But Brother Dusk couldn't be more pleased. I screamed and screamed and allowed a breath to inflate my cold lungs so I could keep screaming because screaming was the only release, screaming made the pain sing a song that blew out, a high and quavering and useless note that I couldn't stop rupturing out of my throat. And Dusk was looking down, folding his arms and relaxing with that grin, a finger even straying up to stroke that soul-path crusted with his blood. Glasses askew but blinking, grinning, blinking, chuckling—

—I felt Soul, like a warm skin of air coasting around me, filling the sleeves of my coat, the legs of my pants, running along my skin like a hot shower's trailing threads of water flowing around the paths of my limbs, the hollow of my throat—his voice running through my head and overlapping, finding gaps where my screaming turned into choked gasping—

Calm down man "…calm down…" *you've got to* "Jesus" *CHRIST WILL YOU—*

"STOP LAUGHING!" Our voices, combined and pouring out with that bizarre wind tunnel distortion of Soul's, not just out of my throat but from my head, from my hands, from the empty socket of my left eye—

—my right registered that there were ripples in the puddles on the floor. Ripples that were rising and verving towards me, not spreading out like ripple circles are supposed to—

—as dust started to shift and make sighing noises in the air, the lights overhead blew out in a spray of sparks and incandescent-hot glass shards. Darkness seemed to collapse in like a dam breaking.

Squalling noises from Brother and panicked whapping noises. He had sparks in his clothes and skin. My right eye's vision went dark as my left but somehow this was okay, even almost soothing. If both eyes were equally dark it didn't matter. It was the asymmetry of the agony that was the worst. A blind man can function, it seemed to me. A half-blind man could only scream.

The pain continued to warble in my skull but there was Soul and there was a cool-hot feeling dancing around in the hairs on my neck and arms.

Where are they?

That troll is still hopping and dancing around in place like an epileptic polka dancer. Wait, he's…it's like he's standing under water—

—that's his thing, yeah. His stage trick. Why you couldn't see him in the alley, I think.

You'd think he was set on fire, he's acting up so much. He doesn't seem to be concentrating it to hide like before. Can you move?

My fingers were clenching and unclenching. I could feel the tips of them like they were each ten miles away but obeying with telegraph efficiency. Bleats of cramp-pain still batted at me from my back and upper arms, but they were nothing next to the hot steam-pound in my skull.

I was on my feet, swaying but standing without falling back onto my face. A shiver of air through my lungs.

Look.

My head drooped down, my eye following it.

I could see again, the vision clear and—

—the coins on the ground.

Three of them were reflecting darkness.

Not seeing. Not my eyes.

Overlap.

The coins that had fallen out of my pocket when Brother had hit me. Next to my comb. But where the other items were lying there in the dark, unremarkable...three of the coins looked like they had infinitesimal sunspots curling and snapping off them. The darkness around them seemed to fall onto their surfaces...then slide away, swallowed and spit and curling out and leaving a greasy sheen of thinner dark around the circles of metal. As we watched, the spit-curl shapes writhed and went thin, then died out completely. The dark swallowed the coins and they were the same as the rest of the ephemera on the floor.

I looked up. Around us, the room was coated in an ocean of moving dust mites, insects, bits of skin and plant matter dead and flaked and blowing around. There were a few angles and curves of objects, unidentifiable in the murk and tangle of piled-up objects, that had strange, soothing turns of air around them—were those magnetic fields? Around weakly-magnetic objects, like old fridge magnets or something?—but overall it was a dead space.

A streak of bright heat shot down to the floor a few feet to my right and I jerked.

It's okay. It was a bird dropping. You're seeing the fresh infra-red heat off it. Relax.

I want out *of here.*

You and me both. But relax a second. We need to orient.

In front of us was a panting, blister-pulsing mass of heat signatures and an oily-twisting, frenetic static-spray of activity.

Dusk.

I didn't yell or give any pain-motivated snarls of victory and battle attack. I simply bulled forward, lowering my head and not caring about stopping myself. Like throwing a good punch, the secret of any good full-body tackle is you need to accept you're going to probably get hurt, too. But with my arms and my back and my eye, my left eye Christ my EYE…what could hurt now?

He half-turned, apparently able to see me better in the dark than I could him, but I had the advantage of surprise. I clotheslined him, missing my target because my balance felt off, my forehead striking his right shoulder and my own shoulder socking into his collarbone, most of my weight plowing into his midsection. My arms loosely bear-hugged against him; even in the fury of it, his smell and sounds revolted me. I didn't want a lot of contact with him, the way you don't want skunk smell on you even if you have to drag a dead one out of your garage and into the trash.

We didn't quite fall over. Those double-joint legs were surprisingly capable at springing with the impact, like the old lotus-leaf shocks on a Model T ford. He sank from me, a shocked cry tearing from his mouth and I couldn't avoid the disgusting crackle I heard close to my ear where the blood dried on his face was continuing to flake and fly. One hand had a stroke of luck and as he flailed it found and boxed me in the jawline. I felt a punky wash of nausea…did he get me close to the ear, something in my inner balance? I huffed through my mouth and tried to get enough purchase on my feet to knee him. But he twisted, and something caught my left calf.

Not something. Someone.

The gurgling-steam sound exploded in my head even as thin fingers hole-punched my calf, through the pants fabric and into the muscle.

I screamed, throwing Brother off me and to the floor as I tried to pivot on the left foot, further grinding the twisting, torn muscles to look down at the blank-faced Cousin Nightsock, hunched down and looking up at me. Her only concession to emotion was her mouth open, bearing tiny little piranha teeth in too-big gums. She had an overbite, one of those crazy details you notice in a bright panic. One hand was buried into my leg, the other was clutched in a child's fist and shaking. I could hear a muffled rattle noise.

I screamed again. This pain wasn't like the left eye. This was vital, pumping, a pack of horses set to run from the leg up to my brain at full-gallop.

Not thinking at all, my right foot kicked out at her free hand. The fingers released, and tiny yellow-pink-white things sprayed like popcorn kernels out of her hand and clacked to the floor.

One of them landed near enough to see. A tooth. Yellow-white, but pink where some of the root nerve was still attached.

"Oh, you've lost her her latest trophy toys!" Dusk tittered from where he gathered himself into an untidy sprawl on the floor. "Cousin will take your other eye for that! She *loves* her toy trophies!"

He had most of his teeth gone, possibly swallowed some.

I snarled and jerked back my left leg. With her grip still tight on it, she was pulled with it, off her hunched position to whump with a gust of expelled breath to the floor.

I didn't even pause. Little girl? Monsters could look like all sorts things. Somehow my eye was still on the single tooth on the floor as I recovered and brought the free foot down again, this time on the forearm attached to the digging, prying little fingers that were knuckle-deep and seeking into my left leg muscles.

Brother Dusk yelled for her. She didn't make a sound as I snapped something in her forearm. All I heard was a teakettle whistle that died away, and her fingers went slack. I pulled away with a staggering back-step, actually sensing the absence of her fingertips, the claws slopping out of the holes in my calf. I couldn't stand steady. Desperate, I fumbled and grabbed at the only thing still upright, the fold-out chair Brother had been using. The uneven leg made it jump but it was more than I'd had. I held it like a too-short walking can and shivered.

"You bastard! You don't hurt one of us!" Dusk was sitting up. I heard a scratching noise and saw through Soul's eyes some furtive extension, a pseudopod of heat and motion from him... reaching for something, anything he could use as a weapon while he hollered. "Trophies scattered, you've...you've broken her arm! You broke Nightsock's arm!" His fake accent had been dropped and instead there was a nasal twang. Distinctly down-home hillbilly dialect, the kind where 'arm' sounded like 'ar-uhm' and 'Nightsock' sounded like 'night-sick.'

"I would've broken...a lot more, if I had time enough."

"You broke her arm! You broke it!" He didn't hear me at all, kept bellowing like a wounded calf in a pasture. The sound echoed off the rafters. I heard a skittering far away. Rats, probably disturbed into running for the fields outside.

Car. He came in a car. Outside. Go...go and see if they left the keys or anyone else with it. No point...running for it...if I can't use it.

Okay. I felt him leave, and as he left I felt as though my skin shrank a couple sizes, and a collapsing, crumpling sensation overtook my lungs, my limbs, even my head. The left eye socket wasn't throbbing as hard. Probably going into shock and adrenaline-junky withdrawal, but my vision of the space around me dissipated as fast as a soap bubble popping on the end of a blade of grass.

"You broke her arm!" Dusk was shifting weight, trying to get back up on those hairy-knuckled feet. "You broke her arm!"

"And you've broken your record, you—"

"Stop talking!" Petulant as a child sent to a time-out corner. His voice shifted position and I could tell he had gained his feet. "Stop talking! You talk and you talk and you *stop talking now!* You broke her arm! You stop talking! Stop talking!" The clownish *plap-slap* as he tried to stomp his feet but the flip-flops simply didn't have the mass to make it sound serious. I pictured him in front of me, stamping a foot in that ludicrous outfit like an angry beach-town tourist yelling at some server in a franchise restaurant because the potato-popper appetizers were cold.

"Stop talking!" I hadn't tried to say anything further, but he was stomping and I heard his voice shift.

He was closer.

I stumbled back in time to feel the air of his swing. and something with a nasty heft to it clung-rang against the tubing of the fold-out chair where I'd been a splitsecond ago. A *whoof* of air from him.

I kept my mouth shut, but another puff of air and this time something clipped my shoulder. Could he see in the dark? Maybe dimly. Better than I could, at any rate. I staggered back another step, leaving the chair and trying to drag my heel back so I could get some slight warning of any obstruction before completing the step. My left leg was useless below the knee. I felt its wet, fresh drips from the wounds but the pain was already dying down. It joined my left eye socket to become a sort of Greek chorus of assaulted nerves.

Clack.

In out.

Sigh-hiss. Gulping, choked sounds to my right. Brother with his club to my left.

Oh no.

Titters to my left. "Oh, dear! Oh dear! You broke her arm and she's not happy about it, not happy at all!" Diseased giggling from the dark. "Not happy!"

A sigh at my ear. *There's nobody with the car outside. The keys are sitting on the hood for some bizarre reason, but not going to argue with the gift-horse.*

Where are they? I can't see!

Nightsock is sitting on the floor. She sat up, she's holding her arm and rocking back and forth, staring at...man...they took his teeth, she was playing with his—

Yeah, I know. What's Brother doing?

He's standing there, swinging what looks like a table leg off some old card table. There's a pile of junk directly behind you, don't step back any further.

Get me out of here!

You need to go back and to your right, around this pile—

A high, flat *bang* that made me freeze. The sound of something clattering right after, like hearing a giant pile of child's Lincoln logs hollow-slapping to the concrete.

"JOHN FLICKER! ARE YOU IN HERE?"

The voice was female, and amongst all the other craziness that had gone on in the last few hours, familiar.

Friend or foe? Lady or tiger? Or…tiger lady?

Brother's stopped swinging his club. He's listening. Nightsock stopped rocking.

Should I call out? Who is that?

I could hear the smile in Soul's face. *I don't freaking believe it, but yeah, call out.*

"I'm here!" I yelled as hard as I could manage, though the exertion made the leg and eye wounds really join in counterpoint, and the end of my yell came out pretty ragged, degenerating into a cough.

Move!

I jerked back and there was that whistle-shove of air as another swing narrowly missed me.

Flashlight beams shot out, spraying across the dusty air like movie premiere spotlights, searching and homing in towards me.

In the gray half-light I could make out the vulture-hunch of Brother's head and shoulders. He was looking back towards the flashlight beams.

I bent over and snatched at the pile of junk behind me, trying to find something that had give, something that wasn't trapped under the pile. I tugged, rejected one thing, tried another. What were these, broken chairs or tables or something? Furniture factory rejects? Something slimy-and-furry, a discarded toy or stuffed doll wet with rain and rot-water. I smeared my hand clear on my jacket, dug again. Found something that felt round and lengthy and snapped free when I pulled at it. It was despairingly light. Balsa wood? Cheap furniture leg? Kiddie baseball bat?

Left!

I dropped left and the club in Brother's hand almost missed, but at the last inch struck the outer edge of my right foot, *cluh-thwang*ing into the floor but leaving that edge, even with the boot on, tingling. I didn't wait for further instructions, but saw the doubled-over form of Brother next to me and swung out whatever was in my hand. I was rewarded with only a woefully light hit that swished more than thunked as I'd hoped.

Brother fell back into the murk and screamed, a slapping noise and then something metal twanging onto the floor.

What the hell?

You had a broken-off piece of wood. With a tip.

What?

Get moving. Go towards the lights. Quick, the girl is trying to get up with that broken arm, move!

The gunshot in the space of the warehouse was deafening, reverberating off the walls and ceiling and coming back like a thunderbolt's understudy, trying out new angles to rupture your ears.

I dropped the piece of wood and limp-staggered past Brother, away from Cousin Nightsock and headed around the vague shapes of piles of broken-down waste towards where I saw the flashlights cutting back and forth, getting brighter as I got closer.

"JOHN FLICKER!"

"I'M COMING! STAY THERE!"

The flashlights stopped sweeping erratically, and as I came around what looked like the back half of a rusted-out hulk of old truck, the beams found me and oriented towards me, pinning me in the glare and my right eye reflexively closed as I stopped, standing and shuddering in the light.

"Gods..." Quiet. Then, calmly: "Mr. Flicker, we received the message. You...you need help."

"No shit." I raised a hand to block the light, and it was politely lowered. I blinked, the movements agitating damaged tissue in my left socket that itched and stung. "Get...there are others...back there...get out of here."

A silhouette, curved and supple, cut in front of one of the beams and approached me. It grew and there was a smell of cardamoms that enveloped me: nutty, aromatic and sweet, a spice smell that was not hot but soft and relaxing. A flawless teak hand took my wrist in supportive welcome.

I blinked my eye at her. "Dhara?"

"You remember me?" Her smile shone almost as bright as the flash of violet that shimmered across her pupils for a beat.

"How can I forget a girl whose neck I broke?"

"I only hope I was your first." The affectation was flat, but the humor was clear enough. She turned and pulled me along with her, gentle but insistent. "Cover!" she yelled to the other flashlight beam.

There was a harsh report, followed by a second that smack-boomed into the wide space. Cover fire, shot neatly into the dark spaces to discourage pursuit. I followed Dhara as obediently as a dog tugged along on a neighborhood walk. The spice smell trailed behind her, and in its wake I almost wanted to cry.

"How did you find me?"

"You were fortunate that we were already looking for you," the vampire woman replied tersely, head twisting back and forth, roving and looking in all directions as she led me outside. We passed through a doorway where I saw the remains of hinged panels lying on the floor—a stock door, torn from its mounting. The clatter-bang noises I'd heard moments ago. There was still a dissipating cloud of dust that caught in my throat when I took a breath to ask another question. I coughed it clear and she paused, letting me have a moment's recovery.

"Looking for me? What?"

"The transition counselor was concerned when you didn't answer your phone or reply to any messages. She sent word to the proper people, and we were dispatched to see if we could locate you. We were not far away when we got a call that your whereabouts were determined."

"How was that?"

"You activated the caller, didn't you? The artifact you were given by the counselor?"

My brain took long seconds to parse out those words. "Wait. The coins? The coins…"

She said drop them if we needed help. Remember how they

had that glow, that fading shadow?

"But how did the coins...how did those work anyway? What were they, some walkie-talkie deal?"

"Simple resonators, set with a particular half-life frequency that is spotted by various beings the community has agreements with. Communication lines. I believe out here...it must have been one of the local amorphoids."

"Amorph—"

"I can answer your questions when we are safely away from here." Outside, parked next to a ratty-looking Suburban with mismatched front panels was a shiny black Escalade with custom rims, engine running. Next to each other, the Escalade looked like a dowager assassin next to a redneck with a jug of moonshine in his lap. There was a circle of gravel that trailed like a comet into a gravel road, leading off into the bushes and presumably a nearby service road past the thin weed-and-tree line of the horizon. The night air was rich with the smell of wild seeds and Dhara's scent in my nostrils. Columbus had its ever-present mauve-and-brown night sky of pollution and cloud cover, but we were far enough from downtown that it was thinned and allowed a few of the brightest night's stars to peek down on us.

She let go of me and I followed as she jogged to the Escalade. "Wait," I called. She stopped, looking back with another panicked flash of violet in her eyes. Were those teeth in her open mouth a little too bright? Maybe a couple of them longer? She sounded confident but I'd met her when she'd been confident about confronting a demon, too. We both learned some humility that time, and I wondered why she was here this time.

"What are you doing here, Dhara? I thought you were an academic in this system."

"No time!" Another bang report emitted from the warehouse, and a shout this time. She opened the driver door. "Come with me, now!"

"Hold up." I saw the keys sitting on the hood as Soul had described. They were attached to something bright yellow and blue. As I picked it up, I saw it was a "South Park" keychain trinket, little Stan with his blue hat.

More than just the car keys. The ring had a hefty weight of various keys, some looked like housekeys, another car key that was a fatter fob, probably one of those with microchips inside to activate the anti-theft device if you tried to tamper with the car without the key. It definitely didn't go to the old Suburban. And a strange cylinder of shiny chrome-steel...a vending machine key, it looked like.

Was this their car? I didn't see Brother Dusk walking into a dealership or a used car lot and haggling. I thought of him, laughing and chuckling at my eye, hopping up and down and interrupting me, yelling "Stop talking!" with an idiot repetition. A nasty, dirty little clown.

Ignoring the pain in my back and shoulders, the grind in my left leg as I gave a good pitcher's twist, pause, and swung my arm as hard as I could.

The keys spun and landed somewhere in the dark weeds, out of sight, making one last muffled jingle before disappearing.

"William!" Dhara yelled from the car. "It is time to leave! *Now!*"

Another shot from the gun, louder as the man holding it ran out of the warehouse door, looking behind him, the flashlight gone. "Get in the car!" he yelled, waving his free hand at us.

I hurried into the passenger seat as our cover-man flung open the rear passenger door and left it open as he half-sat onto the seat, arm straight out and firing once, twice, expertly through the open doorway. Another yell, a bestial thing from inside. Then the Escalade was in reverse, backing away from the other vehicle and roaring down the gravel drive, away from it all. As I started to close my eye, a huge explosive noise jerked me. The rear window behind my seat was rolled down, our cover-man's arm retracting back to the car's interior.

"I took out one of the tires," he explained when I stared back at him. The gun went into a holster at his belt.

"Jennifer put out word that I was missing?" Dhara nodded,

intent on the wheel but constantly glances at the rearview mirror to check the road behind. "But I couldn't...how long was she trying to get in touch with me?"

"You've been unaccounted for a little over fifteen hours, by my estimate."

"Fifteen *hours?*" I blinked and rested back into the plush seat. A *day.* It was dark because it was dark *again.* Missing a whole day...a day. I couldn't get my grasp on that. The seat warmer cradled me and the smell of spicy flowers tickled at my nose again, stronger in the enclosed space. "Why would anything be strange about my being out of touch for a few hours?"

"With all respect, Mr. Flicker," Dhara grinned in the dim light of the car, a slash of light reflected in the rearview across her eyes like a reverse domino mask, "when most people go missing for a day or two, it's not always a problem. When someone like you has been missing for a few hours, clearly something's wrong."

She's got us there.

I couldn't say anything more to that. I let my right eye close and stay closed for a time, not caring about tracking where we went or the turns made. In the silence I listened to little more than the shush of tires on pavement and smooth transmission powering along. After a few minutes, I felt a grin struggle and successfully find space on my lips.

"Is something funny?" Dhara asked.

"I'm picturing Brother discovering his keys are gone."

Neither of them asked for any clarification. The Escalade shushed along.

36.

William leaned forward to bring his head close to Body's. He held out a clenched fist.

"Yours?" As his hand came out, Body extended his. The fingers hovered, opened, and three small, cold chips of metal fell into his palm.

The coins. The pennies that had fallen out of Body's breast pocket: two normal zinc-coppers and that oddball steelhead.

"I almost can't believe these things worked."

William smiled. "There's a way of treating certain combinations of metal alloy. Makes them stand out like lighthouses to certain intelligent parties attenuated to them. Amorphoids see those deployed, they immediately notify us."

There's a shift to them now, not the same as before. I was floating directly over the hand. *Something...*my impressions flowed directly into Body's forebrain.

Oil and feathers, spinning in a tidal circle...rambling bits of broken poetry that left the taste of dust and ozone...*here we go 'round the mulberry bush, a bushel a basket a basket of trouble oh dearie-dear—*

Body blinked, clutching his hand closed on the coins.

William lost his smile. "Are you okay?"

"Yeah," he replied. "Just got a quirky feeling…you're talking about Telephone Birds, aren't you? That's what senses the coins and gets word to your people, isn't it?"

A short moment of frank staring at him. "Yeah. The Birds are pretty universally spread around cities, they make for a very effective grapevine when all else fails."

No kidding. We'd relied on the help of these weird quasi-ghosts myself before. Purported to have been human spirits who in some way mutated into an impish, very fluid and mobile form, Telephone Birds were the magpies and stoolpigeons of the Under.

If you looked carefully at starlings on a phone line, or ravens and crows in trees, occasionally you might spot a twitch, a shiver in the air that shows it's not those birds you're seeing but Telephone Birds, watching and listening and picking up a little of everything that goes on around the city.

If you could get past their strange spinster-maid cackles and demands for flattery to share their gossip, and could keep up in interpreting their stream-of-consciousness ways of describing things like an ee cummings poem played at double-speed, the Birds could be a highly effective form of information-gathering.

William jerked his thumb over his shoulder indicating our past route. "Who were those crazies?"

"A man named Brother Dusk. His Gal Friday was named Cousin Nightsock."

"A cult of some kind?"

"Maybe. He referred to them as *wildeweird*." I looked at Dhara. "Do you know anything about that? I don't."

A shake of her head. "Sorry."

William spoke up. "Maybe Kardas would know, she's pretty smart about all the types running around."

Body put his hand out. "I'm John, by the way."

William stared down at the hand a moment, a hair past normal politeness. Then he grinned and accepted the hand with a firm shake. "William. Bill. Gunderson."

"Thanks for your help."

"Anytime."

He reads as all-clear. Normal reading off his feelings, normal air around him.

"You're a contractor?"

He glanced at Dhara. "What?"

Body smiled. "Don't sweat it. You don't have the usual signs. You're human."

We finally parked somewhere in Upper Arlington. As Body roused himself out of the car seat and got out to look, I recognized it because it was the only part of town where you could still find elderly, grand dignified estate houses cramped up against each others' property lines, and still be under the mauve gauze of the city's night sky.

We were in the circular driveway of a large flagstone house. Body stepped out gingerly to the custom polished-river-stone driveway.

My leg doesn't hurt anymore.

I peered down at it and could see that through the holes in the pants leg, the skin underneath was showing with little pink circles where the flesh was already closed up and almost done healing.

Body reached a hand up to touch his left cheek, afraid to let the fingertips go all the way up to discover the persistent bad news.

It's gonna be okay, man. Relax on it.

Body shook his head. Healing is one thing. I've survived cuts, burns, poisoning, suffocation, drowning...any number of small and large traumas, including my introduction to bullet wounds in recent days. This same eye took a rod of metal punched through it not too long ago. Of course, at the time I was the center of a whirling mass of exploding rage and screeching, burning metal and ash and steam.

I remember. The Jennyripper. Another one of those occasions I hoped I didn't get lost into remembering anytime soon.

The pain of one injury kind of gotten washed away in the larger laundry-load of utter agony that night had been. And I was unconscious for so long after the incident, my damage had mostly healed without my having to be conscious of it.

Guess you got lucky, for what it's worth.

Body bowed his head. *But my eye being gone…I can't seem to get my thoughts away from it. Just looking around, there's a gigantic superimposed blackness that forces its way onto everything I'm seeing, teasing and driving me crazy with the feeling that there's constantly something just around the corner of my right eye's limit of peripheral vision, if only I could. Open. My. Left. Eye.*

Dude, you lost it all of half an hour ago. Give it some time.

Dhara came around to help. She stopped when she saw that he was blinking the right eye rapidly, his left hand raised to the left cheek. "Come inside," she took his left hand tenderly in her own, pulling it from his face to lead him to the front door. "We can help care for that."

"I really…" he swallowed to try and wet his throat, to get rid of the gassy croak that had come out. He coughed.

She could see his difficulties. "Come to the kitchen. I will get you a glass of water, first."

The house was an L-shaped affair with a rounded tower at the center where the front door greeted us. She entered a complicated number into a dim blue-lit keypad at the door and let us in.

We followed her across a long, sumptuously-draped hallway and long sideboards of heavy-dark oak paneling to a side corridor that led into a large chef's dream of a kitchen. Stainless steel shone everywhere with that kind of brushed-squirrely-circle patterning you know is only achieved by manual labor slowly brushing treated steel wool over the surfaces over and over.

She had him sit at one of the eight stools pulled up to the breakfast board buffet island with the deliberately-and-fashionably-rough-edge-cut tourmaline-granite tops, glass-smooth perfect and looking like altars to the gods of cuisine. A perfectly flat-surfaced door of steel that looked like all the other perfectly flat panels of steel next to it was where she withdrew a bottle of water and a chilled crystal tumbler from a side chilling unit set inside the door.

Body managed to cough out one coherent word: "Where…?"

"We thought we should bring you to one of our private community places."

"This…" he coughed again. "A vampire safehouse?"

"This is an installation for our work." She uncapped the water, poured it into the tumbler, the water and crystal meshing perfectly to look as transparent and clear as anything I could hope to see this side of a CERN laboratory clean-room.

The kitchen had something wrong, though. For all the tasteful track lighting and spotlessness…I kept hear-feeling this sort of mellow snap-crackle sense…as if underneath every surface were those tiny wads of firecracker powder kids throw at the ground to make them bang with a little puff of smoke. To me there was a constant flash I couldn't make out, a corner-of-my-eye thing that if I tried to focus on any one point simply disappeared.

"What…safe from?"

"Sometimes a member of another community will come for meetings with our own leaders." She came around the counter and handed Body the glass of water. He had to hold it in both hands at first, with her watching attentively. When the first couple of guzzles of it had wetted the tongue and palate enough to not have them sticking to each other so stubbornly, he smiled and lowered one hand, finishing the whole thing before setting it down.

"Vampire leaders don't have guest space in their own houses?"

Dhara looked down at the countertop as she spoke.

"Sometimes…there are different community…standards and practices, you may call it. Where in one place it is considered the height of rudeness or impropriety to behave in a manner that in another place is…acceptable. Having these neutral places established to accommodate…different community visitors…helps to smooth such uncomfortable interactions."

"Wait…this…you mean this place is for visiting dignitaries who…what? Go buck-wild and crazy and have blood-spraying, gut-churning orgies of feeding here, then they can clean up and go to the big soiree down at the 'Thropes and Throats club?"

The shadow of those jet-black curls fell on her features as she bowed her head, eyes slitted and still looking at the counter. "I would not…describe things quite as…exaggeratedly as that. But you have the principle of it correct, yes."

A picture flashed, unwanted, into my thoughts: a single pink-white-yellow tooth resting on a concrete floor.

Clack. Clack.

Body removed my hand from the counter and glass and let it rest on my thigh.

All of a sudden I didn't want to think about why this was such a wonderful, fully-decked-out kitchen. With easily-cleanable stainless steel and stone surfaces. Why I was acclimating to a very sour, old, faint sensation. Like…old tissues drying in a baking pan full of cow's blood on a hot afternoon porch…metal-oil gone bad…

I think I'm beginning to figure out what's wrong in here. I huddled closer to Body, staying around his shoulders and neck and trying to make myself feel as small as I could, so I couldn't accidentally come into contact with any of those snap-crackle-shiver surfaces…now I was understanding a sort of half-suggested faces, mouths screaming whenever those corner-of-eye flashes hit me from a surface or a shiny panel…

"Are you hungry?" She flicked her eyes up at us, under heavy kohl-lined lids. I saw that there was a bindi on her forehead, a tiny ruby-bright gem pasted between her eyes, above the bridge of her Roman nose bridge.

Body tried a smile but it still hurt too much and she didn't look like she would appreciate it. "No, no…thank you. I don't…I don't need to eat."

She hurriedly collected the glass and left it beside one of the deep, porcelain-spotless sink basins. "Come with me. We will get you fresh clothes and treat your wounds."

"I don't think I need my wounds treated, exactly. This… it'll heal. It just takes a little time."

"Still…you…you may want to freshen up."

I followed her glance at Body's legs and up to his torso, and gave a gander to those hands, turning over from back to front.

Man, you are filthy.

Covered in muck and dirt, streaks of crud on his hands and under the fingernails. He couldn't quite recover enough clear breath through clogged nostrils, but I imagined he couldn't have smelled much better than he looked. Though he doesn't sweat or shed skin or hair cells as far as I know, and as best I can tell even when he doesn't use deodorant or wash for a period of time, bacteria don't seem to collect on Body in the traditional ways they used to to give him underarm smell or bad swampfoot. But those clothes were a loss. Even the jacket, one of my third- or fourth-favorite walking-around coats, was a write-off.

"Follow me, please."

37.

Dhara led me back towards the front of the house and the master staircase. White carpet that looked like an angularly-perfect frozen waterfall coated in a downy layer of snow. A heavily-framed marble-topped balustrade bannister boxed in the staircase against the curving interior wall that had its flock wallpaper pattern broken up by large, unframed modern art works in heavy color-smear abstracts.

The whole staircase was wide enough to have driven a small car the whole way upstairs, but I stayed near the bannister and avoided looking at the paintings. I didn't want to consider what they might be actually painted with, considering the revelations about this place I'd gotten in the kitchen.

The main landing branched off into three different hallways. She took me down the lefthand branch into a dim corridor only lit by a couple of weathered-brass sconces, frosted to make the flickering light bulbs look more like a Victorian gaslight set in modern art deco cuts of crystal glass. We passed a few pairs of double doors until reaching the pair at the end of the corridor.

She opened the doors to admit me, and I entered behind her, feeling a weak swoosh of motion against and through my back.

This suite is bigger than our last couple of residences.

I looked around with faint appreciation. With only fifty percent of my vision, I could take in the details but that infuriating half-black overlay insisting on everything made it seem as beautiful as staring at a furniture store display.

The white carpet of the staircase and hallways stopped at the doorway of the suite, leaving mellow-glowing maple-finished hardwood floors laid out in a herringbone pattern. Area rugs of the same white carpet, cut in whorls and labyrinth patterns made square islands of bright against the wood. Lots of chunky, somewhat Mayan-styled furniture with vague faces suggested in the square facets. Living room area, leading up a single step to a bed-and-bedside tables dais. Potted ferns eating up each corner like crouching predators. Everything had a dark, varnished look of solidity. The huge, frameless bed with an even more huge painting, another of those queasy abstracts, hanging over it. Low, subdued off-track lighting that made me think of the same lighting arrangement in Justin's office, the last time we'd visited there at the 'Thropes and Throats club. Were vampires sensitive to too much direct lighting when in private quarters?

Dhara swept a hand to indicate the open doors ahead of us, where I could see a glimmer of white porcelain and ocean-blue tiling. "The bathroom is ahead. Please feel free to use it as long as you need."

I grunted thanks and was undressing as I walked to the bathroom doors. Coat, ragged shirt...I unbuckled and dropped my pants but then realized that sleepy-kid mistake that I hadn't taken my shoes off first. Had to stop and do a wobbly flamingo stance to work off one boot then another and then use my feet to stomp down on the cuff of one pants leg so as to let the weight of my next steps pull my jeans off. I was naked by the time I thumped through the doors into the bathroom.

Started the shower after a moment's consideration of how to work the faucets: double brass-finished numbers that didn't have knobs but had a pair of big brass push-button affairs. I pressed experimentally and figured out after a few tests that they were pressurized in such a way that as you pressed them the water started and reached varying degrees of mixture of hot and cold. If you pressed the hot or cold button harder, you got a harder spray of hot or cold. It was a square shower stall with thick glass-pane privacy doors that magnetically clinked shut behind me, with a shower-head mounted in all three tiled walls. Finally sussed out the method to get the weakest addition of cold to an otherwise scalding mixture and climbed in.

For long minutes, I didn't move or act to soap myself or anything. Merely stood in the spray of the three converging shower-heads, needling against my skin from head to toe and raising clouds of steam that immediately frosted up the glass doors.

I closed my eyes and turned my head up into the sun-bright overhead lamp.

Strange shower. Strange house. A constant sense on my nerve endings like the feeling of almost stepping out in front of an audience in a darkened theater, but not knowing a single line of the play. Naked in a way that had nothing to do with standing without clothes in a hot triple-shower deluge.

We're getting tangled up in other people's plans a lot more than I'm cool with, lately.

I nodded, head deep in the wash and dribble of the shower. Soul wallowed amongst the billows of steam and vapor coming out from the stall.

When I was finished scalding myself and toweled down, I found a selection of toiletries arrayed neatly on top of a linen handtowel by the sink basin, as courteously set up as any hotel en suite service. Used a brushed-steel finished comb to sweep back the wet hair. Looked into the mirror.

The wreckage of my eye was a horrorshow. The skin had been punctured, the orbital jelly of the eye pulverized and leaked away. A clear seepage of watery fluid with little white flecks sometimes flowing with it trickled down my cheek. I wiped it away with the handtowel. Looking into it revealed various folds of red-pink material I didn't know any medical labels to identify.

There was a dark purple-black shape back there, blurry

and nearly unseen in the shadow of the socket. I looked away when I realized it was probably what was left of the back of the shredded eyeball, maybe a bloody optic nerve stalk.

Soul grunted some agreement, picking up on my disgust with some of his own.

Time for some practical matters.

I reached back to the gold-plated toilet paper stand by the toilet and unfurled several squares. Folded them along their seams then wadded them in double. Looked under the sink counter and found, amongst the various replenishing piles of Q-tips and towels, a first-aid kit. Ace bandage. Surgical tape, the kind that tears off along woven-fiber seams. Shoved the wadded toilet paper against the socket, used four strips of tape to hold it long enough to let me wrap the bandage around my head at a diagonal to hold the whole thing against the cheek socket.

You look like some third-rate actor waiting for a cast call to an episode of "M.A.S.H." *or a World War II playlet.*

I shrugged. Checked my teeth. None missing or loose. Tilted and turned my head. There was a nasty bruise on the nape of my neck. But as I checked the edge was withdrawing, retreating back and leaving reddened, then restored-pink flesh.

Hanging on one of the brass hooks beside the door was a terrycloth robe in a hunter green that looked like it was made of some rich astroturf. I shrugged it on, didn't bother to belt it shut. It was weighty. It felt comforting to be too heavy. Like it gave me a sense as I walked of some sort of real foundation to the world.

Dhara was standing beside the bed. In her hands she had a first aid kit that was a twin of the one in the bathroom.

She set the kit down on the bed. "You already tended to the wound."

"Yes. Thanks for the thought, though." There were various clothes folded and arrayed on the bed. "Those for me?"

She nodded. "I brought you a few of each so you'd have some choice." I nodded thanks as he approached the bed. I let the robe drop to the floor without a second thought. Dhara looked away. I couldn't tell under which emotion she'd turned her gaze. Ultimately didn't care.

I dressed, sitting on the edge of the bed as I finished with lacing up his boots. Dhara didn't move the entire time. Stood up a few feet away, eyes staring at the painting over the bed. The blue jeans and navy-blue T-shirt were fine, though the shirt was a little looser than our usual picks.

"Where's my coat and things?"

"Downstairs. I can go get—"

"No, it's all right. It'll wait."

"Does that...hurt? I can go and get you appropriate medication if—"

"Again, no, thank you. Thank you very much. This is enough."

"Do you need anything?"

"Some time to rest." I reached up and stroked the bandage over the eye. "This should clear up, I'm fairly sure of that. It's inconvenient more than anything at the moment. What I really want more than anything is a few answers about who the hell those monsters were."

"William is acting on that priority even now. He said he would return in an hour or so when he's had the opportunity to recover some information on your abductors. He can properly assess what the response should be in dealing with them."

What?

"What does that mean?"

Dhara's face only raised eyebrows to acknowledge any inner surprise. "To seek proper redress for what they did to you."

Whoa, whoa...no, no. We are not going to have our bills paid, our bails paid, and now our payback paid by Justin and his friends. This is it.

"I don't want any retribution measures taken for me, Dhara. Please."

"We cannot permit—"

"It's not up to you guys, okay?" I stood up. "I'm grateful for you helping me. I really am. If it hadn't been for sheer accident... no, that's not fair...if it hadn't been for Miss Yu's foresight, I would probably still be stuck in that hellhole being tortured by those creeps. But that's the end of it. I don't want any vampiric SWAT teams or werewolf commando packs and whatever-the-hell-else you guys think you should be doing for this."

Dhara was silent for a minute. Then she nodded without another word of argument. "What would you like to do now?"

"Is there somewhere I can simply go and wait until William gets back? I'd like to talk to him about whatever information he gets, before I go any further."

"Of course."

Back down the staircase with the paintings I averted my eyes from catching any lines or blobs of their surfaces. First we stopped at a walk-in closet that was only missing a coat-check girl for size. Dug out my somewhat worse-for-wear trench coat. She muttered an offer to have it drycleaned or replaced but I gave another thankful refusal.

She took me to a sitting room done all in muted charcoals and granites. The effect was of sitting on a bier in a high-ceilinged tomb. She left without another word, not even a good night or a goodbye.

Another sense that I had disappointed someone, failed some unwritten and unannounced test. *To hell with it.*

****

I sat in my chair and waited. Stared into the shadowed corners where huge potted ferns sat in alabaster urns.

I tapped my fingers on the armrests. *Where do we go from here?*

We need to call Sarah. If these crazies have escalated their game to this level, she's in serious danger.

Dug around and found my phone in the coat pockets.

Four rings. Then to a generic voicemail message.

She always answered before.

Three little birds started squawking and fighting over the nest of my stomach. Feathers were tickling my nerve endings with uncomfortable, light irritations.

Damn it. I waited impatiently for the bleep of the

mailbox function.

"I need to get in touch with you as soon as possible. I got... attacked. I'm sorry I've been out of commission today, I was... they had me. But I got out of it thanks to some other local friends of mine. Call me as soon as you get this, it's urgent."

Hung up, dissatisfied. What I wanted to do was call about twenty more times in rapid succession, leaving ever-more-violently-nervous-sounding messages to get her to call back faster. The cellular phone version of people stabbing fingers over and over at an already-lit elevator button.

We should go.

I felt a chill on my fingers, running up my forearms. *I for one am sick of running around and reacting to everything with no clue. If something's happened we have to take the risk that a little while longer won't make much difference either way. We wait for this William Gunderson to come back and when he does, we get whatever info he's got.*

The last time we made a gamble we almost got eaten by a faery monster, and it didn't give us squat.

It confirmed that these crazies following us around were the same ones that had Hope Cambridge and attacked the Scots. So we have that much connection established.

What good is that? I folded my arms against my chest. Stared at my denim-clad knees. *Okay. The freakshows are related to the lead-heads going nuts around town and their hit on the Scots brothers. They've been watching us, maybe for the Believers or who-the-hell-knows.*

The cold moved away, seemed off to my left near the potted fern in that corner. *There are some major freaking pieces of the puzzle missing here, and we don't have even the box lid to show us what it's supposed to look like when it's completed.*

And now we can't get hold of Sarah.

Maybe she's doing a shoot with Hal and has her phone off. You know how Hal gets when a cell phone rings in the middle of a shoot.

I shook my head. *No. She'd keep it around. She knows how deep this shit is getting for both of us.*

So we wait for William. He gives us whatever info he has, maybe some of it helps, maybe not. Then we get a ride back to the Vega, and we start tracking down where the hell Sarah has gotten to and what state she's in. We deal with this. But we stop running around like chickens with heads chopped off.

*Speaking of heads...*I reached back into the coat pockets. Dug. Found a napkin and a folded-up piece of glossy advertising for a local lawn service that was left on the Vega's windshield a few days before. For a panicky second I thought it was gone, until I felt the piece of slightly-waxy photographic paper and withdrew it.

The photo from Hope Cambridge's apartment. I stared at it. Felt the non-breath on my neck as Soul came to look at it with me.

I blinked. The black of the lost eye still disoriented, trying to focus on something and feeling as though I were missing half of a Fisher-Price ViewMaster toy in my head.

What to make of this?

I shook my head. *One of the reasons I want to find out what's happening so bad. Why would Hope Cambridge...no, no, I don't need to know* why *she would have had this photo in her apartment. I want to know* how. Who. *What the hell is all this.*

Chalk that up to one of the questions we'll hopefully get to ask very soon.

Very very *soon.*

****

Gunderson returned and took the seat opposite me, tossing his leather tactical jacket onto the back as he sat, the glow of a smartphone screen in his hand as he beamed at me.

"Forgive me if I seem like a smiling moron," he said, the grin never ceasing as he settled into his seat, constantly re-positioning and adjusting his posture as he hunched in the chair. He made me think of some overstuffed giant toy bear that a little girl kept trying to get to sit upright and stay in place for a tea party seating. "But not only am I still coming down off

the total adrenaline buzz of that rescue, but Dhara said...I...
you're a *doppelgeist.*"

"Also a Pisces, if you're interested."

He laughed, shaking his head, resumed staring at me. "I'm
sorry, sorry, I know it seems weird given who I work for, and
I've seen...last few years, I've gotten to see some really wild
things...I was even part of a *ghost-trapping* last winter, if you
can believe it."

"I believe it."

"But you're...a *doppelgeist.* A real thing. I had heard there
was one and right here in town, but...I read about you, even
thought...a couple times, about...maybe driving by your place,
trying to meet you...but I mean..."

"I appreciate your restraint."

"Can you...I mean, your other, he's—?"

"Present and accounted for," I offered tiredly. "But we don't
do party tricks."

Gunderson's smile snapped shut. "Sorry."

"No offense taken. We're not as impressive as the brochures
make us out to be." I nodded at his phone. "Do you have
anything? On the people I was rescued from?"

Gunderson snorted, shaking his head again.

"Wildeweird."

"I thought I heard that term used, yeah."

"Man, you really have a way of attracting the *worst* classes
of creature, don't you?"

"I'm here with you, aren't I?"

"Smartass." Bill allowed a thin smile to creep back as he
referred to his phone's screen. "Wildeweird are all one giant,
inbred cauldron of seriously crazy shit. They claim to be a mix
of everything, even a few animals. Werewolf, vampire, you-
name-it. What they seem to be nowadays is a bunch of half-
witted freaks and spiritualist crazies, with the occasional *really*
creepy one amongst their number. A whole grab-bag of scary."

I thought of Nightsock, that fish-frog girl of the filthy-black coal
feet...and how she had barely reacted to having her arm snapped.

"Most of the time they stay out of sight," Gunderson went

on. "They don't believe in mingling with anyone outside their shallow end of the gene pool. If you met a wildeweird, there's not any mistaking the experience."

"The modified self-defense spray I used on one seemed pretty effective," I pondered aloud. "The other one, Brother Dusk, had some sort of ability to really hide and melt in shadows. But he seemed more the moronic type you're describing."

"Yeah, there's little to no consistency. When I say 'inbred' I'm not making a flippant insult. They really are one massive family tree with no forks. When one of their brood comes up with a desirable trait, they will put that poor bastard out to stud or as a breed-sow, trying to reproduce the trait in as many others as they can." He waved the phone at me. "I don't have any real facts about whether or not it works. There's no predicting what abilities a given member of the family has until you encounter them."

Brother Dusk. He certainly didn't seem to quite fit with the other two. He acted like the leader but somehow Soursmile and Nightsock were the deadly ones.

Dusk had acted more like a tolerated man-child, playing Boss. Still, the twisted anatomies and weird way he'd tried to sound smarter, talked like he learned everything off children's programming on the BBC...maybe they really were some strange hillbilly assemblage with a satellite dish mounted on a shack somewhere in the middle of nowhere, screwing each other and in between further distorting the family tree's branches catching up on the latest reality television shows to 'better' themselves.

"There seems to be a trio tailing me, hired by parties unknown."

"That's unusual. Wildeweird aren't generally for-hire by anyone, on account of that xenophobia that seems to be the only consistent family attribute."

"I take it they don't advertise in the local Weekly Shopper."

Gunderson shook his head. "They're hard to find unless you know where to look. And no, they're definitely not on Craigslist. I'm surprised they would agree to be in a major city no matter what the enticement. They *hate* masses of people around. The only ones I've heard of in Ohio are all down south, in the Ohio River Valley areas, back in areas even the hardcore moonshiners won't set up shop. They've been around a long time, almost pre-English colonization. There are some up in New England, old upstate hill-folk. Some people think they were Dutch Amsterdam breeds of some original pure bloodline that got mutated and insular after coming to America." He tapped his fingers on the screen. "Vampire communities are told to avoid them. They can be dangerous even to a blood feeder because they really are too stupid to know fear or prudence."

"I haven't met the third one personally, but my counterpart did. Nephew Soursmile. By all accounts probably the nastiest of the three." I recounted Soul's description and the best I could render of his sensory perceptions of Mister Sharkdoll.

"That's a new one on me," Bill replied after I was done. "The wildeweird generally are only known for physical traits. Night-vision, claws, stuff like that. Supposedly there's a rare one that had functional wings. Ever heard of the Mothman down in West Virginia?"

"You're kidding."

"I wish. But these two you described, and the one in the street, this bug-spitter…that's a whole *other* order of crazy. I would suggest that you steer the hell out of their way."

"Would that I could. How were you able to even identify them, if they're so backwoods and secretive?"

"Various ways. Some of it was the description we got… from the connection that alerted us to you."

"Telephone Birds. I know about them. It's cool."

He relaxed a little further. "I don't know how much to go over with you outside of your questions, I'm not really allowed a lot of leeway…I mean, the fact that you're here means they're trusting you a lot more, but—"

"Anything you don't feel is okay to tell me, just don't. You'll probably save us both headaches that way. And if I'm asked, I can honestly say you didn't give away any company secrets, all right?"

"Thanks. Anyways…other than the descriptions, we

have…there's a halfway decent network of contacts, some of whom operate in those areas. The community…my bosses…" I nodded, allowing that I was in the clear on this much as well, "…they like to keep tabs even on the few of their number that live and operate down in those back, out-of-the-way places. Kind of a moonshine grapevine, you might call it. Any strange news or tidbits of odd that come out of those small towns and valley townships. That sort of thing. There are some who…don't like to live in cities or be part of the bigger groups, you know? Anyways, I couldn't point to any place on a map or anything and say 'that's your guys,' but based on the descriptions and what you're telling me now…yeah, it's a fairly good bet they're wildeweird."

"So I've got, what, a whole family of freaks coming after me?"

"Not sure either way. If they were operating on some for-hire basis, they might not be close members of the family. There are even a few cases of exiles. Excommunicated from the brood, if you follow."

I rubbed my eyes.

Terrific. I sensed the shiver across the arms of the chair and down across the carpeted floor, running along the trim at the base of the walls. Just terrific. So we have got either a family of monsters after us, or only the worst of the lot to deal with. That we've pissed off and made this personal.

"One thing at a time…" Gunderson looked puzzled when I opened my eyes. "Not you. Never mind. What about the humans? The ones attacking Sarah and I? The Believers in the Second Freedom? Anything from the grapevine on them?"

"You'll want to stay seated for this one," Gunderson said. His voice had all the warm enthusiasm of an insurance salesman making his ump-thousandth cold call of the day, fully expecting a rude hang-up any second.

"Cut it straight and let me know what I'm dealing with."

"Do you know a woman named Hope Cambridge?"

Here we go.

"Not personally. I was only accused of murdering her yesterday."

"What?"

I gave him a brief sketch of my being brought in for questioning and the discovery of the body at The Nookery.

Gunderson took it in with a faint whistle at the finish. "Wow."

"So what does Hope Cambridge have to do with the Believers?"

He referred back to his screen. "Hope Cambridge was apparently all mixed into it. I was able to get one of our tech-heads to get into her social media sites. Facebook, Twitter, all that. She was a member of a small but highly specific sort of cult." A breath. "And that's the good news."

"Oh joy."

"The bad news is that I wasn't kidding about you wanting to be seated. This group believes that they have only one mission in the world, which is to eliminate an abomination from the face of the earth. Namely: you."

"I had gathered that. But what, you're saying that that's *all* they're about? Wiping me out?"

"We did some digging, found a few darknet forums, did some searches and found hits sifting through very outdated IRC chatrooms and server nets. The Believers in the Second Coming have this warped idea that doppelgeists are not a body and spirit together, but are in fact some kind of punishment by God for rare, unfortunate souls who are meant to provide the Believers with a chance to do God's will and redeem the trapped soul."

"God spare me from the godly."

A chuckle. "Indeed. Here comes the fun bit: they believe that to free said trapped soul, they must do everything they can in their power to see that the 'corrupting flesh' is killed, thereby supposedly freeing that soul to finally go back to Jeebus and all His Chillun,' apparently."

Crap on a pita.

"That's *it*? They don't have any other agenda or foundation of belief than that? You've got to be *bullshitting* me."

"Wish that I was, man. But then again, I'm getting the impression, looking at their last year or so of back-and-forth forum posts and discussion threads on the 'net, they didn't even know of any active doppelgeists for them to 'redeem.'"

"Until now."

"Until you. By all accounts, using some of the online archives and dark net connections I could pull together, these guys didn't even *exist* until a little over a year."

Shit on a shingle.

"Wait…these people…they know doppelgeists exist…so presumably they have at least some knowledge of people like me."

"Sure."

"So don't they also know that they can't really, y'know, accomplish that? *Kill* me?"

"Dude, I can't say how far-gone these people are on the railroad ride between Crazytown and Stupidville. But guns and knives aside, what do you think are your odds if they try, say, coming at you with a machete and hacking you into fifty pieces and mailing each piece to a different state?"

"…I see your point."

"Besides, when did the truly faithful ever let logic or past evidence get in the way of dogged persistence?"

"Again, point taken. Shit."

Gunderson tapped at a few more links in his screen display. He didn't look up as he spoke. "Hey, you've been working for… is it right? This guy Segal?"

"Ceyggan. He's one of the principals of the Faede in Columbus."

"The faeries?"

I nodded. "They asked me to look into an attack on one of their people."

"Does that tie into you getting attacked by the wildeweird?"

"It certainly would seem to. The one who attacked was Hope Cambridge. I was checking out her apartment when those assclowns got me."

"The Faede…I don't know them. Are they cool?"

"They certainly want people to think they are. Yes, they're all right. A bit on the superficial side most times, but overall they're okay. Why?"

"You might want to be careful of dealing with them. I understand they're tricky people. Not trustworthy."

This was getting monotonous so quickly. "Thanks for the

warning. I try to be careful in dealing with anybody asking for my help." I gave him a direct stare that he wouldn't meet but I know he sensed it. "No matter who it is."

"It's just…we don't know much of anything about them. They keep pretty close to the vest."

"And your employers don't?"

"…point taken."

Of course the Faede seemed shallow and simultaneously secretive because of one big, hulking secret they were all keeping. But I wasn't going to start blabbing about the Teaghlach or anything else. The vampire community might be making this all as a calculated effort to further engender our trust and make us feel comfortable debriefing them with anything we knew about anyone else, but I wasn't comfortable. Not at all.

With Gunderson and Jennifer and all previous dealings with them, I was beginning to truly appreciate how extensive their community was invested in all manner of collecting and collating information. The vampires didn't like leaving anything to chance or risk if they could help it. It might be different in other cities and groups, but overall they seemed to really like the advantage of having as many of the cards out of the deck and in their hands as they could arrange. When I'd met her during the Jennyripper investigation, Dhara was some sort of doctorate-level expert in daemonology and electromagnetic research. There were others, vampire and otherwise, who supplied them with everything from historical expertise to scientific research and surveillance on a regular basis.

They'd be happy to provide me with info and help. They had before. But this house and what it did to my nerves made me see that I was racking up a considerable backlog of favors-owed every time I leaned on them.

Another rub at my remaining eye. *I wish I could sleep. God I'm so tired past the point of being exhausted.* "How is Trina?"

"Who? Oh, the girl."

"Yes, the *girl.* I haven't heard from or about her in a little while."

"She's doing fine." Tap-tap, finger-swipe to open a

document. "She's at the transition house, getting some final observation. She should be out within a day or so."

"Good. As long as she's okay, that's what matters."

"You volunteered to be her blood partner?"

"Yeah."

"That's pretty wild. Can you...I mean, do you *have* blood?"

I stared at him. I think my single eye made the proper impression. "Sorry, man." He went back to his screen tapping.

"Can you do checks on people? Not anything deep or intense, but your basic name-social-address kind of thing?"

Another snort. "Hell yeah. I could get you somebody's bra size pretty much just sitting here, without even calling any of our consult offices."

"Good. Can you look up someone for me? Sarah Parley." I spelled out the name. "Don't know her age or address. I know she operates out of Los Angeles. Adult performer. Stage name is Sierra Dunes."

"Don't you do...uh..."

"Yeah, I do. At least, I did. Can you see what you come up with? Nothing deep, like I said. No need to invade social media accounts or anything. Simply the basics."

"'Kay."

A few minutes while I stared at my lap, not thinking of anything. A couple of faint blips from his phone speaker.

"Huh."

"What?"

"There's some gaps in the record. No application for Social Security, though she should be eligible for it. She's a porn star?"

"Yes."

"Does she do, like, 'MILF' porn or granny stuff?"

"Pretty sure no."

"'Cause on the basic records, she's got to be nearly sixty. Not that that means she's ugly or anything, but...this doesn't say porn star. This says actress, but not any adult stuff. Just an IMDB entry for a couple of old horror movies. Low-budget stuff."

"Yeah. She did that years ago."

"Weird. I wonder what it's like when your mom is a porn star."

"What?"

"Health statistic records have her down as having had two kids. Daughters."

A shift of air near my ears, not quite popping them. *Well... that answers one of our pending questions. Sort of. Okay, so far it syncs. But wonder why she didn't mention them before?*

It's not like she was obliged to say anything. Maybe she's not in contact with them anymore. Especially if she wants to keep it from them that she's a doppelgeist.

Not a very good cover, doing porn. I mean, okay, she's not a household name or anything, but that's a pretty public way of hiding yourself, isn't it?

We've done it.

But we don't exactly care about being hidden, do we? And you started doing it simply for the cash, no questions asked. Does she strike you as someone who couldn't make money in other, more behind-the-scenes ways?

No idea.

"Huh."

"What now?"

"I did a basic track on her kids. One of them was Hope Cambridge."

When this plot thickens, it goes straight from oatmeal to Qwikrete, don't it?

He frowned and looked up. "This is all tying together in some weird ways, man."

"No kidding."

Wait...Hope Cambridge was part of the Believers group. Now we find that she's Sarah's daughter?

"Who is her other daughter?"

"All we have is a name and birth certificate entry, Marin County, California. Elizabeth Cambridge. A year younger than Hope. She's thirty-one right now." A few more taps. "Did you know Sarah Parley died?"

You'd be surprised to find out how we do, Soul sighed.

I nodded. "Yeah."

"Says here some sort of drug overdose thing. Not too long

ago, a couple of years. Out in Orange County, at some friend's beach house where she was living. Sleeping pills."

I pictured a kitchen table crowded with little orange-plastic pill bottles. A sleepy face staring forlornly out at a hummingbird feeder. Gave a tiny shake of my head to rid myself of it like cats climbing out of a bath.

I rested my head back against the cushioned upholstery of the chair, thoughts rolling around like a broken carousel. They would rev up and speed, then slow and go choppy, the pull-chains tripping up and steam escaping into random, disorganized confusion.

This has to all go together. It's not making much sense but it's going together in some fashion.

Soul moved around the room, pacing off the corners of the ceiling. *Sarah Parley was a B-horror movie actress. She had two daughters. One of them Hope Cambridge, the other Elizabeth. Okay. Hope moved out here, had a life, got mixed up in the Believers and lead-head addiction. Sarah became a porn star out west, maybe her movie-husband dollars ran out...expensive to live in California, after all...*

I picked up the thread. *She overdoses. Dies. Somehow that makes her into a doppelgeist. She keeps working, business as usual.*

Then the Believers start hassling her, like they've started to hassle us. So she uses her connections to find out we're here and comes out to meet with us, see about maybe joining up for mutual benefit.

I thought about the kiss on my lips. Couldn't argue with the 'benefit' part. *And here we are.*

Soul stopped moving, hovering near the overhead lights. *But it's stupid coincidence, isn't it? Not even right to think of it as coincidence.*

What?

Think about it. All the places in the world, as rare as doppelgeists are, she happens to find that the only other one around for her to meet also lives in the one city *where one of her daughters is? A daughter who happens to be in the same group that's trying to kill her and us? Are doppelgeists suddenly Six*

Degrees of Kevin Bacon for Everything Under?

It doesn't feel right.

No. It doesn't.

There's something else here, though…why can't I focus on it? It feels wrong and I know it's there but I can't think of it…

"Do these Believers have anyone special on Sarah? Maybe those wildeweird were the ones bugging her out west."

"Why would they bug her? Because of you?"

"Because she's a doppelgeist like me. Hell that's probably how these Believers found out about her, through Hope. Maybe Hope knew what her mom had become and was easy pickings when she found this cult."

"There's no talk on their boards about Sarah. Other than a couple of recent posts about seeing you with her at Columbus." A sigh and a glance at the screen. "There's not a lot of these guys, but I get the impression they're somewhat organized."

"No shit. One of them was able to find me at a gallery show that I didn't even know I was going to until about a half-hour before I did."

"Cell phones and text messaging, they're the Elliot Ness of the twenty-first century. Dick Tracy's phone-watch doesn't even cut it does it?" I shook my head.

"So you're with Sarah Parley now? Really?"

"I don't know if 'with' her is how I'd term it. We've met because of this Believers mess."

More staring and swiping at the screen. "Sierra Dunes. Man, if that's her, she's not half bad at all. She's like how my dad used to say: I wouldn't throw her out of bed for eating crackers."

I gave the first genuine chuckle I'd felt in a while. "Yes, she's very attractive."

There was a pressure in my head. It felt like a rapidly-expanding bubble made of glass, cricking and pressing against the front of my skull. My nasal passages seemed to pop along with my eardrums.

Itching. Oh damn it, really?

With a sneer at the discomfort of it, I reached up and snatched at the bandage. It snagged on its own little metal tooth-catches and I used both hands to jerk and tug it free. Tore out the wad of toilet paper, covered in sickly yellowish-red stains, and the surgical tape took away a few eyebrow hairs.

William made a sound, a baby-bird-falling-from-the-nest sound.

I blinked and saw a waxy gauze-lens effect superimposed over him.

Blinked again. Dark-light-dark. Blink.

Very, very fuzzy.

"You...oh man."

You have an eye again.

The eye was watering right away, pained at the over-bright light it was not yet recovered enough to process. I blinked. Water felt down the cheek.

A couple of hours. A couple of hours to re-grow an entire destroyed eye. I briefly pondered if I shouldn't start a records diary of some kind. "Personal Bests" ledger, with to-the-second tracking of all the things cut, restored, regenerated. All the burns, poisons, knives and bullets.

"Does that hurt?"

"I wouldn't know. Where's the bathroom on this floor?" He indicated a direction off the main hall near the kitchen.

Looking into the mirror. I plucked off the remaining sticky piece of tape.

There was an eye there. Blood vessels broken but there. I could see pinpricks of white clearing in the meat of it. From this red sphere looked out the Union uniform blue iris. I found a dimmer switch and reduced the bathroom lights to less than screaming. Blinked away more water as I stared.

The eyelid drooped over it. No amount of tweaking and twisting my face, trying to raise my eyebrows or squinch my cheeks, would open the eyelid all the way. Red, raw flesh. The blue seemed like a sapphire set in cherry Jell-O.

I ventured a fingertip to touch the surface.

Jerked my hand away. The eye felt...spongy. Like pressing into fresh shortcake.

That was...fast. Wow.

"Yeah," he spoke to his reflection. He looked at the wadded pile of bandage and surgical tape remnants. "Think I should re-wrap it until it's healed?"

....nah. Let people feel uncomfortable for a while. Think of it as your street cred scars for another few hours.

I threw the mess of wrapping and soiled toilet paper into the ivory-finished wastebasket before returning to the living room.

William was hypnotized. Unabashedly staring at my face as if watching some rare corpse flower bloom, ten feet high and effluent with a fascinating putrescence.

"Man...you...can you heal from anything?"

"As far as I know, yes. Hasn't failed me yet."

"Could you...could you grow back like an arm or a leg?"

"Not looking forward to finding out. Look, I don't know a lot about it and I'm not really up for a lot of question-and-answer press conferencing on this right now, all right? Maybe another time."

A nod, eyes going to the floor. "Sorry. Sorry."

"S'okay."

William smiled and shook his head. "Maybe you guys are like the porno versions of Dorian Gray, you know?"

"How so?"

"Maybe somewhere out there, there's a video tape of you guys having sex. And every year you guys stay the same while those video-you versions get older and sicker and die out instead."

My spine seemed to lock, from tailbone to brainstem. I blinked.

"Son of a bitch."

William jerked his glance up from the phone screen. "What?"

Oh no. Soul picked up my thought instantly. *Oh yeah. Oh... shit. That...it has to be, doesn't it?*

Yeah. We need to get on this. Now. We need to test it and find out for certain. This stops right now.

"Can you get me a ride to my place? I need to get home and take care of some things."

"Sure." William tucked away the phone and began to

extract a jangle of keychains out of one of his coat pockets. He looked askew at me as he shrugged into his leather jacket. "Is it like schizophrenia?"

"What are you talking about?"

"No offense, I know you didn't want questions, I'm sorry, but...I might never get another chance to ask, never mind being rude. But...your other. You hear and interact with him, right?"

"Yes," Soul replied from my mouth.

He blanched. "So...uh...is it like that? Like schizophrenia, I mean? Is it like having that voice in your head, telling you to do things?"

"No. Well, yes. Technically I have a voice in my head telling me to do things at times. But there's one big difference between being a doppelgeist and being a schizophrenic."

"That being?"

"A schizophrenic can take pills. Get help. The voices in their heads are delusions. *My* voice, if you want to call him that, is real."

38.

When we arrived back at the apartment complex where Hope Cambridge had lived, we passed a police car, visibar lights flashing. It was doing a slow, somewhat predatory cruise of the outer service road that skirted the complex.

At the corridor that led to her apartment, some flaps of yellow police cordon tape. A lot more porch lights were on. I imagined more doors were considerably locked and alarmed tonight.

I'm not looking forward to when Pinney next sees us. I could see the faint blues and whites of televisions on in more apartments than there'd been the night before.

"I would suggest not lingering for anything," William muttered as he slowed behind where the Vega remained parked. He nodded towards our car. "I'm surprised the police didn't impound that or something. Check it against resident records and find it didn't belong to a tenant or a guest, have it dragged out as evidence."

Crap. It very well may have been. Maybe Pinney did some more string-pulling for us.

Or maybe it's Hartsleg. Body cracked his thumbs while and stretched fingers in his lap. He blinked to clear away a few more bits of greasy blurring in my new eye's vision.

Are you seeing any better? The restored eye no longer had a droop of healing eyelid over it, but it still looked an ugly dark pink, with a blot of blood the size of a ladybug planted underneath the iris.

Meh. The parking lot lights have these infuriating haloes in that eye if I look up.

Maybe that cop car cruising around isn't the only police presence out here tonight. Waiting and seeing if the attacker returns to the scene of the crime, like in the television shows. Hartlseg would know that was our car. Might've left it here waiting for a moment exactly like this.

Gunderson wasn't stupid. "Do you want to leave? We could come back another time."

Body rapped his fingers in a short staccato on his knees.

If we sit here too long like this, that's bound to get us noticed by that cruiser when it returns, or if there are any plainclothes waiting nearby and watching the apartment.

Can you go ahead? Look for me?

I pressed through the windshield glass, flowing out, upwards. I soared over the Vega. It had its familiar lime-green-and-bird-turd coloring, a little more faded on the roof—why hadn't we sprung with all the new money to get it repainted? Give the girl a new dress—but then I couldn't miss there was a fishing line of light-pulse that made a noise like a cricket encased in tissue paper. It was emanated from...the ground? I swooped down.

Have William take you for another pass. Go some odd path and come back in a minute, okay?

What's wrong?

Just do it.

The car pulled away and went down to the T-intersection, made a left to take it further into the complex. I saw the taillights come on again before the turn...nice move. To any outward appearances, the slow down, stop, and roll on could be interpreted as simply someone unfamiliar with the complex, looking for the right address. Most likely harmless.

Then I focused on the beam from under the car. Moved, compressed, floated down to the underneath of the vehicle, the chassis and oil pan surfaces...as I pass one of the tires there was a click that might have been a shock absorber settling.

Do you know I'm here, honey? What have you got that's making that funny non-noise in light? It's reddish-orange like a beam of...

Chatter. A steady pulse that was like an epileptic Morse code. Blat-farting in whispers and static stutters. I saw it, tasted the sound as very thin, watery glue.

Attached under the driver's side. I could see short puff-curls of cycling dark green-blue where it met the body of the car's frame. Magnetism, strong but localized. And a black plastic box the size of an Altoids breath mint box. The fishing line of noise-light was coming out of that and beaming off...

...a goddamned tracking device.

I broadcast out along our mental thread. *Get back here. Somebody's lowjacked the car.*

Are you shitting me?

Cute. No need to waste a stakeout assignment when the twenty-first century and GPS can do it for you. I don't know if it was Hartsleg, but it seems his style, doesn't it? Let us drive away and incriminate ourselves, maybe lead him to some new tag and a way to make it stick next time he brought you into the interrogation room.

As their car swung back around and pulled to a stop behind the Vega, I drew in closer to the box.

Magnetically attached. I saw past the sunflare curls that were holding the box to the metal of the car. The fishing line of its broadcast was steady.

I watched it a few moments. Taking in the feel of it, the flavor of its electromagnetic bursts.

Didn't know if this was going to work. Every other time it had been sheer accident. A fluke of the moment's excitement. But for once, trying to consciously will it out, to shape and focus it for a specific effect...

...here's hoping I don't blow all four tires off the rims. Or

make the battery melt.

I imagined the box, seeing it in my mind as resting on a floor. It looked remarkably like the stained and glassy-smooth floor of the Scots' compound.

I let the image truly solidify, become something unmistakable in every detail.

Then I smiled inside myself. And pictured a massive steel-toed boot, almost cartoonishly huge, slamming down and crushing the box. The thought was accompanied by a plume of hard electrical shiver running from the rear of my self-field to the front, towards the box.

A squeal-crack and fart of something breaking. The single LED that had glowed green flared white, then went black. The fishing line of light stuttered and winked out of existence.

The lowjack is no longer an issue.

Body got out of the car, waved thanks to William. That vehicle pulled away fairly quickly to leave the complex before another pass of the cops would wonder why this stranger was still apparently looking for an unfamiliar place in the complex.

Body kneeled down, hand on the door to steady himself. I told him where to reach and he plucked the box off.

He stared at it. Seemed to heft the weight of it to test its reality in his hand.

Then he fished out a paper napkin from a pocket. Rubbed down the sides where he'd held it. Continuing to hold it with the napkin between fingertips and plastic surface, he bent down and returned it with a *thunk* as the magnets re-mounted it to the frame.

What are you doing?

You deactivated it, right?

I think I did a little more than 'deactivated' it.

Body hurried to unlock the door and get the car started. *So the box is still exactly where Hartsleg or whomever put it. We don't have to worry about it tracking us now, but for all intents and purposes the box looks like it's where it was supposed to be. No way to prove that we knew it was there or tampered with it. If we get confronted about it, well hey, Officer Snoop, look at that...*

you put that on my car?

I felt a grin sigh through me. *I dig it. Hey, Officer, I didn't even notice. Must've had something go wrong. Maybe we hit a pothole too deep and crunked it. Maybe the batteries died. By the way, do you have a warrant for putting that on my car?*

You got it. But we need to leave now before they realize it's shut off and have someone, maybe that cruiser out there, start tailing us instead.

He was taking the corners fast, slowing only enough to make sure he didn't hit any parked cars as we left the complex.

Hurrying is no problem. I thought ahead, to what was probably awaiting us within the hour. *Hit the gas and let's get moving. We have some serious questions that need finally getting answers. Just as well the cops aren't going to be able to invite themselves to this shindig.*

****

We got away from the complex, and I kept my non-eyes peeled as much as I could in any direction where we might pick up a black-and-white shadow with its red-and-blues turned off for stealth.

Small favors in being anachronistic in things like our car. The Vega was too old to have any new-fangled OnStar or GPS service or anything that might be satellite-tracked or picked up on a cell tower.

Hrm. A cell tower. That was a worrisome thing. If they were really pushing it, a cell signal could be tracked.

Should you maybe turn your phone off?

No point. Body signaled and we were getting onto the freeway. *Any idiot can wander up and slap a tracker on my car. But for a cell trace they'd have to actually go to a court judge, get a warrant, go through the rigmarole of accessing the cell tower networks to have them try and locate us.*

And you think Hartsleg wouldn't go to that much trouble?

He would. I don't think the law would necessarily let him, though. We weren't charged, and Dario seemed to have whipped them pretty good on the short list of reasons why not to mess with me without proper evidence.

An unnerving inspiration occurred to me with the talk of laws and proprieties. *What if...what if we're wrong? What if the tracker isn't from the cops? What if it's the Believers? They found us at the gallery.*

Body drummed fingers on the steering wheel. *Could be. Then we're even more safe taking off their device, aren't we? And we know that the wildeweird were following us personally, not hiding behind lowjacks.*

Maybe there are Believers in the police department.

Let's deal with one frantically paranoid conspiracy panic attack at a time, shall we?

The cellphone rang.

UNKNOWN.

"Hello?"

"What's wrong? Where have you been? I tried calling you all day. Are you all right?"

"I'm okay now, Sarah. Things are working out okay. But... there are some problems."

No immediate answer. Then, quieter: "What sort of problems are we talking about?"

"Monsters. Getting kidnapped. Attacked. I was narrowly saved by some friends in the local vampire network. Some info was uncovered that I think we should discuss."

"O-okay. Do you want to meet at the coffee shop again?"

"No. This shouldn't be discussed in a coffee shop any more than it should on an open cell phone signal. Come to my bookstore. The Nookery."

"I don't know where that is. Give me the address." He recited it for her.

"Be there as soon as you can. Don't come by way of Third. Use the back road, the rear entrance. That's where my apartment is. I'll expect you. And try to make sure you're not being followed. I think...there are those people still out there, and there's no telling how much they're keeping tabs."

"All right."

He hung up.

Is it safe to have her come to the store? Shouldn't we have her meet us somewhere more out-of-the-way, for caution?

He shook his head. *I want to be on familiar ground again, even if it's just for some minor psychological value. And I need something back at the office besides, for some possible trouble.*

What if trouble follows her to our door, like it already tried to do leaving a body at our back step? Or is already waiting for us back there? The wildeweird know where we live. And I imagine right now if they're still around, they are probably supremely pissed. What if inviting her over to compare notes is inviting all hell to break loose when she gets there?

There was a grind as his hands tightened on the steering wheel.

Truthfully...if we're very lucky...and if we're right with where we're going with all this...I'm hoping that's exactly *what will happen.*

39.

I parked a block away from the store and jogged quickly and quietly to the back entrance. I had lost so much track of time that it surprised me to walk in and see the alarm clock on the desk glowing red with a time well past midnight.

They held us for nearly the day...the vampires getting us free...God, the clock was burning at both ends.

I dug into the desk drawers, but what I was looking for was one of the few things I made sure never to misplace or forget. A small steel key, not much bigger than the kind you use on store strong-boxes or kid's toy safes.

Then I got down on my knees and dug under the cot. There was only a single cardboard box under there where there were a few personal items—a pocket watch from my grandfather, some photos of my family—that I wanted to keep closer than boxing up and leaving moldering in one of the throwaway rooms of the shop.

I removed the plastic gray case from the cardboard box. Set it on the cot and used the key to unlock it.

Inside, set in gray vacuum-formed foam, was the .44 caliber Ruger pistol that I hadn't shot in two years.

It was a gift from a friend, now gone. The only dubious

trophy of when we had helped that same lost friend deal with a leukothrope. The gun still smelled of cleaning oil and machined metal. It had a solid-cast bored cylinder and looked ludicrously large. A Dirty Harry caricature with its seven inch barrel. There was a flick of dried rust that I used a fingernail to scratch off the tip of the barrel.

Hrm. Not rust. I'd missed that somehow in the last cleaning before packing it under the cot.

But when you shoot enough .44-caliber rounds at near-point-blank range into a walking mass of shifting, hyper-intelligent white blood cells trying to extract your bone marrow to use as grist for its brood-sac, I guess it was inevitable a fleck or two of its plasma was going to land on your gun barrel.

Shivers in my hair. *This is what you came back for? Do you think it'll do any good?*

A gun never does any good. It's not designed for that. I picked the gun up and made sure it was still loaded, all six chambers. It might be poor gun ownership, a loaded weapon in the home. Even one in a locked case with the key kept elsewhere. But an unloaded gun doesn't make even a decent club if you're caught short too quickly to load it according to the NRA official pamphlet rules.

My friend had taught me as well as any crash course from a shooting range. *Never assume a gun is unloaded. Handle a gun with its barrel always away and down. Be mindful of the hammer and hold it steady. Squeeze, don't jerk the trigger.*

The number one rule: *never point a gun at anything you don't intend to destroy.*

I felt around under the foam padding to uncover a half-empty box of rounds. About sixteen bullets. Twenty-two counting the ones loaded already.

Too much? Or not enough? The other half of the box was what it had taken to distract the leukothrope.

But more reminders from my old friend.

I could hear him talking in that whispery voice, almost as soft as the cotton cloth he was wiping on his shotgun as he'd talked me through the process of stripping and cleaning the Ruger's works. *A gun is ultimately a really dangerous noise-maker. If you treat it properly, like a tool, then six shots from something like this should be all you need, intelligently used. If not used correctly, if used as a toy or a proxy for your dick, then six or sixty, it won't make any difference what you're trying to do anyway. You'll either overkill or just end up killed. So try and treat it like a tool, not the tool, John.*

Are you going to be okay with that thing? Shouldn't we call...I don't know. Call the vampires back? Get Dhara and some of that muscle she was offering to use for us? Get some help?

I brought the gun's barrel to a forty-five degree angle down, looking across its sight. *Have to keep this contained. I don't want any more people involved than have been already.*

What if we're wrong?

I closed the case, put it back under the cot, out of sight. Got back to my feet. *If we're wrong, then it really won't be any harm, any foul, will it?*

That's assuming that we're right about what we could be wrong about.

I don't feel up for word games.

Neither do I. But better that than you risking shooting your dick off by accident, putting that thing in your pocket like that.

Shoot my dick off? Now I'm a sharp-shooter?

A shared chuckle in my head.

Would you go out, please? As lookout? I want you to keep an eye on the street. See when she gets here. But more important, see if anyone is following. See if trouble decides this is a great time to try and take the upper hand with both of us here.

He flowed out of the space. Leaving me to stand in the middle of the room. I felt like a clown. A rodeo clown, the kind that dress in gunslinger chaps and wear Stetsons, shooting pop-cap guns as the bulls bear down on them and gore them, unless they can manage to leap to the safety of that star-spangled rubber barrel.

I wished I had a barrel.

****

I rooted through the toolbox in the bottom drawer of the desk, managing to find another desired item when I felt the vibrant words in my head, a telegraph wire voice.

She's here. In Hal's other Hummer, looks like.

I closed up the desk drawer. *Alone?*

Yeah. No tagalongs that I see as yet.

Okay.

****

I'd left the door unlocked. She came thumping in and tossed her hat to the armchair before rushing forward to where I stood by the desk and giving me a hard hug.

"You are a really shitty friend, you know that?" She muffled her face in my chest a moment. "A day with no word. You got kidnapped?" She looked up into my face. "What did they— *what happened to your eye?*"

"An accident with a piece of wood. I can explain."

She extracted herself from my arms and stepped back. "Is it—?"

"Healing, yes. You should've seen it at first. Believe me, this is practically a GQ magazine cover shot compared to what it started out as."

"Who was it? The Believers?"

"Maybe. My connections identified them as wildeweird."

A frown on the dusky face. The hat had pulled a few of the reddish curls out of array, almost like two horns sticking out of the left side of her head.

"I don't know that term. What are they?"

"Short answer is, the Under's answer to *The Hills Have Eyes*."

"What did they want?"

"Not entirely sure. The way it happened...it seemed almost more like an act of opportunity, not planning."

"How do you figure?"

"I don't think they were expecting me to go looking where I was, and that surprised them. When I tried to chase one of them down, I got bushwhacked. They're the ones that've been watching this place."

"Watching?" She looked out towards the soaped-over windows. "This place? Why are we here then? We should be a million miles from here. If you got away from them this would be—"

"The first place they'd think to try and track me down. Yeah. That's not entirely out of my realm of expectations right now."

"Going to play Macho Man and doing some flying kicks? Or did you invite us so that we could play cheerleader and watch you go a few rounds with some freaky-deakies from the backwoods?"

"No. I think I might need your help."

She gave an incredulous grin. "What kind of help?"

I reached out my hand. Stared into her eyes with a solemn blankness.

She hesitated. "I get what you're asking, but we...we need to *go*. Get somewhere else. I could call Seppeschal and make some arrangements. Maybe a lodge in Colorado, or out of the country for a while."

I kept my hand held out.

"I'm scared, Sarah. I'm not kidding. I have no idea what we're up against and any time that happens I get scared. But this time it feels much bigger, much larger and scarier than anything we've faced. There's no monster I can track down or hit, no magic words banish the evil to some mystical dimension. I have no clue here, but I know the only way we're going to get through this is together. If you trust me. If we can get to know each other better. If we can really share what we are."

Her grin weakened. "I don't know what to do. I want your help, but we have to...I don't—"

"You know things I don't, maybe I can show you some things. Maybe the four of us can manage to work this out. But at this moment," The outstretched hand shook a little, "I'm scared. " My voice cracked."I don't know if these things can hurt me. Us. I have almost this death-wish craziness. I wanted us here because if they *are* coming here to track me down, I need help. I need support. I want to face these things and get this over with, get them out of our lives for good, I'm tired of being everybody's door prize."

"So let's go and get proper help, call your people and mine and get some experts, get some support for it."

"I can call out all my friends around town. But before we did that, I needed...I needed to feel like we at least were trying to do this together. You haven't had much reason to trust me and I know that's obviously a problem for you. I've seen enough in my own work with Hal, with some of the men and women he's had work for him, who get eaten up by those kinds of things. I'm sure you've seen plenty of it out in L.A. too, like a hack script of clichés. I don't want us running from this or at each other's throats."

"I don't know if I'm any help here..."

"You are. Just by being here. Believe me."

"I'm sorry. I didn't realize this was...hitting you so hard. I guess with the reputation I'd heard of about you, I figured you'd be all hot-shit and ready for bear. I thought...I'm sorry, I was being selfish. I thought I should...that I'd come out here and find you and you could help me. Jesus, John, here you are asking for my help and all I cared about was making sure my own dead ass was going to be safe. I'm..." she swallowed the last syllable. She reached out and took my hand in hers.

I smiled. "It's okay."

I twisted my wrist, bringing her hand, palms up, above mine.

My other hand whipped around with the box cutter—a neon orange twin of the one held as evidence by the police—and sliced a hard, solid cut across the meat of her palm.

She screeched and jerked her hand back, stumble-stepped back until she whammed into the doorframe. Her good hand clutched tight around the injured fist.

"I was hoping you might be able to explain to me why you've been killing people, or why you've been using the wildeweird to watch and terrorize me."

****

"What the fuck?" she yelled at me, stepping sidewise closer to the doorknob.

I had the gun out before she could make a grab for it. "I'd prefer if you'd stay a while."

"Did you go fucking insane in the last twenty four hours or something? Are you possessed or running on a gallon jug of acid right now? *You fucking cut me!"*

"Consider it a down payment for some answers you owe me."

"Answers for *what?* What the *hell?"* Her injured hand shook in the grip of the good one. She tried to make another-step closer to the door and I deliberately shifted the gun, barrel tracking her. She stopped. I waved the barrel the other way, and she took a step back from the doorknob.

"It didn't hit me until someone remarked to me about youth. *The Picture of Dorian Gray."* I peered at her. "You almost had me because of my own idiot optimism." I nodded at her hand. "But I realized I was wrong even before I proved it with the knife."

"What is this insanity? What are you *talking* about?"

"If you died only a few years ago…you'd be an older woman. I don't know everything there is to know about what we are, but I know that when we started out, I stayed the way I was when Flicker died. Same age, appearance, everything. No Fountain of Youth. If you died then, you would've stayed as your near-sixty-year-old self. Not a thirty-something girl."

"We don't know, it's just the way I am, the way you are. There's no—"

"Please cut the horseshit for once. You're not a doppelgeist."

Her face changed. The features went from horrified shock to something calmer. Softer. The eyes narrowed.

"I'm going to call Seppeschal. And your gun is not going to stop me, you know that. And when I tell him what you've done, this crazy shit, he can arrange all kinds of things to make you wish you'd never been reborn."

I couldn't resist the line, or the Jack Nicholson growling delivery.

"I've *been* dead once already. It's very liberating. You might think of it as *therapy.*"

"Put the gun down and talk to me."

"I *am* talking to you. But you're not listening." I waved the gun at her. "Let me see the hand."

"Fuck you."

"Let me see it. I can give you a bandage for it."

"Go fuck your own hand."

"It's not healing, is it?"

The glower of her face gave way then. It allowed the drawbridge of her mouth to lift at the corners. An ugly sickle-smirk. She held the hand up and turned the palm out towards me.

The cut was fresh, unchanged. But not bleeding. There was a glint, a sheen of wetness inside the edges of the wound, but colored nearly as dark as engine oil.

"Congratulations, Sherlock," she growled. "Another case solved by your deductive brilliance."

"Not really. It was mostly stupid luck. For both of us." I slowly put the boxcutter on the desk, then used that hand to reach into a coat pocket, grabbing for the wadded, glossy-finished paper there. "Snooping and coming across a completely lucky piece of junk that put some of it into place."

I pulled the paper out, fingers unwadding it and flattening it out so the glossy side showed out. I held it up at arm's length above the gun so she couldn't miss seeing it clearly.

A photo of two young women who were bookending a third, older woman. It looked like a prom or cotillion photo for the two younger girls. The girls were wearing formal dresses with yellow rose corsages on their right wrists.

One had her arm around the older woman's waist, the other girl had hers around the woman's shoulders. The one on the left side of the photo had auburn hair down to her shoulders. Her grin was crooked but pretty, engaging for its slight flaw. The backdrop of the shot looked like a fairly typical middle-income living room, a couch and old console TV visible behind them.

The girl on the right was a little prettier than her

counterpart, with the same auburn hair streaked with natural sun-bleached highlights in the bangs swept away from her face. At a wild guess from the slight fuzz of the picture's quality and the feathery Charlie's Angels bangs, I speculated it was a picture from the late seventies, early eighties. When I was little enough to probably still wet the bed.

It was the older woman in the middle, allowing for her own feathered bangs and slightly darker hair color, that arrested the attention.

It was Sarah Parley.

I used my index finger to give three slow taps on the photo, over the girl on the right with the doll's red hair.

"You're not Sarah. You're Elizabeth. The other daughter."

Her face went rock still. She didn't confirm it. Not with words. She dropped her hands to her sides.

"What are you after?" I asked

"If you haven't figured out things that far, I'm sure as shit not going to help."

"Oh I could guess, I'm sure I could. I was hoping you didn't have any reason by this point to hide it. I don't absolutely *know* what you are, but I know you're not like us. If I had to hazard a guess...you're a phantophage."

She stared back at me. A minute tick-sighed by as the building around us seemed waiting for the next words.

Quietly: "What would have you thinking that?"

"A few things. But what it really has me thinking is, if I'm right...then you're here...what? To eat Soul? To feed on him like you feed on other spirits for your survival?"

She didn't reply.

"I would further guess that it's your...unique whatever-you-are...that allowed you to nearly pass as another doppelgeist. To communicate with Soul. But it ended up making for a bad show."

"How is that?"

"Your supposed 'soul' half. Mine and I didn't compare notes well enough to see it earlier. When you communicated with Soul, you were barely present or talking to me. Can't exactly do the intangible-ventriloquist stunt, can you? Can't chew bubblegum and astral project at the same time."

"Some of us have to improvise for a living."

"It's the little things. What Thoreau said."

"What was that?"

"'*Simplicity, simplicity, simplicity. Our lives are frittered away by detail.*' When we first talked to each other. You said what a thing it must be, to live in a 'huge' bookstore like this." I looked around, surveying the room around us before looking back at her. "'*All those nooks and crannies.*' But how did you know? How would you know anything about me, if you'd just gotten a name about who I was?"

"Slip of the tongue."

"You made bigger slips."

"Such as?"

"The boxcutter."

"Ah."

"Did you have one of your idiots here plant it when they dumped the body? Yeah, that sounds more likely. That boxcutter. We used that when I ordered a case of printer ink for our printer in the back. Took it with us to the post office. Cut it open in the car to check that the order was filled right. It was left in the glove compartment of the Vega." My eyes narrowed. "And there's only been one person in the car with us lately that could've had any chance to swipe it to use as circumstantial evidence, to get me held up by the cops."

"And I think that's the point in this fairy tale where I take my leave of you."

She turned around, haughty as all get-out, the injured hand held up with the primness of a pageant parade beauty queen in a frozen-elbow twist-wrist wave to the masses. Her other hand grabbed the doorknob and opened the door.

I started to raise the gun. "You're not—"

Stupid.

All it had taken was letting her get as far as opening that door. Signal and opportunity in one swoop.

Soul, yammering from a distance: *From the trees, there's a shadow I couldn't see it right away but the shadows are running down the street there's—*

A flash of white and black.

Hiss-snaps. A string of grubby-light-and-scummy-darkness blurred across the space in time to hit at me. One blow to the chest, while a simultaneous swipe had Nightsock knocking the gun from my hand while I fell back against the desk, narrowly stopping from falling over it heels-over-head.

The girl-thing stood before me. I bellowed some inarticulate fury-noise and moved towards her—

In less than the time to close the space between us, Nightsock bent down, snatched up the gun, pointed it at me and fired.

A second point-blank shot in as many days.

Repetition had not bred comfortable familiarity.

And a soft, cool draft that didn't come from any vent or doorway crossed my palms, blew up and scared away the freezer-burnt condor trying to fly off with my conscious thoughts—

Christ, I can't leave you anywhere, can I?

God…

She shot you. Okay. Turn off the pain, man, I know you can do this.

Easier…said…

I know. But you can do it. I'm sorry…that obscurity…there must be the other here, the one who can do that trick with the shadows, using as cover. One second the street seemed clear then the next at the corner, almost at the door before I knew it, there she was like lightning.

The overlap…the sense of feeling fading even as the intensity of Soul's *presence* flooded down my arms, my legs. Our face felt tingly. The thick oil feeling slid behind my eyeballs, coated my waxy tongue. He was there, everywhere, and I was never so present as in that moment for myself, for everything. We saw the pain still trying to dominate every nerve like a conquering army claiming territories and inwardly grimaced as we pictured hands waving, dismissing them as leaves before a summer wind. The territories were emptying, driving the hordes away but still ravaged in their wake.

I kept a hand pressed to my chest above the wound. The cold trickle at my back went away. I felt nothing of pain or sensation from those rogue nerves any longer.

I looked at her with wide eyes. Soul's vision overlapped to mine was faint. I could see the lines of the air forming around her, the strange liquid masses that gelled and broke apart, like swimming protozoa. The ragged but patterned lines of distant radio signals and heat movements through the thermodynamic air.

Sarah had obviously taken my reaction to the shot as she'd hoped to, how she'd wanted to see me take the hit and not know how to react.

"I don't think you're going to get quite what you wished for," Soul spoke through my lips. Not bound by the limitations of my body needing air to press into service to make words, my own voice added to a razor-filled wind tunnel and passed through a synthesizer to enhance the ragged, whistling notes at the end of the sibilants flowed from my mouth to her. *"You're going to find out in about thirty seconds that this was quite possibly the single stupidest idea anyone's had since 'stupid' was invented."*

"Ah, the intangible son returns home."

The pain hordes were edging in again, trying to flank my rear guard.

Shut the pain out. You can do it.

I can't...oh god...

The feeling was such a violation, such a punch-and-stab that my body couldn't seem to classify the pain. Even having been shot once before to compare, somehow the experience wasn't cumulative. Repetition did not immunize against the experience. My body didn't know what to do. Heal or bleed, scream or suck uselessly at empty air that wouldn't move, wouldn't fill the lungs because of the hole rudely stomped in and through the fibrous tissues. I tasted cold blood seeping into my throat.

"Thank god it's your body I want and not your clothes," she said, eyeing me with a critical eye.

Your body...? So she really isn't one, is she?

No. She...I think we were right. A phantophage. Like the Scots said. But this one is strong. One of those rare ones they said could take a body. And it...I think...

...she wants yours next.

I coughed, managed to push out enough bellows-air to form words in a rapid wheeze. "You really want to go... shooting holes in the body you hope to own soon?"

The smile twisted. "You'll recover. But I think the point is made. You can barely stay on your feet for all that you're regaining."

You're already healing, you know that. This will only take minutes. Calm down. Stop the pain, it's like a light switch, remember? On and off.

Oh god, he was one to talk. He could float around in intangible security but I was meat, I was dead and walking around and sure it's one thing to know you'll recover but a *bullet...*

A bullet was a small metal slug of inexorable reality slamming through all your intellectual presumption...

More bubbling noises. I tried to force a breath, but there was nothing to force. I pressed my hand to my chest harder, thinking I could stop the wound like a child's nursery story about a boy stopping a dam with a little finger. It didn't help. Blood was in the wound. I couldn't stopper it and it was filling in, collapsing even as the tissue was recovering. The copper taste was evaporating from my palate, but god...the pain wanted to keep growing...and there was Soul, that oil-electric feeling trickling and then rippling across my nerves, steadying everything again, harder and harder against the ebb and flow of raw agony.

"I should've stuck to my first instinct that you were too convenient. Too much. A doppelgeist from out of the blue when we seemingly needed help."

"Oh don't act like you haven't gotten something out of this," she sneer. "I showed you things. Things you never even thought to try for yourself. You can speak, you can be *heard*. You don't have to rely on having this *sack* walking around to act as your personal microphone."

"There's more to this than being able to speak."

"You can reside in *memory*, now! You don't even have to spend forever as a bodiless whisper. You can go back through your own memories, re-live a solid life with all the pleasures and old joys. You never have to come back to the present if you don't want to!"

"Another bullshit promise. It's not real." I finally drew in a shallow breath. *"And you don't seem to get it...my memories aren't any place I want to spend much time in if I can help it."*

My hand lifted from my chest. I could feel energy moving through me again. Conscious control. Soul pushed against me and we were no longer overlapping...he was off to a side, out-of-focus from the rest of me. I was back to myself and glaring at Sarah. "It's funny."

"What is?"

"Serendipity. Stupid happenstance." I nodded towards the gun barrel. "You might've managed to pull this off in some fashion, if not for basic crap luck."

"More wisdom? Please enlighten me."

"Your lead-head...your sister. Elizabeth's sister. She was the one that attacked the Faede."

She looked at Nightsock, who couldn't meet her gaze. Her face practically burned like a torch with disgust.

"When you and your cousins went trolling to pick them back up, you fucked up that badly? You let her get out and she attacked someone? Why didn't Dusk tell me this?"

Nightsock merely stared back with stupid malice.

"She didn't attack a Faede. She *killed* one."

"Son of a bitch." She said it as a laugh, not a regret.

"That's what Ceyggan hired me for. To find out who did it and why. Why lead-heads around town were going spastic and violent."

Another disgusted turn of that lighthouse flame of hatred towards Nightsock, who attempted to avoid looking at her by pretending she was intently keeping the gun trained on me.

"I shouldn't have expected any better from a bunch of inbred bucktooths." Nightsock shuddered, fighting responding.

"Indeed. But you know, you might *still* have given yourself away by having these wildeweird idiots doing surveillance on me."

She shrugged. "They were useful to a point. I figured I could make some use of their talents and then eventually drop them. They were the only freaks I could hire on the down-low, couldn't risk showing up on any popular radar or my contractors."

That hit a big zero that clanged like a church bell. I whistled through the mouth: "What?"

"The *Brokerage*. Christ, do you know *anything* about the world? Who I *work* with, who my phant paid to arrange my transplant."

Body-snatchers for spirits. Spectrada negotiations.

Dark stuff. 'Caste-off' Faede managers and flunkies.

"Yeah. If you're rich enough, have enough swing, you can damn well sure make sure there are ways to cheat death. Cryonics? What a joke. What, were me and Ted Williams' severed head going to swap stories on a shelf in the year 3000? Bull-*shit*. I paid for *serious* afterlife. Put me in a new body and with enough cash and grease, it's easy enough to have the Brokerage find someone desperate...stupid enough to agree to be a conscious host. Let me in. Let this run."

"Then feel free and accept my invitation to be happy...with this new body..." That effort was creeping in, to make sound without direct medium. *"...and go take a long dive off...a short fucking pier into an empty swimming pool."*

"Funny."

The door opened again.

"Ah, speak of the lobotomized devil and he shall appear," she spat as Dusk slithered in, skulking like a whipped dog. At the sight of me in my distress, he straightened up with obvious glee.

"Give him the gun," Sarah commanded. Nightsock backed away, eyes never leaving me, following instruction and handing Dusk the gun, whereupon he took up holding it on me. "Go out. Keep lookout on things while we stay cozy here." Nightsock didn't indicate she'd heard, but she blur-shifted and the door slammed shut.

This is getting bigger by the second and already way out of hand.

I blinked, eyes on the floor. *I know. I know.* Air wheeze-kissed the back of my throat.

Soul emerged from my lips: *"Who...who are you?"*

"It doesn't matter. What matters is who I *was*. Someone with the kind of money that I could have had Steve Jobs personally build a go-cart for me if I wanted to. Getting the Brokerage to put me in a new form, that was straightforward enough when they explained it to me."

Of course. What had the Scots said? Phantophages. Major dominant OCD cases of the ghostly realm. It stood to reason: some of the most rarely powerful wills and domineering personalities would emerge from people who'd been pretty much the same as that before death and wanted to damn sure continue climbing up that ladder and stepping on every face that was a rung of it.

"Odd...all that money and the power with it...why not have your pick of whatever body you wanted? Why have...to go with someone desperate? You sound...more like a pimp trolling...for runaways at the bus station."

A shrug. "It's a short-stick contract. You know that old saying, about how the only good compromise in business is one that makes nobody happy? That's what the Brokerage and I worked out. I died, they hooked me up with some loser good enough and dumb enough to have some cash waggled in their face like a stripper getting rained on, and let themselves be hollowed like a Jack o' lantern for me to live in."

"You pay...they delivered. Why are they...what's the unhappy part for...them?"

"Oh, well...that's where it gets clever to be dead, sometimes. Upon my death, a trust was arranged in the deal. Not something anybody could take to court, but that works both ways. Basically a trust fund set up to pay the Brokerage so long as they keep me in bodies. I have failsafes set up from before I first bit the dust, so that each time I have to sign and notify that it's really me to confirm they followed through and didn't try to swindle the fund. If I try anything cute, they can always simply let the contract...lapse."

"That body...with spirits to consume...it won't...last?"

"Of course not." A grumble. "Bodies decompose every second. They rot out. Even faster when they're housing something like me, a dominant spirit that's been artificially crammed into them. But lucky me, in those dire circumstances I can prolong things by...going back to old dietary habits."

She eats them. A phantophage, still able to feed on other spirit energies like always...but now doing it with a human host carrying it around...prolonging how long the body can keep from total burn-out, but generating the energy through feeding...the lead-heads... Wonder what the Scots would make of this.

"The wildeweird—"

"Hope was a basket case, you know that? A real lost girl. Mom died and she thrashed around as a big, bipolar disordered *nothing*. Mom was the pathetic one. No shock that Hope was the same lost case. At least with Dad I lucked out, learned how to live with the other sharks. Hope was trying a little of everything, anything. Booze. Drugs. Religion. Whack-job stuff. Guess who she bumped into on some late-night chat-room?"

"What...did you keep tabs—"

"The Brokerage. They did a fairly exhaustive background screening of my potential bodies-to-be. To check for anyone who might miss them or notice anything. To check for any next of kin."

"Keeping tabs on who would spot the fake? Who would suspect?"

"Eh. More like the way you test family members to see if any of them are compatible to donate an organ to you." She looked down at her shoes, looked back up and smirked at us. "This body won't last forever. The Brokerage is thorough when they have a contract. They made sure they had some options lining up for the inevitable. Family meant a smoother transition. Just like one big, all-in-one-go organ harvest with no risk of rejection, if you follow." The smirk twisted, widened into a ghoulish grin. "They kept tabs on her and I was allowed to read their reports. I was a paying client, after all. When I discovered she was playing with the idea of joining this cult, a group of nuts who somehow worship the idea of erasing you, I had that looked into. They looked into these Second Believer crazies—"

"—and...found us."

"Give the man his bingo money. Finding out what the cult was about—deleting you two from the earth—had me admittedly curious. The further briefing from the Brokerage reports piqued my interest quite a bit further. It was one of those extra jokes that you did porn, like this Sierra slut did."

"Only...part time."

A flap of her free hand, rolling a circle at the wrist. "It was easy enough then to make a call to your buddy Hal, dangle the fruit. It was too good a setup to avoid trying. I mean, c'mon, what could be more perfect to attempt to beat this thing? With an immortal, invulnerable body that so happens to have no spirit currently occupying it? Complete with a floating soul-buffet I could eat as a celebratory snack, no less?"

"Go shit yourself down a toilet bowl."

"But yeah...thing is, this is all necessarily on the Q-T. Very hush-hush. Couldn't ask the Brokerage to help me."

"Oh...of course. You're fucking them over. The Brokerage."

What I'm doing is breaking their contract. Same difference where they're concerned. But screwing over idiot corporate jug-heads like them is how I made a more-than-palatial living my first time around. They act all scary but it's an act, like any other company. I can leave this rot-bag somewhere to be found, *sans* my spirit, and quietly reclaim my hidden caches of funds and live out forever perfectly fine. While they have a null-and-void contract that'll make it look like they screwed up and something went wrong or they couldn't get me a suitable donor in time to take over. No matter what, I'm not paying out what's left of my hard-earned fortunes to some high-rent white slaver trade anymore. But you do not fuck over the Brokerage. No way. I might be rich, but I'm not crazy."

"You might...find them not nearly as much a bluff as you...want to think."

"Pfft. Doesn't matter. What can they do, kill me?"

"Who...were you? Really?"

"Nobody you need to know about. Someone with the money to make all this happen, that's all that should concern you. Better that the real details of all this stay fairly quiet."

That clicked another piece into proper place.

"The wildeweird. Off the radar. Unaffiliated."

"Exactly." A prim nod. "I couldn't use Brokerage people or any community connections. I knew virtually nobody out here and couldn't take the risk that groups like the bloodsuckers would be protecting you." A jerk of the head to indicate Dusk. "At least these inbred apologies to God wouldn't go double-dealing me to anyone, since nobody else in the Under wants to do any business with them if they can help it."

I was recovering some voice. The collapsing drain in my chest was thickening, capable of pushing wind. "You work with...what you can get."

"Next time I guess I'll learn to pay a bit more and get talent that doesn't screw up every tiny, retardedly-simple request." Dusk's eyes blinked rapidly. The gun barrel dipped a beat.

The pain hordes had been rebuffed again. "You came close on a lot of calls. It's like every time you tried to cover tracks or clean up your messes, you only made things worse. Even then, you might have...gotten away with all this...ridiculous horror." The temperature of my voice dropped ten degrees. "But you killed Rod."

"Who?"

"You know goddamned well *who*. The mentalist."

"The pill-popper."

"You didn't need to do that. He was no threat to you. He wasn't a threat to *anybody*. He was a good and decent human being."

"Innocent and decent people die all the time. The way his place looked, I did him a favor. It's called life, and it's an unfair bitch."

"The only bitch I notice around here is standing in front of me."

"Very cute, pretending you comprehend half of this."

"No pretending at all. The timeline didn't work out any other way. You killed Rod shortly after I left him…your wildeweird were tailing me everywhere, like you hired them to."

The bushes. The trees shivering in the dark by Studio 53. Damn it, they really have had that Lovecraft refugee girl following us everywhere.

"After I left, they obviously called you. I guess Rod's living arrangements made it seem like my visiting him meant he was someone seriously important so they should contact you about it. Or maybe you were already there, doing a little shadowing for yourself?"

"They called me."

"So you killed him. But that was a real hurt-on, wasn't it? *He could read you.* It wasn't much, not with your hillbilly hellhounds coming through his door with you at their heels to claim him." A new thought occurred on the tail of this, a spark of inspired connection-making. "The *pills.* The bottles scattered, half a pharmacy in his mouth and down his gullet… he was making a last-ditch effort to kill himself rather than let you do it, wasn't he? It wasn't your flunkies torturing him…why give him painkillers and then torture him? He took the pills. You might've gotten his spirit, but you didn't get shit on him in torture, did you?" I folded my arms slowly. Raised one forearm, pivoted at the elbow, to rest my chin against. A curious Jack Benny posture. "And why would that be, to try and off himself instead of letting you take him? Could it be because he was afraid of exactly what happened, if you'd gotten to him before the drugs could poison him beyond your use of him?"

"Keep going. I love entertaining bullshit."

"Then be entertained. You killed him and consumed him… and you got some of his ability, didn't you? A phantophage… you gained some of his ability to have the minds of the world screaming at you from every direction. Just like he had to live with. Every day."

Soul hummed.

"But by the time you were beginning to realize what a total

dissociative clusterfuck *you absorbed by being the greedy whore you are, your pets had already continued trailing me...to the Scots Brothers. And lo and behold, there's Baby Sis. A lead-head. Drained pretty much to near-empty, but conveniently found just as you were beginning to go absolutely batshit crazy with those voices and screams constantly running through your skull, am I right?"*

"You win a kewpie doll, ass." The frown seemed to eat up the bottom half of the skull, and I wondered how we could have thought that face was ever attractive. How did we not see the hideousness hiding right under that skin? "These idiots," she nodded at Dusk, "I told them to get rid of Hope the first time. I figured they'd do as simple a task as that fairly straightforward. Kill her, bury the body in some unused building site or whatever. Plenty of cornfields outside of this town. But they were *lazy little stupid shits.*" Dusk cringed as her voice stridently slapped him from across the space. "They took her and randomly dumped her on the streets, like any other homeless addict. When I heard, I told them to do it again, and do it *right,* but they *still* screwed up. These Marx Brother *knock-offs* got stuck out of gas, driving out of town to take her somewhere and off her. And those bounty hunter shits got hold of her."

Dusk sputtered. "We thought...it would be better if sthe got herthelf lotht, sthe couldn't..." his goggle-glasses and wispy little chin-beard looking all the more gnome-ludicrous in his cowering. "...she couldn't talk *back*, give uth *away*—"

"Shut up."

"But sthe...we..." The gun swung away, only a moment.

DO IT.

I lunged. But I think the phantophage heard Soul's shout in my head, in the collective aether of the room. That or it merely wasn't a long enough lapse, waving the gun like a baton and forgetting the tool it was for keeping me in place.

I am clumsy.

Some bit of rug—damn it, why didn't I throw it out when it got half-shredded by Trina to begin with?—snagged the tip of a shoe. What was supposed to be a jump-and-tackle turned into a balletically-stupid fall forward into Sarah.

She screamed, and my swinging arms whacked into her. My left hand smacked against her right breast while my right hand knocked into the forearm attached to the gun-holding hand.

Well that much was accom—

Another scream. A fingernail scrawled pain across my forehead. She had enough stance to shove back instead of falling with me, one of those odd moments of human momentum where her shove canceled out my falling and brought me back to a wobbly standing a few inches from her.

I felt something like a nasty electrical shock...more than static, it numbed places in my skin...was this that stunt she'd pulled on the bouncer at the gallery? Lucky it was only grazing—

STEP BA—

She swung her leg out, trying for my testicles but also clumsy in her own attempt. Her foot caught me on the inside of my right knee. Not enough to pop, but it took out a pillar from my foundation. I fell towards the collapsing leg, a squawk from my lips.

As I was mustering some sense of control to regain things, almost going down to the knee like a footballer about to pray before the second half...I saw Dusk had recovered from his surprise and was training the gun on me in goblin triumph.

"No..." she huffed, her face glowing at me with utter loathing. "...no repeat attempts at personal salvation. Or..." she looked at Dusk, practically bouncing on the balls of his hooved feet with happiness, "...he tries any other stunts, blow off his kneecaps to give him something more interesting to think about."

"Forget the kneecaps, Dusk," I growled. "You point that at me to shoot, make it a count. Make it a head shot. Or I'll shove that thing up your ass far enough that you'll be afraid to sneeze for firing it."

"Don't bother with him," Sarah laughed. "He's useless and scared of getting hurt, which is proof of how idiotic he is." Mock sigh. "Ah well. Can't pick the prize every time when you win the contest."

"Sure. But Hope won the booby prize that is having once shared a genetic pool with your host. You were probably in shock. Not in real control, no right mind to keep things in check like normal. Everything could get blown all to hell if you didn't get some mastery of yourself again. The wildeweird led you to Rod and taking him made you wonky. Your flunky here," I glanced at Dusk, and his fear cracked long enough to give me a dagger glare, "he had already figured from tailing me to the Scots that Hope had been re-captured. Had survived being street-dumped like so much garbage by the pure chance that seems to keep intruding in all this. Small world syndrome, right?"

"It's only one world out of many. But it's the only one that matters," she grimaced.

"So let's see...you were recovering from your incredibly *dumbass* mistake of absorbing a mentalist...the wildeweird knew they were in deep shit with Hope still alive...not to mention in the hands of maybe a couple of the hardest cases in the Under for her to have ended up with...so Dusk and company tried to placate you, didn't they? Like a gift offering to make good. They led you to Hope, got her from the Scots... and you at least had a familiar target you could drain—drain *all the way* to dead, this time—and get back enough charge to keep yourself whole once again. Am I getting warmer?"

"Doused in kerosene and lighting birthday candles."

"Cute retorts. You must buy them by the ton. But fuck this noise. You killed Rod, took his power...killed your sister while trying to get more to keep hold of yourself. And you had your losers...get rid of Hope again. A body dump, this time. Much easier to follow basic orders, right?"

"This idiot here," she spat towards Dusk, "had his one good idea of the decade when he slit her throat and said to leave her at your door. Give you some extra pains in the ass to keep you busy."

"You made me sit out a few precious hours in the police sweat rooms. That was it. It was Hope killing one of the Faede royals that really did you in."

Her expression seized, a facial fist clench of features as her mouth turned up with a snarl.

Dusk's happy gleam faded. His eyes darted between me and Sarah with panic. The gun hand dropped a notch.

"You were out of things...your flunkies were taking care of the mess...so you..." I looked to the glint of light in her red hair. Another light dawned. "*Shampoo.* Strawberry mousse."

Mischa. Strawberry Shortcake shampoo. That place...

Soul bubbled out: *"You couldn't do that stunt twice, could you?"*

"What?"

"The memory stunt. You got that from Rod's power. That's why you refused to do it again when I offered to try it willingly. One trick pony, weren't you? The power was gone by then."

"Easy come, easy go."

"You not only took advantage of Hope, you not only drained and killed her and used her body as a prop...you took a shower and used her towels in her apartment, didn't you? You used her apartment as...what? A temporary base of operations? No shock there, I guess."

"It was available. And she wasn't using it anymore."

"Wow. You're a *total* asshole."

"As if I care what a soon-to-be-ex-existing person thinks of my behavior."

I surrendered to a smile.

"The faer folk didn't like the idea of one of their princesses getting killed by a lead-head. They brought me in and asked if I'd look into things, try and find out if it was something personally directed at them or not. They take that sort of thing rather serious."

Her face stopped looking querulous and a flicker of something...yes, that was definitely surprise, some fear there... it registered so clearly it could have been a fire of its own.

"I might be immortal the way you think. But even I have learned to seriously respect how much ass-kicking the Faede represent. You have no idea how badly you messed up with that one."

Too much nonchalance in the shrug of a shoulder. "Ah

well. I can deal with Faede. They're nothing special when you get past that stripper glitter they sweat. *C'est l'vie.*"

"But I don't get this Believers of the Second Freedom. What the hell is that nonsense? I can't fit that anywhere."

"Can't help you there, my friend. They've nothing to do with me. Though they were instrumentally helpful in tracking you down to start this whole clap-trap."

Brother Dusk's face had a bright, sweat-gleamed shine that was hatred polished to a laser-clarity lens directed at me. Every enlarged pore of his bone-knobbed face and rubbery lips faintly pulsed at me as if every inch of him breathed, panting to have release to come at me. There was a dirty swatch of cloth that had been crudely wadded and taped to his right eye socket using a ragged piece of flapping duct tape. A little end of tape holding his glasses together had come loose on the same side, and as he quivered in place both ends, the tape on his glasses arm and the tape end from his wound both made the same frayed swaying, almost as slow and tree-in-the-breeze as his caterpillar eyebrows.

The good eye behind the goggle-thick glasses did its deep-sea clutch-blink much faster, harder, as if having to clear away the lens of dirt with every pass. The black stalk-eye never wavered or twitched but stayed as intent on me as watchdogs having meat waved in front of them.

I looked at the gun. "Seems a rather modern and banal way to threaten someone, for the great family of wildeweird."

"Thop dollking." His lips barely moved. His voice was thick and slurry, sounding like he'd gotten some painkiller at a dental appointment. It made his tongue clip under his overbite. *Stop talking.*

"I'm not thrilled at the idea of getting shot again. But frankly that gun and your lovely new singing voice are not threat enough."

"Thop *dollking*!" Dusk's hand clutched and shook with the gun, making its barrel describe a nervous circle towards me. I felt the backs of my calves stiffen. I didn't want to get shot, that was true…but I was soon getting to the point where that was fast diminishing in its ability to stall me.

"Calm down," Sarah's voice crisply swiped at him. The uninjured hand idly rubbed at the breast that my hand had smacked. The wounded hand wouldn't close its fist completely. Occasionally when she tightened in reflex to anger, she'd wince and the fingers would jerk open again.

"Can't turn your nerve endings off like the real deal, can you?"

"I may not want him shooting you," she replied, "but I don't want you talking any more than he does."

"This won't work."

"And you're the resident expert on the subject of what is or isn't possible?"

"If you could do it, you wouldn't have screwed around with having these morons watching and reporting on me. Or let the Believers attack me." I closed my hands into fists without considering it. "Or go running around with me pretending to be my friend. Or spent the last few minutes giving me all this Bond villain bullshit backstory."

Her eyes flicked down to my hands and back up at my face. "You think I wouldn't look into things first? I may be on the near side of desperate, but I'm not stupid. I had to be sure you were the real thing yourself. It wouldn't be any good to go through all the trouble and risk only to have you turn out to be a bum job."

"You can be sure this was all definitely a waste of your time, no matter how much you think you've checked things out first."

Her smile was punctuated with a tighter squeezing of the wounded fist, causing a few drops of blood to plip out from her grip. "One thing I definitely learned about you," she said, "is that a doppelgeist is clearly not the pants-pissing inducement that everybody else seems to think you are in the Under."

All notions of chivalry had left me with the realization of her connection to the wildeweird, to this whining baby-idiot holding the gun and his freak family that had killed Rod and been spying on me. I would happily have punched that smile backwards.

"If you needed help, you could have asked for it."

"Hardly. More than likely if I'd come to you honestly about what I was, you would've had someone like those twin mercenaries come at me with a blowtorch and needle-nose pliers to see if they could pull me out like one of my teeth." Her eyes narrowed. "I heard how they had the lead-heads. Locked up in a cage like a kennel."

"That wasn't their best choice. They didn't know how to handle them. They tried putting them in a bed and getting them help, but they were too violent."

"I don't see how Hope could have *breathed hard* on those two by then."

"You weren't there."

"Neither were you."

"Yes, but I trust the Scots Brothers. They had to subdue her and she wasn't in any control. Whatever you did the first time you fed on her pushed her beyond just lead-head stupor. She was crazy. Like a meth addict gone over the bend. *You* put her there."

"She was my sister."

Wait...there's a mixture here...it's not all...

"She was *Elizabeth Cambridge's* sister. Not yours. And don't pretend to have any affection for her, since you killed her and dumped her like garbage at my back door."

Her face slackened, eyes widening.

Oh you've caught her on that one.

Soul hum-warbled. *"It's not all you, is it, whoever-you-are? Elizabeth? You're there, aren't you? Burnt down and not in charge, but you're there? You'd have to be, wouldn't you? To be willing to let this fucker into you?"* Then he voiced the question that was in my thoughts: *"How much of that hinting at an awful past you dangled in front of us was the truth? Stage dressing, maybe, but still the truth? How far down did you get after dear Directory Daddy died that this was actually a palatable offer to you? Letting this ghost-maggot eat you up?"*

"Shut up."

"I can't say the Scots Brothers wouldn't have had termination in mind with you." *I sure as hell do,* Soul whispered. "But I'm a different story." I nodded at Dusk. "You should already know that about me if you've had these guys reporting back to you as thoroughly as you claim, not to mention being around me recently or having your Brokerage dinks look into me. I would've tried to help."

"You would've offered me your body freely? Without your producer friend and his cameras to watch?" A snort. "Right."

"I didn't say that. I said I would've tried to *help*."

She leered, releasing her grip on her wrist and lowering her fist to her side. Another drop plopped to the floorboards. "You can help me just fine by standing there like a good boy."

Soul moan-hummed out through my throat: *"The only thing we're going to help you do now is die. Preferably as slowly and painfully as we can stomach. And you're both going, Elizabeth. You know that."*

"Ah, the whisper in the willows talks tough," she laughed.

But her eyes lied. Above the laughing mouth, there was a mouse terror looking out from under the paw of the cat. Elizabeth? Maybe. Or maybe fear was something they shared.

"You were fun, I have to admit," the confident smirk continued. "I imagine you're going to be a decent meal to help me get started in the new ride."

"You're going to choke."

Dusk whine-growled. "Thdop *doll*—"

"Shut up," she snapped at Dusk. He was jittering harder, all but dancing in place on those hob legs. The sweat stains on his khaki shirt were darkening, spreading. A pale oil of sweat was forming weals on his cheeks and forehead, his ears actually twitching with an anticipatory energy. The gun could have fired practically at anything: me or more likely some random point on the wall or ceiling.

"I'll have to leave here and start over, but I've arranged for that." Her disdainful *moue* tilted to the side, a mockery of her former smiles. "Probably start by burning down this dust warehouse. And have your vampire call-girl dealt with too if I can manage it, to cover tracks all the way."

"Wrong choice of words."

There didn't need to be a vote. I took a step forwards, ready to grab for Sarah and this time not let a rug-snag stop me—

Brother Dusk yelped, his arm jerking.

There was that immensely loud and disproportionate snap-crack of the gun going off.

Sarah yelled as I felt the hard wind crisp past my left cheekbone, nearly parting the hair on that side of my head. A spray of mortar and brick chips burst out of a corner of the ceiling. I came to a full stop as surely as walking into a wall.

"Don't do that again without my word!" Sarah bellowed at Dusk, who shrank with Pekingese dog quivering at her words, but managed to nod in whimpery agreement.

I shook my head and my ears rang, but whatever tympanic injury the blast had made was clearing quickly.

"Is this all there is then?" I asked. "The three of us stand here while you, what, make the villain laughs and threats until I vacate my body out of boredom or this dipshit wastes all his bullets in his attempts to hole-punch me enough to put me in a three-ring binder?"

If there are gods, they must get a laugh at the sick sense of timing the Fates practice as they play out the threads of our life. I personally have always pictured that there is the one that pulls out and weaves the thread, the last one who cuts the thread, and the crone in the middle takes bits of them and strings them on a Stratocaster and plays some serious rockabilly on it with our existences.

The door of the store opened.

In walked Nephew Soursmile.

****

I felt the shiver in my shoulders and somewhere down in my chest. *Oh shit.*

Sarah saw it in my face, and glanced approvingly at Soursmile. "You were saying something before, about Bond villains wasting time telling you stories?" She fluttered a hand towards the new arrival. "I see you already know each other. So introductions at least are out of the way."

Soursmile walked past Dusk, who visibly relaxed and started giving me a broad moron grin that showed two teeth missing amongst the corn-yellow nubs. He had the features now of an elated schoolchild who had learned he could burn things with a toy magnifying lens.

By contrast, Soursmile was glacial and showed nothing on his plastic face. He came to a stop in front of them, a few feet from me.

There was a shriveled fingertip of cold wandering up from my diaphragm and along my spine.

This is a problem.

Overlap. A leak of panicked sensations from Soul's perceptions creeping into my own. I could sense the barest hints of motion in the air around Soursmile, hear something that sounded like clicks and electrical arc-snaps from far, far down a long, empty hallway. Soursmile's skull was alive with giddy, gruesome activity,

"From the look on your face," Sarah remarked, "I'm guessing you have some idea of what my associate can do."

Soursmile's mouth parted, showing little gray hints of shark-tip teeth. The nonexistent lips had a sheen like he'd just licked them or applied gloss. The opening was barely more than a breath, as if he was preparing to give a grandchild's kiss on his matriarch's cheek.

"You're right that I was shooting the shit a little with you. On my own, with an unwilling host, even one with no innate soul, I figured I probably couldn't take you. I could fight it... give you a tussle. But I didn't get rich or where I am now by not hedging the bets in my favor before I go put my first buck on the gaming table. This little discovery here...he was a true bonus when I found the wildeweird." An almost admiring look towards Soursmile. "I thought he was merely good at being creepy and hiding in the shadows to watch you. But his real talent turned out to be a real godsend. He has a gift for chipping at people's innards. Cutting away at their essence. I tend to think of as spiritual fly-vomit, digesting them and sucking back the nutrition left behind. But with you, he's going to go full-bore. Hollow you out. And once—"

"Can't do it yourself, can you?"

Her lips froze, caught in mid-sentence. I took the cue to mentally home in for it.

"You *can't*. This isn't another spirit getting eaten up and swallowed like you've done before, is it? You can't reach whatever I am. You might be a threat to some poor poltergeist or house-haunt, but I'm a null value where your ability is concerned. Like Rod. Like how I read as a zero quantity to him, no more than furniture or a car tire."

"It's a shame I can't have the smarts with the suit," she replied, too nonchalant. "But I'll make do. And don't worry, your significant other there will be more than ample eating for me, when he's done."

"Good luck with—"

Soursmile pursed his lips—

MOVE!

—and blew a cold whistle towards me, a teakettle torment.

****

I don't know how much others perceived Soursmile's attacks when he was only doing his on-the-street snacking and tasting as Soul had reported before. Certainly they sensed something wrong, if not outright pain.

But what he spat out towards me struck at my abdomen and neck like someone had swung an armload of concrete mix at me, meaty and substantial enough that I was slammed back into the bookshelves behind me. A couple of books from the top fell and chunked off my shoulders while my body shook.

"Awful" doesn't cover it. That Fate bitch was hitting a serious guitar solo with my thread.

It felt like being kissed and bitten and caressed by the mandible tips of dark, cave-blind things.

I felt a cold burning; it made me think of that horrid hot-white sizzle you feel when you accidentally cut yourself with a shallow papercut nick or breadknife slice, continually flashing across my nerves and working out from where it struck, spreading to my fingers, toes, balls, the hair on my head.

I shook uncontrollably. A worming feeling was making ropy tentacles around my limbs. I wanted to scream and fight back at something, whatever I could, but there wasn't anything tangible. Only the sensations.

Only the feeling of something that reached down, in, taking a hard grip at my spine, at the small of my back, grasping hard and giving my testicles, my head, my stomach a possessive, torturous squeeze. Compression. I felt I couldn't breathe but wanted to, wanted to draw a breath that wasn't there. Boa constrictor pain.

And in my ears a reedy, crickety riot that was waxing and waning with stereo imprecision. Warbling in my ears like trying to sit in the midst of a bee swarm made of electrified hornets, crackling and chittering and drowning everything else.

All around me, like a serpent made of freon gas, Soul was panicking and flitting around, screaming and hollering and telling me to move, to get away.

As he flapped back and forth, intersecting with me at random points, there were spastic resurgences of overlap. I saw heartbeat-steady pulses of cockroach and centipede and shrimp shapes. Bulge eyes that slipped and realigned, staring into me. Spurred into loathsome eagerness.

I felt one particular hard and chitinous sensation slide across my tongue and into my throat. I gagged, gasped, but it dug harder like someone's fingernails carving at my throat lining.

I smelled something like hot, fresh paved tar in summer. Rancid musk, like dirty stray cats in heat yarling and hissing. The tips of my fingers suddenly hurt as if they were going to swell and pop, fever blisters at the ends of my quivering hands.

I almost made it back to my feet. Then I fell to my hands and knees.

*God...oh god...*the hot tar and musk smells, the clattering noise...as my hands slapped to the floor and my kneecaps cracked into the wood, I felt my eyes getting hot and cold in turns. They rolled. I saw the wood grain, but superimposed over it was the mass of eating, swallowing, carapace-snapping things. Fighting over every scrap of my inner self as they spat out their various acids and spirit enzymes, breaking me down.

Then a new terror. A feeling of sinking. A very, very slow version of that nighttime fall-out-of-bed terror that dissipates the second you jerk in reflex. But this falling kept *coming*. I was dizzy. Even on hands and knees I shook, uncertain as to my position, my center of gravity.

"My, doesn't *that* look uncomfortable." Her voice was from some lighthouse a thousand feet away and a hundred feet up in the air. I tried to raise my head but a bundle of nerves in the back of my neck jerk and snapped.

God…jesus CHRIST oh this is—

—get up you have to get up fight this—

—fight like HELL how do I fight—

More overlap. Harsher, a tang of metal across my throat. My feet in their shoes felt as though I'd been walking hot coals, cooking them in oil. The feeling sent ivy vines up my calves, my thighs. My pelvis felt as though it was a giant ball joint in one immense, shaking tractor axis where my upper and lower bodies were helpless, flagging broken motor pieces spewing oil and fuel, burning and peeling…

Get up man if she does this if you go—

—how the HELL AM I SUPPOSED TO DO ANYTHING?

In between blinks of pain and flashes of motion, the noises and clackings, the sensation of falling in on myself over and over, I could see. My skin was fine. Nothing outwardly was wrong with me. I wasn't wounded in any bodily sense, so there wasn't anything to grab, to extract, to bandage, to heal.

This was going to gore me out as clean as a freshly-cut jack o' lantern. Merely waiting for Sarah Parley's inner reality to transplant itself, put its queer and nasty candle light down inside to shine out from my new smile and gleaming eyes at the world.

No. No no…god…

The falling got faster. I thunked my forehead and realized

I'd sunk to the floor, my elbows weak and my arms giving way. Like dozing behind the wheel and hearing the truck horn blare, I snapped up and tried to find some vitality left.

"Watching you fight this is not as interesting as I'd expected." Sarah stepped forward, next to Soursmile. His doll eyes were staring at me with a total lack of any passion or regard. He could have been watching me perform a Broadway solo or reading a newspaper for all that it showed. "I'm told that Soursmile's little…pet-growths can really core someone when they go at it like this."

SHUT UP YOU BITCH

God…

"It won't do any damage to the body, will it?"

Soursmile gave the faintest shake of his head, eyes not leaving me.

"Good. I'd really hate to have anything messed up."

The falling sensation now doubled, trebled…and the crushing, that collapsing-in intensified as well. It was terrifyingly reminiscent of being a child in a large crowd at some concert or big social event, some circus or state fair where the crowds were crushing in, giant and oblivious to my gasping and shoving and crying. All while plummeting to nothing, to a feeling of helpless inevitability.

"How much longer is this going to take?"

Soursmile lifted one shoulder, the minimum approximation of a shrug.

SHUT UP OH CHRIST I WANT YOU TO—

Overlap. But this was bright, sharp as lemon juice and lighting after-images burned on my eyelids.

Overlap. Soul could hear the thing inside her, the thing that was the real being, not this Sarah Parley pretend-thing. It was giggling with a breathless, grossly *erotic* chuffing pleasure as it watched through its stolen eyes.

Freak. Just die and let me have that skin, I'll use it in way more interesting ways than you ever have.

Another freak treating us like a bigger one, another convenience to be used. How stupid and ridiculous had I let us get played, some puppy-eyed idiot thinking I was getting a stroke of luck, a bit of change for the better.

Idiot. Idiot being laughed at and stared at and the screaming, the collapsing and crushing was harder. Colder. I had a deep-space satellite in cold-soak inside my body...it was my lungs, my stomach. My skull felt like it was melting away, sinking into that same pulsar, that forming singularity in the galaxy of my whole failing self.

I felt the doubling, then it settled and my eyes were clearer. But the shapes were brighter, harder and more distinct. Their eyes weren't blind, but white-yellow and lively. The whole mass was coming in and out of my mouth, my pores, my eyes, my ass, my guts, my fingers...everything was assaulted, everything being plundered...for a stilted, nitrogen-plunging splitsecond I wanted my mother, my father to make things right and I couldn't remember what their names had been.

I was going to die. The real dying. Worse, I wasn't going to be allowed to die, to dissolve. I would be consumed. Digested and shucked and then handed over like a suit, like a comfortable secondhand coat. A leather me-costume.

"He's really giving a good fight of it, isn't he?" Sarah smiled down at me from the lighthouse heights. "This isn't too bad to watch after—"

I jumped at her. I couldn't close the space, and I had no balance. This attempt was more doomed than the first. I flopped forward and smacked down on one hand, the other raised in a claw that swiped and missed, only batting at Soursmile's leg as Sarah stumbled back.

A bang-clap that was thunder. A wide wind that didn't quite touch me. More mortar chips and brick dust spat in the air behind me.

"God *damn* it!"

A hard slap and Dusk, crying and quailing. A clatter as the gun was dropped. Snorting and snuffling. I couldn't see. Couldn't focus. Who had the gun? Was it left on the floor this time?

*Have to get up...this...*my stomach *popped*; I swore I could hear it go, a balloon filled with air submerged too deep into the ocean. My ears felt full and numbed with alcohol-soaked cotton that twisted and moved and sent shivering aches through me.

Get up...

"Lively sort."

Soursmile's face. I wanted that plastic to melt. Through a haze of shifting figures and chittering sounds I saw Brother Dusk looking over Soursmile's shoulder, his nostrils flaring and this red-cheeked, panting glee beaming out from him. The kid was enjoying the bug burning in the fuse of his lens.

The red cheeks and the waggling eyebrows, the goggle lenses...Soursmile staring down like a giant wind-up toy gone dead and indifferent...pain...the crackle-crunch in my stomach spreading claws out to my spine, my neck, the top of my skull...

The falling sensation suddenly caught and punched up into me, like riding the roller coaster and the sudden up-swoosh as it drives and catches the track at the last possible moment, all momentum swinging upwards and throwing me back onto my knees, arms out.

"Excitement!" Sarah laughed, and waved her bloody hand at me, a circus ringmaster proudly showing the elephant standing on its hind legs. *Look, everybody, the beast has done a new trick!*

Inside my head, Soul roared and I found my own pain screaming in unison with him.

I wanted that mouth to stop smiling.

I wanted the eyes to quit gleaming with happiness.

I wanted Dusk's idiot-happy face to stop bouncing up and down at my agony.

I wanted to see them burn and shred like so much life-sized paper doll misery. I wanted the collapsing and falling and roaring and flying to stop in my stomach and my head and everything to stop hurting, to stop crushing and dissolving me.

"Maybe cutthin will hath new truphies!" he laughed.

Maybe cousin will have new trophies!

Between my eyes, somewhere in the space between my brain and my sinal cavity, there was a weird pineal-gland sort of focus. A cold and numbing area that, unlike Soursmile's creature-features eating away at me, was collected. Unhurried.

That son of a bitch is too stupid to live.

...agreed...

My eyes were wide open and taking in sight: Sarah, Soursmile, Dusk. The room. The dust motes, the disturbed air. The signals of bleeping and shivering radio beams that were pinging in and around us. The infra-signatures of heat coming off them. The smells of old polish, books, carpet. Skin cells and dust mites and wood grain. My own feelings seemed to suddenly detach and become as watching fish in an aquarium: floating and separate and trapped, away from me.

And around me: the fishbowl trap of the things, the shrimp-crab-cockroach-centipede abominations.

I looked down and saw our hands, fingers opening and closing. A dozen of the things were camped and twisting, an orgy of feeding and pleasure in each of my palms, wrapping up my wrists and playing with my veins, singing around the capillaries and chitter-clacking, snapping and biting and vomiting their little secretions into me. There were these draining, turning *holes* everywhere in me where they'd gone. They seemed to do this floating marine dance in and through the holes, making them wider...shoving and pushing to stretch, to degrade and decompose like termites finding the softest cellulose behind the plaster...eating away the house of me...my attic of thoughts fading and failing, old light bulbs plunking out of light and life with each second...

...disgusting. Grotesque and too disgusting.

They couldn't be allowed any longer.

And it was so easy. Looking at them and feeling my lips curl up in natural repulsion at them.

So easy to feel the motion sick-drunken sway-and-tottering inside my guts quiet down. It was still wanting to roar and shred and crush me, but it was floating away into that aquarium like the rest.

Looking at them, I could see...something else.

Past the lines of heat and cold, the radio signals and

microscopics and oil-slick things beyond the intrusion of these noxious invaders for the moment…

…down there…what were those? Lines?

Not quite. They kept wanting to do their own dance, in and out of translucency. They made me think of very fine hairs, no telephone lines, no…but straight and cutting around and about, zooming off into their own distances and obscurity. Occasionally they brightened, spasming with light that seemed to make the bug-things insubstantial and even less there, vaporous little nothings next to these lines…they vibrated… slowed…merged, then broke apart again, seemingly at random

…I tried curling in my fingers…could I?

*Yeah…let's try that…let's see…*Soul's voice overlapping my own…

"*What…what can I…are these…*"

Sarah was frowning. Soursmile tipped his head in the curious-dog posture. Dusk was still beaming and panting behind them, almost hopping.

Not to be allowed. You are too stupid and gross and idiot and greedy and monstrous. To live. To be tolerated any longer.

Looking at my fingers.

"So easy…*look, that line there, by my pinky…*" It moved a little! Like slowly, gently pressing on a piano wire and as you lift up hearing the lowest, bass reverberation through it…only—

A curl of cobalt fire spat out, curved around my pinky fingernail, and several of the things clutching and digging through me burned. They writhed. We could hear a brief squall like seagulls diving into flame. They spurted, flared and were gone. The gap they left was immediately being filled in with their fellows.

I heard a sound. Another cry?

What was this? Soursmile's face was animate. He had seen it too. No, he couldn't see the lines…the lines were somewhere else, something different…but he couldn't fail to have seen the result of their vibration on those baby-beasts of his…

…I felt a tug from something in some of the lines that intersected with my arms as I brought my hands closer together, the palms facing each other, fingers curled in.

The collapsing sensation...it was less now. Everything in my eyes was more alive, harder and brighter...I wanted a breath to break up the stifled clutch in my throat but I didn't need to breathe...didn't need anything except these lines, their flickers tantalizingly close and so *there*...so much more there than...

...my right thumb caressed a line, and as it twang-thrummed and seemed to bend on nothing, then went around...another blue-white flare that left a lovely violet afterimage...violet, like Trina's eyes...a violet that turned pale lilac, like Jennifer's...very, very far away...I could see into the line as it disappeared under the tension...that attraction, a different sort of miniature falling-in sensation as I looked at it...as if seeing it meant I was traveling, falling away and being taken into it...dark matter...

...what was this? Where was it from?

And where did it go?

What could it do...more things flared and died in the burn. Now the others were noticing. Hungry, helpless, they moved in but I could see some were abandoning me. Floating up and away...trying to go back towards Soursmile and the depleted sphere around him...trying to get away, get safe...somehow having a primitive sense of the danger...

...I smiled.

You people are too monstrous to live. But I don't live.

My/our voice spoke directly to the phantophage inside Sarah's body.

Hello.

...w-what?

Yes. I can hear you in there. Rattling like a bead in an empty spray can. Just as useless.

Screw you.

You should go. Now.

I'll leave when it's your shoes I'm walking out wearing.

I am way more monster than any of you could pray to be. All your money and Brokerage people aren't here right now.

"Now pray for this."

I felt something…was it Soul? Maybe. But I didn't fight it, wanted it to happen too. My arm moved. My left dropped and my right straightened out, palm and fingers stretched and held out towards Soursmile.

Lines…they moved with me…they bent and curved the way you would watch a glassblower slowly heat the red-hot silicon and start to tug, bend, twist at it…

…dark matter…maybe I'm/we're dark matter, too…

…move…press…I felt the faintest resistance from them, but the lines and curves weren't weak. They didn't break… they had *give,* but it was the twist and soft push-back of reconfiguration…they were adapting to my movement…Cat's Cradle…Witch's Broom…old childhood games played between the seats of the schoolbus with string wrapped around my fingers. Swing, loop, pull tight…new configuration.

..could I wish for something without having to move? I thought about the lines turning, becoming a sort of loose grid, moving out…

"What's happening?" Sarah screamed. In her eyes, I thought I saw the impression of something wide-mouthed…Elizabeth? A last vestigial smear of the human being that had sold herself to house this creature?

It didn't matter anymore.

Soursmile didn't answer, only opened his mouth and eyes wide. There were whites around those eyes after all. But only visible when he was terrified.

Good. Terrified is good. Say hello and watch the beast's new trick as the circus gets into high gear, you sick bastards. *Only we'll let you keep your teeth.*

You people killed someone you had no need to, there's never any need but he didn't care he didn't want anything but to be left in the quiet, left alone.

Like I wanted to be left alone. *Just me and my bookstore and my books and my lilacs and rainy-soft warm days in May… you* cockbags…

They took his teeth to play with. They took his teeth and they took his brain and she took his soul and they're trying to eat and swallow me and no god damned way—

I closed my hand into a fist. Squeezed.

The lines, not able to bend or adapt quite so quick, felt like grabbing a handful of stinging roses and thorns, then pop-flashed into a hot bloom. It was the feeling of trying to hold onto a hummingbird heart.

Semi-opaque flame exploded around my hand...and caught the exodus of creatures trying to come off me. I thought of old stories my dad had told me, of him and other kids filling squirt guns with kerosene...follow the trail...follow the fuel...

The flames were not burning, not combustion that I recognized...it was like flame in zero gravity. Like water made of neon and silk...curling around my fist and consuming the writhing, squirming stream of pulsing, things that died and the light followed...followed back to Soursmile...

...as it reached him, I let my smile go wide. This was fun. This was terror and horror and something inherently wrong was going on here, I could tell...but it was still fun. Still the beast rising on its hind legs, look at the trick...

you things *need to be gone now.*

"Go away now," we whispered. The sound was like flat metal fan-blades chopping and spitting it into the room, a wind tunnel shudder.

...as the flickers of light-silk touched Soursmile, first his lips and working up his cheeks and nose...it left nothing.

Dusk dropped his gun and clapped his hands to his hair-choked ears, crying. His glasses shook off and the one good eye-stalk-hole was clasped shut. I could see a bright scarlet ruby-tip of blood-pus squeeze out of the corner.

Nothing but dark.

Soursmile tried to jerk away but it was on him before he could muster any scream...then his lips were gone.

The tongue and teeth behind them already unwinding, falling and being burnt into the fire...I wondered briefly if the sensation was anything like I had felt. The crush-burn-falling and swoop of something eating away before nothingness took over.

From the look on his wide, tear-rimmed eyes before the

light took them and turned them into nothing, it wasn't.
It looked like it felt worse.

40.

Body closed his eyes but it didn't matter.

I could still see it all.

Dark-bright strings…movement…the piano chords of energy…somehow I could see/hear/taste it, the rub of fur being petted the wrong way, static electricity that drained away down a sink-pipe of everything…

Fill up your kitchen sink. Stop up the drain, let it get good and fill, near to the edge. Then pull the drain and shove your hand against the downspout. Don't block the water, merely let it run, draining across the nerves of your hand. The feel was that. The rushing and the pull of it.

I thought very, very quietly. A voice, asking a question of me. Something that was sitting up and noticing me, us. In our tiny corner of a tiny atom-speck in a nothing galaxy in the spinning, expanding universe stew.

But I couldn't hear the question. It was gone, washed out in background static.

Soursmile's head briefly flared like his tiny worm-things. There was a keening eagle-screech, feedback whine in a speaker membrane in the air of the closed room. The silk-bright threads were leaving dark behind…and then as they curled and found more to unweave, to unravel and un-make of him. I could see objects behind his head.

His hands beat at the shapes. But as the fingertips came up and touched the silk-string-line-lights, those tips caught the virus of it and infected the next rows of matter and muscle.

It wasn't eating him away. It was…there is no waste of matter or energy anywhere in the Universe. Everything accounted for in photons and energy and releases and transformations. Light reflected or refracted or infracted back into white purity, into the bright star hearts…

…that question again, but *what* was the question? Soursmile's arms were gone faster…the head had burned away and the candle-wick darkness of it ate down to his shoulders, chest…

In less time than describing it, I could see all of him: heat, flesh, skin and all…gone. Faster than he could fall to the floor.

One last blip of light on the floor when the last of his feet went. I almost wanted to laugh at the association: like an old console television when you turned it off for the night, and the electron-spatter picture momentarily shrank, collapsed into a little star-blip of light just like that.

Lights out.

End of the day's programming.

Cue *The Star Spangled Banner* and stock flag-flap footage.

Dusk was doubled over, rocking back and forth, crying to himself. Utterly lost to everything else.

Sarah lunged towards him Scooped up the gun and held it at us with an authoritative crack of withdrawing the hammer.

"Stop it now or I blow your fucking brains on the wall. And I'll keep blowing them out until something stays stuck to it. I'll get it one way or another, I can make you walk and move even without the top of that head. I'll just wear more hats. Stop and give it up so you can burn out with some dignity."

Body shook his head. The look on our face was regretful, not scared.

"I'd stand right where you are, if I were you." She raised the barrel of the gun so I could see directly into the black hole of its barrel. "I'm a decent enough shot at this short a range to blow half your brains against your favorite movie posters with this."

I could hear myself apologizing to a memory of my old friend. *They took my Ruger away. I'm sorry. I was stupid.*

No. People have guns taken from them. The gun is a tool. A noise-maker. What she's holding is the *tool, not a* tool. *And as long as what she holds is all she thinks to use, you are still wielding the weapons in the room. Stay calm.*

"Somehow I don't think that would be any sort of permanent threat, Sarah. Don't you remember?" I tapped a fingertip on a temple. "Give me an hour or so and I'd probably have a splitting headache and that'd be all. Not even a scar afterwards."

"No, but I understand how the whole head-injury thing works, too." She smiled. The gun barrel did a tight, slow circle that took in head, shoulder, heart, shoulder, back to head. "You can be knocked unconscious. You can be outright killed with a bad enough injury. The fact that you eventually heal is *your* advantage. But that you can be injured in the first place, incapacitated for any length of time, that's *mine*." The barrel dipped a few millimeters.

"You can't scare me," Soul hummed out of my lips. *"You can't scare us and even if you're Annie Oakley with that thing, you only have so many bullets. And I'll still have more lives left."*

I raised our hand again.

"Huh…how *about* that…" More lines. Not quite so many with her, not as refined…somehow the inside of her was bare, like a hollow vase…but there was still the body, the outer casing…still matter…the vase could still be broken even if the water was dried up and the flowers long since dead and powdered…something neat there…tiny shriveled…cat-shadow looming over the mousehole…

…no, wait…this isn't…no…we can't…this isn't…nobody should…*what the hell did we just do to that guy?* What the hell is this?

I turned my hand back to myself, looking down at the palm. The lines on the palm.

Palm lines. Girdle of Venus. Line of Mars.

Lines. Bracelets of Fortune. The Line of Fate. The love-line.

Love. Had I thought there was love with something equally phantasmal inside this...thing? In front of us?

Love. As if there could be such a thing. Ever.

Curving and burnished, copper and argon and flame... something there...was that the question? The question of this... nobody should be able to do this...no one...nothing...no...

Sarah stared at me, watching me peer at my hand. I wonder if she thought I was about to initiate the same thing we'd done to Soursmile on ourselves.

Do you want to know a secret?

I think we were.

"Don't pull any cute hero-suicide shit either, because the second you start that Roman flare on yourself, I'm going out of here and I'll have the whole hillbilly freak clan of these assholes—" jerk of the gun barrel at Dusk "—all over your friends. Your family, if we can find any."

"You can't do anything. There's no family. No friends. Your spirit-eater is gone. Your plan is no longer viable. Go away. Go away and die."

"We can start with your live-in vamp whore."

Here?

Here.

His eyes were crying an octopus of bright green-white tendrils from of each socket, flowing out and wetting the air, burning hard.

His hands came up...I let myself slip around the wrists, into the meat of the forearms...into the will around the shoulders, the tendons of the fingers that tightened...

"Oh...look...you do have lines in there...they're just harder to see...but there..." Our hands turned outwards, facing her...

She pulled the trigger. The gun struck its hammer-slam clap. A tack hammer punched through something down, miles away, inside us.

It made no difference.

We grabbed that etheric harridan in our overlapped grip.

Body had stood there, recovering. Had been listening. Sarah thought so little of her own existence, she had apparently forgotten what she had been risking to begin with.

What did Dhara call us when we first met? Call me?

Pneuma immundus. Unclean breath.

The Benoni Defense. The son of sorrow, tricking others into thinking they'd seen our best and beaten it. The way she'd tried to sneak up on our blind side, our Emperor's Row. To make Court's Betrayal. To get us to give ourselves up, either by force or threat.

The *solidity* was there. My seams had filled in again. The cracks were doing more than knitting back together in a sense of *wholeness;* I was pulling in harder, tighter.

I could feel Body's own integrity increasing, like density in a stone drawing tighter and tighter, almost boiling down and crystallizing, impurities leaving just dense, dense matter behind. Atoms sucking in, the spaces between electrons evaporating, leaving only hard neutral matter in the space where we met.

"What was that you said?" I spoke without Body's throat. *How crazy, I'll have to remember that:* my voice was in the air, around Body's head with no medium needed. My voice filled the room. It *was* the room. It was every dust mote in vibrato time with my words. *"That doppelgeists are the uranium of the Under?"* A whistle of angry steamed air.

We were the walking atomic bomb of all things dark and dim.

When the two halves of an isotope shell meet, the reaction is immediate. Explosive. Radioactive. Louis Slotin at Los Alamos, accidentally slipping his screwdriver and letting two plutonium core-halves touch, achieving criticality, a moment's mindless swing. Touching and dying for that moment's carelessness. We were plutonium halves, beginning to touch...

Synergy.

I addressed the phantophage.

You tried Court's Betrayal. You tried to make me give it all up so you could take Body for yourself.

Her face blanched, confused. All semblance of arrogance blown away as an autumn leaf in a draft. "W-what?"

I'm not the Vassal's Pawn.

Sarah's body jerked at our contact with her, and we were squeezing. Burning. Twisting.

Lines. They curled and fought the bending, but inevitably gave in and let us twist them. Glassblower apprentice skills, clumsy but learning. Learning more every minute.

It was like reaching into a bonfire and finding a still-solid chunk of burning oak. Grasping it, pulling it out, cracking it in two, letting the embers fly out firefly-bright into our own faces. Burning. Twisting. Ripping open and going out, back in...grab a solar flare, crack it like a Pecos Bill rattlesnake-cum-whip.

You are kindling.

Her body fell back to the floor, the legs going rubber as her ass thunked to the hardwood. Her eyes were wide and her mouth was stuck open in a scream that had died for lack of breath before it had a chance to ever make a real sound.

You are not—

"—going to destroy—"

—what little we still have left in the world.

"You should—"

—have left us alone.

She wasn't being cute anymore.

From somewhere, a roar passed through an amplifier and then splashed with hydrochloric acid, letting it scatter as a buckshot blast through her. The echo space hollowed further.

From somewhere? Wait. Christ, that roar was *me*, it was *us*. Floorboards vibrated with it as the sound grew and pounded the air around us.

She had overextended.

She had underestimated.

Meet Ground Zero, you schizo shit.

The burning-twisting-fire-splash was curling out between us, taking shapes of thoughts and intentions, memories and old daydream horrors. For a beat we were seeing a half-shadowed face written in light that was Meghan, laughing at us. The laugh then widened beyond the ears, edge to edge as the face split into a scream and became birds made of holocaust illumination before butterfly-burning into nothing.

Sarah's face doubled, trebled, snarled in the tiger light striping across the walls, the floors, each other. Body looked like the center of a man-shaped wicker fire made of butane fuel and argon, greens and blues blending into whites that were cooking the air itself. The Nookery creaked around us as if it were trying to pull itself away from us., sounds like a ship hull in a growing squall.

Dusk screamed, a spray of red-black blood coming out of his right ear as he fell to his side and rolled back, forth. Oceanic pressures had built up in the room without even realizing it until I started to acknowledge that some of the noise around us had to have been the ceiling and wall beams starting the bend and creak under the invisible pressures...it was getting downright *tectonic*...

Dusk went still.

The phantophage wanted escape. It was trying to get free, get away. Sarah's inner energy was trying to become ropes, twining around and away from the assault. Body and I had the grip too hard, though, to think of getting away. Rats, finding the nearest break in the pipes to get away from the sewer flood. But instead the fire was chasing her lines, flames and shudders of heat chasing after veins of kerosene as I tracked and twined myself into her essence.

Before, she had made it seem like making love, sharing space and crossing energies.

I hated that. I hated *her* for that.

I took that sense of violation and curved it back. What had been intimacy now became a scimitar shift back into her. The once-meeting became a rough, forced shove. What had before been embrace was now iron and shackle, Iron Maiden spikes gouging every phantasmal inch of her into shreds.

The overlap was rich; the feeling was like running zippers up and down, connecting seams, stitching through a hellish sewing machine in cold flames. We were meeting, tearing, re-meeting and re-merging. Over and over, but the same threads were scrambling and flowing out from both of us: hate. Anger. And an exultant joy.

Even burning Spam Tam hadn't felt quite this good, quite this rich and bright and sparkling with malicious, astounding vigor.

Then again, no one had deserved being on the receiving end as much as Sarah, before now.

"Nothing you will ever do will matter again. You will be nothing and no one will remember either of you." We spoke together, and I could hear my own whistling echoes, the dead quality that Body and others remarked was always unnerving when I echo-chambered out of his throat. *"You should have tried to* have *a life instead of trying to take* ours."

But another of those unplanned and unwanted, ugly leaps of thought, as if my thoughts were deliberately trying to jump the train before we reached the end of the tracks:

I'm not a fortune teller.

No...

But I don't have to be, if I can read in the next person's mind that it's the last thing I'm going to read.

Oh damn you. Damn you.

Good luck, John.

Body's lips pulled back. "He *knew.* You were there, you and your flunkies. You were there outside, waiting somewhere... and he *read* you. In some way, deep down maybe you still have something like a real mind and he picked up an echo..." Body's eyes went bright as water collected against them...and I could feel the taste-sting of their lachrymal pools in my own non-mouth...oh damn it...*he was reacting...he was right there reacting to it and we were such assholes, such selfish assholes but he already knew, knew before he'd even closed the door on us...*

Suddenly our hands were releasing, opening as if we were the stage magician setting free armfuls of doves.

I let myself expand. I felt the sense-edges of me thin, expand, then twist and go rock-hard. Smashing.

The windows of the store imploded.

The fluorescent bulbs hanging dark from the ceiling cracked and spat out in powdery glass and old book dust. The room was a cloud of glass that spidered, shattered like high, broken bells…and then flew around.

I saw myself for the first time.

I was seeing the shape of myself in the scatter-chaos of dust, glass shards and energy. The way the fingers of massive hands of wind will show in the grass of overgrown lawns, briefly outlining the invisible.

I was a maelstrom with hands, wings, talons. I merely thought it, and the dust and microscopic glass storms twisted in the currents, becoming my remembered face. Mouths, noses, dark caverns with rudimentary glitters as eyes deep in shadow…

…faces over and over, screaming and as they screamed another head would emerge out from its throat, explode out, and scream to vomit out the next, rolling and crashing into each other like skulls washing up in a tidal wave against a cliffside. Tongues that became arms, grasping and clasping hands, the hands collapsing and melting into skulls with jagged teeth of glass and hot, burning dust. That smell of old televisions turning on after years underneath piles of newspaper and dead dust mites. I could *see* the smell of it and knew it for what it was, could simultaneously smell it through Body's nostrils.

I looked like an idea of hell.

Broken, disjointed…a caricature of something real twisted and blown apart in confusion and mindless motion.

Not quite mindless.

The cloud-me was flying, and both Sarah and Body were caught in the cyclone chamber of it. Dusk's body rolled, clumping into the doorway, trapped against its frame. An arm flailed out and was pinned by glass shards to the wood.

I could hear Sarah screeching, failing. The phantophage dissolving as I found myself joyed at the sound. I was everywhere and in one place, hovering above the two forms. I was tasting the sky, burning the air, every inch of floor, of ceiling beam, of brick texture around us going through and beyond me. The Nookery walls protested with louder groans.

Body was bleeding from cuts and lacerations. He looked up—straight into me—and there was a brief nod as he fell to the floor. Under the sweep of it. That greenish-white-purple tinge of burning power was sloughing off his skin as he collapsed.

Sarah's body jerked upright. I had her in the grasp of the whirlwind.

I looked into the face under those red curls. Kissing lips, smiles. There had been something there. False, pasteboard and betraying. But it had been there for us. For me. For a time.

The things we love, we hate the strongest. Only love can evoke those kinds of passion. To kill as much as caress.

Because I never actually got to kiss the girl, when the bottle spun my way.

Because Trina didn't ask to be what she was, forever and ever.

Because Jerry loved his grandsons and it wasn't their fault they tried to help tried to save everyone and instead lost a hand and a pair of souls and almost everything else you could possibly lose. Not fair…

Because it wasn't Rod's fault that he could do what he could, anymore than it's our fault that we're dead and gone but not gone and can do this, can burn and hate you bitch…not fair not fair ever at *all* ever—

I felt the febrile, shifting, squirming connection, and almost as an afterthought snapped it, cut it as if I still had hands made of mercury and razors. A whisper lost in the gale.

We could hear the phantophage die. It lost that fraying cord to what control it had had to puppeteer Elizabeth's body.

Somewhere I think Elizabeth might have had one last screech in her own defense…but we sang-snatched that away with as much concern as a hurricane has for the straw.

The body dropped to the ground. As it did, something pathetically sparked, like flint against feldspar, from her open mouth and was sucked away like cigar smoke in a wind tunnel.

Burn down. Burn away until Hell is the best place you can go to cool off. Spend your money buying your way out of this. Call your Brokerage to come save you, if there are any phones in Oblivion.

What was that sound? A whistle, a song, something harmonic and humming and passing through me like a sympathetic sine-wave…not sound but the question…

...not right. Not right. I didn't know what it was, but I looked down at Body lying there, at Dusk's body. At the glitter-sea of broken glass and smashed books and the desk and the blue nubbly armchair shoved against the far brick wall...

...not right. What the hell just happened? I saw my face in the glass...I saw the lines and the curves and it was so easy, so easy to reach out and tug and pull, to squeeze and make the burning, to *undo*...

The cosmic DELETE key we had pressed and pressed and pressed, making some god-cursor go backwards and undo... undo Soursmile and undo his things and undo...

As the word 'undo' kept winding back through my thoughts, I lost consciousness. The last thing I saw was a snowcloud of pulverized glass dust, falling to the floor with a floury hiss. Then I passed out.

Which for a bodiless consciousness should tell you something.

41.

"Ceyggan. "
　　"Hey, Jo-Jo, what have—"
　　"Get over here. "
　　"…what?"
　　"Get over here. The Nookery. Now. "
　　"What's go—"
　　"Shut up. "
I hung up the phone.

＊＊＊＊

Ceyggan arrived within twenty minutes. He stepped over the doorframe, expensive shoe soles crunching on glass dust. His face was what I thought I'd seen in black and white photos of American soldiers in German at the closing of World War II, entering the gates of one of the camps. The face of someone seeing a reality they hadn't believed possible. Or hadn't been capable of imagining in the first place.

I stood in the same place where I'd fallen earlier. Not looking at anything, not focusing or paying much attention except to the empty air a few inches in front of my face.

Thinking. Trying to remember a question I thought I had an answer to, like falling asleep hours after a trivia show that you missed a question on but now think you've got it.

I flapped a hand in the direction of the humanoid pile against the far inner wall. Ceyggan went and knelt next to it.

He looked at the face, into the open eyes. Reached a hand out and touched the side of her neck, pressing the index and middle fingers.

He jerked his hand back, curling it back at the wrist, against his chest, as if some dry ice burn had met his touch. His eyes met mine, and for a moment there was nothing but a stark, instinctual terror in those bright orbs.

"She's still alive. "

"Yes. " I stepped over to the blue nubbly-textured armchair, righted it with a single reach-down-and-flip of the arm so it sat with its back three-quarters turned towards him. Sat down in it. "Her name was Elizabeth Cambridge. Also known as Sarah Parley, also known as Sierra Dunes. Now known as nothing. Now take her out of here. "

A breath. Two breaths. I could almost hear the action of his neck as he looked around, as if trying to spot the camera, the obvious candid television stunt gag he was clearly being punked by.

"What?"

"You heard me. She's there. You're here. She's alive. She's the one responsible for Diatha. Take her and do whatever you see fit. "

"Do you mean—"

"I mean take her. " I drummed the fingers of my right hand on the armchair, the left hand balling into a loose fist. As the left's fingers clenched, I almost heard a not-quite-there sound. Something like a knife being dragged lengthwise on a piece of taut piano wire. It whummed and disappeared as the fingertips touched the palm. "Take her and get out of here and I don't want to hear or see anything about this ever again."

"What am I supposed—"

"Do you have a problem hearing me?" My right hand

drummed a little faster, a little harder. "Take her and get her out of here. " I closed my eyes. "Make her disappear. Drop her in the river with stones tied to her ankles, wire her to a car bomb, sell her ass as a comatose whore in some back alley room to rent. I don't care. "

"Good *gods*, Jo-J—"

"*Don't* call me that. That's another stipulation. Don't call me that ever again."

I could hear his breathing, fast and panicked as an overheated hound in miserable shade from a summer sun.

Under that: the much slower, regular tidal shush from Sarah Parley's slack lips. And the rain-drop patter-thump of each of my fingertips making individual *thwaps* against the nubbled cloth upholstering.

"What did you do to her?"

"I have no idea. " No need to give any bluff or bravado when I hadn't the faintest answer. Then anger filled the empty with ease. "And what's more, to repeat myself for the last time: I. Don't. Care."

His voice moved, rose. He was standing directly behind me. "What's *wrong* with you?"

My fingers stopped drumming. My right clutched into a fist to match the left.

He waited.

He waited longer. His breathing calmed but was still hard, harsh as a man fighting to regain some calm after a raging argument. Though his voice never rose above a surprised gasping.

The Faede have been around a long time. But even the Teaghlach wouldn't wait forever for something that would never come. Ceyggan surrendered some time later.

His last question came after a grunt and sigh of effort, the creak of the floorboards. I could sense a shift of mass near me, just at my back. Carrying a weight in his arms.

"Which way?"

I raised my left hand in a dismissive wave towards the door.

I kept my eyes closed as his steps staggered outside. A creak, a swing-cry of unoiled metal and warped wood. A tinkle-clicking of glass shards being stepped on.

I felt a breeze, smelling of lilacs and rain. His footsteps died away down the sidewalk.

I opened my eyes when I was at last sure we were alone.

The hiss in my skull: *He left the door open.*

It'll get closed eventually.

True.

Broken glass. Windowframes are twisted.

True as well. They'll get fixed eventually.

I nodded. Tilted my head as though listening carefully to some sound.

Tired.

You're *tired? I feel as though I've been sifted and sieved and squeezed through a colander made with razor-edged rusty iron.*

She's gone. Done with.

True again.

I'm on a real streak with those statements of the obvious.

When it's obvious, it can hardly disappoint.

A subtle hum across the floor. A shift of air that left my ear canals and moved around. Glass shards shivered lightly, the weak light glints winking off various pieces.

Someone may call the police. Or the fire department.

If they do, we'll deal with it.

How?

I relaxed the fists, let the fingertips explore stretching like cat's paws across the armchairs.

Good question. How would we deal with anything? Anybody? That hole had opened up and the first casualty of its gravity had been any sense of memory or comprehension of events.

I thought random, disassociated things. Lines. Fire. Trails across kerosene dreams. The smell of burnt hair and singed meat. The feeling of a billion paper cuts in the spaces between my mind's fingers. A sense that something had fundamentally changed in us but there was no clear picture of what that meant, none at all. *What happened?*

Looking at all this, I'd say…something bad.

But what happened?

More glints as shards were disturbed. A long, agonized squeal as the door closed itself shut.

A breeze picked up and blew across the broken-teeth edges of the shattered glass in its frame.

I don't remember.

I stared at the fabric of the chair's armrests under my left hand. *Neither do I. I mean, I think I can recall it if I really focus, but…it feels disjointed. Like talking about a movie we saw and not something we did.*

I lost my sense of self. Like blacking out. That hasn't happened before. I didn't think I could pass out. Do you think we were out? Or do you think it's more like we can't stomach remembering? Speaking from the perspective of not having a stomach, I still can't avoid thinking it's the latter.

I think…we broke something. Something…big? Important? I can't tell. Something that can't be fixed. Something…bad.

Soul sighed against the floor.

Is there anything that isn't?

42.

No one called the police or fire department.

An electrical storm knocked out the transformer station two blocks away. No one apparently thought it unusual to hear booms and were more inconvenienced by their temporary power outage. The facts that the power company nor the local weather reports were aware of any such electrical storm didn't stop that explanation from being the wholeheartedly acceptable one.

It was only worth a few moments' consideration, though. Mostly we both appreciated that it was one less thing to deal with.

The next day, the construction crew returned from their weekend off.

Body sat in the armchair. We watched the dark lighten into blue, cloudless sky. The sun rose. Then the sun was outlining Scotty Craig, workbelt slung gunslinger-style at his hip, stepping over the shattered glass of the doorframe.

"Mr. Flicker?"

Body didn't move.

"Are you all right?"

He opened his mouth. Closed it. Furrowed his brow, seeking an answer from some lost file cabinet inside the head.

Finally found a sufficiently short scrap lying on the floor back there and read it aloud with mechanical tones. "I'm fine."

Scotty did a turn. Taking in the room, the glass. He saw a suspiciously ichorous blot near the toe of his workboot and pulled that foot back.

"Oh man...are you...are you sure you're okay? What happened?"

"Nothing that is still happening. Or that you need to worry about."

He stepped back towards the doorframe. "I think...I should call the boss on this one." Outside, the others in the crew were approaching the building and slowing, stopping to take in the sight as they discovered the damage for themselves. Glass splinters everywhere, cracks in the wood frames of the windows. The door askew on disjointed hinges. And the owner sitting alone, to all observation catatonically watching birds and traffic go by.

Scotty stepped back outside, waving down the others on the sidewalk. They congregated and muttered, talked. Nobody looked our way.

I watched them in their group. Cell signals blipped and bloomed from their huddle. Voices moved and slowed, whispered and hesitated. A couple of glances towards the building. A piece of glass somewhere fell and clinked, causing some of their shoulders to jump.

All around them was a cloud of ribboned, twisted gray light, breaking into gelid chunks of gunmetal phosphorescence, fusing and re-fusing. Fear. Fear of something they never thought there was anything to fear from before now.

These guys worked for the vampire community and who knew what other groups. Scotty himself wasn't a wholly human being, we had no reason to think any different of the others. They were used to unusual requests, strange situations, no-questions-asked...but this looked different for even their jaded eye.

Finally Scotty returned, standing at the doorway without stepping over into the apartment. As he stepped away from the group, the fear-ribbons tore and re-merged, pseudopods of the sensations trailing with Scotty as he left the safety of the crew, the odd man elected to do the speaking.

"Mr. Flicker? I'm...I apologize. We don't...the boss has to contact some people. We need okays. This isn't exactly a permit-and-code situation." He tried a thin smile that died as Body didn't respond. "But...he wants us to pull out for today while he checks things out. I'm sorry."

"Okay, Scotty."

Scotty breathed in obvious relief. "I'm sure...we'll get things cleared up. This doesn't look...I'm sure we can be back in a day or so and get things back on schedule for...your kitchen."

"Sure thing." Body's eyes were taxidermy glass, as empty as those set in a stuffed deer or wolf.

The crew left without further commentary. A couple of them paused to take last looks of the destroyed storefront before getting in their trucks and pulling out.

The trees outside continued to sway. Chlorophyll pulsed and solar juice oozed through vascular trunks. Birds chittered at squirrels in eternal turf wars amongst the branches. Cars went by. A couple of neighbors leaving for work at the pastry shop on Third slowed down. Saw Body. One looked like he was going to wave then thought better of it.

The sun had cleared the street skyline across from the store, which meant it was after noon when the phone rang.

Answer it.

Body didn't move.

Answer it. I pulled close, where he'd left the cell lying in his lap since making his last call.

SEGAL GALL

It's Ceyggan.

A hand moved. Tapped the answer button and switched to speaker.

Silence.

Then: "Flicker?"

Silence.

"Flicker...you...they want you. You need to come out."

Answer him.

Body stared at the phone screen, unmoving.

*Damn it...*I saw the cell thread coming out of it, like pumping circles of white-blue. Microwave carrier signals. Radio beams. Heat from the phone's battery. Photon spray from its display.

Lines and curves. It seemed simple enough if you thought of them like drawings on a sheet of paper, things that you could reach out with your pencil, your will as the eraser and the graphite lead...old Warner Brothers cartoons where Daffy Duck was arguing with the omnipotent cartoonist, constantly drawing and re-drawing everything around the duck to drive him crazy...

"*Waaaahhhhhhuuuu...*What. Do..they *www*want?"

Not through Body's throat. But in the cell signal. In the speaker. Only a matter of lines. Lines you could reach out and re-draw, re-curve. Pluck them and play at them with your voice as your fingertips, a piano with the strings percussed by a thought of sound, a memory of words and meaning.

"Uh...yeah...they...you know. They want you to come out. Please. Just this one time."

"*Wuh...hhhh...*why?"

"I don't know. I don't ask."

Body spoke. "I'm not interested in what the Teaghlach want. You jump when they say to. We don't."

"Please. They said they needed...the idea was...they want to tell you something. Something important. But that's all I could get out of it."

"We don't feel like letting them have another try at swallowing us like Jonah in the whale."

"They don't want that. They wanted me to make that clear more than anything else. This isn't about trying that again. Not that. Please, they won't...please."

There was something in the plaintive voice that had me curious. *We should go.*

Body shrugged. *Whatever.* "We'll be there in a little bit."

"Thanks."

****

He found a fresh shirt. *Going to have to buy more, a trip to Goodwill or something,* he grumbled. *All of mine these days are getting bullet-holes that clash with the patterns.*

The blue jeans had survived passably well. He grabbed keys and wallet and we left. The day was warmer than usual, no coat needed. Sunlight and blue sky and that feeling as always...that something had cleared up. That some storm had passed. But it had not done the favor of picking up its debris-strewn disaster area path behind it.

The drive was silent. Even the Vega didn't give any argument.

****

Legs crossed. Carpet. Summer heat. Cut-grass and Strawberry Shortcake Shampoo.

Ah Christ, not this.

What is this? But Body realized what this was fast enough. Mischa. Urging me to spin the bottle.

Mischa. Oh man—

I know, yeah. I know.

Howard Jones on the ghetto blaster outside. *And you waaaant her...aaaaand she waaaants you...*

No...no...don't look, don't do this...traitor fingers reaching, grasping cool glass...a push-twist of the wrist...bottle spinning. Spinning. Stop.

I can't stop...

I know. It's the memory. Ride with it, it'll be...it'll end soon.

I looked up. *Here we go.*

Annie Spartan wasn't sitting across from me.

A girl with honey hair, braided with colored streaks of shining chestnut hanging over her shoulders. The braids met at the crown of her head and formed a kind of amber tiara of hair, a few stray strands caressing the clear forehead.

Eyes that nearly glowed with that white-pink health, the vitality of cut amethysts set in each eye. A smile that was the provocation for poems.

Everything else went still. This girl shared a photograph world with us in that moment. I heard Body choking in the back of my thoughts. I tried to take some lead, some control.

"Who are you?"

Please let this not be another trick, another stunt another trap I can't take it again if—

"I'm here with you now." She said it like someone giving you keys to a car and walking away.

"What?"

"I'm here with you. You can <KEEP/CARE/remember> me."

The flash-fade, the sound-cut from vocals to mind-voice...

...the Teaghlach.

I saw around her a very weak ripple. A heat-haze. *Glamour.* The sparkle of beauty that turned her into something heartbreakingly gorgeous. She was a hundred or she was ten years old. It didn't show in the lineless face, the smile that opened like theater curtains on a porcelain chorus of breathy song.

Body, almost dry in the thought: *so we can see glamour here. In a memory. Strange.*

"Diatha?"

Her grin widened. She nodded.

"Hey," Mischa nudged me with an elbow. Pointed to the bottle. "Have to do it!"

Everything in motion again. I couldn't do this. Not again, not now, what was—

She was already leaning across the space, throwing her weight forward and hinging up on her kneecaps, arms going around my shoulders.

Lips met mine. They tasted like atomic fireball candies and hot lemon tea. Something about her smelled like clove and pepper. Kitchen and home smells. Lovely wildwood.

Opera Creme filling. Christ, that sweet-lemon taste was her lips. Favorite childhood cookies. They don't make them anymore.

Under that, the faintest buzz of cold. Like the low, cool front of pressure above a frozen lake in a hidden thicket of black trees, a ward against summer and everything withering away to time and heat.

Diatha. Lovely Diatha. Lips touching mine. Her eyes open and looking into my shocked ones. Those amethysts mischievous and shining-wet with congealing tears.

She popped her lips from mine and fell back into her Indian-crossed-leg position. A giggle and a tilt of her head.

"Why are you here?"

A shrug. The smile never faltered.

<KEEP/SAFE-KEEP/care/remember/cherish/HOLD>

The fan oscillated. The ghetto blaster outside continued playing tunes. Now it switched to the next one. Crowded House came on.

She kissed me. And it made a larger part of that rusty-metal chunk lodged inside me melt away. I smelled the lingering scent of the clove and pepper on my cheeks and lips.

"Thank you," she breathed.

"For what?"

Hey now...heeeey now...

She shrugged.

Beautiful girl-woman being. Here forever. Where the Teaghlach had put her. To keep this little sliver of her alive in a safe and warm place. To not completely lose and absorb what she had been into its senseless, disorganized mass.

Don't Dream It's Over...

"Thank you," I said to her. She laughed and clapped her hands. For a flash of sunlight through the playroom cut-glass door, I thought I saw a garland of flowers around that gold-amber head. Like a muse. Like a winged and precious thing flitting, a will o' the wisp on a midsummer night.

For <KEEPING/KEEP-SAFE/sake/REMEMBER>.

Yes. I think I understand.

Would you prefer not to <SHARE/have/remember/ HOLD>?

Body replied from somewhere small and warm. *No. This... this is fine.*

It dropped away. Broke apart, falling away into the darkness.

Arms, legs, mouths, shells and wings and membranes, bellow-lungs and massive chimney throats backing, slithering and sliding off into obscurity.

<GIFT/offering>

Thank you/Thanks.

<THANKS/APPRECIATION/applaud/GRATEFUL>

Sunlight.

But for that last whisper as the dark sent us out. A face. Robeyn not-good.

You wouldn't. If you knew what you were giving up.

A pool of light. Body and I on the floor.

If you knew who *you were giving up.*

A hiss of repaired hydraulics. The light from the outside.

This time we didn't need to be told to go.

43.

We came out of the inner chamber and found Ceyggan sitting on the floor at the foot of the stairs. Staring down into his own lap, looking like a puppet waiting to be picked up for the matinee children's show, waiting on the end of the strings.

I stepped up to him. Nudged him in a shin with a toe of my boot.

He looked up. Took a long breath as he brought his head up. Exhaled slowly.

"Is everything okay?"

"Yeah."

"Good." He stood up, pulling himself to his feet with a cat's ease. Patted at his thighs as if to knock dirt off his palms. "What did they want?"

"To trust me with a secret."

"Which was?"

"A secret."

"Oh. One of those." He exposed teeth in a feral, mirthless smile. "They gave you one of their <BOND/HALF/share/SMILE-DIM/love> packages?"

My mouth opened. He chuckled to see it.

"Yeah. We can do it. Not as hard or as powerful as the

Teaghlach. But we're all part of it. A part of the *family*. A part of the whole. The feel-speak thing...it's there all the time. Just not very useful when most of the time you're talking about gallery openings and negotiating getting a blowjob from a girl at a rave."

...they're...it's not a family, it's one being.

As Soul whispered it, I realized it had been a thought coalescing for me as well. The missing aspect that clarified the relationship. The not-birthing/welcoming we'd experienced. The aged but the seemingly ageless, inexhaustible childlike state of the Faede compared to their sire, their creator-figure. Not a creator, anymore than a matryoshka doll's outermost casing 'creates' the smaller dolls that nest within its shell. One into others, the others...

"*It's one being that decided to never specialize, to never split cells or go fissile...the Faede...you're the* larvae, *aren't you?*" Soul speaking through my lips, but parts of his voice seemed to come from the walls. From the electrical wiring, the hum of the overhead fluorescent bars. "*You all are...what? Like scout ants... to bring back experience, to learn and grow and then bring back.*"

Ceyggan nodded, face sober. "No death. Only Oneness. A birth that is the outcropping of a single cluster that we give this or that name that the world sees as a person. The death-time is not death but the dissolve, the break-down time...when each of us returns to it."

They were like botfly larva, the hellgrammite spawn that went out into the world and gained experiences and pleasures and lessons of pain...then at some point were returned to the central mass...

I struggled to retain my perspective, to not lose myself in the vertigo of what that suggested, what we'd only been momentarily in contact with...almost absorbed into becoming part of in its entirety. *They're not a race, they're One...the Teaghlach is the tree of life for all the branches throughout the world...and each branch is still the whole tree. Each can see a different part of the world from where it branches out, but it is all fed to the tree, all cycled in the same immense growth.*

A passage of so many years, the idea of 'years' itself meaningless. No time, only superficial change. Tastes, needs, hungers, feelings that broke away. Not separate species, not species no genus no family no phylum…all one. All a massive One that could break apart and yet retain a One sense of self.

Not children. No future generations, just one breaking then reforming over the years. The father-god Cronus, swallowing his own children over and over.

They go out and they bring back. They are born off and they return when their time is ending and the One must restore that small cluster of cell growths. The body is splintered, the thoughts grow and there is…everything-ness.

"It's really pretty beautiful, as I understand it," Ceyggan said, seeming to pick up on the thoughts. "One day, I'll find out." His smile warmed. "But not today. Not just yet."

"We won't tell."

Ceyggan nodded thanks.

"When your time is done, you return…you become that?"

"No. I *am* that. Always. We all are. It's never a real difference. But yeah, in basic terms, when it's time that I no longer serve any usefulness as something apart, something extended out and touching and grasping at the world for it…the Teaghlach will reclaim me. For whatever reason, my purpose is to be a rave-party, gallery-hop dilettante asshole. And someday all of that, whatever that means, will go back and be added to that massive library of a brain."

"Forgive me, but in some ways…that sounds really damned heartless."

"Just because something is a family doesn't mean it has heart." His voice dropped several degrees, marking the end of the meeting. "And you're not one to judge heartlessness."

"Does any Faede ever…refuse?"

"No."

"Who's Robeyn?"

Ceyggan's features flattened. His ears pulled back as his eyebrows raised. It was the animal response of pricking up ears to hear the approaching predator better.

"Where did you hear that?"

"In the mix, you might say. *Robeyn not-good.* Is he—"

"Robeyn Goode isn't your business either. Forget about it."

He turned away from us, going up the stairs and back to the daylit, day-to-day world waiting. He knew we would follow him.

44.

"I took the liberty of calling the glass service for your windows. The contractors doing the kitchen work will go ahead and take care of some of the wood damage for the frames and your door."

"Thank you."

Jennifer Yu wasn't wearing her fire-engine leather coat and boots this time. She was almost nakedly casual in a pair of khaki cargo shorts and a nicely-fitting Betty Boop t-shirt. Hair tied back in a ponytail.

Another day. The glass contractors were outside with their tools, already quickly and competently cutting and fitting all new sheets of glass for the windows and doorway.

Body spent the day after the last meeting with the Teaghlach, slowly cleaning. Sweeping and throwing out glass fragments. Taking a brush and bucket of water to some of the marks on the floor when the glass was cleared. Pushing some of the free-standing bookshelves from the walls to the front to partially help block the naked holes of the blasted windows.

Righting the messes. The physical ones we could clearly reach and correct, at any rate. If you can't take the spray paint off the walls, you can at least right the crooked frames. The torn-up rug was finally retired, slowly rolled with an almost ceremonial care before being put out in the walled-in alcove by the back door with the trash cans.

Now the next day. The glass contractors had shown up with Jennifer as their spokeswoman to explain their presence. She sat on the nubbly blue armchair in the the shadows of the bookshelves blocking the windows. Legs straight out, ankles crossed in their chunky-soled black hiking boots. The eyeglass corners twinkled in the weak light. Body lay on the cot in another monolith shadow while I hovered over all.

"I hope you don't mind me arranging all that."

"No. Thank you. We needed to get it done. I just...I hadn't been really all-there to get to it yet. It needed doing."

Quiet minutes. The sounds of a portable water-jet saw, precision-cutting glass with a harsh spray-spittle hissing outside. People talking. Birds. Inside: angled shadows and books quietly molding to yellow dust.

"The general rumor mill was that whatever problems have been going on lately...are over with."

"Maybe. Seem to be. For now."

"So..." she sat up, hunched, put her elbows onto her knees. "When can we bring her back? Get your equipment set up? Start training on how to use it?"

"We're not doing it."

She looked down at her phone. "What was that?"

"Practice. Something new. Just a thing."

She looked up at the ceiling, taking in the corners and new strands of cobweb already collecting. "A new gimmick?"

"Call it a new channel of communication."

She nodded. "Learning new tricks every day." Looked at Body. "Maybe you should reconsider."

"We're not. Trina is safer with someone else. Find her a better partner."

"She doesn't want another partner."

"Then talk some sense into her." Body sat up. "Do your job. Counsel her. Transition her. Get her with somebody who isn't a danger to her and everyone else. Get her with someone who isn't self-centered and an asshole, who won't take advantage of her."

"You do realize the massive contradiction in those sentences just now, don't you?"

"Interpret it however you like. Trina can't move back in. This won't work. It was already a failure and now we're sure of it. Find her somewhere else."

"You have an amazing capacity for bullshit." She said it without rancor. "You're so worried about her because you're incapable of worrying about other people? You want her to be treated like an adult, like a real and whole person who should determine her own choices, for maybe the first time anyone's ever let her do that in her life, and yet you want her to start that out by having you or me make all those decisions for her? Maybe *fuck you,* how about that? Maybe she doesn't care about the risk. Maybe it's a risk for everybody to try and be together. Do you really think you're somehow the worst person in the world? The biggest monster that everybody should relegate to loneliness and leave him to his cave in the swamp?"

"Go to hell."

"You want her to stay away, you tell her yourself. Me, I'm just getting your glass fixed and your kitchen finished for you. Trina is your responsibility. And you're hers."

He got up and walked out of the room, back into the bookstore without further remark.

She spoke to the empty air.

"If you get any trouble from any of this mess or what happened, any neighbors that raise a stink or threaten any legal action for whatever unfathomable reason they think they can, call Dario and he'll be able to help you again."

Hold for picture.

Snap. Flash.

And the image finally developed clear.

"Annan is employed by the vampire community?"

"Amongst other groups, yeah. He handles a lot of the civil and occasional criminal cases the community has to deal with."

The vampires sent Dario to get us out of jail.

On the heels of that: I wondered if any of those 'occasional criminal' cases had anything to do with their guest activities at that safehouse.

My voice drew in close. She jerked but then calmed. I spoke quietly but clearly. Dust motes vibrated and carried the sound, the whole of everything around acting as a carrier as I shaped the words.

"Jennifer, I need to be able to trust you to do something, but do it right and for the right reasons."

"This doesn't sound like you're going to ask for me to help you make a phone call or get groceries."

"Not hardly. Though I do want you to help me communicate."

"You seem better at communicating lately already. But shoot."

"You've met me. Us. We're not huge bosom buddies or anything. But I think I can safely guess you've taken your own read of me, am I right?"

"You seem all right. Stupid and slow, but all right."

"Touché. But you saw what we went through. Trina's savaging. The whole mess." She nodded. *"So I want you to take a message back to Justin."*

Her eyebrow kinked up, but she kept her mouth shut.

"Tell him we expect to call on him in the future. I don't know if it'll be the near future. But it will be inevitable. So much so, he might as well chalk off a day for it right between 'Death' and 'Taxes.'"

"Okay."

"We're going to meet, and...we may not be on friendly terms after that meeting. The gist of that meeting will concern primarily the disposition of certain...actions and obligations between us. That we want stopped. Now."

"Nobody expects you guys—"

"Let me finish. I do not like being beholden to him or having little neat dossiers reported on our whereabouts. We can't stop you guys from doing it, maybe, but I sure as hell don't have to be polite or act oblivious about it anymore. We don't put up with credit bureaus collecting our vitals, and we don't need the vampire community with a turkey thermometer up our ass every time we bend over to pick up the paper from the front stoop, either. Am I making myself clear on this point? So you can just as clearly convey it to him?"

She nodded. Slower this time, but nodding.

"Tell him also that we know the kinds of things that must have been going on in this town for who-knows-how-long. Things in places like that convenient safehouse out in Upper Arlington. I picked up enough psychic radio jam out there to make a whole K-Tel series of murder mix-tapes. It was a telepathic slaughterhouse. I don't want to know places like that are operating. This is your community, your rules."

"We can't stop it, I know. But again: we don't have to like it or accept it. You people show your courtesies, you make your obeisance to your occasional out-of-town guests...but if it's this city's people you're preying on, if you're letting the sick kicks get made using locals here, maybe people we know and care about... we won't care about lawyers. We won't care if it was an accident, a crossed phone communication. We will burn down every installation and so-called safe place you people have a lease on. Every corner we can find."

"We're not all like that." Her voice was hushed. Hurt.

"I know," I softened a notch. *"I know that. But you need to hear this because you believe me when Justin might not. Or might think that he can still handle whatever threat we represent. But make it clear to him, as best you can. We don't like being used. We don't like being shit on or screwed over or toyed with."*

"I've never been good at 'forgive and forget.' I'm not a Zen master who can let things slide and walk off without stewing over them. Hell I still remember which bitch on the yearbook staff in high school had to have been the one who got me cut out of the senior book. I still remember a guy who tried to shoplift from this store four years ago and punched me when I caught him. Call it a moral failing. Call it arrested development. I don't care. This time it was Trina. The next time it could be a lot worse. And if there is a next time, there will not be a third. Do you think you can get all that to him?"

"I...yes."

I watched her face. That same absence of body language as always. She couldn't shiver. She stared into the empty air. Her hands gripped the armrest firmly enough that I could hear the fabric beginning to creak in tiny pops.

"I think you should leave." I didn't make it an order or a demand. I tried to sound kind. But I didn't want anyone in the room just then.

She looked into the dust-mote beams of the ceiling. At the dark corridor archway. Seemed to think of going after Body, or saying something. Then shrugged to herself and left.

45.

The next day after that. The glass was all up and the contractors had clearly paid attention. They did the additional courtesies of applying fresh, white soap-paint to the new glass. Two of them even helped me move the bookshelves away and back to their original places.

I was sitting at the desk. Looking at bills without really seeing them. Trying to roughly calculate the little things that added up with the big. Electricity, water, heat. State taxes coming up again for the property. How much would it take to recover the cost of the bathroom, the kitchen remodels...

A knock at the door.

Over my head, amongst the spider webs. The contractors. Jennifer said they'd be returning.

I went to answer the door, my mouth working up the minimal energy to smile and say hello to Scotty or to the boss or any of the workmen who were willing to come back.

Trina stood at the door. Her suitcase held in front of her in her crossed hands. The late morning sunlight found her hair and turned it crystal. Volcanic glass refracting around her. Violets in her eyes.

"Can I come in?"

I stepped back to allow her passage.

She stopped by the desk. Did a turn.

"They fixed it up good. I heard it was a real mess."

"Vampires only hire the best."

She emitted a fake giggle. Kept staring at the windows, at the books back on the shelves. To the bare floor.

"No rug."

"I haven't gotten around to replacing the last one. It was finally put to pasture after the other night."

She put her suitcase down but didn't turn to look at me.

"I don't know what happened. Nobody could tell me. Or would."

"I don't think I'm up to talking about—"

"I didn't want to ask you about it. If it was bad...but you're still here, right? Both of you?"

"As always." Soul's voice was beside her. She pulled away as if a puff of air had graced the line of her jaw, like a baby sighing as you hold it to your breast.

That prompted her to look at me. "He didn't...you don't talk together now?"

"We can. But I'm learning I don't need to."

"Cool." She smiled.

"Trina..."

"No. Let me talk." Another violet flint-spark. I shut my mouth. "Jennifer told me. You don't want me here."

"It's not *want*. We *can't* have this. You can't live here. It's not safe and it didn't work."

"We didn't even try yet. It was only a few weeks."

"And you nearly starved yourself to death or someone else's death. All because we were too caught up in our own bullshit to pay attention to you. That's not right."

"No, it isn't. But you know what I learned as part of the programs? Two wrongs don't make a right. I used to hear that in school but like a lot of stuff it never sunk in what it meant. To really think about it. About giving up and thinking that cutting your losses is the same as taking responsibility for a mistake. It's not."

"I don't want to risk—"

"You can be a real bastard, but so can anyone. It doesn't make you a bad person where it counts. Or...persons, I guess. You can't...this isn't something you simply get to call quits on and walk away. That was the biggest thing they taught me in the transition training. *That there's no leaving what we are.* Changing, growing, but not leaving. No walking away. Not without throwing out the good with the bad. Neither of us can change what we are now, only who we are. But you don't get to say it's too hard and leave me in some apartment with some assigned stranger and figure that solves anything."

"I can't be trusted around anyone anymore." I threw up my hands, practically yelling into her face as she stood unmoving before it. "Do you get what I'm trying to tell you? You tried to *kill* me before when I didn't pay attention to what was going on, but *I've destroyed people in the last forty-eight hours* and I couldn't even tell you *how I did it.* Trina, there's a very distinct possibility that we...that I could simply get *annoyed* with you and that's *it.* Wave my hands or give you a nasty look and... break something. *Hurt* something that won't heal or cure."

"I don't see how that's any different from any other people trying to be together."

Infuriating. God *damn* it! Stupid girl. Stupid situation.

Stupid me for thinking I could do anything different, change anything, even trying to do the right thing meant I was only compounding this farce, this idiotic playing house as if we were still alive, still mattered—

The door glass cracked with a hard, nasty detonation of noise. A splintery dent appeared in the bottom frame. A finger-thick crack shot like frozen lightning down each glass pane of the three-sectioned door, bisecting each pane with a cold, bright snap. Trina jumped, eyes widening.

I waved my hand at the door. "You see?" I pointed my finger at the crack like I was tracing its line down to the floor. *"That's me. That's us. That's what it's becoming.* We don't have any clue about what's going on. That's what I've been trying to find out about all those times we were avoiding you. That's what's been going on the last couple of days. The windows? That wasn't Sarah or her idiots attacking me. That prompted it, but the damage wasn't them, it was me—*us*—this whole thing." I flapped a hand at the broken door. "That's *nothing. That's…* it's starting…it's getting to feel like earthquake season, do you get this at all? It's feeling like sympathetic vibrations. Like that thing, that machine that Tesla claimed he built, the one that could build and build and build up energy until a tiny thing the size of a soda can could shake apart an entire building, or a bridge."

I sobbed. Swallowed a dry throat that felt sticky as duct tape against my palate, choking on the words. "I feel like I'm vibrating harder and harder and faster and it's not going away, *not shutting down—*"

She grabbed me, clutching me so hard that ribs throbbed. My neck ground, vertebrae to vertebrae. Not a kiss but an embrace. Her face socketed into the hollow of my throat. Not a bite, not a feeding, but hunger all the same.

Lips moving against my skin, cold air pushed out of vocal chords that didn't breathe.

"I don't care if you blow up or everything around you does. Everything goes away eventually. Brothers, parents." She forced a breath against me, goosepimple-chilly. Only I couldn't get goosepimples. A faint purse of lips, the barest of kisses bracing on my collarbone. "Everything goes away, that's why we're supposed to be together, some of us, for a little while when we can manage it. Don't quit me, okay? Don't quit me and I won't quit you, okay?"

"I could hurt you. I probably *will* hurt you if we try this."

"So you hurt me. As if leaving me alone in a lousy apartment with nobody else isn't hurting?"

"You'll get over me."

She pulled back and looked up at me, and the fierce violet glint shining from her eyes was enough to make me blink.

"You're a real stupid shit, you know that? I thought you ran a bookstore." She touched my forehead, ran the fingertips down the bridge of my nose, forced my eyes to close as she ran the tips gently across my eyelids, down to my lips. When I looked again, the violet had softened to faded lilac. Dried flowers in the magnifying lenses of her retinas. "I don't *want* to get over you."

"I don't want you regretting that."

"Didn't you say one time that when we regret things, it's for what we didn't do, not what we did?"

"This is not a cute moment to throw back my words at me. You know damned well there are things you can regret because you were warned, because you knew better and did something stupid anyway."

"Yeah. That sums up being in love to me."

"We don't really even know each other. I don't know why I asked Justin...why I simply jumped..."

"Do you pity me?" Her voice was cool and stony. She stared at me with no body movement anywhere in her limbs or face. "Did you offer to help me because you felt sorry for me?"

I thought about it.

"No. I don't pity you."

"Then why did you ask Justin to let me live here? Why really?"

"I don't...it's stupid..."

"It's stupider if you can't tell me, adult to adult, why you wanted me here."

"Because...because I like you."

She blinked. And a red film, like the faintest haze of rose petals...maybe from a Chrysler Imperial...drew over her eyes, folded in the bottom of her eyelids.

"You like me?" A swallow. Her mouth clicked, dry as mine. Her tongue clicked against the back of her upper teeth. Her head bowed, eyes casting down. "You like me? Like to be with me and want...maybe something more?"

I touched her chin with the tips of my fingers. Bent my knees to lower myself to where I could look up into her eyes, which were wincing and a single dark red blood tear had welled and was leaking from the corner of her left eye.

"Yeah. I like you. I may love you."

"We *love you*," Soul chimed.

"We feel that way, I mean. I wanted to be with you. I wanted a cheap excuse to get Justin to let me be with you and spend time with you and get to know you and I was stupid because the responsible thing to do would've been to leave you alone. To go on my own way and let you go on yours and not endanger you with my crazy life. I should've been responsible but I wasn't. I wanted you here and for all the same reasons any person wants someone else."

I grazed my fingers over her lips, the little dents where her upper teeth were biting into the lower lip. "I may love you, Trina. I feel...yes, in our way, though it might change and become other things...right now, yes. We love you. And I want to know more, to love something more. To be with you. For you. Not because of pity or a feeling like I was supposed to, but because I wanted to."

She smiled. Wiped at her eyes. The violet was gone, and I was looking into her natural bright eyes.

"Then there's no good reason for us to not try, stupid."

46.

I gave Trina the summary version of the rules as we entered Greenfriars Cemetery.

"Be polite above all else. But you've probably learned that dealing with Justin." Trina didn't affirm or refute. *"The King is serious business, even if he talks to you like you're his oldest friend in the world. Don't flip him any attitude or you could find out how undead you really aren't."*

"I get it." She said it quietly, and I realized that for her, even with recents events to numb her, driving through the massive tomb-city that is Greenfriars was probably an instant education itself in the gravity of the Under that she was now a small part of. "Is he…is he like a monster or anything?"

How do we possibly answer that one?

"I couldn't tell you either way," Body remarked with all frankness. "He's not scary to look at, if that's what you mean. At least not to me he isn't. Anymore. As for the rest of it, what you can't see up-front…I guess that'll depend on whether or not he likes you. Maybe you should try and remember what someone else told me about him, when I first got to know him."

"What's that?"

"'He can make the dead weep.'"

At her question, I had shifted around in the backseat. There was another question, wasn't there? Something not from Trina but from inside me.

Do you feel something wrong on this?

Body glanced into the rearview mirror, not seeing but acknowledging where I was. *Yeah, but hell if I could tell you.*

A glitter of glass. I thought about Dusk's body. And the thought that Soursmile was probably still out there somewhere, with his Cousin Nightsock and a real desire for some revenge, some time and some night too soon in the future.

I thought about Sarah...no, Elizabeth. Breathing in shallow huffs. Nothing inside. The windows open, the breezes unblocked through the empty house. Where no lights worked any longer.

What had happened? Something and something wrong, but I couldn't think of it.

All I could think was: why was I uncomfortable in some hair-triiger way at the word "monster" spoken in Trina's voice? Or our nearly-glib denial of it?

"What's that mean, anyway?"

"If you are still capable of asking, then you're safe."

47.

"Sarah Parley wasn't a doppelgeist. She was a phantophage. Actually, she wasn't Sarah Parley, but Parley's daughter Elizabeth and this phantophage inside Elizabeth impersonating her. I was fortunate enough to learn before it was too late. It's sort of a super-ghost, the way it was explained to me."

"Yup," the King nodded. "Eats up other spirits. Souls, emotion energies, anything it can get power from to keep getting bigger, to keep going."

"Exactly. She thought in some way that being a doppelgeist, if she could figure out some way to get Soul and I separated, get us in some sort of position where one of us was compromised, then she could finally leave the body she'd been carrying along as a vessel and get mine. And with mine, she calculated she'd effectively be immortal, free of any further hunger or need to feed on other energies to survive."

The Sexton King sat back on the bier in the shade of a massive alder, with the smell of late-bloom honeysuckle filling the air. Every breeze played the grass like baby rattles.

Trina sat on the grass between us, a little triangle within one of the wrought-iron-fenced-in family plots from some Victorian dynasty whose names had all but disappeared from their stones in decades of rains and snows.

I recounted a summary of the rest: the wildeweird, the Brokerage out west arranging for body replacements for some unnamed wealthy client. When I finished on the note of destroying the phantophage, I stopped with a fade of voice. I coughed and tried to sound as though I'd run dry...but in reality, it was just an empty place. We'd done it...I know we had. But it was blank. Smooth and drawn in lines of faint light in an otherwise black infinity in my head. What had we done? It involved that power, that growing sense of what was wrong with us as a being of two-in-one and one-into-two...but I couldn't explain it. Certainly couldn't try putting it into any brief narrative for him that would make it sound any nicer.

He let me cough and swallow while rubbing his chin.

"And all this simply to get a crack at you? At taking up residence in your skin?"

"We're not exactly a dime a dozen, though she certainly wanted us to think so. And I suspect that something was going wrong. Something was beginning to wear out in that body of hers, finally succumb to all that feeding and cycling of energy. The Scots brothers told me that phantophages are usually not that powerful, that possession is something normally beyond them because usually they can't amass that kind of energy."

"I guess she didn't bank on you being so impervious to temptation, hmm? Figured she'd take you to school, did she?"

"It was because of that hint you less-than-subtly gave us that I figured it out at all."

"Hint?"

"Court's Betrayal. You were obviously wanting to lead me to figure out something was wrong and it was with her. Thank you for that, however tricky it was to figure out in time."

The face wreathed in cigarette smoke for a moment didn't look right. There was an immense weight under those eyes, hanging against the cheeks with their sharp jutting edges like the bags of a homeless lottery-winner, all fortunes spent and all hopes gone in that last blast of good luck. Sadness mixed with a bit of rue, like mad Ophelia holding her petal-less little sticks and stems and crying they're the loveliest flowers of the field.

He looked…disappointed? Why? Had we said the wrong thing, somehow, thanking him for his cryptic bit of help?

Ultimately, it was a shade of anguish you see in the most patient and dedicated of teachers. Watching as every student in the room fails the test.

Then the sense left his face, and there was the wrinkle of grin in the corner beside each eye.

"What I said led you to her mess, did it?"

I gave a sour, embarrassed grin. "Court's Betrayal almost worked."

"The Vassal's Pawn nearly got to the tenth square while you weren't looking, huh?"

I'm sorry. I got caught up in the whole thing thinking she was like me. The whole memory-sink thing…

Forget about it. I was just as suckered for my part.

"You don't need to feel bad about it," the King remarked, with his usual eerie awareness of Soul being there. "Better men than either of you have fallen for the gambit. Why do you think Machiavelli tried to destroy the set that he had da Vinci make for him?"

"He did?"

"He developed the variant and commissioned Leonardo to make a set, he was so proud of himself. But he lost when he played a game against Pope Julius the Second. Julie got to talking about Florentine militia arrangements and Niccoló got off-track from the game." The King gave his trademark wolf grin. "Like I told you: sometimes chess isn't about the better player, but about the player who can make the other one stupider for one crucial move."

"I can't imagine he'd try destroying it over one bad game. Especially if he'd gotten Leonardo da Vinci to make the board and pieces."

A tip of the head, a shift of the shoulders. As if destroying masterpieces was as inevitable and predictable as rain in a humid climate. Then again, it probably is. "Tried to smash it, but the stone was too durable. Tried burning it. I guess with da

Vinci, you got what you paid for. He finally dumped it in some merchant's hands, figured it could go out with the bathwater for all he cared for the game by then. But never mind all that. You want to try a round?"

I leaned back against the granite throne opposite the King, which was the marker for the nameless patriarch of this nobody family beneath us. In the corner of an eye, some leaves overhead shook in a way that seemed like maybe the spirit of that buried patriarch was looking on, shaking his head in disapproval. "Of course."

He waved past my shoulder. Following his direction, we looked and saw an altar-stone monument twenty feet off, out of the shade of the tree and in the bright sun. The board was resting there, pieces at the ready.

We got up, resituating ourselves so that he and I took opposite seats in the grass, the low altar stone almost like a dinner table in a Japanese sushi restaurant, the kind with classic tamami mats and cushions.

"So that seems to sum up things, don't it?" The King got down on his bony knees, drawing up those scarecrow legs as he got comfortable.

"Not exactly," I said, getting down to the grass. "I still have the Believers of the Second Freedom after my ass. I don't know about Bill Arrundale, or Steve Dwyer, or whomever else they might have for buddies gunning for me. They're still out there. The phantophage took advantage of their info, but didn't claim any credit for their existence. I'm going to have to be careful for a while."

"Sarah was probably calling Dusk, not her manager, those times on the phone. Helping them keep tabs on us. And don't forget the wildeweird. We've still got Nightsock and Soursmile and who knows however many other sick-ass relatives of theirs to expect to come visiting."

A twinge. *Soursmile?*

Yeah...that name seems rather...off. Was he laughing at us? Or was it something else? Did he have...something with shadows?

The name was there. But it was the disconnected feel of an

amnesiac, all fact with no context.

"Yeah, well...we all have to be careful," the King commented. "But you at least have someone watching your back for you."

"And front, sides, center, and outer space while we're at it."

I stared at the board a moment, starting to chuckle.

"Something strike you hilarious?"

"A little. You said she'd tried to take me to school. School." *What about it—oh. Yeah.*

"Fritz knew about Sarah Parley from her days as a B-movie scream queen. But he couldn't remember every little detail. He'd thought her real name was Sarah Oxford or Sarah Temple, but couldn't remember it just right. Her real name, her name before taking on her stage name, was Cambridge. Just like Cambridge University. Like Temple—"

"—or Oxford," the King finished. I nodded.

Is it me, or did you notice that the board's edges look a little scorched?

"Where'd you find this set, anyway, if I might ask?"

And does the black side Emperor look like his crown is a little chipped, like someone tried smashing it?

Another of those infuriatingly uninformative shrugs. "Found it in someone's trash one time. It's weathered well."

I'll bet.

"What about you there, little lady?" The King leaned to look past my shoulder where Trina leaned against the base of an obelisk behind me. "Care to play a game after I beat Johnny here like a schoolboy schmuck?"

"Maybe." She grinned nervously. She was slowly warming to him. Upon introductions, he had given her the gentlest of handshakes, a little bow as if he were going to kiss her fingers. She had giggled, and he had kept slipping her winks and smiles with a benign flirtation. "I'll watch and see how to play."

"While you're watchin'," he gave a not-unkind half-frown, "you mind maybe sittin' over here with us, and not leanin' against the monuments? It's disrespectful."

She jerked away from the stone column as if it had turned to liquid nitrogen. The sudden fear in her face was not fake.

"I'm sorry."

"S'okay, gal. You didn't know better." His frown turned into a mischievous, sidling smirk. "Although from now on, you *will* know better, am I right?"

"Why didn't you say that to him? He was sitting against that gravestone there earlier."

"He doesn't count. He's dead. The dead are allowed to do whatever they want with a grave."

"That's right," the King ratified Soul's comment. But he gave her a wink and she laughed.

Trina came over and found a soft patch of grass to sit Indian-fashion, where her head only came up high enough to see along the worms-eye view of the chess set between us. She had a flat, wide-eyed look to give back to the Sexton King, and gave a single nod. "Yeah, sir."

"No need to say 'sir.' But that'll do." He picked up the shovel, his scepter with the frying-pan black iron spade-head. "You mind maybe holdin' this for me while we jaw, though?"

She glanced at me. Then smiled nervously, letting him lower it into her open hands.

"It don't bite. Not in the daylight, any rate. Just keep 'im close to you, see he doesn't do any diggin' without me."

She giggled and lay it across her lap when she sat on the grass.

The King regarded me again. "I'm gonna allow that I'm playin' one 'gainst two, but bear in mind that I'll know if you're havin' help to try and play unfair, all right?"

As if I know any more about this game than you do.

The point is made nonetheless.

Besides, you can see where all the pieces are.

Heh. Can you?

The King tilted his head up, letting his hat shadow fall away and revealing that lined, elongated face to the complete sunlight of a warm, false-summer day.

"It's a hell of a day for chess and sunshine," he remarked, eyes closed. He looked as though sunlight smelled of cookies, and the sound of leaves crackling under a squirrel nearby was the rattle of dishes being put out on a family dinner table.

Screen door rattles and cold iced tea. Porch time meditations. Something Ray Bradbury probably wrote about decades before we were all born. "You can't play chess right, when it's too warm or too cold. It's gotta be a day when you don't mind losin' or beatin' a friend."

He brought his head back down slowly, opening his eyes as he returned to earth. For only a moment, even in the sunlight, the shadow of his hat brim falling back across the top of his features, his eyes were pupil-less; jet-black as grave soil and forgotten promises.

"You ready for it, Candleflick?"

"Never ready. But that's never stopped me before."

We're going to lose, you know that.

Like the man said: it's a day when that doesn't matter.

For once.

Yes. I glanced at Trina, who was intent on the battlefield of miniature stone soldiers. *For once.*

I think we should try and stop worrying so much about what we are or if there's some cosmic plan hiding somewhere for us to follow, don't you?

A slow smile as I selected the Vassals Pawn and pushed it forward two squares as Whites opening move. *Agreed*, he answered.

"Well," the King growled, giving Trina another elfin, grandfatherly grin as he pushed his own Pawn forward in answer. "That's all right, then."

****

When I was a boy, I missed a chance to kiss the first girl I ever loved. I chose not to kiss her because I believed in love and romance and meaning, and as sure as I knew you could find winter hiding away in a dark corner of summer, I believed a kiss was not a prize to be given away for the sake of boredom and which direction a Pepsi bottle pointed. I missed that chance and I have always regretted and been miserable to think on it.

When I was a boy, a beautiful, otherworldly-lovely girl-woman kissed me. Kissed me not because I won Spin the Bottle with her but because she was wonderful, and that's what the lovely and wonderful people do in the world. They kiss and laugh. They ache and they see beauty in small things. And one day when it's all over, the only regrets are for those around them for not seeing it sooner.

When I was a man, I stopped regretting being a boy and instead tried to make sure that this time, I kissed the girl.

****

My name is John Flicker.

My name is also John Flicker.

I have learned that to want to be exceptional is not an insult to that which is regular.

I have learned that to let go of the senses does not mean to let go of life. Or of what is truly important to sense in life in the first place.

I am learning that sometimes, when the bottle stops spinning, you should be kissing the girl and worrying less about being embarrassed. Because you'll remember the kiss far better than you can live down the embarrassed regret.

I am slowly learning that whether you are a few months old or more ancient than redwood trees, all life is still to one degree or another about figuring out where you fit in the scheme of things...and maybe realizing there's no scheme to begin with.

Just everybody trying to find a place and be happy fitting into it. Call that hokey, corny, whatever. I can't really stop at this moment on any other note. That's part of it, too.

We are scared as hell that we're going to break something. Or someone. That we care about. Maybe the world. Yet what can we do? Stop existing? There's nowhere on earth you can go to avoid being on earth, after all.

We have learned that something special does not need to be something fragile. Or something awful.

Somewhere out there, maybe closer than we like to consider, are people who would like to see us dead.

But to be honest...we haven't felt this alive in years.

Acknowledgements

As hermetic as many writers want to believe they are, nothing exists in a true vacuum, as Neil deGrasse Tyson might say.

Rod Roscoe really can read minds. And books. And has a lot of scary, precise analytical ability in cutting to the crux of either one. Aside from giving financial and creative support to the previous novel, thus becoming one of the principals of this one, Rod helped me feel more confident in branching out and writing a more diverse and culturally wide world of the Under than I'd previously tried to write. He is one of the main reasons why Everything Under is becoming at least as wide a world of wonder as the real world.

Janet Joseph, my wife's aunt and frankly one of the all-time most incredible women it's been my honor to know. much less have as a relation, put her money where my mouth is and has been a follower of this series since the beginning. There is nothing more dangerously flattering to any author than to have someone sit down and start asking honest, informed questions about your characters and where they're going. Sometimes coming up with an answer to her questions became the answer to many of my own.

Joshua Bates was the only reason I didn't go utterly crazy at my previous job. I lost the job, but I didn't lose the friend he has become. **Jessie Kuntz** is also one of my favorite Vegas people and it's going to be fun to see her in the next novel...

Lastly, but never least, my gratitude to all the others who provided support in both money and spirit to see these books to print. **Bill Arrundale, Hope Moore, Kevin M. Smith, Lucy Snyder,** and **Jennifer Yu** No amount of words, even in this lengthy installment, can express all the gratitude I feel towards you guys.

Ron Horsley is an author and graphic designer living in his hometown of Columbus, Ohio. Between him and his wife they have four cats, three artificial Christmas trees, two cars and one upright piano. He is a graduate of the Clarion Workshop for Science Fiction & Fantasy Writing and spends much of his free time wondering where all his time has gone.

Pick up the Complete Adventures of Body & Soul

"Sin Gorge"   "Jennyripper"

Available on Amazon.com & Other Online Bookstores!

And for More Updates, Visit the
Official Homepage of Everything Under

http://www.Everything-Under.net